The Heretic's Secret

Also by John Wilson

NOVELS

North with Franklin: The Lost Journals of James Fitzjames

The Alchemist's Dream

The Third Act

The Ruined City

Graves of Ice

Shot at Dawn

Where Soldiers Lie

And in the Morning

Germania

Flames of the Tiger

Four Steps to Death

Lost Cause

Lost in Spain

NON-FICTION

Lands of Lost Content: A Memoir

Ghost Mountains and Vanished Oceans: North America from Birth to Middle Age

John Franklin: Traveller on Undiscovered Seas

Norman Bethune: A Life of Passionate Conviction

A Soldier's Sketchbook: The Illustrated First World War Diary of R.H Rabjohn

The Heretic's Secret

Single Volume Edition
(Heretic, Quest, Rebirth)

John Wilson

The Heretic's Secret: Single Volume Edition

Copyright © 2009/10/11 and 2013 by John Wilson.

All rights reserved. No part of this publication may be reproduced or transmitted in any form or by any means, electronic or mechanical, including photocopying, recording or by any information storage and retrieval system now known or to be invented, without permission in writing from the publisher except in the case of brief quotations embodied in critical articles and reviews.

This book is a work of fiction. References to historical places, events and persons are used fictitiously. All other places, events and characters are the products of the author's imagination and any resemblance to actual places, events or persons is coincidental.

Library and Archives Canada Cataloguing in Publication

Wilson, John (John Alexander), 1951 -
The Heretic's Secret: Single Volume Edition/John Wilson

ISBN (paperback) 978-0-9877065-6-0

Cover photography and design by John Wilson

This book contains the entire Heretic's Secret Trilogy: Heretic, Quest and Rebirth.

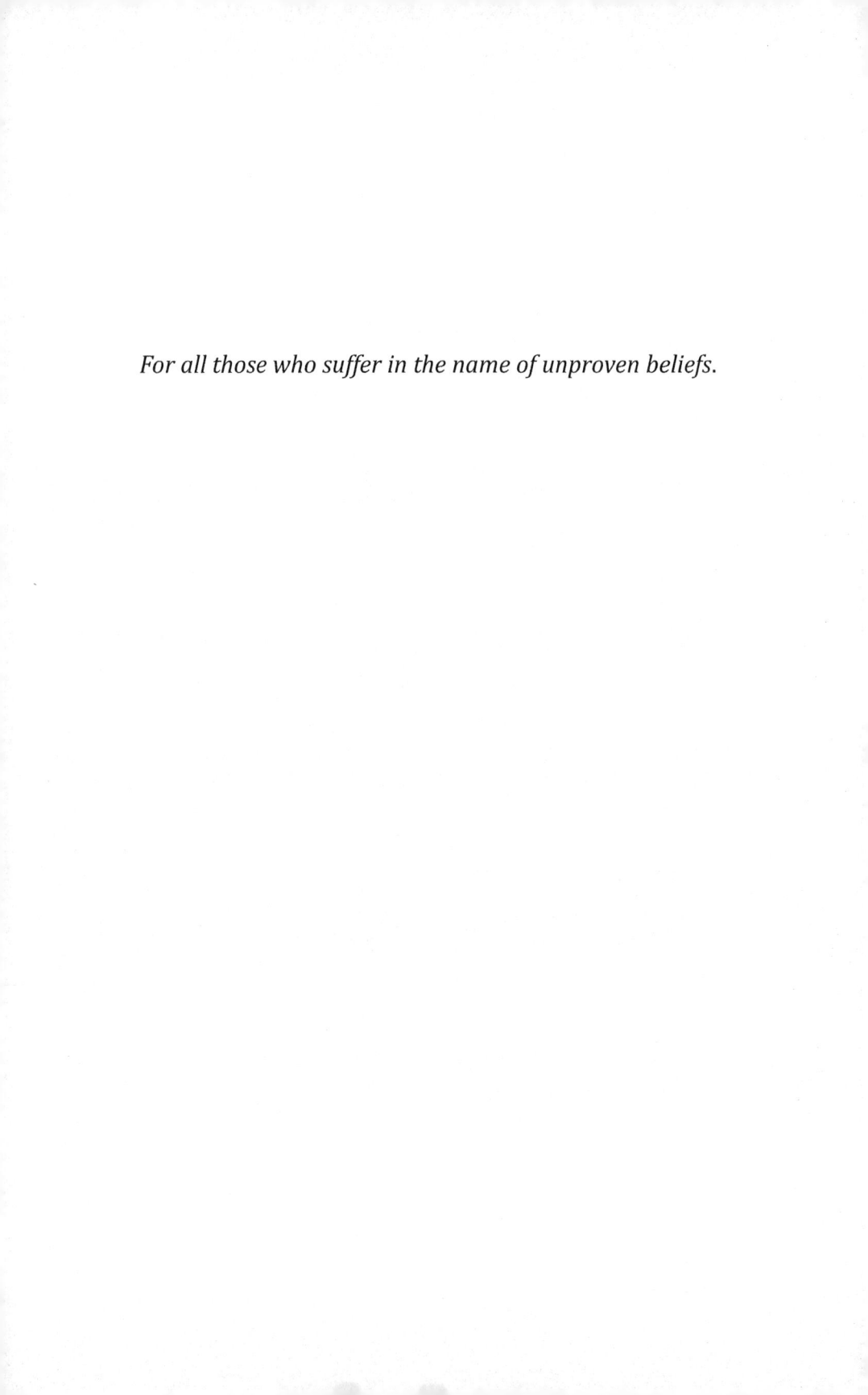

For all those who suffer in the name of unproven beliefs.

*"Such are the heights of wickedness
to which men are driven by religion."*
—Lucretius 99–55 B.C.

A Word from the Author

Lucretius knew what he was talking about. In the two thousand years since he lived, millions of people have died or suffered in religious wars—and there is still no shortage of hatred and fanaticism around the world today.

It is difficult, sitting comfortably in a chair reading a book, to understand what drives an individual to kill in the name of his or her God. How much more difficult is it to understand what motivates entire nations to go to war for their beliefs? Yet, historically, it is not an uncommon occurrence.

Eight hundred years ago, religion dominated most people's lives and guided their actions on a daily basis. People in the thirteenth century weren't scared of cancer or climate change. Instead, they worried about what would happen to their souls after they died. To them, the soul was as real as the body, and they were concerned with it in the same way we might be concerned about what would happen to our bodies after a car crash. The difference is that damage to our bodies lasts only until we can be fixed up in a hospital. Damage to the soul lasted for eternity.

To save an eternal soul, you were entitled to do almost anything to the temporary body. Monks whipped their backs to a bloody pulp to purify their souls. Anyone who put their own, or someone else's, soul in danger could be tortured in unspeakable ways, and then burned alive. The people who supported and took part in these punishments truly felt they were acting for the best.

The soul was so much more important than the body that anything was justifiable to save it, and many Christians fervently believed that it was their duty to go out into the world and forcibly convert non-Christians, or kill them in the process. Time and again, European kings and lords led armies into the Holy Land and to Al-Andalus—the part of what we now call Spain that was ruled by the Muslim Moors—to do battle with people who believed in a different God. The Crusades were popular, and people—from kings and emperors to holy men and children—flocked to them. But not all Crusades were fought in far away places.

In this strange world where belief was all important, thousands of people in Languedoc, a separate country in what is now the southwest corner of France, believed differently. They were Cathars—Christians whose beliefs did not match those of the Catholic Church. In the eyes of the Church, the Cathars were heretics, endangering their own souls and those of all to whom they preached. They had to be got rid of, even if it meant building human bonfires.

In 1208, Pope Innocent III called for a Crusade against the heretics of Languedoc. In doing so, he triggered a brutal war, not in some far off corner of the heathen world, but in the heart of Christendom. It was called the Albigensian Crusade, and it resulted in tens of thousands of deaths and the destruction of a unique culture and language. The war lasted from 1209 to 1244, although the Inquisition's search for individual heretics lasted much longer. The last known Cathar—William Belibaste—was burned at the stake almost a century later, long after the Crusaders had gone home. There is no evidence that any souls were saved.

MAJOR CHARACTERS IN THE HERETIC'S SECRET TRILOGY

* denotes fictitious character

Abdul* —Swordsmith in Toledo
Adam* —One of John and Peter's friends.
Adso* —Soldier and John's friend.
Albrecht* —Expert in siege engines.
Alessandro* —Scribe for King Pedro of Aragon.
Angels —Band of thugs supported by Bishop Foulques in Toulouse.
Armand Gauthier* —Provost of the Abbey at Citeaux.
Arnaud Aumery —Abbot of the Cistercian Monastery of Citeaux and spiritual leader of the Crusade.
Arnulf* —A Falcon.
Beatrice of Albi* —Cathar Perfect and John's teacher.
Bertrand* —Brigand leader.
Dario* —Mysterious artist from Languedoc who drew the new cathedrals being built in the north.
Diogenes* —Hermit living in the hills above Plovdiv.
Dominic Guzman —Travelling priest and preacher. Now known as St. Dominic, founder of the Dominicans and the formal Inquisition. The first nunnery he founded was a copy of a Cathar Perfect House.
Esclarmonde —Raymond Roger's sister and a famous Cathar Perfect.
Eudes III —Duke of Burgundy, Knight of the Crusade.
Fernando-del-Huesca* —Knight who fought on the Moorish side in Al-Andalus.
Foulques —Bishop of Toulouse.
Francesco —St. Francis of Assisi.
Henri* —Monk who works for Arnaud Aumery
Herodotus —Roman historian.
Herve de Donzy —Count of Nevers, Knight of the Crusade.
Innocent III —Pope who called for the Crusade against the Cathar heretics.
Isabella* —Friend of Peter and John in Toulouse.
Jacques* —A spy for Adso and Bertrand.
John* —Boy who gets caught up in the war.
Lucius* —Ancient Roman author.
Marcus Britannicus* —Roman villa owner in Languedoc.
Marie* —One of John and Peter's friends.
Mother Marie* —Abbess of the Priory of St. Anne in Toulouse. She taught John and Peter to read and write.
Muhammad an-Nasir —Caliph of Al-Andalus.
Nasir al-Din* —Librarian at Madinat al-Zahra.

Nicodemus*—Eastern Orthodox monk.
Oddo of Saxony*—Mercenary soldier in the Crusader army and leader of a band called the Falcons.
Olivier*—Abbot of St. Gilles.
Origen—Early church father whose ideas were later rejected.
Paulus*—A merchant.
Pedro II—King of Aragon and Count of Barcelona.
Peire*—Soldier in the Crusader army.
Peter*—John's childhood friend.
Philip*—Cistercian lay brother with the Crusader army.
Pierre of Castelnau—Papal Legate to Languedoc.
Pierre des Vaux de Cernay—Catholic chronicaller of the crusade
Raymond of Toulouse—Count of Languedoc and, before the Crusade, the equal in standing to the King of France.
Raymond Roger—Count of Foix.
Roger Trenceval—Viscount of Carcassonne and Béziers. Liege to Raymond of Toulouse.
Shabaka*—Freed Nubian slave.
Simon de Montfort—Landless lord who took over the Crusade in exchange for the lands he could conquer. His youngest son, also called Simon, is credited with calling the first parliament in England.
Stephen*—Boy who grew up in Minerve.
Ugolini di Conti—Cardinal in Rome and the future Pope Gregory IX. Supporter of Francesco.
Umar of Cordova*—Half Moorish Cathar Perfect.
William of Arles*—Troubadour
William Belibaste—The last known Cathar Perfect.
William of Minerve—Lord of Minerve.

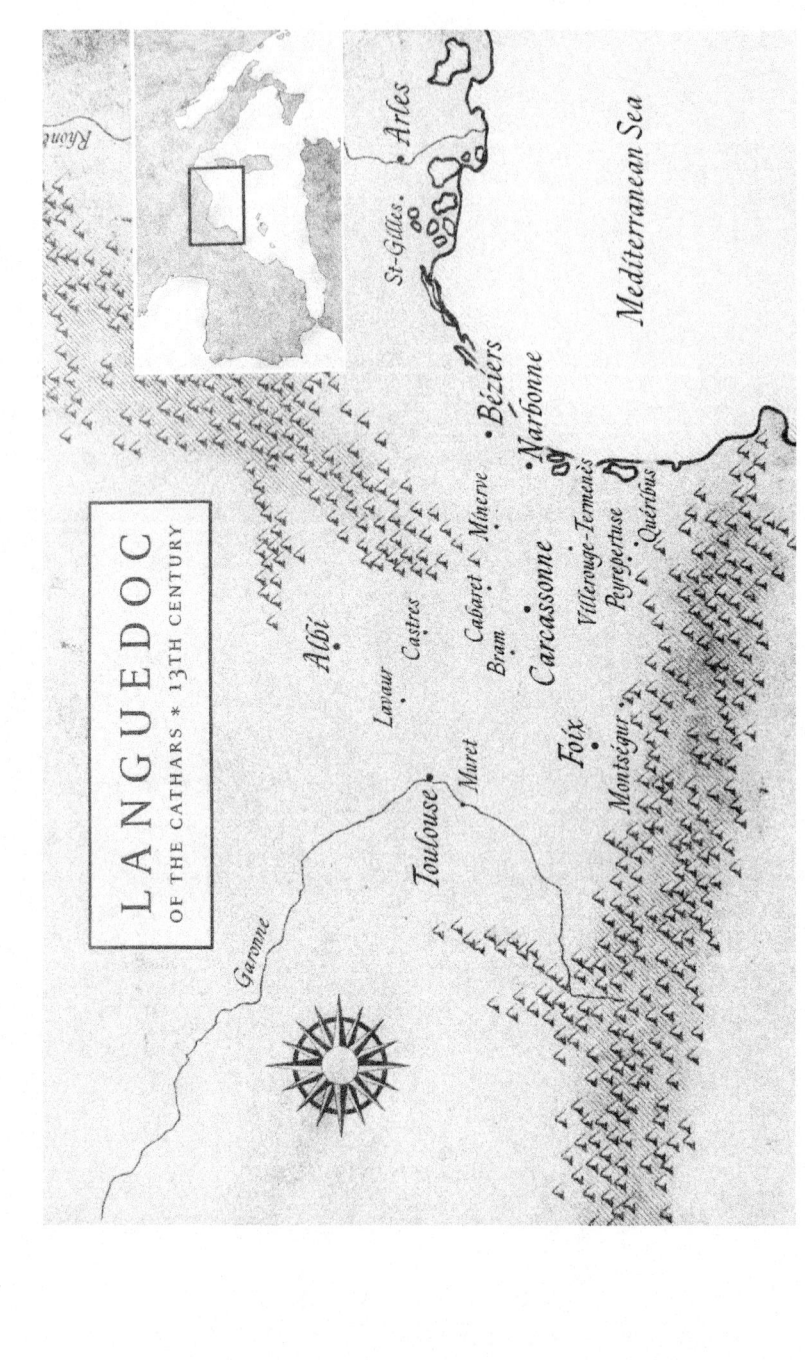

Book I
Heretic

Fire
1321

The Last Heretic

Villerouge-Termenès
August 24

"You will be the last to die," the black-clad priest said almost gleefully. "There are no more. Once you are dust, this land will be free from your foul heresy."

William Bélibaste forced his shattered mouth into a parody of a smile. "What you say, Master Inquisitor, may be true," he slurred, "but it has taken all the might of the Catholic Church more than one hundred years to kill a few thousand of us. Does that not show you the power of our ideas? When you examine your mind, is there not a tiny piece that says, 'Perhaps they were right?'"

The priest shook his head. "A hundred years is but a blink in God's eternity."

"And the momentary pain I face is nothing compared to the paradise to which I go. It is you I pity, facing endless repetitions of an ignorant life in the cesspit of this material world."

"We shall see what your pity is worth on the bonfire," the priest responded, angrily pushing Bélibaste forward through the archway into the bright courtyard of the castle at Villerouge-Termenès.

Bélibaste squinted in the sharp light, closed his eyes and raised his head to feel the sun's warmth on his face. He drew in a deep draft of air and caught a faint smell of lavender. It reminded him of his childhood, tending his father's flock of sheep among the limestone hills around his village. They had been happy days, before a life of loneliness, running and hiding. But he was content now, too.

If William had one regret, it was that he had not lived one hundred and fifteen years ago, before the armoured knights of the crusade and their compassionless inquisitor priests had thundered down on his people. It was difficult to imagine those wonderful days when men and women of the Elect could walk openly, meet and minister to their congregations; when they were welcomed everywhere, from the simplest village hearth to the court of the most powerful lord. It must have been as close as this evil, corrupt world had ever come to paradise. But it was a vanished world. The priest was right: William Bélibaste *was* the last of the Elect.

A push in the small of his back brought William back to the present. He opened his eyes to see the stake in front of him, surrounded by neatly tied bundles of dry logs, straw and vine cuttings. To one side, a hooded executioner stood holding a burning torch.

William stumbled on the rough cobbles, not through fear, but because his crushed left foot was twisted in at an awkward angle. Every hobbling step sent needles of pain shooting up his leg, but he would not give the priest or the watching crowd the satisfaction of showing it. He wore a coarse woollen tunic that stretched from his neck to his ankles and hid the livid scars where red-hot irons had seared his flesh. His arms were tied behind his back, but there was no need—both his shoulders had been so seriously dislocated that, even had his arms been free, he would not have had the strength to lift a spoon and feed himself. William also suspected that several of his fingers were broken.

As William approached the pyre, he was intrigued to see that the builders had thoughtfully shaped the bundles of sticks into a short staircase up to the stake.

"Do you renounce Satan and all his ways?" the priest intoned.

"Of course I do," William said, through his broken teeth. "I renounce Satan and all this worldly filth. And I renounce Satan's minion in Rome—the Pope and his corrupt Church."

A gasp ran through the watching crowd.

"So you admit, as you face an eternity of the torments of hell, that you are a Cathar Perfect, and that you have led others into this abominable heresy?"

"You call us 'Cathars' and the Elect 'Perfects', but to ourselves we are simply Good Men and Good Women, struggling to bring light into this darkness."

William found strength as he spoke. He forced himself to stand taller and look his inquisitor in the eye. "Together, we are Good Christians, preserving the old ways and offering hope. Your degenerate Church is putrid at the heart. It offers nothing but suffering and damnation."

William raised his gaze to address the men and women gathered behind his questioner. "You think you eat the body of Christ at Communion? How big was this Christ that his body can feed so many?"

The crowd shifted uncomfortably, but William heard a choked laugh and saw a few heads nod in agreement.

"You bow and scrape to priests and cardinals who drown in the filth of the material world. How can they lead you to anything but depravity? You worship idols and—"

"Enough!" The inquisitor's voice cut William off. "Enough of this evil! The Holy Inquisition is done with this verminous devil. I place him in the hands of the secular authorities to do with as they see fit."

The Mayor of Villerouge-Termenès stepped forward nervously. He would rather not do this, but he had no choice. The Inquisition could investigate, but it could not condemn. Although that decision was left to the secular authorities, it would be a brave man who refused to do the Inquisition's bidding.

"For the crimes of heresy, denying the divinity of Christ, consorting with devils, and seducing others into your evil ways, I sentence you, William Bélibaste, to death by burning."

Two men stepped forward and half led, half carried William up the pyre to the stake. There they bound him around the waist and chest so that he remained upright.

The men hurried down, leaving William alone.

"I shall pray for your misguided soul," the inquisitor intoned.

"And I yours," William replied.

The mayor nodded to the executioner, who walked around the pyre, thrusting his torch in among the dry kindling. Tiny yellow flames grasped eagerly at the straw and grew. They turned orange as they began to eat at the sticks.

William shivered. He began to recite the only prayer the Elect recognized.

Our Father who art in Heaven,

The flames gathered strength and moved toward William's feet.

Hallowed be Thy name.

His feet were burning, the skin blistering, the pain shooting up his legs.

Thy kingdom come,

The inquisitor's mouth was moving in prayer, but William heard only his own voice and the crackling of the hungry flames.

thy will be done on earth as it is in Heaven.

The pain moved higher as his robe burned. Searing, blinding pain.

Give us this day our supplementary bread,

William concentrated with all his might. The pain was transitory. It would pass. It *would* pass.

and remit our debts as we forgive our debtors.

William knew what he had to do. It had been drummed into every member of the Elect. He must wait and endure the agony as long as possible. And then, when the pain became too great, he had to breathe in the fire as deeply as he could. That would hasten the end.

And keep us from temptation

The bright flames raced hungrily up William's body.

and free us from evil.

His hair was alight.

Thine is the kingdom,

He closed his eyes and threw his head back.

the power and glory

Wait! he told himself.

William's heart was racing.

Wait!

He had stopped sweating and felt oddly cold.

Wait!

The agony engulfed him.

for ever and ever.

Wait!

Amen.

William thrust his head forward into the flames and drew them into his body with a single deep breath. The shock stopped his heart and he slumped forward. The charred ropes holding him upright gave way and his body collapsed into the roaring heart of the fire. The crusaders and the Inquisition had won—the last of the Elect was dead.

PART ONE
Old Friends

Debate

Toulouse
August 15, 1206

"That was as much fun as watching a group of travelling players," John said with a laugh. "Bishop Foulques is such a fool, it's not surprising that the Cathars won."

John and Peter stood in the square in front of the imposing bulk of St. Sernin Cathedral in Toulouse. It was August 15, the feast of the Assumption of the Virgin Mary, the day when Christ's mother ascended, body and soul, into heaven, and there was a party atmosphere in the air. It had been a hot day, and although the sun had already dipped behind the surrounding buildings, heat still radiated uncomfortably from the uneven cobbles underfoot. People stood in small knots, animatedly discussing the debate that had just finished in the cathedral. Pairs of black-robed Cathar Perfects, both men and women, strolled through the crowds, stopping to talk to those who hailed them.

"The point is not to have fun," Peter replied, staring seriously at the cathedral, "and it's not a question of winning or losing. Only God can win."

John looked hard at his friend. Lately, it had become almost impossible to have a light-hearted conversation with him. Peter took everything John said so seriously, and he seemed to have suddenly developed a certainty that he knew better than John what God wanted.

John shrugged. He wasn't going to let Peter's new-found pomposity spoil his fun on his favourite feast day. "All right," John conceded, "the debate was a serious matter, but even you must admit that the Cathars were a lot more popular with the audience."

"Popularity is fleeting. Souls are eternal, and it is *their* well-being that the Church must address."

"Of course the Church must look after our souls," said John, stifling a sigh of frustration, "but must it not also win over the mass of the people to convince them that it *can* save their souls?"

"You think too much of what happens in this world, John." Peter turned and looked gravely at his friend. "It's the next world that's important. Look at all the time you spend on your drawing. Where does it get you?"

"What's wrong with my drawing?" John asked indignantly.

"Art is only important as a way to glorify God," Peter said, his voice taking on a lecturing tone. "Look at the magnificent golden paintings of the saints in the cathedral."

"But they're not real! They have no depth, no life." John could feel himself growing angry. It was one thing to disagree over the debate, quite another for Peter to criticize the thing John loved more than anything. Peter opened his mouth to object, but John held up his hand and continued. "I agree that art in the great cathedrals should glorify God, but why can't that be done with realistic paintings?"

"Because God does not wish it," Peter said, his eyes gleaming with conviction. "He does not want us to dwell on this world, but to give our minds over to contemplation of the next."

John shook his head in annoyance.

"Look at all the hours you have wasted trying to draw things," Peter went on, oblivious to the irritation he was causing. "You've learned nothing! Your sketches of animals, people and buildings are just the same as they were when you began years ago. And why? Because God does not wish you to draw these things. If you want to be an artist, then accept the way things are done and work to glorify God."

John took a deep breath. Losing his temper wasn't going to help, and he did want Peter to grasp what was important to him about his drawing. "I don't understand why God does not wish me to draw more realistically. Surely I can glorify Him that way, too! Imagine—paintings that showed the Crucifixion, the Annunciation, or the lives of the saints realistically, as they actually were. Would that not amaze people and draw them even closer to God?"

"It's the same as these Cathars trying to make themselves popular with the people," Peter said, ignoring the rising excitement in his friend's voice. "Only God matters and, obviously, He does not want you, or anyone else, to draw the way you imagine must be possible."

"Then why did God give us the power to think and the free will to try new things?" John asked, struggling to make Peter see. "Surely it is partly to find new and better ways to glorify Him. Look at the cathedral." He waved his hand to indicate the west front of St. Sernin. The wall that loomed over the square was plain and unornamented except for a round window and two doors, deeply set into the thick walls. "It looks like a fortress. The walls are plain and must be the thickness of a man lying down."

"The inside is painted to glorify God," Peter objected.

"Exactly, and you can barely see the art because the windows are so small."

"You know it has to be that way. The walls must be thick to support the roof and to put in more windows would weaken the walls. Do you want the roof to crash down on our heads as we pray?"

"Of course not," John said, forcing himself to stay calm and develop his argument, "but I hear stories of churches that are being built to the north—churches where impossibly thin columns soar upward with nothing more substantial between them than coloured glass. Surely God must be happier with all His light flooding in to illuminate the paintings that glorify Him?"

"Indeed," Peter said in a puzzled tone, "but what does any of this have to do with your scribbling?"

"Things change," John explained patiently. "One day, someone, somewhere, decided that the old way of building churches wasn't good enough. He thought and worked and planned until he came up with this new way of building churches and glorifying God. A way that allowed more light in to illuminate the paintings inside. That's exactly what I want to do—find a new way of doing things, a better way to draw and paint."

The two boys fell silent. John wondered how they had grown so far apart. For thirteen years, they had been as inseparable as twins. Neither had known his parents and both had been abandoned as infants, only weeks apart, on the steps of the Priory of St. Anne. Whether their parents had died in one of the fever epidemics that regularly swept through the overcrowded streets of St. Cyprian, beneath the towering walls of Toulouse, or whether they had given their child up because it was simply one mouth too many to feed, no one knew.

The boys had grown up together, playing, studying and dreaming, under the care of the old abbess, Mother Marie. She had taken to the pair and decided to teach them both the rudiments of reading and writing in hopes that they might seek a life of devotion in the Church. It had worked well enough with Peter—who saw knowledge only as a tool, a way to advance in the world—but with John, her teaching had unexpected results.

The more John learned, the more he wanted to learn. He craved knowledge for its own sake. For him, knowledge brought one closer to truth and, therefore, to God. John didn't think the Church should limit knowledge. It should be available to everyone.

In the days when the friends could discuss things without annoying each other, John had been fond of quoting Peter Abelard, who had written that doubting was good because it encouraged enquiry and enquiry led to truth.

Peter would counter with Anselm of Canterbury, who said that belief was more important than doubting because only through belief could someone understand. They had laughed about it and joked that one day Peter would be Pope in Rome, and John would be his advisor on all matters complex and arcane. But now, with Peter's growing certainty that he knew God's wishes, John doubted if his friend would need any advisors at all.

"If God is stopping me learning how to draw realistically," John said, breaking the silence, "why didn't He also give the bishop and the priest arguments this afternoon that would have convinced the people? Then the Cathar Perfects would have been defeated, and everyone would now be standing out here glorifying God."

"I don't know," Peter said with a frown. "God does, sometimes, work in mysterious ways. Perhaps he is testing us. Perhaps—"

The boys' discussion was interrupted by a commotion at the cathedral doors—the Church delegation was leaving. They were led by Foulques, Bishop of Toulouse, surrounded by fawning priests and lay brothers. Foulques was a fat man and beads of sweat glistened on his plump cheeks and forehead in the late afternoon heat. His large body was completely covered in sumptuous robes, richly embroidered with silver and gold thread. His jewel-encrusted mitre sparked in the dying light.

As Foulques appeared on the steps, a ragged cheer rose from a crowd of rough-looking men standing to one side. A few of them were dressed in dirty white robes with black crosses crudely drawn on the front. Foulques acknowledged them with a half smile and a nod.

"That must be one of God's more mysterious ways," John said, looking at the men. "For a bishop of the Church to control a bunch of thugs who wander the streets robbing and beating up whomever they choose—and call them Angels—is a disgrace."

"His intention, to control heresy, is commendable," Peter said, "but I agree his lack of control over them *is* a disgrace."

Foulques had been appalling in the debate. The fat man had blustered mightily all afternoon, but had not said anything intelligent. He'd misunderstood what the quieter, thoughtful Cathars had said and had had no reply to their reasoned arguments.

Much more effective had been the short, scrawny, olive-skinned priest who stood on the cathedral steps in Foulques' shadow. He was dressed, like the Perfects, in a simple black robe that was travel-worn and stained. He was bare-headed, wore practical walking sandals, and held a knotted staff in his left hand. He was surrounded by a small group of similarly dressed priests.

The man's name was Dominic Guzman and, in a voice heavily accented with his native Castillian, he had held his own against the Perfects. Foulques' rants were always made against a murmur of background conversation, but when Guzman spoke, silence fell over the audience. He had argued for a return to the uncomplicated life of the early Church and for orders of itinerant priests who would own nothing and wander the land, as he did, preaching to the people.

It was similar to what the Perfects did, and John could see that the idea resonated with the people much more strongly than Foulques' overblown bluster and rich life.

The debate, like the many others that were being held all over Languedoc these days, had been inconclusive. Neither side had convinced the other of its point of view. In the end, though, John knew that the Catholic Church would view it as a defeat. It was they, after all, who were trying to eradicate the Cathar religion. The Perfects were happy to merely carry on the way they always had.

Foulques waved to the crowd, which largely ignored him, and swept down the steps toward his ornate litter as Dominic Guzman quietly disappeared into the gathering gloom of the narrow streets surrounding the cathedral.

John noticed that Peter's eyes had been following Guzman, not Foulques.

"He's quite an extraordinary man," John said. "It must be very hard to live the life of itinerant poverty that he is sworn to. And he has a power when he speaks that makes people listen."

Peter absently nodded agreement.

"In fact," John continued, "Guzman lives his life much like the Cathar Perfects."

Peter turned to John, ready to argue, but stopped when he saw his friend's mischievous smile. "You say these things just to annoy me," he said, his expression softening.

"I do," John admitted. "There's so much we don't know in this world—how can we take it too seriously? I know you don't think fun is important in God's grand scheme of things, but let's not argue about it. We've been friends all our lives. Let's not lose that just because we have different ideas."

"You're right," Peter said with a weak smile. "Our friendship's important to me, too."

"Good," John said, clapping his friend on the back. "Now let's go over to the Château Narbonnaise. Count Raymond and Countess Eleanor have invited the troubadour from Arles to perform tonight in the square."

Peter didn't answer right away, and John could see the doubt written on his face. Peter didn't like troubadours. He thought their love songs frivolous, and the jokes they sometimes made about the Church annoyed him. But

John didn't want to end the evening with their argument still fresh in their minds.

"It will be one of the last times we will all be together," John encouraged. "Adam leaves in a few days for the court at Foix and Marie is betrothed to that dolt down in Carcassonne. We are all at an age when the world beckons and life will allow few enough opportunities to continue the carefree days of this summer."

Peter looked uncertain.

"And Isabella will be there," John added, teasingly. "You know she never misses a troubadour."

A smile flashed across Peter's face, and John knew that his words had hit their mark. Isabella was one of Countess Eleanor's attendants. She was the same age as the boys and often spent time with them and their friends, singing or playing games. Like Dominic Guzman, she was from across the mountains and had the dark eyes and olive skin of her people. Peter was totally smitten. Whenever the crowd of friends got together, Peter gravitated toward Isabella and engaged her in conversation. He always tried to partner her in the board games they played.

John thought it a very odd match. Isabella was high-spirited—always laughing at some joke or clever song or listening with interest to the stories John told—and she was very beautiful, with a high forehead and long dark hair that she wore in elaborate styles or simply tumbling down over her shoulders.

In contrast, Peter was serious and often missed the point of jokes—and no one had ever called him handsome. He was tall and gangly, like a tree that has sprouted too fast, all angles and sharp corners. His face was long and thin and his pale skin seemed to be drawn too tightly over his skull; his high cheekbones made his eyes appear deep-set and worried. John used to tease his friend that God had run out of flesh and bone when he made Peter and had to fall back on sticks and string. But whatever the reason, John was pleased at the feelings his friend had for Isabella. Perhaps her sense of humour and exuberance might act as a balance against Peter's increasing religious certainty.

The mention of Isabella had the desired effect. "All right," Peter said, "I'll come with you, but I'm not going to stay late."

John laughed at his friend's transparency as they set off through the darkening streets.

* * *

The huge square was a riot of sights, sounds and smells. Everyone seemed to be dressed in their brightest clothes, and colourful banners almost covered the red brick walls of the Château Narbonnaise, where Count Raymond and Eleanor lived and held court. Anyone who thought they could make a few sous from the feast-day crowds was there. Jugglers and acrobats performed wherever there was a foot or two of empty space; vendors with trays of food, trinkets and rolls of garish cloth worked the crowd, screaming the benefits of their wares to anyone who would listen; and fortune tellers, beggars and musicians struggled mightily to make themselves heard over the background noise. In one corner, a ragged, mangy bear danced lethargically on the end of a chain while its owner cracked a short whip and small boys darted as close as they dared to taunt it.

Near the centre of the square, three entire pigs—a feast-day gift to the people from Count Raymond—roasted on spits, their fat dripping and sizzling onto the wide bed of deep-red glowing coals beneath. A large, sweating man in a bloodstained leather apron busily carved slices of meat and passed them out to the crowd. A nearby table groaned under the weight of a pile of spiced loaves in a bewildering variety of shapes and colours. John breathed deeply. The delicious smell of roast pig and freshly baked bread filled the air, almost covering the pungent odour of hundreds of sweating, unwashed people.

"Come on," John said, his mouth watering, "let's get something to eat." Pushing through the seething mass of humanity, he led the way to the roasting pit and accepted a large, greasy slice of meat and a hunk of green parsley loaf. Barely waiting for the meat to cool and oblivious to the fat running down his wrists and dripping into his clothes, John tore off chunks with relish as he headed out to the less busy fringes of the crowd. Working more neatly and slowly, Peter followed him.

John had almost finished his meat and bread, and was looking around for some beer or watered wine to wash them down, when a cheer from the crowd made him turn. The troubadour and his musicians were strolling out onto the wide platform at the top of the steps leading up to the doors of the château. On the flag-draped balcony above the musicians, Count Raymond and Countess Eleanor, dressed in all their finery, stood smiling amid their almost equally colourful courtiers.

William of Arles, a short, skinny, middle-aged man with a mop of straggly light-brown hair, was dressed in a bright, multi-coloured tunic that sported wide cuffs and ended below his knees in a ragged fringe. He wore blue boots of soft leather with tiny golden bells sewn around the tops. Other bells, on the edges of his tunic, tinkled lightly as he moved to the centre of the platform. He carried a tambourine.

Four musicians milled around the troubadour, dressed identically in bright green tunics and caps with flaps that hung down over their ears. One played a flute, one the bagpipes, one the tabor drum and the last turned the handle of a hurdy-gurdy.

"Welcome my lord and lady," William said, bowing to the group on the balcony. Raymond acknowledged him with a nod. "And to you, good folk." The troubadour turned to the crowd, who responded with an enthusiastic shout. "I trust that you are in a mood to be entertained." Another shout. "And I hope my songs and stories will be worthy of your time."

The troubadour's voice was high-pitched and carried well over the hubbub of the crowd. "I am William of Arles, here with my companions to transport you on this fine summer's eve with tales of knights and ladies, war and peace, love and death. And"—William leaned forward conspiratorially and jerked his thumb over his shoulder toward Count Raymond on his balcony—"the foibles of the high and mighty." Laughter rolled around the square. "But first," William stood straight and banged the tambourine against his thigh, "I will sing of the troubadours."

The musicians set to work and William began to sing, all the while dancing lightly from foot to foot:

"I sing of the glorious troubadours
And the wonderful styles they espouse.
There's Roger of Bram
A most wonderful man—"

One of the musicians to William's left interrupted with

"Like an oyster dried out in the sun."

As the crowd laughed, William turned theatrically and glared at his companion, who affected to look as innocent as possible.

William continued:

"There's Bernard of Nime
Of most hearty esteem—"

Again the musician interrupted:

"With a voice like a young piglet's squeal."

William glared once more. And so it went on, William introducing every well-known troubadour of the day, only to be interrupted by a rude comment from the musician. The crowd was delighted at the insults and, during one of William's glaring pauses, someone shouted, "What of William of Arles?"

William looked at the crowd. "I see you have impeccable taste," he said, smiling and giving a mock bow.

"This William of Arles.
The master of all—"

He stopped and stared pointedly at the troublesome musician who stayed silent this time and worked extremely hard at playing his instrument. William continued:

"He plays with such skill,
That the valley and hill,
Both resound with the sound of his music.
His verse is so sharp,
When accompanied by harp,
That his listeners are held in a thrall.
His voice, I've heard tell
Is as clear as a bell—"

The musician jumped forward:

"Like a frog that is trapped in a well."

The crowd roared its approval as William chased the musician around the courtyard, brandishing his tambourine.

"Look," Peter said, grasping John's arm and interrupting his laughter. "There's Isabella and the others. Let's join them."

The pair worked their way through the crowd until they joined their friends on the steps in front of a small church on the opposite side of the square. As they approached, Isabella looked up, smiled broadly at John and pushed the boy beside her over to make space. John smiled back, thinking as he did so that someone as beautiful as Isabella should be dressed in finery and sitting beside some great lord in a palace instead of being a handmaid who hung around with the likes of him and his friends.

John stepped aside to let Peter take the seat. He thought he saw a flash of disappointment cross Isabella's features before Adam, on the top step, shouted to him, "John, come and tell us of the debate. Did Foulques make a fool of himself?"

"He did," John said as squeezed in beside the others, "and he had a gang of his Angels with him."

"Those thugs," Adam said. "Raymond should do something about them."

"He should," John agreed, "but for all his corruption, Foulques is a powerful man. He manages to keep in with the Pope. There are many Cathars in Toulouse. Raymond has to be careful."

"I suppose, but we're a long way from Rome. Does the Pope really care what happens here?"

"He sends enough priests and legates to debate with the Cathars," John said.

"But that's just words," Adam said with a frown. "He'd never actually do anything."

"You're probably right," John said. He was tired of talking about debates and Popes. He just wanted to eat, drink and enjoy the evening. He looked down. Isabella, her expression very serious, was talking earnestly to an unhappy Peter. John wondered what was going on.

Across the square, William of Arles and the musicians were launching into a spirited rendition of the epic "Song of Roland and the Battle of Ronceval."

> *"Charlemagne, our lord and sovereign,*
> *Full seven years hath sojourned in Andalus,*
> *Conquered the land, and won the western main,*
> *Now no fortress against him doth remain,*
> *No city walls are left for him to gain."*

John was getting drawn into the troubadour's tale when he felt Adam fidgeting beside him. He turned his head and noticed his friend staring down at Peter. John followed Adam's gaze, half expecting to see Peter and Isabella in the midst of an argument. Instead, he saw Peter twisted round and staring up at them, his mouth open, his face pale and his eyes wide in horror.

"What's the matter?" John asked, suddenly alarmed.

Peter ignored his friend and continued to stare. Slowly he raised his arm and pointed a skinny, shaking finger at a spot above John's head. "Look," he managed to croak out.

John spun round, half expecting to see a gang of Foulques' Angels bearing down on him, but there was nothing behind him except the doors of the church and a few people watching the entertainment.

"What is it, Peter?" he asked, turning back.

"Don't you see them?" Peter gasped. "One stands behind each of you."

Now everyone glanced nervously over their shoulders.

"There's no one there," John said, as calmly as he could.

"It is Death that stands behind you all," Peter said. "Each wears a cloak of grave clothes and carries a scythe and an hourglass. Can't you see them?"

John shook his head.

"See! They remove their cowls—skulls, grinning—and they look at me. What does it mean? Am I to die this hour?" Peter shivered violently. "I am so cold."

John leaned forward to comfort his friend, but Peter drew back and turned to Isabella.

"Do *you* see them?" he asked.

Isabella shook her head, as puzzled as the rest.

"What do they mean?" Peter asked again. "If only I can see, it must be that..." His voice tailed off. His lips were trembling and beads of sweat had broken out on his forehead. For the little group on the stairs, the sound of the crowd's chatter and the troubadour's singing seemed very far away.

Peter continued to stare at Isabella, whose worried frown had turned to a look of fear.

"What is happening, Peter?" she asked. "Why do you stare at me so?"

Peter slowly drew back, his hands clenching and unclenching convulsively.

"Your face..." he began. "The flesh..." Peter struggled to find words. "Rotting. The grave opens." His mouth hung open, and drool spilled down his chin.

"Oh, God! Oh, God!" he exclaimed at last, waving his arms as if trying to push Isabella away. "The worms!"

With a sudden violent lurch, Peter attempted to stand, but his co-ordination was poor. He tumbled down the steps, bumping into the legs of a group of young men standing at the bottom. They all cursed, and one aimed a kick at him. The boy ignored them and, struggling to his feet, pushed his way through the crowd, heedless of the curses that accompanied him.

Peter's progress across the square was easy to follow thanks to the disruption it caused. Eventually, even the troubadour and his musicians noticed, but they were professionals and used to disturbances in their audience.

John stood up and glanced at Isabella. Stunned, she stared up at John, her eyes wide and questioning. A desire to go and comfort her swept over John, but he pushed it back. His friend needed him more.

John followed Peter to the far side of the square, where he sat on the bottom step of the Château Narbonnaise, to the right of the musicians, arms wrapped around his knees. He rocked rhythmically back and forth, and low moans accompanied his movements. John sat beside his friend and placed an arm around his shoulder.

For a long time the boys sat in silence, letting the song of Roland's final battle wash over them.

"Marvellous is the battle in its speed,
The Franks there strike with vigour and with heat,
Cutting through wrists and ribs and chines indeed,
Through garments to the lively flesh beneath;
On the green grass the clear blood runs in streams."

Eventually, Peter stopped his rocking and calmed down.

"What happened?" John asked.

"I saw Death." Peter lifted his pale face to look at John. "I am to die. He was a hideous skeleton and stood behind each of you!"

"That doesn't mean that *you* are to die," John said, trying to comfort his frightened friend. "It simply means we will all die eventually."

"Yes," Peter replied. "Death stands behind us all, and eternal suffering awaits our immortal souls. We play and frolic without a care, but we are all damned."

John could not have disagreed more with Peter's grim view of the world, but he kept silent. It was not the time to argue.

"But then I looked on Isabella." A violent shudder passed through Peter's body. With a great effort, he went on. "She's so beautiful! I suppose I hoped her beauty would chase away my visions."

"What did you see?" John encouraged, gently.

"It worked! I looked at her face—her smooth skin, high forehead, that wonderful half smile she always wears, as if there is some joke we cannot understand—and I felt calmer. She is the most beautiful thing I have ever seen, a true angel. But then it happened."

Peter took a deep breath and continued. "Her face began to change. The glowing, smooth skin became grey and pocked with rot, the hair lank and the flesh sagging. Before my eyes, the beautiful creature of my dreams decayed—the flesh fell from her, bones thrust through her skin and maggots and grave worms crawled from her blank eye sockets and lipless mouth. She faced me—a corpse from the grave—as she would be on the Day of Judgment."

Peter looked down, and John saw tears on his cheeks. He tightened his grip on his friend's shoulder. He didn't know what to say. He'd heard of hermits and priests having visions, and he knew the stories of St. Anthony's temptations, but he'd never had a vision himself, nor witnessed a person having one. The power of what Peter had seen, or thought he'd seen, was frightening.

Gradually, John became aware of a shadow above him. Half expecting to see the cowled figure of Death, he looked up. William of Arles had moved along the steps until he stood looking down at John and Peter. He was still singing, but the "Song of Roland" was drawing to a close.

"The Count Roland, beneath a pine he sits,
Turning his eyes toward Andalus, he begins
Remembering so many lands where he went conquering.
And Charlemagne, his lord who nourished him.

He cannot help but weep and sigh at this.
He owns his faults, and God's forgiveness bids.
Over his arm his head bows down and slips,
He joins his hands: and so is life finish'd.
Roland is dead; his soul to heav'n God bare."

With a final stare in John's direction, the troubadour danced away.

Peter sniffed loudly and looked up. "I know what I must do," he announced.

"What?"

"I must give myself to God." Peter grabbed John's tunic and stared into his eyes. His expression was almost pleading. "I see it now. We have a choice: transient earthly pleasure or eternal heavenly bliss. Earthly pleasure is easy and seductive"—for a moment, Peter looked uncertain, then his expression hardened—"but eternal bliss must be our goal. I shall become a monk this very night."

John had often thought that Peter might enter the Church, and the time was certainly coming for all of them to make decisions about how they would find their way in life, but the abruptness of his friend's pronouncement, and the frightening way it had come about, shocked John.

Peter made a move to stand, but John held him down.

"A monk? Now? Is there no middle way? Your vision, or whatever it was, is over! Come back to our friends. They'll support you. The evening's young. We'll play some games and tell jokes. An evening of fun and a good night's rest, and these strange occurrences will seem different in the morning."

"No!" Peter tore himself from John's grasp. "You don't understand! Death was telling me there is little time. I must go and pray."

Looking about wildly, Peter rose and stumbled up the steps onto the platform where William was finishing his song. Oblivious to the gestures of the musicians or the shouts of the crowd, Peter crossed the stage and disappeared into the darkness at the edge of the square. John sat and watched him go. He thought of following his friend, but had no idea what he would say.

"Your friend looked distressed." John looked around to see William of Arles beside him. The public performance was over now and the musicians were moving toward the château, where they were to perform later at Count Raymond's dinner.

"He is," John said. "He has had disturbing visions."

"Tell me," the troubadour asked, gathering his multicoloured tunic and sitting beside John.

"Why should you care?" John asked, slightly annoyed that the man saw fit to barge in on his private worries.

William laughed. "Because I am a troubadour and am interested in the world I wander through. I don't sing only of nonsense about my colleagues and of ancient battles. I pass on news as I travel and tell tales of our world, its troubles and its stupidities. We live in unsettled and dangerous times. Many have visions and, if you are willing to share, I would learn your friend's."

John thought for a while. It was an odd request from someone he didn't know, but John instinctively liked William and his thin open face and easy manner. Besides, maybe if he told someone about Peter's strange behaviour, it might make more sense.

William listened intently and, when John finished, nodded gravely. "I thank you for sharing your friend's distress," he said. "There is much that is strange and worrisome in our land today. God seems to be coming down to interfere in our daily lives more often of late." William stood to leave as he spoke, but John had questions of his own.

"So you will turn Peter's story into a song and sing it on your travels?"

"Perhaps. Or I may incorporate it into a larger tale of visions and troublesome occurrences."

"You're a storyteller as well as a troubadour?"

"They are the same," William said with a smile. "It is simply that some of my stories are put to music."

"You must see some fascinating places on your travels."

William tilted his head and regarded John carefully. "I see many wonders and I see many different places that are all the same. You wish to travel?"

"More than anything."

"It is a hard life. You forsake home and hearth for uncertainty and discomfort, not to mention the dangers of the road. Why would you seek that?"

"I wish to know everything."

William laughed loudly. "Youth has the arrogance of gods!"

John felt his cheeks burn with indignation. "You mock me!"

"No! No." William held up his hands in supplication. "I am sorry. I intend no mockery. Tell me, why do you wish to learn so much?"

"Because I cannot escape the idea that the world is more complicated than the priests would have us believe. I wish to see for myself, to read books, to talk to wise men and women but, mostly, I want to draw."

"To draw? That at least is easy. Simply enter St. Sernin and copy the paintings until you can do them as well as the original artist."

"You don't understand." John shook his head. "I wish to show the world as it is, not as the priests wish it to be. I want to be able to look at a drawing or painting and feel that I could walk into it and live the scene I see."

"That is a tall order, indeed."

"I know. And that is why I must travel, and learn everything."

This time, William did not laugh. Instead, he looked thoughtfully at the boy on the steps before him. John was beginning to squirm uncomfortably under the man's gaze when the troubadour finally spoke.

"What of your family? What do they think of your wish to desert them for learning?"

"I have no family. I was taken in at the Priory of St. Anne when I was but an infant. Mother Marie and the nuns are my only family, but I am of an age where I must leave and find my own way in the world."

"Very well," William said, after another pause. "You seem an intelligent boy and you did tell the tale of your friend with some talent and wit.

"I and my musicians leave from the Narbonnaise Gate tomorrow at cock crow. Think on what you wish tonight and, if you are there, you may accompany us and see how you like the itinerant life. It will be hard. I will make you work and, if you are troublesome or do not earn your keep, I will abandon you as easily as I would discard a worn out shoe. You will sleep rough in fields when we can find no benefactor and there will be times when you will wonder at your sanity for undertaking this life, but you will meet a multitude of interesting people, learn the art of storytelling and have ample opportunity in the places we stay to search out wisdom in men's minds or in their books. And perhaps, when you are a famous artist, you will do me the honour of portraying me with such skill that people will wonder at my immortality!"

John stared at William in shock. The troubadour's offer had taken him completely by surprise. Yes, he wanted to travel, but leaving tomorrow? Peter, he might already have lost, but saying such a sudden goodbye to all his friends—to Adam, Isabella and the others, to Mother Marie and the Priory where he grew up? To leave Toulouse, the only place he had ever known, and go off into an uncertain world he knew nothing of? It was frightening.

"It's so sudden," John said.

"It is," William replied, "but sometimes life's opportunities are thrust at us. Some seize them, some do not. Perhaps your friend's visions are his opportunity. In any case, think on what you wish and meet me tomorrow—or not. For now, I must keep Count Raymond waiting no longer than necessary. I bid you good night."

William turned and walked toward the château, leaving John in a turmoil. He felt as if he were at a crossroads: the decision he made tonight would determine the rest of his life. John stood and looked across the square at his friends. They were talking to each other and fooling around. Only Isabella returned his stare, her brown eyes still serious with the memory of Peter's visions. John was about to go over and tell her what had happened when two other boys whirled her up and into a wild dance. John didn't feel at all like dancing, but he hoped the music and the movement would cheer Isabella. With a shrug, he set off in search of Peter. Deep within himself, a tiny kernel of joy was forming. John knew that when the cock crowed tomorrow, he would be at the Narbonnaise Gate.

PART TWO

Gathering Storms

Reunion

St. Gilles
January 13, 1208

"Peter!" John shouted as he ran down the arched corridor of the cloister, his leather shoes slapping loudly on the stone tiles. It had taken John a minute to recognize his friend dressed in the brown, sleeveless habit of a Cistercian lay brother and with his hair shaved in a tonsure, but there was no mistaking the gangly frame.

John threw his arms around Peter. "What have you been doing? Why are you here?"

Gradually, John became aware that his embrace was not being returned. He looked up. Peter seemed embarrassed. Several other lay brothers and a monk, in his white habit and black apron, stared disapprovingly.

"I'm sorry. It's been two years since I've seen my friend," John explained to the monk, thinking back on that last night in Toulouse. "I didn't mean to create a scene. I was surprised to meet him here, that's all."

"It's all right," Peter said, recovering his composure and smiling. "You took me by surprise, too. What are *you* doing here at St. Gilles?"

"I'm here with Count Raymond's delegation," John said proudly.

"You work for the count?"

"Not really," John admitted. "His nephew, Roger Trenceval, the Viscount of Carcassonne, brought me here as a scribe because I can write and read some Latin."

"The same reason I am here," Peter said.

John glanced at the nearby monk. "You are with the papal legates?"

"I am here to do God's work," said Peter. "As I hope you are? This Cathar heresy that has taken root *must* be eradicated. Count Raymond is much too soft on the heretics. It has angered His Holiness. The legates are here to see that Raymond undertakes his duty as a Christian and excises this evil canker from his lands. There are to be no more half measures."

John frowned. He'd heard that Peter had joined the Church after his disturbing visions in Toulouse, but this person before him sounded unbearably pompous and self-important. And why this extreme, violent hatred of the Cathars? John had never paid them much attention. They'd always been around, a part of Languedoc life as long as anyone could remember. True, they believed differently from most, and the Church disliked them, but there had never been any violence other than the occasional shouting match at a debate.

But perhaps Peter had to say these things when the priest was listening. "We must talk," John said quietly. "There's so much to catch up on! Can we go into the courtyard?"

Peter looked over at the monk and John followed his glance. The man was not attractive. He was short and rat-like with narrow features, a pointed nose and thin lips pulled into a permanent sneer. But what startled John most were the man's eyes. They were wide open and staring, like those of a corpse, John thought with a shudder. As John stared, the eyes blinked, but the action did nothing to change the effect. There was no expression, simply a penetrating glare that both accused and missed nothing. John was transfixed. To his relief, the monk blinked again and nodded almost imperceptibly to Peter.

"Thank you Father Aumery," Peter said as the monk turned and strode off down the corridor with the other lay brothers scuttling after.

"Let's talk. The meeting is not due to begin for some time." Peter led the way through a rounded arch into the small courtyard that lay against one wall of the Abbey Church of St. Gilles. It was square and surrounded by a colonnaded cloister. In the centre was a small fountain, and John and Peter sat on the low wall that surrounded it.

"Did you become a monk because of your vision that night?" John asked as soon as they were settled.

"No. For one thing, I'm not a monk yet, I'm just a lay brother. We do all the mundane work so that the legates can concentrate on prayer and doing God's will—but one day I hope to be fully ordained. And I didn't join the Cistercian brothers because of the visions, they were simply Christ's way of opening my eyes. I joined to glorify God and do His work."

John took a deep breath. He had hoped that Peter would relax once he was away from the monk, but he still seemed serious and distant, almost as if there were a curtain between them. The ease of their old friendship was gone.

"Did you stay in Toulouse?" John asked, resolving to stick with safe topics.

"For a year, yes. I studied at the brothers' house there."

"Did you see Mother Marie at the Priory? How is she?"

"She has gone to Christ," Peter said matter-of-factly. "She passed on about three months after you left."

"I'm sorry to hear that. She was a good woman." John felt a pang of sadness at the news. Mother Marie had been an extraordinarily gentle woman who'd gone out of her way to help John and Peter. They both owed whatever they had and might achieve to her.

"She rests with the Lord, awaiting the Judgment Day," Peter said.

John felt a momentary flash of anger, but he pushed it down. "And Isabella, how was she when last you met?"

Peter looked suddenly uncomfortable. "She is godless," he said.

"Godless?" This time, John could not hold back his feelings. "Is that not harsh? True, I could not see her joining Holy Orders, but godless? Did you talk with her after your visions?"

"I did not."

John frowned. It was odd that Peter, who had been so smitten with Isabella, should not have at least talked to her about the strange visions and his plans. John opened his mouth to question his friend further, but the expression on Peter's face made it clear than any more talk about Isabella would not be welcome.

"How did you get in with the papal legates?" John asked, changing the subject.

Finally, Peter smiled. "I was blessed to be introduced to Father Arnaud Aumery, the abbot of the monastery at Cîteaux, four months ago, when he stayed at the brother's house in Toulouse. He saw the spark of God in me and offered a chance to accompany him on his travels to convert the heretics."

"He has strange eyes," John commented.

"God has seen fit to give him such, yes," Peter continued, "but Father Aumery is a holy man, as is the senior legate, Pierre of Castelnau. Like yours, my reading and writing has proved of use, and I take notes that the legates use in their reports to Pope Innocent."

"You've done well."

"Yes." Peter's eyes glowed with pride. "And one day I hope to go to Rome itself!"

John smiled at his friend's enthusiasm, but inside he was worried. Peter seemed devoted to Aumery, but John had instinctively distrusted the man.

"But I am being rude," Peter said. "What have you been doing these past two years?"

"Much," John said. "I searched for you that night in Toulouse—at the Priory, in St. Sernin, and through the crowds—but you were nowhere."

"I needed solitude. I left the tumult of the feast and sat by the river, pondering what God wanted of me. I too looked for you after I had been accepted as a lay brother, but you had left by then."

"I left that very morning in company with William of Arles, the troubadour at the feast. You remember him?"

"I do. A godless man, I recall."

John wondered if everyone was godless in his friend's eyes. He ignored the insult and continued. "I travelled with him for more than a year, and learned much. William knows all the history of Languedoc and told it to me, either in songs or in tales around the evening fire. We visited the courts of the lords of Foix—where Adam now works for the count—Comminges and Béarn, and I had chances, never long enough, to study their libraries. I even had time to practice my drawing, copying the pictures in the margins of the books."

"So you still scribble and struggle to find God through earthly pursuits?"

"I still try to perfect my drawing and seek to learn all I can," John said, swallowing his anger once more. "And that is how I ended up here. The library at Carcassonne was particularly interesting and I decided to stay when William moved on. I told myself I could catch up with him later, but my interests came to the notice of Roger Trenceval and he offered me work as a scribe on this venture."

"So you work for a heretic."

"Viscount Roger is not a heretic!" John said. "He is young and clever and trying to do the best for his people. And he attends Mass regularly."

"He supports heretics and allows them to flourish in his cities. In God's eyes that is as bad."

"There are heretics all over!" John was about to defend his employer when he was interrupted.

"Indeed there are," Arnaud Aumery said as he appeared out of the cloister's shadows. His voice was high-pitched with a heavy accent that John recognized as originating across the Pyrenees Mountains in Castille or Aragon. "And that is why we are here at St. Gilles, to stop the spread of this pernicious evil before it corrodes the very heart of Christendom.

"The meeting convenes. Peter, you must take up your quill. And you"—Aumery stared coldly at John—"must run to your master."

Aumery turned and strode out of the courtyard. Without a word or a backward glance, Peter rose and hurried after.

John watched their retreating backs in confusion. He had been so excited when he first caught sight of his old friend in the cloister. As children, they had been so close, sharing everything, including their dreams of the future. John knew that they'd been growing apart even before Peter's visions, but now the gulf between them seemed unbridgeable. Peter was so sure and inflexible! Was that the influence of the strange Arnaud Aumery or did Peter simply need certainty to feel comfortable with the uncertain world in which they were living?

Shaking his head sadly, John walked slowly into the abbey church. Meeting Peter and the legate had turned what John had hoped would be an exciting adventure into something else—something darker. He couldn't help but feel perhaps more than his childhood friendship was at risk.

Threats

St. Gilles
January 13, 1208

The confrontation between the papal legates and Count Raymond's delegation promised good entertainment value and the abbey church of St. Gilles was busier than it ever was for Mass. The nave and aisles were packed to capacity, and the crowd overflowed out of the three ornately carved doors into the square. The late afternoon sun, appearing fitfully between threatening clouds, sent shafts of light through the rose window above the doors, illuminating the restless crowd and the tables set up on either side of the altar. It would make a wonderful painting, John thought, if only the life and depth of the scene could be captured on a flat surface.

At length, the murmuring of the crowd lessened as the principal actors in the drama entered and took their assigned places. Count Raymond led the way and took his seat at the centre of the long table to the left of the altar. He was a large, bluff man, sumptuously dressed in a deep purple, fur-lined cloak, and he appeared relaxed, chatting lightly with the young Viscount Roger Trenceval on his left. As befitted his lower station, Trenceval was not as lavishly outfitted as Raymond; still, his youth and open, smiling face made him stand out among the more serious members of the retinue.

On Raymond's right, being pointedly ignored by the count, sat Bishop Foulques of Toulouse, looking just as well fed and self-satisfied as John remembered him. Years of good living had given the bishop several chins, which spilled over the richly embroidered collar of his vestments. His bishop's mitre, sparkling with jewels, balanced precariously on top of his large head.

Foulques was the archetype of the corrupt churchman so hated by the Cathars. He lived a life of unbridled luxury, financed by the tithes charged to the poor. Even worse, he allowed his priests to marry, as well as embezzle money at will, and sell indulgences—providing that they paid him his share.

John recalled a popular song that William of Arles had composed about Foulques:

He loves Christ so much
This man of the Church
That he eats and drinks all
'Till his belly shall burst
So there is nothing left
To tempt his poor flock.
He lets his priests marry
So that all girls so fair
May not walk the streets
To seduce the young men.
You see he loves Christ
This pig of Toulouse.

John smiled at the seating arrangements. Foulques was rabidly anti-Cathar, yet because of his position as bishop of Toulouse, he was not sitting to the right of the altar with the papal legates, but next to Count Raymond, who was in trouble for protecting heretics. William would appreciate the irony.

The legates took their places, surrounded by monks and lay brothers. Arnaud Aumery concentrated deeply on some parchments, and Pierre of Castelnau sat by his side, stern and aloof.

John knew a little about Pierre of Castelnau from stories he'd heard on his wanderings with William. For five years, Pierre had been travelling the countryside, sometimes with Aumery and sometimes with the Spanish friar Dominic Guzman, preaching against the Cathar heresy and seeking converts. His failure—John had heard of no more than a dozen illiterate peasants who had renounced the Cathar faith—was due to the man's unyielding stance that allowed for no compromise. He would not deviate from his strict interpretation of the Gospels, an attitude that did not compare well with the much more open discussions the Cathars encouraged.

Pierre's mission was probably not helped by his unpleasant personal appearance. Even if he did convince someone of the rightness of his arguments, John could not see many people wishing to set this legate up as a role model. Pierre was a remarkably ugly man. His skin was pitted with pox marks, and one eyebrow was pulled down by a livid scar that gave him a perpetual disapproving scowl. His nose was large and squashed flat against his face and it sat above a pair of fleshy lips that surrounded a mouthful of rotted, yellow teeth. John had heard tell that Pierre's breath was so foul it could make even the strongest stomach churn. John couldn't help thinking of a vulture, sitting ready to plunge its head into a rotting carcass in search of delicacies. It was probably an image of which Pierre would approve, since he saw himself as plunging into the vile body of heresy to find savable souls.

John and Peter sat at the far ends of their respective tables with quills and ink at the ready. Around them, and to the front of the crowd, local dignitaries and monks from the abbey settled themselves as best they could. The mass of curious onlookers gathered behind, straining for a view.

Finally, Bishop Foulques stood and raised his hand for quiet. Gradually, the crowd fell silent. "We are met," Foulques began in a simpering voice, "to resolve the difficulties between my Lord Raymond, most honourable Count of Toulouse, his nephew Viscount Roger Trenceval of Carcassonne, and the Holy Mother Church of the glorious Pope Innocent III, as represented here by his blessed legates, Pierre of Castelnau and Arnaud Aumery, Abbot of Cîteaux.

"We fervently pray that God will look down favourably upon our conclave here this day and guide our steps as we undertake His divine mission. We call for His blessing upon His Holiness' legates"—Foulques smiled ingratiatingly across at Pierre and Arnaud—"and pray that my Lord Raymond comes to see the error of his ways."

Count Raymond grunted loudly and shifted in his chair, but made no comment. Foulques ignored him and continued. "The problem of heresy in our fair land is a serious one, and our lords have failed over many years to eradicate it from the bosom of the Holy Church."

Raymond sat forward and seemed about to speak, but Pierre's voice rang out first. "Enough of this nonsense," he thundered, standing and thumping the table before him. "His Holiness has given Count Raymond every chance, and the count has sworn, on numerous occasions, to carry out Rome's requests.

"Has he done so? No. The vile canker continues to grow and spread. I read here from a letter written by the blessed Innocent himself: 'Are you not ashamed of breaking the oath by which you swore to eradicate heresy from your dominions? Are you so mad that you think yourself wiser than all the faithful of the universal Church? If we could pierce the wall of your heart, we would enter it and show you terrible abominations you have wrought. What pride has swollen your heart, what madness, wretched man, has seized you, that you ally yourself with the enemies of Catholic truth? You feed on corpses like a crow. Are you not ashamed?'"

A gasp ran through the crowd. John looked up in shock at Pierre's violent outburst. He had expected the discussion to be calm and civilized—like the debates he and Peter used to listen to back in Toulouse. He watched as Foulques sat down abruptly and Raymond struggled to contain his anger.

It was Arnaud Aumery who spoke next, his voice soft and calming.

"Perhaps my esteemed brother in Christ goes too far. We all wish only that —"

"Do not presume to tell me how far I may go." Pierre rounded on his colleague. "I am senior legate here! I am the voice of His Holiness the Pope, and I shall determine how far to go."

John glanced up from his furious writing in time to catch the look of utter hatred that Aumery gave Pierre. Almost immediately, though, the look was replaced by a fawning smile.

"My apologies, brother," Aumery said. "I meant nothing."

Raymond rose then and leaned forward, his fists clenched before him. "How dare you! You come into my lands as a guest, to discuss a problem that plagues us both, and instead of a civilized discourse, I am insulted most foully in my own house! What gives you the right—"

"God Almighty and the Holy Mother Church give me the right," Pierre shouted back. "The time for discussion is long past. We are tired of your dissembling and delays. Burn the evil from the heart of your land at once or suffer the consequences."

For a moment, John feared that Raymond was going to leap across the table and strangle Pierre with his bare hands. Instead, he took a deep breath and spoke in a quieter voice, thick with venom. "You pox-scarred, drooling idiot. You and your carrion brotherhood presume to come into my lands and, in the name of a distant Rome that knows nothing of our situation, order me about. How dare you!"

"In the name of the Pope and the Holy Church," Pierre intoned, "I order you, this instant, to take arms against this Cathar heresy that gives birth continually to a monstrous brood, by means of which its corruption is vigorously renewed, with the offspring passing on to others the canker of its own detestable madness."

Both men were standing and speaking at once. The crowd was straining forward, staring from one to the other in an attempt not to miss a word. John scratched frantically with his quill, trying to get down as much as possible. A brief glance at Peter showed that he was doing the same.

"I came here in good faith," Raymond yelled. "Yet all I have received are orders and insults. What kind of discussion does your master in Rome consider that?"

"For your abject failure to eliminate this harmful filth from your lands, in the name of Pope Innocent III, I pronounce a sentence of excommunication upon you, Raymond of Toulouse."

Pierre's words hit everyone in the church with the power of a mailed fist and shocked even Raymond into silence. Everyone listened in horror as the legate continued in a quieter voice.

"I declare you shunned and deprived of all your lands and properties. No man shall owe you allegiance and all debts outstanding to you are hereby forgiven. Any man who takes arms against you shall do so with the blessings of the Church and, should you die before this sentence is lifted, you may not enjoy the sacraments or last rites. You may not be buried in consecrated ground and your coffin shall lie in the open, a feast for the rats and crows. May God have mercy upon your soul."

The silence in the church was almost a physical thing. Excommunication was a final resort and, if rigorously applied, could destroy the wealth and power of the mightiest lord, not to mention condemn his soul to eternal damnation. This was a much better entertainment than the crowd had hoped for.

"The Lord's work here is done," Pierre said eventually. "We shall leave this night and return and report these proceedings to His Holiness. I shall pray for you, Raymond of Toulouse."

Arnaud Aumery and the lay brothers stood and collected their parchments. Raymond blinked, his face red with fury.

"Do not think you can escape this place with such ease," he said coldly. "I shall watch for your departure whether you go by land or by water, and you shall die before me, Pierre of Castelnau."

With the threat hanging in the air, Raymond turned and strode from the church. A hubbub of conversation erupted behind him.

John looked across at Peter, hoping to catch his eye, but his friend had already gathered his writing equipment and all John saw was a retreating back. John gathered his own quill, ink and parchment and slowly made his way out of the church into the cloister. He was sitting on the wall, trying to gather his thoughts, when Roger Trenceval approached. John jumped to his feet.

"Sit," Roger said with a smile. He was a young man, only a few years older than John, but since the death of his father in 1194, when Roger had been only nine years old, he had controlled large swaths of land and the cities of Carcassonne and Béziers. He ruled easily, without the violence of so many of his kind. As long as the populace kept the peace and paid their taxes he allowed them to go about their business unhindered. As a result, the young viscount was immensely popular with his subjects. His court was famous for its jollity, and the most renowned troubadours in the land came to perform on feast days. John could imagine no one for whom he would rather work. The only difficulty was that Roger's laxity created a haven for heretics, who now preached and worshipped openly in the streets of Béziers and

Carcassonne.

"That was quite the entertainment, was it not?"

"Entertainment?" John asked.

"Of course! You do not imagine anyone took it seriously, do you?"

"But the legate excommunicated Count Raymond!"

Roger laughed. "Not for the first time, and probably not for the last. I shall tell you what will happen. That weasel Aumery will write a report to the Pope denouncing Count Raymond and, most probably, me as vile protectors of heretics. Count Raymond will also write, complaining that the legates gave him no fair chance to comply with their demands, swearing that he will do his utmost to eradicate the foul heresy from his lands and bring his people back to Christ. The Pope will lift the excommunication, Raymond will make a few gestures, and things will go on as before. That is how it has always happened in the past and I see no reason for it to be different this time."

"But the legate was so..." John searched for the right word.

"Arrogant. Violent. Stupid. Ugly. Take your pick. He is not a pleasant man, either to look at or to listen to. But he is the Pope's creature and will do as he is told. As long as Raymond can keep direct channels open to His Holiness, we need not worry about Pierre of Castelnau or Arnaud Aumery. But I sought you out for a reason. I believe you know one of the lay brothers?"

"I do. Peter. We grew up together in Toulouse."

"Splendid. The papal party will leave within the hour. I should like you to go with them. Your friendship with Peter will give you the excuse. You can say you are catching up on old times or that you are fed up working for such a friend of heretics as I. I care not. What I wish is that you keep close to the legates, hear what gossip circles them and, if possible, acquire from your scribe friend a copy of the letter Aumery will undoubtedly send to the Pope. Count Raymond and I should much like to see it and, if you think it manageable to wait for the Pope's reply, I should much like to see that as well. Would you be willing to attempt this?"

It was a question, but John knew he had little choice. Roger Trenceval was his lord and he had an obligation to obey any request made, just as Roger had an obligation to reward John once the service was done.

John had the uncomfortable feeling that his life was beginning to spin out of control. Was he now to be a spy? A part of John wished he were still leading the carefree life of a troubadour. But another part of him was excited. He was at the centre of things, associating with the men who had the power in this land. And, maybe, he would be able to rekindle his friendship with Peter.

"I am willing," John said.

"Excellent! Then I suggest you gather a few belongings for the journey. I fear you must walk, as to give you a mount would attract too much attention, but I wish you well." Roger reached into a leather purse that hung from his belt. "Here are a few coins for your keep on the road. I trust I shall hear from you in due course. Good luck."

Placing the pennies in John's hand, Roger favoured him with one last smile and disappeared into the shadows.

Arguments

Near Arles
January 14, 1208

John sat on a cold, damp rock, chewing on a hunk of heavy black bread. In front of him the broad, murky waters of the Rhône River swirled past and the boatmen struggled to propel the flat-bottomed ferry toward him. On the far bank lay Arles, William the Troubadour's home town. It wasn't an imposing place; only three square church towers and the walls of the Roman amphitheatre rose into view above the squat city walls. To the left of the city the weak early morning sun was struggling to rise above the horizon, a pale, colourless circle through the mist and cloud.

In the nearby trees birds called out warnings, and a rabbit screamed as a weasel ended its life. John pulled his leather jerkin tighter around his shoulders. It had been a miserable night. First there had been the abrupt departure from St. Gilles and the dark walk to the river. Then the long, cold wait for dawn and the ferry. It would be here soon now. Perhaps there would be time to stop for some hot soup in Arles, but John doubted it. Neither Pierre of Castelnau nor Arnaud Aumery struck John as men who had much time for luxuries like hot soup. They probably wouldn't even enter the city, choosing instead to skirt the walls and continue north to Avignon.

John stood, stretched his aching limbs and stuffed the remaining piece of bread into the leather pouch that hung from his waist. It would do for lunch on the road. Remembering his purpose—to gather information for Raymond and Roger—he turned to examine his companions. To his right, three Cistercian monks were kneeling at their morning prayers looking, in their white habits with the black aprons hanging behind and in front, like a flock of large, slow-moving magpies. Behind them, a half dozen lay brothers, in their brown sleeveless robes, scurried around, taking down tents, packing bedding and loading mules.

Slightly apart from the activity, the thin-faced Arnaud Aumery also knelt in prayer, hunched forward like a large rodent. His habit was pulled down to his waist and his scrawny hands twisted together in front of his chest. His left hand held a heavy knotted rope and, after each fervent prayer, the hand would break free from its companion and snap up, arcing the rope over the right shoulder and across the skinny back. It must have hurt, yet each time the hard knots dug into the flesh, Aumery jerked his head back and John saw the monk's face twisted not in pain, but in ecstasy. John had heard of monks scourging themselves to rid their lives of sin, but he had never imagined that they enjoyed it.

To John's left, Pierre of Castelnau sat aloof on a black mule, watching Aumery with an expression of distaste. John wondered how the two legates could be so different, and yet so equal in their lack of appeal as advertisements for the Catholic Church. It was easy to see how the Cathars had gained so many converts.

"So, you have come with us!" John turned his head to see Peter walking toward him. "Are you thinking of entering monastic orders?"

"I would have preferred a monastic cell last night to sitting in the open by the river," he retorted. Despite the differences that had grown between them, John was glad to see his old friend. "Or a place in one of the monk's tents."

"Then become a lay brother. Join us in doing God's work."

John gently shook his head, not wishing to start another argument. "It's not for me. I enjoy the bustle of court life and the songs and stories of the troubadours. And I want to be free to learn everything, to read whatever books I wish and know whatever they might teach me. And do you know the strangest thing? The more I learn, the less clear everything becomes. For every black there is a white and countless shades of grey between. There is so much I need to learn!"

"John, John," Peter said. "You approach the problem the wrong way! Clarity comes not from dwelling eternally on the details. Our purpose here on earth is to adore and glorify God. We worship for His sake, not our own. If you come to know God, you know everything and the details fall into place as a part of His grand scheme. Remember how I used to quote Anselm of Canterbury, 'I believe so that I may understand'?"

"I do," John said with a smile. "And do you remember how I used to counter with Peter Abelard's 'By doubting we come to enquiry, through enquiry to truth'?"

Peter nodded and smiled back. "I remember our debates fondly, even if you were wrong."

John's smile broadened at the gentle dig. "I am glad our paths are crossing again. I have many stories to tell you of my travels." Perhaps they could still recapture the easy friendship of their childhood.

"I am glad, too." Peter said. His smile faded and he looked seriously at

John. "You are as close to me as a brother, and I am thankful that God has given me another opportunity to show you the error of your ways."

John frowned. It was as if Peter had relaxed for a moment, but now that old curtain was once again coming down between them. He tried to keep the tone of the conversation light.

"I hope correcting my error doesn't involve whips," John joked, inclining his head toward Aumery.

"That is Father Aumery's way," Peter said seriously. "We must each find our own path to God."

"I agree," John said, worried that his joke had misfired. "It's just that my path is through learning. If God created all that is in the world, He placed truth here too. By searching for that truth, I can come to know God better."

"If!" Peter's voice rose to a near shout. "Do you doubt that God created all?"

"Of course not!" John said hurriedly. "It's just an expression." Clearly his attempts at levity had failed. "I agree with you, Peter, we all need to find our own way, but I doubt if freezing by this river, or hitting yourself with knotted ropes, brings you closer to God. Personally, I would have been much more inclined to dwell on the Lord if I had been warm and well fed last night."

"Father Aumery is a holy man," Peter said indignantly. "He scourges the body to cleanse the soul."

John sighed. He knew he should change the topic to something less controversial, but Peter was sounding pompous again and it annoyed John. He could avoid a fight with Peter only by slavishly agreeing to his friend's unquestioning certainty. He wasn't prepared to do that.

"Like the Perfects do?" John asked provocatively.

"There's an eternity of difference between the heretics and Father Aumery." Peter spoke angrily. "The Cathars are doomed to the fires of hell, and he will sit with the blessed saints at Christ's feet. You can't possibly believe all this nonsense those Perfects preach!"

"But aren't there a lot of similarities?" John went on. "Both Father Aumery and the Perfects believe that the spiritual realm is the important one and that the physical body is evil, correct?"

"There are *no* similarities." Peter's voice was rising and his cheeks were reddening. "Father Aumery believes, as all true Christians should, that the flesh is weak and that we must be continually on our guard against sinful temptation put in our way by Satan. But the body, like everything around us, was created by God. The heretics believe that the body, and the entire material world, is the creation of Satan and since that is the case, anything you do in this life is all right because the world is by its very nature corrupt.

That simply encourages debauchery and sin." Peter made the sign of the cross in the air before him.

John cast a look in Aumery's direction. "I wonder how God looks on the way Father Aumery is treating His creation? It can't be that simple, Peter! A lot of what the Perfects say *is* strange, but it's not all nonsense. And it seems to me that, with their vows of poverty and their itinerant life, they are much closer to the ordinary people than the likes of Bishop Foulques, bedecked in his jewels and finery."

"Do you see Pierre or Arnaud bedecked in jewels?" Peter waved his thin arm toward the two legates.

"No," John allowed. "No one could accuse either of being seduced by the material world, but the church they serve is undeniably rich and some of its members seem to enjoy the wealth too much. Remember the debate in St. Sernin?"

Peter nodded.

"The Perfects won that day because they talked about things that ordinary people could understand—the unfairness and harshness of a world filled with random cruelty. They explained why life is difficult and unfair, why children die, why soldiers suddenly appear and rape the farmers' women, steal their possessions and burn their crops. The world *is* evil, created by Satan. That is how most people see things—a cruel, hard life—followed by death. The Perfects understand that and offer hope: do the best you can in this corrupt world until death comes to release your spirit to an infinitely better place."

John took a deep breath. He knew he should stop, but it was too late. He was angry now and, in any case, a part of him wanted to see how far Peter's new certainty could be pushed.

"On top of that, the people know the Perfects," John continued. "They live among them, simply and without pretension. They live in ordinary houses, not splendid palaces; they conduct services in the common language, not a foreign tongue few understand; and they pray wherever there is need, not in churches that look as though they have been dipped in molten gold. The Perfects live with the people, owning nothing, consoling the sick and answering questions that trouble people frankly and clearly.

"What does the Church offer to counter that? Stories about a far-off day when all the dead will rise out of their graves to be judged on how they have lived their lives. No wonder the Perfects laugh."

"Heretic!" Peter's shout was loud enough for several nearby lay brothers to look up nervously.

"Peter, I'm not a heretic—you know that. I'm simply trying to explain why the legates are failing to win the people. What happened to the days when we could discuss anything and argue for the joy of it?"

"There is no joy in propounding heretical ideas," Peter said loudly and quickly. "Your masters, Count Raymond and Roger Trenceval, tolerate and encourage heretics. These black-clad vermin spread like rats through the streets of our towns, and no one dares stop them. They must be eradicated. You praise the heretics because they own nothing, as if there were virtue in poverty for its own sake. There is not."

"Christ was poor," John replied.

"Christ lived far from here twelve hundred years ago. We have advanced since then, and it is the cardinals, bishops and the Holy Church whom the Perfects mock so much who have led us so far. Without the Church to create order and spread the word of God, you would still be a pagan, living in animal skins and huddling in terror at the unknown noises of the night. Would your Perfects have us return to that?"

"Of course not!" John said, angry at the way Peter was twisting his words. "They argue that, since the world is imperfect, it cannot have been created by a perfect God. Therefore it must have been made by another—by Satan."

"Dualism!" Peter's voice was almost a scream now. "There is only one God, who created all. All else is Satan whispering in our ears."

"Peter," John said softly, trying to calm his friend. "I do not believe in two gods, but even you must admit that there are things within the Church of Rome that need reform. Why should a privileged few live in luxury and control all knowledge of the Holy Book? Surely Christ himself spoke directly to the masses?"

"Of course he did, and were Christ still walking the earth, I would be the first to say let us go and hear him. But he is not." Peter spoke fast and harshly. "Christ lives in our hearts and, since we are imperfect, we need the Church to ensure that his words remain pure for all and not simply what every individual understands or remembers. The Catholic Church was established by the disciples and therefore its words are the closest one can come to knowing God's wishes."

The pair stood staring at each other. Peter was breathing heavily and his fists were clenched. John could think of nothing to say that would relieve the tension. He lowered his eyes to gaze at the ground between them.

"Beware, John," Peter said. His voice was quieter now, but still filled with anger. "You put your mortal soul in jeopardy."

Peter turned and stalked off before John could think of a reply, leaving him to suddenly wish that he were back at St. Gilles with Roger Trenceval. He raised his eyes and noticed Arnaud Aumery staring at him icily. More immediate than any threat to his mortal soul, John thought, was the need to beware of that man.

Murder

Near Arles,
January 14, 1208

John's attention was drawn by the shouts of the ferrymen as the boat drew near the shore. The lay brothers had finished packing and the monks were rising from their prayers. As he scanned the riverbank one last time, John noticed that Pierre of Castelnau, still sitting on his mule, was beckoning him. Puzzled and a bit nervous, John walked over to Pierre and stood by the mule's head, stroking its muzzle. They were some way off from the activity by the ferry dock and close to a thick stand of pine trees beside the road. The trees' lower branches were moving in the breeze, but there was something odd about the way they swayed.

As he waited for Pierre to speak, John studied the pines, trying to see into the darkness between the trees, but he could make out nothing other than meaningless, shifting shapes. His attention was drawn back to the legate as Pierre leaned forward and exhaled a disgusting breath in his face. It was all John could do not to pull back, but Pierre's stare held him in place. His eyes were a pale, washed-out grey, and their piercing, unforgiving gaze made John feel guilty, regardless of anything he had actually done. The fact that Pierre might have heard Peter call John a heretic made John's guilt ten times worse.

"You must do penance, boy," Pierre hissed, spraying spittle toward John.

"Penance?" John asked, tightening his grip on the mule's bridle.

"Aye, penance. Your masters are sinful men and will pay the price. If you wish to avoid their sin, you must cleanse yourself. Become a lay brother. Peter tells me you have some reading and some knowledge. That is a good thing—in the service of God. You must leave the path that the arrogant Raymond refused to reject and find the true way."

John listened in shock. Why did *he* have to do penance? Yes, he worked for Roger and Raymond, but that did not mean he shared their sins—did it?

Before he could form a reply, John was distracted by increased movement in the trees. He squinted hard to try to make out the moving shapes.

"Pay attention to me, boy," Pierre ordered.

John ignored him. Suddenly, the moving patterns in the branches made sense.

"There's someone in the trees," he said.

"What are you saying?" Pierre said angrily. "I am talking about your immortal soul and the fires of hell, and all you do is look at trees!"

"But—"

The knight on horseback broke from cover in a burst of noise. He was mounted on a massive charger whose great hooves pounded the ground like distant thunder. The knight was dressed in a long leather coat that was split front and back so he could sit comfortably on his horse. Countless overlapping steel rings were sewn onto the coat to create a protective layer of chain mail. He wore a pointed helmet, designed to deflect sword or axe blows aimed at his head. A nose guard descended from the helmet and was attached to two broad cheek plates, completely obscuring the man's face except for the eyes. He carried a shield on his right arm and a lance tucked beneath his left, but wore no identifying coat of arms either on his shield or on the saddle cloth that hung over his horse's sides. As he spurred his mount forward, the knight aimed his lance at Pierre's back.

To John it seemed as if the world had become a tableau in which only the knight retained the power of movement. For several seconds, everything hung in the balance, until finally, seeing the look of shock on John's face, Pierre began to turn his head. Gripping the mule's bridle, John tried to haul the beast out of the way. He was too late.

The lance entered Pierre of Castelnau's back slightly to the left of his spine. It tore through his heart and shattered his sternum. John watched in horror as the lance point, bloody and evil, ripped out the front of Pierre's chest. The force of the blow hurled the legate out of the saddle and the terrified mule reared, knocking John to the ground. The hooves of the knight's charger thundered past inches from John's face and threw clods of wet earth over him. Rolling aside, John saw the knight retreat at a gallop back up the road toward St. Gilles.

For a moment there was an unearthly silence, then shouts and screams rent the air. John scrambled to his feet, pushed the distraught mule out of the way and knelt over Pierre. The legate lay partly propped up by the lance that still impaled his body, his head oddly twisted to one side. Already his habit was soaked in blood. The dying man's pale gaze met John's as he attempted to speak. He managed one word that sounded like "forgive" before the blood welled over his lips and his eyes glazed.

In shock, his heart pounding and his hands sweating even in the cold air,

Heretic

John stood, unable to think what he should do next.

"Murderer!" Arnaud Aumery's shrill voice came from over John's shoulder. John assumed the legate was shouting at the knight, who had all but disappeared into the morning mist. It took him a moment to realize that Aumery meant him.

"What?" he asked, bewildered.

Aumery pointed a finger at John. His thin face was twisted with hate and his expressionless eyes stared. "You are the worm in the heart of our group! You held the mule steady while Raymond's spawn slaughtered the blessed Pierre, even turning the beast so that the lance would do its foul job more efficiently."

"No!" John shook his head in confusion. "I was trying to pull the mule *away*. I was trying to save him."

"Then why did you pull him to the left? You pulled the mule left and the knight was left-handed. You pulled Pierre onto the lance and made the stroke more certain."

"I didn't have time to think. I just pulled."

"Why were you there at all? Your standing by Pierre was a signal, part of a devilish plot hatched by Raymond in the halls of St. Gilles."

"The legate beckoned me over," John said weakly.

Aumery laughed derisively. "I saw no beckoning," he spat.

John noticed Peter standing behind Aumery. "Peter, tell him I didn't do anything! Tell him I wouldn't kill anyone!"

Peter's glance darted between John and Aumery, but he remained silent.

"It was all planned," Aumery ranted, kneeling by Pierre and cradling his bloody head. "Raymond admitted as much with his threat last evening. His soul is lost. He has sold it to Satan. He never intended to obey His Holiness. He is a heretic and worse, a protector of heretics! And this pup is his servant, sent among us to make the murderer's task easier. I have no doubt that, had the lance missed, this demon in human form would have finished the job himself."

A murmur of agreement swept through the crowd of shocked monks and lay brothers who had gathered round Pierre of Castelnau's corpse.

"No! It's not like that!"

"I even heard"—Aumery drowned out John's protestations—"our own dear brother in God, Peter, call this one a heretic. Is that not so, Peter?"

John looked imploringly at his friend, but Peter simply lowered his eyes. "Yes," he said quietly.

Some of the lay brothers stepped forward toward John.

"Seize him," Aumery ordered. "Fire is the lot of heretics."

A hand grasped at John's sleeve. John swung his fist wildly, felt it connect with flesh and heard a groan of pain. The hand let go of his sleeve. John turned and ran, barging past the lay brothers who were not quick enough to move out of his way.

He had no idea where he was running, he just ran, past the surprised ferrymen and along the river bank—away from the sounds of pursuit, away from the screaming Arnaud Aumery and away from Peter and his past.

* * *

John ran unthinkingly, until he could run no more. The muscles in his legs burned and his agonized lungs threatened to explode from his chest. Then he collapsed, face down on a bed of moss between the roots of a broad willow tree.

Gradually, his breathing slowed to normal and the pains in his body eased. The sweat that soaked his clothes cooled and he shivered. Rolling over, he stared up through the bare, black branches of the tree. It was beginning to rain and large, fat drops plunged to the ground around him—as if the tree itself were weeping.

John sat up and looked around. He had no idea how long he had been running, but his surroundings were completely unfamiliar. He was still close to the river, but there was no sign of Arles on the opposite bank. John listened hard, but heard only the rain pattering on the ground around him. He had escaped, but for how long? And what had he escaped from? Certainly Aumery's wild accusations of murder, but he had also abandoned his past. Aumery's abuse John could take, but Peter's silence was harder. His friend hadn't lied—he *had* called John a heretic loud enough for Aumery to overhear—but he hadn't spoken up in his defence. A calm voice of reason might have defused the situation before it got out of hand, but Peter had stayed silent, and John would have trouble forgiving him for that.

What could he do now? The way back was closed. Aumery would undoubtedly take the body of the murdered legate back to St. Gilles. Even if Count Raymond and Roger Trenceval were still there, they could not protect John; they would be having enough troubles of their own. Yesterday Raymond had been excommunicated, and today he would be accused of organizing the murder of a senior papal legate. Whether he was guilty or innocent, Raymond would hardly have the time or the inclination to protect a page who had been in the wrong place at the wrong time. John was on his own.

There was one hope: Béziers, the closest large town where John could lose himself. Arles and Avignon were actually closer, but they were not a part of Raymond's domain and John would be an outsider. Béziers was familiar, and it was on Roger Trenceval's land. Perhaps the young viscount, who had sent him on this mission in the first place, would shelter him. Maybe, by the time he got there, the situation might even have resolved itself. After all, Viscount Roger had said things would go on as normal. But would they? Or had the murder of Pierre of Castelnau changed everything? John suspected it might have, but he had no choice. He stood and walked away from the river.

An Offer

Near Arles
January 14, 1208

Peter stood in utter shock, staring at Pierre of Castelnau's blood-soaked body. The sudden outburst of violence and Arnaud Aumery's accusations had thoroughly confused him. What *had* happened? The papal legate was certainly dead and his killer had escaped, but what part had John played? Yes, Peter had called him a heretic, but that had been in the heat of an argument. He hadn't meant to suggest, as Aumery had, that John was in some way capable of aiding a murderer.

Aumery knelt over the body, mumbling prayers and making the sign of the cross. A few of the lay brothers had given chase to the fleeing John, but it had been a halfhearted effort and they were now returning to mill about uncertainly. One was leading the dead Pierre's mule.

Peter was glad John had escaped. Still, he doubted they would ever again be friends as they had once been, not after this. Partly it was John's fault—he had developed so many worrying ideas of late—but Peter knew he shared the blame. He regretted the argument they had just had by the river. He had gone over intending to be friendly, but as soon as John had started to disagree with him, he had fallen back on the Church's teachings. He knew he had sounded pompous, but he couldn't help it. He hated being wrong, being made to look foolish, and taking refuge in what the Church told him was true was a comfort when he felt challenged. And it worked with most people, who were too ignorant or scared to disagree with him, but not with John. John kept questioning and pushing and Peter just got more angry.

"You!" Peter was jerked out of his thoughts by the realization that Aumery was pointing a skinny finger at him.

"Yes, Father."

"Come and give me a hand. We must remove the lance from the blessed Pierre's body. Hold him down."

Hesitantly, Peter moved around and crouched by the legate's head. Blood ran from his mouth and nose, and his eyes were wide—very like Aumery's,

Peter thought with a shudder. As gently as possible, Peter leaned over and closed the eyes.

"Pierre is already seated with the Lord," Arnaud Aumery said. "Closing the eyes to prevent the escape of the soul is a pagan habit. Are you a pagan?"

"No!" Peter exclaimed in fright. "I am a good Christian."

"Hah! That's what the heretics call themselves. Perhaps you are a heretic like your friend?"

"No! He's not my friend. I mean, I'm not a heretic."

"I don't believe you are. You're just a stupid boy. How are we supposed to combat evil with material such as you? Now, hold the body's shoulders, firmly."

Peter did as he was told, although it was all he could do not to bring up his meagre breakfast. The dead man's clothing was soaked in blood and his fleshy body beneath the fabric already felt cold and limp.

Aumery pulled on the lance, but it remained stuck. He pulled harder. Pierre's body slipped out of Peter's hands.

"Hold him tight," Aumery ordered. "It's wedged in his ribs."

Peter felt his stomach heave, but he clenched his teeth and held on. Bracing himself, Aumery jerked hard. The lance came free, accompanied by a soft sucking sound. Peter turned away and retched.

"Good." Aumery threw the bloody lance aside. "Now load Pierre on his mule. We are returning to St. Gilles."

Peter looked up from wiping his mouth, surprised that they should be returning to the scene of so much argument yesterday. "Will we be welcome there?" he asked.

"I doubt the heretic count will still be there, but it is no matter. We are doing God's work and we have the body of a holy martyr with us—a saint to be, I have no doubt. God will see us trample over our enemies."

Peter wasn't certain. If someone was prepared to kill Pierre, what was to stop them killing the rest of the party? It was a worrying thought, but even more disturbing was the expression of excited triumph on Aumery's face. The man looked almost gleeful as the body was strapped across the mule's back.

* * *

The long walk back to St. Gilles was a sombre affair. Peter was mostly occupied with leading the mule, which was upset by the smell of blood from the body on its back, but his task didn't prevent him from reflecting on the morning's events.

He felt sorry for John, and regretted calling him a heretic, but until his old friend discovered God, as Peter had, he would be open to the work of the

Devil. As Peter walked, he decided that he would pray for God to send John a revelation as powerful as the one that had changed him in Toulouse. Things would be so much better if John would just accept the truth: all that was good and worthwhile in this world was a gift from God, and it was the Holy Roman Church's duty to uphold that. The Church stemmed from the word of God as given to man in the Old Testament and through the lips of Christ. To deny that, or even to question it, opened the door to chaos at a time when the Church was beset on all sides by unbelievers.

Judgment Day, when the graves would open and the righteous ascend to heaven, could not come until the entire world accepted Christ and his teachings. The crusades to Jerusalem and Al-Andalus were spreading the faith, but to have heresy rearing its head in the very heart of Christendom was the work of the Devil. Surely John would see that! The Church had to be strong and unified if it was to succeed. This was no time for doubts.

Peter could almost hear John's objections in his head. Undeniably, there was rotten fruit within the Church. Bishop Foulques of Toulouse with his sinning priests and vast wealth was one example, but that did not mean that the Church as a whole was corrupt. Pierre of Castelnau—Peter crossed himself at the memory—and Arnaud Aumery were holy men who denied themselves almost all pleasures to be close to God. In time, men like them would root out evil in the Church and restore it to its former glory, and Peter wanted to be a part of that. He dreamed of being ordained and devoting himself to holy work. He would work hard, convert the ignorant masses and save countless souls. That way he would rise, perhaps to become abbott of his own monastery, or even a cardinal in Rome, or even...

Peter's musings were interrupted by the mule bucking violently and twisting Pierre's body to one side. Peter calmed the beast and was readjusting the body when Arnaud Aumery approached.

"You have an education, boy?" he asked.

"Yes," Peter replied as he wiped the blood off his hands. "John and I were taught by the nuns of St. Anne in Toulouse."

"John is the heretic who helped the knight murder Pierre?"

"No!" Peter said. He was calmer now and better able to defend his friend. "John wouldn't do that. I am certain he was doing what he said, holding the mule while Pierre talked to him."

"Hmm," said Aumery, nodding thoughtfully, "but he is a heretic?"

Peter hesitated. "No."

"Yet you called him such."

"He's not a heretic, of that I am certain," Peter said, more firmly this time. "I think he simply questions too much."

"And you do not?"

"It is not up to me to question the Church. We must be strong to combat heresy."

"You can read and write well?"

"A little."

"Latin or this corrupt Occitan language that is spoken hereabouts?"

Peter hesitated. The question was strewn with potential pitfalls. It was forbidden to read the Bible in Latin unless you were ordained in the Church. To admit being able to read Latin, unless you were a notary, judge or highborn, was to invite that charge. Yet, to read only Occitan marked you as a Languedoc provincial.

"Mother Marie, who taught John and me to read, was most holy," Peter said hesitantly. "She taught from a copy of St. Augustine's Confessions."

"You are familiar with Augustine! He was a heretic."

"And a pagan," Peter returned. "He also fathered an illegitimate child."

"Not a very good background for a central figure in our Christian thought." Aumery looked slyly at Peter.

"On the contrary," Peter replied, warming to this battle of wits. "It gave him a knowledge of his enemies that better enabled him to defeat them."

"Indeed, and you have a knowledge of this Cathar rabble?"

Peter saw the trap. "Only in so far as it is impossible not to, growing up as I did in the midst of their evil. Could I have chosen the place of my birth, I should have selected Rome."

Aumery laughed. "Birth in Rome is no guarantee of holiness. But what should the Church do when faced with a heresy that it cannot defeat by reasoned argument or example?"

"Listen to St. Augustine: 'Should not the Church use force in compelling her lost sons to return, if the lost sons compelled others to their destruction?'"

Aumery nodded approvingly. "So you *do* know your Augustine. Do you wish to become ordained?"

"More than anything, Father."

"And do you wish to devote your life to the Lord and His work?"

Peter hesitated. The easy answer was yes, but what would he be committing himself to?

"Hesitation is all right. You have not yet been called to service."

"But I have," Peter interrupted.

Aumery looked at his young companion sharply.

"I had a revelation two years ago," Peter went on.

"A revelation," Aumery reflected. "Tell me about it."

Peter told the story of his vision—of how he felt about the beautiful Isabella, of Death pointing at him and of Isabella's decay before his eyes—as Aumery listened intently. After Peter finished, the legate turned his strange eyes on the young lay brother.

"You are lucky," he said, a hint of envy in his voice. "God has blessed you with absolute certainty. For the rest of us, the struggle is harder."

Peter found it hard to imagine Arnaud Aumery struggling with anything less than certainty.

"I too was in love once," Aumery continued.

Peter stumbled and almost fell. The idea of Aumery loving someone, or of being loved in return, was utterly strange.

"You cannot imagine a man who has dedicated his life to God, as I have, being in love?"

Before Peter could think of an answer, Aumery continued. "My father was a prosperous wool merchant in Aragon, and I was to follow in his footsteps. At age twelve, I was betrothed to Dolores, the third daughter of the local count. As was the custom, I had never met her, but I had seen her from a distance and was smitten by her beauty. The future looked bright and I was happy." Aumery turned and favoured Peter with a wintry smile before continuing.

"One day, as my father and mother returned from the local fall fair, they were set upon by bandits and slaughtered. I had pleaded to accompany them, but father had insisted I stay home and study."

Peter thought he detected a catch in Aumery's voice, but the legate coughed and continued. "After I buried my parents, I went, in the company of an aged uncle, to the count to finalize the betrothal arrangements. I met Dolores in the company of one of her ladies in the courtyard. My heart leaped to my throat, and I hurried forward and bowed low.

"'I come to pay my respects to you and your father,' I stammered.

"Dolores laughed, harshly. 'To what end?'

"'So that our betrothal may be finalized.' I looked up, hoping against hope that I had misheard the scorn in her voice, but her beautiful face was twisted in disgust.

"'Do you honestly think that my father would consent to our marriage, or even that I would wish such a marriage, now that you are nothing? Already, your father's business crumbles, and what can you, a child, do about it?'

"'But I love you,' I blurted out desperately. Dolores' hard stare made me feel lower than a worm.

"Do you think I, the count's daughter, could love you, a skinny rat-faced child with the courtly graces of a slug? Go and find a peasant to rut with.

That is all you are worth.'

"Blinded by tears of shame, I fled back to my empty parents' house.

"I swore a thousand kinds of revenge on Dolores and her family, but she was right. My father had been deeply in debt to local moneylenders who immediately called in what they were owed. I was soon near penniless."

The legate was a difficult man to feel sorry for, but Peter came close as he listened to his tale of rejection. Even Aumery's grating voice seemed to soften as he spoke of Dolores. A sharp pang of regret stabbed Peter as he remembered his feelings for Isabella.

"In the depths of my despair," Aumery continued, "God sent to me a travelling friar who taught me the ways of the true Church. I threw myself into my learning and devoted my life to finding and eradicating sin from our unclean world."

"What happened to Dolores?" Peter asked.

Aumery shot Peter a sharp glance. "She married an empty-headed young knight. Their house became a noted place of sin and debauchery. At length, their activities came to the notice of the Holy Inquisition, and the woman was investigated. She was found to be in an adulterous carnal relationship with a non-Christian, and both were put to death. Even in her final moments, she was unrepentant and died cursing the Holy Church and me."

"You?"

"Oh, did I not mention?" Aumery turned to Peter, a smile on his face. "I was the inquisitor who brought the charges against the witch."

A chill ran down Peter's spine. Aumery had seemed almost human as he told his story, yet here was evidence that he had harboured a grudge for years and exacted a terrible revenge.

On the other hand, wasn't Aumery's determination to overcome and suppress his natural human instincts admirable? Perhaps, Peter reflected, he too might learn to rid his mind of the painful memories of Isabella that struck when he least expected them.

Aumery's eyes gleamed. His hands clasped and unclasped in prayer as he stared at Peter.

"So God wishes us both to do his work. Are you prepared?"

"I hope so."

"You will need more than hope, but I shall help you. Stay close by me. We have much work ahead, and the Church needs intelligent and dedicated soldiers such as you."

"Stay close?"

"You are much above the stupid peasants who fetch and carry, but you must learn to control this habit of asking questions before you have let your mind work.

"Pierre's death today is a blessing," he continued. "He will become a saint, and Raymond will be damned in all eyes for his role. This tragedy is exactly what is needed. This summer I shall travel north and help preach a great crusade in the name of the martyred Pierre and Pope Innocent. In the following year I shall return at the head of a mighty host and root out this evil from these lands with no mercy. Do you wish to accompany me and do the Lord's work?"

"I do."

"Then learn to hold your peace and stay close."

Aumery strode away, leaving Peter to walk on alone, his head crowded with thoughts. Aumery had obviously been impressed enough by Peter's vision to open up, but why? Peter was certain that the legate did nothing without calculated intent. His intent here must be to mentor Peter and bring him to an important position in the Church. And what was wrong with that? Peter would do as Aumery asked—accompany him to preach the crusade, and be ordained as well. It was a chance to realize his dream, and he would seize it. With friends as powerful as Aumery, Peter saw a life of service in the Church stretch out before him—all the way to Rome.

PART THREE
Crusade

Perfect

Béziers
July 22, 1209

John stood on the battlements above Béziers' west gate looking out at the narrow humped bridge over the river Orb. The July sun had already risen with the promise of another hot, dusty day, but the shadow of the massive bulk of St. Nazaire Cathedral behind him protected him from its glare.

After the murder of Pierre of Castelnau, John had travelled a long, roundabout route, over swollen winter rivers and through freezing rain, to the safety of this city. News of the legate's death had preceded him, but Roger Trenceval had welcomed the details of it and sworn to protect his informant. Opinion was divided over whether Raymond had ordered Pierre's assassination by the mysterious left-handed knight or not, but to Roger, it mattered little.

"If Pope Innocent wishes to use the murder to crush the Cathars," he told John, "he will do so, regardless of whose idea it was."

"Will he call a crusade?"

"Quite possibly, but don't be alarmed. Northern knights agree to serve the Pope for forty days in return for remittance of sin and assurances of a place in heaven. Béziers is well supplied, well armed and surrounded by imposing walls. The crusaders will soon strip the surrounding countryside bare of provisions and turn their camp into a foul cesspit. We will sit in comfort and watch them disintegrate into a starving, diseased rabble. The forty days will pass, they will go home, and life will go on."

John hoped Roger was right, especially after the viscount asked him to stay in Béziers and report back to him at his main court in Carcassonne.

As 1208 progressed, word came down that a crusade against the Cathars *was* being preached in the north by Arnaud Aumery. John wondered if Peter was part of it. Most people agreed with Trenceval that the crusade, if it even got as far as their city, would be only a minor disruption of the comfortable life they had led for decades. Besides, Languedoc, even with its population of heretics, was not the heathen east or Al-Andalus. It was a Christian country, and no crusade had ever been called against Christians.

But as the spring of 1209 progressed, news filtered in about an immense host moving in triumphant procession down the Rhône River. Refugees brought tales of local lords, terrified by the size of the army, scurrying to pay tribute and swear allegiance to Aumery and his knights. Bézier's walls would be the invaders' first real test.

John raised his gaze and looked at the crusader army as it awoke. It lay, sprawled along the far bank of the river, like some vast, colourful beast. Bright identifying pennants fluttered from luxurious red, blue and gold pavilions while the blood-red cross of the crusade emblazoned shields and tunics everywhere. Between the pavilions, John could make out servants polishing armour, repairing surcoats and chain mail, sharpening swords and lances and preparing meals. Voices echoed in the morning air, calling on pages to bring food and clothing for the day. Beneath a rising haze of dust the destriers—huge, powerful war horses, specially bred to carry the weight of an armoured knight and his weapons into battle—snorted and stamped as grooms hurried to feed and tend them.

The crusade had arrived at the city gates only yesterday, and it would be several days before they were ready to mount a concerted assault. Siege weapons—trebuchets, catapults, mangonels, towers, battering rams, scaling ladders—had to be constructed, and miners had to try to dig trenches and tunnels up to and beneath the walls before work on breaching the city's defences could begin.

The knights' bright pavilions, interspersed with the plain tents of the monks and lay brothers, sat back from the river on slightly higher ground. On either side of the camp were tethered the thousands of small work horses, mules and oxen that carried those who could afford to ride and pulled the carts laden with everything the army needed, from food and cooking pots to tents, personal weapons and dismantled siege engines. They stretched in a seething, snorting, stinking mass almost as far as the eye could see.

In front of the knights' city and hard up against the bridge lay the much less colourful bulk of the army. Housed in crude lean-tos and rough tents or on the open ground, and already beginning to smell in the warm weather, the infantry managed as best it could. Some belonged to the knights and had come as part of their duty to their lord, but most were mercenary bands—soldiers for hire from all over Europe: brutal, savage and unconcerned by death.

Around and mingled with the infantry lay the host of camp followers. In the morning sun, several thousand pilgrims, freebooters, hangers-on and bored opportunists scratched and began to wonder how they might profit from the day, for profit was the reason they followed this holy army. Some sought spiritual profit from the indulgences the Pope had promised all those who undertook God's blessed work, but most had more material aims. Many, like the tinkers, fortune tellers, jugglers and whores, profited directly from their proximity to the army. Others sought easy plunder as the army devastated the country it passed through or, hopefully, reduced the fortified cities it besieged.

So far there had been precious little plunder for either the mercenaries or the camp followers, but Béziers held promise. The hilltop city was rich, its normal population swollen to well over ten thousand by refugees who had brought with them every valuable they could carry. The problem was getting at the plunder, which was secure behind the impressive collection of ditches and walls that fortified the town.

"The army of the Devil."

John turned to see a female Cathar Perfect standing behind him. The sight itself was not unusual; more than two hundred Perfects, many of them women, lived openly in Béziers. The Perfect leaned on a rough walking staff. Her face was thin from age and from a lifetime of wandering and relying on others' generosity. Her skin, drawn over her narrow features, was weather-worn and wrinkled, yet the effect wasn't hard. A gentle strength seemed to emanate from the slight smile and pale blue eyes. A cascade of snow-white hair lay over the woman's shoulders in dramatic contrast to the black habit she wore. John experienced a sudden urge to draw this woman's interesting face.

John had meant to learn more about these Cathars, who were the source of so much hatred, but he always seemed to be running some errand for Roger or reporting to the court at Carcassonne and had not had much contact with them. He knew little more about the Cathars now than when he'd argued with Peter a year before.

"You think everything is the work of the Devil," John responded.

The Perfect smiled and nodded. "Indeed, and it must be so. Do you think God would create something that will cause as much destruction and misery as this?" She swept her cloaked arm wide to encompass the view of the army.

"They will not destroy Béziers," John countered. "They will sit out there in the sun for a few weeks then lose heart and go home."

"That may be, but in the meantime, there will be much suffering. To feed itself, the army will destroy everything for leagues in all directions, battles will be fought beneath the walls, and disease will sweep through the city as well as the enemy camp. Even after they are gone, there will be no crops for the farmers to return to. It will be a hard winter, whoever wins here."

John watched the Perfect as she talked. Her eyes sparkled and she looked almost delicate, even when talking of death and destruction. She spoke with an intensity that made John uncomfortable, yet the soft cadence of her voice was calming. He had the impression that what she was saying, even though he had heard it many times before, was unutterably wise.

"What's your name?" he blurted out.

"Beatrice," the Perfect said, her smile broadening. "Your next question will be where am I from, and the answer is Albi."

John had never met anyone, especially a woman, so self-assured and confident.

"I am the daughter of James," Beatrice continued, "a lord of Albi and protector of many Good Christians. I grew up with Good Men and Good Women as teachers and took the *consolamentum* many years past."

"The *consolamentum*?" John said.

"It is our dedication to God. Every Good Christian must take it before death if he or she is to enter paradise. But some of us take it early in life and try to live as God would wish. We are the ones you call Perfects.

"But I have told you of me, what of you?"

"My name is John. I was born in Toulouse and I serve as a page for Viscount Roger." John hesitated, wondering whether he should mention being present at the murder of Pierre of Castelnau.

He was saved from making that decision by a commotion in the street below. A rabble of several hundred townsfolk, armed with rusty swords, pitchforks and assorted clubs, was clamouring for the gate to be opened.

"You see," Beatrice said. "Already the common folk, who normally would be living peaceful lives, are lusting after blood. The enemy cannot get in here, so they are prepared to go out there to kill and maim."

With a loud groan, the gate was slowly pulled open and the townsfolk, shouting loudly to keep up their courage, poured out. They ran down the slope and stood, yelling curses at the mercenaries and camp followers at the other end of the bridge. Encouraged by their fellows and confident that they could strike a blow at their enemies before they were organized, other villagers rushed from their houses, waving any crude weapon they could find, and joined the melee.

"What are they doing?" John asked.

"They are proving that they have more of the Devil in them than their enemies," Beatrice answered.

"But it's pointless! They're not going to defeat the crusaders. And it's stupid to leave the protection of the walls."

"Would God create such stupidity?" Beatrice asked.

Across the river, an equally disorganized rabble was gathering and the two groups began yelling insults back and forth. One of the mercenary soldiers— braver, or stupider, than most—ventured onto the bridge. He stood in the middle, waving a sword and hurling curses that John could only imagine through the tumult.

Suddenly, half a dozen townsfolk broke away and sprinted onto the bridge. Taking the mercenary by surprise, they dodged his sword swipes and dragged him to the ground. Other rushed to join in and after a brief flurry of blows, the soldier's bloodied body was raised and flung off the bridge into the racing waters below.

Enraged, the man's companions swarmed across the bridge. A brief scuffle erupted on the Béziers' side before the townsfolk, less inclined to fight with swords than words, began retreating up the hill. As more and more mercenaries crossed the bridge, the retreat became a panicked flight.

John glanced down at the gate where more townsfolk, unaware of the events at the bridge, were still rushing to join their companions. Already people were falling as the two groups milled chaotically and jammed the narrow entrance.

"Close the gate!" someone yelled above the noise.

The soldiers tried, but the confused crush of people stopped them. Already a handful of mercenaries was at the gate and more were swarming up behind them. One man in particular caught John's attention. He was taller than the others and dressed in chain mail, although in his rush to battle, he had neglected to put on a helmet. His tunic was emblazoned not with the crusader's cross but with a blood-red falcon holding a black axe in its talons. The man carried a similar axe in his left hand. John noticed that several others near the big man also wore clothes marked with the falcon crest.

Instead of trying to push through the crowd into the city, the tall man headed for the guards who were still trying to close the gate. The first one he reached never knew what hit him. He collapsed in a pool of blood, his chest split open by a single blow.

"To me, Falcons! Kill the guards. Keep the gate open!" The mercenary was screaming at the top of his voice as he hacked about him. Others quickly obeyed and, at their onslaught, the surviving guards fled into the city.

"They must close the gate," John shouted, moving toward the steps that would take him down into the street. Only Beatrice's light touch on his shoulder stopped him.

"It is wrong to kill," she said. "Besides, I doubt that you, one unarmed boy, could make a difference."

John hesitated. He looked down at the tall man, who was now fighting through the crowd, swinging his deadly axe indiscriminately. There was something familiar about him, something about his looks, or the way he moved. All at once, John realized what it was: the axe in the man's hand. The mercenary was left-handed! It was the same helmeted knight who had killed Pierre of Castelnau and got John into this mess. John had never seen the man's face before, but he was certain he was the one.

As John stared, the man raised his head and looked straight at him. His face was weather-beaten and cruel, splattered with blood, and featured a long scar running across his right cheek. He smiled broadly, as if he hadn't had so much fun in a long time.

"Come! Now!" Beatrice's voice was urgent as she began moving along the battlements.

As if to underline Beatrice's order, a crossbow bolt slammed into the wall with sufficient force to shower John with rock chips. Without the faintest idea of where he was going, John hurried after the Perfect.

Soldiers were beginning to pass the pair, hurrying from town into the developing battle, but John suspected they would be too late—already the noise of fighting was spreading along the streets. Béziers, the fortress that was supposed to break the hearts of the crusader army against its impregnable walls, was doomed.

Kill Them All

Béziers
July 22, 1209

Peter stood to one side of Arnaud Aumery, patiently awaiting the outcome of the debate going on before him. All the nobility of the crusade were gathered here in this tent at a council of war. From outside, a group of monks chanting holy verses provided a background noise:

White was His naked breast,
And red with blood His side,
Blood on His tragic face,
His wounds deep and wide.

Stiff with death His arms,
On the cross widespread,
From five gashes in His side
The sacred blood flowed red.

Few in the tent were listening. These were warriors who preferred battle and plunder to prayer and forgiveness. Some would even rather have been fighting each other than the heretics.

Eudes III, Duke of Burgundy, detested Hervé de Donzy, Count of Nevers. Both were arrogant and powerful and the disputed borders of their lands had been the scene of open conflict for many years.

"Damn it all," Eudes, a large, bluff, red-faced man, said angrily. He was dressed in his padded under-armour, although he'd covered it with a tunic bearing the Burgundian arms, three alternating diagonal blue and yellow stripes surrounded by a red border. "Order the attack for today! The longer we wait, the better their defences."

"And the better our preparations." Hervé was the opposite of his enemy—thin, precise and fastidious in his dress and manners. He wore a long silk cloak, emblazoned with the Nevers symbol, a yellow lion rampant on a blue background. "We need three days at least for the carpenters to construct the trebuchet and collect rocks large enough to breach the walls. Then we can talk about an attack."

"Three days while you sit simpering in luxury in your tent. And how many more to make the breach? We came here to fight, let's get on with it!"

"Better sitting in a tent than watching our knights be slaughtered on scaling ladders that are still too short to reach the battlements."

"Our knights shall not be slaughtered." A third man stepped forward between the two arguing barons. He was of medium height and build and around middle age, and was dressed for practicality rather than show in a stained and patched leather jerkin, dark blue leggings and scuffed boots. His coat of arms, a white leaf on a red background surmounted by a bleeding dragon, was nowhere to be seen. His greying hair did nothing to soften the hard lines of his face.

"And what makes you so certain of that, Simon de Montfort." Eudes spat the name with obvious disdain. De Montfort ignored the insult and addressed his remarks to Arnaud Aumery.

"It's simple," he said. "We don't send our knights in. Begin the attack with the mercenaries and the camp followers. The former will go for riches and the latter in hopes of salvation. No one cares if they are slaughtered. If they succeed, we will follow. If they fail, we will bury them."

"You cannot listen to him," Hervé sneered. "He's merely a landless fortune hunter. What does he know of honour and knightly battle?"

"I do not know if he is as honourable as you," Aumery replied with a smile, "but I do know he has taken the cross in the Holy Land, where he sent many of God's enemies to hell. That is more than either of you gentlemen can claim. I, for one, would listen to more of his plan."

De Montfort nodded, but before he could speak, a commotion at the tent flap distracted everyone. A priest was struggling to get past the armed guards at the entrance.

"Let him in," Aumery ordered.

The priest rushed forward crossing himself frantically. "God has opened the gate. It's a miracle," he shouted.

"Be calm, my son," Aumery counselled. "What do you mean? What has God done for us?"

The priest fell to his knees in front of the legate, panting excitedly. "The townsfolk came out of the city on a sortie! The mercenaries chased them back, and God held the gates open."

"The gates are open?" de Montfort asked, stepping forward. "Are any of our men in the city?"

"They stream through the gates now, your Lordship. It is a miracle! God

Heretic

has delivered us the city of the heathen!"

"We must move at once," Eudes shouted. "That rabble will strip the city bare before we can get in."

"I remind you," Aumery said, "that you are here with the blessings of Pope Innocent to do God's work, not to line your pockets."

"But the possessions of the heretics are ours by right."

"Indeed."

"You told us," Herve said in sly voice, "that heretics may be distinguished by their reluctance to take any oath or accept the holy sacrament."

"That is true."

"How, though, if the walls are already breached and the rabble running through the streets, are we to distinguish in the space of a sword stroke the Christian from the heretic?"

Aumery stood silent for a long while. The knights fidgeted uneasily, eager to be away to battle. Peter watched Aumery's face. It was hard and uncompromising. Eventually, he spoke.

"Kill them all! God will know his own."

Peter let out an involuntary gasp. Kill them all?

"As you wish," Eudes said with a smile. With Aumery's brutal injunction ringing in their ears, the nobility of France streamed out to prepare themselves to do God's bidding.

Aumery turned to Peter. "You do not approve?"

"It's not for me to question, Father," Peter said. "But there must be many thousands of honest Catholics in the town. Must they, too, die?"

"Yesterday, as you may recall, Bishop Reginald of this very city entered his town, held a Mass in the cathedral and advised the council of citizens to surrender and give up the heretics from within their walls. Do you remember the response he brought back?"

"The Bishop brought back a list of the names of known heretics."

"Two hundred names out of ten thousand? Is that the extent of heresy in this land? I think not. Besides, remember the words of the council. They took no more note of Bishop Reginald's advice than of a peeled apple and claimed that rather than submit to our holy demands, they would eat their own children. Well, it has come to that. Let their children suffer!

"Besides," Aumery continued coldly, "I merely follow the scriptures, with which *you* should be more familiar. In Timothy it says, 'The Lord knoweth those that are His.' And in Numbers, 'The Lord will show who are His and who are holy.' We need not trouble ourselves with that aspect of God's work."

"And a goodly pile of corpses will serve our purposes admirably, I think."

Peter turned to see that Simon de Montfort had not left the tent with the others.

"That is indeed true, my lord," Aumery said with a smile, "but our young novice may require further explanation."

De Montfort stepped forward and regarded Peter closely. His face didn't have the reptilian coldness of Aumery's, but Peter had no doubt that he was staring at a man who would not hesitate to commit the most horrendous acts if he believed they would further his aims.

"Even with our miracle this morning," de Montfort explained, "Béziers is but the first of many strongly fortified towns and keeps scattered across this godforsaken land. Even the smallest of them can delay us past the forty days our noble knights have signed on for. An example here will…"—de Montfort hesitated, searching for the right word—"encourage many Languedoc garrisons to see sense and surrender rather than suffer the fate of Béziers."

"But the innocent—" Peter began. De Montfort's laugh cut him off.

"Innocent? Who is innocent in this world? We arrive sinners and die the same way. Only on the Day of Judgment will we be accounted and cleansed.

"But think on this too, young monk. Those who die this day do so that countless others will be spared in years to come." De Montfort, finished with his explanation to Peter, turned his gaze on Aumery.

"We are undoubtedly blessed, Father. If Béziers falls today then all the land round about, and perhaps even Carcassonne itself, will be ours in a matter of weeks. But Toulouse and the mountain fortresses will not fall so easily. To root out the evil of heresy as the Holy Father wishes, this war must be continued over the winter and after the likes of Eudes and Hervé have departed. Someone must stay behind to hold the conquered lands until the next wave of crusader knights arrive next year."

"And you, as a landless baron, would be the one to stay." Aumery finished de Montfort's thought.

"Neither Eudes nor Hervé will allow the other to return and ravage their unprotected homelands."

"Indeed," Aumery agreed. "My thoughts have run along similar lines. But you are not as close to the king as Eudes and Hervé, and the role of protecting our victories must be offered to the highest first."

De Montfort nodded acknowledgement before Aumery continued. "Though, I suspect with much bluster and apology, they will decline the honour. I must then look to a third." Aumery smiled broadly. "But these details must await the fall of Carcassonne. We will talk more."

"We shall, Father." De Montfort bowed to the legate. "But for now I must see to your instructions in Béziers."

Peter watched the knight turn and stride out of the tent. That was how important things were done, he thought. Understandings quietly reached in private with no specific agreements written down, or even expressly stated. Eudes' bluster and Hervé's slyness were in the open and thus easily countered. Aumery and de Montfort held the real power.

Peter had a sense of being privileged to be part of the inner circle of this venture. Gradually, he became aware of Aumery's eyes on him.

"You begin to see how things are done, young Peter?"

"Yes, Father."

"The Lord works in subtle and, sometimes, mysterious ways. All we can do is keep the ultimate goal in sight and work toward it as best we can.

"Now, you need to see more than the workings behind the scenes. You must see the cutting edge of our holy work. I must write tomorrow to His Holiness the Pope, telling him of our great triumph. I wish you to be my eyes and ears on this day. Go with the knights and return to tell me what things happen in the city."

Peter hesitated. He was being asked to enter a holocaust. It was not fear of his personal danger amidst the bloodshed that gave him pause, but he suspected that the sights he must witness would be too strong for his stomach.

"It is God's work," Aumery said. "Would you deny it?"

"No."

"Then go. I will talk with you later. Now I must scourge this loathsome body in thanks for our great miracle."

As Aumery turned away dismissively, Peter exited the tent into the bustle of the knights preparing for battle.

A Hiding Place

Béziers
July 22, 1209

John gasped for breath as he followed Beatrice through Béziers' narrow cobbled streets. Despite her age and the walking staff, she set a blistering pace and John had trouble keeping up as they bumped and pushed through the crowds.

Word that the walls were breached had spread like wildfire and panicked people were running in all directions. Some, clutching whatever valuables they could carry, were seeking sanctuary in the nearest church while others simply ran about aimlessly. Still more, trusting that the speed with which the city was falling would protect them from the fury of the crusaders, kept to their houses and peered out into the street with frightened eyes. Here and there, Perfects stood praying and comforting the Credents who knelt around them. All about, almost drowning out the screams of the terrified people, every church bell in Béziers tolled a funeral knell.

Eventually, Beatrice arrived at the square before the great doors of the church of St. Mary Madeleine. John stopped beside her, panting. The square was filled with people, swarming toward the church. Men stumbled along with cloth-wrapped bundles of valuables clutched to their chests. Women, carrying screaming infants, tried to herd their scared older children in the right direction. Everyone glanced fearfully over their shoulder.

"Are we taking sanctuary?" John asked.

"There is no sanctuary for me," Beatrice replied, "or, I fear, for anyone this day."

"Then where are we going?" Although he had only just met her, John didn't question that he should follow Beatrice. She seemed an island of calm in the midst of all the chaos.

"Whatever happens here, there will be no safe place in Béziers for a Good Man or Woman. Many will die, and those who have taken the *consolamentum* are ready. But some of us must escape. There are things to be done. Will you accompany me?"

John hesitated. He had a duty to Roger Trenceval, but dying in Béziers wouldn't help that. If Beatrice could get him out of the city, then at least he would be alive to go to Carcassonne and report.

A sudden commotion at the far side of the square distracted him. People were screaming in terror and struggling away from a narrow alley. As he watched, a group of mercenaries burst into the square, swords swinging in all directions. The group was led by a tall man wielding a bloodstained axe in his left hand.

"I will accompany you," John said hurriedly.

"Then come," Beatrice ordered as she slipped into the alley beside the church and resumed her punishing pace.

They were heading across town, away from the river and against the flow of people. Everyone seemed to be heading toward the churches, either the cathedral or Madelaine. John supposed they felt safer in familiar surroundings and assumed that their churches would protect them. He wondered if he should be joining them instead of heading off into the unknown with this strange heretic woman. Perhaps he was putting himself in greater danger by following her. After all, unless there had been a particularly long and brutal siege, the rules of war protected women, children and civilian men. Their property could be seized and their valuables taken, but there was no point in killing them. And John had no valuables to lose. For a brief moment, he considered turning back. But then the image of the left-handed knight swinging his bloody axe swept into John's mind. Somehow, he didn't think the normal rules were going to apply today.

Eventually, Beatrice led them to a small gate at the end of a stinking alley. The gate was open, but there was no one in sight.

"Good," Beatrice said. "It looks as if they haven't found this gate yet. It is a blessing that they did not have time to organize a proper siege and block all exits."

"Perhaps God wishes us to escape this way," John suggested.

"Hah!" Beatrice laughed. "We need work to make you a Good Man. The world and all in it are the creation of the Devil. If there is a purpose to this gate being left open, then it is his."

Beatrice smiled at John's worried expression. "But I think there is a more worldly explanation. I had planned to depart this evening, but I see that my co-conspirator has reassessed the situation as well as I have." Putting her fingers to her lips, she whistled three times.

A man, a dozen years older than John, appeared through a doorway to the pair's left. He was filthy, dressed in rags and wore a sullen expression on his broad face.

"'Bout bloody time you was 'ere," he said. "All 'ell's breaking loose back there." The newcomer jerked a thumb up the alley.

"John, meet Adso," Beatrice said serenely. "He has agreed to help us escape."

"Not if you don't get a move on. An' I only agreed to one. 'Oo's this? Another of your...Good Men?"

Adso managed to make the expression sound obscene, but Beatrice showed no sign of taking offence. "Two travel as easily as one, and you will be paid in Carcassonne," she said. Then, turning to John, "As you see, Adso is not a Good Christian. Sadly, I suspect he is closer to the pagan than anything else."

Adso spat derisively onto the filthy cobbled street. "Well, we can stand 'ere jawing until they come an' skewer us or we can go." Adso spun on his heel and stalked toward the gate. After cautiously peering around it, he disappeared. Beatrice followed quickly and John slipped through after her.

Once outside, John felt a curious sense of relief. Instead of being cooped up between the smoke-stained walls of the city, he was out in the open. A rocky slope, covered in small bushes and cut by irregular gullies, stretched gently down to a wide, flat plain dotted with small villages and patterned into long rectangular fields. About two miles to the east, along a completely straight road, John recognized the large, regular shape of what had once been, eight hundred years before, an extensive Roman villa. The regular lines of an olive orchard spread out behind it.

To John's right, a number of people were frantically scrambling down the slope. Others who had left the city earlier were already spread out over the flat fields. A noise behind John made him turn just in time to avoid being bowled over by a short, dumpy man carrying a sack over his shoulder.

"Close the gate," Adso ordered, harshly.

John obeyed, heaving the heavy object shut on its rusted hinges.

"Fools," Adso said, spitting onto a nearby rock.

"Why?" John couldn't help asking. "Aren't they doing the same as us?"

Adso regarded John as if he had the intelligence of a slug. "Can you outrun a man on 'orseback?"

John shook his head.

"Neither can they." Adso waved an arm at the fleeing people. "Now, shut up an' follow me."

Meekly, John followed Beatrice as Adso led them around the foot of the palace wall until a deep, narrow gully barred their way. The smell of human excrement was so strong it made John feel weak.

Adso stopped and looked at John. "Through that wall," he said, patting the stones beside them, "is where the rich folks live. This 'ere's the wall of the Viscount of Béziers' palace. 'Course, 'e ran away to Carcassonne long ago, but 'is lords and ladies is still there, unless the butchers 'ave broke the door in already."

John wanted to defend Roger Trenceval—to tell this crude Adso that the young viscount hadn't run away—but he kept silent.

"Thing 'bout rich folk is, they smell just as bad as poor folk." Adso pointed to the wall two feet above the head of the gully. A downspout protruded some six inches from the surface, and the wall below it was caked in a disgusting brown mass that spread into the bottom of the gully.

Adso laughed at John's grimace. "That's the thing that separates the rich from the poor—fancy toilets." With another laugh, Adso jumped down into the gully.

"I can't go down there," John said in horror.

"I fear you will have to if you want to live." Beatrice pointed back the way they had come. A group of crusaders was running over the hillside, hacking at the refugees who had fled out the gate.

"All the world is excrement," she said cheerfully and followed Adso down.

John took a last look behind him, where he saw the dumpy man who had almost knocked him over hold his arms up in a futile attempt at protection. The sword took the man's hands off as if his arms were made of butter. He only had a second to stare in horror at the bloody stumps before the return swing of the blade sent his head bouncing down the slope. John took a deep breath and stepped off the edge of the gully.

Holocaust

Béziers
July 22, 1209

P eter entered Béziers through the West Gate and, unsure of exactly what Aumery wished him to do, decided to head up toward the cathedral, whose blocky profile dominated the town. He could hear the sounds of fighting in the distance but, with the exception of the occasional knight hurrying to find some plunder, this area of town was deserted—at least by the living. Bodies from the earlier fighting around the gate lay all about in their bloodstained clothing. Most were soldiers and some still clutched weapons in dead hands.

As Peter worked his way uphill, the number of unarmed civilian corpses increased. The majority were men, but many lay on their faces with sword or spear wounds to their backs, as if they had been cut down while fleeing. Here and there a Perfect in a black habit lay surrounded by the bodies of Good Men and Women.

The doors on both sides of the street had been ripped open or shattered by axe blows, and the contents of the dwellings ransacked. A few piles of bloody, dishevelled clothing showed where the occupants had not fled to safety rapidly enough. Several house were on fire, forcing Peter to hurry past on the far side of the street.

Toward the cathedral, the smoke in the air thickened and the number of bodies increased. Peter began to hear the noises of ransacking and the occasional scream coming from the houses around him. Soldiers staggered past loaded down with sacks of loot. But even with everything he had seen on his journey, Peter's first view of the square in front of the cathedral came as a shock.

The square was large and dominated by the imposing west front of the cathedral, behind whose squat archways and round windows deep red flames were already flickering. It was like a backdrop for a scene from hell.

Amid the swirling smoke, figures ran in every direction. Men, women and children fled aimlessly until caught and cut down by rampaging soldiers.

The killing was random and callous. Peter saw two women and a man burst out of the cathedral's main door to escape the flames and be cut down before they had even reached the bottom of the steps. No one was paying attention to any rules of war; the innocent died as easily as the guilty.

The acrid smell of burning wood filled the air and caught at Peter's nostrils, as the clash of weapons and screams of the dying assaulted his ears. Between his feet, a trickle of blood ran down the drainage gutter from the body of a young man not ten feet in front of him. Was this truly God's work?

Peter stood in shock for several minutes before he noticed a group of knights off to his right. One was Simon de Montfort. Peter made his way over, assuming they were discussing how best to stop the massacre and restore order.

"It is a disgrace," de Montfort was saying, "and must not be allowed to continue." He was talking to a tall man whose tunic was soaked in blood. He carried an axe over his left shoulder. Behind him a rabble of equally bloody killers stood, each wearing a tunic emblazoned with a falcon holding an axe in its talons. Many carried booty in addition to their weapons, several items of which, Peter noticed, had obviously come from churches.

"My Falcons and I broke through the gates," the big man was saying in a heavy, foreign accent. "We took this town for your precious crusade. It is ours by right of conquest and we shall do with it as we wish."

"Yes, you conquered, but in the name of God and only by His grace. The crusade marches and fights under the cross and you will obey the Holy Church."

"Perhaps God will open the gates of Carcassonne, but I think you would do better to trust in my Falcons. They obey me and they fight for what they can get. If they are paid to kill heretics," the man shrugged, "so be it. A sword guts a heretic as swiftly as a Catholic.

"This war will not be over this summer, and someone will have to stay over the winter if this year's work is not to be lost. That someone"—the big man stared hard at de Montfort—"will be well advised to keep some good fighters near him and not be too fussy about how they earn a few extra coins."

Simon de Montfort stood silent for several moments. "Very well. You and your men may keep what you have, but you must, from now on, work with me in preventing any more looting. All valuables must be taken to the camp and their disposal determined by Father Aumery."

"We are at your service," the mercenary said sardonically.

With a shock of disgust, Peter realized that the knights had not been discussing how to stop the killing, but how to share out the spoils. He was

Heretic

about to step forward and say something when a mighty roar drowned out all talk. Peter spun around just in time to see the cathedral roof crashing in on the nave beneath. Violent bursts of flame, sparks and smoke boiled out of doors and windows. Figures, some engulfed by the fire, were thrown into the surrounding streets. For a moment afterwards, apart from the roiling smoke, the scene in the square was a frozen tableau as everyone stood in awe. Then the violence began again.

"So much for their refuge," the big man said with a laugh.

"But there must have been hundreds of innocent people in there," Peter blurted out. Everyone turned to stare at him.

"Who are you?" the big man asked, lifting his axe from his shoulder.

"He is one of Aumery's underlings," de Montfort answered for Peter. "No doubt here to see that everything is done as it should be."

The mercenary smiled, but there was no warmth in it. He pushed his axe forward, poking Peter in the chest.

"Little monk, you go and tell Father Aumery that God saw fit to smite the unbelievers in His cathedral. Tell him also that God's work saved Oddo of Saxony from repeating the work he has already done in the Madeleine."

Peter couldn't move. His eyes were fixed on the bloodstained axe in front of him.

"So," Oddo went on, "you wish to be introduced to my friend, Britta?" The axe pushed harder, forcing Peter back a step. "She has been busy today. I have introduced her to many new friends—some you would call innocent, but Britta doesn't care. Guilty, innocent, it is all the same to Britta. Is that not so, my dear?" The axe forced Peter back another step. The men behind Oddo laughed.

Peter was terrified. Sweat poured off him and the smell of the fresh blood on the axe made him gag.

"But you are not being polite," Oddo said. "You have been introduced to a lady. Should you not kiss her hand?"

Peter stayed silent.

"Answer!"

The sheer violence of Oddo's command forced a response. "Yes."

"That's better. Now kiss Britta." The mercenary turned the axe so the flat of the blade lay inches from Peter's face. The sharp edge tickled his throat. Half-congealed blood was thick on the blade and a tuft of dark brown hair clung to the edge.

"Kiss Britta!" The command was accompanied by a slight twitch of the axe that cut a thin line in Peter's neck. Closing his eyes, he bent his head forward and kissed the cold blade. The blood was sticky on his lips. Stumbling backwards, Peter collapsed to his knees on the cobbles, retching. The sound of laughter from Oddo's men was deafening.

Struggling to his feet and frantically wiping at the blood and vomit on his face, Peter ran from his torturers.

"Oh, leaving so soon, little priest? Britta will miss you."

Peter fled blindly through the chaos and slaughter, tripping over bodies and slipping in pools of blood. Tears burned his eyes as he barged into cursing soldiers and screaming victims.

At length, he found himself in a square in front of another large church. Bodies and discarded treasures lay around, but there was not a living soul in sight. The wide church doors were thrown open, but no one entered or left, and Peter could see no movement in the dark interior. After the noise of battle, the silence was eerie.

Peter moved forward, drawn by the open doors. Perhaps, at last, he had found a refuge. It took a moment for his eyes to adjust from the bright sunlight to the gloom in the church. At first, he could not make out what the shapes covering the floor of the nave were. He stepped forward, and his foot slid out from under him. He would have fallen heavily, except that his landing was broken by a body. In fact, several bodies were piled around the foot of the marble font. Peter pushed himself away and his hand landed in the puddle that had caused him to fall. It was sticky and smelled sweet. Blood.

With rising horror, Peter struggled to his feet and looked about. The church was a charnel house. Hundreds of bodies—men, women and children—lay piled in the aisles, side chapels and round the high altar, where they had huddled in terror. All were covered in blood and many showed the signs of having been hacked at in a frenzy long after death.

Peter was frozen to the spot, breathing heavily. Here and there a voice groaned for help. Suddenly, Peter felt something clutch at his ankle. He stared down to see a bloodied hand reaching out from the pile of corpses beside him.

"No," he screamed, kicking at the hand and fleeing back into the square. Peter ran aimlessly, tears blinding him. The church must be the Madeleine that the foul mercenary had mentioned, but Peter didn't care; he wanted only to escape the cruelty and horror. But he knew there was no escape. He could run forever, but the scenes he had witnessed in the last few hours were burned into his brain.

At last, Peter found himself back at the West Gate. Staggering through, he collapsed, gasping, on the hillside.

"Are not the workings of Divine vengeance wondrous?"

Peter peered up to see Arnaud Aumery standing before him. "They're killing everyone," he choked out. "The corpses litter the streets, the cathedral has burned down, the Madeleine is filled with the dead!"

"Is that not appropriate?" Aumery asked. "Today is the feast day of Marie Madeleine and, if you knew your history, you would also realize that the only truly Catholic viscount this citadel of the Devil has ever had was foully murdered by these citizens on this very day, forty-two years ago. Our Lady is taking her retribution through the strong arms of her crusaders."

"But the women and children! No one is being spared."

Aumery sat down beside Peter. "Have you already forgotten what we talked of earlier this day? God offered the citizens of Béziers a chance to deliver up the heretics from their midst. They did not; therefore, they are equally guilty and deserve their fate."

Peter sat glumly gazing at the dirt between his feet, images of death replaying in his mind. Without question, they had the power to shock and horrify him, but it was the embarrassment of his encounter with Oddo that kept bubbling to the surface.

Aumery placed an arm comfortably across Peter's shoulder. "There is something more on your mind?"

Peter nodded bleakly.

"Then tell me, my son. I have seen much of the world and will understand."

Peter took a deep breath. "I met de Montfort by the cathedral. He was with Oddo of Saxony, one of the mercenary soldiers. I thought at first they were discussing how to stop the killing, but they were merely talking about sharing the loot."

"The spoils of war are sometimes important to motivate the likes of these men to do God's work."

"But Oddo was so powerful!"

"The Lord needs strong arms."

"Not just physically. His will dominated de Montfort, and when I complained, he brushed me aside like a dry leaf in autumn, and his men laughed. He forced me to kiss the bloodied blade of his axe. The man is a brute! He strides through the world as if he owns it, taking what he needs and doing what he wishes. No one can stop him."

"And you envy him."

Peter jerked his head up and looked into Aumery's weirdly staring eyes. He was right; the power that Oddo flaunted so openly was seductive—what *would* it be like to have no restraints, no, limits on what you could or could not do? Not to have to work to make people like you, but have them respect you simply for your power?

Peter nodded miserably. "I *do* envy his strength and power. I'm not worthy to become a monk."

"No, you are young and insecure," Aumery said gently. "You do not believe that you are worthy of anyone's respect. So, when you come upon the strong of this earth, you feel weak and uncertain. You lose sight of anything larger than your own worries."

"It's true, Father. If I am honest, the sound of Oddo's men laughing at me caused me more distress today than the horror of the Madeleine. But what can I do? I will never be physically strong. Look!" Peter held out an arm and pulled back his robe. The bones of his wrist and elbow stood out through his pale skin like pebbles under a blanket. "Sticks and string," he said, recalling John's jest about when God had made him. "And as for strength of will, what power can I possibly have to support me?"

"Pierre of Castelnau was one of the most revolting men I have ever met," said Aumery. "Yet he had power, and nobles did his bidding. He is no more and now I have his power."

"You have the power of God."

"And you shall too, once you are ordained. But I have something more immediate. Something that, unfortunately, carries more weight with the likes of de Montfort and that mercenary. I have the authority of the Pope. I can threaten eternal damnation and the fires of hell, and I can call excommunication. Do you know what that means?"

"The excommunicant is cast out from the Church."

"Yes, but all his debtors are released from their debts, his lords are released from their obligations to protect him, and those under him no longer owe him allegiance. At a stroke, I can destroy anyone who challenges the authority of the Holy Mother Church, and that Church is represented through me. That makes even the most troublesome lord sit up and take notice of what I say. They do not have to like me, but they do have to respect my power.

"Your way to power, young Peter, lies through the Church and through me as your mentor. Why do you think I chose you?"

"You chose me?"

"Of course. We are mortal but the Church is eternal. I fear those who say this crusade will last many a year might be correct. Others must follow in my footsteps once I am become dust. I would wish you to be one."

"I would be honoured."

"Do not be honoured too quickly. It will be a hard road and I will not be a gentle taskmaster, but I will teach you the ways of power, how to acquire it and how to wield it. I will teach you how to use the authority of the Church so that the likes of de Montfort and Oddo will do *your* bidding."

Aumery stood and stretched. He looked back at the city on the hill. "I fear the enthusiasm of this morning has gotten even more out of control."

Peter followed Aumery's gaze. Thick columns of dirty smoke were rising from behind Béziers' walls. Large areas of the city were already ablaze and the fires were spreading rapidly through the dry wooden houses. Knights, laden with treasures, were heading back toward the crusader camp.

"It appears God does not wish anything to be left of this abominable city," Aumery said. "I fear not even treasure will survive that holocaust. Still, I do not think there is much treasure in this town."

Peter frowned. There was a vast amount of treasure in Béziers and Aumery knew that. Yes, much would be lost in a fire, but the crusaders would salvage a lot, as well. He was about to ask Aumery to explain when the legate spoke again. "Come, young Peter, let us go and see what de Montfort *has* managed to salvage."

Peter followed the priest across the bridge. Aumery was right: the Church was the answer to Peter's problem. With the power of the papacy behind him, Peter need never feel weak again.

Destinations

Outside Béziers
July 22, 1209

"It looks as if there might be a cave behind that bush down there," the first voice said somewhat uncertainly. "We should check it out."

"Might be's not good enough to get me down there," a second voice replied. "I came to this godforsaken city for plunder. I can get covered in excrement anywhere. Let's go find us some heretics to skewer."

John held his breath as he listened to the two men work their way over the stony hillside. His first breath made him gag, but he loved the smell. It had saved his life.

John, Beatrice and Adso sat huddled together beneath an overhang in the stinking gully beneath Béziers' walls. A couple of half-dead bushes pulled over the entrance did little to hide them, but meant that someone would have to come down into the gully to look into the deep shadows and, as they had just seen, few were prepared to do that.

Adso lowered the evil-looking dagger he had been holding in front of him. "I'm almost sorry they didn't come down," he whispered. "Though I doubt you two'd 'ave been much 'elp."

"You know I refuse to take any life," Beatrice said.

"I know, and your friend's got no weapon. Fine pair you are."

"Why do you refuse to take life?" John asked Beatrice. "Those men would have killed us if they could."

"All souls are trapped in their bodies," Beatrice explained. "Death releases them, but to heaven only if the body has undergone baptism by the Holy Spirit in the *consolamentum*. Otherwise, the soul remains trapped on earth in another body, either human or animal."

"Reckon I'd 'ave been doing those two a favour, sending their souls to live in a couple of frogs."

"So you would have sat calmly awaiting death had they discovered us?" John ignored Adso's comment.

"I would," Beatrice replied. "Death is a blessing for those who have taken the *consolamentum*."

"You would not have acted to save either mine or Adso's life, even though our souls are as condemned as the other two?"

John sensed a hesitation. "I would struggle to protect you, but not to the extent of endangering another life."

"Fat lot of good that does," Adso murmured.

"So, if death is such a blessing, why do you flee from Béziers?" John asked.

"Aye," Adso added, "there's plenty back in the city 'oo'd 'appily give you your wish this day."

"I have a task to perform yet."

"And if you wish to live to perform it, we'd best be silent and rest. It's many 'ours 'til the sun goes down and it'll not be dark long. We need to be far from 'ere afore day breaks tomorrow."

* * *

All day the trio huddled uncomfortably in their disgusting refuge. Occasional screams reached them, and twice they held their breaths as footsteps passed nearby, but no one dared brave the filthy gully to search for survivors. As darkness finally fell, they dragged their aching limbs into the open and moved cautiously away from the devastated city. Fortunately, although the night was cloudless, the moon was new and their progress went unobserved.

After several hours of nerve-racking travel, during which John jumped at every sound in the darkness, the three stopped in a small stand of willows by a stream. They washed off as much of the gully's residue as possible then sat on the bank to rest in the warm night.

"How far is it to Carcassonne?" John asked Beatrice.

"I'm not going to Carcassonne," Beatrice answered. "I'm heading to Minerve."

"Minerve!" Adso exclaimed. "No, no. My agreement was to get you out of the city and take you to Carcassonne."

"No," Beatrice said quietly. "The agreement was that you would be paid in Carcassonne. And so you shall be. You need merely go to the Good Christian's house by the main gate and they will pay you what we agreed."

"An' extra for 'im?" Adso jerked his finger at John.

"Of course," Beatrice said. "I am in your debt, Adso."

Adso grunted. "As long as I'm paid."

"One day," Beatrice said, "you will see that money is but the Devil's tool."

"I daresay." Adso stood and stretched. "Until then, I'll use the Devil's tool to buy an 'ot meal and a soft bed in Carcassonne. You coming with me, lad, or you off to that nest of crazy heretics?"

John hesitated. Was he still bound by his responsibility to Roger Trenceval in Carcassonne? He had agreed to keep Trenceval informed of what happened in Béziers, but Béziers didn't exist any more. The viscount would discover that soon enough without John. And John was frightened. Carcassonne was the next obvious destination for the crusader army and escape might not be so easy a second time.

John also had to admit to a fascination with the calm, gentle Beatrice. She was the first Cathar Perfect he had a chance to really get to know, and the part of his mind that craved knowledge wanted to find out more about her and her strange beliefs. Her mention of a mysterious task also intrigued him.

"I'm going to Minerve," John said.

"You're both crazy. Carcassonne won't fall as easy as Béziers. The foreigners'll work their forty days, take their indulgences and go 'ome. Everything'll be back to normal in a month." Adso shook his head. "But if you insist, 'ead west for a day or two. Keep the black 'ills on your right. When you reach the Cesse River follow it into the 'ills to find Minerve. And stick to the low ground—there'll be crusader foraging parties all over this country soon. I wish you luck."

The leaves rustled as Adso strode away in the darkness. John felt strangely lonely in the silence that followed. Adso may have been crude and abrupt, but he knew what was going on and they owed their escape thus far to him.

"I wish him the best," Beatrice said, rising slowly and with some discomfort, "but we should get moving."

John jumped to his feet and offered his hand. Beatrice took it.

"Thank you. I am not as young as I used to be, and sitting on the damp grass stiffens the muscles. I don't suppose I should be running around burning cities either!"

"Why are we going to Minerve?" John asked as they set off along the bank of the stream.

"Because I have things to do there, and Carcassonne will fall, if not this year, then the next. After that happens the crusaders will move out north and south from the cities. Minerve, Bram, Terme, Laveur and Toulouse will fall eventually."

"Toulouse?"

"Especially Toulouse. Count Raymond may argue with the Church and stall as long as he can, but the crusaders, and that fat slug, Bishop Foulques, will demand Toulouse be cleared of heretics. Either Count Raymond surrenders or he fights. Either way, Toulouse will fall. The Catholics will not give up, even if it takes a hundred years. They hate us passionately."

"But why?"

"Because we exist and thrive in the very heart of Christendom. To them, we are a canker that must be cut out and burned. We threaten them because we follow the old ways. We keep alive the form and intent of the original Christians and of God himself, from a time before the Church was corrupted by Satan. They hate us for that, but deep down, they know we are right and they are wrong. They cannot change—that would mean giving up all their power—so they must destroy us, root and branch. They will not, as Adso and so many others fondly wish, give up and go home. They will stay and more will come until this land is destroyed and the last Good Christian is hurled into the flames of the last bonfire."

John was silent for a long moment, contemplating the bleak picture Beatrice had painted. If she was right, there was nowhere to run. But John didn't need to run. He wasn't a heretic. He wasn't a particularly devout Catholic either, but if he went somewhere, kept a low profile and attended Mass regularly, he would probably be ignored. Perhaps Minerve was as good a place as any.

"What is in Minerve?"

John sensed that Beatrice was weighing her options, deciding on how much to reveal. "Books," she said eventually.

"But books are material things—the work of the Devil, no?"

"So you've been listening." John could hear the smile in Beatrice's voice. "It's true, all material things *are* the work of Satan and we, as immortal souls trapped in this corrupt world, must reject them. But God's work is spread through the world as well. Wood is material, yet fire, which consumes it, is immaterial and hence pure. Our bodies are evil, yet our souls are trapped within them. Books are corrupt, yet the wisdom within them—wisdom that comes from our souls—can be pure."

"So the books at Minerve contain wisdom?"

"Of course! And Minerve is not the only place with books. But they are all in danger. The Church of Rome excels in the destruction of all knowledge that does not accord with its own ideas. For example, you know of the four Gospels?"

"Of course: Matthew, Mark, Luke and John. Everybody knows them."

"What if I were to tell you that these are not the only, or even the most accurate, gospels? There are others, about eighty in total, written by disciples and by other holy men, that preserve so much more knowledge than is in the Catholic Testament. There are Gospels by St. Thomas, James and Barnabas. There is even one by Judas."

"I have heard of such things, but aren't they forgeries?"

"Some, but not all. Eight hundred years ago, the founders of the Catholic

Church sat down and decided which gospels were to be in the Testament. They chose not for authenticity but for congruence with their ideas. The rest they destroyed or suppressed."

"And these are at Minerve?"

"Some, and other things as well. Mankind's soul has been trapped for a very long time, and the wisdom of God has struggled for release in many different ways. Wisdom is not the preserve of a single time or place."

Despite his exhaustion, John felt excitement building at the thought of the library at Minerve. How he would love to read through the knowledge that was collected there.

"So we are going to Minerve to read?" he asked eagerly.

"And other places. There are books in many libraries scattered over this land, and as many as possible must be saved before the army of Satan finds and destroys them."

"Where will they be taken that will be safe?"

"That's enough questions for now."

"I want to help." John barely had time to think about his words before they were out of his mouth, but he knew his offer was genuine.

"Then you shall. I can use a pair of strong arms and the company will be welcome. In exchange, I shall teach you something of our ways."

"And turn me into a heretic!" John said with a laugh.

"No. Turn you into a Good Christian. But tonight, we will turn into corpses if we do not stop chattering and keep moving."

For the rest of the night, to the regular rhythm of Beatrice's staff hitting the ground with each step, John's mind whirled with the possible wonders he might discover in the lost books. What scholarship and enlightenment did they contain?

Truce

Carcassonne
August 14, 1209

Peter answered the summons to Arnaud Aumery's tent with some trepidation. In the three weeks since the fall of Béziers, he had been kept busy, but not in the way he had hoped. Despite Aumery's promise to teach Peter the ways of papal diplomacy and prepare him for ordination, the days had been much the same for Peter as for the other lay brothers.

Since the army had left the smoking ruins of Béziers, he had helped pack up Aumery's tent and its contents each morning and reverse the process at the end of the day's march. He had tended the mules and horses, fetched water, helped cook meals, and cleaned and repaired equipment and the large collection of relics and religious artifacts that always accompanied the Holy Crusade. What unpleasant job had Aumery found for Peter to do this time? True, there was less to do now that the army was camped outside the walls of Carcassonne, but many of the tasks, such as cleaning out the mule lines, were even less pleasant.

Oddo had been right: the gates of Carcassonne had not fallen open as miraculously as Béziers, and a prolonged siege had ensued. But, after seventeen days, everyone felt that some kind of resolution was approaching fast. The forty-day term of service for the crusader knights was almost up, and many would soon begin to drift home. On the other side, conditions in the overcrowded city must be dire. It was a question of which side could hold out the longest.

"Ah, Peter, good of you to come."

Peter was taken aback by the cheerful tone of Aumery's greeting. Nevertheless, he pushed into the tent and stood before the legate. As usual, Aumery was flanked by two lay brothers, but Peter was surprised to see de Montfort standing to one side.

"Remove your clothing," Aumery ordered.

"Remove..."

"You wish to be ordained into holy orders, do you not?"

"Of course, yes!" Peter's heart was suddenly racing. Was this what Aumery had summoned him for? "But I have not studied."

"These are exceptional times, Peter. The Lord will understand our need for haste. Now, remove your lay robe that you may be ordained."

Peter did as he was told, feeling weak and vulnerable as he stood naked before these men.

"Now lie on the ground."

Peter did so.

"Do you repent of all your sins and renounce all your past life?" Aumery intoned.

"I do."

"Do you renounce all sins of the flesh?"

"I do."

"And as you are reborn into the holy order, will you devote what remains of your earthly life to the service of God and the performance of the seven holy sacraments of Baptism, Confirmation, Eucharist, Penance, Extreme Unction, Ordination and Matrimony?"

"I will."

"Will you abide by the Rule of the Blessed St. Benedict and the laws of the Cistercian Brotherhood?"

"I will."

"Then stand."

Peter stood and Aumery made the sign of the cross on his forehead with holy water from a small vial at his waist. "Now be reborn in Christ and receive the power to offer sacrament in the Church for the living and the dead, in the name of the Father, and of the Son, and of the Holy Ghost."

Aumery, the two lay brothers and Peter said, "Amen."

One of the brothers stepped forward and draped the white habit of the Cistercians over Peter's head.

"Welcome, Brother Peter," Aumery said, embracing him.

As thrilled as he was at the unexpected event, Peter's stomach churned with uncertainty. Normally, ordination was preceded by a long period of training in a monastery, during which one learned the forms and rituals of the priesthood. Peter had been looking forward to this time—to the opportunity to study his calling. He felt unprepared for the work at hand, but as Aumery had said, these were extraordinary times.

"That's just what we need," de Montfort said, stepping forward, "more monks."

"We can never have too many soldiers working in God's army," Aumery replied.

"Well, they're going to have to work in *my* army if this damnable town doesn't surrender soon."

"It is in hand," Aumery snapped at the knight. "Now, Brother Peter, God has a task for you. We need an emissary to go into the den of Satan and suggest terms for an end to this siege."

So that explained it—Peter's perfunctory ordination. Nothing was ever straightforward with Arnaud Aumery.

"Why me?" Peter asked. "Should this task not be entrusted to someone more important?"

"Do you question that God has chosen you?"

"No, of course not."

"Then be glad you can do his work. Besides, you speak some Latin and this local Occitan language. You will go under a flag of truce and meet with the heretic Roger Trenceval. You will offer him the following terms: if he surrenders immediately and hands over all heretics in the city to justice, then his city and its inhabitants will be spared the horrors of Béziers."

"He will want guarantees," Peter pointed out.

"You will tell him that you are empowered to give him safe conduct and escort him to this tent to discuss the details. Make sure that you offer only safe conduct *to* this place."

"And if he quibbles about the heretics' fate," said de Montfort, stepping forward, "you may say that *all* the inhabitants of the city may walk free as long as they leave everything behind."

"God and the Holy Church cannot agree to that." Aumery turned on the knight. "You had your earthly example of the power of the crusade at Béziers to encourage your men. Now the Church needs a spiritual example. The heretics of Carcassonne must burn."

"Trenceval will not agree to hand over the heretics. Too many high-placed persons in his city are involved, and he is not yet defeated. We have not come close to breaching the main walls, and he has food and water enough. If Carcassonne holds out for another week or two, my knights will begin to go home—then where will your crusade be?

"If, on the other hand, the city falls by storm, there will be massacre and looting to make Béziers seem as if it were a child's game," de Montfort continued. "I need an intact city if I am to hold this land for the winter. If I do not get it, then all we have achieved this year is lost and we must begin again next spring. How many of your forty-day knights will flock next year to repeat the work of this? Your precious crusade needs this city unburned. Carcassonne is worth a few heretic lives. In any case, you will catch them next year or the year after. Do you want to see your treasure go up in smoke?"

The venom in Aumery's stare shocked Peter. How he must hate the idea of letting the heretics go, but de Montfort's logic was unassailable. If Carcassonne burned, then this year was a waste and Aumery would have to be the one to tell Pope Innocent that his crusade had failed.

"Very well." Aumery turned to Peter, all traces of the cheery note with which he had welcomed him gone. The voice was cold and hard. "If Trenceval refuses to submit his heretics to the Church's justice, you may offer him what de Montfort wishes. But do not give it easily. You will take these two lay brothers and go now. I want Trenceval here before sunset."

Slightly stunned by the sudden rush of events, Peter left the tent, followed by the two lay brothers. Outside, a squire wearing de Monfort's colours stepped forward and offered him a large white flag on a stout pole. Peter took it and in silence the three marched through the crusader camp toward the walls of Carcassonne. It was only as they entered the city gate that Peter recalled de Montfort's final, intriguing words, "Do you want to see your treasure go up in smoke?"

* * *

Peter's walk through Carcassonne was very different from the one through Béziers. The steep, narrow streets, lined with timbered houses that leaned over to almost meet above Peter's head, were crowded, filthy and stinking, but there was life in them. Signs of the siege were everywhere: Skinny mules and dogs wandered about, scavenging what they could from the piles of refuse lying all around. People stared hard at Peter in his fresh habit, their wide eyes betraying strain. But there were no bodies cluttering the streets, and the looks the people gave him were defiant. De Montfort was right, the city was suffering, but it was not collapsing.

The trio was led into the viscount's palace and made to wait in a sumptuous room whose walls were covered with fine, brightly coloured tapestries that showed scenes from the troubadours' songs. Eventually, Viscount Roger Trenceval entered.

Word had obviously reached the viscount of their approach, and he was dressed in a long cloak bearing the Trenceval arms and bordered in blue and gold. He was followed by an equally well-dressed page and troubadour. Peter was surprised at how young Trenceval was—only a few years older than himself. Despite the man being an enemy, Peter immediate liked his broad, open face, which broke into a smile as he stepped forward to introduce himself.

"Welcome to Carcassonne! I am Viscount Roger Trenceval of Carcassonne and Béziers, and I assume you are envoys of Father Arnaud Aumery?"

Heretic

"I am sent by him," Peter said as formally as he could manage. "I am Peter and I am authorized to offer…"

"Before all that, let me offer you, as guests, some refreshment. Just because we are at war does not mean that we cannot be civilized." Roger Trenceval clapped his hands and a servant bearing a silver tray of wine goblets appeared as if by magic from behind a tapestry.

Peter had the goblet of dark red wine in his hand before he wondered if it was the right thing to do. Did accepting this hospitality somehow undermine his position? Both lay brothers refused.

Roger seemed unconcerned and took a long swallow with obvious relish. "Now, let us hear what you are authorized to offer."

"I am to tell you that you, your people and your city will be spared if you surrender and give up the heretics in your possession."

Peter was startled as the viscount let out such a loud guffaw that he spilled some wine on his cloak. "That is where we were at the beginning of this affair! Let me make you a counter proposal. I will let your crusader army pack up unmolested and return home before disease takes hold in the ranks, starvation follows on from the ravaging of the countryside, and the forty days of service for the papal indulgence are over."

"I cannot accept that."

"Of course not. And I would not expect you to, but you must have come to me with something else. Let us put all our cards on the table."

Peter glanced nervously at the other people in the room. Roger Trenceval smiled and clapped his hands again. His page and troubadour stood. Roger waited expectantly.

"Would you please leave us?" Peter asked the lay brothers with as much authority as he could muster. The brothers looked hesitantly at each other, but eventually stood and followed the page and troubadour out of the room, leaving Peter and Roger alone.

"Now we can speak openly," Roger began.

"If I am to speak openly, then you must too," Peter said. "It is true that the forty days are almost up but, as you can see from your walls, our camp is well situated. We control the entire countryside from Béziers to here. Narbonne and every castle, keep and town hereabouts have sent envoys to pay homage and promise support." Peter was surprised at how easily the words came once he began. "There is no disease and we are well supplied. It is only August; enough knights will stay past the forty days as long as the weather holds and there is hope of plunder. You must still have water and food, else I would not have seen mules and dogs in the streets, but the people have the look of hunger in their eyes. By September, how much water will you have left? How much food? And will Carcassonne look like Béziers when it does fall?"

"I do not worry about your last point," Trenceval said thoughtfully. "Your army wishes Carcassonne preserved as much as I do. However, you are correct in the rest. The desire for plunder is a powerful force and makes dangerous enemies. It will keep enough men here to maintain the siege past the point where I can offer effective resistance. But for all that, I still cannot accept your terms."

"Why not? You keep your lives. All you lose is your treasure, which will be taken eventually in any case, and a few heretics."

"The treasure I do not care for overly, but I am loathe to see the Good Men and Women thrown onto a bonfire."

"Are you a heretic?"

"Sometimes I think we are all heretics, so narrow are the Church's interpretations and restrictions." Roger smiled again. "But no, I go to Mass like every other good Catholic. But it is my job to rule this land, just as it was my father's. It is the Church's job to save souls. I will not go into my subjects' houses and tell them what to say in their prayers to the Almighty. If enough of them keep the peace, pay their taxes and answer my call to arms when we are threatened, I am happy and my subjects adjudge me a good and fair ruler. If the old, fat bishop of Toulouse would rather sit in his palace surrounded by his fine possessions and corrupt priests than tend to the souls of his flock, is it a concern of mine?"

"The army camped outside your walls this day and my very presence here would suggest that it is."

"Indeed, but these ones that you call heretics are my people. Many of my liege lords are Good Christians and their wives and daughters are Perfects. Am I to cast them into the flames to save my skin? And were I to do so, would it help me? I have offered to submit, to give up my lands, to pay homage to Rome and do public penance. Arnaud Aumery dismissed me like a peasant. He wishes blood."

"What if there is no blood?"

"No blood! You think this can be resolved without that payment?"

"It might be possible. De Montfort needs your city and he is prepared to allow heretics to live to acquire it." Peter felt strong as he negotiated. Aumery was right, this was real power, not Oddo's blood-stained axe.

"Go on," Trenceval encouraged.

"If you surrender the city and all its contents, your people will be allowed to go wherever they wish."

"Heretics as well?"

"Yes."

"And what is to stop de Montfort's knights rounding up everyone in a black habit after the surrender and slaughtering them?"

"Nothing, if they are wearing black habits."

"The Perfects will never agree to hide in ordinary clothes."

"Yes, but de Montfort wants everything left in the city when the inhabitants leave. If that were to include clothing, the Perfects would not refuse, and who can tell the beliefs of one naked man from another?"

Trenceval smiled. "You are clever for your age." He thought long and hard, his hands clasped before him as if praying.

"And how does Simon de Montfort propose to undertake this surrender?" he asked eventually.

"I do not know, but I am authorized to offer you a safe conduct back to our camp to discuss the details."

Trenceval thought again. At length he said, "Very well. I do not trust your masters, but I trust you. If it will save my people, I shall return with you into the lion's den. But first I must prepare and inform my knights of what is afoot." The viscount rose and left the hall.

The thrill of having succeeded at such an important task, his first, swept through Peter. The only worm of doubt in his mind was that, in suggesting a way for the Perfects to escape, he had overstepped Aumery's instructions. But shouldn't a negotiator have some leeway?

Peter imagined where this might lead. Perhaps he would become the negotiator for the crusade, travelling ahead of the army and persuading impregnable fortresses to bow before the might of God. Think of all the lives he would save—all the lives he had already saved here in Carcassonne, not least of which was Roger Trenceval's! The young viscount reminded him of John; he had the same open mind and broad interest in the world. It may have been misguided, but it was nonetheless attractive. Where was John now? Peter wondered.

"Let us go and see what fate has in store." Roger's return interrupted Peter's reverie. The viscount had changed into a simple suit of brown leather breeches and a deep red tunic that bore his coat of arms on the breast. He was accompanied by the page who had been present earlier and two sullen, yet unarmed, knights.

"You walked here, as befits your station as a monk, but I shall ride, so as not to seem to be surrendering. At times, appearance is more important than reality."

On the way back through the streets of Carcassonne, Roger led with Peter at his stirrup. The page, the knights and the two lay brothers followed behind. The streets were crowded, yet strangely quiet. People stood and watched the small procession pass. It was almost as if everyone were holding their breath, wondering what this new turn of events meant. Peter noticed a number of heretic Perfects amongst the crowd. He felt a momentary qualm. Had he, perhaps, just saved the heretics' lives? And if so, was that a mortal sin?

* * *

"So, if I agree to surrender the city and all its contents, everyone will be allowed to leave unharmed?" Roger Trenceval seemed relaxed, even when faced with Arnaud Aumery and the crusader knights. The negotiations for the surrender of Carcassonne had been swift—Simon de Montfort needed an intact city, and Roger Trenceval wanted to save lives. Peter was pleased. He didn't want to see more bloodshed.

"That is the agreement, yes," de Montfort said.

"Everyone?" Trenceval stared directly at Aumery, who glanced over at de Montfort, but nodded. "Yes. Everyone."

"Very well then. I hereby surrender the city of Carcassonne and all its material contents to the army of Arnaud Aumery and Simon de Montfort and I pass my people into the care of his Holiness Pope Innocent III."

"Excellent." Aumery's voice was flat.

Peter stepped forward with the document he had been preparing from his notes. He placed it on the top of the large trunk between the two parties. Aumery, de Montfort and Trenceval crowded round to read it. Peter prayed that he had not made any serious mistakes.

"What's this?" Aumery asked, pointing a skinny finger at a paragraph halfway down the page. "All will leave the city wearing nothing but their sins."

"All possessions are to be left in the city," Trenceval said.

"And without clothing, no one will be able to hide any valuables as they leave," Peter added.

Aumery shot Peter a sharp look, but before he could say anything, de Montfort burst out laughing. "He's a clever one, this little monk of yours. This will save a lot of searching."

De Montfort picked up Peter's quill, dipped it in ink and signed the bottom of the document. Roger Trenceval followed suit. Arnaud Aumery hesitated, but eventually signed. A wax block and lighted candle were brought forward and small pools of red wax dripped onto the parchment. Each of the signatories pressed his ring into the wax to seal the deal.

"Very good," Aumery said, lifting the document and waving it in the air to dry the ink. He turned to Peter. "You offered the viscount safe conduct *to* our camp?"

"I did."

"Good. Seize him!"

Two knights stepped briskly forward and pinned Roger Trenceval's arms to his sides. The young man didn't resist. His two unarmed knights stepped forward but were met with a wall of drawn swords.

"What are you doing?" Peter asked, shocked.

"Arresting a notorious protector of heretics," Aumery replied.

"But I promised!"

"You promised him safe conduct *to* our camp. He is here now. You did your job well."

"But—"

"Do not argue with me, boy! I will not have this man free as a rallying point while so many heretics still roam openly in this land. Bind him well and guard him until we can place him in one of the city's dungeons."

Crusader knights dragged Roger Trenceval out of the tent while others guarded his escorts. The viscount did not struggle but, as he was being pulled away, he looked straight at Peter and smiled.

Trenceval knew, Peter thought. He knew that in coming here with me, his freedom, and possibly his life, were sacrificed. He was prepared to give that up to save his people. Peter felt stupid that he had not seen Aumery's ploy. His dreams of becoming a famous negotiator vanished.

"Make copies of this," Aumery said to Peter as he handed him the signed document, "and have it nailed to every church door in the city." He turned to de Montfort and the other knights. "Tomorrow at dawn, the population may leave unmolested, taking, as my young friend said so eloquently, only their sins. Your knights will plunder nothing on pain of excommunication. All valuables will be brought here, piled up and guarded. They will pay for the continuing crusade. Escort Trenceval's page and knights back into the city."

The knights filed out, leaving only Aumery, de Montfort, Peter and a few lay brothers.

"So now you have your intact city for the winter and a base for your expeditions next summer." Aumery addressed de Montfort.

"And you have one of the main protectors of heretics in chains," de Montfort responded.

"I do, but I would rather your men were building a bonfire for tomorrow."

"Patience. There will be bonfires a plenty in the summers to come. But what has our young monk here got from the day?"

"Nothing," Peter said bitterly. "I was just a tool."

"But a tool in a righteous cause. And that will take you closer to God. Is that not so, Father Aumery?"

"Indeed, and I believe he has learned yet one more lesson in the art of diplomacy. He has learned much in a short time and will learn more in the coming winter months. He may yet be of service to you in your work here."

"Perhaps. But for now, I must see to our prisoner." De Montfort strode out of the tent.

"And you must to your rest," Aumery said. "Tomorrow you begin to study what you should have learned before your ordination."

Peter nodded and left. Darkness was falling, and the first stars were showing themselves. Word of the end of the siege had passed swiftly through the crusader camp and the sounds of revelry were already beginning.

It had been a strange year, Peter reflected. He could recall every moment of his troubling encounter with Oddo. The image of Oddo's scarred face and Britta's bloody blade still caused shudders of embarrassment, but it also strengthened his resolve to never again be so powerless that a thug like Oddo could humiliate him. Today, he had been a tool in a shameful deed, but his reward, so Aumery and de Montfort seemed to promise, was to be learning over the winter and a place on next year's crusade. As Peter made his way through the dark to his own tent, it seemed a good exchange.

Remembering

Minerve
July and August 1209

"We shall be safe here. At least for the time being," Beatrice said.

It was a hot late July day and Beatrice and John were sitting on opposite sides of the rough wooden table in the kitchen of the Perfect house in Minerve. The room was rectangular and the table ran almost the length of it. John sat with his back to the huge stone fireplace where pots of all shapes and sizes hung in a hearth large enough for John to stand upright in. The opposite wall was broken by doors leading to pantries, upstairs rooms and a small courtyard. Above John's head, the roof beams were black from the smoke of cooking fires and below his feet, the beaten earth floor was covered in a fresh, thick layer of dry threshed hay mixed with herbs. The smell of wild sage and rosemary filled the air.

The kitchen was also a dining room and meeting place for the twenty Perfects who slept on the floors of the upstairs rooms, but the two new arrivals had it to themselves this afternoon. Beatrice slept upstairs, but John had been given a nook by the fireplace. It was comfortable, but the location meant that he didn't get much sleep—he couldn't retire until the evening service was done, and he had to be up before the morning meal was served, shortly after the sun rose.

After Adso had gone his own way, the five-day journey to Minerve had been tiring but uneventful. The farther they travelled from Béziers, the less chance there was that they might stumble on a crusader patrol foraging for supplies or plunder.

In the days after their arrival, Beatrice had been closeted with the other Perfects, leaving John to wander the steep, narrow cobbled streets of the small town and fend for himself. As soon as it became known that he had escaped from Béziers, John was the centre of attention. For a few days, he couldn't take more than a few steps in any direction without someone approaching him and asking if the stories of the atrocity were true, but things had quietened down now and he'd had a chance to explore.

Minerve was an extraordinary place, surrounded on three sides by deep gorges and joined to the surrounding countryside only by a neck of land some thirty feet wide. The gorges, which held the torrents of the Cesse and Briant rivers in winter, were almost dry in summer. John had even ventured down onto the sandy bed of the Cesse and explored the high, broad caves where it ran underground.

The neck of land at Minerve's north end carried the only road into town and was blocked by the imposing walls and tower of the castle. Walls grew from the top of the gorge and completely surrounded the town. A few determined defenders with enough water and supplies could hold this town against any army in the world.

"Is anywhere safe after what happened at Béziers?" John asked.

"In the long term, no," Beatrice responded, "but Carcassonne should hold them up for a while."

"It might stop them altogether. They might go home."

"I don't think so. The crusaders will try everything to capture Carcassonne as soon as possible so that they will have a winter haven. And, remember, the example of Béziers will encourage surrender sooner rather than later."

"Will they get to Minerve this year?"

"No. Next year, maybe the year after. There are many castles and the crusaders will have to lay siege to each in turn. If the defenders are stout, it will take a long time to subdue this land. But the Church will subdue it. The hatred is too great, and the Pope has deep pockets. Good Men and Women will fuel many fires before this is over."

"Why don't the Perfects flee?"

"Where to?" Beatrice shrugged. "We will be hunted to the ends of the earth."

"And you won't resist." John thought back to Adso's comments as they'd hidden outside Béziers.

"No Good Christian will take up arms and fight, but there are many lords who will battle to save what they think is important. And, although I think all their worldly concerns are foolish, I am glad of the time it will give us."

"Time for what?"

Beatrice stared hard at John, who began to feel uncomfortable. "What books have you read?" she asked, eventually.

"Only the ones the nuns had in Toulouse. St. Augustine mostly."

"Nonsense," Beatrice said dismissively. "He would have done better to remain an ignorant pagan than write all that rubbish that the Catholics take so seriously. Anything else?"

"There was one other, in Latin. It was a history by an ancient Roman called

Herodotus."

"Do you remember any of it?"

"My favourite bit was the story of Leonidas and the three hundred Spartans. They held a pass against the invading Persians and they all died."

"Yes, but do you remember any of the words?"

John's brow furrowed as he struggled to recall the text.

"So the barbarians under Xerxes began to draw nigh; and the Greeks under Leonidas, as they now went forth determined to die, advanced much further than on previous days, until they reached the more open portion of the pass.

"There's another bit in here that I can't remember, but then it goes on.

"Now they joined battle beyond the defile, and carried slaughter among the barbarians, who fell in heaps. Behind them the captains of the squadrons, armed with whips, urged their men forward with continual blows. Many were thrust into the sea, and there perished; a still greater number were trampled to death by their own soldiers; no one heeded the dying. For the Greeks, reckless of their own safety and desperate, since they knew that, as the mountain had been crossed, their destruction was nigh at hand, exerted themselves with the most furious valour against the barbarians."

John shrugged. "I remember a few other bits as well."

"You remember the violence and excitement—the bits about the battle," Beatrice said with a smile.

John lowered his eyes in embarrassment. "I suppose so. It's what interested me."

"That's what we find easiest to remember, what is of interest. But how do you remember?"

John looked up. "I don't know. I just read and reread the interesting bits until I knew them."

"You didn't place them in your mind?"

"I don't understand."

"There is a way to train your mind to remember. It is called the memory cloister. Have you heard of it?"

"No." John could visualize a long, arched cloister, but how that helped your memory was a mystery.

"It takes training, but the idea is to think of your memory as a cloister with alcoves off each side. The alcoves contain what you wish to remember. Thus, if you want to remember the scraps of your Herodotus book, you imagine it placed in, say, alcove number thirty-five on the left. When you wish to retrieve it, you return your mind to alcove thirty-five and imagine pulling the manuscript out and reading it."

"It sounds easy," John said.

"It's not. It requires much concentration, discipline and practice, but the memory cloister can be used to memorize entire books. The possible complexity is endless. Each alcove can become an entrance into a new cloister, which in turn may have other cloisters spreading from it. Even the pillars of the arches can be used to remember specific important facts or lists. I have met adepts who have built cloisters in their minds in the shape of mazes with rooms and branches off almost every archway."

John struggled to visualize what Beatrice was describing. He understood what she was saying, but couldn't see how it would work. On the other hand, the idea of having all he learned from books organized and easily found excited him.

"Would you like to learn the memory cloister?" Beatrice asked with a smile.

"I think so," John said uncertainly. "It sounds very useful. But why would you teach me? I don't know many books."

"Remember on the road here I told you that we had to preserve books for the wisdom within them?"

John nodded.

"We have collected the physical books, and scrolls of parchment, papyrus and vellum, and placed them in many libraries all over the land—"

"Here at Minerve?" John asked.

"We have only a few here. Most are in high fortresses in the mountains— Quéribus, Peyrepertuse, Montségur—places that are either unassailable or too remote to attract attention. But our libraries will not be ignored forever. The Pope knows of our collections and the crusade is instructed to find and destroy them all."

"Destroy books!" The idea horrified John. He had always regarded books as almost magical things that contained all the knowledge he craved. "Books are precious! I thought the crusaders wanted to burn heretics, not books."

"Books *are* precious," Beatrice agreed, "but the knowledge within them can also be dangerous. The Catholic Church has spent untold energy over the past one thousand years building a single version of the truth. From the vast literature available, they have selected what fits with their story and with it, constructed their religion. They have suppressed the rest, burning the books and the people who have spoken against them. They have listened to Satan whispering in their ears and created a religion that exists in the material world. In the process, they have forgotten the spiritual. But they have been overwhelmingly successful. Satan now sits in Rome and no one notices."

"But the Pope is powerful and the Perfects few."

"That is true, but his power is material and, like all material things, can crumble and fall with remarkable ease. The Perfects *are* few, but our knowledge is vast."

"And, as you said, dangerous."

Beatrice nodded.

"What is this knowledge that the Pope fears?"

Beatrice studied John hard.

"What if Christ were not divine?" she asked, at length.

John's mouth dropped open in shock. This was blasphemy.

"God is perfect, infallible; therefore He cannot create something which is less than perfect," Beatrice explained, slowly. "He created our souls, which *are* perfect, but not our bodies or the material world in which we exist. That is corrupt and fallible and was created by Satan. If Christ was made of flesh and blood, He was corrupt and therefore could not have been of God."

"Perhaps His body was an illusion, so that we poor humans could see Him?" John suggested, struggling to keep up with Beatrice's arguments.

"A clever idea, but if Christ's body was an illusion, that makes a mockery of the Crucifixion and the suffering that the Church makes so much of. And, if God is infallible, how could Christ have failed?"

"Failed?"

"Yes. Even in the Gospels of Matthew, Mark, Luke and John, Christ says that the end of time is coming soon. He says specifically that He is bringing it, and that it will arrive while some of the people who listen to Him preach are still alive. That was more than one thousand years ago."

Beatrice fell silent and watched John. His thoughts were a turmoil. If Christ was not the son of God, where did that leave everything he had ever been taught?

"I don't know what all this means," he said helplessly.

Beatrice smiled. "Of course you don't. If it were that easy to convince people of what I have just told you, then the Church would have crumbled long ago. All I ask is that you open your thoughts. Reread the Gospels with what I have said in mind.

"For now, though, simply assume that what I say is true, or at least that many people fear it might be. Now, imagine a book that told the story of Christ's life as if he were an ordinary man. A man who had an ordinary birth, married, had children of his own, preached and was crucified but survived to realize his ministry was a failure—that all he had taught of the imminent arrival of God on earth was a sham, an illusion placed in his mind by the Devil. What would the Catholic Church think of that book?"

This was almost unimaginable heresy indeed! John knew he should walk away—leave Minerve and Beatrice and find somewhere he could live and not think of all this. Where he could attend Mass with everybody else and live an ordinary life. Where he could forget about the crusade, and the Church, and heretics. But he was fascinated, drawn in by the sheer outrageousness of what Beatrice was suggesting. He had to go on and see where it led.

"The Church would say the book was a forgery," he said.

"And burn it?"

"Certainly." John began to see why burning books might be so important to the crusade.

"And if the book were true?"

"It would destroy the Church."

"Yes. The entire corrupt, material edifice of the Pope's domain would collapse like a castle made of sand when the tide rolls in. Bishop Foulques, Arnaud Aumery and countless others cannot, will not, allow that to happen. If they found such a book, they would destroy it and everyone who had ever heard of it."

What Beatrice said made sense to John, but was she just making a theoretical point?

"Does such a book exist?" John asked, far from certain that he wanted to hear the answer.

Beatrice's shrugged. "I simply give an example of how the knowledge in but a single volume could have the power to destroy the entire Church. And we have hundreds of books in our libraries. If even a quarter of them contain a mere shadow of what I have just told you, then the Pope will never rest until every page is consumed in fire."

"So, that is why you keep your libraries in such inaccessible places. But you said that, sooner or later, every castle and keep will be destroyed by the crusade. Does that not mean that your libraries are doomed?"

"It does, yes. On the road you also asked where we will take the books for them to be safe. I did not answer."

"I remember."

Beatrice tapped her head. "*This* is where we keep the books. That is why we teach the memory cloister."

"To memorize the books!" With a rush of excitement, John realized what he was being offered. The memory cloister was not simply a way to organize what little John knew. It was, when filled with the things Beatrice was talking about, a path to almost untold knowledge.

"Exactly. The physical pages of a book or a scroll are nothing. Parchment and vellum are scarce. It takes a long time for a scribe to copy even a small book. Yet fire can destroy the largest book in minutes. The wisdom that resides in a book is all. A book may be found, read and thrown on a bonfire, but none can know what is in a man's or a woman's mind unless that person chooses to tell."

"So, the Perfects learn the books and preserve the knowledge?"

"That is the way it has been. Some Good Men and Women know the lost knowledge and have kept it safe, but now it is no longer safe in their heads. By the time the next century is passed, if there are any Good Christians left they will be a scattered, hunted remnant. None will be allowed rest until they are dead."

"So who will preserve the books?" It felt to John as if Beatrice's gaze was stabbing right through him.

"You will," she said softly. John began to protest, but Beatrice raised a hand to stop him. "Not only you. There will be others, enough so that the knowledge can be passed on and spread throughout the world in the generations after the last Good Christian is ash.

"That is why I offer to teach you the memory cloister. You have a love of learning and, I believe, will make a suitable vessel for our wisdom. If I am wrong, say so now and go upon your way. If I am right, then I will teach you the memory cloister, and you can travel the land placing all manner of wondrous books in your mind."

"I'll do it," John volunteered.

"Do not answer so quickly. Aside from the risks of having such dangerous knowledge, there is a heavier price. To be able to come and go as you please in these troubled times, you must be invisible. That means that all those who accept this role can never receive the comfort of the *consolamentum*. You will not be able to join the Elect and therefore, you will not, unless you are lucky enough to find a member of the Elect on your deathbed, be able to enter paradise. Your soul will be condemned to wander this evil earth until the end times come. It is not a sacrifice to be taken lightly."

John sat in silence, contemplating the offer. The idea of his soul wandering the earth was worrying but, according to the Good Christians, that was what his soul was doing now, and it wasn't so bad. He only had the sketchiest idea of what the Cathars believed, but that was probably why Beatrice had chosen him—unlike the Elect, John had no concept of what he might be losing. And, if he didn't know much about Catharism, the crusaders could hardly call him a heretic. These were frightening times whatever he chose to do, and the idea of developing his memory in the way Beatrice suggested was attractive. On top of that was the access he would get to all kinds of rare and forbidden books.

"I'll do it," John repeated.

"Good." Beatrice's face broke into a gentle smile. "But I must give you one more warning. If you become an adept, there will be consequences. Releasing the memory is like digging for stones in sand. You collect the stones, but you also collect a lot of sand. As you put books in the alcoves, the experiences of everyday life, like the sand, comes too and it sticks to the walls of the cloister. Every carving, window, painting, down to the tiniest mark on the cloister wall, takes on significance. Each triggers a memory from your past life. Eventually, if you become good enough, you can forget nothing."

"That is wonderful," John said, thrilled at the idea of such a powerful memory.

"Perhaps, but it has its cost. There are always things we would prefer to forget, are there not? Memories we would rather lock away or erase than continually be reminded of? You will not have that luxury. If you learn well, you will remember everything you see and do, even that which you would wish not to."

"It doesn't matter," John said, unable to think of anything he wanted to forget.

"Very well then. There is a small collection of books here that we can use for training before you go out to the libraries. We must begin immediately."

* * *

In the two weeks since Beatrice had begun teaching John the memory cloister, he had barely slept. Every waking moment had been spent reading and performing mental exercises to train his memory. John was amazed at the progress he was making. His memory, it turned out, was vastly more powerful than he had imagined. All it had required was the discipline. Now John could read large chunks of text, consciously file them in an appropriate place, and there they were, ready to be recovered in their entirety whenever he wished. At the same time, the Latin he had learned as a child was improving by leaps and bounds and there was little now that he could not read.

Sometimes pieces of text would go missing or John would search a specific alcove and find nothing there, but, like his Latin, his memory had improved immensely—and the things he was learning were amazing. Gospels, some only fragmentary, that he had never heard of; Roman histories and descriptions of all manner of wonders; strange documents from Al-Andalus and the Christian states of Aragon and Castille. It was a whole new world, richer and more complex than any he had ever imagined. John was so excited that he begrudged even the few hours of sleep Beatrice forced him to take. There was so much to learn.

"You are learning faster than I had hoped." Beatrice and John were sitting once more in the kitchen. "You have a natural talent for remembering."

"I love it," John said. "I want to know everything."

"That is good." Beatrice smiled broadly. "But beware two things. Be careful that you do not confuse facts with wisdom. Wisdom comes only through having a place to put the things that you learn. Otherwise, the facts are useless and you fall into the trap of arrogance. That is a sin.

"Also, beware the Devil. He is subtle and knows how to use our weaknesses. Satan is always as clever as the one he is tempting. He places many things in books to mislead us. That is not an argument, as the Catholics think, for destroying books, but it is a reason to gain the wisdom to tell what is false from what is true. And that is a much greater task than mere remembering. For example, the Gospel of Thomas that you read yesterday. It says—"

Beatrice was interrupted by a loud knock on the door to the street. Before she could rise to answer, the door swung in and a ragged figure stepped over the threshold.

"Adso!" John exclaimed, jumping to his feet.

Adso was filthy and looked as though he hadn't eaten or slept properly in days. His cheek bones protruded and his eyes were dark-rimmed and sunken. He was followed by an old man dressed in beggar's rags. The old man was small and hunched over, making him seem no larger than a child, yet his face was deeply lined and his skin as dark as old leather.

John helped Adso to the table while Beatrice assisted the old man and then went to the pantry. She returned with a loaf of bread, a hunk of dry cheese, an orange and two cups of watered wine. She broke the bread in two and gave the cheese to Adso and the orange to the old man.

The old man picked at the bread like a delicate bird, but Adso demolished everything before him in seconds, drained his wine, wiped his mouth on his sleeve and said, "Weren't nothing that good in Carcassonne, nor on the road 'ere."

"What happened at Carcassonne?" John couldn't contain his questions any longer. "Has there been another massacre?"

"No killing this time, least not other than the knights, whose job it is to kill and die. Town surrendered three days past."

John wanted to know the details of how the battle had gone, but Beatrice spoke first.

"And the Good Men and Women. How did they fare?"

"Well," Adso responded with a smile, "weren't no bonfires."

Beatrice frowned. "Why?"

"Not certain. We was 'olding out well. Still plenty water and we 'adn't sunk to eating the mules and rats yet. De Montfort 'ad attacked several times, but that only left piles o' bodies in the ditches below the walls.

"One day, a damned monk comes into the town, a tall skinny kid, all arms and legs, and talks with Viscount Robert. I expected—"

"What did the monk look like?" John interrupted. The description had made him think of Peter.

"Like I said," Adso replied, puzzled, "tall and skinny."

"Did you hear his name?"

"I didn't learn the name of every monk—no wait, I did 'ear this one's name mentioned. It was one of the apostles, Philip? No, Peter. That was it. Why d'you care?"

"I knew him once," John said. Part of him was glad to hear news of Peter, but the other was sorry that he seemed to have risen to such an important place in the invading army.

"D'you mind if I go on with my tale, now?" Adso asked. "I expected Trenceval to send this friend of yours packing"— Adso flashed a sharp glance at John—"but, instead, what does 'e do? 'E goes off into the lion's den with 'im. Never comes back. Story is they threw Trenceval in the dungeon—never mind 'im being under a flag of truce."

John gasped at the news. Then a wave of guilt swept over him. He had abandoned his responsibilities to Roger Trenceval to follow Beatrice to Minerve. He had been so wrapped up in his own activities since then that he had barely thought about the young viscount.

"Just as well you didn't go to Caracassonne, lad, else you might be in that dungeon with 'im," Adso said, looking at John.

"But I let him down," John said.

"Don't worry yourself. You made the smart choice. It doesn't pay to put your faith in lords and princes. Trenceval would 'ave made 'is own decisions, whether you was there or not. But what's this Peter to you?"

"I grew up with him in Toulouse," John said. "He had a strange vision one day and went off to become a monk. He was with Aumery at St. Gilles before Castelnau was killed."

"Doesn't surprise me. He must be well in with that devil Aumery to be made a negotiator.

"Anyway," said Adso turning back to Beatrice, "whatever 'appened at the truce, the next day there's these notices on all the church doors, saying everyone's to leave the city but that they cannot take anything—'carry only your sins' was 'ow it were put. No mention of giving up the Good Folk for burning. I was just appreciating my good luck when this old man comes up and demands that I bring 'im 'ere. Seems I'm making an 'abit of escorting Good Folk round this country. Brought 'im all the way here without a word of thanks—barely a single word of any sort as it 'appens."

"I told him to seek you out should he ever need help." Adso and John stared at Beatrice.

"You told 'im I would 'elp?" Adso asked.

"I knew you would never refuse."

"Huh!" Adso grunted. "What makes 'im so important?"

"He is Umar of Cordova," Beatrice said, as if that explained everything.

"He is a Moor?" John asked.

"And what is wrong, might I ask, with being a Moor?" The old man stared at John, a glint in his eye that belied his age. "The Moors, as you call them, know more of the world than you can imagine. And I"—Umar sat up straighter—"am descended directly from Abd ar-Rahman, greatest of the Umayyad caliphs of Al-Andalus."

John had no idea what the old man meant and was beginning to feel uncomfortable under his penetrating gaze. Fortunately, Beatrice broke the silence. "A Moor on one side only, and that your mother's, a serving girl four hundred years removed from the great Caliph."

Umar shrugged agreement and went back to his orange.

"His father was Gregory of Foix, a Good Christian who led many debates against the evils of the Church."

"This is all very interesting," Adso broke in, "but no one has yet told me what is so important about the old goat and why I should 'ave risked my life to bring 'im 'ere."

The three stared at Umar, who was concentrating on carefully peeling his fruit.

"What?" he asked, as he became aware of the attention.

"Adso wishes to know what is so important about you," Beatrice explained with a smile.

The old man waved his hand dismissively. "There is nothing important about me. I am but an old, cracked vessel that will soon release another soul to a better world."

"We could 'ave released your soul in Carcassonne and saved ourselves this trip," Adso said.

"I dare say," the old man said, "but then I wouldn't have been able to pass on the books, would I?"

"Books?" John asked, looking to see if the old man had carried a satchel in with him. "You don't have any books with you."

Umar cackled roughly. "Can you see the air around you?"

"No," John said.

"Yet you know it is there with every breath you take. Seeing is not all. Beware of trusting only what you see. Your eyes show you material things, and they are the Devil's toys."

"The memory cloister!" John exclaimed with a flash of insight. "You have the books in your head."

Umar nodded and placed a segment of orange in his mouth.

"Books. Books. Books! It's always about books with you people." Adso rose and fetched another piece of cheese and refilled his wine goblet.

"Perhaps you are not as stupid as you look," Umar went on, staring hard at John. "Yes, I have the books in this old head. Are you the one I am to transfer them to?"

"He is," Beatrice said before John could respond. "And you should have been here weeks ago. It was not the plan to have you trapped in Carcassonne."

"These eyes are not what they once were. And there were so many books." Umar spoke to Beatrice, but he never took his eyes off John.

"You were only supposed to get one—*the* book."

John's heart leaped at the emphasis on "the." Could this be the book Beatrice had suggested could bring down the Catholic Church?

"And I have it. And I am here. So all is well. What is your name, boy?"

"I'm John."

"Well, John, we must get to work, if we can get rid of these annoying chatterers." Umar glanced at Adso and Beatrice.

Beatrice nodded approval. "So Adso," she said, standing, "I assume you and Umar are not alone in coming here?"

"Indeed not," Adso agreed. "There's plenty near-naked and 'ungry people streaming up the valley be'ind me. It'll take more than a few 'unks of bread and cheese to see to them."

"Then we must make ready. Adso, if you are sufficiently refreshed, go to the city gates to direct any people who need help to the square outside the church of St. Etienne. I shall go to the houses about town and arrange places to sleep and food to eat."

With that, she was gone. Adso looked at John. "The adventure continues," he said with a sly smile.

"But how will it end?" John asked.

Adso's smile broke into a laugh. "That's the question, and only God—or the Devil—can answer it. I shall leave you with this Good Man."

"Let's get to work," Umar said as Adso left. "Are you adept at the memory cloister?"

"I've only just begun," John explained. "Beatrice has been teaching me and I am learning, but I have some way to go yet, I think."

Umar shook his head and sighed. "It's not like the old days. I remember when people took things seriously. Now it's all rush and bother, and no one takes any notice of what's important. The Devil defeats us by swamping us in trivia so that we lose sight of what's significant. You mark my words: one day no one will care about anything at all. And then where will we be?"

Umar fell silent and stared at John with his watery eyes. John had no idea what he was supposed to say. "I agree," he ventured at last.

"Nonsense!" Umar exclaimed. "This is exactly what I mean! You cannot agree with something if you haven't thought about it. You have a brain with immense God-given power. Use it!" He slapped his hand loudly on the table. John jumped at the noise and Umar grimaced in pain. He massaged his hand.

"Well," he went on eventually. "I suppose we must work with what we have, imperfect though it may be. Sometimes I wish I were back in Cordova. At least there, they appreciate learning."

"You have been to Cordova? Have you seen the Mezquita? Is it the wonder they say?"

Umar shook his head. "You chatter on like an angry squirrel. How will you have room in your head for the important things if you fill every moment with useless nonsense?"

John dropped his gaze to the tabletop. Already he had disappointed this strange old man.

"But yes," Umar went on, his voice almost wistful. "I have been to the Mezquita and it is even more wonderful than any can say. It is a forest of more than a thousand pillars, of jasper, onyx and marble, many taken from the long-vanished temples of the Romans. When you first cross the orange groves and enter, as your eyes adjust to the dim light, it is as if the pillars go on for ever. As if you can walk and walk through this stone forest of trees for the rest of your days and never see two the same."

Umar fell silent for a minute. John was about to ask another question when the old man jerked himself out of his reverie and continued in a much more business-like voice. "But we must continue. There is work to do. Please do not distract me again." Umar closed his eyes and breathed deeply. *"Inasmuch as it pleaseth God the Father, I shall set down my life so that others may learn from it after I am gone to join Him.*

"In the beginning it was..."

"What is this? What are you saying?" John asked in confusion.

Umar opened his eyes and glared across the table. "You have never done this?"

"What?"

"Transference. Learned a book from the recitation of another?"

"No. I have only learned from reading."

Umar sighed heavily. "Such coarse clay with which to work. Now, listen carefully. The process is the same. Create a space to accept the words, close your eyes and listen hard.

"*Inasmuch as it pleaseth God the Father.*"

"Wait," John said. "What is it I am learning?"

"You truly know nothing," Umar said in amazement. "How long have you been a Good Man?"

"I'm not," John said helplessly. "Beatrice is teaching me the memory cloister *because* I am *not* a Perfect. She says it is safer that way because the crusaders will not stop until all the Good Christians are burned."

The old man gazed thoughtfully at John, drumming his fingers on the table. "So you know nothing of us?"

"I know that you believe that the material world is the realm of Satan, that you don't take oaths, that you believe the Catholic Church is corrupt, that Christ was just a man, that..."

"Enough." Umar stopped John's recitation. "But you don't know of our origins?"

"Not much, no."

Umar rubbed his eyes. "Such strange times," he said more to himself than to John. "I hope Beatrice knows what she is doing." He sighed again. "Very well. I shall tell you something of the burden we Good Christians carry. In doing so, I shall be passing some of that burden on to you. Can you bear it?"

"I can," John said as confidently as he could manage, although he had not the slightest idea what the burden might be.

"Hmmm..." Umar rubbed his chin. "Our beliefs stretch far back, as far before the Christ as we are after, to ancient Persia and a prophet called Zarathustra. He taught the Five Truths: all are equal; all living things deserve respect; nature is to be celebrated; hard work and charity is the way to heaven; and loyalty is required to all family, friends and clan. He also taught of two Gods, Auramazdah, the God of truth, good and creation, and Angra Mainyu, the God of lies, evil and chaos. Humans are the battleground between these Gods, our souls and all things spiritual from Auramazdah, our bodies and the material world from Angra Mainyu. Do you follow?"

John nodded, although he was far from certain.

"Good," Umar declared. "Unfortunately, over the centuries, Zarathustra's words were forgotten or changed, and his followers began arguing and fighting amongst themselves. They started to worship other, false gods. The last texts of Zarathustra perished when the armies of Alexander burned the great library at Persepolis, three hundred and thirty years before the Christ.

"A few survivors spread through the world and kept the faith alive as empires rose and fell around them. You know of the Magi?"

"Everyone does. They visited the Christ child at his birth in Bethlehem."

"Nonsense," Umar scoffed. "The Magi *were* wise men from the east, followers of Zarathustra, but they did not come to pay homage at a baby's crib—that is a story for children. They came much later, after Christ had begun preaching and word of his ministry had spread. They came to talk with him as equals to discuss the philosophy of God, but that has been removed from the Gospels you know."

"How do *you* know this?"

"Patience," Umar snapped. "One group of Zarathustra's followers fled to the land of the Bulgars, others, over many hundreds of years, through Greece and Italy to here. They were the first Good Christians.

"Yet others survived in the new world of Islam and moved with the armies around the Mediterranean Sea to Cordova where they lived and studied. I myself studied there with the great scholar Nasir al-Din, God bless him, in his library at Madinat al-Zahra.

"The material world is evil, but it is also transitory. Manuscripts decay, libraries burn, even carvings on rock flake and disappear with enough time. The only thing that survives intact is the human mind. That is why we memorize everything, why we train adepts in the memory cloister. As long as one remains with the accumulated knowledge of the ages locked in his head, Auramazdah will not pass away."

Umar took a sip of wine and looked at John, who was frowning as he struggled to understand both the history and what was being asked of him.

"So," he began tentatively, "you will transfer the books of Zara..."

"Zarathustra."

"Zarathustra. You will transfer his books to me?"

"Yes. What remains of them, but much more besides. The battle has been going on for millennia, and countless tyrants and priests have burned all manner of books and scrolls. The task increases with each passing generation and each forbidden book we can rescue from the flames of ignorance and prejudice.

"For example, the book I was beginning to transfer to you is not of Zarathustra. It is much more recent, but in this time and place, it is of immense power and import. To give you but one example: your friend Adso could not understand why Roger Trenceval accompanied the priest you seem to know out of Carcassonne to negotiate with Aumery and the crusaders, even though he knew it meant the surrender of his city and, most likely, his own death. Trenceval went for one reason only—to save my life."

"Your life!"

"Well, not my life, that is of no importance, but what is in my head is. Trenceval knew that the young priest offered the only chance for the Good Christians of Carcassonne to avoid the flames. They would have gone willingly, and I would have too, but what I am about to transfer to you would have been lost, and there are few of us left who know it. Beatrice was right, I should not have stayed so long in the library."

John's mind was whirling. What as so important in this old man's head that Roger Trenceval would sacrifice his life for it? What was Peter's role in all of this? "What is it that is so important?" John asked.

Umar studied John for a long moment. "It is a gospel."

"I have read some lost gospels," John said. "Thomas, the Apocalypse of Paul, even the one said to be by Judas."

"That is good, but this one is different. This gospel was written by the Christ."

John sat in silence as the meaning of Umar's words sank in. The Gospel of Christ himself! Not just a few stories and parables, but an entire book in the words of the founder of Christianity. Beatrice hadn't made it up! She had been hinting at something real.

"Is it authentic?"

Umar smiled. "That is what everyone asks, at least those whose first reaction is not to cast it or its bearer into the flames! It *is* true, and what is in this book in my head, if it were ever to become known and accepted, has the power to bring down the whole corrupt edifice of the Catholic Church in a single morning.

"You see now why they wish to burn us all, and why Roger Trenceval sacrificed himself?"

"Yes," John gasped, still stunned. A gospel written by Christ. These would be the most powerful words in all of Christendom. He was being offered nothing less than the power to change the world. It was awe-inspiring—and terrifying. If anyone found out that he knew about this, the entire weight of the crusade would fall on him.

"Are you prepared for this?" Umar's voice interrupted his thoughts.

"Yes," John said. How could he not? This was the knowledge, perhaps the ultimate knowledge, that he had sought in all his readings.

"Very well. Now concentrate.

Heretic

"Inasmuch as it pleaseth God the Father, I shall set down my life so that others may learn from it after I am gone to join Him.

"In the beginning it was..."

* * *

It took John three days to learn the Gospel of Christ. Three days in which he barely slept and simply took in food as fuel to keep himself going. By the time it was done, both he and Umar were exhausted.

"Do you have it all?" Umar asked as the pair sat in the kitchen by candlelight on the third day.

"I think so," John replied. He had just finished running the words through his mind before returning them to alcove thirteen in the cloister. He had concentrated so much on individual words and phrases that the full import of the gospel had passed him by. Now that he was done, the work lay complete in his mind. "Is it true?" he asked once more.

"Yes," Umar confirmed. "The original, long lost now, was written on vellum in Aramaic, the language the Christ spoke. It is older than any of the accepted gospels."

John shook his head in wonder.

"For many years," Umar explained, "a copy lay in the library of a rich Roman landowner, Marcus Britannicus. He lived not far from here on estates that produced some fine wine that was in high demand in Rome. When the empire collapsed, the library was dispersed and some books, the Gospel of the Christ included, were preserved by a Visigothic lord who wished to emulate the glories of Rome. His family kept it safe when the darkness of ignorance descended and the land became a battleground between Christian and Moor. Eventually, upon their arrival from the east, some Good Men found the document and began the remembering. By that time, the manuscript was in sorry shape and, I believe, was finally lost in a fire some three hundred years past.

"But we are not yet done. You now have the most important of the books in my head, but there are many more. Some preserve more of the truth of the early Church and support what you have learned these past days. Others are even older and contain knowledge and wisdom that is lost to our world. You must learn and remember them all. We have a busy winter before us, young John."

"There is so much we do not know!" John felt overwhelmed by the task before him. Only now was he beginning to fully understand what his promise involved: a lifetime of learning. It was exciting, but exhausting.

"Indeed," Umar said sadly. "What we preserve is but a tiny part of all that there was. I once heard of a map, a wondrous representation of the entire world, which showed it to be far vaster than the one we know, with continents, known and unknown, and wonders we can barely imagine scattered across it. I fear it is lost and may never be recovered."

Was this how he would end up, John wondered, an old man with a head full of marvels striving to pass them on to someone else before he died?

"But, Beatrice tells me that you are something of an artist." Umar broke in to John's thoughts.

"I scratch a few drawings in what spare time I have."

"And do you do it well?"

"As well as I can. Drawing has always fascinated me. I used to love the work that illustrated the few books the nuns possessed in Toulouse, even though many of the pictures in the margins were not of religious subjects. Often, they showed ordinary people at work and play—the farmer in his fields, the blacksmith at his forge or the miller at his wheel. Sometimes mythical animals, fire-breathing, winged dragons for example, writhed around the text."

Umar nodded encouragement.

"I used to sneak away from my duties or studies whenever possible and visit the great churches of Toulouse. I adored the brightly painted murals of saints and scenes from the Bible, the play of light on the blues and reds and the luxurious shine of the gold that made the holy men's haloes."

"Rubbish," Umar scoffed.

"The content may have been," John said, "but the form had a beauty that I admired. The problem I had was not with what the pictures represented, but with the way they did it. Despite the detail and the accuracy of many of the scenes, there was something about them that was dissatisfying."

"What was it?"

"I don't know." John struggled to explain. "They seemed flat and lifeless. In some ways, I was more drawn to the painted statues of the saints and holy men that adorned the doorways. The figures were long and serious—less accurate in many cases than the paintings—but their carved reality gave them a depth that was missing from the murals."

John shrugged helplessly.

"Once, many years past," Umar said, "I saw a book in Cordova that you would find of interest. It talked of different ways of painting and of representing our world, and it contained some strange drawings. I do not agree with this interest of yours, but I do understand some of what you say. Some drawings in the book were of such exquisite beauty that they made men breathless."

"Did you learn this book?" John asked with rising interest.

"Some, but it was not easy. Words are easy, drawing not so. How do I tell a drawing? I cannot."

"Where is the book now?"

"I do not know. Perhaps it is lost. The Moors do not treasure the representation of life. For them it is a sin that offends God. They prefer designs, so they would not care for such a book. If it still exists, it would be at Madinat al-Zahra in Nasir's library."

"Nasir is still alive?" John had assumed that Umar's teacher was long dead.

Umar shrugged. "It is possible; he was not all that much older than I. In any case, his library would still be there. Shabaka would know."

"Shabaka?"

"A Nubian, with skin so black it glows. A most interesting person. He is devoted to Nasir. When I was last in Cordova, it was Shabaka who took supplies to Nasir in his library at Madinat."

"But I ramble on. It is a sign of age and exhaustion. I must to bed if we are to work more tomorrow."

Umar stood and stretched stiffly. "And you should sleep as well."

"I will," John said, "but I must calm my mind first."

"Very well. I bid you good night."

Umar picked up one of the candles and shuffled out of the room. John remained seated in the flickering light, staring into the darkness. His body ached with tiredness, but his mind would not let him rest. The things he had learned, and their possible consequences, sat in is mind like great weights.

He had just managed to convince himself that, despite his racing thoughts, he should lie down and try to sleep, when the door to the street opened and Adso entered. John only just managed to protect the flickering candle flame from the draft.

"Well, well," Adso said cheerfully as he went to the pantry and grabbed a piece of bread. "Finished work for the day?"

"Yes," John replied, glad to see his happy-go-lucky friend after the intensity of his time with Umar. "I've learned some incredible things."

"No doubt," Adso said. He sat at the table and broke off a piece of bread. "That old Umar 'as been around in a lot of places for a lot of years. 'E must 'ave picked up all manner of things. What is it you 'ave been so wrapped up in these past days?"

John hesitated. Should he tell Adso? Was the book he had learned a secret from everyone, or just those who did not support the Cathar cause?

"Was it that Gospel of the Christ?" Adso asked through a mouthful of bread.

"You know about that?"

Adso shrugged. "I keep my ears open. A lot of folk certainly seem to put a lot of store in it."

"It could change the world."

"The world'll change for sure, with or without your memory books."

"But this book is in Christ's own words," John explained eagerly. "It turns what the Gospels say upside down."

"Much turns the Gospels upside down. Nothing new in that. I doubt the cardinals in Rome'll pay it any mind."

"They'll have to," John said. "This book proves that Christ did not die on the cross, that he was taken down alive and nursed back to health by Mary Magdelene. He did not want to live on in this world and felt that his time here had been a failure. The End of Days had not arrived with him, and people were going about their business wrapped up in their petty cares, just as they had before he preached and was crucified."

John felt the words rushing out of him. It was a relief to tell someone about the burden he had been given.

"Mary and Jesus travelled and learned. They read and talked with holy men of all faiths, trying to understand. Jesus pondered much on what he had discussed with the wise men from the east. He came to appreciate the ancient wisdom they had talked about. He collected books and with Mary came here to Languedoc to study and think. At the end of his long life, his ideas were very close to those of the Cathar Perfects."

"Good story," Adso said.

"Good story! Is that all you can say? This book undermines the entire Christian faith. Christ was a Cathar—the first heretic. If it gets out, the Catholic Church will collapse. This is the most important book in the world!"

"Per'aps. Per'aps not. For a start, 'ow do you prove that it's true and not just some tale made up to cause trouble? And even if you can do that—" Adso held up his hand to prevent John's interruption—"even if you can prove it to be true, do you think the likes of Arnaud Aumery will ever allow it to become known? 'E, and plenty others like 'im'll move 'eaven and earth to destroy that knowledge. The bonfires of books and men and women will make this crusade seem like a picnic.

"And, even supposing that you are right and the Gospel is true and believed and not wiped out by the Inquisition, and the edifice of the Church comes crashing down around all our ears, the world'll go on."

"How can you say that?" John asked indignantly. "Without the Church in some form, where would we be?"

"Somewhere. Look, John, you think too narrow. I 'ave heard tell of a god, far to the east, who 'as six arms and in each of them he carries a weapon that can destroy the world. I doubt *that* god'll worry too much about your Gospel.

"I even met a man once," Adso continued, "'airy he was and from the north where it's dark for 'alf the year and the snow lies to the rooftops. 'E believed in an ancient god what carried a war hammer and an 'eaven where warriors went to wench, drink and fight after they died. That's a god I could believe in.

"Point is, there's a lot of gods out there in this world. If one falls, even if it's yours, the others'll go on doing what they've always done and so will the people who believe in them."

"You don't believe in God?" John asked, horrified.

"I wouldn't say that. I'm just a simple man who 'as precious little time for anybody's god or devil. If all the brilliant men and women in the world cannot decide what God's like, what chance do I 'ave? Best to just get on with life. There's enough 'appening every day to keep us busy without looking for trouble, and there's enough trouble in the world without killing those what thinks different."

Adso stopped speaking and broke into laughter—so hard that he collapsed in a fit of coughing and choking. John jumped up and poured him a goblet of wine. Adso took a long draft and calmed down.

"You looked so comical," he said eventually, "better than a travelling jester! But don't be so shocked, I'm not about to try and convert you to my 'eathen beliefs, and I won't be 'ere long enough to give Beatrice a chance to convert me. My strength's almost back. A few more days and I'm off."

"Where to?" John felt a pang of regret that his friend was leaving so soon.

"Bram, Cabaret, down that way. There's plenty of bands roaming the country, just waiting for a few of these northern jackals to stray too far from their castle walls. Should be some good plunder." Adso winked broadly at John.

"You'll become a robber."

"In a manner of speaking. Tho' I don't see it as robbing. These crusaders came down 'ere uninvited. They wish to burn our towns and slaughter innocent people. They deserve whatever they get, I say. Better to do something and 'ave fun doing it than sit around worrying if God'll approve.

"But I think I've upset you enough for one night! I'm off for some sleep. The shed out back's not the most comfortable, but at least I don't 'ave to get up at the crack of dawn to pray. I bid you good night."

Adso took a candle off the mantle, lit it from the one on the table, and retreated through the house. Again John was left with his thoughts.

Adso's view of the world was the opposite of Beatrice and Umar's, but there was an attraction to what he planned to do. Adso would be free, roaming wherever he wished—and he'd be doing something active to fight the invaders. John was certain that preserving the ancient writing was important and he was looking forward to the other books Umar could give him, but what if Adso was right? What if it all made no difference in the grand scheme of things? One part of John craved the clash of swords and the life of adventure. Another wanted to head straight down to Cordova and try to find the drawing book of which Umar had spoken. But John had made a promise to Beatrice and Umar. He would have to follow that through.

Yawning hugely, John stumbled over to his alcove and fell into his bedding. A good night's sleep was what he needed.

PART FOUR
War

Angels

Toulouse
March, 1210

Despite the familiarity of the surroundings as he walked through the narrow streets of St. Cyprien at Arnaud Aumery's side, Peter didn't feel as if he were coming home. It was the place he had grown up, and he had many happy memories but, as Aumery had pointed out, the Holy Mother Church was now his only home. Peter wasn't here to relive old times; he was here simply to pressure Count Raymond to weed out the heretics in his city.

No one had found any evidence to link Count Raymond to the murder of Pierre of Castelnau and, since he had recanted the angry statements he'd made at St. Gilles and done penance, his excommunication had been lifted. The count had promised to support the crusade and drive all heretics out of his lands, but so far he had done nothing. While the crusaders had been dying under the walls of Carcassonne, Raymond, as reported in numerous harsh letters from Bishop Foulques, had allowed Cathars to meet and worship openly in Toulouse. Over the winter, he had stalled and delayed on his promise to send knights to help Simon de Montfort subdue the land around Carcassonne and now, as Foulques reported, things had degenerated to the point where there was almost open civil war in the streets between Raymond's followers and Foulque's own Angels.

As he looked around, Peter could see few signs of war. St. Cyprien looked much as he remembered it: not wealthy, but not dirt poor either. The houses were well maintained, the streets relatively clean, and the smells of humans and animals no worse than in any crowded city. The people were well enough dressed and they watched the small party of monks and lay brothers pass through their neighbourhood with only mild interest.

Peter knew that pride was one of the seven deadly sins, but he couldn't help holding his head high and hoping that someone in the watching crowd recognized the poor orphan boy returning as a full Cistercian monk. Peter had studied hard over the winter and now felt able to perform some of his duties—hear confession, perform baptism, administer last rites. He was still a long way from leading a full Mass but that was not a major part of his duties. Mostly, all that was required was a quick blessing of the knights as they prepared for battle.

In any case, the most important learning Peter had done recently had nothing to do with blessing knights or comforting the dying. It had come during the long, cold evenings when Peter and Aumery had sat in the legate's tent and spoken about wielding power. Aumery had done most of the talking, telling Peter long stories of his work as Abbot of Cîteaux and his visits to Rome. Peter's lessons were continuing now as the pair wended their way through the narrow streets.

"If there is one thing you need to remember at all times," Aumery said, repeating the winter's main message, "it is that, no matter how powerful a lord may seem, every man has a weakness. Find that weakness and, when the time is right, exploit it. And be ruthless. Be like a terrier who, once it gets hold of a rat, may be beaten senseless before it lets go. If you are right, and if God is with you, you will triumph."

"And yet," Peter responded, "the negotiations at Carcassonne allowed the heretics to escape. Had de Montfort been more of a terrier, would we have won both an intact city and the heretics?"

"Possibly, Peter," Aumery said thoughtfully. "Maybe I miscalculated there. I thought that sending you in to the city would do no harm. I did not expect Trenceval to submit so easily. Why do you think he did?"

"To save his subjects the slaughter of Béziers?"

"In part, but he could have done that by giving up a few score heretics to the fire at the beginning of the siege."

"Then it was the heretics that were important to him?"

"That is what I have come to believe. Have you heard of the Cathar Treasure?"

"I have heard some wild tales," Peter said, hauling old bits of gossip into his mind. "Some said it was riches beyond our wildest imaginings. Others that it was the Ark of the Covenant itself. Some said that the heretics brought the treasure with them from the east or from the Holy Land."

"And what did you think of these tales?"

"That they were just imaginings. The heretics never struck me as ones who would hoard treasure."

"My thoughts exactly," Aumery said. "The heretics set little store by material possessions. They have no chests of gold or precious stones, but what if they have a small treasure of immense power?"

"Like what?"

"What is the holiest object in Christendom?"

Peter searched his memory. There were countless relics of saints that were associated with miracles—he'd even heard that a church in Rome possessed the preserved head of John the Baptist—but the holiest object would have to be something from Christ himself. It couldn't be his body as he ascended to heaven, and the cross on which he had suffered, or a large piece of it, was said to lead the crusaders into battle in the Holy Land, so it couldn't be that. There was only one other alternative. "You mean the Grail?" Peter asked.

"I mean nothing else," Aumery said, smiling broadly. "The holy cup from which Christ drank at the Last Supper."

"And you really believe the Cathars possess this?"

"It must be. It is the only thing small enough to be easily hidden and transported."

Peter was thrilled at the idea that the Grail might exist, and even be close by, but there was a problem. "Why would the heretics preserve the Grail? They do not recognize the divinity of Christ."

Aumery stopped walking and stared at Peter with his strange eyes. "They do not preserve the Grail because *they* worship it. They preserve it because *we* worship it. Think of the Grail's power! What could we not do if the Pope possessed the Grail? It would revitalize the church and sweep the corruption of those like Foulques away. With the Grail at their head, the armies of Christ would sweep triumphant across the world! Heathens would bow down and Christ would reign in glory! It would herald the Judgment Day. The tombs would open and the dead rise to stand naked with their sins before Christ."

Aumery's voice rose and his eyes gleamed with fervour. Passersby were stopping to pay attention.

Peter was caught up in the odd monk's enthusiasm. "Could it be true?"

"It is! It is the only answer. I have read the holy books in Rome and talked with the greatest minds in Christendom. I am in no doubt. The Cathars possess the Holy Grail. And *that* is the real purpose of this crusade, to regain the power of the Grail for the Holy Mother Church."

A horrible thought struck Peter. "Could the heretics not simply destroy it?"

"They would not dare!" Aumery exclaimed. "The Grail has power. It has touched the lips of Christ Himself. The heretic rabble fear it. They will do their utmost to hide it from us, but they will not destroy it. And one day, in one of their pitiful castles, I shall find it and announce the coming of the End Days, just as is foretold in the Revelations of St. John."

Aumery strode along the street and Peter had to hurry to keep up. He felt an extraordinary thrill. This was better than his wildest dreams! He was at the forefront of the battle against evil, and he was going to win. When Aumery found the Grail, together they would use it to remake the world.

Aumery slowed and his breathing eased. He began talking again, almost as if to himself. "Clues that I had collected over the years led me to believe that the Grail was in Carcassonne, but it was not. As you arranged, the heretics left with nothing but their sins, and a thorough search of the city has turned up nothing."

"Then the clues you followed were wrong?"

"Perhaps. Or there is another explanation. The clues could refer to the key to finding the Grail rather than the holy object itself."

"But the key could be anything, a book, a map, a scrap of paper."

"Yes, and perhaps those exist, somewhere," Aumery reasoned. "But we know the Cathars left the city naked. Therefore, they hid the key, destroyed it, or else they did take it out and we never saw it."

"How?"

Aumery tapped his forehead.

"Of course," Peter said in sudden realization. "One of them knew the location."

"That is what I suspect," Aumery mused. "Probably an old, respected Perfect. I regret not being able to apply some persuasion to the heretics in order to flush this Perfect out—if indeed there is only one—but we will find him or her again.

"In any case, the Grail must be at one of the heretics' remoter strongholds, perhaps Minerve, Peyrepertuse or Montségur. In the long term it is of little consequence. We have time and, eventually, every Cathar will burn and the Holy Church will recover its most treasured relic."

"But," Peter said, "the Cathars are fanatical. They may be willing to die without revealing the location of the Grail."

"That is true. In which case, it is God's wish that we do not find the Grail yet. Perhaps the Church is not ready. All we can do is try, and in the process, cleanse Christendom of this rabble."

Peter was silent as the implications of Aumery's speech sank in. To discover the Cathar Treasure, Aumery, with the blessings of the Pope, was prepared to conduct a war that might last decades and kill everyone tainted with heresy. Even if the Grail was not found, the land would be cleansed of anyone who might know something dangerous to the Church. It was a huge task, but a noble one. "It will take years," Peter said.

"Indeed. It will not be easy, and it may not be completed in our lifetimes, but the Church deals with eternity. And if only a few dedicated souls, such as you and I, devote our lives to the task, it will be completed and a day will dawn when not a single heretic will wake to see the sun."

Peter thought about what Aumery had said. The idea of finding the Holy Grail excited him, the thought of spending his life chasing down every last ragged heretic in this remote corner of the world less so. That hardly seemed the best way to achieve power within the Church. Peter had looked forward to triumphing rapidly. Even without the Grail, a few speedy victories at Aumery's side might result in a more important position, as an abbot of a small monastery, for example. That would be the first step on a ladder that, with luck, could lead anywhere. Peter would have to be careful not to become wrapped up in the ever more difficult hunt for an ever smaller but increasingly elusive number of enemies.

But that was not the only thing on his mind. He was quickly learning that nothing came without a cost. The ways of wielding power were not always as clean as one would wish. The betrayal of Roger Trenceval, even if the man had been complicit in the process, had been one such example. Peter had been sorry when news of the young viscount's death in the dank dungeons of Carcassonne last November had reached him. There had been talk of murder, but it was much more likely that the man had succumbed to bad food, cold and filth.

"You must harden your heart to do God's work," Aumery had said at the time. "The Devil often wears a smile. You liked Trenceval, that is understandable, but behind that smile was a demon doing Satan's work. Had he undertaken his Christian duties and rooted out the vile heretics from his domains, he would be alive, sitting today in Carcassonne, basking in the blessings of His Holiness."

Peter understood that, but it was hard. He had liked Trenceval, yet the man had been doing the Devil's work. He hated and feared the cruel Oddo, yet he was on the side of righteousness. What if it was a friend who was corrupt and doing the Devil's work—say John, or Isabella?

He pushed these unpleasant thoughts out of his mind as the party crossed the bridge over the Garonne River and approached the gates of Toulouse. The walls above were hung with brightly coloured banners bearing the coats of arms of the city's important families. Flags and pennants snapped in the wind from the battlements of the towers on either side of the gate.

"Bishop Foulques' Angels are waiting to welcome us," Aumery said, waving his arm to indicate a group of men standing on either side of the gate. They were dressed in white with a black-outlined cross on the chest. "Foulques calls them his White Brotherhood, but the common people call them his Angels."

Peter shuddered. He had known the Angels as a boy and they had scared him then. On one occasion, three Angels had attacked him and John as they had walked home at night. Peter had been terrified into immobility, but John had taken on the largest attacker and knocked him to the ground. The three had fled, and the boys had been spared a beating. Afterwards, Peter had felt ashamed and inadequate and had fought with John over something insignificant. The memory made him very uncomfortable.

Peter took a deep breath. Why was he so bothered by an old memory? He wasn't a scared boy any more. He was a servant of Rome with the power of the Catholic Church behind him. He need never fear the ignorant rabble again.

He took a good look at the Angels. Most were pox-marked and many exhibited the white lines of old battle scars. Each man carried a club, several of which had nails or other irregular pieces of iron hammered into their surfaces. These Angels looked more like the scum of the worst taverns as they gazed sullenly at the approaching monks.

As Peter watched, a side gate opened and Bishop Foulques stepped through. He was dressed in sumptuous robes embroidered with in silk threads and precious stones that glittered in the March sunlight. As he threw his arms wide in a theatrical welcome, Peter was distracted by a commotion on the walls above. A group of figures, young boys, as far as he could see, were struggling to manhandle three large pots onto the battlements.

"Toulouse! Toulouse!" the boys cried as they tipped the pots. "To hell with the Bishop's Angels."

Foulques skipped back under the gate's archway in time, but his men were caught by the full force of the pots' contents. A yellow waterfall of urine, mixed with excrement and rotting animal intestines, cascaded down on the Angels, soaking hair and staining robes. Pulling Peter's arm, Aumery moved to one side of the road.

The boys on the battlements were laughing uproariously and flinging insults down. The Angels were swearing and hurling curses back as they struggled to organize themselves. Several were on the ground, having slipped on the piles of glistening entrails.

Eventually, the Angels managed to get to the gate and, waving their spiked clubs, poured through in an attempt to catch the boys, who vanished along the top of the wall.

From his safe position on the side of the road, Peter struggled to sort out his feelings. A part of him was shocked at the disrespect shown to the bishop's men, but he also felt a thrill that they had been humiliated so easily. On top of it all was relief that they were gone.

"My apologies, my apologies!" Bishop Foulques remained under the arch.

"You see what we must endure from the Cathar rabble that Count Raymond refuses to eradicate from the bosom of the Holy Church. But rest assured that my White Brotherhood will find and suitably punish the perpetrators of this outrage."

Aumery, Peter and the others carefully picked their way through the disgusting debris, lifting the hems of their habits to avoid the worst of the mess. Once through the gate, everyone relaxed.

"Again, my apologies," Foulques said. "Come to the Château Narbonnaise. I have had a lunch prepared that I think you will find to your liking."

"We did not come for lunch, your Grace," Aumery said. "We wish to meet with Count Raymond as soon as is convenient."

"Of course, of course. I shall see to it." Foulques turned to a short priest who was hovering at his side. "Please take my compliments to Count Raymond, and ask if he would be so good as to attend the meeting at the Château two hours earlier than we had previously discussed."

"*Tell* him!" Aumery ordered.

The priest looked confused.

"We carry the authority of His Holiness Pope Innocent III," Aumery went on. "We require the count's attendance at *our* pleasure, not his."

The priest still hesitated until a nod from Foulques sent him on his way.

As the group walked to the Château Narbonnaise, Peter realized that his mentor had just taught him another valuable lesson. Aumery had told him that the best way to handle Bishop Foulques was through flattery, but the incident at the gate had exposed one of the bishop's weaknesses. Foulques had chosen to meet the delegation at the gates rather than wait in the Château because he wanted to show off his White Brotherhood and their power. It had backfired horribly. The boys' attack had shown, in the most dramatic way, that Foulques did not control the streets of Toulouse and it had left the bishop deeply embarrassed. Aumery had taken full advantage of that, dropping the idea of flattery in favour of flaunting his own power and ordering the bishop to change his plans. At least for this visit, Aumery had the upper hand.

* * *

Peter felt a pang of nostalgia as he turned the corner into the square in front of the Château Narbonnaise. Here was where he had seen his vision, where he had turned away from Isabella and John, and where his life had changed forever. Only three years had passed since that night, yet he was returning at the side of a papal legate working to recover the most holy relic in the Church. Peter strode confidently across the square at Aumery's side.

The Château Narbonnaise was more a fortress than a palace. It was constructed of red bricks and built into an angle of the city walls. Round towers, dotted with threatening arrow slits, rose above the squat walls. Only the entrance made any allowances for decoration, the round arch being surrounded by carvings of shields and armour. Above the arch the largest shield bore the cross of the counts of Toulouse. It was a strange design, a complex cross with arms of equal length. Each arm ended in three points and all twelve points ended in a nob of stone.

"It is said," Aumery commented, seeing Peter's gaze focused on the cross, "that the present count's ancestor, who went on the First Holy Crusade to recapture Jerusalem from the heathen, brought the design of the Toulouse cross back with him for his family's coat of arms."

"But if Raymond is a heretic, he would not allow a cross on his coat of arms," Peter said. "The heretics hate the cross in any form. They say it is merely an instrument of torture and that our Lord Christ did not die upon it." Peter crossed himself as he mentioned this heresy.

"Indeed, but remember, Count Raymond says he is not a heretic, and that may be true. He may simply allow them to preach their evil sermons. But also consider this. Some say that this is not a true cross. They say it has a pagan origin from long before the suffering of our Lord. See, it is not a solid carving, but merely a carved outline—a hollow cross—and the twelve points on the arms represent the signs of the pagan zodiac."

"So, it may be a heretic symbol after all?"

"It may. Do not be too ready to take things at face value, young Peter. The Devil continually conspires to trick us in new ways."

The party climbed the steps and entered the courtyard of the château. It was small and dark, surrounded as it was by the high brick walls.

"The count gave me the château last year," Foulques said, waving his arm to encompass the buildings around.

"A bribe?" Aumery asked, acidly.

"No, no." Foulques went on with no sign that he had taken offence. "Merely as a convenient place from which to undertake the Lord's work."

As they stood, a group of musicians entered the yard from a doorway opposite. Peter was surprised to see William of Arles, the same troubadour he had seen on the night of his vision and with whom John had gone travelling. As the musicians began, William banged his tambourine and began singing in his high-pitched voice. The language was Occitan.

"I go to her with joy
Through wind and snow and sleet.
The She-Wolf says I am hers
And, by God, she's right:

I belong to her
More than to any other, even to myself."

Bishop Foulques smiled at his arranged welcome, and despite there being nothing religious about the song of longing and lost love, Peter found his foot tapping to the tune. Aumery stepped forward, however, and Peter stopped his tapping, expecting a violent diatribe. Instead, to everyone's complete astonishment, Aumery began to sing in Latin. His voice was surprisingly deep and quickly drowned out William, who fell silent. To the musician's tune, Aumery sang:

"It's hard to bear it
When I hear such false belief
spoken and spread around.
May God hear my plea;
Let those, young and old,
Who cackle viciously
Against the law of Rome
Fall from its scales."

As Aumery finished, William stepped forward and acknowledged the legate's performance with a nod of his head and a sweep of his arm. "I am William of Arles and I bow before such a voice. Should you ever leave the Church, you could make a fine living as a troubadour."

"I am Arnaud Aumery, Abbot of Cîteaux and legate to Pope Innocent III, and I use the gifts that God gave me to do His work and praise His name. You would do well to consider a similar path rather than wasting your life on frivolous nonsense that encourages debauchery and sin."

Aumery pushed past the troubadour and scattered the musicians as he strode up the steps into the hall. For a moment, Peter found himself standing before William. The troubadour stared at Peter for a moment, then nodded in recognition. "Your visions gave you a hard taskmaster," he said with a smile.

"God is my master," Peter replied, striding after Aumery.

* * *

Peter's stomach grumbled noisily when he saw the sumptuous meal laid out on the long oak table in the château's main hall. The centerpiece was an entire roast boar, and it was surrounded by an assortment of pies, plates of quail, eggs of all sizes, and breads. Servants stood respectfully to one side, holding decanters of wine, and the rich smell of roasting meat wafted through from the archway that obviously led to the kitchens.

Aumery approached the servants. "Clear this away. Leave only the bread and wine," he instructed.

The servants hesitated, but at a nod from Bishop Foulques, they sprang into action. In no time, the table was clear except for loaves of bread, decanters of wine and goblets. Aumery sat and bowed his head in prayer to bless the food. The others joined him.

"You live well, Bishop," Aumery commented as he broke off a piece of bread.

"I find," the Bishop replied between swigs of wine, "that living at a certain standard engenders respect among the upper classes. And, without them, we cannot hope to combat this pernicious heresy."

"I think you will find that God's help is of more use in our struggle than a few minor lords whose wives are, probably, closet Perfects."

"Of course, of course. But I think you misjudge them."

"And how many heretics have they, or you, converted of late?" Aumery asked.

"Such things are hard to judge," Foulques said. "The Perfects, it is true, will never change their corrupt ways. However, there are many plain folk who were sympathetic to the heretics and now greatly favour us."

"Those would be the boys who emptied the contents of chamber pots on the heads of your Angels?" Aumery asked sarcastically. "Perhaps, as we speak, those very Angels are now subtly converting them to the true faith with the clubs they carry?"

"Come, come," Foulques blustered. "The situation is not as simple as—"

The bishop was cut off by a commotion at the door. Peter turned to see Count Raymond enter the hall. As host in his own territory, he was more sumptuously dressed than he had been at St. Gilles. Raymond was a tall man, and his presence was accentuated by his clothes. He wore an ankle-length tunic of startling blue, decorated with a diamond pattern picked out in gold thread. In the centre of each diamond, a golden Toulouse cross glinted. The tunic was bound at the waist with a heavy chain of gold, and from a lighter chain around Raymond's neck hung a large medallion with the Toulouse coat of arms in cloisonné. The clutch of retainers who followed the count were almost equally well dressed and a small whippet, wearing a collar of red velvet, frolicked at their feet. The count had obviously designed his entrance to say: "Here is a lord the equal of the King of France."

"My dear Aumery," Raymond said as he reached the table and held out his hand to the priest, "I see you declined Bishop Foulques' generous repast. Probably wise. I always find that the mind works more clearly on an empty stomach."

Out of the corner of his eye, Peter saw Foulques grimace at the implied insult, but his attention was held by Raymond. The count was unrecognizable from the blustering, threatening man he had seen two years before. Obviously, he could play games as well as Aumery.

"Count Raymond." Aumery stood and clasped the count's hand in both of his. "So glad you could accommodate our schedule. We have little time. The battle against the Devil is ceaseless."

"I am certain it is," Raymond replied. "And I can think of no one who is better fitted to lead that struggle than you."

The insincere pleasantries over, the two men sat at opposite sides of the table. A page poured Raymond a goblet of wine, which the count sipped appreciatively.

"In deference to the pressures of the continuing struggle against evil," Raymond said, wiping his mouth with his tunic sleeve, "we should get down to business. To what do I owe the pleasure of this visit?"

"Since your pledge to support the Holy Crusade and root out the vile Cathar heresy from your lands, His Holiness has written to me on a number of occasions, requesting details of the actions taken. Unfortunately, I have been unable to provide him with any."

"His Holiness must understand," Raymond said, smoothly, "that the situation here is not simple. I have had only a few months to address this complex situation, and my power over the city itself is not absolute. I have made the city fathers aware of your request to give up the heretics within our walls for interrogation, and they have complied." A page placed a document in Raymond's outstretched hand. "I have here a list of the known heretics in Toulouse." He slid the document across the table.

Aumery scanned it. "I thank you, but this is not satisfactory. There are a mere score of names here. Do the city fathers expect His Holiness to believe that that is all there is in this hotbed of heresy?"

Raymond shrugged. "I can speak for neither the expectations of the city fathers nor the beliefs of His Holiness."

Peter watched, fascinated, as the two men sparred. He knew that they detested one another. Yet they hid behind politeness and the wishes of the Pope and the city fathers.

"What is de Montfort's position?" Raymond asked.

"He is sworn to carry out His Holiness' orders. To that end, a mighty army from the north is assembling."

"And to what use will this army be put?"

"It will be a righteous sword that will sweep through the nests of heretics, *wherever* they may be found."

If Raymond heard the veiled threat to Toulouse in Aumery's statement, he gave no sign. "And I shall aid this noble cause to the fullest of my capabilities. Perhaps Bishop Foulques might offer the services of his White Brotherhood to the crusade?"

Foulques looked startled, but recovered quickly. "Of course, of course. They should be honoured. But they already fight in the cause, battling the heretics at their heart, in the streets of this very city."

Aumery smiled. "Very generous of you, but I am certain the Brotherhood are performing God's work admirably here in Toulouse.

"But, as to the matter of handing over the heretics: His Holiness has instructed me that you have six weeks in which to submit them—their bodies, not simply their names on a piece of parchment—for interrogation and punishment."

"And if this should prove impossible?"

"Then Toulouse and all its inhabitants shall be placed under an interdict. All places of worship shall be closed, Mass will not be said and no sacraments—baptism, marriage, confession or last rites—given."

Peter stifled a gasp. Aumery was threatening the excommunication of an entire city. Raymond showed no reaction, merely gazed thoughtfully at Aumery.

"I believe that to be harsh," he said eventually, "and I shall petition His Holiness directly on the matter. However, I shall attempt to carry out his instructions. I thank you for informing me of them.

"Now, if there is nothing else," said Raymond, standing, "I shall attend to my business. You are welcome to stay as long as you wish. Perhaps you would consent to say a Mass in the Cathedral of St. Sernin this afternoon? I am certain Bishop Foulques would be happy to arrange it."

"Thank you for your hospitality," Aumery said as he also stood. "It has been a most instructive meeting." He kept his smile in place as Raymond and his entourage left the hall.

"I would be honoured to arrange a Mass," Bishop Foulques said.

Aumery's smile vanished as he turned to face the bishop. "I do not wish to perform a Mass in a half-empty church while heretics mock us in the streets," he said angrily. "You would do better to persuade the city fathers to give up the heretics. When the interdict takes effect, you will be a bishop with no power and no flock.

"Now, I wish to cleanse myself and pray. Please show me to a cell. Peter, fetch my scourge and attend me."

Peter followed Aumery and a servant to a tiny bare room with only a single narrow slit high in the wall to allow light. Aumery knelt and prayed briefly. Then he loosened his habit. Peter shuddered at the intricate pattern of knotted white scars that covered his back.

"My scourge," Aumery said, holding out his hand. Peter passed him the knotted rope he had collected from one of the lay brothers.

"There is so much evil in the world," Aumery said sadly as he swung the rope hard over his shoulder. Tiny flecks of blood showed on his pale skin where the coarse rope hit.

"Peter, why did we come here today?"

Peter was momentarily confused by the question. "To force Count Raymond's hand?" he guessed.

"Only partly." The rope swung in another arc. "Our main purpose was to humiliate Bishop Foulques."

"But he is a bishop of the Church," Peter said.

"A corrupt and weak one." The rope arced and the spots of blood on Aumery's back grew. "Raymond will pretend to do something while doing nothing. He will appeal to His Holiness and attempt to delay the crusade with words. As long as he does so, de Montfort, even when he is strong enough, will have no excuse to attack Toulouse. However, should Toulouse fall into chaos, both de Montfort and Pope Innocent will be forced to act.

"If Foulques feels threatened, as surely he is by the possibility of an interdict, then he will fight for the only thing he cares about—his own power. He will use his Angels to spread fear through the streets. The heretics —not the Perfects but the common herd—will respond, as you saw this morning they already do. There will be bloodshed and violence. With luck, Raymond will be unable to control it and we shall be forced to step in. De Montfort will mount a siege with His Holiness' blessing and the heretics will burn on the banks of the Garronne River."

Aumery's plan was becoming clear, and once again, Peter found himself amazed at Aumery's resolve. He was fomenting uncontrollable violence to get his way. "But at St. Gilles, when Pierre of Castelnau met with—"

"Do not mention that man's name in my presence." The rope swung in a wide arc. "He was weak. Were he still alive, there would be no crusade, and I would not lead it."

"But he is a holy martyr."

"He was a fool." The rope slashed into Aumery's back with particular force. Drops of blood sprayed onto the floor. "He deserved to die."

"Deserved?"

"You have not yet learned to think things through, Peter. Do you imagine it mere chance that the murderer knew exactly where we would be camped?"

Peter was too stunned to reply. Had Aumery told the knight or Count

Raymond where Pierre could be found so that he could be murdered? Certainly, Aumery had benefited by the deed. He had used it to raise the crusade he now led. In two years he had risen from a junior papal legate to one of the most powerful men in Christendom. Arnaud Aumery was devious, yes, but would he stoop to murder?

"What do you mean?" Peter stammered.

"I mean just what I say," Aumery said dismissively. "Now leave me. I would pray."

As Peter closed the cell door, the last sounds he heard were the soft thud of the rope digging into Aumery's flesh and the sigh of satisfaction that escaped his thin lips.

* * *

Peter walked back through the narrow stone corridors, his mind crowded with thoughts of the day's events. There were times—many, lately—when he felt that he understood Aumery, his ways and his goals. At other times, though, like today, he wasn't so sure. If Aumery had truly arranged for the murder of Pierre of Castelnau, how was that God's work? He knew that Aumery worked toward God's goals, but murder as a way to get there? Peter was startled from his thoughts by a figure stepping out in front of him. It took him a moment to recognize who it was.

"Isabella," he said, taking a step back.

"Hello, Peter. I saw you at that strange monk's side. You've done well since last we met."

Peter's mind was a chaos of conflicting emotions. For three years, the only contact he had had with the world from before his visions had been his fraught meeting with John. He had deliberately pushed down all memories of the games, jokes and songs of his friends, and all thoughts of Isabella. Now, with no chance to prepare himself, here she was, standing an arm's reach in front of him, as darkly beautiful as ever and with that mysterious half smile playing around her mouth and eyes, that used to make his knees go weak.

"I do God's work now for Father Aumery and his blessed Holiness, Pope Innocent." Peter silently cursed himself. Once again he was falling back on the self-important phrases that had so annoyed John.

Isabella's smile broadened. "Are you happy in this work?"

Peter hesitated. He'd never asked himself that question. Doing God's work was a reward in itself; happiness had nothing to do with it. "The work of rooting out this foul heresy in the heart of Christendom must be done if we are to prepare for Christ's coming."

Isabella nodded, but her smile faded. "Have you had more visions since that night in the square?"

"God has not seen fit to favour me with more."

"As I recall, it did not seem much like a favour at the time, but"—Isabella hurried on to prevent Peter's interruption—" I have wondered many times since then if the visions were my fault."

"Your fault?"

"If you recall, our conversation on the steps that night was not to your liking. You declared your love for me and, I believe, were about to ask that we become betrothed."

Peter didn't say anything, but it was true. That night—troubled by the debate and his discussion with John, excited at the festive atmosphere in the square and undecided as to his future—Peter, when faced with Isabella's beauty, had babbled on inanely about love. And, yes, had Isabella not interrupted him, he would have asked for her hand.

"I said that I was not ready for such a declaration of love," Isabella went on. "I was young and had led a sheltered life. I wanted to see more of the world. I wanted desperately not to hurt you and was about to suggest that we remain friends and see what the future would bring, but you were not listening. Your visions of death held you in thrall by then.

"What I have often wondered is whether you saw my response as rejection and if this, in some way I do not understand, caused thoughts of death to overcome your mind and allow Satan in to corrupt your sight."

"Satan!" Peter was taken aback. "It was *God* who sent me those visions. They caused me to become a priest and fight the Holy Crusade against heresy. Is that what Satan would have wanted?"

"Only if the crusade is wrong."

Anger flooded through Peter. "The crusade *cannot* be wrong! It is Christ's work, blessed by His Holiness himself. This vile canker in the heart of Christ's earthly kingdom *must* be burned out, else how can we defeat the heathen overseas? You put your soul in mortal jeopardy by even thinking such thoughts."

All traces of Isabella's smile were gone now, replaced by a sadness Peter could not recall ever seeing on her features before. "I am sorry," she said. "I was wrong to doubt your visions. I do not wish us to part with bad words between us."

Peter breathed slowly and tried to calm himself. He didn't want bad words between them either. He wanted to sit down as they had years before and just talk, but he couldn't. Talking brought out ideas, and ideas could be dangerous. That was John's problem—he put no limits on what he thought, simply allowing any and all ideas to surface and giving them equal weight. It was much easier, and safer, to be certain, to build a shield of the correct doctrine to protect yourself from hurt and embarrassment. But some people didn't seem to understand that.

"I am truly glad that you are doing well on the path you have chosen." Isabella's smile had returned to her lips, but it didn't reach her eyes. "Have you seen John since that night?"

"Our paths have crossed."

"He is well?"

"It was some time ago, but his body was well enough." Peter's mind went back to the last he had seen of John, fleeing for his life down the riverbank after the murder of Pierre of Castelnau. How did *that* fit with what Aumery had told him a short while ago? "I fear for his soul, though. He worked for the heretic Roger Trenceval and consorted with all manner of Cathar filth."

"Do you know where he is now?"

"I don't, but why should you care?"

The sad expression flitted across Isabella's face again.

"If you see him," Isabella said, "greet him for me."

"I doubt I'll see a heretic like him."

"You never know," Isabella said, her mysterious smile back. "You met me. But I must be off. Go well, Peter."

Before Peter could ask what she meant, Isabella was gone.

Leaving

Bram and Cabaret
March 1210

John tramped along the dead straight road to Bram, his shoes slapping on the wet stone cobbles laid by Roman legionnaires more than a thousand years before. It was only March and the bitter winds from the mountains still blew strongly. At least the last rain squall had stopped before it had soaked through to John's tunic and trousers, but his dark-red woollen cloak was saturated and heavy. To its weight was added a large satchel, hanging from his shoulder and balancing on his left hip. In his right hand, he carried a long, knotted walking stick with which he marked his strides. He shivered as another icy gust chilled him. Although he knew they would be sparse, John looked forward to the companionable comforts of the Cathar house at his destination.

To dull the discomfort of his present state, he thought back over the events of the previous winter. It had been a busy time learning from Umar. The old man was a hard taskmaster; nevertheless, the winter had been one of the most peaceful in John's life. Minerve had been quiet and its inhabitants protected from the violence sweeping the surrounding countryside. For more than half a year, John had been comfortable: not living in luxury, but safe and fed adequately, and all he had to do in return was learn. It was a good life, but a tiny worm of discontent wriggled in the back of his mind.

What was Adso doing? As he had promised, he had left Minerve a few days after he and John had last spoken, heading south to find a band of robbers to join so he could seek plunder and harass the invaders. He had gone cheerfully and John had envied him a little. What an adventure it would be, living rough with a close band of companions, attacking the crusaders when there was an advantage and disappearing into the forests to rest and await another chance. Beatrice and Umar were wonderful and very wise, and John loved the life they had given him. Still—

There had been fighting all around Carcassonne most of the winter. Simon de Montfort, and those crusaders who had stayed with him, had made sure that anywhere within easy marching distance of Carcassonne was subject to raids. De Montfort had surprised everyone, not least Beatrice, by continuing his campaign into the previous autumn. He never had enough men to mount a serious siege of a major castle or town, but the few knights who had remained, led by Oddo and his Falcons, had rapidly gained a reputation for ferocity. Through a combination of rapid movement, brutality and the memory of Béziers, they had forced the surrender of Fanjeux and Montréal. Even Toulouse and Albi had paid at least token homage. On the other hand, with not enough men to garrison his new conquests, de Montfort had had to rely on the promises of local lords, and many had reverted to their old ways and allegiances as soon as the crusader knights rode over the nearest hill. Had Adso been involved in all that?

"De Montfort will have to reconquer all the small fortresses again come the spring," Beatrice had prophesied only a few days ago, "but this time he will have a new army from the north and he will wish to teach his faint-hearted vassals a lesson."

"Will he come to Minerve this year?" John had asked.

"He will first subdue the land around Carcassonne," Beatrice explained. "He will probably begin by making examples of a couple of minor castles, but, to be secure next winter, he will have to reduce a major fortress and that means Minerve. We are probably safe until late summer, but by then, water will be a problem for a besieged town swollen with refugees, and de Montfort's task will be easier. You must go before then."

"Where?" John had asked.

"De Montfort cannot attack every stronghold. He will concentrate on the ones that are big enough to hold sufficient knights to mount raids when he is occupied elsewhere. Small castles like Montségur or Quéribus are virtually impregnable, but they cannot support a large garrison and are too remote to threaten him directly. Many of the smaller fortresses have books that must be rescued."

"And memorized."

"Indeed." Beatrice smiled at her pupil. "You have done better than I could have hoped this winter. You have learned all of Umar's books?"

"All the ones in languages I can understand," John said proudly. "But there is one he has told of but does not have—a book on drawing."

"I have heard of it."

"Do you know where it is?"

"If it is anywhere, it is in Al-Andalus."

"Umar says he has seen the drawings in it and would copy some down for me, but he delays. He says there are more important books, and copying drawings is harder than reciting words."

"And in that he is correct, but there is another reason. Umar is very proud. It is not a good characteristic for a holy man, but he comes from a proud people. In any case, his hands pain him greatly. You have seen how they are twisted and how he rubs them constantly?"

"I have."

"He fears that he has not the skill left to copy the drawings from his mind and he does not wish to seem weak before you, so he hesitates. He will do it eventually."

John hoped so. The religious books were wonderful and undeniably important, but he craved what the drawing book might teach him. He still practiced whenever he could, attempting to draw the streets and buildings of Minerve, but learning books took all his energy and it was hard to find the time or the materials. It was exasperating and John looked forward to the day he would have time to sit down and practice. Maybe one day he would even go to Al-Andalus himself and search for the mysterious drawing book.

Despite the rain, the cold, his sore feet and his frustrations at not having enough time to draw, John was happy. The memory cloister sat in his mind, loaded with wonders and ready to receive more. He thought over all that Umar had taught him. The Gospel of the Christ had been the most important and the most shocking. Despite Adso's disparaging comments, John still believed in the power of the work. Not only did it undermine the whole Catholic faith, but the issues that Christ wrote about as an old man in Languedoc greatly supported the idea that the Cathars were the ones who preserved the true Christianity. John believed that the Gospel was true, but he struggled with how it would be possible to convince enough others of its authenticity. Although it didn't really matter if it were true. True or false, Adso had been correct in saying that the Church would stop at nothing to suppress the Gospel's contents.

John looked up and caught a glimpse of the walls of Bram on the horizon. It was a small, not particularly well-fortified town, one that Beatrice thought de Montfort would pick off easily before he tackled the harder nut of Minerve. That was why John was on his way. There were two books in Bram that needed rescuing.

One had been written by a man called Origen, a mystic who had lived some two hundred and fifty years after Christ. Using texts that were old even in his day, Origen had written that the early Christians believed that every soul came from God, and that through reincarnation, each soul came closer to returning to God. Origen's writings had been popular once, but the

Emperor Justinian had been convinced by the Church cardinals that they were heresy. They said that every soul could not be direct from God, because that made them equal to Christ and, if reincarnation was the way to become closer to God, what was the point of Mass and going to church? Many of Origen's most controversial writings had been burned, but a copy of one was preserved in Bram.

The other book was not religious. It was a copy in Latin of a Greek book on mathematics by Aristarchos of Samos, who had lived some three hundred years before Christ. It was said to prove that the earth was a sphere and that it travelled around the sun rather than vice versa. Understandably, the Church, which believed in the idea that the earth was a mirror of heaven, a flat land with Jerusalem at its centre, would not take kindly to it.

John would reach Bram that evening and begin reading immediately. To keep his mind active, he went to the memory cloister. John closed his eyes as he walked and looked inward. He saw a heavy oak door that swung open easily at his touch, revealing a long corridor of stone. Arches led off on either side. John walked a short way along the corridor and stopped beside the thirteenth archway on the left. Within it was a shelf and on the shelf lay a book. John lifted the book and looked at the title: The Gospel of the Christ. He opened the book at random and began reading:

Chapter 8: 1. Had I not been so near to death, I would not have permitted it. In the hours on the cross, my doubt had blossomed.

2. At first I attributed it to the works of Satan, but as time passed and my Father remained hidden, I began to believe that I had misled myself, that I was forsaken. I looked down upon the people coming and going below me, soldiers, peddlers, the curious. To them, as they went about their mundane and worldly pursuits, I was simply one prophet among many—and a failed one at that.

3. I had preached as I believed was my duty. I had done all that my visions in the desert had required of me. I had healed the sick, preached to the multitude and offered myself as the door through which heaven would prosper on earth. And yet the End of Days was not here. The earth had not opened and released the dead, the sun had not been extinguished, Satan had not been defeated in the final battle, the world with all its petty cares went on.

4. Perhaps the holy men from the east, with their ancient beliefs in an eternal struggle between Good and Evil, had been right and I misled. I hung my head and awaited death. But I was not even to be allowed that luxury.

5. At the coming of dark, Mary and the women came and took me down from the cross. I knew nothing of it, otherwise I should have made them leave me to my solitary, defeated fate. But they wrapped me in cloth and took me to the house of a friend where they tended me back to health.

6. They put around the tale that I had been buried in the stone tomb that had been prepared, and attempted to keep my continued presence in the city a secret. It was not possible. The curious went to the tomb and found it empty. Thomas, the doubter, stumbled upon me. He tried to persuade me to continue preaching, but I was too sick in body and mind.

7. As I lay on my cot and as Mary mopped my brow, I decided that I had to leave Jerusalem as soon I was strong enough. I would preach no more, but instead I would travel and learn. The world was much larger and more complex than I had believed living in this small corner. Somehow, I had misunderstood the message God had sent me in the desert.

8. Perhaps my labour upon this earth was to learn all things. Perhaps only through discovering my own inner peace and what those from the east call Enlightenment, could I understand what was required of me by God.

9. And so I began my travels. I first went east to—

"Hey! Watch where you're going."

The book slammed shut and flew out of John's hands, back into the alcove. He opened his eyes to see a band of soldiers standing in the road before him. They were dressed in a motley assortment of armour, chain mail and helmets and carried a selection of long pikes, axes and the occasional sword. John's first fearful reaction was that he had been captured by a crusader party, but none wore the red cross on their tunics. They were more likely either soldiers from Bram or common robbers.

"Where are you heading?" The leader was a short, stockily built man. His face was round and his features bulbous and pox-scarred except for his chin, which was cleft and jutted forward aggressively.

"Bram," John replied.

"You must know the way well to be able to walk there with your eyes closed." The men behind the leader laughed.

"I was thinking," John said defensively.

"Ah, a thinker. Well, I think too. Do you want to know what I think?"

John stayed silent, but the man went on anyway. "I think you might have something worth stealing in that bag of yours."

"I don't." Instinctively, John raised his staff.

"So you want to fight for the bag," the robber said, smiling and hefting his axe. "*Must* be something valuable in it." He stepped forward.

"Bertrand. I know 'im."

John peered past Bertrand to see who had spoken. One of the soldiers stepped forward.

"Adso!" John exclaimed, delighted to see his friend.

"Still doing Beatrice and that old Moor's bidding?" Adso's smile undermined any insult there might have been in the question.

"They have taught me much," John said.

"I have no doubt. Beatrice is a very clever woman and old Umar's 'ead contains more knowledge than the library in Rome. 'E escaped with me from Béziers last year and 'e works for the Good Christians," Adso said, turning to Bertrand. "'E's no crusader and he won't have anything worth stealing."

Bertrand looked disappointed and spat pointedly in the dirt. Then his face broke into a smile and he made a mock bow to John. "Then let us escort you to Bram," he said.

As they walked, Adso and John talked.

"The autumn was 'ard," Adso said after John had told him about the winter in Minerve. "De Montfort 'ad knights everywhere. They call themselves Falcons and are led by this brute of a man called Oddo."

"He's left-handed and his men wear the crest of a falcon clutching an axe."

"'Ow did you know that?" Adso asked. "Not in one of your books."

"I saw him at Béziers. He led the charge through the gates. I didn't know his name was Oddo, but the falcon's his symbol. I think he may also be the knight who killed Pierre of Castelnau and started all this."

"Then 'e 'as a lot of blood on 'is hands," Adso said thoughtfully. "'E'll be an 'ard man to stop and no mistake. 'E even led an attack on Cabaret for de Montfort, but 'e weren't strong enough for that one. 'Ad to go 'ome with 'is tail 'tween 'is legs.

"After that it got better for us—good pickings. We ambushed a party of knights back before Christmas. Turns out the leader was Bouchard de Marly, one of de Montfort's most trusted lieutenants."

"Did you kill him?"

"Naw, 'e's sitting rotting in a Cabaret dungeon. Thought at first we could swap 'im for Trenceval, but we was too late."

"Roger Trenceval is dead?"

"November last's what I 'eard."

"How did he die?" John was saddened by the news that his protector in Carcassonne was dead. He also felt a returning pang of guilt at the way he'd abandoned Trenceval after Béziers, although he couldn't see how anything *he* could have done would have made any difference.

"Murdered, most like. De Montfort and Aumery wouldn't want 'im lingering on as a symbol for the rest of us."

"That's terrible."

Adso laughed out loud. "Terrible, is it? You've a lot to learn, lad. War's a brutal business and this one's worse'n most. We 'ad two men captured this February past."

"What happened to them?" John asked.

"Tortured," Adso said bitterly. "These damned priests said they was 'eretics and cut up their faces something dreadful. Then they burned them. Seems if you think someone's bound for an eternity in 'ell, what you do to their bodies in this world don't matter. Mind, we sent a few of them to their 'ell in exchange."

"Beatrice says a new army from the north will gather this summer."

"Sooner than she can imagine. De Montfort 'as met it near Béziers. Word is, they're already on the way back to Carcassonne. After that, who can say? De Montfort'll want a quick victory to begin 'is year, and Aumery'll be craving some Cathar flesh to roast. They won't be ready to take on Minerve yet, but they could take any one of a dozen smaller castles."

"Bram?"

"Could be, if 'e comes west, Cabaret if 'e goes north, or Aguilar if 'e decides south. Only time'll tell. My guess is 'e'll go in all different directions, try to clear around Carcassonne. The towns in most danger'll be the ones closest in, Alairac for example, but where 'e goes first only 'e knows."

"How long can Bram hold out?" John asked, worried at how little time he might have.

Adso shrugged. "For a time. But a lot of folk want to surrender. They think de Montfort'll spare them if they do. And they might be right, 'least the regular folk, but anyone 'oo doesn't swear allegiance to the Pope's doomed."

"And you? What will you do?"

Adso looked at John. His smile was firmly in place and his eyes sparkled. "You know me, I'm not one for regular Mass, but I'll bend a knee to the Pope if it'll save my skin.

"Look, you thinkers worry too much. Did Christ say this? Does God wish us to do that? Whatever God wants from us, 'E's doing a good job of keeping it a secret from regular folk, and I don't know that the rich bishops in all their finery or the 'oly Perfects are any closer to knowing the truth than I am. Oh, I'd rather sup with Beatrice than Bishop Foulques, although I dare say I'd be better fed by the bishop, but I'm not about to throw myself on either an' say, 'Oh yes, you're right. Tell me what to do.' All a man *can* do is look after 'imself and those 'e cares about the best 'e can, and 'ope that that's enough for whatever God 'e chooses."

The pair lapsed into silence as they trudged toward the walls of Bram. Adso was right, John thought, most people *didn't* care about the things Aumery or Peter argued for, or what Beatrice had told him over the winter. The day-to-day struggle for existence took up all their energy. Still, in the face of the brutal crusaders, preserving the knowledge in the old books was something worthwhile, wasn't it?

* * *

"You might not 'ave time," Adso said as he and John walked the odd, circular streets of Bram. Built on a low hill, the town featured streets that ran in ever increasing circles around the central church, like ripples on a pond.

"It will take three or four days to memorize the books. Surely we have that long." John had found Origen's book and the other one exactly where Beatrice had said they would be, in the cellar of the Cathar house near the centre of town. The Aristarchos book was small, no larger than a slim prayer book, but it was full of symbols and complexities that would take time to learn. Origen's work was simpler, but it was a massive tome. Its memorizing, even with all the practice John had, would be a larger, and he feared, duller, task than he had expected.

"The refugees are saying that de Montfort's only a day or two away and 'e's certainly coming 'ere first rather than Cabaret or Alairac. Bram's not the strongest fortress, but it might be able to 'old for a week or two. Bertrand's got more'n a hundred knights 'ere. Problem is, if de Montfort arrives tomorrow, you'll be trapped, and then what use'll all that learning in your 'ead be?"

Adso made a good point. If John took the books to Cabaret, fifteen miles to the northeast, he would have time to read and learn them in safety, however long Bram resisted. He would also be almost halfway back to Minerve.

"I'll leave tomorrow morning."

"Good idea. Leave the fighting to soldiers." Adso smiled, displaying his broken teeth.

A thought struck John. "If Bram's not very strong, why is Bertrand committing his knights to defending it? Wouldn't he be better to take to the woods and harass the crusaders from there, as you did last winter?"

"Maybe we'll make a soldier of you yet. That's exactly what I argued for. But Bertrand'd 'ave none of it. Seems 'e 'as sworn some sort of oath to Raymond of Toulouse and at least 'alf 'is knights are Raymond's men. Don't 'old with oaths myself, but what can you do?"

"But that means you'll be trapped when Bram falls."

Adso laughed. "Don't worry 'bout me. Remember Béziers? I'm not one to get trapped anywhere. You 'ead off to Cabaret and learn Beatrice's books. You've got a strong 'ead, so you're a scholar. I've got a strong arm, so I'm a soldier. Our paths'll cross again. Now go and read."

John watched Adso head down to the town walls. He knew what he had to do, but he still felt that he was deserting his friend. He hoped Adso was right, and that they would indeed meet again.

Heretic

* * *

Cabaret was the most northerly of three small keeps spread along a rocky ridge. They looked impressive and each was an independent fortress, but the lower slopes of the ridge were cluttered with the houses and workshops of a small village. Cabaret had been an important place for centuries, and an ancient, Roman path ran along the opposite valley side, linking several small iron mines. Agricultural terraces were scattered across the surrounding hills and there was a continual bustle of people tending to them or fetching water from the streams in the valley bottom. John could see why de Montfort had failed to subdue the place the previous year. It would take a huge army to seal off all approaches to the community and there was precious little flat ground where siege engines could be located.

After the long walk from Bram with his bag of books, John had found a warm welcome in a Cathar house beneath the walls of the keep. The mention of Beatrice's name ensured that he was given a quiet corner in which to work and was allowed to join the Perfects at their vegetarian meals. He began reading immediately and, after three days, finished Origen's book. Despite its imposing size, it had proved unremarkable and had contained little John had not read elsewhere.

On the afternoon of his fourth day at Cabaret, John was struggling with Aristarchos' book when he was disturbed by a commotion at the door.

"I'm told that young John of Toulouse is within," a familiar voice said. "Tell him that the greatest troubadour in all of Languedoc is here to see him."

"William!" John exclaimed, jumping to his feet and running to the door. The pair embraced. "But you are alone," John said, a trace of a smile turning up the corners of his mouth.

"I am. I could not feed my musicians in these troubled times. What of it?"

"Where is the great troubadour of whom you spoke?"

William burst into gales of laughter and playfully punched John on the arm. "I see you have not learned manners in your months away from me," he said when he had calmed down.

"And you have not learned modesty," John replied. "But sit, have some bread and wine."

The pair seated themselves at the table and William poured them both a goblet of wine while John broke off a couple of pieces of bread.

"What brings you here?" John asked when they were settled.

William's face became serious. "Hard times. I was on the road from Toulouse, where Count Raymond and that fat slug Foulques paid me too little for too much work. I was headed for Pamiers and Foix, where they say men are not yet killing each other and still appreciate good songs. But I ran into some crusaders north of Bram and was forced to spend a night singing Catholic dirges in Latin for the legate Aumery."

"Aumery is at Bram?"

"Aumery, de Montfort and an entire army are at Bram. There was also a young priest friend of yours I seem to keep bumping into."

"Peter!"

"Indeed. A humourless lad, I thought, but in a weak moment he did ask me to pass on his greetings should I run into you on my travels."

"Peter is well?" John asked.

"As well as anyone can be who is forced to spend their days with Aumery. The man has a beautiful voice, but he has the face of a surprised ferret and the soul of a rabid fanatic." William paused and shook his head. "But I also have a message from a much more pleasant friend."

"Who?"

"She approached me in Toulouse and asked how you were and if I knew of your whereabouts. It seems she was there the night we first met."

"Isabella?"

"The very same, and with looks that could turn the head of even that rat-faced Aumery."

"How is she?"

"She is well, and showed uncommon concern for your well-being. Personally, I do not think you worth the effort, but she seemed determined to make me tell what I knew of your story since last you two met, and I have never been one to resist such beguiling eyes."

"Tell me how she is," John ordered. He found himself strangely eager to hear news of Isabella. He had thought about her a lot on his travels; if he were honest, she probably crossed his mind more than Peter, but he had assumed their paths would never again intersect.

"She is well," William repeated with a sly smile. "I told her of our adventures that first year, but despite my witty relating, your recent doings appeared of greater interest. I did not know you were here, but I had heard on my wanderings that you had escaped the unpleasantness at Béziers with Beatrice and that she had established herself in Minerve, so—"

"You told Isabella that I was in Minerve?" John felt a thrill pass through him.

"You didn't want me to?" William asked innocently.

"Of course I do, I did! I don't know! Why should she care?" John babbled in confusion.

"For a smart boy who is learning so much, you sound perilously close to a village idiot. Even I, a mere scribbler of musical entertainments, would guess that she cares for you."

"But she cares for Peter."

"Your stick friend? If she did, I doubt she does now. The young lady did not strike me as one who is attracted to visions of death and religious certainty. In fact, when I saw her, she was living in a Cathar house."

"She is a Perfect?"

"No, but I think she might be called a Good Christian."

John felt strange. Did Isabella care for him? Did he care for her? He had never asked himself either question. Isabella had been one of the group of friends and Peter had been utterly smitten by her. John would be happy to see any of his old group of friends, but this happy? John felt like hugging William for bringing him this news.

"You came all the way here to tell me this?" he asked with a silly grin on his face.

"Don't flatter yourself," William said. "The affairs of a couple of puppies who barely know their own minds are no concern of mine. I came here because Bram will fall soon. The attacks on the walls are brutal and ceaseless. The ditches are filling with blood faster than water in a storm. Word is that after Bram, they will head for Alairac and then, maybe, south to Aguilar. It seemed to me that the north would be a safer place for one of my talents to seek a living. I shall head to Minerve, where I can at least have a sensible conversation with Beatrice, and then, who knows. Too far north and they don't appreciate a troubadour's talents. Perhaps I shall go to Aragon—I hear both Good Christians and good singers are still welcome there."

"Then you had better become a Good Christian," John said playfully. Then, more seriously, "So, de Montfort is not coming to Cabaret?"

"Not this year, it seems. I suspect his failure last winter rankles, but he cannot afford too many such." William paused and his eyes narrowed in worry. "But Aumery did say a strange thing."

"What?"

"He said that there would be a gift for Cabaret when Bram fell."

"What did he mean?"

"I cannot imagine."

"Your presence is gift enough," John said. "Will you stay and entertain us for a few days?"

William drained the last of his wine and stood up. "I am honoured by your flattery, even though I suspect you are more pleased with my news than my presence, but I must move on. I had not intended to stop here at all, but I fell into conversation with a Good Man and from his description of the ugly boy who had suddenly appeared to scrounge a bed and meals, I assumed it must be you."

"I see I did not learn flattery from you!" John rose to stand beside his friend.

William bowed in mock gratitude. "But tell me, do you still draw? You have not forgotten your promise to immortalize me?"

"I have not forgotten my promise, although I fear it will take more than mere human skill to create a work that will match your opinion of yourself. I practice when I can, but those times are rare these days. I fear my skill is not improving much."

"Maybe you need a worthy subject. Someone of Isabella's beauty, perhaps," William said slyly.

"That would certainly be a more pleasing task than attempting to capture your sorry face on a wall, but what I need is a book. I hear there is one in Al-Andalus that contains wondrous pictures."

"There are many wondrous things down that way."

"You've been there?"

"I have. There are few places I have not been in search of stories and songs. If things get much worse here, perhaps it will not be long until I am seeking refuge down there again. At least the Moors appreciate talent, but for now I must be on my way." William moved toward the door.

"I am glad you dropped by," John said. "Say hello to Beatrice when you are in Minerve and tell her I am near done and shall return in a few days."

"I shall do so," William said as the pair walked outside. "Do not read too much. It strains the eyes and the brain. And do not spend your hours dreaming of that girl in Toulouse. I do not doubt you will meet again and, perhaps, by then you will have learned to draw well enough to do her beauty justice."

"I shall try. Travel well, William. I hope we shall meet again in happier times."

"As do I, young John. And when we do meet again, you must tell me of the mysterious gift from Bram. Perhaps it will be worthy of a song."

The pair embraced once more and John watched the troubadour head down the rough path across the hills to Minerve. It had been good to meet his friend again and, although the news from Bram was disturbing, John was happy as he returned to the table. Both Peter and Adso were at Bram, but the first was safe enough beside Aumery, and the other's skills and cunning would serve him well in a crisis. Isabella was in Toulouse and was asking for him—that was the thought that spun happily around John's brain. He sighed contentedly and returned to his book.

* * *

The candle flame spluttered out in the final pool of melted wax. It was still dark outside, but the sounds of birdsong announced that dawn was near. Soon the Perfects would rise to begin their devotions and eat their meagre breakfast. John sat in the darkness, his mind a turmoil. He had finished Aristarchos' book more than an hour before and he was tired, but his brain would not allow sleep. New ideas—literally new ways of looking at the world—were swirling around his head.

Aristarchos' mathematics had been beyond him, but the ideas behind it were earth-shaking. As Beatrice had suggested, the book held that, instead of the sun travelling around the earth, which was what everyone knew to be true by simply looking in the sky, the opposite was the case. The earth was not the centre of God's universe, the sun was, and the earth and the other planets were merely objects spinning around it. What's more, the moon was simply a lesser object spinning around the earth. And the stars were not set in a crystal sphere above the earth at all, but were points of light almost immeasurable distances away.

The Church would scream heresy, but what if it were true? Would that not be as shocking in its own way as the Gospel of the Christ?

John looked down at the book in his hands. He could see it now without the candle flame; the pale light of predawn was filtering in through the window. Above him, he could hear the sounds of the Perfects beginning their day. Soon they would be down to set the fire. John didn't want to be caught up in that. He needed time to think—and to draw. Strangely, the urge to draw had been growing since William's news, two days before, that Isabella was asking after him. He wanted to draw the world around him, yes, but mostly he wanted to draw Isabella. Her face hovered in his mind as clearly as if he had seen it yesterday and he wanted to get it down on parchment. But the Perfects of Cabaret had no parchment, or even ink or quills.

John turned the mathematics book over in his hands. The back cover was fine leather and blank. He went to the hearth and the black remains of yesterday's fire. He selected a suitable piece of burned wood and made a few experimental lines on the cover. They took. Stuffing the small book into the pouch at his waist, John collected several more pieces of charcoal, wrapped himself in his fur-edged cloak and let himself out into the morning.

* * *

John walked along the ridge and then down the path that followed the narrow valley in the direction of Bram. The sky was clear and it was the first day in weeks that the rain had stopped, but the wind coming off the hills was knife-edged and the ground beneath his feet muddy. He pulled his cloak tight around him, but he still shivered whenever he stopped walking. His feet and legs were soaked and filthy almost to his knees, and he was beginning to lose the feeling in his toes, but it was good to be outside.

John followed the path for nearly a mile, until the valley widened out before him. The weak sun bathed the landscape and mist rose in thick swirls from the wet ground. He stopped at a rock half as tall as he was. Long before, it had tumbled down from the surrounding hills and come to rest by the path, providing a spot sheltered from the wind. He sat down.

The view toward Bram was empty as far as he could see, except for some distant travellers winding up the valley toward him. John looked up at the sun and tried to envisage the solid earth beneath him moving around it. It certainly seemed as if the opposite was happening. The sun was moving through the heavens but, if the earth were turning, he supposed the effect might be the same. He took out the mathematics book and began making tentative marks on the cover. As the sun rose, he sketched the shape of Isabella's face with her dark hair cascading down on either side. He drew in her high forehead, narrow nose, eyes and mouth. John got the proportions right, but it looked nothing like the image in his mind. The eyes were lifeless and his attempt at giving Isabella her mysterious smile simply made it look as if she had eaten something distasteful. The face was the same as all the mosaics and paintings in the churches, magnificent if you painted it in bright colours and surrounded it with gold, but nothing like a real person.

In frustration, John smeared out the charcoal lines and stuffed the book back in his pouch. He wished once more that he had the drawing book Umar and Beatrice had mentioned. Maybe it would teach him how to draw what he saw the way he saw it.

He would also have to study the mathematics book more. He knew its conclusions, but not how Aristarchos had come to them. Maybe John could find a mathematician who could explain some of it, but who? Peter had always understood figures and numbers, but he would probably just say the book was heresy and burn it.

John frowned. Would Beatrice and Umar be any happier with his questions? They obviously thought the mathematics and drawing books were much less important than the gospels they had given him to learn. Would they approve of him spending his time trying to understand Aristarchos' ideas, not to mention drawing? Probably not. The earth and the sun were material things and thus the Devil's work, and certainly Umar would regard further study as an unnecessary distraction from John's main purpose, which was to fill the memory cloister.

But was that what John really wished to devote his entire life to? To fill the pot of his memory with ancient books? It was without question a noble thing to do, and John was completely in favour of preserving books that people wanted to burn, but there were so many other things! John still wanted to see the world, he wanted to master drawing, if he ever found the book, and he wanted to understand the world and the sun and all that the strange book in his pouch seemed to promise. And there was more. John wanted the free life Adso led and he wanted to do his part against the crusaders who were ravishing his land. Yet, it was impossible to do all those things and still be what Beatrice and Umar wanted him to be.

The thought of Adso made John wonder how his friend was doing and what was going on at Bram. He desperately wanted to know, to get up and walk down the valley, past the winding procession that was much closer now, all the way to Bram. There he would find Adso and Bertrand, learn what was going on, and fight beside his friend to rid the land of its invaders.

John leaned his head back against the rock and felt the warmth of the rising spring sun on his face. It was an impossible dream. He knew he had to go back to Beatrice in Minerve. But once he was back, would he ever escape? Beatrice's soft voice and calm logic would convince him that his idea of joining Adso was nonsense. She would say that fighting was never the answer and simply played into the Devil's hands. The only way to truly fight the crusaders was the path she had pointed him on—collecting, learning knowledge and wisdom so that, whatever happened here, future generations would have the chance to see the truth and learn from the mistakes being made now.

John sighed and lowered his head. A song thrush, lured into the open by the sunny weather, sat on a nearby branch. "What should I do?" he asked the bird. The thrush tilted its head and stared at him curiously. "You're right not to answer," John went on. "It's my decision and, in any case, I *know* what I should do. I should get up from this rock, have some breakfast at Cabaret and set off for Minerve.

"But I *want* to go to Bram." his raised voice startled the thrush and it hopped up to a higher branch. John's gaze wandered to the road. The travellers were closer now. It seemed to be some sort of procession, but exactly what sort, he couldn't make out as the walkers appeared and disappeared around corners.

"Bram is where the action is. Maybe Beatrice is mistaken. Maybe the crusaders can be beaten and driven home. I should go and do my bit to make that happen. I wish I could fly like you. Then I could just fly to Bram and see what is happening to Adso and Peter."

John lapsed into silence, vaguely embarrassed that he had been talking to a bird. He watched the procession wend closer. There was something odd about it. A line of figures in single file, so close to each other as to be almost indistinguishable, and all with their heads down. Perhaps they were religious penitents; there were lots of people with strange ideas around at the moment.

The procession entered a stand of stunted pines and disappeared from view. John gazed at the puffy white clouds scudding across his view and let his thoughts wander. Lucky people were those who were certain about things. Beatrice and Aumery were lucky—both were certain. About different things, but that didn't seem to matter. Now even Peter seemed to be acquiring certainty. Was John destined to live his life questioning? But how did one know what to be certain about? Maybe God would appear to him one day in a blinding flash of light and tell him.

John shivered and stood. It was time to get back; some hot wine by the fire sounded good.

The figures were emerging from the trees. As he took a final look at them, the leader stumbled and fell. A low moan rose from the group and reached John on the wind. The rest stopped and began turning their heads as if looking around. But they weren't looking at anything. And there was something wrong with their faces. Curious, John began walking down the track toward them. The thrush took off in a flutter of wings.

The leader of the procession was back on his feet and had resumed his stumbling progress. There were dozens of people in the line. Each had a hand reaching out onto the shoulder of the one in front. John broke into a run. Realization of what was coming dawned slowly, but he forced it back. It couldn't be. It was too awful.

Eventually John reached the shuffling men and stopped in horror. At the sound of his skidding feet, the leader raised his head. It was all John could do not to collapse on the path. The man's bare feet were caked in mud and blood, and the skin, where it showed, was white with the cold. He was dressed in a padded, bloody tunic that John recognized as the sort knights wore beneath their chain mail. But it was what was left of his face that made John's stomach churn. Someone had deliberately mutilated this man almost beyond recognition. His ears and nose had been sliced off. His lips too were gone, leaving a bloody hole that exposed his teeth. One eye socket was just a black, blood-filled hole. From the other, a bloodshot eyeball stared at John.

John glanced at the man behind the leader. He was the same. No, he was worse, both eyes had been removed. The rest in the line that stretched back into the trees were the same, blind and hideously mutilated.

John looked back at the leader. Despite the man's mutilations, he recognized him. The cleft, jutting chin was distinctive.

"Bertrand?" John asked.

The man inclined his head painfully. These were the knights of Bram. A gift from the crusaders—a hundred mutilated and blind, led by a one-eyed man. A warning: if you resist, this will happen to you.

"Adso?" John asked with a sick feeling in his stomach.

Bertrand shrugged. The effort almost caused him to fall over.

John stepped forward and placed Bertrand's arm over his shoulder.

"Come on," he shouted to the rest of the line. "You're almost at Cabaret. People will help you there."

A low groan rose behind him as the procession started moving again. A host of emotions swarmed through John as he took Bertrand's weight and staggered forward. Rage that human beings could perpetrate such an atrocity on others. Anger that Peter might have been a part of it. Worry that Adso could be one of the helpless wrecks behind him. But there was, finally, certainty too. Beatrice could take the way of peace, but he could not. He could no longer hide in books. He had to fight, to resist the monsters that could perform such a horror. He would go back to Minerve, he owed Beatrice that, but then he would find a knight who would teach him the arts of war.

A Mission

Alairac

May 1210

Peter stared at the pile of twisted, naked bodies in the field below the walls of Alairac. There were about a dozen of them, stripped of their chain mail and weapons and piled unceremoniously in a heap that could be seen from the muddy road leading north. It was early May, but it felt more like January. The fifteen-day siege had been in the teeth of a raw, howling gale, but the castle had fallen the night before. Realizing they were doomed, the defenders had tried to sneak away under cover of darkness. Oddo's Falcons had had a fine hunt in the darkness and the results formed the pile that Peter now contemplated.

The gale had finally died down, but freezing rain was blowing in from the west in bitter sheets and Peter felt unutterably miserable. Apart from the trip with Arnaud Aumery to Toulouse, accompanying Simon de Montfort on the spring campaign against the heretics had been brutally hard work. Perhaps one day Peter would rise to a position of great power and sit in a comfortable abbey, but for now he was a lowly monk, given a host of grinding tasks. Aumery's distrust of luxury in any form meant that the monks had to work hard and devote their spare time to prayer and contemplation.

Not that Peter objected to the prayer. It was, after all, what monks did and was a vital conduit to God, and he also found it strangely relaxing. Even in the black pre-dawn, kneeling on the frozen ground and shivering in the wind, the monotonous repetition of the memorized words took Peter out of himself. Aumery said that, during prayer, a monk's mind should focus on a love of God and the sacrifice and suffering of His only son on the cross, but Peter found that by concentrating his mind on the words of the prayer, everything else left his head. Eventually he found that he could, for brief moments at least, experience an extraordinary sense of peace and well-being. The sense of loneliness he also felt was a bit frightening, but the peace convinced him that the place he went during prayer must be somewhere closer to God than the brutal world in which he spent his days. He wondered if Aumery's scourging his back with the knotted rope was the priest's way of searching for that same place.

"That's one more castle we won't have to worry about." Peter turned to see Simon de Montfort standing beside him looking at the bodies. He was wearing a red cloak against the weather and held the reins of large horse. A heavy cart, loaded with timbers for a siege engine, lumbered past, splashing mud over Peter and de Montfort's legs. The crusader's horse stamped in annoyance, but the man ignored it.

"There are too many damned castles on hills in this country."

"And too many heretics," Peter ventured.

"And not enough bonfires, according to Aumery." De Montfort looked up at the leaden sky. "Even God would have His work cut out getting a heretic to burn in weather like this. This is truly a godforsaken country. At least in the Holy Land we were always warm."

"That must have been wonderful, to go on a crusade against the infidels."

"Wonderful? I don't know if that is the correct word. Bloody, exciting, frustrating, holy—it was all those things and more—and those infidels are damned fine warriors. We could never get them to stay in one place long enough to fight a proper battle—always raiding our knights, killing one or two and then disappearing over the next hill. We were fine as long as we sat in our castles or ventured forth in strength, but too small a party was inviting disaster. At least the Moors of Al-Andalus fight our kind of war." De Montfort wiped the rivulets of rain off his forehead. "Still, God knows best, so we must move on."

"Where to now?"

De Montfort regarded Peter with his cold eyes. "I am tired of these minor outposts and spending our time burning wet villages. More knights from the north join us every day. We will spend another month clearing the country around Carcassonne and then we will be strong enough to attack a major fortress."

"Which one?"

"Minerve. Aumery will have his bonfire." The pair stood in silence before the bodies for a moment. "Have you always wished to be a monk?" de Montfort asked at last. "Did you have a message from God instructing you to lead this life?"

Peter was startled by the abrupt change in topic. "All who do the Lord's work are called by Him in one way or another."

De Montfort laughed. "You are young, but already you have learned the art of playing with words. I am not seeking to trick you, I simply wish to know what draws you to Aumery. He cannot be an easy man with whom to work."

"Father Aumery is very holy."

"I do not dispute that. I have seen how his back bleeds for the love of Christ. I merely observe that you do not appear to be one who is drawn to such mortification of the flesh."

Peter thought for a long moment. De Montfort was right, he had no desire to beat himself into ecstasy as Aumery did, but how much was it safe to tell this man? "I believe there are other ways to get close to God."

"And if those ways should advance you in this world, so much the better?"

Peter stared at his feet.

De Montfort laughed. "Don't worry, young monk. All of us advance ourselves as best we can. Oddo does it through sheer, naked power. Aumery uses the mysticism of God. Both, I believe, have the same end in view, personal advancement, although I suspect Oddo will settle for what advancement is possible on this earth, while Aumery has his eyes set more on the next.

"You have done well for one so young. That was a heavy load Aumery placed on your shoulders at Carcassonne and you carried it. You are intelligent and you learn quickly. I may have need of you in the future. Would you be prepared to serve if I called?"

"If the duties did not conflict with my calling to God." Peter answered carefully, but inside he was excited. De Montfort was powerful and being close to him might advance Peter's ambitions.

"You are a difficult man to tie down!" de Montfort said with a nod. "That is a good characteristic. It means you can keep secrets, and that means that people will tell you things—valuable things. Knowledge is power, never forget that. But you have not asked how I strive to advance my own cause."

"It is not my business."

"Of course not, but you will listen if I tell you. I do not seek selfish power such as Oddo craves. He enjoys watching others cower before him, and that is a transient pleasure at best. Nor do I seek the uncertain comfort of a position in the next world.

"Oh, do not look so surprised. I am convinced there *is* a next world, it is simply that there are many competing paths toward achieving a position in it and I am not sure which is the most certain.

"My hopes for immortality lie with my son, Simon. I have been deprived of my lands in England by the king, so I must rebuild. That is why I chose to remain here and lead this venture last winter when no one else wished to do so. It has been a hard season and there will be others, but now the knights flooding south for their forty-day indulgences must bow a knee to me. It will take many years, but if I can secure this land, I will have something worthwhile to pass on to my offspring—a power base from which he can build without the struggle I have been subject to."

De Montfort fell silent and gazed again at the pile of bodies. "That is how we are all destined to finish," he said eventually. "Does your God make the prospect easier? Certainly, the heretics seem happy enough to embrace their end. I will go naked to the tomb if I have something to pass on to my son.

"But"—de Montfort roused himself from his reverie—"for now we must be on our way. Power must be exercised, else it becomes rusty and of no use. And I would ask a favour of you."

"If it is within my power," Peter replied.

"It is not a large thing, and it might greatly ease our work later. However, it will entail removing your monk's habit for a short time."

Peter remained silent.

"What I need," de Montfort said, staring hard at Peter, "is a spy. As I said, when summer eventually arrives, we shall attack Minerve. I know something of its situation and it is formidable, at least on the outside. What I need to know is if there is a softness at the centre. Is there disaffection with the lord, are the granaries full or empty, where does the town's water come from? Those are things I need to know if I am to capture the town without destroying my army on the ramparts. Will you help?"

Peter pondered what he was being asked. It would certainly be more exciting than the long trudge north with the army, and it didn't sound too difficult. There were refugees all over the land this year. If he shaved his head to remove his distinctive monk's tonsure, it would be easy to pass himself off as one more displaced person. In addition, doing a favour for de Montfort would place the knight in Peter's debt, and there was no telling how useful that might be in the future. The only difficulty was Aumery.

"I will need to talk with Father Aumery," Peter said.

"Of course," de Montfort replied with a smile. "I foresee no difficulty. Speak with Aumery and then return to talk with me. I would wish you to leave soon."

The crusader hauled himself into his war horse's saddle. "You will go far." De Montfort turned his horse's head and moved away up the track.

Peter watched the retreating back and recalled de Montfort's words: knowledge is power. Aumery had often told him the same thing. The trick, he assumed, was to acquire the right knowledge. Perhaps this task for de Montfort might be one way to do just that.

Return

Minerve
May 1210

The clang of metal on metal rang through the warm, late-May air and echoed across the gorge below Minerve's castle walls. Sweat poured off John's forehead and stung his eyes; dark patches stained the back and the underarms of the padded jerkin he wore for protection. It was becoming increasingly difficult to wield the heavy sword, yet his opponent showed no signs of tiring.

John swung his sword low across his body and parried a blow that would have taken his left leg off below the knee. Remembering his training, he twisted his sword up and over, trying to force the other man's weapon out of his grip, but his adversary was clever. Almost faster than John could see, he transferred his sword to his left hand, pushed John's sword wide and away and moved in close. John could feel the man's breath on his face—it smelled strongly of wild garlic—and see the glint in his eye. He was about to push him away when he felt a prick on his neck. The man smiled. "You're dead," he said.

John looked down to see a narrow, evil-looking dagger in Adso's right hand. He sighed, dropped his sword and sat down heavily on the dusty ground. "Damn," he said. "You always have another trick!"

Adso joined John on the ground, replaced the dagger in the sheath by his waist and took a long draft from the wineskin beside him. "If you're not big or strong enough to overpower your enemy, tricks is what'll keep you alive," he said, offering John the skin. "Remember, in the 'eat of battle, most soldiers just rush forward and 'ack about madly. It might be frightening, but there's no skill to it. You can always out-think a man like that."

The pair sat on the low hill at the opposite end of the narrow neck of land from Minerve's castle and caught their breath. Below them was a hive of activity. A small group of soldiers was practicing with crossbows, while others sweated to deepen the ditches beneath the castle walls. A continuous stream of carts, loaded with sacks of grain, barrels of olives and squealing pigs, rumbled up to the gates and were admitted.

John had arrived back in Minerve from Cabaret two weeks before. To his delight and relief, Adso had beaten him by a full day, having snuck away from Bram the night before it fell.

"It was obvious what was going to 'appen," Adso had said after John told him of meeting Bertrand and the others. "The defences of Bram never 'ad a chance of standing up to the siege engines de Montfort 'ad with 'im. Massive they were. I told Bertrand that our only chance was to try and fight our way out, but 'e says no. Said 'e would rely on the rules of chivalry and throw 'imself on de Montfort's mercy after they surrendered." Adso laughed bitterly. "For a rogue, old Bertrand is stubborn in his belief in honour and rules. I suppose 'e 'as paid more'n enough for 'is mistakes. Seems there's no rules in this war."

John had persuaded Adso to teach him all he knew about fighting, and they had been outside the city walls every day since. Those two weeks had been a chaos of fevered preparation for the town. No one doubted that de Montfort and his crusader army would soon arrive, which left two choices: either flee or prepare to fight. Most chose the latter and set to with a determination firm in the belief that Minerve was one of the strongest fortresses north of the Pyrénées. Rooftop cisterns were filled with water, and food was stored everywhere. The earthy smell of the farmyard hung over the town as farmers brought their animals in from the surrounding countryside. It was becoming increasingly difficult to walk the steep, narrow streets without having to kick pigs, goats and chickens out of the way. Refugees from outlying villages camped in every spare room and open space, and more knights, many escapees from Carcassonne, trickled in each day to offer their services.

"How long until they arrive?" John asked, eventually.

"Week or two at most," Adso replied. "Word is they're moving north from Alairac, but slow. De Montfort's in no 'urry. The longer he takes to get 'ere, the bigger his army gets, the more subdued the countryside be'ind him is, and the more strain there'll be on us with all these extra mouths to feed. But that also gives us more time to prepare a welcome that'll break the crusader army once and for all."

"That's what you said about Carcassonne."

"And I should 'ave been right. If Trenceval 'adn't given up the city for that old man and his books, we'd still be there. Minerve'll be different. Even after Béziers, people didn't take the crusade seriously. Everyone thought they'd get tired and go 'ome 'fore they got to 'is village. Last winter and Bram changed all that. Now everybody knows they're 'ere until we beat them and force them to go 'ome. Minerve's where we'll do that."

John wished he could be as optimistic as his friend, but the tales told by refugees from other towns made it hard. "What about the siege engines?" he asked. "Bram's walls only held out for three days against them."

"They'll make life unpleasant, no doubt about that, but Minerve's much better situated than Bram. Siege engines or not, de Montfort will have to assault us eventually, and the only way in is along this causeway. As long as there's twenty men with crossbows left alive, that'll be suicide. We'll break the crusader army's spirit right 'ere. One serious defeat and that army'll melt away and the Pope'll make peace."

John fervently hoped Adso was right. A part of John's mind was thrilled to be learning to fight, and he was proud of how good he was getting, despite the fact that every time he mastered something, Adso had a new trick to get around it. But the rest of John's mind wouldn't let go of the strange books he had read and the knowledge they seemed to promise.

Despite Beatrice's injunction to leave the books behind once he had memorized them, John had brought the mathematics book with him to Minerve. He had all the words in the memory cloister, but there were many numbers he didn't understand. The book was important, John realized, and he wanted to master all of its secrets.

"Well, come on then," Adso said, getting to his feet. "There's still time left today to learn that trick with the dagger."

John jumped up. That was something else that had changed. Two weeks ago, after a hard day's training with Adso, John's muscles would have ached horribly. Now they simply responded as he required. His body had hardened with the work.

"Right," Adso said. "Left 'anded swordsmen always 'ave an advantage 'cause they come at you different than you expect. Why do the stairs of a keep always spiral to the right?"

"So a defending swordsman has the space to swing against an enemy coming up."

"Exactly, if the swordsman is right-'anded."

John thought for a minute. It was true, keeps were built to be defended and the advantage always lay with a right-handed man if he were uppermost on a right-handed spiral stair. A right-handed man fighting his way up the stairs, or a left-handed man defending, would be at disadvantage. His sword arm would be crammed up against the pillar at the centre of the staircase, and he would be continually bumping his arm against the wall.

"I 'ave 'eard tell," Adso went on, "that there's a family up north where the lords are always left 'anded. They had a keep built with the stairs going the opposite way. They say the keep's never been taken.

"Now, I'm not left-'anded, and I'll never be good enough on that side with a sword to take a natural left man, but I've practised and I can perform passably well. Certainly well enough to confuse my opponent when 'e's tired and not thinking too good. Just 'cause God gave you a good right 'and, don't mean your left's useless."

Without warning, Adso swept up his sword in his left hand and attacked John. John managed to parry the blow only because he had been expecting something like this. The first lessons he had learned were to never let your guard down with Adso and to always expect the unexpected.

The swords clashed loudly as John tried desperately to parry Adso's swings with his left hand. It was hard work and Adso often got past John's defences. The swords were round tipped and blunt, but a blow in the heat of combat still hurt, even through the padded jerkin. Adso's lessons were written in the patchwork of bruises, in various states of healing, on John's arms, legs and sides.

"So you're a soldier now." Both John and Adso stopped and turned to see Beatrice standing beside the road.

"I'm trying to be," John said sheepishly.

To John's surprise, Beatrice had barely attempted to persuade him not to learn to fight. In a sense, that had been worse than if she had shouted at him and called him stupid. Then he could have gotten angry and stormed off to do what he wanted, but it was impossible to get angry at Beatrice. She never gave cause. Still, John had guiltily avoided her as much as possible since his return from Cabaret.

"Well," Beatrice said with a smile, "if you learn the art of soldiering as well as you learned the memory cloister, I'm sure the crusaders will be in trouble."

John felt himself blush at the compliment. "I'm sorry," he mumbled, dropping his gaze.

"Never be sorry," Beatrice said. "I offered you a path through this life. You chose another, but paths sometimes wind in ways we cannot anticipate. Perhaps one day your two paths will meet."

"Enough talk of paths," Adso said. "My path now is to a cool spot and some of this food that we seem to 'ave so much of."

Adso picked up his wineskin, sheathed his sword and strode toward the town. John hesitated. He felt he needed to explain what he was doing to Beatrice.

"I *do* appreciate all you have taught me," he said, eyes fixed on the ground, "and I shall remember all I have learned. I can be a soldier *and* work with the memory cloister."

"It is hard to serve two masters," Beatrice said softly. "You have a good mind, John, and now it contains things of value. I understand why you need to fight by Adso's side, but be careful. Try to stay alive. I have a sense that your mind may yet do some good in this world, and it would be a pity to lose it to some mercenary's crossbow bolt or sword."

"I will try." John raised his head and looked at Beatrice. "Do you know which of all the wonders you and Umar have told me of is the one I crave most?"

"The book on drawing?"

"Yes! I know you think the material world is evil and that we should not be seduced by it, but if the Devil created the entire world about us, why did he make some of it so beautiful?"

Beatrice remained silent.

"A sunset over the mountains that turns the sky to fire can uplift the spirit to wondrous heights," John continued. "The ruins of the ancient Roman temples and villas, grown about with vines and scented with wild herbs, capture a lost past so strongly that it brings a lump to my throat. The stained glass windows in the cathedral of Toulouse were made by the Catholics you so despise, yet they are a wonder to behold even to the pagan eye. Would the Devil put these things in the world when they would give us poor mortals such comfort?"

"The Devil seduces in many ways."

"Perhaps. Or perhaps God slips a little beauty into the Devil's creations to give those who can see it some comfort as they struggle through their lives. If that is the case, then the ability to recreate that beauty in art on a wall or a page would be a great gift. It would spread the beauty before the eyes of many and increase the good in the world. I think, if the book Umar talks of can teach me to draw, then, through that, I might bring some hope into the world.

"Oh, I will remember the mystical texts of Zarathustra and the Gospel of the Christ and the others, and wherever I see an opportunity, I shall pass on that knowledge and try to use it to confound the plans of these crusaders and their minions. But I want to understand the world and to draw it."

John fell silent in embarrassment after his outburst. He had never really thought all this through before, it had just come to him as he spoke. Even though he had begun by trying to explain how he felt so that Beatrice wouldn't be angry with him, he was afraid that he might have horribly offended her. But Beatrice was still smiling.

"You have a fine mind, and that is something that comes from God. I think you are mistaken, but I do not regret teaching you. Perhaps you have been given the tools to come to the right conclusions on your own." The smile faded. "I am sorry I shall not be here to see that happen."

"You are leaving?"

"I have things to do."

"Are you afraid that we will lose here?"

"I cannot say, I do not have a military mind. Perhaps Adso is correct and you will win. What I do know is that winning or losing here is of no importance. In any case, I wish you luck and hope that our paths cross in the future."

"I do too."

With a final smile, Beatrice tapped her staff on the ground, stepped onto the road and set off against the flow of traffic.

John watched her back until it was lost in the dust. He was so intent on watching Beatrice that he didn't notice the ragged refugee with the shaved head who hesitated and stared at him for a long moment before continuing on into Minerve.

The Spy

Minerve
June 1210

Peter trudged up the narrow cobbled streets of Minerve. On either side of him, the rough limestone walls of the houses reared like castle battlements, broken only by small, deeply set windows. People going in both directions jostled past him and skinny goats bumped his legs. The town was crowded, but so far Peter had discovered nothing that would give his masters any comfort. There was plenty of food, the cisterns were all full of water, despite there being no evidence of communal bucket wells or pumps in the streets, and the inhabitants seemed determined. The Perfects he frequently saw walking the streets were comfortably accepted by the populace, and the services they held in their houses were well attended.

Peter had been in Minerve almost a week and May had turned to June, but so far no one had questioned him. He was dressed in rags and sheltered behind a story about being a refugee from Carcassonne who had been wandering and begging around the countryside all winter. His only worry was that he would bump into John. Seeing him as he had arrived at the city gates had been a shock, but so far there had been no further sign of his old friend.

Peter would have to leave soon, whether he had any information or not. Simon de Montfort's army had to be close by now and the last thing Peter wanted was to be trapped in the besieged town. Unfortunately, he had fulfilled neither of his tasks. After his conversation with de Montfort outside Alairac, Aumery had agreed to the spying idea. He agreed so readily, in fact, that Peter suspected that the two men had been discussing it before he was even approached. Aumery blessed Peter's task, making only one condition to releasing him temporarily from the priesthood. While in Minerve, Peter had to try to find out all he could about the Perfects within its walls. How many there were, how popular they were with the townsfolk and whether there were any who had arrived recently and were held in special regard by the others. "Look for a Perfect, probably aged, who travels from town to town,"

Aumery had advised. "That may be the one who knows the location of the treasure."

Peter was slightly concerned that he was spying for two masters, but resolved his worry by reasoning that they were all on God's side. He was also thrilled that the Grail might be in Minerve, even though Aumery didn't think so. How wonderful it would be to find it, or at least be the one who discovered where it was!

But Peter had found no weakness in Minerve's defences nor any clue as to the location of the Cathar Treasure. He wondered how he would explain his failure to Aumery and de Montfort. He desperately hoped he could find something out; to return with nothing wouldn't help him curry favour with either.

Peter turned a corner and froze. John was heading toward him down the hilly street. He was carrying a yoke over his shoulders, from which swung two large, empty buckets, and he was having trouble negotiating the crowded thoroughfare with his unwieldy burden. He was also deep in conversation with an old Perfect who scurried along by his side, tapping a gnarled staff on the cobbles.

Peter hunched over and moved to the edge of the street, where several beggars were loitering, half-heartedly holding out their hands for alms. Out of the corner of his eye, he watched John approach. It felt odd to see him again after so much had happened. Peter almost wished he could step forward and swap stories with his childhood friend.

John and the old Perfect passed without even glancing at those around them, and Peter fell into step behind them. He followed in part because he was curious about his friend, but also because John appeared to be on his way to collect water. The source of the town's seemingly endless water supply would no doubt interest de Montfort.

Following John and his companion was easy in the crowded streets and the pair soon arrived at an old metal gate in the town walls, near the southeast corner. The gate was open onto a set of steep stairs that descended into a dark tunnel. John spoke a few words to the Perfect and disappeared down the steps.

Peter waited a few moments and then approached the old man, who had settled himself against the wall to one side of the gate.

"Hello, Father," Peter said respectfully.

The Perfect looked up, squinting against the bright sunlight.

"Good day. Are you here for water from the well?"

"No," Peter said, crouching beside the man and doing his best to hide his excitement. A well! "I am just taking the air."

"As am I. I find being cooped up indoors causes the mind to become dusty. Fresh air blows away the cobwebs. Are you from here?"

"No. I am from Carcassonne. I left when it fell last year and I have been wandering ever since. My name is Peter." Peter had told the story so often that it came easily.

"I am Umar. Are you a Good Christian?"

Peter hesitated for a moment. "Yes," he said. It was all right to lie if you were doing God's work.

Umar nodded thoughtfully. "And have you sworn the oath to defend Minerve and her inhabitants with your life?"

"I have," Peter said, although he had not heard of such an oath. It seemed a harmless enough lie.

"Excellent," Umar said. "We need all the fighters there are to combat the evil that comes to attack us. You have my blessing."

"Thank you," Peter said, uncertain whether he should bow. He knew better than to cross himself—heretics never did that—but he didn't know what they did. "Are you from this town?" he asked.

"I am not," Umar said. "Like you, I am a recent arrival."

"Where are you from?"

"I am from everywhere," Umar replied with a smile. "I travel much from town to town."

Peter's heart leaped. First the well and now this—an old Perfect who travelled a lot. Did he hold the location of the Cathar Treasure in his head? "You must learn many things on your travels."

"Indeed. I see much of the Devil's work as I venture through this corrupt world, as you must have over this past winter."

"Yes, of course, but you must also see wonders."

"Ah, yes, but worldly wonders are nothing—books are my great joy. I have been blessed with frequent opportunities to read many books and I have learned wondrous things." Umar tilted his head and looked slyly at Peter. "It is gratifying to have one so young take such an interest in an old man."

Peter's pulse raced. Had he made a mistake? Was the old man suspicious? But Umar went on calmly. "Do you read?"

"A little," Peter replied.

"That is good. There are some books at the Good Christian house by the town gate. Perhaps, if the forces of Satan give us enough time, you might like to visit and I would gladly show them to you."

"I should like that," Peter said. He was nervous. He was certain that he had found a Perfect who knew at least a part of the secret of the Cathar Treasure, but he knew that if he talked much more, sooner or later he would make a mistake. Also, he needed to check out the water supply.

Peter nodded toward the gate. "I think I shall visit the well. A cool drink would be good."

"Indeed. Go in safety. Perhaps we shall meet again."

"Perhaps."

Peter headed toward the gate, pleased with himself. At last he might have something to tell de Montfort and Aumery.

The steps—worn and slippery with spilled water—led down a short tunnel and then levelled out to a covered path along the base of the town wall before descending steeply once more. Peter moved cautiously, sticking close to one side where he could touch the cold stone of the wall and keep out of the way of anyone going up. The steps were mostly carved out of the rock of the gorge wall, but in some places they had been built up or repaired. The walls and roof of the tunnel were man-made from large blocks of local stone, and light was let in through occasional narrow windows cut in the walls. The effect was of going from bright light by the windows to almost complete darkness between them, and Peter's eyes were continually adjusting. This was good as it meant that, should he run into John coming back up, it would be unlikely that he would be recognized.

Peter assumed that he was climbing down to the river bed and that the tunnel was to hide and protect the route from observers and enemies across the gorge. This explained the lack of wells in town and might prove to be a weakness.

The stairway took several sharp turns as it descended, but eventually, Peter arrived at the bottom. The tunnel opened into a low, dark room with a stone floor. The gloom was normally broken only by the light from four narrow windows, but a heavy door in the far wall was open and a broad shaft of light illuminated Minerve's water source. The air was cold and damp, and the walls and floor were covered in slippery moss. Peter stood by the wall at the base of the stairs and took in the scene before him.

On the rock wall to Peter's left, some three feet above the ground, a spring of clear water bubbled out of a fissure in the limestone. The water ran down into an artificial pond from which John and a couple of others were filling buckets.

So this was the town's water supply. If it was the only source—and Peter had certainly seen no other—it might be possible to capture or destroy it. At this time of year the river was almost dry. If some men could force their way in and hold the area for long enough, they might be able to somehow contaminate the well or pull down the walls around it. Without water in the dry summer, Minerve would not be able to hold out long.

Peter turned to ascend the stairs before John was finished at the well. Instead, he found himself face to face with the old Perfect, leaning on his staff and watching him curiously.

"Are you not going to have a drink then?" Umar asked. "The water is fresh and cold."

"I... I'm not thirsty any more," Peter stammered.

"I think that's only one thing you are not. No Good Christian would ever take an oath, even a fictional one to defend Minerve, and calling me Father proves that you are a Catholic. Do you come here to spy on us?"

"No! I mean, I am a Catholic. I was scared." Peter floundered, trying to think of a convincing story.

"Well," Umar interrupted him, "perhaps on your travels over the winter, you have seen something of the crusader army and might be willing to tell us of it. John," Umar raised his voice to call to his companion and stepped toward the pond.

Peter panicked. John knew he worked for Aumery. He didn't think that anyone in Minerve would hurt him—least of all John—but they certainly wouldn't let him leave. If he was going to escape, he had to escape now.

Peter's choices were limited. He could run back up the stairs, but that would just take him back into the heart of the town and there was only one way out. John would follow and raise the alarm. A couple of guards on the gate and Peter would be trapped.

His other choice was to get out the door onto the river bed. He knew that one branch of the river ran underground nearby. There must be at least a few places where he could climb the gorge walls. His choice was made.

Umar was waving at John, who had put down his buckets and stepped toward the old man. Others were watching curiously.

"I think I have found a spy," Umar was saying. "He is too young for me. Do you think you could apprehend him?"

It was now or never. Peter lunged toward the door. He took one step and his foot landed on a patch of slimy moss. His leg shot out from under him and Peter fell painfully to the rock floor. His sliding foot caught the old man in the middle of his shin and catapulted him over. Umar spun around and fell heavily, his head hitting the rim of the pond with a sickening thud that echoed in the confined space.

For an instant, silence descended. Umar's limp body rolled to a stop and Peter scrambled to his feet. Pushing people out of the way, he made for the door. John grabbed at him, but recognition dawned on his face, and he hesitated just long enough for Peter to shove him aside and leap through the door.

The bright sunlight hurt his eyes after the gloom of the tunnel, but Peter didn't stop. Glimpsing water to his left, he turned right and ran. His feet sank into wet sand, but he kept going. No one seemed to be following.

Eventually the walls of the gorge met above his head and Peter found himself in a broad tunnel. This one had been carved ages before by the river and was much larger and brighter than the stairs. Peter stopped to catch his breath.

His course was obvious: follow the dry river bed until he could find a way out and then make his way south until he met the army. Peter was elated, partly because of the adrenaline in his body after the excitement of his escape and partly because he had succeeded in his mission. Even so, he was upset about the old man. He hadn't meant to hurt him and he hoped he wasn't dead. Aumery would certainly be interested in the secrets Umar carried in his head.

Taking a deep breath to calm himself, Peter set off over the sand. There was no sound of pursuit. If he kept a steady pace, he would be back with de Montfort and Aumery in a couple of days.

The First Casualty

Minerve
June 1210

John stood stunned, staring at the bright doorway, the empty water buckets rolling at his feet. The figure who had pushed past him had been Peter, he was certain, but what was he doing here? Why had he run? Was he the spy Umar had called to him about?

Umar! John turned to see the old man's body, small and fragile, crumpled beside the pond. One arm was raised and rested against the wall, the hand groping feebly for purchase, as if trying to haul the body upright.

John knelt and cradled Umar's head. Blood seeped from a deep wound in his temple where his skull had cracked against the wall. Umar's eyes were open, but his gaze was unfocused. The other people at the well crowded around John.

"Move back!" John shouted. Umar seemed to hear John's voice and struggled to fix his gaze on him. His lips moved and John leaned forward, trying to catch what Umar was saying. It took a moment, but eventually John understood: the old man was repeating a single word over and over, almost as if it were a chant: "Remember."

When John drew back, Umar's eyes were closed. His lips had stopped moving, but his chest rose and fell shallowly and the blood continued to flow. John stared at the blood, transfixed. The old man's head was crammed full of all manner of wonders, collected over a long and varied life, yet they were all seeping away with the blood. What was being lost? John had been taught some of it, but there must be so much more.

"What did he say?" someone asked. The question brought John back from his musings.

"We must get him up to the Good Christian's house." John put one arm under Umar's shoulders and hooked the other under his knees. He stood. Umar was incredibly light, much easier to carry than two full water buckets. John noticed a young man standing beside him. He was wearing a coarse wool scarf around his head.

"What's your name?"

"Stephen," the man said.

"Hold your scarf against the wound in the Perfect's head, Stephen," John ordered. "We will take him up the stairs." The young man obeyed and they started the long climb.

As John struggled up the stairs, his confusion and anger grew. Was Peter in Minerve to spy for de Montfort and Aumery? The way he'd run suggested that he was, but did it make any real difference? There were so many people coming and going through Minerve these days that any number of them could be spies, but what was there to spy on? There was no horde of gold here or library of forbidden books to discover. Once more, John was reminded of the benefit of holding books in the memory cloister.

But somehow, Peter spying seemed more of a betrayal than had it been some stranger from the crusader army. And there was the disturbing fact that, wherever his old friend showed up, someone died—Pierre of Castelnau at St. Gilles, Roger Trenceval at Carcassonne, and Peter had even been present at the hideous mutilation of the knights of Bram. But Umar wasn't dead. John looked down at the old man's head. He was unconscious and the scarf that Stephen was holding against his head was soaked in blood. It wouldn't be long. John felt tears well up. He had grown to love Umar and his books and stories.

John realized that Peter probably hadn't meant to hurt Umar, but still. Why did Peter have to take the side of the crusaders? Even if they weren't the Devil incarnate, as the Cathars believed, they were still so obviously wrong! Wrong to invade John's homeland, wrong to slaughter and mutilate the inhabitants, and wrong to force an unpopular religion on the people. How could Peter not see that?

As John moved out of the tunnel and into the streets of Minerve, people began to gather. Word of Umar's injury spread quickly through the small, crowded town and everyone wanted to see what had happened. Even though Umar was light, John was tiring, and now he had to push through the curious crowds.

"Come on! Make room!"

John couldn't help but smile to see Adso bustling through the crowd toward him. Without hesitation, he took Umar from John's arms.

"You, keep that cloth against the Perfect's 'ead," he ordered Stephen. Then, looking at John, "Can't let you out of my sight without you getting in trouble. What 'appened?"

"I don't know," John said, both out of honesty and a desire not to get into details about Peter. "We were at the spring and there was a scuffle. Umar fell and hit his head. He said something about a spy."

"Wouldn't surprise me. De Montfort'll 'ave men all over checking out our defences. But we can't do anything about that now. Let's get Umar back to the 'ouse. 'E don't look too good."

John nodded and stretched his aching limbs. The small, sad group pushed through the curious onlookers.

The Bad Neighbour

Minerve
June 1210

A group of five men stood on the vineyard-covered slopes above the River Briant and gazed across the gorge at the grey walls and red-tiled roofs of Minerve. Peter knew three of the other four—Arnaud Aumery, Simon de Montfort and Oddo—but the fifth, a stocky, tough-looking man dressed in stained leather, was a stranger.

In the month since Alairac, a hard spring had given way to a hot summer and the June sun shone from a washed out blue sky. It had been a long circuitous trek north, but the crusader army had grown as it travelled and now a force of some seven thousand men was gathering around this major heretic stronghold.

"It will be a tough nut to crack," de Montfort remarked.

"God will find a way," Aumery answered.

Oddo snorted.

The stone houses of Minerve, clinging to the slopes of the promontory, seemed impossibly far away across the deep gorge. Simon de Montfort stared to his right, to where the tower of the castle dominated the narrow neck of land.

"The only point where we can attack, unless we learn to fly like falcons," de Montfort mused, "is from the north along the causeway, and I doubt even you, Oddo, could get through those fortifications."

"That is true," Oddo replied. "The castle will not allow engineers to get close enough to undermine the walls and, in any case, those walls are too thick even for the largest siege engine. It will be a bloody business."

"You say they are well supplied with food and water?" De Montfort turned to Peter.

"They are," Peter replied. "It is difficult to find a room in which to lay your head for piled sacks of grain, and impossible to walk the streets without tripping over livestock. Every water cistern is full to overflowing."

After his escape, Peter had followed the Cesse for almost a mile, along the gorge and beneath arches and through tunnels of limestone before he had found a place where he could scramble up onto the plateau. There had been no pursuit, and Peter had had no trouble heading south and finding the crusader army only four days' march away.

"There." Peter pointed at the line of heavy masonry snaking down the side of the gorge from the southeast corner of the town. It was barely distinguishable from the surrounding rock. "That is the tunnel covering the steps down to the spring."

"And you say, boy," Oddo said gruffly, "that there is a door by the spring that leads to the gorge bottom?"

"There is," Peter said, guessing where Oddo's thoughts were heading, "but it would be difficult to get through it and fight up those stairs."

Oddo ignored Peter's comment and turned to de Montfort. "If you can get someone into the town to ensure that the door is open, my Falcons and I will travel along the gorge and, despite what our military expert here says," Oddo sneered at Peter, "fight our way up and into the town."

"God shall bless your endeavour," Aumery said.

De Montfort stood silent, looking across the gorge. Eventually he said, "I think, Oddo, that our young monk might be right this time. *If* you can travel undetected along the gorge beneath the town walls. *If* we can ensure that the gate at the spring is left open. *If* you can fight your way up the stairs. All the defenders need do is close and lock the iron gate at the top and you will be trapped like rats. And the stairs are long. They will have plenty of warning."

Oddo grunted in annoyance.

"But the spring may be the key, nonetheless," de Montfort went on. "This is Albrecht." He indicated the stocky stranger by his side. "He hails originally from some savage forest on the fringes of the world, but he travels so much in order to sell his skills that he no longer has a home. Most recently, he has been working in Brittany."

"What can he do that we cannot?" Oddo asked.

"Albrecht is most adept at building machines," de Montfort said with a smile.

"We have machines. Our trebuchets shattered the walls of Bram in three days. Minerve is not so far off that we cannot send rocks into the town. What is so special about his machines?"

"At Bram we could get close and we had a complete wall to aim at," de Montfort explained. "Here we cannot get close because of the ravines, and our target is very small."

Oddo looked puzzled, but de Montfort ignored him and pointed at the covered stairs. "Albrecht, can you build a machine that is powerful enough and accurate enough to destroy that line of masonry running down the edge of the gorge?"

De Montfort's logic was becoming clear. Peter watched as Albrecht, stroking his beard, studied the gorge.

"I think, yes," he said at last. "It will be a long business and much money, but it can be done. I shall build for you a trebuchet such as has never been seen. For them"—Albrecht swept his arm wide to indicate Minerve—"it will be a *Mala Vezina*—a Bad Neighbour."

"All very well," Oddo said. "You may be able, in enough time, to destroy the way down to the spring and, assuming it is their only source of water, cut it off. But we have heard that every cistern in the town is filled. If they are careful, they will have enough to last until the rains come at summer's end."

"You have solved that problem yourself, Oddo," de Montfort said. "We have other trebuchets and mangonels that are eminently capable of hurling rocks into the town. They may not be as accurate, or as powerful, as Albrecht's bad neighbour, but I am certain that, over the next few weeks, they will destroy or damage many of the rooftop cisterns. *Mala Vezina* and the hot dry weeks of summer will do the rest."

Attacking not the town itself but its water supply would be a lengthy process, Peter thought, but it should work.

"And we have young Peter to thank." De Montfort smiled and patted Peter on the back. "Without his spying, we would not have solved this puzzle nearly so quickly. But come, Albrecht must begin and, Oddo, we must see if we can find some work for your Falcons in the surrounding country."

The three men walked back toward the camp, leaving Peter with Aumery.

"You have done well," Aumery said. "De Montfort is in your debt and he is a powerful ally."

"Thank you," Peter said.

"And the information you brought me was of use as well," Aumery continued. "I had not realized there was such a cluster of the Devil's host in Minerve. We shall have a wonderful pyre when the town falls."

Peter was disturbed by the gleam in Aumery's eyes as he spoke about burning the heretics—Peter could reconcile killing as a necessity in God's name, but not enjoying it. He said nothing and let Aumery talk on.

"And I think you might be correct in assuming that the old man you met, Umar, held secrets in his head. I have heard others mention that name. He is an important heretic. Do you think you killed him?"

"I didn't mean to hurt him," Peter said. "I bumped him by accident, and he fell and hit his head."

"No matter. You did God's work, however He arranged it. The pity is that I should have liked to talk to this man, although our methods of persuasion do not work well with these fanatics. I think I shall go and pray."

Peter watched Aumery follow the others back to the camp. He felt pride in what he had achieved and pleasure at the compliments he was receiving, but he hoped he hadn't killed the old man and lost the secrets in his head.

Then there was John. Peter thought about him often and wondered if he had become a heretic. Seeing him with Umar suggested so. Did that mean John was evil? He was probably still in Minerve, trapped by the surrounding army, and Peter had helped find a way to destroy the town. Was Peter, then, causing his own friend's death? Why did God make it so difficult to tell the difference between good and evil? Not for the first time, Peter found himself wishing for Aumery's certainty.

* * *

"Stand clear!"

A man swung a large hammer, knocked out a holding pin and released the long arm of the mangonel. The arm of the siege engine shot up and came to rest with a shuddering crash against a cross beam of solid oak. Peter and Aumery stopped walking to watch a large rock arc through the air and crash into the centre of town, sending up a thin column of grey dust. Moments later, the dull sound of falling masonry reached their ears.

The mangonel crew set to work rewinding the arm of the catapult. It was back-breaking work, hauling the arm down against the tension of the twisted ropes attached to the arms of the crossbeam, but all the men were large and well muscled. Four others were busy manhandling a rock from the pile behind the mangonel so they would be ready to load when the priming process was complete.

"Leave the rock," the foreman of the crew shouted. "We'll give 'em the donkey this time."

The men groaned and left the stone where it was. They disappeared behind a nearby limestone outcrop and returned dragging a rope net on which lay the rotting carcass of a donkey. A thick cloud of flies hovered above the body. Even from where he stood, several yards away, Peter could smell the sickly odour of decay.

"Why do they throw dead animals?" Peter asked Aumery.

"Three reasons," Aumery said casually. "First, there is little more disheartening for a defender than to have rotting animals fall from the heavens. Of course, it would be better to send some prisoners over the wall, but we haven't taken any yet.

"Second, there are a lot of people crammed inside Minerve. A few dead donkeys will spread a fine smell and, if we're lucky, some disease."

Aumery stopped as the foreman shouted at his crew, "Come on, you lazy lot. Put your backs into it. The sooner we get this donkey loaded, the sooner the smell'll be someone else's problem."

"You said there were three reasons," Peter prompted.

"Indeed there are," Aumery said with a smile. "Can you think of a better way to get rid of our waste?"

Peter and Aumery continued on their way. Peter never tired of watching the siege engines at work and often came to observe them hurl their missiles against the town. There were four engines spread around the town—a trebuchet to the north that could fire rocks along the neck at the main gate, and mangonels to the west, east and southwest. Peter and Aumery had been watching the eastern mangonel.

They had all been busy lobbing rocks onto the unfortunate inhabitants and, Peter hoped, their water cisterns, for three weeks now. There was little obvious sign of the damage done, but Peter knew that the rocks landing in Minerve were probably injuring and killing people. The effects of the siege engines didn't bother him; watching them was far less personal than watching soldiers hack away at each other with swords. Safely out of crossbow range, Peter could admire the workmanship of the machines and the skill of their operators. But he hadn't accompanied Arnaud Aumery this sunny morning just to watch another mangonel at work. Today was special—*Mala Vezina* was ready for her first shots at the covered stair.

The giant trebuchet was set up in the midst of the vineyard where Peter and the others had first observed Minerve. Under Albrecht's direction, it had taken twenty-five days to build *Mala Vezina*, and the finished product was awe-inspiring. If the mangonel was a catapult, the trebuchet was a slingshot. Where the mangonels were squat and powerful, relying on tension and brute force to hurl objects at their targets, the trebuchet was slender and elegant, like some immense, exotic animal.

Mala Vezina consisted of a long arm, set on a pivot supported more than thirty feet in the air by a spider web of beams thicker than Peter's body. The arm was not pivoted in its centre. The short piece was the length of a tall man, and the long portion was thirty feet from pivot to tip. A vast, enclosed box filled with tons of rubble and sand hung from a second pivot on the end of the short arm. A complex weave of ropes ran from the long arm to winches on the ground, which were being worked by pairs of sweating men under Albrecht's supervision. With painful slowness, the long arm was being winched down and the heavy box was rising in the air.

"Behold," Aumery said with a theatrical wave of his hand, "God's arm, ready to send destruction to the heretics."

"And show them the error of their ways," Peter added.

"Certainly," Aumery said silkily. "And all in Minerve, however misled and misdirected, shall be given a chance to see the true light. But these devils will not take it. They are mired too deep in sin and would rather face the flames than renounce Satan. Well, let them." Aumery's eyes gleamed at the thought. "The fire will cleanse their evil."

The tip of the trebuchet's long arm had been winched down until it was almost at the ground. Men were busy attaching a twenty-five-foot-long rope sling to the end. Others were rolling a massive rock toward it. They placed the rock, which weighed several hundred pounds, Peter guessed, in the sling and hooked it onto the end of the arm.

"Stand clear!" Albrecht shouted.

Men scurried in all directions. Peter and Aumery were far enough away to be safe, but the looming size of the machine made them step back farther.

Albrecht stepped forward and raised a huge hammer. With one swing, he knocked out the pin holding the winch ropes to the long arm. With a mighty groan, the weight on the short arm fell. The long arm shot into the air, whipping the sling after it.

Above the creaks of the shuddering machine, Peter could hear the whistling of the sling. At the top of its arc, Peter estimated the rock in the end of the sling must have been almost a hundred feet above his head.

When the weight reached its lowest point, the upper end of the arm slowed, but the sling kept going. It whipped past the vertical, releasing one end from its hook and sending the rock on its way. Peter watched in fascination as the boulder arced across the gorge and shattered against the far wall, some thirty feet to the right of the covered stairs. Large blocks of limestone and fragments of the boulder crashed into the riverbed below.

"It missed," Peter said, disappointed that the stairs had not been destroyed at the first attempt.

"It did," Aumery agreed, "but that is not the main problem. Albrecht will make adjustments and with a rate of throw of two rocks an hour, he will expect to hit the stairs several times a day. What is more worrying is the way the rock shattered on impact. Such a blow will not easily destroy the masonry covering the stairs. We may need to bring in firmer stones from some distance away. It all takes too long!"

Even though the counter weight was still swinging, a man was already scrambling up the structure. Timing his jump perfectly, he leaped onto the long arm and began climbing. He had a rope wound around his waist and, when he was halfway along and despite the fact that the arm was swaying frighteningly, he attached the rope to the arm and signalled to his companions on the ground. Gradually, they brought the swing under control and started the long process of winching the weight back up in the air.

Peter looked over to see Albrecht standing among a pile of rocks, hitting them with his hammer to select the best one for his next shot.

"Well," Aumery said, turning and starting off back to the camp, "it will be a long campaign, but the end will be worthwhile."

Peter hoped so.

Besieged

Minerve
July 1210

John and Adso walked down the narrow cobbled street, carefully stepping around the occasional piles of rubble. Their water buckets hung empty on either side of them, but it was not a problem. There were few people about these days. Three weeks into the siege, most preferred to stay indoors. Partly it was fear of the bombardment, but partly it was simply that it was cooler behind the thick stone walls now that the summer heat of July had arrived.

The two friends were making their daily trip to the spring to refill the cistern on top of the Perfect house. Most cisterns were still intact, being situated in the centre of houses, but people had become sloppy about keeping them topped up. It was a chore to fetch water from the spring every day, and most preferred to wait until they ran low and then spend a morning filling up. John made the daily trek because he wanted to do something in return for his keep, and most days he persuaded Adso to accompany him.

"That's one on our side," Adso said, pushing John against a house wall. The thud of the mangonel's arm hitting the crossbeam was clearly audible all over town. Adso had learned to distinguish each machine and knew where they were located. The ones on the far side of town were not a problem, they couldn't reach this far, but the one on the east bank could.

John didn't see the rock, but he heard it crash into a building behind him.

"Missed," Adso said cheerfully as they set off again.

"It hit something," John said.

Adso shrugged. "They make a lot of noise, but the 'ouses are sturdy enough to withstand anything but a direct 'it on the roof. Look, they've been 'urling everything they can find at us for days, and what's the result? A couple of dead, some broken bones and piles of rubble in the streets. People'r frightened, but there's little real 'arm being done."

"I suppose so. I just wish there was something to do. It's so boring just sitting waiting! Won't they attack?"

"Listen to you," Adso laughed. "You learn a couple of moves with an old blunt sword and you want to take on the 'ole crusader army. Patience! Remember, they're just as bored as us, an' if they get bored enough they'll do something stupid like attack us, else they'll go 'ome. We can 'old out 'til doomsday."

The crash of the mangonel sounded again.

"Busy this morning," Adso said as he moved to the shelter of another wall.

John looked up to see if he could catch the flight of the rock. What he saw was a shock. Arcing down toward him was some sort of creature, legs and head wobbling stupidly as it spun through the air. The grotesque thing landed with a sickening thud on the street just up the hill from John and Adso. The bloated stomach split open with the force, spilling glistening entrails over the cobbles.

"What was that?" John asked in horror.

"Looked like a donkey to me," Adso replied. An evil smell wafted in on the morning breeze. "And it's been dead for some time," he added, wrinkling his nose. "We'd best get on. Perhaps we might take a different route back."

"Why on earth are they throwing dead donkeys at us?"

"Showing their contempt, maybe, or trying to spread disease. I've 'eard of that being done."

"It's disgusting."

"It's unpleasant, certainly, but every donkey they send over is one less rock. I'd rather dodge dead donkeys!"

The pair reached the gates at the top of the stairs and began the long climb down. Every time John reached this spot, he remembered the trip with Umar. The old man had lingered for two days after John and Adso had carried him back to the house, but he had never regained consciousness. The Perfects had celebrated when he died since, having taken the *consolamentum*, Umar was guaranteed a place in paradise. They had no interest in Umar's body because it was of the material world and was, therefore, merely a trap within which the old man's soul had been enslaved. Now that his spirit was free, the body was simply waste. John was not comfortable with just leaving Umar's body out in the open for the vultures and wolves, so he enlisted Adso and persuaded the Perfects to allow him to take the body outside the walls and bury it. They shrugged and let him do as he wished.

John and Adso had buried Umar beneath a stunted tree on the edge of the gorge. There was not much soil, but John hoped they had piled enough rocks on top of the body to discourage wild animals. John had not said anything at the graveside, Umar would not have wanted that, but he did mumble

Heretic

goodbye as he left. The next day de Montfort and his army arrived and Minerve was under siege.

It was dark at the spring these days, since the door that led out to the riverbed was always kept closed and bolted. Two men in chain mail stood guard at all times. John nodded to them.

"Coolest place in town down 'ere," Adso commented.

The two men were silent. John and Adso filled their buckets and started back up the stairs.

"Good talking to you," Adso called back over his shoulder. As if in reply, the whole tunnel shook. Vibrations thrust up through the rock steps, making John stumble and drop his buckets. Dirt and small pieces of masonry fell from the roof.

"What was that?" John asked.

"My guess," Adso said, "is that our visitors across the gorge 'ave finished their little construction project. That, my friend, is what a trebuchet can do. Let's go and take a look."

John refilled his buckets and followed Adso up the stairs. Back in full daylight, they carefully placed the buckets by the wall and climbed the nearest tower.

The sun was still low and they had to squint to see the trebuchet clearly, but it was obviously preparing for another shot.

"Let's 'ope it's a donkey," Adso said wryly.

Several people had come to the wall to see what was happening. One had a crossbow and fired it speculatively in the direction of the crew resetting the trebuchet. The bolt made it over the gorge but fell short of the men.

"Waste of a good bolt," Adso said. He was leaning out as far as he could over the edge of the wall. "That's where the last one 'it, to the left of the stair."

John stared where Adso was pointing. He could just make out a scar on the rock wall of the gorge.

"They're way too low," John said. "The mangonels are doing more damage in the town."

"They're not aiming for the town," Adso said thoughtfully.

"What?" John asked, but Adso had leaned back and was watching the trebuchet.

The machine, looking like some huge animal grazing amidst the vines, was almost ready. John watched as the rock, as big as the men who were manhandling it, was placed in the sling. John heard the metallic clang as the pin was knocked out and the trebuchet's arm began its long swing up. It seemed slow and almost stately from this distance. The sling whipped over the top of the arm and the rock arced toward them. Instinctively, everyone ducked, but Adso kept upright, watching.

With reverberations that John could feel even this far away, the rock shattered against the cliff some fifty feet below the battlements and twenty to the right of the stairs.

Some of the people on the battlements laughed nervously and began shouting taunts at the trebuchet crew.

"Is that the best you can do?"

"We're up here."

"Are you trying to wear down the cliff?"

Adso looked pensive. "That one was closer."

"It was no higher than the last," John said.

"They're not trying for height. That thing could send a rock the size of a house over our heads and into the town with ease. They know what they're doing. It's adjusted to shoot low. They're not aiming for us, they're aiming for the stairs—and I reckon it'll only take another three or four attempts before they hit them."

"The stairs!" John said. Suddenly, Peter's presence at the spring and Umar calling him a spy made sense. Peter had been in town to spy out the water supply! It was because of the information he had escaped with that the trebuchet was targeting the stairs. If the crusaders could destroy the route to Minerve's only source of water, the town was doomed.

John kept his thoughts to himself and stared out across the distance, listening to Adso's musings.

"The tunnel is strong and those rocks they're throwing break too easy. But if they bring in some better rock, sooner or later the tunnel will be so collapsed that it'll be the devil's own job to get to the spring. And anyone clambering back up in the open with two 'eavy buckets'll be a sitting duck for crossbowmen on the far rim."

"What can we do?"

"Well, there's some things we might do. Even with that beast, it'll take a good long time to collapse the tunnel completely. The first thing we need to do is make sure all the cisterns are filled, and kept full. Come on."

Adso climbed down from the wall and retrieved his buckets. John followed, deep in thought. This changed things. Now they couldn't just sit and wait the siege out. They would have to do something, but what?

* * *

The group of twenty men gathered in the dark by the iron gate at the top of the stairs. All were dressed in dark clothing and were lightly armed, mostly with swords and daggers, although one man carried a crossbow slung across his back. Most had bundles of tar-soaked sticks and straw strapped to their bodies, and two had earthen pots filled with glowing coals. John wore the old sword he had been practising with, honed now to a razor-sharp edge. Adso carried a pot of coals and had his dagger tucked into his belt. It was ten days since the trebuchet had opened fire on the stairs and the group was setting off to destroy it.

"We travel in silence," Adso said in a low voice. "Stephen," he said, nodding at the young man who had helped with Umar and now hovered by the group's edge, "will lead us up the other wall of the gorge. With luck, the infernal machine will be unguarded and we will be able to set the fire unmolested. If we are discovered we retreat as quickly as possible. Do not get into a fight. We will lose. Travel as quietly as you can and good luck."

Stephen led the way through the gate and onto the stairs. At first the going was easy, but about a third of the way down, they came to the first place where the roof had collapsed. They had to scramble into the open and find a way over the steep pile of rubble. The night sky was clear, but the moon was new, so the darkness in the gorge was impenetrable. John had to feel his way along, following the heavy breathing of the man in front. Soon his shins and hands were scraped and bruised. He just hoped he wouldn't catch an ankle in a crevice between two boulders and break something.

Even with the poor-quality rocks the crusaders had been using, the trebuchet had scored so many hits that the tunnel was badly damaged in several places and completely collapsed in two. It was still possible to get to the spring and back, but it was much harder work and the open spaces were dangerous. Few people were inclined to make the journey often and the cisterns in the town were low.

Even more worrying, the day before yesterday had seen the arrival of a train of heavy carts from the north. Each cart was pulled by a team of four huge oxen and was loaded with boulders of hard, black volcanic rock. The first of these to be fired had shattered the tunnel roof and enlarged one of the collapses. In a day or two more, the stairs to the spring would no longer exist.

The night raid to destroy the trebuchet—their one chance, John thought—had been Adso's idea, but it had not been difficult to recruit men. No one wanted to surrender to the crusaders. Since there had been no raids on the crusader camp, the hope was that the guards might be complacent and give Adso's group a chance to set a large enough fire to destroy the machine.

Slowly, the group made its way down to the gorge floor. Stephen, who had lived in Minerve all his life and spent his childhood scrambling up and down the gorge walls, knew every rock for miles around. He led them through the shallow water of the Briant to the foot of the gorge wall. To John's surprise and relief, the climb was not too steep or dangerous. The route followed a wide crack in the limestone, and the rock was rough and provided plenty of handholds. There were even a few stunted bushes that were well enough anchored to bear a man's weight.

At the top, the men crouched and gathered their breath. In the distance, a few patches of orange showed where cooking fires had been allowed to burn low, but there was no sign of life. The trebuchet was easy to see, even in the near blackness. Its looming bulk blacked out the stars near the horizon, and its soaring arm caused others to blink in and out as John moved his head.

"Stay here," Adso whispered.

Dropping his pot of coals, Adso disappeared through the wrecked vineyards. John followed a short way and listened. He could hear the soft rustle of Adso moving, but it was little more than the sound of a breeze in the dead leaves. Eventually, even the rustling stopped.

John cocked his head and stayed motionless. He was rewarded with a grunt, followed by a thump. After a few minutes, Adso returned. He held his dagger in one hand.

"Only one guard," he said. John could see the white of Adso's teeth as he smiled. "Let's go."

Working as quietly and quickly as possible, the men stacked their bundles around the base of the trebuchet. Up close, even in the dark, John was awed by the size of the thing and by the effort that had gone into its construction and operation. For the first time, he understood Beatrice's belief that the crusaders would never give up.

Adso and the other man carrying the coals were busy igniting the bundles that were in place. Already the tar in several had caught and bright flames were dancing up. The closest tents were about thirty feet away, but there was still no sign of life apart from a dying fire outside one. If only they were given enough time for the fires to join, the heat would be so intense that no one would be able to put out the flames, and the trebuchet would be doomed.

John's own bundle was burning fiercely now, and the flames were catching on the wood of the trebuchet's frame.

"To arms! To arms!"

The shout was almost deafening after the enforced silence. John looked toward the tents. By the light of the spreading fires, he could see a man, dressed only in a long linen nightshirt. He was yelling and waving his arms frantically.

There was a thud and a crossbow bolt whistled past John. The shouting man staggered and held a hand to his throat. His whole body shuddered and he slipped to the ground. But it was too late. The man's cries had woken others, and several armed men were coming out of nearby tents to see what the commotion was about. They were confused and rubbing sleep from their eyes, but one large figure was already heading for the trebuchet. The sight of the axe in the man's left hand made John's heart miss a beat.

"Get back," Adso yelled, "back down the gorge."

The men began to retreat as more crusaders appeared. Stephen and Adso stayed by the trebuchet, frantically stuffing coals into bundles that had not yet ignited. Oddo was running now, his axe raised.

"Adso!" John shouted. "Come on." His friend ignored him.

John unsheathed his sword and moved forward. The pile of sticks Adso was working on burst into sudden bright flame, and John could see Adso smile as he stepped away. But Oddo was at his back.

"Behind you!" John yelled. The axe was almost over Adso's head and beginning its descent. At the last minute, Stephen flung himself to his right, shoving Adso out of the way. Adso cursed and John saw the blade of his dagger glint in the firelight as he fell.

The axe swept down, almost disappearing in Stephen's side and embedding itself in the trebuchet's wooden frame. John screamed and leaped forward over the burning pile of sticks. Blinded by rage, he forgot everything Adso had taught him and simply lunged at the big man.

Oddo punched hard with his right hand, catching John on the jaw, knocking him backwards and scattering coals and burning sticks. By the flickering light, John watched as the big man struggled to release his axe. Stephen's body, almost cut in half, lolled stupidly with each tug.

Out of the corner of his eye, John saw Adso struggle to his knees. The axe jerked free and Stephen's body slumped to the ground. Oddo turned toward Adso, the deadly axe poised for a swing. Without thinking, John grabbed a handful of red hot coals in his left hand and flung them at the knight's face. Two pieces caught him on the cheek below his left eye and another hit his forehead. Oddo roared in pain and staggered back. Adso reached up and plunged his dagger deep into the man's thigh.

John reached over and grabbed Adso's tunic. "Adso, come on, we've got to get out of here." Already men from the tents were working to extinguish the fires on the other side of the trebuchet and other figures were rushing toward them. Several wore coats emblazoned with a falcon.

John's left hand was a mass of pain and he could smell his own burned flesh. Oddo clutched his thigh, dark blood welling up between his fingers. In the firelight, his face was a mask of hate, made more horrible by the patches of red, blistering flesh where the coals had struck him. He raised his axe and attempted to stand, but his wounded leg gave out and he slumped down. He stared at John.

"Do not think I will forget you, boy," he snarled. "The next time we meet will be your last moment on this earth."

In a stumbling run, Adso and John made it back to the gorge edge and slithered down into the relative safety of the river bed. A couple of Falcons attempted to follow, but a crossbow bolt thudding into a tree by their heads discouraged the effort. The nineteen survivors made it across the gorge and up the stairs without hindrance. John remembered almost nothing of the journey except the pain in his hand.

* * *

For five days, John lay in the Perfect house by the town gates as the rocks from the mangonels crashed around him. The Good Christians put salves on his hand, bandaged it as best they could and gave him what little water and food he wanted. The pain in his hand was intense, as if it were still on fire, and the sight of the red, blistered, suppurating flesh was frightening, but gradually he improved. Adso visited frequently.

"Thank you for saving my life," he said on several occasions. "That was quick thinking."

"It was no thinking at all," John said with an attempt at a smile. "After all the tricks you taught me, all I managed to do was burn my own hand."

"There's always new tricks. It's a shame we didn't manage to kill that brute, Oddo. At least 'e'll be limping for a while."

John nodded.

"Our efforts were all in vain," Adso told John on another one of his visits. "The fires never had a chance to join, and the trebuchet was back in action that very day. I fear we have but little time left."

"So, Minerve will fall." It was more a statement than a question.

"It's certain, and in not too many days."

John wondered aloud whether the citizens of Minerve would be massacred like their counterparts in Béziers.

"I think not." Adso shook his head. "Count William is trying to arrange a truce to talk terms. I fear the Perfects are doomed though."

The thought of all his Cathar friends being burned at the stake pushed John into a pit of misery. He was lying down, on the afternoon of the fifth day, thinking of that and feeling sorry for himself, when he heard the door open.

"Self-pity is one of the Devil's emotions."

The familiar voice startled John into sitting up. "What are you doing here?"

he asked.

Beatrice smiled gently. "I came to see how much trouble you had got into."

"But how did you get in?"

"Along the dry riverbed and up what is left of the stairs. No one is looking for people trying to get into Minerve. The trick is getting out."

"But now you're trapped here."

"Being trapped or not is a matter of outlook. I know men who have the freedom of entire kingdoms, and yet they are trapped more certainly than we are. For myself, I have been trapped in this body since I first came screaming into the world."

"But Minerve will fall any day now! You must escape. You said yourself that Aumery will not rest until all the Elect are burned."

"Then there is not much point in running, is there?" Beatrice's smile widened. "Do not worry about me. I heard about your adventure. How is your hand?"

"It hurts fiercely, but it is getting better. What worries me most is that the fingers are curling in and I cannot straighten them. I fear I may have to live with a claw."

"The Devil's work," Beatrice said. "I hear that Umar's soul has gone to a better place."

"Yes, he fell and hit his head. It was a tragedy."

"Not for him, so we should not think of it as such."

"But all the wisdom in his head! It is lost now," John said.

"To us. Do you not think it selfish and arrogant to wallow in regret for our own loss, when we should be happy for Umar's soul?"

John felt a pang of guilt.

"He was not alone in knowing secrets," Beatrice went on. "His work was done. It was time for him to rest. He passed on much." Beatrice delved into her habit and produced a small parchment volume. "I have brought you three presents, material things and the Devil's work, but you may find something in each to aid the spirit."

"Another book for me to learn?" John asked.

"If you wish. I found it in the library at Montségur and thought it might interest you."

John accepted the book as graciously as he could. The cover was of faded leather with a one-word title picked out in barely legible gold letters: *Scultura*. John opened the book and let his eyes scan the first words. They were written in Latin.

"*My name is Lucius of the Macrinus family and I respectfully write this modest volume as a companion to my treatise on the art of drawing. The drawing system I presented in my other work, if studied and applied with rigour, allows the recreation of the real world around us on a manuscript page, wall or board with a fidelity that few can imagine. I aim here to show how this can also be achieved with a statue hewn from a rough block of stone."*

With a thrill, John realized what he was holding. "It's a book on sculpture by the same Roman who wrote the lost book on drawing!"

Beatrice nodded. "I am sorry I could not find the drawing book, but perhaps this will aid you in your quest for beauty and its representation. If I am honest, I must admit that I think it a waste of time, but I do find some of the pictures within pleasing."

John carefully thumbed through the fragile pages. Several contained illustrations of statues and they certainly did look much more lifelike than the ones he was used to seeing flanking cathedral doorways.

"Thank you," he said. "I shall work at copying these pictures."

"And this will help." Beatrice said, handing John a second book. This one was about the same size as *Scultura*, but it was roughly bound and made of paper instead of parchment. The pages were blank.

"It is from the Moors in Al-Andalus, where they use this paper instead of the animal skins we write on. Umar used to say that paper holds the ink much better and does not allow it to run. I thought it might be good for you to practice with, if you are set on this drawing."

"It must be very valuable," John said, feeling the smoothness of the pages.

"Money is the Devil's tool."

"Thank you, again," John said.

"You are welcome. Perhaps when you have satisfied this passing phase, you will return to the memory cloister and what is truly important."

"Perhaps," John said with a smile. It was the first time he had felt like smiling since the raid on the trebuchet. He swung his legs out of the alcove where he had been lying. He had to admit it felt good to be on his feet again.

"I will practise my drawing with great care," he said.

"That is good, but I suspect you will have to wait. This afternoon a delegation will meet with de Montfort to discuss surrender."

John nodded. It was inevitable. The sooner the surrender was worked out, the greater the chance that the population would be spared.

"You must escape tonight," John said.

"Must I?"

"Yes! You told me yourself that they will burn every member of the Elect they can find."

"And I have also said that leaving this world is to be welcomed. But there is another reason I cannot leave. There are a number of Credents who wish to take the *consolamentum* before the surrender and I must perform that this evening."

"Couldn't someone else?"

"Yes, but should I pass that responsibility to others while I flee to safety?"

John didn't answer. It was obvious that nothing he could say would change Beatrice's mind.

"Will you come to the ceremony?" she asked.

"I thought outsiders weren't allowed."

"Their presence is not encouraged, but no one is banned from our activities. In any case, it would be one more thing for you to remember. I fear there will be fewer and fewer *consolamentum* ceremonies in the coming years."

"I should be honoured."

"Good. And there is one more thing I would ask. As a member of the Elect, it would not be wise for me to attend the negotiations. My presence might set the priests off on a tirade. Would you attend and tell me what transpires?"

"Will I be allowed?"

"I shall clear it with Count William."

"Then yes." John could think of no reason to refuse.

"Thank you."

John remembered something. "You said you had brought three things."

"Indeed I did, although the last one is not a thing." Beatrice smiled and left the room. Puzzled, John watched the door. The stone floor shuddered as a rock landed nearby, and an earthenware pot crashed off the mantle above the fireplace. John bent to pick up the pieces.

"A tidy mind is a good thing."

John looked up to see Isabella standing in the doorway. Her dark hair cascaded over her shoulders, and her almost black eyes stared at John while a half smile played on her lips.

"Isabella!" he exclaimed, standing up and catching his head a painful glancing blow on the mantle.

Isabella laughed lightly, a sound that even through his embarrassed pain sounded to John like golden bells in the wind.

"Are you all right?" she asked.

"I'm fine, but feeling stupid," he said rubbing his head with his healthy hand. "You look good."

Isabella's smile broadened in acknowledgement. "How is your hand?"

John looked down at his bandaged claw. "It hurts less now. But why are you here?"

"You don't want to see me?"

"No! I didn't mean that."

"Let's sit down." Isabella moved into the room and sat at the table. John sat opposite. "I came to see you."

"Me? Why?" John was thoroughly confused. He was happy to see Isabella, happier than he thought he could be, but they'd had no contact for years. Why had she suddenly shown up?

"John, you are the most foolish clever person I have ever known!" Isabella smiled, and John's knees felt so weak he was glad he was sitting down. "In all our years as friends in Toulouse, did you never notice that I sought you out and sat next to you whenever possible? Did you never wonder why I continually asked you about the books you were reading? Did it never once cross your mind that I had feelings for you?"

"Peter was your close friend."

"No. He was the one who sat beside me and sought me out to engage in conversation. Oh, I liked Peter, but he was too intense and lacked your inquiring mind. I talked with all our friends equally but, I fear, Peter misread me."

"What do you mean?"

A frown replaced Isabella's smile. "On that last night in Toulouse, Peter declared his feelings for me. I could not return them and before he could ask me to be his betrothed, I told him so in the gentlest way I could. I was also going to explain my feelings for you, but he was taken by his terrifying fit of visions. I thought for the longest time that I was to blame in some way, but Peter thinks not."

"You have seen him?"

"He was in Toulouse some months ago with that monster Aumery. In any case, after the visions, everything happened so fast. The next day Peter was becoming a monk, and you had vanished with that troubadour."

Isabella fell silent and John pondered what she had said. It made sense. He remembered the way she had always sought him out to ask about books. He had been happy to tell her and pleased to be in her company, but she had been just a friend.

"I never realized."

Isabella's smile returned. "I know. That's why I came to look for you. It took me a long time to decide this is what I must do and, for much of that time, I had no idea where you were. But these are troubled times, and I fear if we do not seize what we wish, it will be lost."

"How did you know where to find me?"

"Peter told me you were with Beatrice, and William the troubadour said he had heard that Beatrice was in Minerve. I was planning on coming here on my way to Aragon, and perhaps Al-Andalus, when I heard that de Montfort was besieging the town. Then Beatrice arrived in Toulouse. Apparently William had stopped in Minerve and told her where I was and how he surmised I felt about you. When she said she was coming back to Minerve, I decided to come too. The journey was fun. Mostly we had to travel by night."

"You have just passed through an enemy army with a Perfect that they would burn on sight, and you say it was fun?"

Isabella laughed. "It was."

"On your way to Al-Andalus?" Something Isabella said suddenly struck John.

"Yes," Isabella's face darkened. "I left when I was an infant and an orphan like you. But it is where my family is from, and I would like to..." Isabella hesitated as if deciding what to say next. "See the land," she finished weakly. John was about to ask if there was anything else she meant, but she hurried on. "Besides, I hear that King Pedro is sympathetic to Good Christians. From Aragon it is but a short step to Al-Andalus, and I should like to see the world our Moorish neighbours have created there."

"You're a Cathar?" John asked.

"I am, and one day I hope to take the *consolamentum*, but for now I wish to learn what good this corrupt world can teach me."

"I want to go to Al-Andalus too," John said, thinking of the drawing book that might be in Cordova. "Umar, an old Perfect who was here, mentioned a book I should very much like to see in the library at Madinat al-Zahra, outside Cordova. The old librarian, Nasir al-Din, was Umar's teacher and there is a black man, Shabaka, who helps him." John found the details he stored automatically in his memory useful but, sometimes, he couldn't help letting everything pour out.

"Then we should travel together," Isabella said. "I wish to spend time in Aragon, but I would be happy to go south after that. We could—"

The door flew open and crashed back against the wall. "Satan's spawn are coming under a flag of truce," Adso said. He stopped and stared at Isabella. "Beatrice said she had brought a lady from Toulouse, but she did not say you were beautiful." Adso bowed theatrically. "And you came all this way to see 'im," he jerked a thumb at John. "When there are plenty noble and 'andsome knights about to choose from?" He stepped forward and kissed Isabella's hand. "I daresay there is no accounting for taste.

"But, before you two lovebirds sneak away to sit in a bower and recite courtly poems to one another, there is work to be done. As I said, the Devil is at the gate. It is time to go and meet the enemy."

Who Lives, Who Dies

Minerve
July 21, 1210

Peter watched the small procession approach along the causeway from Minerve. It was led by William, Count of Minerve, who was attended by a scribe and two pages. All were brightly dressed in tunics that bore the count's coat of arms. Peter was surprised to see John following a step behind them. He had not seen his childhood friend since the night of the attack on the trebuchet. He'd awakened and gone out to see what the commotion was about, arriving just in time to witness four figures fighting in the firelight. He had seen one man struck down and a second, whom he recognized as Oddo, wounded and driven back. As the two attackers turned to go, Peter realized that one of them was John.

As the fires on the trebuchet had been brought under control and extinguished, Peter had heard Oddo roar out his anger and hoped that the man who had humiliated him in Béziers, and whose power he still envied, was dying. He wasn't. Several Falcons half carried, half led their leader away. Oddo's face was badly burned, and the wound in his thigh was deep, but the bleeding had stopped and, if no infections set in, he would survive to fight again in de Montfort's crusade.

Now Peter stood between Arnaud Aumery and Simon de Montfort, a step or two behind them. Both were dressed simply, and the only bright colour other than the red cross on de Montfort's tunic was the red ecclesiastical cloak worn by Bishop Foulques, who stood on Aumery's other side.

William stopped several paces in front of de Montfort and nodded slightly. Peter stared at the count so as to avoid catching John's eye.

"I have come," Count William said formally, "to offer the surrender of my town and all my lands in keeping with the rules of warfare."

"I accept your surrender," de Montfort replied, "and will abide by the rules governing the submission of a brave enemy."

"Very well," William said, his face a stern, unreadable mask. "At dawn on the morrow, I shall throw open the gates of Minerve and welcome you to the best of my abilities. You shall be known as Count of Minerve, and all those who owe fealty to me will do so to you. At the same time, all those presently within the walls will be allowed, should they so choose, to leave unhindered to go about their business."

"I thank you," de Montfort said with a faint smile, "but I cannot accept your final condition. There are, within your walls, a number of heretics we know as Cathars."

"Filthy vermin," Foulques spat.

"We come in the name of Christ," de Montfort continued, ignoring the interruption, "and with the blessings of His Holiness Pope Innocent III, to rid this land of foul heresy. We cannot allow these people to leave and spread their lies. They must be handed over to Father Aumery for investigation."

"I cannot agree to that." Count William's voice hardened. "Heretics or not, these are my people and I have a sworn duty to protect them. I shall honour that duty."

"Then I suggest you return to your town and prepare to defend it as best you can," de Montfort said.

"I came here in good faith, to stop suffering, but I am not defeated yet. There are still a wealth of crossbow bolts in Minerve to pierce many crusaders' hearts."

"Gentlemen. Gentlemen." Aumery stepped forward and spoke in his silkiest voice. "There is no need for all this unpleasantness over such a trivial matter. I am the voice here of Pope Innocent, and I see no difficulty with William's request."

Everyone stared at Aumery. The most avowed heretic hater in the land, the man who had launched the massacre at Béziers, was offering to let the heretics go.

De Montfort stared hard at Aumery. "Go on."

"I have no objection," Aumery said with a smile, "to letting everyone go about their business freely. It is not my wish to cause undue suffering and pain to honest Christian folk. Let all live—"

"This is preposterous," Bishop Foulques interrupted, his face scarlet with anger. "One hundred and fifty of the worst sort of vermin, in our grasp, and you propose to let them go! It is a disgrace!"

"Let all live," Aumery repeated calmly, "who will be reconciled with and obey the orders of the Church. If any hold contrary opinions, they need only convert to the Catholic faith."

"So the Devil's children need only bend a lying knee to go free?" Foulques asked angrily.

"Indeed. But I think, my dear Bishop, that you do not know your enemy as well as you should. You will search long before you find a Perfect heretic who will 'bend a lying knee.'"

De Montfort was smiling broadly. "Are these terms acceptable, Count William?"

"They are." The count let out a sigh, and his features relaxed. He looked suddenly exhausted and his eyes carried a look of terrible sadness. There was nothing more he could do. He had secured for all his subjects a way to survive. He could not do more to protect the unrepentant heretics without drawing suspicion himself.

"Very well, then. At first light tomorrow, we shall approach the gates and expect them open." De Montfort turned and strode back toward his camp.

Peter was smiling at the clever way Aumery had resolved the difficulty. He glanced up before William and his delegation turned to leave and briefly met John's eyes. He shuddered at the look of hatred he saw there.

"Come," Aumery said. "There is much to do. We will need a large fire to accomplish God's work tomorrow."

Consolamentum

Minerve
July 22, 1210

John stood on the battlements above the town gates, staring morosely over the causeway at the victorious enemy camp. It was past midnight, but fires still sparkled among tents. On the cool breeze, he could hear the sound of music and singing and smell the odour of roasting pigs and goats. The crusaders were celebrating. And why not? The greatest heretic stronghold had fallen in a matter of weeks with barely any casualties. De Montfort was established now and there was no chance that these foreign knights would simply go home.

John's eyes drifted to a flat area of ground lit by a ring of torches. In the centre of the ring, several priests were busy adding the finishing touches to a huge mound of wood and straw. It seemed Aumery was certain that Minerve's Elect would not even attempt to escape the flames. He was right. None was prepared to lie about his or her faith, and John had noticed that several seemed almost eager for the next day. A few were even preparing to take the *consolamentum* this night so that they could walk into the fire in a few hours. John shivered at the thought of flames blistering skin and heat searing lungs. His hand still ached from his own encounter with fire, and he tried to imagine the pain of that wound spread over his entire body. He couldn't conceive of having the strength to walk voluntarily into the flames.

As figures moved in and out of patches of light, John strained to see if Peter was working on the pyre. He caught a glimpse of one tall, gangly figure, but the distance was too great to be sure. John had been surprised at the surge of hatred he'd felt toward Peter when he saw him standing smugly beside Aumery as Count William had been forced to give up Minerve's Perfects. Ever since his vision, John realized Death *had* been at Peter's shoulder—striking down those around him.

Anger boiled up inside John. If the Devil was abroad in this land, he was out there with the crusaders. Reflexively, John's good hand clenched around his sword's hilt. If Aumery were magically to appear before him now, John would have no trouble cutting the evil man down. And Peter? Would he kill Peter, too?

John sighed and slumped against the battlements, his anger gone as fast as it had arisen. What was he to do? It seemed only yesterday he was a naive boy thrilled at a world overloaded with wonderful possibilities. Now he was a soldier wishing for a chance to kill his best friend.

"They look like devils walking through the fires of hell." The soft voice startled John. He turned away from the battlements to see Isabella standing behind him. She looked peaceful in the light from the nearby torch. John swept his arm wide to encompass the camp and the pyre.

"How can they be so cruel?" he asked, desolately.

"It's the Devil in them that creates cruelty. Is Peter cruel?"

"What he's doing is cruel, and I am beginning to hate him for that."

"He was never cruel when we were all friends in Toulouse," Isabella said gently. "Maybe he isn't now. Beatrice would say he is misled and that it is the Devil seducing him into the arms of a corrupt Church."

"Is that what you would say?" John asked.

"Beatrice could forgive the Devil himself." Isabella smiled sadly. "I do not have her mercy." She fell silent for a moment, then said, "I was tempted in Toulouse to take the *consolamentum*."

"Why didn't you?"

"I do not have Beatrice's certainty either. I admire the Perfects, and I *am* certain that they are closer to the truth than Aumery and Foulques, but I am not ready to renounce the world, even if it is the work of Satan. There is too much to discover."

John nodded. "That's how I feel, but sometimes, I wish for certainty. I envy Beatrice"—John hesitated—"and even Peter. They both know they are right. It must be simple for them. I always doubt."

"Maybe we are meant to doubt," Isabella said with a shrug. "Look where certainty has led Peter and Beatrice, one builds a pyre and the other must climb it. In any case, this land is corrupted now and, if we do not wish to take the *consolamentum* and die with the Perfects, our choices have narrowed—accept what the crusaders are doing and all the hatred that goes with it, or fight. Either way, the result is death and destruction. That's why I am going to Al-Andalus. I want to go somewhere where learning is still possible. Did you mean it when you said you wanted to go, too?"

"I did," John said firmly. "I have to escape before I become as cruel as them." He pointed at the funeral pyre. "And there are also things I want to learn. Cordova might be a good place to begin."

"Then we should travel together. I should like to show you Aragon, and see it for myself." Isabella lowered her gaze and, for a moment, looked terribly sad. "No one will know me," she said.

John was about to ask what she meant, but she looked up and continued. "Anyway, the Perfects say one should never travel alone. The bond of companionship is a consolation and a strong protection against Satan whispering in an ear." Isabella's smile returned, overwhelming any questions John had.

"I would like that." John spoke calmly, but inside he was wildly excited. Isabella's sudden appearance in Minerve and the revelation that she had always had feelings for him had been a complete shock. But the more he thought about it, the more he realized that he had also had feelings for Isabella; he had simply ignored them or pushed them into the background because of Peter. But now Peter was on the other side in a war and Isabella was suggesting that they travel together to a place he desperately wanted to go. A dream John had barely realized he had was coming true.

"Will your friend Adso come with us?" Isabella interrupted John's thoughts.

"I don't think so. He is set on continuing the fight against de Montfort and the crusaders. But I can protect us."

"We shall protect each other," Isabella said with a slight laugh. "And I have a small bag of coins saved. That will protect us when we are hungry or cannot find a pilgrim's roof in a monastery."

"It is good to hear laughter this night." The pair turned to see Beatrice standing nearby. "It is something they have forgotten." She gestured toward the crusader camp. "I think it might be our strongest weapon yet."

For a long moment, Beatrice stared out at the growing pile of wood across the causeway. "We are ready for the *consolamentum*," she said, turning back to John. "Do you still wish to observe?"

"I do," John replied.

"And you?"

"If I may," Isabella answered.

Beatrice nodded. "Then let us go."

"Don't you ever doubt?" John blurted out.

Beatrice smiled and shook her head. "There is no need. I believe the Good Christian way is the true way. All else follows from that."

"But the crusaders don't doubt either," John said.

"Some are certain they are right, that's true, but look at the consequences of their certainty—death, suffering and destruction. The trick is being able to recognize the Devil's seductions."

"But I doubt all the time," John said helplessly.

"Perhaps one day you will find certainty," Beatrice said gently.

"And if I don't?" John asked.

"Then you will do what the rest of humanity does—the best you can."

"How will you have the courage to face the flames tomorrow?" Isabella asked, all laughter vanished and her voice choked with emotion.

"I do not need much courage," Beatrice said, placing a hand on Isabella's shoulder. "My courage is only a small part of the bravery of all those who will walk out there when the sun rises. Nothing need be withstood alone. We are all of a like mind, and in our certainty there is great strength. I shall be fine tomorrow. I am old and tired and I look forward to the release. But what will you do? Where will you go?"

"John and I will go to Aragon to see my homeland and then to Al-Andalus," Isabella answered.

"I am glad that you've found each other and that you're leaving this sad land. When you are tired of searching in this world, think of the next."

Beatrice faced John. "Will you continue to fill the memory cloister?"

"I will," John said. "We plan to go to the great library at Madinat al-Zahra, and I shall fill many empty alcoves there. Perhaps I will teach Isabella."

"That would be good." Beatrice's face became serious in the torchlight. "You have a gift and I am glad you will not waste it. You're the best student I have ever taught and you've learned much very fast. But remember, with a gift comes responsibility. You have things in your mind that are important and very dangerous, not only to you but to many others as well.

"Tomorrow, you will walk out through the crusader camp, free to go where you wish. But be aware that there will be many around you who would kill you without a second thought for simply having the Gospel of Christ in your head. Keep it, and the other books you have and will learn, safe. When you meet someone who you think will understand, pass on the wisdom you have accumulated. That is the responsibility you carry with you."

John nodded, slightly overwhelmed at the seriousness of Beatrice's words. Since Adso had begun to teach him soldiering, he hadn't given much thought to the memory cloister, but Beatrice had been right when she'd first explained the cloister—he couldn't forget anything that was stored within.

"I'll do my best," John said.

"Good." Beatrice's face relaxed. "So, travel, learn, teach and beware the Devil's seductions. Perhaps you are right to believe that God has placed beauty in the world to help us on our journey through the Devil's domain. If so, I wish you luck with your dream of portraying that beauty. I hope you find the book you seek."

"Thank you," John said.

Beatrice placed a hand each on John and Isabella's foreheads. "Be consoled as you journey through this corrupt world by wisdom, each other and the Holy Spirit."

John felt oddly calm at this strange woman's words and touch.

Beatrice lowered her hands and smiled. "And now we must go to the *consolamentum*."

* * *

John and Isabella followed Beatrice off the battlements, through Minerve's streets and into the main hall of Count William's castle. The hall showed signs of the siege—everything was covered in a thick layer of dust, the walls were bare stone where the tapestries had been removed, and one corner of the roof was open to the night sky where a rock from a mangonel had crashed through. It was full of Elect standing in their hoodless black robes. A small group of five Credents stood at the front by the huge ceiling-high fireplace. They looked nervous at being the centre of attention.

Beatrice ushered John and Isabella to a bench carved out of the side wall where they would be out of the way but could still watch what was going on. Then she walked to the front. The hall fell silent. Without preliminaries, Beatrice raised her hands and began. Her voice was soft, yet it carried to every corner of the room.

"Christ says in the Gospel according to St. Matthew, 'Wheresoever two or three are gathered together in my name, there I am in the midst of them.'"

John counted those in the hall. In addition to the five Credents, there were one hundred and forty-five Elect. Would they all die willingly in a few hours?

Two of the Credents were women, wives of men killed in the siege; two others, one so seriously wounded that he had to be supported by his companion, were knights; and one was a local baker. All wore simple clothes —tunics, shirts, leggings—and all were barefoot on the cold stone tiles. Four appeared calm, but the baker fidgeted continuously and looked around the hall nervously.

"'Seek ye the proof of Christ who speaketh in me.'"

They are going to become living saints, John thought in wonder. Would I ever have the certainty to do this? To die for my beliefs?

"Lo, I am with you always, even unto the end of the world."

After each recitation the congregation affirmed by nodding. John was fascinated to see this ritual, the holiest of the heretics', but his mind kept wandering to the pyre on the plain. Is that what the baker was thinking? He was a fat man and John could see his chins quivering with fright.

"'If ye forgive not men their trespasses, neither will your Heavenly Father forgive your trespasses.'"

John Wilson

Beatrice beckoned the Credents forward. As they stepped up, she recited the only prayer that the Elect were allowed to say.

Pater noster qui es in caelis,
sanctificetur nomen tuum.

Our Father who art in Heaven,
Hallowed be Thy name.

Her voice was gentle, almost mesmerizing.

Adveniat regnum tuum.
Fiat voluntas tua sicut in caelo et in terra.

Thy kingdom come
Thy will be done on earth as it is in Heaven

John focused on the words. He could hear Isabella softly repeating each line under her breath.

Panem nostrum supersubstancialem da nobis hodie.
Et dimitte nobis debita nostra sicut et nos dimittimus debitoribus nostris.

Give us this day our supplementary bread,
and remit our debts as we forgive our debtors.

Did the Credents realize what each step took them toward?

Et ne nos inducas in temptationem

And keep us from temptation

Step. The baker hesitated, but moved forward.

sed libera nos a malo.

and free us from evil.

Step. The baker stumbled.

Quoniam tuum est regnum

Thine is the kingdom,

Step. One of the women took the baker's arm and steadied him.

et virtus et Gloria

the power and glory

Step. The baker turned and smiled at the woman.

in secula.

for ever and ever.

Amen.

When the Credents reached the front, Beatrice told them, "We deliver you this holy prayer and the power to say it all your life, day or night alone or in company. You must never eat or drink without first reciting it. If you omit to do so, you must do penance."

Together the Credents replied, "I receive it of you and of the Church." The baker's voice was thin and reedy, and his replies came a split second after everyone else's.

One by one the Credents bowed at Beatrice's feet. One by one, she asked them, "My brother, do you desire to give yourself to our faith?" Each answered, "Yes." The baker hesitated a long time before he spoke.

"Then God bless you," Beatrice said to them all, "and bring you to the good end."

At the mention of tomorrow's inevitable conclusion, the baker visibly shivered.

"All is vanity. Hate the solid garment of flesh."

John had a sudden vivid image of the baker's ample flesh, blackening and falling off his bones. Why was he forcing himself to do this? He could just walk out of Minerve tomorrow. In his mind, John knew that the soul was what mattered and that it was immortal, imprisoned for only a brief moment in this world, but he could not understand either the cruelty of the Inquisition or the level of belief that impelled the baker to undergo such self-imposed torture.

"Do you promise that henceforth, you will eat neither meat, nor eggs, nor cheese, nor fat, that you will not lie, that you will not curse, that you will swear no oath, that you will not kill, that you will forsake luxury, that you will forgive whoever wrongs you, and that you will hate this world and all things in it and never abandon your faith for fear of water, fire or any other manner of death?"

"Yes," the Credents answered.

"Love not this world. It is corrupt and lustful. The world passeth away and the lust thereof, but he that doeth the will of God abideth forever."

Beatrice stepped forward and placed her hand on each Credent's head in turn. This was the heart of the ceremony, the passing of the Holy Ghost from an Elect to a Credent through the laying on of hands. As she touched each head, Beatrice said, "He that believeth and is baptized shall be saved, but he that believeth not shall be damned. Receive ye the Holy Ghost."

As she reached the baker, John thought the poor man was about to pass out. Oddly, as Beatrice placed her hand on his head, he quieted. His shaking and his nervous glances stopped. As she recited the words, he looked up at her. It was as if his fear was draining out of him, being pulled away by Beatrice's blessing. Suddenly John understood. The baker was no longer alone. Now he was supported by all the others in the room. He was no longer one person, but a tiny part of something much larger. That was what *consolamentum* meant. It was a consoling—a comfort to the spirit trapped and alone in a corrupt body. The baker need never be alone again. John remembered the strange feeling of calm when Beatrice had blessed him and Isabella on the battlements.

"For all the sins I have ever done in thought, word and deed," the Credents recited together, turning to look on the Elect, "I ask pardon of God, of the Church, and of you all."

"By God, and by us, and by the Church, may your sins be forgiven, and we pray God to forgive you them," the Elect answered as one.

"*Adoremus, Patrem, et Filium et Spiritum Sanctum.*"

The Elect surged forward to congratulate the five. Even the baker was smiling from ear to ear.

Beatrice made her way over to John and Isabella.

"I was watching the baker," John said. "He was terrified, but when you laid on your hands, he grew calm and suddenly became happy."

"That is the power of the *consolamentum*. That is what the Pope and his minions fear and hate so much."

"But tomorrow all will die a hideous death."

"All die," Beatrice said. "Life is but a flicker in eternity. Is one brief death better or worse than another?"

John shrugged. He didn't have an answer.

"Now I must say farewell," Beatrice said. "I would go to meditate in the few hours before dawn."

Isabella stood and embraced Beatrice.

"We *will* meet again," John said desperately, tears welling up in his eyes.

"Certainly," Beatrice responded, "but I doubt in this world. Find your own way. I wish you both luck on your journey."

"Thank you," John managed to croak out.

"Goodbye." Beatrice turned and walked out of the room, her staff clacking hollowly on the stone floor.

"Goodbye," John said after her. "And thank you." For a moment, he was utterly alone and confused. Then he felt Isabella's arm around his shoulder. He looked up at her through his tears. Her dark eyes were clear.

"It is her choice and her way," she said. "We should feel happy."

John supposed so, but even with Isabella's arm around him, he couldn't feel happy about Beatrice's coming death.

"We should go and prepare for the morning," Isabella said. "It's a long walk over the mountains to Aragon."

Rome and Al-Andalus

Minerve
July 22, 1210

Peter shivered in the pre-dawn chill. It reminded him of the cold morning years before when he had stood waiting for the ferry to take him, Arnaud Aumery, Pierre of Castelnau and John across the Rhône to Arles. Much had changed since then: John was lost to the heretics, Pierre was murdered and Peter was an ordained monk with considerable power. Aumery, who was standing beside Peter on the low hill outside Minerve looking down on the monks putting the finishing touches on the pyre, had had a part in all of those events.

"This is one of the things I came for," Aumery said. He was rubbing his hands together in front of him. Peter could not tell if it was in gleeful anticipation of the bonfire or because of the cold. "One of my tasks is done. The Holy Crusade is finally established and the first batch of heretics will burn before the sun is risen an hour. It will be a long, hard struggle and I may not live to see the end of it, but it is well begun."

Peter was not looking forward to the mass burning with the same enthusiasm. Secretly, he hoped that the Perfects of Minerve would accept Aumery's offer, convert and live, but he knew that hope was slim. At least John would survive.

"What is the other thing you came for?" Peter asked.

"You know." Aumery turned his head and the first rays of the sun glinted off his peculiar, staring eyes. "The Cathar Treasure, the heretic's secret, the Holy Grail that touched Christ's lips at the Last Supper. The cup that, in the hands of the righteous, will transform our sorry world and usher in the Last Days. The Judgment is coming, Peter. Are you ready?"

"I am," Peter replied, although he was far from convinced that he was. "You're still certain that the Treasure is the Grail?"

"It can be nothing else. It is a well-kept secret, but I shall discover it. These heretical vermin have had a long time to conceal it and it is better hidden than I had anticipated. That is why you must go to Cîteaux."

"Cîteaux?"

"Of course! You have progressed rapidly and performed well, but you have much to learn. Our struggle against the heretics and our quest are long. There is time for you to learn all that is required of a full monk in the Cistercian brotherhood. A year at Cîteaux, my home abbey and monastery, under the guidance of Brother Armand Gauthier. You will be of more use to me once you are fully trained. Perhaps then I shall send you to Rome."

Peter's heart leapt at the mention of Rome. That was where he wanted to go, the seat of Catholic power, and Aumery was talking of sending him there in only a year.

"The crusade will carry on here," Aumery continued. "Oddo and his Falcons and de Montfort will capture more castles and burn more heretics, and I shall make sure it is all done in accordance with God's will. But I do not have enough lifetimes to await the capture of every castle and search every hidden nook and cranny. I underestimated these heretics. To combat them I must find out more about them and their ways.

"The heretics accuse us of burning books, and they are right, but we only burn the books so that they may not fall into the hands of those who cannot understand them and would be misled. Many are preserved in Rome for the eyes of only those who can comprehend them through true belief. Perhaps you will find clues as to the location of the Grail in those books."

"I should be honoured," Peter said.

Aumery grunted an acknowledgement and returned his gaze to the pyre.

"When do I leave?" Peter asked.

"Tomorrow," Aumery said. "I shall prepare a letter for you to take to brother Gauthier. But now"—he turned and looked down the other side of the hill where knights were congregating beneath the unfurled banners of the crusade—"we must go and see to the fire."

* * *

Despite the sun only just having risen over the eastern hills, most of Minerve's population was awake to see the victors enter the town. They lined the battlements or leaned from windows and watched in silence as Arnaud Aumery and Bishop Foulques led the way through the narrow streets. They were followed by a group of priests and lay brothers carrying a large wooden cross and lustily singing the *Te Deum*. Behind them, below their colourful battle standards, came Simon de Montfort and the lords of the crusade dressed in their war finery.

John, in his travelling cloak and with his satchel slung over his shoulder, watched despondently as the group crossed the main square and entered the church of St. Etienne. The Elect, including the baker and his four companions, were already there, standing silently in the nave. John pushed through the sullen crowd into the church, where he stood at the back. Aumery and de Montfort stood side by side in front of the altar. John noticed Peter with the other monks off to one side.

"God is merciful," Aumery said in his high-pitched voice. "I come with the authority of His Holiness, Pope Innocent III, to offer you all salvation. Even though you have transgressed these many years past and sunk deep into the ways of Satan, the Church will still welcome you back with open arms if you only renounce your errors. All you need do is convert to the Holy Catholic faith, the one true faith, and you will be blessed on the Day of Judgment. Otherwise, the pyre is ready beyond your walls."

Several Perfects shouted out replies:

"Why do you preach your filth to us?"

"We want nothing of your corrupt Roman faith."

"We renounce your evil ways."

"You labour in Satan's name in vain."

"Neither death nor life can separate us from the beliefs we hold."

Beatrice stepped forward and the crowd fell silent. "You know so little," she said, almost sadly. "You have fallen so far from the Word of God and corrupted so much with your arrogance and debauchery that you have condemned countless thousands to eternal damnation.

"You offer us conversion to the Devil's work or the momentary pain of the flames. I offer you a chance to save your eternal souls from the torments of this degenerate and depraved world. Renounce the sins of this world and join us as Good Christians."

"How dare you," Bishop Foulques shouted, spraying spittle over the nearest listeners. "You are nothing but filthy swine who pervert the natural order by denying the divinity of Christ and undertaking all manner of disgusting and deviant behaviour. You deserve to rot in hell in eternal torment."

"And eternal torment they shall undoubtedly have," Aumery added, cutting off Foulques' tirade. "But their fate is no longer in our hands. We have offered them the infinite mercy of the Mother Church and they have spurned it. It is for the secular authorities to determine their fate."

Aumery glanced at de Montfort, who stepped forward. "You will not admit the error of your ways and return to the fold of the Church?"

"Had we committed an error," Beatrice said, "we would gladly admit it, but we have not. We renounce your Pope, your Church and all its works."

"Then I have no choice. I condemn you in the name of the Holy Crusade to suffer death by burning. May the fire cleanse your souls."

An almost imperceptible shudder passed through the crowd, but no one said a word. In silence, every member of the Elect followed de Montfort out of the church and down the hill to the gates. John followed behind, as did many of the townsfolk. Several wept silently.

"Are you a heretic now?"

John looked to his right to see Peter in his priest's habit walking beside him. His eyes met Peter's for a brief moment, but he looked away before answering. "If hating those who would kill so many good and gentle people means I am a heretic, then yes I am."

"That is not what I meant. Do you hold with their beliefs and worship the Devil as they do?"

Anger swept over John. "What do you know of the Devil or these people's beliefs? All you do is follow that rat Aumery and wallow in his hatred. Do you really think God judges people simply by what prayer they mouth or which arrogant bishop they fawn over? Does being good and doing good count for nothing if you bend your knee to the wrong idol? I want no part of that God."

"I could have you thrown on the pyre with your friends for saying that," Peter said quietly.

"Go ahead. That's all your precious crusade can do, destroy what it cannot understand."

The pair walked in silence for a while. Eventually, Peter said, "How have you grown so far from what we were both taught as children by the sisters?"

"Because I have kept my mind open. I am grateful to the sisters for what they taught me, but it was not everything. The world is a much larger place than even your Church. I intend to discover what I can of it."

"Even if that search leads to heresy and the condemnation of your soul?"

"If, as the Good Christians believe, the Devil created the material world, then what I do in it makes no difference. If, as you believe, God created the world and all the infinite wonder in it, how can He condemn me for wanting to discover the beauty of His work? He gave us free will. How can He then condemn us for using it?"

As he passed through the gate, John unbuckled his sword and threw it on the pile of weapons being collected by a group of Falcons; no one was allowed to leave the city with a weapon. The crowd walked over the causeway toward the pile of wood and straw. The route was lined with armed men, and others, several holding lighted torches, surrounded the pyre.

"Does that not trouble your soul?" John asked, pointing to the pyre.

"The land must be cleansed," Peter said. "That is the only way we can reach the kingdom of God."

"Even if it means climbing over mountains of charred bodies?"

Peter didn't answer.

"You have become trapped in a system that allows no thought," John said. "You are doing well and have risen fast. If that is what you want, you will continue to prosper and I wish you well, but it is not for me."

"What will you do?"

"I am going to Al-Andalus."

"The land of the Moorish heathen?"

"A different land where there is much to learn." John ignored the sneer in Peter's voice. "And you?"

"I am going to Cîteaux, to gather true learning, and then to Rome," Peter said proudly.

"So we are both leaving our homeland in opposite directions," John said sadly. "These are indeed strange times. We are not the children we were. This war has changed us, and I suspect it will change much more before it is done. I wish you well."

"And I you," Peter replied. "I shall pray that you come to see the true light."

"Hello, Peter."

The pair turned to see Isabella and Adso standing nearby, both dressed in travelling cloaks. Isabella had cut her black hair short for the journey and carried Beatrice's knotted staff. In different circumstances, the look of horrified recognition that crossed Peter's face would have been comical.

"Your visions of death are coming true," she added coldly, glancing at the pyre.

"Why are you here?" Peter asked, struggling to keep the emotion from his voice.

"I came to seek out John," Isabella replied.

"John?" Peter looked back and forth between his two childhood friends.

"Yes," Isabella said. There was not the slightest trace of a smile on her lips. "He seeks answers through enquiry and learning, not through the thoughtless repetition of a corrupt belief."

Isabella's words hit Peter like hammer blows. Tears ran down his cheeks and he appeared to shrink into himself. "I—" he began, but he choked on the next word and, turning away, stumbled roughly through the crowd.

"That was cruel," John said. "He was very fond of you once."

"No," Isabella said, moving to John's side. "What I said was true. That"— she pointed at the pyre and the line of black-clad Perfects walking silently toward it—"that is cruel. Peter cries for me and an impossible dream he had years ago. He should be weeping for what is happening this day."

"There'll be no shortage of weeping today," Adso said, moving up beside his friends, "and in many days to come."

"We cannot persuade you to come with us?" Isabella asked.

Adso shook his head. "This is my land these people are raping and my friends they are burning. I must fight them as best I can."

"They will not give up and go home as you once believed," John said.

"I must fight nonetheless. You and Isabella go to the land of the Moors and find your learning. Come back with knowledge, although I would prefer you came back with an army."

"Be careful," John said.

"Always," Adso said, "and you watch out, too. It's a long way you go. But I must leave now—I 'ave no wish to see this fire."

The three embraced for the last time before Adso slipped away through the crowd.

John looked toward the pyre. It was in the form of a large raised square, more than twenty feet on each side and higher than a man. Crude stairs had been built on one side and, already, Perfects were clambering up. The soldiers stood by threateningly, but they were not required. The Perfects went voluntarily to their fate.

Beatrice stood at the foot of the steps, helping those who stumbled. She offered a hand to the baker but he shrugged it off with a smile.

John counted. There were one hundred and fifty men and women on the pyre. Many were holding hands both for comfort and to help keep balanced on the uneven bed of logs and sticks. A few embraced.

Beatrice was the last to ascend. At the top, she turned and looked over the crowd. John thought for a moment she was going to address the assembled townsfolk and soldiers, but she said nothing. At last, her eyes came to rest on John and Isabella. She smiled.

Tears flooded John's eyes, blurring the scene, but he could still see the shapes of soldiers stepping forward and thrusting their torches into the pile. Sharp hearts of bright flame caught eagerly at the dry sticks and straw and a low moan rose from the crowd.

Aumery was chanting something but John ignored him. He rubbed his eyes and watched as the flames grew and coalesced. Smoke rose and thickened, swirling across the view of the Perfects standing still and silent. Beatrice was looking at John and smiling. Slowly she raised her hand and waved. John returned the gesture as a cloud of smoke obscured her.

Bowing his head, John took Isabella's arm and pushed through the crowd. The pair found the road and turned south without looking back. Behind them, the crackling of the flames drowned out Aumery's voice.

Book II

Quest

New Beginnings 1211

Adso

near Lavaur
May 4

"I really wish you'd cover that up," Adso said with a shiver, staring at the hideously scarred face before him. "At least put a patch over the 'ole where your eye used to be."

"Oddo's damned Falcons did this to me," Bertrand said, twisting the tight scar tissue of his face into a parody of a grin. He spoke slowly so that the slurred speech coming from his lipless mouth could be understood. "I can't forget and I don't want them to. I'll kill every one of those devils I come upon, and I want my face to be the last thing they see as I send them to hell."

"Fair enough," Adso said with a sigh, "but it's 'ard on the rest of us when there's no Falcons about. You didn't 'ave a face the troubadours'd sing about *afore* they took a knife to you."

In the year since Bertrand had led the hundred mutilated knights from Bram to Cabaret, his face had healed well and knots of livid red scar tissue had formed over his wounds. He had grown his hair long to cover his disfigured ears, but he couldn't hide the teeth beneath his missing upper lip or the deep, black hole where his left eye had been. His nose was a shapeless mass with two small, irregular holes through which the air whistled when he breathed. Nevertheless, Bertrand was one of the lucky ones. He had been left with one eye so that he could lead his blinded companions away from Bram. The others, if they hadn't died agonizingly after infections ate away at their ravaged faces, were completely blind and reduced to a pitiful begging existence on the streets of Toulouse or Carcassonne.

Bertrand maintained that it was his fiery hatred for Simon de Montfort's crusaders, and in particular the mercenary Oddo and his Falcons, that had kept him alive the previous summer. It had also driven him to persuade Adso to help gather a band of twenty landless knights—men from Minerve, Cabaret and Carcassonne, whose lords had surrendered or been defeated and who did not wish to swear allegiance to de Montfort—and lead them to ambush and kill any knights, priests or merchants who aided the crusade. The band killed indiscriminately, but Bertrand ordered that one victim be left alive in every attack. The survivor was to be mutilated, as Bertrand had been, and sent on his way to tell the tale.

For two months now, since the fortress at Cabaret had surrendered in March, Bertrand, Adso and their men had been living in the wooded hills east of Toulouse. They had little trouble supplying themselves with food, either through hunting or from sympathetic villagers, and the limestone walls of the deep gullies were riddled with caves that provided dry, comfortable shelter. The pickings on the roads had been good too, as knights travelled to join de Montfort's army besieging Lavaur, twenty miles northeast of Toulouse. Today, in the warm afternoon sun, Adso and the others were waiting for a small band of men whom scouts had spotted heading east from Lavaur along a little-travelled track at the base of the hills.

"Where in 'ell are they?" Adso grumbled as he shifted his position on the steep hillside. Below him, the narrow path was empty. "Should be 'ere by now."

"They'll be here," Bertrand said. He was sitting beside Adso, his back against a wide oak tree. A loaded crossbow lay across his knees and he stroked the weapon lovingly.

"You're more fond of that crossbow than a woman," Adso remarked.

"Saladin doesn't care about my looks and with only one eye, I'm no good with a sword or axe."

"Why d'you call it Saladin? Weren't 'e a Saracen out by Jerusalem?"

"He was, and that's where my Saladin comes from. Look." Bertrand held up the bow and pointed to the crosspiece, which was bent sharply back by the taut string. "That's the prod. It's where all the power comes from."

"I know that," Adso interrupted. "I don't need a lesson in 'ow a crossbow works."

"As a rule, crossbows have a wooden prod—yew or ash, mostly," Bertrand went on, ignoring his companion's comments. "Look closely at this one."

Adso bent forward and stared. "It's built up in layers."

"Exactly. It's called a composite prod. Not just wood, but alternating layers of horn, sinew and wood, glued together and shaped. Much more powerful than wood alone. Makes it hard to draw, which is why it's got this foot stirrup on the nose." Bertrand put his right foot into the triangular piece of metal that hung from the nose of the bow. "After I've fired, I put my foot in there, grab the string and simply stand up. It's hard on the hands, but faster than most crossbows, and this bow can kill a man a hundred yards away."

Adso nodded appreciatively.

"But mainly," Bertrand went on, "I call it Saladin because he was a great warrior who killed seventeen thousand enemies at the Horns of Hattin. Both Saladin the Saracen and my crossbow are great crusader killers."

"Well," Adso said, "it's a nice weapon, but sword 'n dagger's good enough for me. I knew a man once who—"

A soft whistle from the trees—a signal that the enemy was approaching—silenced Adso. Bertrand sat back, rested his crossbow on his knees and peered along it at the path. Adso moved to one side and unsheathed his sword.

The approaching group was led by a red-haired, mounted knight wearing a chain-mail suit that covered his arms and hung over his legs on either side of the horse. A sword dangled from his belt on the left side, a shield was slung on his right and a helmet was attached behind his saddle. His equipment glinted as he rode through the beams of sunlight that stabbed through the new leaves on the surrounding trees. He wore a surcoat over his chest, which was emblazoned with a blood-red falcon clutching a black axe in its talons.

"A Falcon," Bertrand whispered with grim pleasure.

The knight was followed by half a dozen men on foot. They were dressed in short, sleeveless, leather tunics, leggings and simple helmets. Each carried a sword and had a crossbow hung over his back. Adso was relieved to see none of the bows were loaded and ready to fire. A young lay brother, leading a pair of heavily-laden donkeys, brought up the rear.

Adso watched as the party approached. They were relaxed. It was a fine day for travel, not too hot or cold, and a light breeze rustled the branches above, as birds bustled back and forth searching for insects and grubs to feed their demanding young. The men were confident, part of an invincible army besieging and capturing towns and fortresses one after the other across the land. Lavaur would surely be next.

The knight was almost level with Adso. "Come on, Bertrand," Adso breathed to himself. Above his head a squirrel chattered a complaint. The knight looked up, straight at Adso. He opened his mouth to yell just as the crossbow bolt caught him in the centre of the chest, driving his chain mail through his rib cage and cartwheeling him backwards off his horse.

Adso was up and running before the man hit the ground. As he pounded down the slope and other figures rose from the trees, the knight's companions began to react. Some reached for their swords; others unslung their crossbows. One man almost had his crossbow drawn when Bertrand's second bolt caught him in the throat. Then Adso and his companions were in among the survivors, slashing left and right.

It was all over in moments. Adso stood breathing heavily amid the torn and bleeding bodies of the crusaders. A couple were still alive, but they were quickly dispatched with swift dagger thrusts from Bertrand's men. The only one still on his feet was the young lay brother, who stood, eyes wide with terror, between the donkeys.

Bertrand arrived, Saladin slung across his back, and stood looking down at the dead knight. "Strip the bodies, get this knight's horse and collect the pack donkeys," he ordered. "We need to get back into the hills before anyone else comes by. And bring that monk over here."

Adso dragged the lay brother over to Bertrand, where the young man fell on his knees, bowed his head and clasped his hands in prayer. "Sir Knight," he pleaded, "show mercy to a man of God."

Bertrand laughed unpleasantly. "A man of God, are you? Look at my face, you snivelling worm."

The lay brother forced himself to look up at Bertrand's mutilations.

"This is what the servants of your God did to me, and worse to others."

"Please don't kill me," the young man begged, tears streaming down his cheeks.

"I'll not kill you," Bertrand said, drawing his dagger. "You'll take a message back to your masters, but you'll look like me when you do it."

Bertrand stepped forward as the lay brother fell to one side and tried to scramble away.

"Hold him!" Bertrand ordered.

Adso hesitated. He felt stirrings of pity for the boy. He was about the same age as John had been when Adso had helped him and Beatrice escape from the massacre at Béziers. Adso grabbed the boy and hauled him to his feet, but he held a hand out to Bertrand. "'Ow much revenge d'you want?"

Bertrand looked up at his friend, his knife close to the terrified boy's face. "I want all I can get. Oddo's Falcons killed a lot of good men in the name of the god this blubbering baby worships."

"But 'e's still just a blubbering baby, and I don't 'old with killing babies. Besides, 'oo's going to pay attention to one maimeded lay brother? I've got a better idea for a message."

Bertrand nodded uncertainly and lowered his dagger.

Adso dropped the boy, drew his sword and strode over to the dead knight. In one swift movement, he grabbed the body by the hair, hauled it up and cut off the head.

Holding the gruesome prize in his left hand, Adso turned to Bertrand. "Cut up this one 'til he looks as good as you, then wrap 'im in 'is surcoat. The boy can take 'im to Oddo with the message that this's what'll 'appen to 'im and all 'is Falcons." Adso swung his arm and the head arced over to Bertrand, bounced once and came to rest at his feet.

Bertrand stared down at the bloody object for a long time. Then he laughed. "I would give much to see Oddo's face when he unwraps our gift." He looked at the wide-eyed lay brother. "This is your lucky day, boy," he said, before crouching down to do his work.

The boy stumbled over to Adso. "Thank you, sir. Thank you," he whined, grasping Adso's hand.

Adso shook himself free. "What's your name, boy? You're not from 'round 'ere."

"No, Sir. My name's Philip. I'm from up north—Orleans."

"Well, you and all your kind should've stayed there. But listen, what's the tale from Lavaur?"

Philip's eyes widened even more. "You haven't heard?"

"Course not, else I wouldn't 'ave asked you. What 'appened?"

"Lavaur fell yesterday."

"Not a surprise," Adso said thoughtfully. "It weren't the strongest fortress. What of the defenders?"

Philip dropped his head and mumbled something.

"Speak up."

"De Montfort ordered every knight found in the town hanged from the walls."

"How many?"

"Eighty."

Adso sighed. The waste of eighty knights defending a worthless town against overwhelming odds made him angry. With those same men in the hills, he could have made Oddo pay a heavy price.

"What of the Perfects? Were there many in the town?"

"Four hundred," Philip said softly.

"Four 'undred!" Adso exclaimed. "And…?" he asked, already knowing the answer.

"They walked willingly into the flames. All except for the Lord of Lavaur's sister, Giraude. She was cast, screaming and weeping, down a well and stoned to death."

Adso cursed under his breath, the memory of Beatrice and the others climbing the pyre outside Minerve was vivid in his mind.

Bertrand finished his work, stood up and carried the mutilated head over to the body. He removed the Falcon surcoat and wrapped the head in it.

"We must be quick now," he said to the knights who had collected the dead men's weapons and added them to the donkeys' loads.

"The legate, Arnaud Aumery," Adso asked Philip, "was 'e at Lavaur?"

"He was," the lay brother replied, "but he left this morning."

"Coming this way?" Adso asked hopefully.

"No," Philip said. "He goes north to help raise an army to fight the heathens in Al-Andalus."

"Does 'e?" Adso said, pensively. "Not content with one war, 'e wishes to begin another."

"Come on," Bertrand said, thrusting the bloody bundle at Philip. "Do you know who Oddo is?"

"Of course. Everyone knows the leader of the Falcons."

"Good. Then take this to him and tell him that it pays for one of the men he mutilated at Bram."

Philip took the bundle and, with a final nod to Adso, scuttled off down the road back toward Lavaur.

"We'd best be going," Bertrand said. "I want to be far from here by the time Oddo receives his gift."

Leading the donkeys and the knight's horse, the small party headed into the hills. Adso brought up the rear, occupied with his own thoughts. The mention of Al-Andalus had made him think of John and Isabella. He had wished them goodbye almost a year ago outside Minerve and he hoped their search for knowledge was going well. Some people were born to learn, others to fight. John and Isabella belonged to the former group. It made sense that they had escaped the war while Adso remained. Unfortunately, it looked as if the war was expanding. If Aumery was planning on heading south with an army, John and Isabella's refuge in Al-Andalus might not turn out to be as secure as they had hoped.

John

Cordova
May

The drop of sweat seemed to fall in slow motion through the hot air. Silently it splashed on the open book in John's lap, soaked into the paper and vanished. John groaned and looked up. "What must the heat be like in summer? How do people manage? I feel as if I'm a wet cloth that is constantly being wrung out."

Laughing, Isabella reached a hand into the fountain pool behind them and splashed her compnion with the cool water.

"Be careful of the book," John said, joining in her laughter "But that does feel good." He placed the book to one side, removed the scarf from around his throat, soaked it in the fountain and squeezed it out over his head.

"Remember," Isabella said, "the Moors came from a land even hotter than this. They know how to live here. They plant lots of shade trees and build fountains and high, cool rooms, and they don't go wandering about in the hottest part of the day."

"You're right," John acknowledged. "I do like it here despite the heat, and the Moorish robes *are* comfortable. Even after all this time, though, I still feel out of place. I get tired of being stared at. Fair hair and skin are not very common sights down here."

"You're too sensitive. Everyone's friendly and there's no war going on like there was back home."

"But when we passed through Aragon last winter, all the talk was of reconquering this land from the Moors."

"True, but I doubt King Pedro will ever be strong enough to expand Aragon much to the south."

"Maybe he'll go north then," John said. "He can't be happy about de Montfort and Oddo thumping about in his backyard. Perhaps he'll invade Languedoc."

"We certainly met a lot of Good Christians in Aragon," Isabella observed.

The mention of Isabella's birthplace prompted John to change the subject and bring up something that had been bothering him for a while. "In all our time in Aragon, you never made an attempt to find any relatives."

"I told you"—Isabella spoke sharply and her brow furrowed with irritation, but John detected an underlying nervousness in her tone—"my father was killed in 1195 at the Battle of Alarcos when I was only two years old. My mother was sick and dying, and sent me to live in Toulouse. You know the rest."

"But there must be other relatives—aunts, uncles, cousins—still alive in Aragon. We could have found someone."

"Well, we didn't," Isabella snapped. "I wanted to see the land I was born in, but I have no interest in the people."

"All right!" John held up his hands in mock surrender. "We're just a pair of orphans with no pasts."

Isabella relaxed. "And another thing. If you *really* want to fit in," she scolded John gently, "don't call the wars that the Christians fight in Al-Andalus a reconquest. This land has been Moorish for over five hundred years. The Christians have only been in Aragon for two hundred. The people the Moors took it from are not the same people who are trying to conquer it now."

"You always see the other side of things," John said, relieved that Isabella was no longer upset.

"Because there always *is* another side."

John laughed and splashed water in her direction. "Sometimes I think you just argue for the sake of it!"

"And you don't?" Isabella asked in mock amazement.

"No," John said seriously. "I'm always right."

Isabella sent a large wave to soak John's back.

"Watch the book," John repeated, grabbing it off the edge of the fountain.

"Well don't be so arrogant," Isabella said with a smile. "How's the drawing coming along, anyway?"

"Same as always," John opened the book and showing Isabella what he was working on. "I can't get it right."

The sketch showed the view before the, the grove of orange trees with the ornate wall of the mosque behind. On the right, the tall minaret from which the faithful were called to prayer five times a day soared into the empty sky. John had obviously spent a lot of effort on the trees, carefully drawing leaves and individual branches, and on the ornate carvings around the door of the mosque.

"It's very good," Isabella said. "You've spent a lot of time on the details."

"No, it's not very good!" John said despondently. "The details are easy, they just take some care, but look at the view." He swept his arm wide. "It's real, we can get up and walk into it. I want to capture *that* in my drawings."

"Maybe it's not possible. The page you draw on is flat. You *can't* walk into it. How could a drawing show that?"

"I don't know, but I'm certain there's a way. As soon as I find Lucius' *Perspectiva*, I'll know. Umar and Beatrice both said the secrets to the way I want to draw are in that book." John paused thoughtfully. "Peter also said what I was trying was impossible. He said God didn't want me to draw a different way."

"Whether it's possible or not, I'm certain it's not because God wants or doesn't want you to succeed." Isabella trailed her fingers through the water. "Where do you think Peter is now?"

"I often wonder that," John said. "I suppose he's still with Aumery and de Montfort, fighting for the crusade. I wonder about the others as well. Is Adso still fighting against the crusaders? Is William still singing? I miss them."

"I miss our home. I wonder if the crusade will ever end and let us go back and live in peace." Isabella sighed. "But sitting here being miserable won't help, and we have to find your book first. Speaking of which, I think it's probably time to meet the guide who's going to take us to the library."

In the weeks since they had crossed from Aragon into Al-Andalus, John had found the mention of Umar's name in the right places had brought them much help. It had led to this meeting today with a man named Shabaka, who was to take them to the library at Madinat al-Zahra. John glanced up at the sun, high overhead. "You're right. He must be in the mosque by now. I'll go and meet him."

John stood and tucked the drawing book into the satchel he'd slung over his loose robes. "I won't be long." He walked through the orange grove, removed his shoes and entered the mosque.

As always, the view inside took his breath away. A forest of more than a thousand marble pillars, surmounted by intricately carved double-round arches, stretched away into the distance. The walls on either side of John were covered with complex patterns, many inlaid in gold. The whole interior was lit by an ethereal blue light from the glass windows in the ceiling.

John regretted for the hundredth time that women were not allowed into the main body of the mosque, and that Isabella could not see this for herself. He struggled to put an image of this wonderful place into his memory so that one day, he would at least be able to draw it for her. It was difficult to hold an image in his mind—the memory cloister that Beatrice had taught him was designed to hold words and books, not pictures—but John had worked hard and thought he had managed.

"Of all the thousand mosques in Cordova, the Mezquita is the most magnificent, no?"

John turned to see a tall man standing beside him. He was dressed in a typical Moorish robe, but his skin was so black it almost shone in the pale light. John had trouble guessing how old the man was. His skin was unwrinkled, but there were flecks of grey in his short, tightly curled hair. He stood very straight and bore himself regally, but a smile played around his eyes and seemed ready to explode and engulf his whole face. John had never seen anyone like him before. He couldn't help but stare.

The man's smile spread, exposing a set of remarkably white teeth. "You were not told to expect a black man?" he asked.

"Yes, I was," John said hurriedly, afraid that he might have offended him. "It's just that I've never met anyone *so* black before."

The man burst out laughing, a deep sound that seemed to come from the depths of his chest and echoed through the mosque. "I am used to being stared at," he said, holding out his hand. "I am Shabaka, from the lands of Nubia, to the south of Egypt. We were burned black by the desert sun in the far distant past when the great Nubian kings conquered and ruled Egypt as the famous black pharaohs. I am named for one of them. We were rulers then, but now Nubia is merely a poverty-stricken land and a source of slaves prized by the Arabs for their strength and the novelty of their appearance."

John was struck by the angry passion in Shabaka's voice. He pitied anyone who became this man's enemy.

"You must be the northerner, Johan, who wishes to see the library at Madinat al-Zahra."

"John," John corrected, taking Shabaka's hand. "Yes, I wish to see the library. You speak very good Latin."

Shabaka flashed his dazzling smile. "I was taken as a slave and sold to a rich merchant when I was but a child. He treated me well and gave me freedom on his deathbed. I travelled much with him and have continued since. I find speaking many languages a useful talent for a traveller, and Latin is understood by many of you northerners. I am pleased to meet a friend of Umar. How is he?"

"I am afraid Umar is dead. He died at Minerve a year past."

Shabaka turned and began strolling between the pillars. John walked beside him. He was wondering if he should say something else when Shabaka broke the silence. "I am sorry to hear your news. Umar was a very wise man. But he had visited this earth for a long time. I hope he rests with his god." Shabaka stopped and faced John. "Why do you wish to visit the library?"

"Umar told me about it, and there is a particular book I'm looking for."

"I hope it is still there," Shabaka said. "The library is not the great place it once was, but Nasir will know."

"Nasir is the librarian?"

"He is, although I fear he will be the last."

"Why the last?"

"I will tell you the story of Nasir and the great library of Madinat al-Zahra as we travel, but we must go now. It is a long journey."

"Yes," John replied, taking one final, longing look at the pillars of the mosque.

Outside, the sun was blinding, but John managed to lead the way to the fountain where Isabella waited. After introductions, Shabaka led them out of the orange grove to a narrow alley where three donkeys were tied.

"They are not the most sociable of beasts," Shabaka said as they mounted, "but I prefer that their four legs and not my two do the walking. It is five miles to Madinat al-Zahra and the afternoon is hot."

Peter

Cîteaux
June

"Peace. Pray. Work." Softly, Peter repeated the three words that now ruled his life. It was mid-afternoon and he was sitting in the sun on the rough wall that surrounded the monks' cloister for a few moments of solitude before the None bell called him to prayer. Behind him was the abbey church and on the other sides of the cloister the monks' dormitory, refectory and storage rooms. Farther away lay the work buildings—the barn, the fulling shed and the tannery—and in the distance the monks' fields, either planted with various crops or filled with placidly grazing cattle and sheep. It was the picture of order and prosperity and, in some respects, the past year had been the happiest of Peter's life.

For the first time since he had left the priory of St. Anne in Toulouse, Peter felt he was a part of something. The monastery at Cîteaux was set up like a family; the abbot was the father and the monks all brothers. Outside the community, they owed allegiance to no one but God. It was a stable world and Peter liked that.

As Arnaud Aumery had intended, Peter had studied the practices and responsibilities of an ordained monk, but he had learned much more. The Cistercian community at Cîteaux existed separately from the world, but that did not mean they were unworldly. They followed the rules of St. Benedict: they lived in peace with each other; their day was organized around eight visits to the church where they prayed, said Mass and sang every three hours from midnight—Matins, Lauds, Prime, Terce, Sext, None, Vespers and Compline; between, they worked, ate, slept and contemplated God.

Peter found the pattern comforting and he thanked Aumery daily in his prayers for sending him here, but a part of him was dissatisfied. He could live here comfortably and, perhaps one day, aspire to be abbot of the community, but he couldn't shake the idea that all he would be doing was hiding. Peter had tasted power, both the seductive thrill of wielding it at

Aumery's side and the gut-wrenching fear of being dominated by it at Oddo's hands. Much as he enjoyed life here, he wanted more.

"Good day, Brother Peter." Peter looked up to see Armand Gauthier coming toward him across the cloister. Gauthier was Cîteaux's provost and in charge of the day-to-day running of the community while Abbot Aumery was away at the crusade. He was not an imposing man to look at—he was short and his ears stuck out rather alarmingly—but there was something about his quiet manner that commanded attention and respect.

"And good day to you, Father Gauthier."

Gauthier sat down on the wall beside Peter. "It is almost a year since you joined us."

Peter nodded. "I have been very happy here and I have learned much."

"But now you must leave?"

Peter looked questioningly at Gauthier.

"Oh, I am not throwing you out," Gauthier said with a smile. "You have fit in well and would be welcome to stay and make your life here, but I sense a restlessness. For example, you say you *have been* happy here, not you *are* happy here."

Peter returned Gauthier's smile but stayed silent.

"I know that Abbot Aumery wished you to come here to learn, and you have done that well. Is it time for you to return?"

Peter hesitated. "Perhaps. I don't know." Aumery had talked of possibly sending Peter on to Rome after his time at Cîteaux, but no word had arrived.

"You seem troubled," Gauthier said gently.

Peter closed his eyes and sighed. Gauthier was right. As his time at Cîteaux had progressed, Peter had begun to wonder if his life was on the right path. "I have begun to doubt," he said.

Gauthier said nothing and Peter opened his eyes. The provost nodded encouragement. Something in the calm eyes of this man made Peter want to open up.

"I had a vision," Peter began, thinking back to the terrifying evening with his friends in Toulouse. "I saw Death stand behind every one of my friends, and I witnessed the corruption of one who was very dear to me." Peter felt a stab of anger at the way Isabella had rejected him for John, but he pushed it back. "I knew I must dedicate myself to God and He led me to Arnaud Aumery. I have been fortunate to be a part of the Holy Crusade against the Cathar heretics, and my heart soared when I saw the Perfects climb the funeral pyre at Minerve. But I have seen other things too: the devastation of the countryside I passed though on my travels, the suffering the crusade has caused innocent people and the hatred."

"But there is more?" Gauthier asked softly, as Peter lapsed into silence.

"Yes," Peter said, lowering his gaze. If he wanted this gentle man's help, he couldn't hold anything back. "There is a man, Oddo, who commands a group of mercenary soldiers. The man is a callous brute, a devil I would say were he not doing God's work. I hate him, I fear him." Peter closed his eyes and he was back in the square at Béziers, awed by Oddo's power and forced humiliatingly to kiss his blood-stained axe. "But I envy him his strength and power."

The words came out in a rush, and Peter was surprised at the immediate relief that came with confessing his doubts. He took a breath and continued.

"Father Aumery taught me that true power comes from God through the Church and that Oddo's earthly power is nothing compared to that. I am grateful to be a part of God's work. I will go to Rome or I will return to the crusade if that is what Father Aumery wishes, but, recently, a tiny voice in my head has begun to say, 'You do this for yourself, Peter. The power of God is not something you should seek because you envy the likes of Oddo.' What should I do?"

"The way forward is not easy and the Devil puts many stumbling blocks and false signs in our path." Gauthier hesitated a long time before he continued. "Let me tell you how I came to the Church. My father was a man of business in the city of Dijon and required that I follow him into a life of commerce. For the most part I was content with that lot. I had many friends, and played and travelled without a care. One morning, as I staggered home the worse for too much wine and revelry the night before, I stumbled over a pile of rags in an alley. As I struggled to my feet, the rags moved and I saw it was a leper. I don't know what he was doing in the city and not in one of the colonies—perhaps he was put there by God. In any case, the man's fingers were mere stumps and his face was half eaten away by his affliction. As I recoiled in shock, the man looked at me. His eyes were the most piercing blue I have ever seen, and they seemed to look into my very soul. As long as those eyes were on me, I was incapable of movement. Then what was left of the man's mouth moved. I suppose I expected him to beg for alms, but he didn't. The leper said to me, 'Bless you, my son.' Then he closed his eyes and I was released. I fled home, but I could forget neither the eyes nor the blessing. If a man in such a hideous predicament as that leper could find it in his heart to bless me, then how superficial was my faith, and what was my comfortable life full of material advantages worth?"

Gauthier smiled at Peter. "It took much agonizing, but I decided that I would dedicate my life to helping the poor. I joined the Cistercian brotherhood, and now my days are spent redistributing the profits from our lands and other enterprises as alms to the poor of the district."

"But your vision was simple," Peter said. "Christ, through the poor leper, asked you to help the afflicted and you do. My vision was much less clear."

"But was my vision so clear?" Gauthier's expression became serious. "From the many possible ways I could have helped the poor, I chose an easy route. As you have discovered, we live a simple yet comfortable life here. Yes, we work hard and distribute the products to ease the lot of the less fortunate, but sometimes, as I lie in the darkness awaiting the Lauds bell, I wonder if I deliberately misunderstood my experience and if God is displeased with me."

"What else could you have done?" Peter asked.

"Perhaps God was asking me to minister to the poor souls in a leper colony."

Peter shuddered. To voluntarily go into the midst of all the wrecked bodies of a colony and risk becoming infected yourself—it didn't bear contemplating.

"I can see you are as horrified by the idea as I was," Gauthier said. "So, did I choose the easy course and ignore the real message?"

"I don't know," Peter said helplessly.

"Of course you don't." Gauthier's smile returned. "And neither do I. You see, visions, dreams, messages from God—they are never simple. Perhaps only a very few of us make the right choices."

"What could my vision mean?" Peter asked.

Gauthier shrugged. "That is for you to see, not me, but one day it will become clear. In the meantime, all you can do is live by the scriptures and obey your superiors in the Church."

Peter supposed Gauthier was right. But if he was to devote himself to achieving Aumery's goals, he had another question. "Do you believe the Grail that Christ drank from at the Last Supper exists?"

"I believe it existed. Whether it still does is something else."

"Father Aumery believes that it does still exist, and the Cathar heretics either possess it or have knowledge of its whereabouts. It is their treasure," Peter explained. "He also believes that the Grail, in the right hands, has the power to revitalize the Church's mission, and hasten the Judgment and bring about the Last Days. He has made it his quest to find the Grail and I am a part of that."

"And you are not certain that this is the path your visions mean you to take?" Gauthier asked quietly.

Peter nodded.

"I cannot tell you what to do. Personally, I do not believe that the Grail, if it still exists, is a magic answer to the Church's difficulties. I believe the answer lies in here." Gauthier patted his chest over his heart. "Christ taught that every one of us must find a way to God on his own, and that only when enough of us have done so will the Day of Judgment come. I do not think he would place in the world such an easy answer as the Grail. We must each work on finding salvation in our own ways.

"But," Gauthier continued with a shrug, "who can say what God's purpose for you is? Perhaps this search you are undertaking will have a consequence that you cannot anticipate, a consequence that has nothing to do with the Grail or even Abbot Aumery."

"So what should I do?"

"The best you can," Gauthier said. "When you are given a task by your senior in the Church, carry it out to the best of your abilities, but always be open to hearing God's voice."

The None bell sounded and the pair stood.

"Thank you," Peter said.

"I think it is well we had this conversation," Gauthier said, "and I hope I have been able to help with your doubts. However, my reason for seeking you out was more mundane." He reached inside his habit and produced a small elongated package. "This arrived for you with a traveller this morning. I believe it is from Abbot Aumery."

Peter took the package and examined it. It was wrapped in a piece of vellum and tied with twine. There wasn't time to look at it now—cowled monks were hurrying past to prayer. Peter tucked the package into his habit and followed Gauthier into the abbey church.

* * *

Peter sat on the church steps and untied the string on his package. All through the prayers and psalms of None, he had been aware of its bulk against his waist. Why had Aumery sent it? The abbot had written Peter only two letters over the past year, inquiring about his progress. Both had been terse and had offered no information on the progress of the crusade or Aumery's search for the Grail.

As the final twist of string came away, Peter removed the vellum wrapping and looked at the scroll inside. It was heavily stained and very old. The edges were ragged and black, as if it had once been in a fire. As Peter turned it over gently in his hands, he noticed writing on the back of the vellum wrapping. He smoothed it out to find a letter from Aumery, longer than the others he had received.

Greetings, Peter, from your brother in God, Arnaud.

By now you must be nearing the end of your apprenticeship with Father Gauthier and the brothers at Cîteaux. I wish I could say the same of our task here, but, despite the best labours of de Montfort and his knights, and pyres outside every town, the vile heresy of Catharism continues to hold the gullible in its evil sway. So we must gird ourselves and continue unquestioningly to undertake God's divine wish. However, by God's grace, the quest of which we spoke before your departure, I believe, progresses on apace.

You will see that the scroll I sent you is a map, or I should say a fragment of a map.

Peter placed Aumery's letter aside and unrolled the singed scroll. It was indeed a map, but not like any Peter had ever seen. It was divided into land, with sketched mountains, rivers and towns, and sea, dotted with scattered islands and tiny ships, but it represented no part of the known world that Peter recognized. Not that Peter was an expert, but one of the books in the convent where he had grown up had contained a map. The sister who explained it to him and John had pointed out various places of interest: Jerusalem and the crusader lands at the centre; the irregular boot shape of Italy with the Holy City of Rome; Greece; and Al-Andalus. None of it had looked anything like the map he held now.

The scroll was about a foot long and half that in width. The land was arranged in long strips, separated and surrounded by narrow seas or wide rivers. The towns were represented by small, square fortresses and were joined by thin red lines that Peter assumed were roads. Latin script beside the towns appeared to give names, but those he could read—Trimondium, Brindisium, Appollonia and Dyrrachium—meant nothing to him. Puzzled, Peter turned back to the letter.

I rescued this from a fire in Lavaur where, by God's grace, we burned four hundred heretics. The Perfects attempted to burn a collection of scrolls and books and had, in the main, succeeded. A few fragments, including what you hold in your hands, survived.

I do not know what part of the world the map represents, but I am convinced of its relevance to our quest. As you will notice, the town or city of Trimondium is circled in a hand later than the original map. Since the map was obviously of great import to the heretics, it is possible that this marked location may have bearing on what we seek. Whether or not it is there or was at some time in the past, I believe it worth investigating.

My belief is supported by the words of a Perfect I held back from the flames of Lavaur. Using the instruments of the Holy Inquisition, I questioned her in some detail. She told me little before she died, but one thing she blurted out in her agony, as I examined her about the map, was "the eighth of seven hills."

On the surface, it is nonsense—there cannot be an eighth of seven things—but as you know, Rome itself is built on seven hills, so I take what she said to suggest that the answer to our quest, or at least a signpost to the next road we must follow, can be found there.

Therefore, I charge you to take this fragment to Rome and search the great library in the Holy City. In addition to books, you will find maps of many strange and diverse sorts, and some may contain clues as to this one.

If you are fortunate enough to discover the location of this city of Trimondium, I leave it to your judgment whether to go there to pursue the quest or return to me and report.

I should go to Rome myself, but the Moors of Al-Andalus are becoming restless. I believe a crusade is to be called to protect the Christian lands there, and I must play my part.

I also do God's work here in pursuing the forbidden books the heretics keep in their fortresses and in their minds. Piece by piece I collect fragments of knowledge that I hope God will see fit to place in a larger picture. There is one particularly damnable volume, an odious forgery supposed in heretic circles to be a gospel written by Christ himself. I have clues, but their meaning slips through my fingers like water from a fountain. I must persevere in many God-given tasks and, thus, I entrust this quest to you.

Go with God.

Arnaud Aumery

Peter put down the letter. His heart was pounding. He looked at the map and noticed that there was indeed a thin line drawn around Trimondium. Did it mean the Grail was hidden there? It seemed unlikely and, even if Trimondium *was* the location, he had no idea where the city was located. But he would find out. And what about "the eighth of seven hills?" Was it anything more than the gibberish of a tortured and dying Perfect?

Peter stood and rewrapped the scroll in Aumery's letter, his hands shaking with excitement. *This* was his chance. He was going to Rome, the centre of all the power in Christendom.

"Find the eighth hill."

The voice rang out in the quiet evening air. Peter spun around to see who was speaking to him, but he was alone. "Who's there?" he demanded, but there was no answer from the empty silence around him.

"Find the eighth hill," the voice repeated. It was a man's voice, clear and deeply resonant, and it seemed to come from all around.

Peter spun wildly, fear mounting. "Who is it?" he demanded desperately, but again there was no reply. He sat down heavily. What was happening to him now? Sitting on the steps of this church in Cîteaux, with his heart pounding in his chest, he couldn't help but remember his vision in Toulouse. But this was different. He wasn't terrified now; he was completely confused. A voice was speaking to him, but whose voice was it? A saint, Christ, God—the Devil?

Peter shivered. He closed his eyes and listened hard but there was only silence. The voice was gone. Gradually, Peter's heartbeat slowed to normal. Someone or something was giving him instructions. He had no idea who, or to what purpose, but did that matter? He was going to Rome to find out what the odd map meant, and a part of that search would be to find any clues that might fit with the statement made by the Perfect. For the time being, at least, the voice and Aumery seemed to want the same thing.

Peter stood and moved slowly toward his cell. Maybe, he thought hopefully, the voice was God, beginning to make His wishes clearer. Perhaps he would no longer have to agonize over what his visions meant. In any case, there was nothing he could do except wait and see if the voice returned. In the meantime, he had a long journey ahead.

PART ONE

Adso's Story

Betrayal

Rouairoux
June, 1212

"There's too many of us," Adso said. Squatting on the edge of a sloping forest clearing, he was sharpening his dagger on a stone. The morning sun had just reached the tops of the surrounding trees and the day was beginning to warm. Bertrand sat beside him, polishing his beloved Saladin. "Sooner or later, they'll find us. We can't move fast any more. Look." Adso swept his arm to encompass the clearing. "We're more like a small town than a military camp! It takes us 'alf a day just to break camp and move anywhere."

The twenty knights of the previous year had grown to a community of over a hundred. Word had spread about the band of knights who fought the hated crusaders from the security of the mountain caves and forests. Refugees sought them out and begged to join. Bertrand rarely refused, but the problem was that many of the newcomers, while eager, were not military men. Adso seemed to spend most of his time training men in the basics of handling a sword, instead of planning and carrying out raids.

And he was right about the clearing not looking like a military camp. Ragged tents and lean-tos were scattered about and equipment lay everywhere. Men who didn't possess a helmet, shield or piece of chain mail lounged about beside smoking fires. There were even a small number of women and children who had accompanied their men into the forests.

"We're deep enough in the forest," Bertrand said. "No knights'll come up here—it's too steep for a man in armour on horseback. Besides, the more soldiers we have, the more damage we can do."

"I'd agree, if we 'ad soldiers, but most of them that you welcomed with open arms last winter wouldn't last an 'eartbeat against any of Oddo's Falcons. All they're good for is finishing off the wounded and plundering the dead."

"We'll train them," Bertrand said, grimly. "One day, we'll have an army that'll be able to take on the Falcons and defeat them. That'll weaken de

Montfort, and all the minor lords who cravenly bow a knee to him will come over to our cause. Then we can defeat the crusade and drive it out of Languedoc."

"I'd like nothing better," Adso said, "but you're dreaming if you think this lot'll do it. They'll never be an army"—Adso scanned the shambles of the camp—"but even if they could be whipped into shape, we've tried taking on de Montfort on equal terms. Remember, it was your idea to stay and fight in Bram, and look what that got you—a face to terrify children."

Bertrand grunted.

"This army idea makes me nervous," Adso went on. "I felt much better when we were a leaner group of just soldiers. We 'ad only ourselves to worry 'bout then."

Bertrand remained silent and concentrated on polishing his crossbow.

Adso shook his head. The changes in Bertrand over the past year were hard to take. Before Bram, he had been a simple fighting man, good at what he did and, for the most part, sensible at judging when the odds were in his favour. Now he was a cold-blooded killer, interested only in how many crusaders he could slaughter. Not that Adso thought that was a bad thing, but Bertrand's obsession clouded his judgment. This attempt to build a large army was senseless and would only lead to trouble for all of them. He would rather take fifteen or twenty of the best fighters and abandon the rest. They would kill Falcons, but one or two at a time instead of trying to take them all on at once.

Adso complained, but he stayed with Bertrand out of loyalty. "Well, you stay 'ere and dream of a mighty battle. I'm fed up playing nursemaid to this lot. I'm off to Les Cardines to see if there's any news. Per'aps I'll 'ear of some crusader army we can attack."

Bertrand grunted again, but said nothing.

"I'll be back this evening," Adso said, standing and sheathing his dagger. He walked over to his lean-to, set up in the trees away from the camp. He picked up his leather tunic and a satchel containing some bread and a pouch of berries and set off down the slope.

The slope wasn't steep enough, despite what Bertrand thought—that was something else that bothered Adso. In the early days, they had lived in caves cut into the almost inaccessible sides of remote, rugged gorges, and they had moved every few days. Now they camped in pleasant forest glades and stayed for weeks on end. It was only a matter of time before they were discovered. Too many people knew where they were.

But Adso couldn't talk to Bertrand any more: the man had become hard and unmovable. Adso suspected that his old friend's injuries went deeper than the scars on his face.

Adso reached the valley bottom, where the horses and donkeys were kept. They had quite a number now, ranging from pack animals to high-spirited war horses. Not that they were much use in the forested mountains, but they were part of Bertrand's dream. Adso picked a donkey, more surefooted and reliable than a horse in this country and much less likely to attract attention, and set off toward the hamlet of Les Cardines.

* * *

Les Cardines was a collection of half a dozen rough houses scattered along a dirt track on the valley bottom beside a tributary of the Arn River. The families who lived here existed by running sheep and goats on the high pastures and selling the meat and wool at the markets in the larger towns farther down the valley. It was a hard life in the winter, but in the summer, when the hunting was good and a few crops grew on patches of ground beside the river, life was agreeable.

The recognized leader of the community was a thin shepherd called Jacques. He was the only person from Les Cardines who had ever made the forty-mile journey to Béziers, and he commanded immense respect because of his stories of the great market, large stone houses and vast churches he had seen there.

Jacques was neither a strong Catholic nor a Cathar—his confused religious beliefs were more a leftover from an ancient pagan past, when people worshipped trees and forest sprites—but he resented the presence of the northern crusader knights in his land and had been shocked at the destruction of Béziers. He seemed happy enough to pass on any information he collected on the movements of knights along the roads through the local market towns in exchange for the small share of the booty that Bertrand gave him.

Adso didn't much like Jacques—his eyes were shifty and his only loyalty was to his extended family in Les Cardines—but he was useful, and as long as Bertrand kept paying him he would continue supplying information.

"Jacques around?" Adso asked the woman carding wool outside the largest hovel in the hamlet. She wore a long, brown woollen dress, frayed at the hem and smeared down the front with the grease stains from many meals.

The woman looked up and spat into the dirt beside her. "Pig's gone to Rouairoux," she said.

"Why Rouairoux? 'Tisn't market day."

"Didn't say." The card paddles in her hands, rough wooden boards with coarse metal teeth sticking out of one side, flashed back and forth as she untangled a clump of wool and shook out any pieces of dirt. "Reckon 'e's got a whore there. The pig's al'ays 'ad ideas 'bove 'isself since 'e went to the city."

Adso was continually amazed at the narrowness of these village people. It had been at least ten years since Jacques had made his one and only trip out of the valley to Béziers, yet it still made him the most important man in the place and created resentment that he might see himself as better than the rest.

"Them things you give 'im don't 'elp," the woman went on sullenly. "'E puts on a rusty piece o' chain mail and thinks 'e's the bloody Count Raymond 'isself."

"When'll 'e be back?" Adso asked, hoping to end the conversation quickly and escape.

The woman shrugged. "'Morrow. Next day. Who cares? I'll tell you this, though." The woman looked up at Adso with a malevolent gleam in her eyes. "'E'll pay for 'is fun when 'e does get back."

"Thank you," Adso said as he retreated along the track to where his donkey was waiting. Now he had a choice. Waiting in Les Cardines for the wayward Jacques to return didn't seem like an attractive option. He could head back up to the camp, but then he would have achieved nothing, and the camp, and Bertrand's mood, annoyed him. The third option seemed best: head the six miles down to Rouairoux and find Jacques. It wouldn't likely be difficult. Rouairoux was bigger than Les Cardines, but it was a lot smaller than Béziers or Carcassonne. Besides, a visit to a larger town with decent ale and food would be welcome. Bertrand could wait a day or two.

Whistling tunelessly, Adso mounted and rode down the valley.

* * *

Adso drained the last of his second mug of ale, wiped the residue from his lips with his sleeve and burped satisfactorily. The mutton had been stringy, the sauce watery and the bread coarse, but the ale had been strong and dark, and all in all it was the best meal he had eaten in weeks. He debated ordering another mug of ale, but the afternoon was getting on. He had travelled at a leisurely pace from Les Cardines and lingered in the tavern. If he was going to find Jacques today, he should move. There would be plenty of time to relax later.

Standing up, Adso dropped a few coins on the table and smiled at the serving girl, a fair-haired northener with an attractive turned-up nose. She smiled back. Perhaps he would offer to buy her a mug of ale this evening.

Quest

The cobbled square outside the tavern was much larger than the sixty or so rough stone houses of Rouairoux would suggest was needed. But on market day it would be a bustling place full of crude stalls selling everything from fine woollen blankets to live goats. The air would be rich with every imaginable animal and human smell, and alive with the shouts of the vendors and the bargaining of the villagers come to town from the surrounding hills. And, once a year after shearing, there was the wool fair, when merchants came from as far away as Toulouse and Montpellier to trade in live sheep, fleece, spun wool and finished clothing and blankets. For two weeks, Rouairoux had the life of a much larger town, and it was hardly possible to fight your way across the square or hold a conversation above the shouts and bleats. But when Adso blinked in the brightness outside the tavern, the square was all but deserted. That was why he saw Jacques so easily.

The man Adso had come to find was sneaking out of a small house across the square. "So that's where you keep your fancy woman," Adso muttered under his breath. He considered shouting to attract Jacques' attention, but didn't want to draw too much notice. As Jacques slunk into a narrow alley, Adso set off across the square.

The alley stank. The house on one side was backed by a pen where a couple of large, semi-wild, hairy pigs wallowed. One lunged viciously toward Adso as he passed close to the low stone wall that hemmed it in. On the other side, four skinny goats stood tethered to a tree. A filthy, naked child sat in the tree, idly throwing pebbles at the goats.

"Jacques," Adso said as soon as he got close to the man.

At the sound of his name, Jacques jumped a full foot in the air and spun around. For a moment, Adso thought he was either going to flee or faint.

"It's all right," he said reassuringly as he walked up to Jacques. "I'll tell no one 'bout your woman 'ere, though your good lady wife does seem to 'ave suspicions of 'er own without any 'elp from me."

Jacques' eyes darted from side to side.

"Don't worry," Adso said, stepping forward and putting a comforting arm around the man. As he did so, he felt the bulge of a purse and heard the muffled clink of coins. He reached down and hefted the bag hanging from Jacques' waist.

"Got some good coin there. Where'd it come from?"

"Done some business," Jacques said sullenly.

"Good business, by the feel of it. What's paying these days?"

"Sold some sheep."

"That's a lot of sheep."

"Not just mine." Jacques grew calmer as he got into his explanation. "And them crusaders pay good money for nice fatty mutton."

Adso slipped his dagger out of its sheath and held it in front of Jacques' face. "You wouldn't be playing both sides of the board, would you, Jacques?"

"Course not!" Jacques shook his head emphatically. "You know how I hate them crusaders for what they did to Béziers. But you can't blame me for trying to make some honest coin from them."

Adso nodded. "I suppose not, though I don't know as you'd recognize an 'onest coin if one jumped up and bit you. Just remember—you sell me out and I'll slit your belly open and tie your guts 'round a tree."

Jacques quaked visibly and sweat broke out on his forehead. "I wouldn't sell you out, Adso. You know that."

Adso smiled and put his dagger away while Jacques babbled on.

"But it's lucky I ran into you. I was heading up to see you the morrow. I got news."

"What news?" Adso asked.

"Party of knights—Falcons—is heading down this very road day after morrow."

"How many?"

"Only five, but Oddo'll be one o' them." Jacques tilted his head and leered at Adso. "That should be worth some coin."

"Maybe," Adso said. "'Ow'd you come by this tidbit of information?"

"Were a Falcon drinking here in the tavern last eve. Had a bit much of that fine ale and loosened his tongue to his new drinking companion." Jacques winked dramatically. "Seems he was sent on ahead to arrange some meeting in Narbonne. There's a crusade happening 'cross the mountains and Oddo wants to be a part of it. Good plunder down that way, I've heard. Anyway, that's what the meeting with the archbishop in Narbonne's about. You planning to ambush them?"

"Of course."

"Where 'bout?"

"Usual place," Adso said casually "Back up the road at Valtoret. Thanks for the information."

"What about some payment?"

Adso shook his head. "You'll get paid out of what we take from the knights, as always." He turned and strode down the alley. There went his night in the tavern. He'd have to get the donkey and head out onto the road now. He wouldn't make it all the way back before dark, but Bertrand would be excited at the possibility of ambushing Oddo, however late he heard the news.

Adso also felt a thrill at the thought of finally killing Oddo—the mercenary's death would be a major blow to the crusade—but a tiny worm of doubt wriggled in the back of his mind. Despite Jacques' explanation of where he had acquired his bag of money, Adso was suspicious. He wouldn't put it past the man to sell them out, and the crusaders would pay well to get rid of the knights who were making the roads dangerous for them. One thing was certain, though, wherever they planned the ambush, it wouldn't be at Valtoret. If Jacques *had* betrayed them, the net set to capture them would come up empty.

* * *

"So, we ambush them *before* they get to Valtoret," Adso said. He and Bertrand were sitting hunched together by the dying fire. It was late—the journey back to the camp had been long—but Bertrand had insisted on hearing Jacques' story several times. "That way, even if there's a trap, we'll be long gone before they have a chance to spring it."

"Oddo," Bertrand slurred happily. "I've dreamed of this day ever since his Falcons took a knife to my face!"

"Well, don't get too excited yet. I don't trust Jacques as far as I can throw 'im."

"I don't either," Bertrand said, the teeth in his mutilated mouth gleaming in the firelight, "but if it is a trap, Oddo's the bait. He'll be there and I will kill him. Then I can die a happy man."

"Don't rush into this dying, old friend. I aim to live a good few years yet. But you're right. Oddo's the bait—'e'll be there."

"And so will Saladin and I."

"All right. You sit up all night dreaming of what a wonderful world it'll be with Oddo dead, but I'm going to sleep. We've got a lot of preparation tomorrow and it's a long way to the ambush site. Throw a couple more logs on the fire afore you turn in."

Adso pulled his blanket around his shoulders and lay down. Around him fires crackled and men snored. Somewhere in the darkness a child cried. Adso was glad to see Bertrand so happy, and he would be delighted if Oddo died in two days' time. The plan should work, even if Jacques had betrayed them, but the worm at the back of Adso's brain was still there. Was it too easy?

* * *

Fifteen of Bertrand and Adso's best knights lay hidden on both sides of the trail in the mid-afternoon sun. The land was flatter and more open here than Adso would have liked, so he had pulled the knights in closer to the path and hidden them as best he could behind bushes and trees. All were armed with crossbows, and Adso's hope was that the first volley would kill or disable Oddo and his knights and prevent any escaping on horseback. He hoped Jacques was right about there being only five in the party—many more and the ambushers would be outnumbered and too close to the road to escape back up the hill to where their horses were tethered.

"Come on. Come on." Bertrand was lying beside Adso, pointing his beloved crossbow down the path.

"Patience," Adso counselled. "They'll be 'ere. Don't you go firing off at Oddo afore the whole party is in the trap. We don't want no one escaping."

"They won't escape," Bertrand said.

All yesterday, as they had travelled here and set up the ambush, Bertrand had been as taut as his bow string. It worried Adso. He understood Bertrand's hatred of Oddo, but he knew it was always much better to go into battle dispassionately—you made fewer mistakes. On top of that, Adso's doubt wouldn't go away. Infuriatingly, he couldn't grasp it. Try as he might, he couldn't shake the vague sense that everything was not as it should be, although what specifically was wrong eluded him. He hoped it was just nerves. A soft whistle came from down the path. To anyone else, it sounded like a bird call, but it was a prearranged signal. Oddo was coming. Adso felt Bertrand tense even more beside him. He squeezed himself flat to the ground and watched. He didn't have a crossbow, but he held his unsheathed sword by his side.

It seemed like an age before the five riders came in sight. At the first glimpse, Adso heard Bertrand draw his breath in sharply. The man leading the way was big and prepared for trouble. Like those behind him, he was dressed in full chain mail, complete with a gleaming helmet that covered his face. Each man wore a surcoat with a falcon emblazoned on it, and those behind the leader carried swords. The leader held his war horse's reins lightly in his left hand and clutched the handle of a huge axe in his right. The men continually scanned the surrounding undergrowth, almost nervously, Adso thought. They travelled painfully slowly, and Adso prayed that Bertrand would be able to wait.

As the party approached the point where Bertrand had agreed to trigger the ambush, Adso's worry grew. They were travelling too slowly, even for men expecting trouble, and the more Adso looked, the more nervous they seemed. Oddo and his Falcons had never struck Adso as nervous men before. And there was something about Oddo himself.

Quest

Realization struck Adso like a physical blow. Suddenly he knew why they were travelling so slowly, why they looked so nervous and what was wrong with the man at the front. Oddo was carrying his axe in his right hand.

"It's a trap," he hissed at Bertrand, but he was too late. His last word was drowned out by the thwack of Bertrand's crossbow firing.

The bolt caught the big man full in the chest and catapulted him out of his saddle. Immediately, a flurry of bolts flew through the air. Men yelled and horses screamed as the travelling party dissolved into a chaotic welter of bloody bodies and limbs. Before they could recover, Bertrand's knights were in among them, hacking and stabbing. Bertrand didn't even have a chance to fire off a second bolt before it was all over.

"We got him!" Bertrand exclaimed gleefully as he leaped to his feet and set off toward the carnage. "Leave Oddo," he yelled. "His head's mine."

"Wait," Adso shouted, getting slowly to his knees. "It's not Oddo."

Bertrand either didn't hear him or didn't understand. Adso scanned the surrounding landscape. Everything looked quiet. For a moment, he wondered if perhaps he'd been wrong, but deep down he knew he wasn't. The dead men on the path weren't Oddo and his Falcons. They'd been dressed up to look like them, but they were too nervous, and Oddo was left-handed, not right. Adso narrowed his eyes and peered harder through the sparse trees. Had they been moving slowly so that men travelling off the path could keep up? Bertrand's trap had likely sprung the Falcon's own.

Adso turned back to look at the path. "Bertrand," he called. "It's a trap. We've got to go. Now!"

Bertrand was crouching over the fallen figure of the big man who had been leading the party. He had severed the head and was working on removing the helmet. When he was done, he paused. He stood, the bloody head swinging from his grip, and looked up at Adso. "It's not Oddo," he said.

The crossbow bolt hit Bertrand on one side of his head and exploded out of the other in a spray of blood and bone fragments. Bertrand, still clutching the severed head, slumped to his knees and fell over.

Immediately, other bolts began thudding into the rest of the knights, who were looking around in stunned horror. Men in Falcon surcoats were pounding toward the path, screaming and waving swords and axes. Six or seven of Bertrand's knights who had survived the crossbow assault unwounded were standing to face the charge, but they never had a hope.

Most of the attackers were on the far side of the path from Adso where the trees gave more cover. Everyone was focused on the band of knights fighting for their lives on the path and, for a fleeting second, Adso considered joining them. As soon as he thought it though, he rejected the idea. The men on the path were doomed. Turning away, Adso faced the attackers on his side. Selecting the largest Falcon pounding toward him, he screamed a curse and charged.

Convinced that the lone, yelling idiot running toward him was no threat, the Falcon barely slowed as he raised his sword to split Adso in two. At the last minute, Adso ducked low to his left, swept his sword around and up in a broad arc, and severed his attacker's sword arm at the shoulder joint. The arm, still clutching the sword, tumbled over Adso's head and a warm spray of blood bathed his face. The man, not yet aware of what had happened, continued past him.

Rolling once, Adso was on his feet and sprinting uphill through the thickening forest. If anyone attempted pursuit, he never knew. Keeping his head down, he ran until his aching lungs felt as if they would explode. Gasping for air and bathed in sweat, he launched himself into a thicket of thorny bushes and, oblivious to scratches and cuts, burrowed in as deep as he could.

As he regained his breath, Adso assessed his situation. Jacques *had* betrayed them, but it had been a much more sophisticated trap than he had imagined. Five men, probably common soldiers, had been bribed—or, more likely, threatened—into dressing up as Oddo and a band of Falcons. With the lead group travelling slowly, the real Falcons had been able to keep pace some distance from the path. Bertrand's ambush set things in motion. As soon as Bertrand and the others had been drawn down onto the trail, the Falcons had attacked. It had worked perfectly, and Adso knew that he would be dead too if the niggling doubt in his mind hadn't made him examine the situation so closely.

So common sense and luck had kept him alive, but what would he do next? Bertrand and the best of his knights were dead. Adso knew he was safe where he was until dark. After that, he would travel back up to the camp and warn those left behind to disperse. It would only be a matter of time before the poorly defended camp was found. Once he had seen to that, he would settle his own score: he would go to Les Cardines and kill Jacques.

* * *

Adso sat, slumped against the rough wall, at the entrance to the alley across the square from the tavern in Rouairoux. A pair of Falcons passed within three feet of him, but paid no attention to the filthy, drunk beggar dressed in rags, whose face was covered in scabbed cuts and scratches. Adso's back and legs ached from sitting in the same position for so long, but he was patient. He'd already waited three days for his revenge—he could wait a few hours more.

Jacques had not been at Les Cardines, and Adso had been forced to come to Rouairoux, where he knew the traitor would be spending his ill-gotten gains. Adso had seen Jacques enter the tavern hours before, so it was simply a question of waiting for his victim to come out.

The square was sinking into twilight before Adso saw Jacques stagger from the tavern and relieve himself against the tavern wall. Weaving an unsteady course, Jacques crossed the square and stumbled into the alley. He paid Adso no more attention than anyone else had that day and, mumbling a vulgar drinking song, he entered the shadows. Adso rose silently and followed.

The deepest shadows in the alley were next to the pig pen behind the house Adso had been sitting against. It was the perfect place to carry out his plan.

"Jacques," Adso said softly as he caught up.

The drunk man took a moment to realize that someone was talking to him. He turned unsteadily and gazed uncomprehendingly at Adso's face.

"It's me," Adso said with a smile, drawing his dagger from the fold of his rags. "I'm the Devil, come to send you to 'ell."

A frown crossed Jacques' drink-besotted face. Over the man's ragged breathing, Adso could hear the semi-wild pigs rooting about in their pen, disturbed by the two men leaning on their wall.

Jacques' frown vanished, replaced by wide-eyed terror. He opened his mouth to shout, but before any sound emerged, Adso stabbed his dagger downward, pinning Jacques' tongue to his lower jaw. A surprising amount of blood welled up over the shocked man's lower lip and spilled down his chin, soaking his grubby tunic. He struggled to speak, but all that came out were odd gurgling noises.

"Don't want any company," Adso said. "This's between you and me. I know you betrayed us."

Jacques attempted to shake his head, but the dagger in his mouth prevented it. He had to hold his head forward so that the blood ran out of his mouth and down his front, rather than back into his throat where it would drown him.

"You don't need to say anything," Adso went on. "I just want to make sure you know why I'm going to kill you."

Jacques twisted, but Adso had no difficulty holding him.

"The Falcon's trap worked almost perfectly. Bertrand's 'atred of Oddo made sure of that, and now 'e's dead. I'm the only one 'oo escaped. I swore to kill you and, if the ambush were all that 'ad 'appened, you'd be dead by now, but it wasn't.

"You see, after I escaped, I went back up to the camp in the 'ills to warn the others, but I was too late, Jacques, wasn't I? Someone 'ad told Oddo where the camp was, and 'is Falcons, or maybe just some brutes 'e payed to do the job, 'ad got there afore me."

Adso hesitated and clenched his teeth to hold back the tears. Behind Jacques, the pigs, unsettled by the smell of blood, snorted and rummaged about restlessly.

"The knights we left be'ind had tried to fight, but they never 'ad a chance. Their bodies were stripped and mutilated, left in a pile by the camp fire. Then the crusaders 'ad their fun. Women, children, old men, it didn't matter. There were bodies everywhere. Some were cut up pretty bad, some 'ad suffered afore they died. I 'ad to chase off a lot of animals, wild pigs and the like, but that gave me an idea.

"A few women and children had run off in time and survived. I took them down to Les Cardines. Your wife was happy to 'elp look after them once I told 'er what 'ad 'appened. She also volunteered where I might find you."

Jacques struggled weakly and tried desperately to speak. His gurgling noises sounded as if he were trying to say "kill," but Adso had no idea whether it was a threat, a plea for mercy or a request to end the suffering.

"*I'm* not going to kill you," Adso said as if he were speaking to a child. "That wouldn't be fair. After all, you didn't actually kill Bertrand and the others. You gave them to the Falcons. Now, falcons are noble birds, much too good for the likes of you. I reckon pigs is more your standard."

Adso forced Jacques back until he was leaning over the low wall of the pig pen. With one last twist, he tore the dagger out of the man's mouth. A stream of blood gushed into the pen, catching one of the pigs on the snout. The beast snuffled and began licking the blood from the ground. Its companion moved closer and reached up to sniff at Jacques' blood-stained shoulder. The man struggled and whimpered, his eyes bulging with horror.

"I considered slicing the backs of your knees so you couldn't stand and rolling you into the pen, but not even you should 'ave to go through what some of those at the camp suffered. I just wanted you to know what's going to 'appen to you."

Adso hit Jacques as hard as he could on the side of his head. The body went limp and Adso tipped the legs up and into the pen, where the pigs snorted with anticipation. Wiping his dagger clean on his rags, Adso set off into the gathering darkness.

Rhedae

The Dragon's Head
October, 1212

Adso awoke with a scream, the nightmare fresh in his mind. At first it had been a pleasant dream: Bertrand stood in front of him, his mutilated face twisted in what had passed, in life, for a smile.

"Hello, Adso," he said. "We had some good times, didn't we?"

"We did," Adso replied, happy to see his old friend again. "And we'll 'ave good times once more."

Bertrand groaned. "I don't think we can."

"Why not?" Adso asked.

"I'm dead," Bertrand went on in his slurred voice, "and I'm not revenged. I cannot rest while Oddo lives."

"I did revenge you," Adso said, worry growing in his mind. "I killed Jacques. 'E was the one 'oo betrayed us."

"You killed the traitor, but he was not the evil one. Oddo is the Devil. You must kill him."

"I can't," Adso said, a sick feeling gripping his stomach. "'E's off fighting the Moors in Al-Andalus. There's only a few Falcons left 'ere with de Montfort."

"You abandoned me on the path," Bertrand snarled, suddenly furious. "I thought you were my friend. You *must* make amends."

"I didn't abandon you," Adso said, defensively. "I tried to shout a warning, but you wouldn't listen. If I'd gone down, I'd be dead too."

"And you should be," Bertrand's voice boomed. "I shall only allow you rest once Oddo's shade stands beside me in the afterlife. You must kill him."

Adso shuddered. He felt utterly helpless. "I can't kill Oddo. 'E's too strong."

"And you are too weak," Bertrand retorted. "Too weak. Too weak. Too weak." As Bertrand spoke, he gradually changed. His clothes fell away and his face healed until it was Jacques who stood before Adso instead, his eyes shining unnaturally.

"You killed me," Jacques said calmly.

A chill passed over Adso as beads of sweat broke on his body. "You betrayed us. Bertrand and the others died because of you."

"No," Jacques said. "They died because of Oddo. I did what I did because of Oddo. And you fear him too. Are you any better than me?"

Several large pigs materialized out of the dark beside Jacques and began eating him, ripping off large chunks of flesh and chewing with relish. Jacques didn't seem bothered. He continued to stand and smile at Adso. Adso wanted to rush over and beat the pigs off, but he was paralyzed with fear.

"I...I *am* better than you," Adso managed to croak out through his fear.

Jacques laughed as the pigs continued their work. Eventually, all that remained of him was a skeleton with rags of skin hanging from the bones and the eyes still gleaming from their deep sockets. The hideous figure raised a bony arm and pointed silently at Adso. The pigs moved forward, slobbering with anticipation.

Adso sat up, covered in sweat, and shivering uncontrollably in his makeshift bed. He looked around wildly, half expecting to see the pigs coming for him. There was nothing, just the grey ashes of the fire he had built the night before and the pale dawn sun filtering through the trees.

Adso sucked in a huge breath and tried to calm his pounding heart. He stumbled to his feet and dragged himself down to the stream on the other side of the trees. He lay down and thrust his head into the deep pool by the bank. The shock of the ice-cold water revived him. He sat up and shook a spray of drops out of his hair.

What was happening to him? This was the tenth time in the past month that he had had the same dream. What did it mean, and why had it started in September, more than a month after the failed ambush and Jacques' death? Adso shook his head and thought back to June, before the attack and all that had followed. He had been cheerful and confident then, a soldier revelling in what he was good at. Now he was unsure of himself, plagued by nightmares and scared of shadows.

For the past two months, Adso had drifted aimlessly around Languedoc, taking care to avoid the cities and crusader patrols. It had been a quiet summer—many of the knights were in Al-Andalus and no great numbers had come this year from the north—but de Montfort still had enough to keep his war going. Adso had heard from other travellers that Auterive had been burned, and there had been massacres at Ananclet and Hautpoul. In fact, Raymond of Toulouse could now only call three places of any size—Moissac, Montauban and Toulouse itself—his own, and Adso had heard that Moissac was already under siege.

Quest

It seemed as if the crusade was almost over and everything was lost. Hundreds of Cathar Perfects had been burned, and most of those left had taken refuge in the remote mountain fortresses. The vast majority of the heretic believers were keeping a very low profile. Yet the war—Simon de Montfort's war now—continued. As far as Adso could tell, the man was trying to carve out a kingdom for himself and his son, consolidating his power so he wouldn't have to rely on the uncertain stream of crusader knights coming south every summer. He had even laid claim to Foix and Comminges, both of which Adso knew owed allegiance to King Pedro of Aragon.

Adso gathered up his few possessions and set off through the trees onto the narrow road that ran south along the valley toward Quillan. He'd passed through Limoux the day before, but he had no specific goal in mind. The mountains here were dotted with cliff-top castles—Montségur and Puivert to the west, Peyrepertuse, Quéribus and Puilaurens to the east—that seemed to have grown naturally from the rock rather than been the works of man. Many of these castles sheltered Perfects, but the Holy Crusade had, as yet, shown no interest in them. They were too small and remote to be a military threat and too inaccessible to be easily subdued. It was much more profitable for de Montfort and his knights to concentrate on the cities to the north, so this tiny corner of the land was quiet.

Adso trudged south. He had no wish to fight any more. His companions and friends—Bertrand, Beatrice, John, Isabella—were lost or dead and his cause seemed doomed. Let de Montfort have his land and the Inquisition its bonfires. Adso just wanted peace and quiet, and this remote mountain land seemed to be the place to find it. But his nightmares were worrying. Peace and quiet were all very well during the day, but no use if his nights were tortured by Bertrand's demands and the horror of Jacques' death. And what if the dreams didn't stop? What if Jacques' ghost, or whatever it was, wouldn't let him rest until he had killed Oddo? Would the slavering pigs get him? More likely, in desperation, he would find Oddo and die then.

"Bertrand," Adso said out loud, trying to shrug off his misery, "don't torture me. I can't kill Oddo anyway. 'E's in Al-Andalus. You can't expect me to go down there."

"He does God's work."

Adso spun around at the sound of the voice behind him. His first impression was that the young man was a Perfect, but his black habit was hooded and a rough wooden cross hung from the rope belt tied at his waist. The monk was smiling at him.

"Oo're you?" Adso asked gruffly, embarrassed at being caught talking to himself.

The monk's smile vanished and he stared hard at Adso for a long time.

"Don't stand there like a tree," Adso said. "'Oo are you?"

"Don't you recognize me?"

Adso studied the young man intently. He was clear-skinned with no pox marks on his pinched face and had the narrow nose and thin lips that Adso associated with northerners. He wore plain sandals and stood leaning on a rough staff. There was something vaguely familiar about him, but Adso couldn't remember ever meeting a monk from an order that wore black habits. "No," he said uncertainly, "but I can't remember every young pup I meet."

"But you don't save all of their lives," the monk said, his smile returning.

Adso's brow furrowed in concentration. Then it came to him. "Good God!" he exclaimed. "The ambush more 'n a year back. You were the boy with the mules. Old Bertrand wanted to make you look like 'im and send you back to Oddo."

"And you stopped him."

"Instead we carved up the Falcon's face and sent 'is 'ead back. 'Ow did Oddo like that?"

"He didn't. I thought he was going to kill me when I told him what had happened and showed him the head. I'm glad to run into you. I can thank you at last. My name's Philip."

"Don't thank me," Adso brushed off the gratitude. "I just thought the Falcon's 'ead would be a better present for Oddo than a snivelling kid. I'm called Adso."

Philip stepped forward and the pair continued along the road.

"What's that black 'abit you're wearing?" Adso asked. "Except for the 'ood it makes you look like a Perfect. I've not seen the likes of that afore."

"I'm not a heretic. It's the habit of the Dominican friars."

"And 'oo might they be?"

"A new order, founded by Father Dominic Guzman in Toulouse."

"'E were that skinny fanatic that walked all over arguing with the Perfects."

"Yes, he preached in this land for many years and debated with the heretics before the blessed Pope Innocent called the crusade."

"So this Dominic Guzman 'as founded 'is own order, 'as 'e?"

"We're not officially recognized by the Pope yet," Philip said, a bit sheepishly, "but we're dedicated to travelling the land and preaching. We own nothing and live from the generosity of virtuous Christians everywhere."

"Beggars, are you?" Philip looked hurt, but Adso went on before he could say anything. "That what you're doing down 'ere, preaching?"

"I preach at every opportunity, but that is not my main reason for this journey. Father Aumery sent me—"

"Aumery," Adso scoffed. "That pop-eyed fanatic."

Philip looked shocked. "Are you a heretic?"

"I'm no 'eretic, boy," Adso said. "Although the path of a true Christian seems a narrow one to follow these days. I'm simply a soldier 'oo's tired of fighting. I've seen all my friends travel to foreign lands or die and now I just want some peace and quiet."

"You must follow the will of God," Philip said pompously.

"The will of God!" Adso turned on his young companion, who shrank back at the violence in his voice. "Is it the will of God that de Montfort's 'ired brutes come down 'ere, burning and destroying until all that's left is scorched earth and bloody wilderness? I've seen some of the gentlest people I've met burned alive, my friends 'anging from battlements or with their faces mutilated and their eyes gouged out. Is that what your God wants?"

Philip wisely didn't answer and Adso strode off down the road. Philip followed a step behind. Eventually, Adso spoke over his shoulder. His voice was gruff but the anger was gone. "If you're not down 'ere to preach, what did that slug Aumery send you for and wher're you going?"

Philip took a hurried step forward to draw level with Adso. "I am going to Rhedae."

"And what's there?"

"A book."

"A book! What's Aumery want with a book? 'Part from the Bible, 'e don't strike me as the reading sort."

"He's not," Philip agreed, "and I must admit to being surprised at his request, but I did not question him."

"Wise of you."

The talk of books made Adso think of Umar, Beatrice and John, and their love of books—or at least the wisdom that books might contain. When John had begun memorizing books, Adso had thought it a waste of time. He was a man of action and was certain that fighting the invaders and killing crusaders was the only way to free his land. But he'd tried that, and all he'd achieved was a lonely, depressed existence in a remote mountain valley. Not one thing he had done had even slowed the course of the crusade. Maybe John's way, preserving knowledge in his head, was better after all. "What book's 'e so interested in?"

Philip hesitated. "Father Aumery swore me to secrecy."

"'E would."

"He made me take an oath, and Oddo swore to kill me if I broke it."

"Oddo?" A chill ran down Adso's spine. "'Ow can that be? 'E's in Al-Andalus."

"No longer," Philip said. "He has returned to complete his work here. Oddo led his Falcons into Moissac at the end of the siege, hardly a month ago."

Bertrand's voice echoed in the back of Adso's head, ordering him to kill Oddo. Adso swore and shook his head to bring his focus back to the conversation. "So Moissac 'as fallen. Was there a slaughter?"

"The good citizens surrendered because the grapes were ready for harvest and they did not wish to lose this year's vintage. They paid one hundred gold marks to avoid the sack of their city."

Adso spat derisively. "Damned farmers. They care more for their crops than their country. I 'ope their vintage turns to vinegar. I meant was there a massacre of Perfects or knights?"

"Knights only. There weren't any Perfects in the town."

"At least the Perfects 'ave learned not to sit bottled up in towns waiting for Oddo to come and get them. 'Ow many knights?"

"Three hundred. Count Raymond had sent them from Toulouse."

Adso sucked in a long breath. "Those vultures won't rest until anyone 'oo can oppose them's dead." An image flashed in Adso's head—of Oddo hurling curses at him and John as he stood in the flickering light of the fires burning on the trebuchet at Minerve, his face blistered from red hot coals and blood running down his leg where Adso had stabbed him. It was a vision of the Devil himself.

"And Oddo was with Aumery when 'e swore you to secrecy?"

"He was," Philip said. "It was he who insisted on an oath."

"When the Devil swears you to secrecy, does it count?" Adso said, his voice laden with sarcasm.

Confusion and doubt registered on Philip's young face. "It is true that Oddo acts much as if the Devil were in him," he said, "yet he does God's work for the Holy Crusade and has the blessing of Abbot Aumery."

Adso shook his head. This young monk was completely out of his depth dealing with Aumery and Oddo. That was Philip's problem, but the thought that there was something nearby that was important to his two superiors intrigued Adso. If he could get his hands on this book before Aumery and Oddo, perhaps he could use it to hurt them.

"Young Philip," Adso said, putting on his most reassuring, friendly voice. "You are innocent in the ways of the world and no match for the likes of Oddo or Aumery. Might I offer you my assistance in your search?"

"Why would you do that?"

"Many reasons," Adso said pleasantly, "but mostly for the adventure. I 'ave no goal in life now. I'm alone with no companions. I'm defeated. The crusade 'as been won. What'm I to do, drink myself into a stupor in some flea-bitten tavern in Quillan? I'd rather 'elp you see what this search uncovers. You're not like the others, you seem 'onest and straightforward, and remember, I saved your life. Our fates are bound. You owe me! 'Ow can you refuse me this one small favour in exchange?"

Philip thought for a long moment. "Very well. I cannot see what harm telling you would do and, to be honest, I have been daunted by my task and would welcome the help and company you offer. Do you know about Rhedae?"

"Never 'eard of it," Adso said.

"It was a villa one thousand years ago, owned by a rich Roman called Marcus Britannicus. I'm told little remains of the villa now, and even its exact location is uncertain. After the Romans left, a people called the Visigoths came and built a town over the villa. It was their capital before the Moors swarmed over the mountains from Al-Andalus and sacked it. Now there is little more than a ruined castle on a hill."

"Don't sound much like there's a library there," Adso said.

"Oh, there's no library. The book I seek is hidden, perhaps in a vault beneath the villa."

"But if there's nothing left of the villa, 'ow do you know where a vault might be?"

"Father Aumery found a clue."

"I bet 'e did, and I bet some poor 'eretic suffered on the rack for it."

Philip looked uncomfortable and lowered his eyes to stare at the path.

"So," Adso went on, "*if* this clue leads to the vault and *if* there's a book in it, what would it be and why's it important?"

Philip's face creased with worry as he wrestled with what to tell his new companion.

"Look," Adso said. "A book in a buried vault. Sounds to me like a lot of digging, even if Aumery's clue works. You're welcome to do that on your own, but if you want my 'elp, I'll need to know what I'm sweating for."

"The Gospel of the Christ," Philip whispered.

"What!" Adso exclaimed.

"The Gospel of..."

"I 'eard you," Adso interrupted, "I just didn't believe you. A copy of the Gospel of the Christ exists?"

"You know of it?" Philip asked with a worried frown.

Adso realized his mistake. It probably wasn't a good idea to let Philip, and so possibly Oddo and Aumery, know how much he knew of the books in John's memory cloister. He tried to backtrack. "Everyone 'as 'eard of the Gospel of the Christ, but I thought it were just a story."

"It exists," Philip said. "Of course, it is a foul forgery written by heretics to try and discredit the true Church, but some simple folk believe it is true."

"So, you've been sent to find it and take it back to Oddo and Aumery?"

"I think so," Philip said uncertainly.

"You *think* so," Adso said. "You're not certain what to do when—if—you find this gospel?"

Philip looked uncomfortable. "Oddo and Father Aumery disagreed about what I should do. Father Aumery instructed me to bring the book back and give it to him. Oddo flew into a rage and ordered me to destroy the book the instant I discovered it. They had a violent argument. Oddo said that the book was too dangerous to survive and Aumery said that the Inquisition needed to know what was in it in order to fight heresy. Eventually, Father Aumery invoked the power of Pope Innocent and Oddo had to back down, although he did so with bad grace."

"Grace, good or bad, is not Oddo's strength," Adso said. The pair walked on in silence, Adso deep in thought. He knew John had memorized the Gospel of the Christ from Umar and was glad that his friend was far from Oddo and Aumery's dangerous prying. Adso had scoffed at the Gospel's import, claiming that there was no way John could prove it was genuine and hence no one would take it seriously. However, if there *was* a surviving copy of the Gospel in its original language, it would convince a lot of people that it was true. A discovery like that would rock the Catholic Church to its very foundations—and the book in John's memory cloister would become much more important and dangerous.

Something else bothered Adso. Why did Aumery want the book saved? Oddo's view that it should be destroyed as soon as possible seemed to make more sense.

Whatever the reasons, Adso was convinced of one thing: the Gospel had power, and if he could get hold of it before Aumery or Oddo, he might be able to cause the crusade some problems.

There was almost a spring in Adso's step as the valley widened out into neat, cultivated fields and pastures rich in well-fed sheep and goats. In the centre of valley stood a small, rough stone priory. The war had obviously not reached here yet, and Adso felt happier than he had in months. He was so wrapped up imagining the prospect of a decent meal and a bed for the night that he failed to notice the two knights sitting on horseback at the summit of the last hill they had crossed. They were watching the two travellers carefully, and each wore a falcon on his surcoat.

* * *

"So what's this clue of yours?" Adso asked. He and Philip had been welcomed by the prior and given a pilgrim meal of bread and bean soup. Now they sat beside the river watching the sun sink below the line of hills to their west. To the east, bathed in the last of the sun's warm glow, lay a long, sinuous ridge of rock and behind it a higher hill surmounted by the ragged ruins of Rhedae castle.

Philip looked around nervously to see if anyone was within hearing range. Then he closed his eyes and recited, "Abandon hope to Eve's temptation below Rhedae. Beyond the dragon's head in the serpent's tail, I lie." He opened his eyes and stared at Adso.

"That's it? That's your precious clue? What the 'ell does it mean?"

Philip shrugged apologetically. "That's all Father Aumery told me. He did say that there might be more to the clue, but that was all that he could find. He wished me luck."

"Well, we're fine then," Adso's voice dripped with sarcasm. "Aumery's luck is all we need." His lips moved as he recited the lines to himself. "Dragon's 'ead, serpent's tail, Eve's temptation..." Eventually he said, "It's all nonsense. The only bit that makes sense is 'abandon 'ope.' As far as I can see that's all we can do. Trust Aumery to send you off on a wild goose chase."

"It must mean something," Philip said.

"Oh, I'm sure it does, but can you make sense of that gibberish?" Adso spoke more harshly than he intended. It wasn't Philip's fault that this was a waste of time. Adso had got himself involved because he had seen a possible way to embarrass or hurt Aumery or Oddo. It hadn't happened, and that was disappointing, but at least he was no worse off than before. He looked over at Philip, who was staring miserably at the ground.

"God has blessed us with a beautiful evening," the prior said cheerfully as he came up behind the seated pair. He was a short man, almost as wide as he was tall and his round cheeks glowed with good health on either side of a bulbous nose shining red from too much rich wine. The prosperity of the valley was no illusion.

"'E 'as indeed," Adso replied.

"Are you pilgrims on the road to Santiago?"

"No," Adso replied. "We're merely 'onest men trying to escape from the war."

"A terrible business," the prior said. "Mind you, the heretics brought it upon themselves. The Holy Mother Church tries to bring all into her fold, but some are determined to deny."

Unwilling to enter a theological discussion, Adso attempted to change the subject. "'Oo's the patron saint of your priory?"

"One perfectly suited to these difficult times," the prior said, his round face wreathed in smiles. "It is St. Jude, the patron of lost causes. That is why we named the priory Esperanza, to give hope to those who have lost it. As I am sure you know, the apostle Jude, or Thaddeus as he is sometimes known, was martyred with Simon the Zealot in the year of our Lord sixty-five, and…"

Adso had stopped listening. At the mention of Esperanza, Philip's head had snapped up and the pair stared at each other.

"Esperanza means 'ope in the language of the southerners over the mountains, doesn't it?" Adso asked slowly.

"Yes. Yes," the prior said enthusiasm. "You see, the priory is hope for those who have lost hope."

"Or abandoned it," Adso whispered to himself.

"What?" the prior asked.

"Nothing," Adso's mind was racing. Suddenly things were beginning to fall into place. "Is there a serpent around 'ere?"

"Oh, many," the prior said, clapping his hands together at the prospect of another topic to expound upon. "These mountains are full of them. Most are harmless, but you must beware the viper. Its bite is most deadly. You can recognize it by—"

"I'm afraid you misunderstood me." Adso cut off the flow of information. "I meant a physical feature that might look like a serpent."

The prior didn't seem the least bothered by the change of topic. "Oh yes, silly of me. It's right there." He pointed a chubby finger over Adso's shoulder.

The two travellers spun around so fast they almost fell over. The sun was painting the hill on which Rhedae stood a glorious warm orange, and below the hill the last rays had caught the sinuous ridge. A slight bulge, like a head, at its nearest end made the ridge look like a long snake, winding its way down toward the river. Philip gasped.

"I imagine," said Adso, trying to keep the excitement out of his voice, "that there are caves in them 'ills."

"Riddled with them," the prior said. "Sheep and goats are always disappearing into them, and no one will go in after them. Superstitious folk around here say the caves are haunted by ancient monsters. Rubbish, if you ask me, but they *do* go deep and it *is* easy to get lost."

Quest

The prior stood up, his corpulent form jiggling from the movement. "Well, I must be off. You are welcome to join us at our prayers when the bells ring. Rest well and God bless you."

"And you, Prior," Philip said.

"And thank you," Adso added.

The pair sat in silence, staring at Rhedae as the sun sank behind them and the serpent and the ruined castle darkened. It was Adso who said what was on both their minds. "Abandon 'ope means leave Esperanza."

"And Eve's temptation is the apple in the serpent's mouth," Philip added.

"And there's your serpent below Rhedae." Adso waved his hand toward the dark hill.

"The serpent's tail I can guess, but the dragon's head?" Philip said.

"I don't know," Adso said thoughtfully, "but I'll wager a solid gold piece that there's a cave up there somewhere that'll answer that question."

Darkness thickened around the pair as the prayer bell chimed. "I must go and pray," Philip said, standing up.

"Pray for good luck tomorrow and get plenty of sleep. Something tells me it'll be an 'ard day."

Philip nodded and headed toward the small church. Adso sat for a bit longer. He was excited about what they might find in the hills. For the first time in ages, he felt his life had a focus. Perhaps the dream wouldn't come tonight.

He rose and stretched. A monk's cell wasn't much, but it was the first roof he would have had over his head in a while. Adso yawned and headed to the priory. Behind him two pairs of eyes watched from the darkness of the trees.

* * *

Adso woke from his dream just as Bertrand was ordering him to kill Oddo. That was odd; he'd never yet woken before the horrifying end. Then he realized what had woken him—a footstep sounded in the corridor outside his cell. His first thought was that it was one of the monks going to pray, but there had been no bells and the monks either went barefoot or wore sandals. They didn't wear a knight's riding boots.

Adso slipped silently off his cot onto the cold stone floor. He carefully unsheathed his dagger and crawled toward the door. The faint moonlight coming through the high window allowed him to see the outline of the other cot, on which Philip lay snoring softly, and the wooden door. The door was swinging slowly open. Adso stood behind it and waited.

The man entering led with a long sword that gleamed pale in the moonlight. He was bareheaded and wearing a padded leather jacket. As soon as he was fully in the room, Adso launched himself forward, hurling the intruder against the wall. The sword clattered to the floor as Adso grabbed the man's hair with his free hand and slammed his head repeatedly against the wall. After three blows, the man went limp.

At the sounds of the brief fight, Philip woke. "What's happening?" he asked groggily, struggling to untangle himself from is blanket. He had barely placed both feet on the floor when a second man burst into the cell and lunged forward to plunge his sword into Philip's chest. The boy fell back, dragging the attacker on top of him. Before the man could free his sword, Adso was on him. He pulled the intruder's head back and slashed a deep gash across his throat. As the man gurgled and warm blood rushed out of his neck, Adso dragged him aside and bent over Philip. He was lying half off the cot with the sword still protruding from his chest. His eyes were blinking rapidly and his mouth was working but no sound emerged. He was dying.

"The book," Philip managed to say at last.

"Don't worry," Adso said. "I'll get the book. You rest."

"What in God's name?" The prior bustled into the room. He was carrying a flaming torch and stared at the carnage in horror. The man Adso had stabbed was lying across the blood-soaked bed. The other was groaning in the corner.

"We were attacked," Adso said. "See to the boy." He moved aside to let the prior in. The prior knelt beside Philip. "Do you wish me to hear your confession?" he asked.

Philip nodded weakly.

The man in the corner was struggling to stand. There was blood matted in his hair and running down his face. Adso grabbed him and hauled him out into the corridor where several wide-eyed monks retreated in shock. Seizing a flaming torch from the closest startled monk, Adso pushed his captive to the ground, knelt on his chest and held the torch in front of his face. The man twisted away from the heat.

"'Oo are you?" Adso demanded.

The man remained silent. Adso lifted his head and let it drop on the stone tiles of the floor. The man groaned. "My name's Arnulf."

"A northerner. Why're you 'ere? 'Oo sent you?"

"I'm a Falcon," he said, strength returning to his voice.

"That's bad luck for you then," Adso said. "Your dead companion, was 'e a Falcon too?"

"Yes."

"Why're you 'ere?"

"Oddo sent us."

"Well, that's just double bad luck. Why?"

Quest

Arnulf stared sullenly at his tormentor. Adso let the flames from the torch lick the side of the man's face. He twisted away, but the smell of singed hair wafted up. "I've seen better people than you burn," Adso snarled.

"We were told to follow the black-robed monk. If he found anything, we were to destroy it and kill him. If not, we were just to kill him."

"So why kill 'im tonight, before he had a chance to find anything?" Adso asked.

"We didn't plan to kill him, just you. You weren't supposed to be here, you made it more complicated. We overheard some of what you talked about last night and decided to kill you and force the monk to find the book."

Adso leaned forward until he was almost lying on top of Arnulf with his mouth beside the man's ear. "You failed, didn't you," he said as he slipped his dagger up underneath the Falcon's ribs. Arnulf twitched and his body arched but Adso kept him pinned down. The man let out a long stinking breath and went limp. Adso pulled his dagger out and stood up.

"'E's dead too," he told the stunned monks.

The prior came out of the cell. "Your companion has gone to sit with Christ in a better place."

"Almost anywhere's better than this corrupt cesspit," Adso said bitterly. He had come to like Philip and his naive view of the world. Now he was just something else good that Oddo had destroyed. "Will you bury 'im 'ere?"

The prior nodded. "Of course, and we will pray for his immortal soul. What of the others?"

"Don't waste your prayers on those devils. Feeding them to the crows is too good for them."

"But all have a chance at redemption and forgiveness."

"I wouldn't count on it," Adso said, "but do what you must. I'll leave at first light." He turned and went out into the darkness to sit alone with his black thoughts. "You don't need to visit me in the night any more, Bertrand," he said under his breath. "I swear on all that's 'oly and on the souls of all the good men and women I've seen slaughtered by the brute, I shall search out and kill Oddo, or die trying."

* * *

Dawn found Adso clambering up the slope toward the head of the serpent. He carried a satchel of food, a full wineskin and a tightly bound brush torch soaked in pitch. In his head he carried Philip's clue and a burning desire: he would find the Gospel of the Christ and use it to destroy Aumery and Oddo.

The slope was rough, fallen rock thickly covered with low bushes and small scrub trees. Adso was soon sweating freely as he cut his way forward with his sword, but he kept working his way up. By mid-morning he stood at the foot of a small cliff. He took a long drink and looked around. "So this's the 'ead of the snake," he said to himself. "Somehow I 'ave to get in and go toward the tail, but what and where is the dragon's head?"

Adso spent the entire day scrambling about at the foot of the cliff, crawling over boulders, cutting vegetation away and examining every crack in the surface that might be a cave. He studied every oddly shaped rock from every angle to see if he could possibly visualize it as a dragon's head, but nothing looked like anything other than a piece of rock.

Adso was exhausted. It was surprisingly hot, even late in the day with the sun sinking toward the distant mountains. He was filthy, aching and covered in scrapes and cuts from his clambering, and on the verge of giving up for the day and finding somewhere to make a camp when he felt the breeze. There had been breezes all during the day, but this one was cool and it was coming from an entirely different direction. Adso traced it back until he came to a narrow crack in the face of the cliff. He tried to remember if he had passed this way before. It was hard to tell. This crack looked no different from dozens of others that he had passed, and he would not likely have paid it any attention—it was far too narrow for anyone to get through. But the breeze suggested that there must be a larger cave behind it. The question was how to get in?

Adso looked up. The crack narrowed as it rose until it was no more than a line in the rock. Downward, it appeared to widen, but before it was wide enough to crawl through, it was blocked by fallen rocks, dirt and bushes. Adso sighed and began hacking at the bushes and pulling rocks out of the way. His muscles protested, but the cool breeze kept him going.

After about an hour's hard work, Adso had created a hole large enough to squeeze through. The sun had set and twilight didn't allow him to see anything inside the hole, but he doubted he would have been able to see much even in broad daylight. He had two choices: either come back tomorrow and try to enlarge the hole or go into the unknown now.

Adso looked at the hole again. The rocks he would have to move to make the hole much bigger were large. It would be a lot of work and it might not reveal much more. Adso kicked a stone into the hole and listened. It rattled down a slope into silence. At least there wasn't a sudden drop off, but who knew what happened a few feet in.

"Damnation," Adso muttered to himself. He took out his flint, clutched the torch and pushed himself feet first into the hole. The darkness overwhelmed him almost instantly. At first he had to push himself along, but the slope gradually steepened until he was sliding with increasing speed. He tried to dig his elbows in to slow himself, but it made no difference. Then, for a sickening moment, there was no slope beneath him at all and he was falling. An instant later he crashed painfully to the ground.

It took Adso a moment to realize he was still alive. Gingerly, he sat up. Holding the torch between his knees, he forced his hands to stop shaking and struck the flint. On the third try, a tiny yellow flame appeared on the torch, and soon the head was blazing cheerfully.

Adso sighed with relief and looked around. The slope he had come down and the drop at the end were surprisingly small. He even thought he could see a slightly lighter patch of sky that marked the cave mouth. On either side, the walls danced in the flickering torchlight, but above and ahead they narrowed into darkness. Adso stood and moved forward. His leg hurt where he had landed on it at the bottom of the slope, but at least the floor of the cave was smooth—packed earth, it looked like.

Farther along, the walls drew in and the roof lowered. Eventually, Adso was on his hands and knees, crawling forward. Ahead, the gap was no wider than his shoulders and so low he would have to turn his head to the side to fit. He couldn't go through that. He had no idea what, if anything, was on the other side and if he became stuck, which seemed likely, he faced a long, slow death from starvation.

This couldn't be where Philip's clue led. Cursing, Adso pushed himself backward until he could sit up and rubbed his eyes. He had been convinced that he was on the right track, but all his hard work had only led to disappointment and exhaustion. There must be another cave somewhere. Adso sighed and looked around. He might as well stay here until morning, at least he'd be warm and dry.

He turned around and began crawling back. A dragon's face in the flickering torchlight made him gasp with fright. The snout loomed toward him and dagger-like teeth threatened to tear him apart. Adso lunged backwards, catching his head painfully on the sloping wall of the cave. The dragon didn't follow him.

When Adso's heart slowed, he looked at what had given him such a shock. Embedded in the rock wall across from him was the largest set of jaws he had ever seen. The jaws were fully as long as his forearm and each was studded with curved teeth as big as his middle finger. Tentatively, Adso crawled over and touched a tooth. It was cold, hard stone, but darker and smoother than the surrounding rock. Adso's fingers traced the rounded snout, the fearsome teeth and the jaw as it widened back into a massive skull that disappeared into the cave wall.

"A dragon," Adso breathed. The final bit of the clue made sense. He had entered the snake's head and been crawling toward the tail. His goal lay beyond the dragon's head. He looked back at the narrow entrance that had turned him back. That was the way he had to go. He took a deep breath, undressed and piled his satchel and clothes beneath the rock dragon. Taking only his dagger, clutched in his teeth, and the torch, pushed ahead of him, he crawled back to the end of the cave. Cursing Oddo, Bertrand and Philip for getting him into this, Adso began wriggling into the hole.

It was hard not to panic as the rough stone roof lowered until it began to scrape the skin off his back. Adso couldn't help thinking of the vast weight of rock that seemed to be pressing down on him. The walls were so narrow that he could progress only by edging his body forward a fraction of an inch at a time. He dug his toes and fingers into the earth to try to help pull himself along. To make matters worse, hot pitch from his torch rubbed off on the ground as he pushed forward, burning his chest and belly as he moved over it.

Adso's nose itched uncontrollably and he couldn't even bring his hand back to scratch it. The slightest narrowing of the tunnel or lowering of the roof and he would be stuck—forever. I'm in my grave, he thought miserably. Shuddering and pushing the thought to the back of his mind, Adso forced himself forward, his only focus the next inch.

After what seemed like hours, the torch flickered. At first Adso thought it was about to die and leave him without the only tiny bit of comfort he had, but as he edged forward, he sensed instead the tunnel widening out ahead of him. Soon the weight of the roof on his back eased and he could crawl more freely. Suddenly, there was room to get up on his hands and knees.

Adso sat up, removed the dagger from his mouth and gave a fervent prayer of thanks to whichever god put dragons in rocks. He was shivering in the cool air and his breathing was shallow and rapid. Gradually he calmed down and looked around. He was in a second cave, smaller than the first, but after the tunnel it felt like the nave of St. Sernin Cathedral. Where he had entered the cave, the roof was high enough to sit up, but it sloped away to meet the ground about twelve or fifteen feet in front of him. The walls were smooth and far enough apart that Adso could reach out his arms to either side and touch them. Carved out of the rock, about half way along the left wall, there was an alcove. In it lay a grinning, mummified body.

The mummy was a man of medium height, dressed in the fragments of what had once been an ankle-length robe and with dark hair that spread over his shoulders. The dry air in the cave had prevented the man's skin from rotting, but it was dark and wrinkled, like old leather. His closed eyes were sunken and his lips had drawn back from a mouthful of yellow teeth. His nose was prominent and hooked. The figure lay on its back, arms crossed on its chest. The hands held a blackened scroll, and a crude earthenware cup stood by his head.

Adso stared. Was this what Aumery had sent Philip to find? All the clues seemed to fit, but there had been no mention of a body, only a book. Could that be the scroll in the mummy's skeletal fingers?

"'Oo are you?" Adso asked. Hearing his own voice was comforting in this silent tomb. "'Ow long 'ave you been 'ere? Are you Marcus Britannicus or some forgotten Visigothic lord or someone even more antique? I've 'eard that there were ancients who lived 'ereabouts and painted wondrous pictures of strange animals on cave walls." Adso swung the torch around to see the roof and walls, but they were bare. "Are you a man from before the Flood? 'Oo buried you in this cave and why?" There were no answers.

Adso reached out and touched the man's face. The rough skin was cool and dry, and he could feel the stubble of a beard. His gazed drifted down to the scroll in the corpse's hands. "Is that the Gospel of the Christ you carry? Will you let me 'ave it? It's very powerful and I shall use it to do good."

Adso carefully placed his torch against the wall and laid his dagger on the ledge beside the mummy. Slowly he leaned forward and grasped the end of the scroll. It crackled softly beneath his hand. Very gently, Adso pulled. Nothing happened: the withered hands held the scroll firmly. Adso let go and looked at the hands again. The brown fingers were interlocked around the parchment. Tentatively, he took hold of the middle finger of the right hand and pried it up. With a soft snap, the finger broke at the first joint and came away in Adso's hand. Cursing under his breath, he tried another finger with the same result. He tried to pull the hands apart, but time had frozen the dead man's grip. He returned his attention to the scroll. Holding the end as gently as he could, Adso pulled again. The end of the scroll disintegrated in a cloud of fine dust and a scattering of black fragments. "No!" he shouted, sitting back on his heels.

Now a good half of the scroll no longer existed. Adso picked up a fragment and it turned to dust between his fingers. He groaned. Even if he could get the hands apart, there was no way the scroll would survive, let alone be readable. All the effort, the deaths down at the priory, the struggle to get here, were a waste. If this scroll was indeed the Gospel of the Christ, it was worthless now.

Adso felt like weeping. He had invested all his hopes in Philip's quest. He had imagined that a copy of the Gospel of the Christ would destroy Oddo and Aumery, send the crusaders home and free him from his nightmares. How stupid to think so! Philip's search had been simply another lost cause, and even St. Jude had let him down.

A large drop of burning pitch dropped from the torch to the floor. He wouldn't even have light much longer. There would be plenty of time to feel sorry for himself once he was back through the tunnel.

As Adso reached forward to grab the torch, he noticed a carving in the rock below the alcove. He held the torch close and squinted at the inscription. Some of the letters were vaguely familiar from paintings he had seen in churches. Others looked like letters he had seen in books, but he had no idea what the words meant. Was it important? How could he copy it? He had the dagger, but nothing except his skin to scratch it on. Then his eye caught the cup by the body's head.

"So your companions left you something to drink on your journey to the other world. Not much for the time you've been travelling." Gently, Adso reached over and picked up the now empty cup. It was a goblet with a short stem and a round base, smooth on the inside but rougher on the outside. It was a simple everyday earthenware cup. "'Ooever you were, you weren't no prince." Adso leaned the fading torch against the wall beside the writing and, using the point of his dagger, carefully scratched the strange letters around the outside rim of the cup.

Χριστός ο άνθρω_ος ο ריקא

When he was done, Adso sighed and sat back. As he did so, his foot knocked the bottom of the torch, tilting it to one side. He grabbed for it and managed to catch it, but as he did so, the flame sputtered. A drop of burning pitch flew off and landed on a fragment of material hanging from the mummy. With terrifying speed, tiny yellow flames raced up the cloth onto the body. In seconds, the mummy was a blazing inferno.

Adso pushed himself back from the heat as the acrid fumes from the fire caught the back of his throat. He half closed his eyes against the stinging smoke and searing flames. The flames grew and raced along the dry corpse. In seconds, all that remained was ash and cracked bones.

Adso coughed and spat in the swirling smoke. He was sure he had learned all he could from the mummy, but he was sad nonetheless. Crawling through the tunnel, he had come close to joining this ancient, unknown man in his dry tomb. "Well, 'ooever you were, you're finished now," he murmured. With a final flicker, the torch died.

Oddly, the painful journey back through the tunnel was easier in the dark, or perhaps it was that Adso now knew he could do it, even holding the goblet in front of him. Feeling his way along the wall, he found his pile of clothes and dressed, then crawled slowly back through the large cave to the bottom of the entrance slope, where he collapsed miserably into an exhausted sleep.

Rescue

Foix
December, 1212

Adso lay in the stinking alley as a chilling rain soaked his tunic and puddles of filthy water formed around him. He tried to ignore the pounding in his head, his painful cough and the hard ground digging into his skinny body, but he couldn't ignore his loneliness and guilt. The rational part of his mind knew that his miserable isolation was of his own making and that he had no reason to feel guilt. In wars, people betrayed one another and died violently; there was nothing Adso could do about that. However, it seemed that everywhere he went, death followed *him* in particular. All his friends were dead: one even haunted him from beyond the grave.

The nightmares still tortured Adso, at least when he wasn't lying in a filthy alley in a drunken stupor. The hope that Philip's quest might provide him with a way to attack Oddo and Aumery had vanished with the flames in the cave above Rhedae. All that was left was his oath to Bertrand to kill Oddo, and his friend's shade wasn't about to let him forget it.

Adso rolled over and heard a loud crack from the tattered pouch he wore at his waist. Thinking through his aching misery that it might mean some food or even money that he had forgotten about, he struggled to undo the knot. Fragments of pottery fell out into the puddle beside him.

Adso stared at them uncomprehendingly for along moment before memory slowly returned: it was the cup from the mummy in the cave. Well, it was no use now. He moved his shaking hand aimlessly through the broken pieces. The largest had the letters Adso had scratched from the tomb. With difficulty, and without really knowing why, he returned that piece to his pouch. He tried to get up, but the effort was too much and dizziness swamped him. With a pitiful groan, he slumped back down. A passing merchant cursed and kicked Adso's legs out of the way as he dragged his loaded cart down the alley.

Adso groaned, rolled over and vomited onto the wet ground. He was a dismal failure. All he tried to accomplish ended in tragedy and death. Dying would have been an escape, but he had even failed at that. After leaving the cave at Rhedae, he had set out to find and kill Oddo. It seemed the only thing left for him to do, and the only way to stop his nightmares. At any rate, that's what he told himself. In truth, he could see no hope for the future even with Oddo dead and his nightmares gone. The Holy Crusade had won. Only Toulouse, Foix and a few inaccessible fortresses were still free. Perhaps the easy solution was to find Oddo, challenge him and die in the fight. At least that would be a quick end followed by the peace of death.

Adso had travelled extensively seeking Oddo, but every time he came close, his prey and his salvation slipped away. Either Oddo had been there the week before and was now gone, or else the man he found wasn't Oddo. As the harsh winter weather settled in and the chance of killing Oddo remained just as remote, Adso sank further and further into depression and misery. Bertrand's relentless message of revenge, combined with the exhaustion of never having a restful sleep, wore him down until he was a physical and mental wreck. He awoke every morning with one goal: to drink enough during the day to sink into a dreamless stupor that night.

In his increasingly rare sober spells, he still tried to find Oddo, but only half-heartedly. Begging food and drinks, he had spent several weeks in Toulouse, avoiding Bishop Foulques' Angels and trying to discover where Oddo might be. Eventually, a merchant told him that he had seen Falcons in the south and Adso had drifted down to Foix.

Foix, dominated by its castle and surrounding an ancient abbey, was one of the very few refuges left in Languedoc. Nestled against the foothills of the Pyrénées, the town had never been besieged by Simon de Montfort. The lord of Foix, Count Raymond Roger, existed in a complex web of allegiances that made him a vassal of both Count Raymond of Toulouse and King Pedro of Aragon and, therefore, dangerous to cross. He was also a vicious man, known to have murdered priests if they displeased him and whose sister, Esclarmonde, had taken the *consolamentum* and become a famous Cathar Perfect. Those Cathars who had not taken refuge in one of the inaccessible mountain fortresses such as Quéribus or Montségur, sought sanctuary in Foix.

But there was no sign or news of Oddo in Foix, and Adso knew he would have to move on if he were to continue his quest for death. Yet every day he found one more excuse to stay for just a short time longer. In desperation, he had sold his sword and entered a tavern intent on getting himself his first decent meal in weeks, cleaning himself up and leaving. He had woken up three days later in a ditch outside the town walls, bruised and penniless, and with no memory of what had happened. Miserably, he had returned to a pathetic life of begging and drinking.

Yesterday had been a good day: he had managed to lift a silver coin from a distracted merchant's purse. It had been enough to drink himself into oblivion before he had been thrown out of the tavern in the early hours of the morning. Now his silver coin was gone and he was huddled, cold and hungry, in the alley with a pounding headache and a feeling of disgust that he still lived.

Adso coughed harshly and rolled stiffly onto his side on the rough cobbles. "I've got to kill 'im," he mumbled to himself without conviction. He said the same thing every morning, not because he believed it any more—once he had been good with a sword and dagger, but the drink and near starvation had reduced him to a shaking skeleton that wouldn't last a minute against Oddo—but because his only remaining goal was to find Oddo and a quick end.

As the sky lightened, people began passing along the alley. They ignored the crumpled form, thinking him dead already, unless they happened to witness his body being wracked by another fit of coughing. Several kicked him as they passed and one man jabbed him painfully in the ribs with his staff.

Eventually, Adso summoned the motivation to begin the day's begging. He struggled to his feet and leaned against the wall. He felt dizzy and nauseous, and sweat was breaking out all over his body. With a huge effort, he began to move along the wall toward the street.

At the end of the alley, he stopped and retched some pale, burning liquid. In front of him, the square bustled with activity. At first all the commotion puzzled his aching brain, but then the answer surfaced—market day. That meant hope. Many people would come into town with coins in their pouches. Heartened, Adso launched himself into the square.

Walking without the support of the wall was harder than he had expected. He wove through the crowds, trying to keep a straight line, but frequently staggering into people and stalls, and suffering curses and blows in return.

"Money," he mumbled, holding out his hand whenever a figure swayed into view. "Alms for a poor soldier 'oo needs a drink. 'Ave pity." He was battered, empty-handed and barely able to take another step when he became vaguely aware of a commotion ahead of him. Hoping his luck would change, he lurched forward and crashed into a soldier who swore loudly and hit him across the cheek with the back of his hand.

Adso collapsed to the ground and curled into a protective ball. The soldier kicked him a couple of times and moved off. He rolled over painfully and looked up at the laughing faces round him. He didn't care; the only thing he saw was the back of the large man leading a group of soldiers away. The men weren't wearing armour, but each was dressed in the padded jackets that knights wore beneath their chain mail. They had swords hanging from their belts and one of the men at the rear turned to look back at Adso He was wearing a surcoat emblazoned with a red falcon carrying a black axe. The large man was obviously the leader and he carried an axe over his left shoulder.

"Oddo," Adso croaked, but no one heard him. He tried to stand and failed, groaning with frustration as his tangled limbs kept him on the ground. He had to catch Oddo and kill him, or die.

Mumbling wretchedly, he crawled across the wet square through the forest of legs. People kicked out at him but it meant nothing. He had lost sight of his quarry, but he had to keep going. If he didn't either kill Oddo or be killed by him, he would never know peace.

Adso crawled amid the kicking feet for what seemed an age. "'Elp me," he pleaded, "I 'ave to kill Oddo," but the only reaction he got was laughter and more blows. Eventually, he reached the far side of the square and collapsed, tears of frustration rolling down his cheeks. Every square inch of him ached.

"I can't do it," he said, helplessly. "I can't kill 'im. I'm doomed."

"We're all doomed," a familiar voice said in his ear. "Who is it you wish to kill?"

Through his pain and misery, Adso could just make out a figure leaning over him. He couldn't see the features, but he knew the voice. "Oddo. I 'ave to kill Oddo."

"A tall order indeed, I would say," the voice said, "but certainly worth a song if you manage it." Adso felt a cool hand on his forehead. "Killing Oddo is a fine goal, but I don't think you will manage it today. You have a fever, more cuts and bruises than you deserve, and you look like you haven't had a good meal in weeks. I know somewhere you can rest. And clean up," the voice added. "Even for the inhabitants of the gutter, you stink."

Adso was hazily aware of arms reaching under his shoulders and lifting him. He tried to help, but his legs didn't seem to want to obey his commands. Eventually, he stopped struggling and just let the man drag him wherever he wanted. The swirls of passing people and buildings made Adso dizzy. Just before blackness overwhelmed him, he recognized the voice. "William of Arles," he said softly and passed out.

* * *

Quest

Adso woke up with only fragmentary memories of the previous few days. Dreams and reality had fused into a baffling mixture of fevered visions. Even the Bertrand nightmare seemed to have retreated to let the fever do its work. He was lying on a rough cot in the corner of a large kitchen. Two figures sat at a table in the centre of the room, talking quietly. He sat up and instantly regretted it. The room swam around him and a racking cough rose from the depths of his chest. He slumped back and lay gasping like a stranded fish.

"Your fever broke last night, but you are weaker than a newborn calf."

Adso struggled to see who was talking to him, but the black-clad figure kept drifting in and out of focus. His first impression was that it was Beatrice come back to life, but the voice was wrong and the hair wasn't white. "'Oo're you?" he croaked.

"My name is Esclarmonde," the woman said, "and you are in a safe room of my brother's palace. Do you feel strong enough for some soup?"

Adso nodded weakly and Esclarmonde went over to the fireplace where a large pot hung over the glowing coals. The room was simple and unadorned and reminded him of the Cathar house in Minerve. The other figure at the table raised a hand in greeting.

"William," Adso said, "what're you doing 'ere?"

"I go wherever there are stories and songs and wherever I am welcome to sing them," the troubadour said, rising and coming over to sit at the foot of the cot. "Unfortunately, there are few such places left. But why are *you* here?"

"To kill Oddo."

"Ah, yes," William said. "You talked of little else in your delirium, but it strikes me you did not plan your assassination very well. I doubt if crawling drunk, starving and sick across the square after him would work, unless of course your plan was to lull him into a false sense of security." William smiled and Adso felt ridiculously happy. It was the first friendly smile he had seen in months.

Esclarmonde came over holding a wooden bowl and spoon. William propped Adso up on the cot with his back resting against the wall, and Esclarmonde slowly fed him soup while William talked.

"These are certainly difficult times. I have travelled all across this land in the past two years and have seen nothing but suffering and distress—and it is not only the so-called heretics who feel the anger of the crusade. Crops are burned or stolen and livestock slaughtered or driven away to feed de Montfort's armies. The world suffers and there are precious few islands of sanity like this one."

"Is this a Good Christian 'ouse?" Adso asked.

"No," William replied. "They exist now only in the most remote of places. This is a room at the rear of Count Raymond Roger's palace. He walks a fine line between bending a knee to de Montfort and protecting those like his sister." He gestured toward Esclarmonde. "Even then, he only still has such freedom of action because he owes allegiance to Pedro of Aragon, and de Montfort does not wish to antagonize King Pedro."

"'Ave you 'eard word of John and Isabella?" Adso asked.

"I have not. They went to Al-Andalus in search of books, but I have heard nothing since. I hope they managed to avoid the fighting down there."

"Oddo was in Al-Andalus."

"So we get back to him," William said with a smile. "Yes, he was. He took a band of Falcons down to join that fanatic Aumery in the Christian cause." William's smile broadened. "It seems God is not overly choosy about whom He gets to do His work for him."

Adso finished the last spoonful of soup. The hot food had tasted wonderful but exhaustion was overwhelming him and it was hard to keep his eyes open. "Thank you," he said to Esclarmonde.

"You are welcome," she said with a smile. "Now you must sleep." William helped lay the invalid down.

Before he drifted off to sleep, Adso heard William and Esclarmonde return to the table and talk in low voices. "Do you think he will be up to it?" Esclarmonde asked.

"He needs feeding, both in body and mind, and rest," William replied, "but I think he will do it, if he can overcome this mad idea of killing Oddo."

"I wish you luck then," Esclarmonde said. "I must leave tonight. This parliament that de Montfort has called in Pamiers makes it too dangerous for any of my kind to be in this area."

"I will talk with Adso when he wakes tomorrow. I wish you a good journey."

* * *

"Oddo need not fear you yet," William said, "but a few days of rest and good food have performed miracles."

Adso had to admit that his friend was right. The pair were sitting at the table and Adso felt better than he had in a long time. His strength was returning gradually and his cough easing. Even the nightmares seemed less insistent.

"And I see your appetite has returned," William added as he watched Adso tear off another piece of bread to go with the round of cheese he was busily demolishing. "Are you ready to hear Esclarmonde's proposal?"

Quest

"I am, as long as it involves no fighting. I fear I'm not up to swordplay yet, and first I'd like to know more of this woman. You're a storyteller, tell me 'er story."

William laughed. "And Esclarmonde has a story that one day I shall put in a song. As Raymond Roger's sister, she was an important woman who married well and bore three powerful sons. However, after she was widowed, a dozen years past, she took the *consolamentum* and became a Perfect. She led debates against that black-clad monk, Dominic Guzman. He was the only one of them who could come close to defeating her in argument. She also oversaw the rebuilding of the castle at Montségur into the impregnable fortress it is today, and she founds schools and hospitals wherever she goes. It is said that de Guzman copies her in setting up houses for his Catholic nuns. She is the most important and powerful Perfect still living."

"But she cannot live openly."

"Indeed not. She moves a lot, mostly at night, and takes refuge in the still secure mountain fortresses. So far, she has been lucky, but it cannot last forever and that is why she asked that I talk with you. Since Esclarmonde cannot move around the land freely, she must have eyes and ears who can, and who are willing to pass what they see and hear back to her. She wishes you to be one of those."

"Are *you* one of those?" Adso asked.

"I am," William replied, "although not the most effective. Troubadours are not as welcome in the palaces of our new Catholic rulers as we once were in the courts of Carcassonne and Toulouse. No matter; I do what I can. You, on the other hand, can go where you wish. You can drink with soldiers, talk with merchants and eavesdrop as you seek absolution for your sins from monks."

"But what use will the snippets of information I glean be to Esclarmonde?"

"Who knows?" William said with a shrug. "But all information helps build knowledge, and knowledge leads to wisdom. If we hear where some drunken crusader is headed next, we may gain knowledge of their plans and derive the wisdom to act accordingly.

"This past year has been quiet. Many knights have been in Al-Andalus, but as you saw in the square, they are back now. Does de Montfort intend to use them to attack Toulouse, or is he content to consolidate his power? As we sit here, there is a parliament in session at Pamiers, a mere dozen miles from here. I am told"—William winked broadly at Adso—"that the counts and bishops there have confirmed de Montfort in his lands, reaffirmed the primacy of the Catholic Church and ordered everyone to attend Mass on

Sundays. The search for heretics is to continue, so the fires will not be put out, but we can expect fewer sieges. All mercenaries are to be sent home. In future, de Montfort's army will come from his vassals."

"That means Oddo will leave," Adso said.

"Possibly, though I suspect de Montfort will find a way to keep him. In any case, I have not told you the most important element. Foix and the lands about were included in de Montfort's empire. And since Foix owes allegiance to King Pedro of Aragon, technically, de Montfort is now Pedro's vassal."

"De Montfort'll never accept that."

"Exactly. And Pedro will not allow de Montfort to continue building an empire at his expense."

"What will 'e do?"

"No one knows," William said. "Probably he will send emissaries to the Pope in Rome. They will argue that it is de Montfort and Aumery's role to search out heresy, and that they are overstepping themselves and upsetting the God-given order of the world in demanding sovereignty over lands from lords who owe allegiance to other Christian monarchs."

"How will the Pope react to that?"

"We do not know, nor do we know what de Montfort and Aumery will argue in return. That is why we need people like you to discover as much of their thinking as possible in the coming months. This war against the Cathars may not be as close to being over as some think."

Adso thought for a long moment. He was excited by what William had told him. Perhaps things weren't as bleak as they had looked. Pedro of Aragon taking an interest in Languedoc affairs was a new twist. He was a Catholic monarch, so wouldn't be too friendly to the Cathars, but he was powerful, and if he felt his lands were threatened, who knew what he might do. For the first time in many months, Adso felt a tiny spark of optimism. Doing something to fan that spark into flames would give him purpose again. There was just one problem.

"I gave an oath to kill Oddo."

"Indeed," William said. "Oaths get us into all kinds of trouble, but it need not prevent you undertaking this task. Rushing into a fight is not the only way to kill a man. Collecting information that may harm the crusader cause will be killing Oddo a little at a time. Think of it as tiny sword thrusts that weaken your enemy until you may administer the *coup de grace*."

Adso thought for a long moment. "I shall do what I can to 'elp you and Esclarmonde, but there's one condition. If on my travels I see a chance to kill Oddo, I'll take it, regardless of what other work I may do."

"Very well," William said with a smile. "Let us hope that King Pedro will do something to help you in that task."

The pair sat in silence for some time, William deep in thought and Adso eating. At length, William reached into the pouch hanging from his belt and produced a fragment of pottery. He laid it on the table between them. "I found this on your person when you first arrived and we were working to clean the smell of the gutter off you."

Adso picked up the fragment and studied the mysterious signs. It was all that remained from his adventure at Rhedae.

"I found it in a cave to the south," Adso said. "Do the words mean anything to you?"

"Some," William said. "The first words are in the language of the old Greeks. I am not very familiar with it, but I think it says, '*Xristos anthropos.*'"

"What does that mean?"

"'Christ and man' or 'man of Christ,' I'm not sure. It must be part of a prayer."

"That'd fit. It was carved into the rock by a body. What is the last word?"

"I don't know. The language is not Greek. I've never seen it before."

"Well, per'aps it'll bring me luck," Adso said, putting the fragment in his pouch.

"Perhaps," William agreed. "I fear we will need all the luck we can get in the coming year."

PART TWO

John's Story

The Library

Madinat al-Zahra
May, 1212

John sat in the shade of the orange tree and sipped his scented tea while Nasir dozed against a neighbouring tree. This past year had been the happiest of John's life. It had been quiet and uncomplicated. He had spent it surrounded by books, in the company of Isabella. Nasir had been nearby to teach him, and Shabaka supplied them all with food and brought them news of the distant outside world. John smiled; he would be happy enough never to return to that world of betrayal, war and death in Languedoc.

When he had brought them to the library from Cordova a year ago, Shabaka had talked non-stop for the entire journey, telling stories of the land and its people. The stories were fascinating—Shabaka was almost as good a teller of tales as William of Arles—and John had almost managed to forget how uncomfortable it was to ride over rough ground on a bad-tempered, stubborn donkey.

Madinat al-Zahra had been built three hundred years in the past by a great caliph, Abd ar-Rahman III. "It is said," Shabaka had told John and Isabella, "that he built the city for, and named it after, his favourite concubine, the beautiful al-Zahra. The Caliph had an immense statue of al-Zahra built with the most magnificent pink marble ever seen and mounted it above the gate into the city.

"The less romantically inclined say that, despite her great beauty, al-Zahra was a scheming, shrewish woman who used her power over the great man to enrich herself and her friends. To prove her power, she commanded the Caliph to build a new city that would be the envy of the entire world and immortalize her name.

"For eighty years the city was one of the wonders of the world. Even the most jaded traveller could not fail to be awed by its splendour: sculptures of amber and pearl, doors of ivory, walls of gold and gardens filled with every exotic creature that swam in the oceans, walked the earth or flew in the sky. The Caliph's audience chamber contained a pool of quicksilver. In the midst of an audience, a slave would slip in and disturb the surface of the pool, sending brilliant lances of reflected light dancing off the polished marble pillars and golden walls."

"What happened after eighty years?" John had asked.

"It is said that one accumulates enemies as fast as one accumulates wealth. A tribe from the south—Berbers, a hard desert people—attacked the caliphate, which had become soft with too much luxury. They defeated the Caliph's army and sacked Madinat al-Zahra. Since then, the city has been abandoned, its treasures lost and its buildings mere quarries for local builders."

"If Madinat al-Zahra's abandoned, why are we going there?" Isabella had wondered out loud.

"Because not all the treasures were stolen. The Caliph's wise man persuaded the Berbers to leave the great library. They had no interest in books and scrolls, so they let him have his way. Since then, the descendants of that wise man have kept the library.

"Nasir al-Din is the great-great-grandson of the original wise man. He is also the last of his line and already extremely old. When he dies," Shabaka had told them, "there will be no one else to tend Madinat al-Zahra's books."

John remembered the first time he and Isabella had met Nasir as clearly as if it were yesterday. Nasir had been sitting exactly where he was now, his eyes closed, his beard white, straggling and long, and with pieces of his most recent meal embedded in it. John had barely been able to believe that someone as deeply wrinkled and obviously ancient could still be alive. Perhaps, he had thought, the old man was dead and his body preserved by the sun, but then Nasir's eyes had sprung open and regarded his visitors brightly.

"Greetings," Nasir said in a voice that called to mind two rough pieces of stone being rubbed together.

"Greetings," John and Isabella replied in unison.

"We would like to see the library," John added.

"We would like to see the library," Nasir repeated. "The world has come to this. Once, a visitor here would bring a delicacy and we would sit and drink tea and talk of the world. Now it is simply, 'We would like to see the library.' Well, there is the library before you. Look all you wish."

Nasir waved a grizzled arm vaguely at the building behind him and closed his eyes.

John and Isabella stood in the hot sun, exchanging glances and feeling stupid.

"We're looking for a book," John said uncertainly.

"There are many books in Cordova," Nasir replied without opening his eyes. "Find one there."

John felt himself getting angry. They had travelled a long way and were tired, and now this old man was dismissing them out of hand. He opened his mouth to try again, but Isabella silenced him with a wave and stepped forward. "We humbly apologize for our rudeness. In the north we did not learn your ways. But even as far away as we were, the fame of the library of Madinat al-Zahra, and of Nasir al-Din who keeps it safe, was known to all."

Nasir opened his eyes and stared at Isabella. "You are a liar," he said, "but you understand flattery and the need an old man like me has of it. And you have a beauty that would turn the head of the great Abd ar-Rahman away from al-Zahra herself. What is it you and your coarse companion seek?"

Isabella smiled acknowledgement of the compliment and turned to John.

"I, too, am sorry..." John began a stumbling apology, but Nasir interrupted.

"You have neither beauty nor honeyed words. Say simply what you wish."

John took a deep breath. "A book on drawing by a Roman called Lucius. It is a companion to one on statues called *Scultura*. Umar told me it was in your library."

"Umar!" Nasir suddenly became animated. "The old fool still lives? Why did you not give me news of him sooner?"

"I'm afraid it is not good news," John said. "Umar is dead."

Nasir slumped back down. "How?"

"It was in Minerve, before the siege. He slipped by a well and hit his head." John didn't mention that it was his friend, Peter, who had pushed the old man.

"And such a head," Nasir said, thoughtfully. "Umar had some strange ideas about God, but his head was full of many wonders. The world will be a sadder place without him." Nasir fell silent and his gaze drifted over the dry landscape. John shuffled his feet uncomfortably and coughed.

"You are impatient," Nasir said, returning his stare to the new arrivals, "but you are young and from the north. I suppose you have no choice. How goes the war there?"

"Badly," John said. "The crusade is killing many good people."

"As always in war," Nasir agreed with a nod. "It is so often the best who are taken first. And I feel the winds of war gathering here. I do not think I shall live to see it, but it comes nonetheless. But you were telling me of Umar."

"Before he died," John said, "he passed on many of the books he had memorized to me."

Nasir stared at John with something like respect. "You have the memory palace?"

"Memory cloister, we call it, but yes, I do."

"It matters not what you call it." Nasir waved a hand dismissively. "What is important is that you have preserved at least some of Umar's knowledge." The old man turned to look sadly at the doorway to his library. "I fear much more knowledge will soon be lost.

In the days of my ancestors, Abd ar-Rahman's library held over four thousand books. Now there is but a tenth part of that left."

"What happened to them?" John asked.

Nasir turned back to look at the pair. "Many things," he said with a wry smile. "The Berbers took some to fuel their cooking fires when they destroyed the city, and over the many years, others have plundered as the mood took them. Neither I nor my predecessors have had the strength to prevent such desecration. All we have been able to do is prevent the rats from gnawing at the books that are left. We have always had to rely on our remoteness and most people's sad disinterest in learning. Umar, and now you, have saved some.

"Do you have the memory palace?" Nasir asked Isabella.

"John has taught me. I find it hard, but I try."

"That is all we may ask," Nasir said with a smile. "Will you save some of what is left before I pass over and the rats have their final victory?"

"Yes," John and Isabella said almost simultaneously. They turned and smiled at each other. Then John frowned. "If they are in a language we can understand."

"Such youthful enthusiasm," Nasir said, "to agree without thought. But you are in luck. Many books were burned for their value as fuel, but those stolen were most often taken by Moors, who took works in their own language. Many of the remaining works are from the pagan days and are in Greek or Latin."

"Has Lucius' work on drawing survived?" John asked.

"*Perspectiva*, the book is called. It is long since I have seen it—we have few Latin scholars visit. I fear my eyes are weak and my joints pain me now, so I have been remiss in my duties, but it may still be here." Nasir struggled to his feet. "There are few luxuries out here and it is a lonely life, but while you learn and search, you will have an entire city, albeit a ruined one, to yourselves."

Nasir had shown them around the library that day. John smiled to himself as he remembered how Isabella had stepped forward and offered her arm when the old man stood up. The wrinkles around Nasir's mouth had deepened even more when he grinned. "Thank you," he said. "It has been many a year since I took the arm of a beautiful woman."

John often thought of the succession of men who had devoted their lives to preserving the library and of what would happen to it and the city after Nasir died. He remembered what Beatrice had said about it taking only a moment to destroy a book in a fire and he was determined to place as many books as he could in the memory cloister.

Madinat al-Zahra would survive much better. John imagined travellers in the far distant future wondering at the ruins, what they meant and who had lived there. They would see the three long tiers of the city on the hillside long before they reached it, its broken white walls gleaming in the sunshine. They would ride through the ruined gateway and, if the story was still remembered, wonder if this was where Abd ar-Rahman had placed the statue of the beautiful woman he loved.

Once in the city, the visitors would have to dismount and walk through the rubble that clogged the streets. They would wonder at the fallen pillars with their intricate carvings and the broad sweeps of the overgrown gardens. Undoubtedly, they would recognize the imposing ruined entrance to the Caliph's audience chamber as being part of an important building, but the library would be long empty, and they would probably not recognize the unremarkable square building that barely protruded from the hillside as the wondrous seat of knowledge it had once been.

John scanned the ruins, looking for Isabella. She had worked to learn some of the books, but she much preferred wandering the ruined city, scratching around and collecting odds and ends that had been missed by generations of plunderers who had been here before her. Right now, she was probably on her hands and knees in some filthy, dark corner, digging up a fragment of gold from some inlaid throne or a precious stone fallen from a royal sword.

John stood and stretched. It was time to return to the library. There wasn't much left for him to work with, just a few old maps and drawings that he had kept until last because they were much harder to memorize than books. He hadn't found Lucius' drawing book, but he had memorized several interesting scrolls.

He was also sad that their time here was coming to an end. Sitting beneath a tree as the sun set, with the air filled with the scent of oranges and his stomach filled with exotic delicacies, John had imagined succeeding Nasir as Madinat al- Zahra's librarian. It would be a good place to grow old, but John wasn't old yet, and this wasn't his land. Sooner or later, he and Isabella would have to return home. It would be hard to leave Nasir and the library to their fate, but all John could do was postpone the inevitable for as long as possible.

* * *

The monster's heads seemed to twist angrily as John tilted the vellum manuscript in the angled sunlight streaming through the library door. He had discovered some unusual drawings in his explorations, but this was easily the strangest.

Unrolled, the vellum was a square about a foot on each side. It was of very high quality and held an extremely detailed drawing of some mythical beast. From a bulbous mass to the bottom left of the page, seven heads writhed and intertwined. Each had a single, glaring red eye, beside which was inscribed a letter: D, A, R, H, E, K and E.

The bulbous mass was attached to a large body, on the back of which rode a woman with flowing robes and hair. The creature's legs were stretched out behind as if it were running. The back end appeared to lose definition and sprawl all over the page, ending in two tails, one of which hung down toward the bottom right corner while the other swept up and over the creature's back toward the woman, threatening her with a gaping serpent's mouth.

The illustration was brightly coloured—the monster was scarlet and the woman's cloak was delicately decorated in red, purple and gold. In her hand she carried a golden goblet set with many-coloured precious stones, each carefully drawn. Seven golden dots were spread over the beast's legs and belly, and each was accompanied by a Roman numeral. There was writing above and below the drawing. Above were the words "*septumdecim denique libri*," and below "*ungere qua oculus et septem opportunus*."

"Seventeen of the final book. Anoint where the eye and seven meet," John translated under his breath. It meant nothing to him, but the quality of the drawing was so fine he wanted to examine it more. He didn't get the chance.

"John! Come quickly. It's Nasir." Isabella's worried voice came from outside. He rolled up the scroll, stuffed it into the pouch hanging from his waist and rushed into the sun.

The heat hit him like a physical presence and the glare temporarily blinded him. He stopped and rubbed his eyes. He felt Isabella grab his arm and lead him aside. Blinking rapidly and with sweat already breaking out all over his body, John stood in front of the shade tree where Nasir habitually sat. The old man was in his usual position, his back against the trunk, hands crossed on his lap and eyes fixed on the flat plain below the ruined city.

"What's wrong?" John asked, but as soon as the words left his mouth, he knew. Nasir's eyes didn't move to look at him, but kept staring straight ahead.

"Nasir," John said, reaching out to touch the old man's shoulder. It was almost as if his touch released something and Nasir slumped into a heap on his side. The eyes remained open, staring blindly at the sky.

"He's dead," Isabella said unnecessarily.

John crouched and gently closed Nasir's eyes. "The last of the librarians of Madinat al-Zahra. We should not mourn him. He spent a long life doing what he loved. If whatever God is up there is indeed worthy of our prayers, he will welcome Nasir al-Din with open arms."

"We should move him out of the heat," Isabella said.

John threaded his arms under Nasir's shoulders and knees and lifted. The old man's body weighed almost nothing. It reminded John of carrying the dying Umar up the steep streets of Minerve.

John carried Nasir into the main hall of the library and laid the old man gently on the cool marble floor. "What is to be done?" he asked, returning outside. "I don't know what Nasir would wish for his body."

"Shabaka is due here this morning with supplies," Isabella said, sitting in the shaded doorway. "We'll ask him. But what will *we* do?"

John sat beside Isabella and gazed out over the plain. Although it was not yet noon, the land already appeared burned. The reddish-brown earth was broken by patches of green only where irrigation allowed a field of crops or a small stand of trees to flourish. The landscape shimmered in the heat and John had to screw up his eyes to make out the scattered buildings that appeared to have grown from the dried earth rather than being formed by the work of men.

John was sad, he'd grown very fond of Nasir in the time they'd spent here. The man carried an amazing wealth of information in his head. On the surface, Nasir's world was limited—a few hundred old books scattered through the darkened rooms of a deserted library in the middle of a ruined city—but John had come to see that it was much more. Each of those books was a doorway to another world, a world of Greek philosophers, Roman poets, Arab mathematicians. Even with only four hundred books left, Nasir's world was almost limitless. What must it have been like when there were ten times that number?

Nasir was a Moor, yet he reminded John of the Cathars he had known. He had the same open-minded interest in the world, unfettered by the blind dogma that limited Peter's thinking and contributed to the death and destruction in Languedoc. John promised himself that he would never become so wrapped up in a single idea or belief that he would ignore another opinion, or worse, persecute the person who held it.

Some of John's favourite times at Madinat al-Zahra had been sitting in the cool of every evening, sipping tea and talking with Nasir. Sometimes Isabella would join them, but often she was off exploring the ruins that stretched along the hillside. Now and again, they talked of the small mathematics book by Aristarchos of Samos that John had learned in Bram and still carried with him.

Nasir knew of the book and could explain many of the complex symbols, but he could also take the ancient information and lead John in new and sometimes frightening directions. He painted pictures of a universe so vast it was barely imaginable. At its centre was the sun, a great eternally burning ball of fire, and around it the planets in orbit. The moon spun around the Earth and in doing so, caused the tides. The millions of other stars visible on the clear desert nights were like the sun, but so far away as to appear tiny.

The ideas fascinated John, as did most of what he and Nasir discussed. One evening, however, the old man went further and suggested something truly shocking—a new heresy.

"Suppose," Nasir had said, "that Aristarchos was correct, which mathematicians with much better minds than I say he is. Suppose the balls of fire that are the distant stars are like our sun."

John nodded agreement.

"If they are like our sun, might they not be surrounded by planets like the ones you call Mercury, Venus and Mars?"

"I don't see why not," John said.

"And Earth?" Nasir added with a mischievous glint in his eye.

"Yes," John said hesitantly.

"And on that far Earth, might there not be a you and an I, sitting beneath a tree looking up at the tiny, distant glint of our sun in their sky?"

"No!" John said instinctively. "God created our earth for us. He put Adam and Eve in the Garden of Eden."

"But you agree that there are other suns and planets and earths. Is it not arrogantly presumptive of us to assume that God created this great majestic universe simply to give us some twinkling stars to look at on a summer night and provide poets with a subject for their verse?"

"I don't know," John said and Nasir laughed.

"That is the thing about knowledge," Nasir said. "One piece leads to others. As long as you believe, like your Christian church teaches, that the stars are mere dots of heavenly light shining through pinpricks in a fixed crystalline sphere, all is simple. The moment you expand the universe to include millions of suns uncountable miles away, any thoughtful mind is led to the sorts of conclusions I have just outlined."

"Led into heresy," John said.

Nasir tilted his head in agreement. "That is why some believers, in my religion as much as yours, wish to prevent us seeking knowledge and questioning the universe."

John nodded thoughtfully. The ideas were fascinating and exciting, but almost any one of them would have him thrown on a bonfire back home if he spoke of it to the wrong people. He thought of Peter. His friend was intelligent, but he was afraid of where questioning like this might lead. He took the easy way and embraced the beliefs of the Church so he didn't have to think too hard. Sometimes, when he came upon some new and radical idea, John envied Peter's certainty. But it wasn't for him. John had to keep seeking, even if he never found the answer.

John loved the loneliness of Madinat al-Zahra. There was knowledge all around him and no one to tell him which ideas he could think about and which he could not. His mind was free.

"I've been thinking we should leave here." Isabella's voice broke into John's memories.

"We haven't found Lucius' *Perspectiva*," John said instinctively.

"It isn't here," Isabella said. "You've looked at all the books—you'd have found it by now. And you've memorized all the important books. All that's left are a few minor works, books in a language we don't know and some sketches.

"Our time here has been remarkable, and I would not exchange it for a chest of gold, but it's time to go. The world is moving on around us and Shabaka says there is trouble brewing. If a war breaks out, we will be on the wrong side. And what is happening back in Toulouse and Languedoc? I want to know. I want to go home."

John knew Isabella was right. Their time here *had* been wonderful, but staying longer was simply avoiding the world, in the same way that Peter's unquestioning belief in the Church was his way of avoiding difficult ideas. It *was* time to go.

"You're right," John said. "I don't want this time to end, but I—"

John was interrupted by Shabaka rounding the broken wall behind the orange tree. He was covered in dust and leading three unladen donkeys. John and Isabella stood up and stepped into the sun.

"Hello, Johan and Is'bella," Shabaka shouted as he drew close. "Where is the old man?" He nodded to Nasir's usual spot beneath the orange tree.

"Nasir died this morning," John said.

"Aaaaaahhh," Shabaka let out a long, low groan. "May his soul rest with the angels. Where is he?"

"In the library," Isabella said. "We didn't know what he would want done with his body."

"He thought of that. Long past he had me dig his grave high on the hill above Abd ar-Rahman's audience chamber. It is a pleasant spot with good views and it faces Mecca. We shall bury him there and then I must talk with you. But first we must wash and prepare the body."

* * *

"We created you from it, and return you into it, and from it we will raise you a second time." Shabaka spoke the proper words over the fresh mound of red earth on the hillside. He had been right: it was a beautiful spot, surrounded by the shade trees that Nasir had loved, yet with spectacular, panoramic views over the wide plain of the Guadalquivir River.

"Goodbye," Isabella said, wiping a tear.

"And thank you," John added. "You were a great librarian and, whenever I pass on one of your books, I shall tell of you, the last of the librarians of Madinat al-Zahra."

"And now we must talk," Shabaka said, leading the pair over to a shady spot and passing round a goatskin of wine. "It is appropriate that Nasir should die this day. He would not have wished to see the war he knew was coming, and he had grown fond of you. He would miss you and it is not good for an old man to be lonely."

"Miss us?" John asked, puzzled.

"You must go," Shabaka said plainly. "That is why I brought no supplies and two extra donkeys. They are for you. Tomorrow as the sun rises we will leave."

"Tomorrow?" John asked, frightened by the suddenness of the decision.

"The caliph Muhammad an-Nasir has assembled a mighty army, some say four hundred thousand men, at Sevilla, and the Christian kings Alfonso and Pedro have finally united. They wait with a host of knights at Toledo. Alfonso has not forgotten his humiliation at the Battle of Alarcos and is eager for revenge."

John glanced at Isabella at the mention of the battle that had killed her father. She was staring at Shabaka, her face creased with worry.

"Soon," Shabaka went on, "there will be a great battle, one of the greatest in history, and it will decide the fate of Al-Andalus for all time."

"But this battle won't be here," Isabella said. "We're safe."

"No one will be safe. Al-Andalus has a great history of tolerance. Christians, Jews and Muslims have all contributed their strengths to this land and freely shared their wisdom and knowledge with one another, but I fear those days are fast vanishing. The Caliph has said he will conquer Toledo and drive every Christian out. If he wins, he will attempt that. If he loses, he will take his revenge on any Christians he can find. Either way, this summer no one with fair hair"—Shabaka looked pointedly at John—"will be safe here. There is still time to travel to Toledo and your own people—many Christians are on that road—but we must leave tomorrow. Once the fighting begins, those caught on the wrong side, innocent or not, will suffer."

John thought back to the suffering of the innocents in Béziers. Was the hatred of the crusade about to explode here?

"You're coming with us?" Isabella asked.

"Part of the way, at least. I have been here too long and my feet itch for the road." Shabaka frowned. "Besides, there is a task I have long promised myself I would attempt and now is the time."

"Will we be safer in Toledo, if that is where the Caliph is headed?" John wondered out loud.

"Maybe, maybe not," Shabaka said with a shrug. "But you will be with your own kind. It is said that there are knights from the north in Alfonso and Pedro's army, sent here by the Pope. And, young scholar," Shabaka continued, looking at John, "Nasir told me you seek a book that was here but is no longer."

"A book on drawing, yes."

"A few years past, a band of monks from Toledo came here and took five donkey loads of books away with them. Nasir could do nothing but wish them well: it is the curse of all the librarians of Madinat az-Zahra to watch their beloved charges be taken and scattered. The monks took the books to Toledo where they planned to translate them. I do not, and neither did Nasir, know if the book you seek was on one of those mules, but it is possible. The book is no longer here and few northerners, other than these monks, have visited here in recent memory."

John felt his heart speed up with excitement. It had been a disappointment to discover that Lucius' *Perspectiva* was not in Nasir's library, but here at least was another clue to follow.

"It's possible, yes," he said. "Thank you."

"But I shall let you talk," Shabaka said, standing. "I have brought food and shall prepare us a meal. All journeys go best if one is well fed at the start."

"Looks as if our decision's made for us," John said when Shabaka was gone. "I wonder if Lucius' book is in Toledo."

"I don't want to go to Toledo." Isabella's statement took John by surprise.

"But *you* suggested we leave here."

"Yes, but I want to go to Toulouse. I don't want to go to Toledo."

"Why not?"

Isabella hesitated, as if deciding on an answer. "I don't want us to get caught up in the war," she said eventually.

"But we can't stay here, and Shabaka has offered to guide us. It'll be much safer travelling with him." John was confused. Isabella was normally clear in everything she said, but her reasons for not going to Toledo seemed weak. John thought back to the worried look he had seen on her face when Shabaka had mentioned Alfonso of Castille and Pedro of Aragon and their knights being at Toledo. Did that have something to do with it?

Isabella had been a bit strange during the time they had spent in Aragon on the way to Cordova. For the most part she had been her usual cheerful self, showing John the sights and telling him stories from Aragon's history, but as soon as he brought up the subject of her family or where she was born, she became silent and withdrawn. Something had been bothering her then and John wondered if it was connected with her reluctance to go to Toledo now. He wanted to know, but now wasn't the time to try to find out.

"We won't stay long," he said. "I'd like a couple of days to see if the book is there, but then we can set off north. The alternative is to go off on our own and try to find our way north without going through Toledo. I think that way we'd be in a lot more danger of getting caught up in this war."

John watched as a range of emotions played over Isabella's face. Confusion and doubt dominated, but John saw flashes of fear too.

Eventually, Isabella closed her eyes and let out a long sigh. "You're right," she said, opening her eyes and looking at him sadly. "We don't really have a choice. I know that. But let's not stay long. Let's move on quickly."

"Of course." John put his arm around her and Isabella leaned against him and rested her head on his shoulder. He stroked her hair. "It'll be all right. We'll be back in Toulouse before you know it."

For a long time the pair sat on the hillside beside Nasir's grave. John thought back over the almost two years since they had set out from Minerve. It had been a happy time. Isabella and he had developed an easy relationship. Both enjoyed travelling, discovering new things and discussing what everything meant. Both were fascinated by the past, but John's interest was in the minds of those who had gone before, whereas Isabella was drawn to how they had lived and the things they had left behind. John was never happier than when, in the evening, wherever they were, they sat together and talked over what they had found during the day.

Isabella took a deep breath and lifted her head. She was smiling, but her eyes were uneasy. For a moment, John hoped she was about to tell him what was troubling her, but then her face relaxed and her smile became less forced. "I found something," she said, reaching into the leather satchel she carried.

She took out a package wrapped in a dirty piece of cloth. She unwound the cloth to reveal a square of ivory about twice the size of the palm of her hand. One side was intricately carved with wonderful swirling patterns of branches and leaves, surrounded by tiny birds. Each vein on a leaf and feather on a bird was picked out in lines of pure gold and the birds' eyes were minute precious stones. More sparkling gems were inlaid in an intricate pattern around the border.

"It's beautiful," John gasped. "Where did you find it?" Isabella had dug up a number of interesting things that had been missed by looters. They kept a pouch of the smaller, more valuable items, mostly broken pieces of gold and silver jewellery and precious stones that had come out of their mountings, but nothing was as complete or as striking as this ivory tile.

"I was digging around in the audience chamber and it was under a pile of dirt in a corner. I think it was once a panel in a larger box or casket. It was probably broken up by looters who missed this piece." Isabella handed the square to John. "I want you to have it."

"It's so beautiful and valuable. Thank you. I'll carry it with the other pieces, but it's ours."

"Keep it safe," Isabella said, and John thought he saw a hint of sadness pass over her face, but then it was gone.

"I found something interesting as well," John said. "I'd like you to have it. It's not as beautiful or valuable as your find, but the workmanship is exquisite." He pulled the vellum out of his satchel and unrolled it. "What do you think it means?"

Isabella leaned over the picture. "A monster with seven heads," she said thoughtfully. "That sounds familiar. What does the writing say?" She tilted the page to see better. "*Septumdecim denique libri*."

"Seventeen of the final book," John translated. "It doesn't mean anything."

"Yes, it does!" Isabella said triumphantly. "I remember where I've heard of the monster—it's from the Book of Revelations of St. John. Seventeen must be the verse number."

John entered the memory cloister and went to the alcove that housed the Bible. He visualized the end. "You're right," he said closing his eyes and reciting the bits that seemed relevant to the drawing. "'And there came one of the seven angels. And I saw a woman sit upon a scarlet coloured beast, having seven heads and ten horns. And the woman was arrayed in purple and scarlet colour, and decked with gold and precious stones and pearls, having a golden cup in her hand. And I saw the woman drunken with the blood of the saints. And the angel said unto me, behold the beast that was, and is not, and yet is. The seven heads are seven mountains, on which the woman sitteth.'" John opened his eyes. "That must be it."

"Yes," Isabella agreed, "but what does it *mean*?" She read the writing underneath the beast. "*Ungere qua oculus et septem opportunus.*"

"Anoint where the eye and seven meet," John translated again. "It makes no sense! There are seven eyes—how can they meet?"

"And what do the letters by the heads mean? Or the seven numbers by the golden dots?"

"They're not consecutive numbers," John observed. "See, there are two of number I and no number VI, but only one each of II, III, IV, V and VII. It's a mystery."

"Indeed," Isabella agreed, "but it is a wonderfully done piece of work. I don't suppose we'll ever know what it means. Thank you." She kissed him lightly on the cheek. "But come on. We should go and eat before Shabaka burns our supper."

Isabella stood, rolled up the picture and headed down the hill. John rewrapped the ivory and gently placed it in his pouch. He stood watching his friend, a worried look creasing his brow. Suddenly, things seemed to be happening very fast.

Auramazdah

Toledo
June, 1212

"Come in, sir, and see the finest blades in all of Toledo. My ancestors made swords for the Roman legions. The great warrior emperor, Hadrian, carried one of these very blades."

John hesitated and peered over the rough counter that bordered the street. The blacksmith's shop was like a scene from hell. It was open to the sky, but even on a June afternoon John could feel the blast of heat from the forge. A large man wearing little more than a leather apron and bathed in sweat was beating a long rod of glowing steel with a hammer that John wondered if he would even be able to lift. Each blow was deafening, and sparks flew in all directions.

"Toledo steel." A small man, carrying a wickedly curved scimitar, stepped from the shadows. "The most excellent steel in the world. Made in a way that has been kept secret for a thousand years. Soft enough to bend without breaking"—he flexed the thin scimitar blade—"yet hard enough to take and hold the sharpest edge." The scimitar became a blur in his hands and sliced through a fat candle standing on the counter. The candle appeared undamaged, but the man leaned over and lifted the top half up to reveal a perfect cut. He laughed. "And it will do the same to your enemy's neck. I see you are a discerning man. Try it, sir." He offered John the handle.

"I'm not a knight or a squire." John shrugged apologetically. "I have no money." That wasn't strictly true. He had the fragments that Isabella had found, but they were for living expenses. The jewel-encrusted ivory tile was undoubtedly worth a lot, but he would only sell that in an emergency.

The small man's head bobbed from side to side. "You have a lucky face, sir. Perhaps one day, when you have made your fortune, you will remember my humble forge and return for your blade. I have marked it, see."

The man pointed to a pattern stamped into the steel blade by the handle. John puzzled over the strange arrangement of lines and triangles. "What does it mean?" he asked.

"It is the name of the sword."

"But it's not in any language I've ever seen," John said.

"It is a very ancient language," the blacksmith explained. "It is spoken no more, but some remember it. Such a sword as this carries the name of a god. Try it."

John passed his satchel to Isabella and, gingerly, took the sword. It was surprisingly light and the handle, although simple and unornamented, fit his hand comfortably. He twisted it experimentally. It was a superb weapon, designed for speed and skill rather than the crude slaughter of a northern sword or Oddo's axe.

John tested the curved blade and a spot of blood appeared almost magically on his thumb. He pressed the sword against the candle and it disappeared into the solid wax with no resistance. How Adso would love a blade like this!

John handed it back. "It's beautiful."

"One day, when you are rich, you will come back." The small man smiled. "When you do, ask for Auramazdah."

A jolt ran through John. He knew that name. Umar had told him about the ancient dualist religion from which the Cathars had received their ideas that there were two gods—Angra Mainyu, the god of lies, evil and chaos, and Auramazdah, the god of truth, good and creation—and that mankind was their battleground.

"Your name is Auramazdah?" John asked in wonder.

The man laughed. "Not me. I am Abdul, a humble blacksmith. Auramazdah is what is written on the blade. It is the sword's name."

"We have to go." Isabella's whisper was urgent in John's ear.

"What?" He turned to where Isabella stood behind him. She nodded down the street. It was narrow and sloped steeply up to the Alcazar, the Moorish palace of the caliphs before Toledo had been conquered by the Christians more than a hundred years before. There were several knights in view, strolling or examining weapons at the various blacksmiths' shops. None was in armour, but most wore a surcoat emblazoned with the red crusader cross. Only one knight was different, and he immediately caught John's eye. Instead of the cross, the man's surcoat bore a falcon clutching a black axe in its talons.

"A Falcon," John said under his breath. The knight wasn't paying them any attention, but he was coming closer. "Is Oddo here?" A surge of fear darted through John as he thought of the man whose face he had scarred and who had sworn to kill him in revenge.

"I don't know," Isabella said, "but we can't take the chance. We must go."

John nodded. He murmured his thanks to the blacksmith and the pair set off hurriedly up the hill.

"Why are Oddo's Falcons here?" John wondered a soon as they had put some distance between themselves and the knights. "I know Pope Innocent has called this crusade against the Moors, but the Falcons are sworn to de Montfort and he would never leave his new lands until they're completely conquered."

"Maybe he's the only one," Isabella said hopefully.

"Maybe," John replied, unconvinced.

The pair continued up the hill. They had almost reached the Alcazar when Isabella broke the silence. "I hate this place," she said. "Let's leave now."

John wasn't fond of Toledo either. It was certainly a beautiful city, sitting on a hill in a curve of the Tagus River and dominated by the old Moorish Alcazar, but it was where Alfonso and Pedro's mighty crusading army was gathering to await the Caliph's next move, and the streets were full of knights, monks and rough mercenary soldiers. On the other hand, they'd only been in the city for two days and John hadn't yet managed to track down the monks who had visited Nasir's library at Madinat al-Zahra. There were a lot of monasteries, both in the town itself and scattered through the surrounding countryside.

John was torn. He was desperate to find Lucius' book, but Toledo made him nervous and Isabella had been short-tempered and edgy ever since they'd left Cordova. Shabaka had escorted them to the mountain pass that led down to Toledo and marked the border of Moorish Al-Andalus. He had wished them luck and turned back south, talking mysteriously about something he had to do and complaining that he had no desire to be stared at like a carnival oddity because the crude northerners did not know enough of the world to realize that it was populated by people of a whole range of skin tones.

On top of everything else, Toledo was an expensive place to be. Every merchant had doubled or tripled his prices to take advantage of the crusader host, and all the religious houses that offered free cots and simple meals to pilgrims were filled to overflowing. Even the money they could get from selling the bits and pieces in John's pouch wouldn't last them long. They would have to be on the road north soon enough.

"I haven't found the book yet," John said as he strode around a corner beside the Alcazar. There was no immediate answer from Isabella. John turned to look for her and crashed into a group of monks heading down the hill. Flustered, he began to apologize, but words deserted him as he looked into the face of the leading monk. The staring, emotionless eyes seemed to reach out and hold him.

"Aumery," he gasped.

"Ah," Arnaud Aumery said as a smile of recognition curled his lips. "The young heretic who helped murder the blessed Pierre of Castelnau. I have often wondered what became of you." The monk looked John up and down. "And dressed in Moorish robes. Do you have a new master now?"

"N...no. I...I...I'm not a heretic," John stammered, although he knew that by Aumery's rigid standards he probably was. "I had nothing to do with Pierre of Castelnau's death."

"That will be for the Holy Inquisition to decide. Seize him."

Two monks, a lay brother and a knight wearing the crusader cross grabbed John. He wrestled but they hauled him to the ground.

"Take him to the Alcazar and lock him in one of the cells," Aumery ordered. "I shall examine him later."

John protested as he was dragged up the hill, but no one listened. He was scared and suddenly lonely. As he was being dragged away, he had seen no sign of Isabella.

* * *

The cell was cold and damp and the only light came from a tiny barred window high on one wall. The heavy oak door also had a window, but it let in no light; the corridor outside was as dark as the cell. The floor was covered in a thick layer of stinking, damp straw, in which John could hear the rustle of rats. He had been locked in the tiny room for only a few of hours and he was already terrified and depressed, his mind full of questions. Where was Isabella? How long was he to be kept here? What was Aumery's plan for him? His last question was answered first. A flickering light illuminated the window in the door and the rusty hinges groaned in protest.

"I must apologize for the standard of the accommodation." Aumery stood in the doorway, holding a blazing torch. He was smiling. "Space is at a premium with the crusade here, but you need not stay here any longer. Come, I have something to show you."

Reluctantly, John followed Aumery and an armed guard out of the cell and along the stone corridor. After a couple of turns, they stopped outside another door. The guard unlocked it and pushed it open.

"Wait here. I will call if I need you," Aumery ordered the guard as he ushered John into the room and closed the door.

The room was considerably bigger and cleaner than the cell John had been in. A fire blazed welcomingly in the hearth and torches were mounted in brackets along the walls. Despite the warmth and light, John shivered—the room was filled with instruments of torture.

"This is the examining room for the Holy Inquisition," Aumery said almost cheerfully. He placed his torch in an empty bracket and began showing John around with evident pride. "The Devil is cunning, and sometimes the Inquisition is forced to use persuasion to find the truth."

Torture, John thought, but he said nothing.

"We are forbidden by the Holy Scriptures to shed blood, so you will find no crude axes or swords here. Fire we use"—Aumery waved an arm casually at an array of pokers in a rack by the hearth. One was already placed in the flames and its head glowed a dull red—"because heat seals a wound and prevents bleeding. Fire is also a great purifier."

"However, I find the strappado most successful." Aumery pointed to a large iron hook embedded in the roof. "The heretic's hands are tied behind them with a rope that is then passed over the hook. When one pulls on the rope, the heretic is lifted from the ground and the shoulders become dislocated. I am told it is very painful and that weights may be added to the feet to increase the effect."

John was utterly horrified, as much by the calm way in which Aumery described the torture as by the methods themselves.

"Of course, there are many other refinements: the rack may be applied to the entire body; screws may be used to crush thumbs, hands and feet; and iron chairs may be set above a fire. The trick is to use a method of persuasion that suits the constitution and moral strength of the heretic being examined. Children usually require little more than heating of the feet, and women most often cooperate before men.

"Were I to assess you"—Aumery turned to look at John. His eyes stared coldly and all pretence of a smile vanished—"I would judge that you are strong and we should need the hot irons and the strappado."

John felt the blood drain from his face and his legs weaken. He reached out to steady himself against the nearest wall.

"You look pale," Aumery said, suddenly concerned. "Do not misunderstand me. I have no wish to apply these methods to you. Besides, your trial will not be by the Church. You are accused of a civil crime, aiding in the murder of Pierre of Castelnau, a papal legate to His Holiness Innocent III. You will be tried by the civil court and, if found guilty, you will be hanged.

"Of course," Aumery continued thoughtfully, "were you to be accused of heresy, then that, as a crime against God, would have precedence and the

Inquisition would have to become involved. But there is no need of that. I wish merely to talk with you."

"About what?" John managed to ask in a whisper.

"Our mutual friend, Peter, told me of the unfortunate accident that befell the old man, Umar, in Minerve. Whatever happened to him?"

"He died." John concentrated on breathing regularly and his racing heart slowed.

"I suspected as much, since he was not among those who climbed the pyre after the town fell. Such a shame! I would have liked to talk with him. But *you* talked with him."

John nodded. As he grew calmer, he began to think more clearly. What was Aumery after?

"What did you talk of?"

"Many things," John said warily. Was Aumery after the books in the memory cloister? "Cordova, Al-Andalus, places he had been. Umar was a much travelled man."

"Indeed. And you talked of books, I imagine."

John tensed. How much did Aumery know? "Some books," John said. "Umar had read many in his journeying."

"Hmm." Aumery scratched his chin thoughtfully. "All of this," he said, sweeping his arm wide to encompass the instruments of torture, "is of little use with the Cathar Perfects. They suffer happily for their misguided faith, but there are those who are not so certain. I have had the pleasure of talking"—Aumery's smile sent a chill down John's spine—"with some of them."

"Do you read a lot?"

John was startled by the abrupt change in topic. "There were not many books in Minerve," he answered uncertainly.

"No," Aumery agreed, "but there are many in Al-Andalus."

"So I have heard, but most are in the language of the Moors."

"Yes, and we must work to translate them. One in particular, I heard tell of from a woman at Lavaur. She claimed to know the whereabouts of a gospel supposedly written by Christ himself."

John clenched his jaw and blinked at the runnels of sweat stinging his eyes. He couldn't prevent himself from glancing at the strappado hook in the ceiling. The memory cloister felt like a lead weight in his head.

"A forgery, of course, if it even exists," Aumery said companionably. He was smiling, but John couldn't meet his eyes. "The Devil in his malevolence sends many forgeries to attempt to confound us. Unfortunately, the weak are sometimes tempted, do you not find it so?"

"I suppose so," John managed to croak out. Was he going to be tortured for the Gospel of Christ? If so, how long could he last before he told Aumery everything he knew?

"I hope you are not weak," Aumery continued.

John could only shake his head.

"Did the old man in Minerve ever talk to you of the Cathar treasure?" Aumery asked, abruptly changing the topic once more.

John hesitated. He felt Aumery's piercing eyes studying him. "I'm not sure," John stalled. "What is the Cathar Treasure?"

"Something of great value," Aumery said. "Do *you* know what it is?" He leaned forward eagerly.

"No," John said, too quickly. "Why would Umar tell me of treasure? I hardly knew him."

"Liar!" Aumery almost screamed the word and John staggered back against the wall. "I saw you flinch when I mentioned the treasure and you were close to the vile Perfect, Beatrice. The old man and the Perfect are both dead. You are all that's left, and you *will* tell me what I want to know."

"I don't know anything about the treasure," John said.

"We'll see." Aumery relaxed and leaned back. "Ultimately, it matters little what you tell me. I have other means. For example, your gangly friend, Peter, is this minute following a clue I discovered, which may lead to the treasure without your assistance."

"Where is Peter?" John asked.

"That is not your concern." Aumery's smile returned and John was reminded of a snake preparing to strike. "I have to admit that I lied to you as well. I guessed that you would need the hot irons and the strappado to encourage your cooperation. That's not true. I think you will tell me what I want to know before I have even crushed your thumbs."

John's knees went weak. He was relieved he was still leaning against the wall.

"It's an interesting thing. We think of our bones as strong because they hold us up." Aumery reached out both of his hands and took one of John's, the one that had healed twisted after he burned it throwing hot coals on Oddo's face outside Minerve. John shuddered at the touch, but was surprised at its gentleness.

"But bones and the joints between them are *not* strong." John winced as Aumery slowly bent his thumb back.

"The joints give first, of course," Aumery said, as if casually explaining the workings of some machine. John tried to pull his hand away, but Aumery held it firmly. The pain was increasing and sweat returned to John's forehead.

"But with the skilful application of enough pressure..."

John gasped. It felt as if his thumb was about to come out of its socket. The pain was excruciating.

"Any bone in the body can be turned to little more than a thick porridge."

John let out a low moan. He couldn't stand much more of this.

"It's quite amusing," Aumery said conversationally, "how a thumb, or any limb that we consider solid, will flop around like a dead fish once the bones in it are crushed."

Aumery suddenly let go of John's hand. "Guard," he shouted.

John cradled his hand against his chest, trying not to cry with relief.

"You will go back to your cell and think on what I have said and what you have seen and felt here," Aumery said. "I must go and have your crime registered as heresy. Then you will be mine and we can talk much more freely."

The guard opened the door.

"Take him back to his cell," Aumery ordered. "I shall come for him later."

When John didn't move, the guard grabbed him by the arm, dragged him along the corridor and threw him onto the filthy straw of his cell. John lay there quietly, nursing his sore thumb and worrying. He doubted he could last long under serious torture, but the truly terrifying thing was that he didn't even know if he possessed the information Aumery sought. He could tell him about the Gospel of the Christ, but that would only convince Aumery that John had to die to prevent others learning of it.

John had heard Beatrice and Umar mention treasure, but neither had told him what it was or where it was hidden. Aumery would torture him until he was a helpless, pain-wracked, gibbering wreck before he was convinced that John knew nothing. John shut his eyes to stop the tears, but he couldn't hide the image of his broken body hanging from the strappado while Aumery gleefully applied red hot irons to his twisting limbs.

* * *

John had no idea how much time had passed before the flickering light of a torch illuminated the corridor outside his cell. *No! It's too soon*, his mind screamed. *Why couldn't he be a rat and simply disappear into the foul straw?*

"John." The voice was only a whisper, but it hauled John to his feet in an instant.

"Isabella?"

"How are you?"

John clutched the bars and peered out. Isabella was standing only two feet away, holding a flaming torch. She was dressed in rough travelling clothes and her long hair was tied behind her head. The light flashed in her dark eyes. To John, she had never looked more beautiful.

"What happened to you? Where did you go?" John forced his forearm through the narrow space between the bars. Isabella reached over and took his hand.

"I was a couple of steps behind you when I saw Aumery. You were too close to him for me to warn you. I just ducked into an alley. I don't think he saw me."

"What are you doing here? Did they capture you too? Are they accusing you of heresy?"

Isabella glanced nervously back along the corridor where the guard was leaning against the wall, leering in her direction. "No. I came to the Alcazar to talk to King Pedro."

"Talk to King Pedro! Why? How?" Isabella had always been fearless, but talking to kings!

"I can talk to Pedro because he is my uncle. Now, we don't have much time. If you stop asking questions, I'll tell you a story."

John nodded, too stunned to respond.

Isabella closed her eyes and took a deep breath. When she opened them, she began. "I lied to you when I said my father was killed at the Battle of Alarcos. He wasn't. In fact, he's still alive."

"What—"

Isabella's look silenced John.

"He *did* fight at Alarcos"—Isabella hesitated and her eyes flicked down —"but on the Moorish side."

John struggled to stay silent.

"My father's name is Fernando del Huesca. My mother was Leonora, sister to Pedro. Before I was born, when King Pedro's father, Alfonso, ruled Aragon, Fernando del Huesca was a young knight at the court. He was strikingly handsome and a favourite with all the ladies, but he had a cruel streak. He was arrogant and believed that whatever he wished should be his by right.

"Fernando set his sights on Leonora, even though he knew that Alfonso had plans to wed his daughter to the Count of Montpellier to strengthen his claims to the lands across the mountains. But Fernando persisted and secretly turned all his considerable charm on Leonora. At first she resisted him, but she was a child, younger than I am now, and she could not withstand the approaches of the handsome, worldly Fernando for long. He seduced her and, once he had achieved his goal, abandoned her and moved on.

"My mother was devastated at losing her honour, but worse followed. As the weeks passed, Leonora realized that she was pregnant. Now it would not even be possible to keep her shame secret. She wrote a letter to her beloved brother Pedro and fled to a convent in the mountains, where I was born."

Isabella paused, as if gathering strength.

"My mother sickened in the harsh conditions of the convent. The sisters did all they could, but she died when I was only a few months old. However, before she died, she gave the sisters all the money she had managed to bring with her, a letter telling me the story of my birth and a letter to her distant cousin, Count Raymond of Toulouse, begging that he give me a home and allow me to be brought up at his court.

"The good sisters took care of me until I was old enough to travel and then placed me in the care of a pious merchant who was en route to Toulouse. The count took me in, arranged for my upbringing and trained me as a handmaid to his wife. The rest you know."

Isabella looked so sad that John's heart ached. He wished more than anything that the door between them would vanish so that he could hold and comfort her. She was like the tragic heroine in one of William of Arles' songs, he thought, born to royalty but denied her right by a cruel fate that killed her mother and left her estranged from her father.

"What happened to Fernando?" he asked gently.

"Pedro was a headstrong young man," Isabella continued her story. "When he read my mother's letter, he flew into a rage and swore to kill my father. Somehow Fernando got word of this and fled the court before Pedro caught him. Since nowhere in the Christian kingdoms was safe from Pedro's wrath, he went south to Al-Andalus, where he gathered a group of disaffected knights around him and offered his services to the Caliph.

"The following year, Fernando led his knights at the battle of Alarcos, and some say they turned the tide in favour of the Moors. Pedro has never forgotten this, nor Fernando's slight against my mother. His hatred is alive and well, and he will try anything to revenge himself on my father."

Isabella fell silent and John's brow furrowed as he tried to take in all of this new information. Now he knew Isabella's story—and he was grateful for that—but how did it relate to his situation?

"Why are you telling me this now?" John asked.

"For two reasons," Isabella replied. "I have to go away and I wanted you to know the story." She squeezed John's hand to stop him interrupting. "The other reason is that I have bargained for your release. After Aumery took you away, I went to the Alcazar and demanded to see Pedro. When he heard who I was, he summoned me immediately. I told him that in exchange for your freedom, I will go south and find my father. When I do, I will try to persuade him to change sides. I am to say that Pedro has forgiven him and wishes to meet him in secret."

"Has Pedro forgiven him?"

"No. Pedro will never forgive him. If my father goes to the meeting, he will be arrested and killed."

"And if he refuses?"

"Then I will kill him."

Isabella's voice was so matter-of-fact that it took John a moment to register what she was saying. "Kill him!"

Isabella nodded and looked down. "I have dreamed of it many times. He dishonoured and killed my mother and abandoned his child. He deserves nothing less."

"You can't do this!" John exclaimed. He had never known his own father, but as a child he had often imagined him as a noble knight who had fallen on hard times. John knew it was nonsense, an orphan's dream, and that Fernando was far from an ideal father, but kill him? It was horrifying.

Isabella looked up. Her eyes were narrowed with anger. "What I cannot do is leave you here in the hands of that monster Aumery. My father is a traitor and a coward. You are the kindest, most interesting person I have ever met. I would exchange him for you in a heartbeat."

John shivered and clenched Isabella's hand. He felt on the edge of tears. He loved Isabella, he was certain of that, but to hear her say coldly that she would kill her father to save his life was overwhelming. Would he do something similar for her? Yes.

"I love you," John said.

Isabella smiled and visibly relaxed. "And I you. But take heart. It may not come to that. These times are chaotic. There will be a battle soon, and who can say what the outcome will be. My father may have had a change of heart. I may not reach the Caliph's army in time. Anything might happen. The main thing is that you are to be released tonight. I think you should go north as quickly as possible."

"I want to go with you," John blurted out.

Isabella's smile broadened. "And I want you to come with me, but it is not possible. I have a horse and an escort of soldiers waiting outside. I should not even have come here, but I could not leave without saying goodbye, or giving you this." Isabella slipped John's pouch of broken jewels and the gilded ivory tile through the bars of the window. "The guard has your satchel with your mathematics book and the strange drawing in it, but I did not want to leave these with him."

"But won't you need them?"

"King Pedro has given me money for my journey, not much, but enough, and I do not think I will need money once I find my father. Sell what you need to get back to Toulouse. I will find you there if I can."

"Isabella," John said helplessly.

"I must go." Tears sparkled in the corners of her eyes. She lifted his hand, kissed it and let it go. "Goodbye."

Isabella turned and walked slowly down the corridor toward the guard. "Be careful," John shouted after her. "I'll find you. I swear."

John squinted through the small, barred window until the last flicker of the torch was gone and the corridor sank back into gloom, then he slumped down against the door. He was incredibly thankful that he wasn't going to be tortured, but what had Isabella sacrificed for him?

John sat for a long time, thinking over what had happened. The tiny patch of blue sky he could see through the window in the far wall faded and the shadows in his cell thickened. The dark shape of a rat poked out of the straw in the last corner of pale light. It tilted its head and watched John.

"You're all right," John said. "You can hide.

"So can I," he added. "I can go to Toulouse, disappear into the crowds and wait for Isabella.

"But I'm not going to," John said, making a sudden decision. He stood up and the rat darted back into the straw. "War or no war, I'm going to follow Isabella. I can't let her kill her father because of me, even if he deserves to die. We'll go back to Toulouse together."

John jumped as the cell door creaked open.

"Come on," the guard said.

"Where to?" John asked, nervously.

"You're the luckiest man in Toledo," the guard said. "I'm to escort you to the town gate and tell you to be on yer way—orders of Pedro himself. Now come on afore anyone changes their minds."

* * *

John knocked on the heavy door as loudly as he dared. It was still an hour or two until dawn and few people were about, but he didn't want to take the chance of attracting unwelcome attention.

True to his word, the guard had taken John to the north gate and let him go. In the dark, John had stumbled away until he heard the gate creak closed behind him. Then he had backtracked, worked his way around the city walls and re-entered Toledo by another gate. It had taken him a long time to find the blacksmith's shop down the hill from the Alcazar, and every step along the unlit streets had been nerve-racking, although the only people he had met had been the occupants of the many taverns, most of whom were in no condition to cause him any trouble.

John had thought about circling Toledo and immediately heading south after Isabella, but he knew he wouldn't make much progress on an unknown road in the dark. Besides, he needed a weapon. John was setting off into a war to find Isabella, who was being guarded by Pedro's soldiers. Who knew what dangers he could face? A weapon might get him out of a tight spot. He also couldn't get the scimitar the blacksmith had shown him out of his mind. It was beautiful, and what an extraordinary coincidence that it should be named for the originator of the Cathar heresy—the very thing that had gotten him into this situation in the first place. John couldn't shake the feeling that he was meant to have the sword.

John repeated his knock on the door and heard a shuffling noise behind it. A bolt was drawn and the door opened a crack.

"Who is it? What d'you want at this ungodly hour?"

John recognized the voice of the skinny blacksmith, Abdul. "I've come for Auramazdah," John whispered.

There was a long silence, then the door swung open. "I don't suppose tomorrow, when civilized men do business, will do?"

John stepped through the door.

"I thought not," Abdul said, pushing the door closed behind John. "Apparently, you have come into funds more rapidly than you expected. Follow me."

John followed the blacksmith toward the smithy, where yesterday's coals still glowed in the forge. Abdul pumped a set of bellows. The glow grew and flames leaped up, casting wild, flickering shadows on the walls. Then he reached down behind his counter and lifted the scimitar. The blade shone dark blood-red in the firelight. "What can you offer me for it?"

"These." John opened his pouch and tipped everything into Abdul's outstretched palm.

The blacksmith put the sword down, leaned toward the fire and bent to examine each piece of gold and precious stone.

"It's not enough," he said, straightening up. "Auramazdah is worth more. Do you have anything else?"

John hesitated for a moment, then sighed. He was committed now. He pulled the ivory tile out of his satchel. "I have this."

Abdul gasped as the gold and stones on the tile glinted in the light. "This is remarkable," he said, taking the tile carefully and looking hard at it.

"Magnificent workmanship. It must have been the property of kings or caliphs. How did you come by it?"

"My friend found it in Madinat al-Zahra."

The blacksmith looked thoughtfully from the tile to John and back. "Very well." He picked up the sword and handed it to John. "Auramazdah is yours."

John held the scimitar. It felt right. "Thank you."

"Where do you go that you need such a blade?"

"South."

"To the war." Abdul tilted his head and gazed at John. "I shall not ask why one who seems as intelligent as you should wish to become involved in this sorry mess, but I shall say this: you are dressed like a Moor yet you have the fair hair of a northern Christian. A good way to get killed by both sides, no?"

John reached up and fingered a lock of his hair. He hadn't given it a thought.

"Now, since you seek me out in the dead of night and pay for a fine sword with broken jewels and a remarkable piece of ivory and gold, I would guess that you do not wish too many people to see your comings and goings, or at least not realize it is you they see. Wait here."

Abdul lit a small torch from the fire and disappeared through the back of the shop. He returned a moment later carrying a scuffed scabbard, a jar and a bottle.

"First," he said, taking the scimitar from John and sliding it into the scabbard, "any soldier worthy of the name will recognize a good and expensive blade when he sees it. Keep Auramazdah in this until you need it and no one will know what a treasure you possess.

"Second, that fair hair will get you killed faster than a crossbow bolt." The blacksmith undid the lid of the jar. It contained an oily, thick ointment. "Run this grease through your hair and it will be as black as that of the Caliph himself. Rain will not wash it out and you will either be safe or dead before the fairness grows back."

John took a palmful of the ointment and began working it into his hair. It was greasy, but no more so than his hair normally was. "Don't forget the eyebrows," Abdul warned.

"Third," he continued, handing John the bottle, "rub this liquid on your skin. It will darken it enough that you will be able to pass for a light-skinned Moor. It will fade after a few days, so take what is left with you and repeat the process. When you are done, you will be able to join the Caliph's army—as long as you don't open your mouth."

"Why are you helping me?" John asked as he finished his hair and began applying the liquid from the bottle to his cheeks.

"You paid me well for Auramazdah, and I am fond of that weapon. I should not like to see it fall into the hands of some crude mercenary too soon. And I am a romantic." Abdul smiled broadly. "You are here alone and yet this afternoon you were accompanied by a lady of great beauty, a lady whom, as the sun set, I saw being escorted down this very street by two of King Pedro's soldiers."

John stopped rubbing in the liquid. "You saw Isabella?"

"An attractive name," the blacksmith said, "but yes, if that was your companion. They were headed for the south gate and, since that is the direction you seem intent on going, I assume that you, like a chivalrous knight in a troubadour's song, are set upon rescuing her."

John nodded. He replaced the stopper in the glass bottle, slid Auramazdah into his belt and slung his satchel over his shoulder. "Thank you."

"Go safely," Abdul said, leading the way to the door and heaving it open. "I hope Auramazdah serves you well."

"I do too," John said, stepping out into the dark street. "And thank you again for everything." With the comfortable weight of Auramazdah on his belt and the first glimmerings of dawn lighting the sky to his left, John set out toward the south gate.

Battle

Las Navas de Tolosa
July, 1212

For three weeks, John managed to stay one step ahead of the crusader army. The morning he left Toledo, he noticed unusual activity in the camps outside the city walls, and later that afternoon, a rising cloud of dust behind him told him that the army was on the move. On several occasions since, he'd had to hide behind rocks or walls as scouting or hunting parties rode past, but he was still a few hours in front of the main body.

He had no idea if he was catching up to Isabella, or even if he was heading in the right direction. He knew only that he was heading south toward the Moorish army, and that was where she had said she was going. Once, in a tiny village, an old man had told him he had seen a beautiful woman and a pair of soldiers pass through several days before. He seemed to be on the right track, but he was falling behind.

As he travelled south, the landscape became more mountainous and the road more crowded. Many travellers were Moors who thought it better to keep away from the crusading army. No one paid much attention to John and when someone did approach, John put on a mime show, pretending he couldn't speak.

On the twenty-first day of walking, footsore and filthy, John was approaching the village of Castroferral when a soldier sitting by the roadside holding the reins of two small horses addressed his companion in Occitan. "Where d'you suppose the heathen's heading? Think he's a spy for the Caliph?"

John was so deep in thought, convinced he would never catch up to Isabella and wondering what to do next, and the man's voice reminded him so strongly of home, that he answered automatically. "I'm no spy and I'm heading south."

"By God!" the soldier exclaimed. "The heathen speaks Occitan." He stood up and passed the reins to his companion, who stayed seated on a rock and watched disinterestedly.

"Come here. How do you know our language?"

John felt the blood drain from his face and he shivered, even in the summer heat. He'd made a huge mistake. His mind raced to think of a way out.

"I meant no disrespect, kind sirs," he stammered. "I spent many happy years at the court of your illustrious Count Raymond in Toulouse. I learned a little, but speak unwell." John deliberately stumbled over his words.

The soldier who had spoken laughed. He had a cheerful, open face and ready smile, and John felt himself relax. "I had heard Raymond kept some Moors in his palace. What're you doing down here?"

"My mother in Cordova sickens and Count Raymond, bless his name, released me to go to her."

The soldier's companion snorted. "Touching," he said morosely. John glanced over at him. The man was the opposite of his cheerful friend. His skin was swarthy and his thin lips sneering. His heavy, dark eyebrows joined in the middle, giving the impression that the man was continually peering out from shadows.

"Pay him no mind, my Moorish friend," the cheerful soldier said. "God's seen fit to give him a jaundiced view of this world. He was miserable when we were safe back in Toulouse and he's miserable now that we're in the middle of a war."

"I ain't miserable," the man said miserably. "I just don't share your stupid belief that everything'll always work out for the best. I seen too much death and destruction to believe that."

"Well, we're still here, aren't we?" The standing soldier winked broadly at John. "Seems to me that's the best we can hope for these days."

His companion grunted.

"Anyways," he continued, addressing John again, "you didn't pick a good time or place to go visiting. You've gone and got yourself stuck between two armies."

"Armies?" John put on the stupidest expression he could manage.

"See that dust?" the soldier waved his hand to the north. "That there's the crusader host coming down from Toledo. All the armies of Aragon, Navarre, Portugal and Castille, not to mention a few of us poor slobs from Languedoc who got caught up in it all.

"Over there"—the soldier swung his arm to encompass the dry mountain peaks to the south—"across the pass at La Llosa, the Caliph's sitting with his army, waiting. Now, I'm no king or prince, but I'd wager all the plunder in Cordova that the Caliph's guarding that pass and it'll be a bloody business to get through. 'Course, it won't be for a few days yet—it'll take that long to get our army here and organized—but when it happens, there'll be one almighty battle hereabouts. If you don't want to get caught in it, you'd be wise to head in any direction but north or south.

"Then again," the soldier added thoughtfully, "being a Moor and all, you should have less trouble than us getting across the pass. Mind you," he added, leaning close to John and lowering his voice conspiratorially, "word is we won't be going by *that* pass. Supposed to be another over to the east, Despena...something or other. Only known to the locals hereabouts. Get the army over *that* and we'll take the Caliph by surprise."

"That's right," the seated soldier said with a sneer, "tell this Moorish spy all our secret plans so that the Caliph can slaughter us as we come down out of the pass at Despeñaperros."

The soldier in front of John shook his head. "I'm getting so sick of your misery. This boy's no spy. He's a neighbour from Toulouse, isn't that right?"

John nodded vigorously.

"You see," the soldier said. "Anyways, I don't see why we should be killing each other in the first place. Live and let live, I say. And it's no secret. Everyone hereabouts knows about the other pass and I'd wager there'll be no shortage of guides for our army as soon as a bag of gold is waved about."

"And you honourable men are part of the noble crusade?" John felt the need to change the subject. He was having trouble absorbing all this information while still concentrating on the role he was playing. Besides that, the seated soldier was glaring at him malevolently.

"You could say that," the cheerful soldier said. "We were happily enjoying the pleasures of Toledo—at least I was." The soldier winked again and jerked his thumb over his shoulder at his silent companion. "Then, all of a sudden, we're told to escort some woman down here. Fool's errand, if you ask me."

John felt his heartbeat speed up. Could this be Isabella's escort?

"She were good looking, right enough," the soldier went on, "but she didn't speak much to the likes of us and we were under strict orders to be polite."

"Why did you bring the fine lady to this place if there's to be a battle?" John struggled to keep the eagerness out of his voice.

"You've got me there, friend," the soldier said. "We took her up to La Llosa, least as close as we dared, and sent her on her way, straight toward the Moors. Makes no sense, if you ask me, but I'm just a simple soldier who does as he's told. And I reckon that's what I'll do in a few days, whichever pass we're told to climb. But I certainly do wish I was back in Toulouse.

"Take my advice and keep out of it. Find a nice quiet cave and hide out until it's all over, one way or the other. Then sneak away and visit your mother."

"Come on you miserable, lazy sod." The soldier walked over to the horses and prodded his partner. "We'd best be off if we're to rejoin the army afore dark."

Grumbling, the second soldier stood and stretched. He gave John an unpleasant look and swung up into his saddle. His companion mounted and the pair rode slowly north toward the approaching crusade.

For a long moment, John stood deep in thought and watched their retreating backs. So, Isabella was on her own now and probably already with the Caliph's army. John shivered. Had she killed Fernando del Huesca, or worse, been caught and killed herself?

John had hoped to catch up with her before she reached the Moorish army, but now he would have to cross the mountains and find her among the soldiers. That wasn't going to be easy. He was going to have to trick his way past the Moorish garrison on La Llosa Pass or find a route around it. Either way, he was going into the lion's den on the eve of a major battle. The prospect was frightening, and John didn't have a lot of information to go on. He had Isabella's father's name and the hope that del Huesca and his daughter would be easy to find amid the Caliph's horde. As for protection, all he had was Auramazdah and his stained face and hair. On top of all that was the question of what to do when he found Isabella. With a sigh, he turned and headed into Castroferral.

* * *

John trudged up the mountain road in the fading light—still unsure but having at least decided to face his task head on. In Castroferral he had asked about ways across the mountains. As the soldier had told him, there were two: the main, direct route across La Llosa Pass, and a longer, minor track across Despeñaperros Pass. As far as anyone knew, the Moors were not guarding the latter, but using it would require a long detour west. John was in a hurry, and whether he ran into the Caliph's army in La Llosa Pass or on the plain beyond, the problems would be the same. He had decided on La Llosa.

John stopped to catch his breath and turned to look out over the valley behind him. Already the cooking fires of the crusader army were flickering in the countryside around Castroferral. The friendly soldier had been right about it taking time for the army to assemble. There were very few fires compared to the numbers he had seen around Toledo, so the crusaders had to be strung out over a great distance. It would be days before the army collected here, and days more before the move to Despeñaperros, if they even decided to take that route. John would have time, but for what?

If he could find somewhere to sleep soon, he could head through the pass in the early daylight. The Moors would still be sleepy when they saw him coming. He guessed that one man wouldn't pose much of a threat and if he put on his mute and stupid act, his dyed hair and face might be enough, if he was lucky, to get him through. Then he would just have to hope for the best, find Isabella and pray they could escape. It wasn't much of a plan, but he couldn't think of anything better.

The darkness was thickening rapidly; he would have to hurry if he wanted to find somewhere to sleep while there was still some light. He took one last look around the valley. The campfires were still there to the north, and the dark orange of the setting sun marked the western sky, but there was something else. Off to the east, where it should have already been completely dark, a faint glow reflected off the scattered low clouds. John frowned and squinted. They were far off, but John thought he could make out more camp fires. They stretched into the distance behind some low hills —and that was where the glow was coming from.

John's brow furrowed. That many fires could only be from a large army, but whose? The Caliph was across the mountains behind him and most of the crusaders were still on the road to the north. Unless…Realization swept over John. The crusaders *weren't* to the north. They'd sent a small band to camp around Castroferral to make the Moors think that's where they were coming from, but the bulk of the army was going to cross the mountains by the Despeñaperros Pass! By the look of the fires, their plan was well in hand: the army was already at the entrance to the pass. Perhaps they even planned to cross tonight and attack tomorrow. John stood stock still, staring into the distance. This changed everything! Isabella would have no time to find her father—either to tell him of Pedro's offer, or to kill him—and she, a northern girl, would be caught in the middle of the Moorish camp as a battle raged around her.

Taking a deep breath, John turned and hurried up the road, far more nervous than when he'd stopped. As he progressed, his fear increased. With every step, he expected the shadows on either side of the path to resolve themselves into wild Moors charging at him with swords swinging. He nervously clutched Auramazdah's handle, but nothing happened and he eventually calmed down a bit.

Keeping to the rough road in the pitch dark made travel slow, but after an hour or two the moon rose, full and majestic above the surrounding peaks, to cast a weird silver glow over everything. The road wound through the mountains, sometimes clinging to steep hillsides and sometimes descending into valleys, only to rise again to the next pass. With no one to talk to and no signs of life, John couldn't help but feel he was the only person left in the world.

As the road began to wind consistently downward, John started to feel that dawn couldn't be far off. All at once, he rounded the shoulder of a hill and saw the plain of Las Navas de Tolosa spread out before him. The sight took his breath away. In the moonlight, it was as if he were looking down on a ghostly city. The tents and camp fires of the Caliph's army covered the valley floor as far as the eye could see. John had observed the crusader army outside Béziers, and the one camped around Toledo; this army was six or seven times that size!

John's first reaction was that the crusader army was doomed, whether it launched a surprise attack through the Despeñaperros Pass or not. As he stared out over the plain, he fought off an insane urge to laugh. It was madness to attempt what he was about to take on—but what choice did he have? Isabella's life was at stake: he had to try.

John hurried down the track, a new sense of urgency in his steps. How was he going to find Isabella among all those tents? And more importantly, how were they going to escape? But first things first. If he could just—

John's thoughts were interrupted as rough hands grabbed him and threw him to the ground, and a babble of Arab voices rose and fell around him. Someone brought a flaming torch out of the undergrowth. By its light, John saw a band of wild-looking warriors. They were dark-skinned; they wore coloured turbans and flowing robes cinched with bright cloth belts into which were tucked an assortment of swords and daggers. One man held a small, strongly curved bow. When they saw that John was alone and looked Moorish, they smiled, stepped back and let him stand. The man with the bow, the only one of the group who was bearded, spoke to John.

John didn't understand a word, but he was relieved that the man seemed friendly. He was about to launch into his mute act when a thought struck him. He could act dumb and probably get past these men, but what good would that do? He would be alone and unable to communicate, still searching for Isabella and her father in whatever short time remained before the battle. His only chance was to find someone who spoke Latin.

John took a deep breath. "I don't speak your language," he said slowly. "I need someone who can speak Latin."

Quest

His captors' friendly smiles dissolved into suspicious stares and, John was disturbed to see, a couple of the men began fingering the hilts of their swords.

"I come from Toulouse," John hurried on, hoping that they wouldn't kill a man who was talking, even if he was babbling in a foreign tongue. "I've been to the crusader camp." John waved an arm back over the mountains. He remembered the story that Shabaka had told him about the Moorish victory at Alarcos and the current Caliph's desire to replicate his predecessor's triumph. "I have important information for Caliph Muhammad an-Nasir."

The mention of the Caliph's name obviously confused John's captors. They began a hurried conversation among themselves. John prayed that they were deciding not to kill him in hopes that he was more important than he seemed.

Eventually, the man with the bow stepped forward and grabbed John roughly by the arm. With the torch-carrier leading the way, John was dragged along the road to a small hut. He was pushed inside and the door closed firmly behind him. He sighed, happy to still be breathing. The hut had a dirt floor; it was windowless and totally dark. It was small—barely two strides across in either direction, and not quite high enough for John to stand up straight in. John guessed it was a storage hut, empty now. He slumped down on the packed earth against one of the cold stone walls. He was still alive, but he was no closer to finding Isabella and he didn't know what his captors had in mind for him.

Time dragged interminably in the darkness and John had no idea whether hours or minutes were passing. He clenched his fists in irritation. He had escaped one prison in Toledo only to end up in another here. Beatrice had been right, he thought, when she had offered to teach him the memory cloister—there were responsibilities involved that he couldn't avoid. True, he and Isabella had escaped the horrors of the crusade in Languedoc. They had even found real happiness with Nasir and Shabaka at the library in Madinat al-Zahra, but it wasn't enough. Holding the dangerous Gospel of the Christ and a host of other forbidden works in the memory cloister weighed heavily on John's mind, and he was no closer to finding the book on drawing that he craved.

As he sat miserably in his new cell, John gradually realized something: it might be possible to escape physical danger, though he and Isabella hadn't been very successful at that, but it wasn't possible to escape what he carried in his mind. Just knowing something as important as the Gospel of the Christ carried with it the duty to use it. His conviction that there was a new and better way to represent the world in drawings imposed on him the obligation of trying to discover that way. Whatever peace and quiet John wished for, he couldn't have it. He would never be truly content until he at least tried to use the Gospel of the Christ for good and searched everywhere for the book that held the key to his dream of drawing reality. He was trapped by his past.

John pounded the dirt floor beside him in frustration. Nothing was as simple or clear as he had hoped all those years before when he had stood outside the cathedral in Toulouse with Peter, debating whether God meant for him to draw in a new and different way. All he had wanted then was to draw and learn, but God or fate or something had had a different plan. John sighed. His childhood dreams of a peaceful life seemed naive now. Memory cloisters, heretics, secret gospels, strange drawings, battles—all of these had taken him so far from where he'd started.

John clenched his eyes shut and shook his head despondently. On top of everything else, he seemed destined to lose everyone he cared for. First Peter had had his strange visions of death and embraced the crusade's fanaticism, then Beatrice had willingly climbed the steps of the pyre outside Minerve. Old Umar and Nasir were dead, and where were Adso and William of Arles? Even Isabella, to save him, had been swallowed by an army on the eve of battle. The thought of Isabella brought John back to the present. Before he worried about anything else, he had to save her, but how?

* * *

The sound of the door scraping open and a shaft of light from a torch woke him. Rubbing his eyes, John struggled to his feet, wondering when he'd drifted off and how much time had passed. He squinted at the figure in the doorway. It was a man, holding a torch. He was dressed the same as the warriors who had captured John, but his skin was black and it gleamed in the flickering light.

"Shabaka!"

The newcomer stared hard at John for a moment. Then his mouth broke into a wide smile, exposing a gleaming set of teeth. "My friend, Johan. I would not have recognized you. You have darkened so much in the sun." Shabaka laughed. "Even your hair."

John laughed with relief at seeing a friendly face. "What are you doing here?"

"You wish I were not?" Shabaka asked.

"No, of course not!" John said hurriedly. "It's wonderful to see you."

Shabaka nodded. "I think what *you* are doing here should be more a question that I ask of you. It seems you have been careless and lost the beautiful Isabella."

"She's here somewhere," John said. "I've come to find her. We went to Toledo to search for the drawing book, but I was arrested as a heretic before we could find it. I was going to be tortured, but Isabella bargained for my freedom." The words rushed out of him as the tension from his journey and the night's events relaxed. "Her father fights for the Caliph and she has come to persuade him not to. But there's hardly any time! The crusaders are coming over Despeñaperros Pass, not La Llosa. They could be ready to attack by this morning!"

The smile faded from Shabaka's face. "Do not rush on so! First, who is Isabella's father?"

"Fernando del Huesca," John said.

Shabaka's gasp was audible, but before John could ask if he knew him, Shabaka went on. "And how do you know the crusaders are coming tonight over Despeñaperros Pass?"

"I *don't* know that they're coming tonight. But as I started out over La Llosa last night I saw their camp fires to the east. They had no reason to be there if they are coming over La Llosa. They must be heading for Despeñaperros. I don't know if they are ready to cross yet, but they will be soon."

Shabaka stroked his chin thoughtfully. "You told the men that you wanted to see the Caliph. Why would you tell him that his enemy comes over Despeñaperros? Do you not betray your own kind? If the Caliph sets a trap and the crusade is destroyed, the deaths will be on your head."

"They are not my own kind," John said, realizing for the first time how true that was. Images of Bertrand and the hundred mutilated knights of Bram and of the torture chamber and the glee with which Aumery had shown it flashed through his mind. "The crusaders who are coming here have destroyed much of my homeland. They have killed thousands, mutilated hundreds and committed scores of the gentlest people I have ever met to the flames. Their minds are closed to everything but their own narrow beliefs." An image of Peter sprang unbidden into John's head. It was true as well—even his childhood friend had to bear responsibility for the horrors the crusade had unleashed on Languedoc.

"There's going to be a battle here," John said. Saying it out loud made it real, and the thought seemed to sap all his energy. "Tens of thousands of men are going to die. I can do nothing about that. I do not care if the Caliph or the crusaders win. All I care about are the people who are important to me and right now, that is Isabella. She's in danger and I will do anything to find and rescue her."

Shabaka nodded again. "If she seeks Fernando del Huesca, finding her should not be difficult. But rescuing her—that is a different matter."

"Who is del Huesca?" John asked.

"A devil." Shabaka spat out the word with unexpected bitterness. "After he and his knights helped the Caliph's father win at Alarcos he was declared a favourite. Since then, he has been at the forefront of every battle, both here in Al- Andalus and across the water in Africa. Now he commands the Caliph's personal bodyguard. Isabella will not have difficulty finding him, and if we find him, we find Isabella. However, it means venturing into the very heart of the Caliph's army."

"Then that's where I will go," John said.

"And how close to the Caliph's tent do you think you will get? You can pass for a Moor on a deserted road at night, but already your fair hair begins to show and the instant you open your mouth, you are lost."

"I've managed this far," John said, feeling anger rise in him. "I don't need your help. I will find Isabella on my own."

"Calm yourself, my young northern friend," Shabaka said. "I do not recall your asking nor me offering help. But"—he hurried on to prevent another outburst from John—"I shall help. I will be your mouthpiece and together we shall enter the presence of the Caliph."

Shabaka's mouth curved into his habitual smile as he spoke, but John couldn't help but notice that his eyes were cold and filled with hate.

"Thank you," John said, calmer now. He looked once again into his friend's eyes. "Why are you here, Shabaka? You said that you were going travelling."

"There are many Nubians here in the Caliph's camp," Shabaka said enigmatically. "But come, we must hurry. Dawn approaches and if what you say is accurate, we do not have much time."

** * *

Close up, the Moorish camp was much more impressive, and frightening, than it had been from the hill by moonlight. Dawn was beginning to lighten the eastern sky as Shabaka led John through the vast army toward a great tent on the summit of a low hill. All around them the Moorish host was awakening and preparing for the day. Fires were being rekindled, food eaten and prayers mumbled. The smell of wood smoke filled the air and the clank of equipment and weapons, the stamp of horses' hooves and the shouts of men giving commands provided an ever-changing backdrop of scent and sound.

John took in his surroundings with a sense of awe. He had never been in the midst of a real army before. He had only seen them at a distance, when they looked and acted like a single unit controlled by a few men. From inside, John could see how an army was composed of individuals, and the overall impression was one of random chaos.

Few of the soldiers whom John passed wore any recognizable uniform, although all wore coloured turbans of some sort and most sported beards. Many wore long robes like John's own, but several had shorter tunics, and the closest thing John saw to armour were short, sleeveless, padded jackets. Favoured weapons were curved scimitars similar to Auramazdah, although there were a lot of small, curved bows and lances around, and everyone appeared to have a round shield decorated with brass shapes and tufts of horsehair. This was a much more lightly armoured force than the crusader knights, John realized, but one that was flexible and could probably move very fast.

John noticed the ground rising and the number of tents increasing as they progressed. It seemed as if the bulk of the army slept in the open, although tents were scattered throughout. Most were small and some were little more than awnings supported by poles, open on every side. Others, obviously the property of officers, were brightly coloured and elaborate. The large one on the top of the hill was easily the most impressive. It was the size of a house and circular, with a peaked roof from which a pole extended bearing a green banner. Embroidered patterns embellished the roof of the tent, and the sun, which was just now appearing over the eastern hills, glinted off the golden threads. The tent was surrounded by a black fence, with guards stationed every few paces along it.

As they approached, John began to notice odd things about the fence—it was irregular and almost appeared to be moving. He raised his hand to his brow and squinted against the low sun. With a rising sense of horror, he realized that the fence was composed of people, black people tied together in a continuous line.

"They're Nubians!" John exclaimed.

"Slaves," Shabaka hissed under his breath. "Chained together as a human fence that any enemy will have to slash their way through before they will be able to attack the Caliph."

"But that's brutal," John said, lowering his voice to match Shabaka's.

"They're only worthless slaves," Shabaka said bitterly. "What does it matter if they die, as long as the Caliph lives?"

John looked over at his friend. His jaw was set as he strode forward, his eyes fixed on the Caliph's tent. John remembered that last afternoon in Cordova. There was something he had to do, Shabaka had said.

"Why are you really here?" John asked.

"To help you find Isabella," Shabaka said.

"No." John grabbed Shabaka's arm and pulled him to a stop. "That's not the real reason. You came here to rescue the other Nubians, didn't you?"

"They cannot be rescued," Shabaka said, staring hard at John. "They are chained and guarded night and day by del Huesca's men. At the least suspicion of unrest, they will be slaughtered. Del Huesca can easily find more slaves."

"Then why?"

"I came to kill the Caliph."

For a moment John was silent, struggling with the implications of Shabaka's confession. "You used me," he said at last, his voice rising. "You don't care about rescuing Isabella. You just wanted to get close to the Caliph so you could kill him. You're just like everyone else in this damn war—out for yourself and to hell with the rest."

Shabaka glanced around nervously, but no one was paying them any notice. "It is true that the news you brought over the mountains offered a chance to get into the Caliph's presence, but it is not true that I do not care. You and Isabella are good, interested in learning, and you see beneath the skin when you look at people. But you are young—you do not understand the harsh bitterness of the world, nor how history can designate one people free and another slave.

"Moorish traders have used my continent as a source of slaves for hundreds of years and my people have been particularly prized. I was fortunate that the trader who took me saw me as a human being and taught me. These men and women"—Shabaka waved his arm at the human fence—"are simply valueless lumps of meat and bone to be used and discarded at the Caliph's whim.

"I cannot save my people, but I swore many years ago that, one day, I would kill the Caliph as a warning to all those who would enslave others. That is why I came to Al-Andalus, but the Caliph was far off in Africa surrounded by his Berber horsemen. By the time he returned, I had committed myself to Nasir and his library. As long as he lived, I could not leave. But now Nasir is dead and I am free to fulfil my vow.

"As for Isabella"—Shabaka held up his hand to stop John's interruption—"if it is possible, I shall help you rescue her, and I shall not deliberately place either of you in danger, but my vow must take precedence. I hope you understand."

John wasn't sure he did understand, but the intensity of Shabaka's expression convinced him that his friend was deadly serious.

"Do you have a plan?" John asked.

Quest

"Just follow me and speak only when you are addressed," Shabaka said. "When we are—"

"What're you doing here?" A guard stepped forward and challenged them. He was a northerner but was dressed in armour made of scales instead of chain mail, and his head was covered by a round helmet with a leather flap hanging down the back of his neck. He wore a curved sword on his belt, and his hand rested casually on the hilt. He blocked their way forward and stared aggressively at them both.

Shabaka began speaking rapidly, but before he had finished a man emerged from the nearest tent. He was tall and wore scale armour, but he was bareheaded, so John could see his long fair hair and beard. The man walked with a certain arrogance and John assumed he was an officer, but something about him was puzzling. He had never seen this man before, and yet he looked familiar.

"What is this black slave doing here?" the man asked unpleasantly.

Before the guard could reply, Shabaka clasped his hands in front of him, bowed his head and spoke in a fawning voice. "Esteemed sir, I bring a traveller from across the mountains"—he waved a hand at John—"who brings news of the infidel army for the Caliph."

"He does, does he?" The fair-haired man transferred his stare to John. He had piercing dark-brown eyes that John felt were studying his very soul. He looked away. "And who is this ragged traveller that he knows something that the great Caliph does not?"

"Just a poor traveller, sir," Shabaka said hurriedly. John was surprised at his companion's new subservience. He had always seemed so confident and secure. "He crossed the pass last night and discovered the infidel's plans to cross by Despeñaperros."

"Why should I believe a slave and a peasant? Perhaps this man has been sent by the crusade to spy on us and spread false rumours, perhaps even attack the Caliph when he is ushered into his presence. The Caliph has his own spies. I doubt this boy knows anything that they do not."

John looked up. The man was still staring at him.

"Be glad," he said, "that I do not have you flogged for your presumption. Be off. And you,"—he looked at Shabaka—"you can go where you should be. Guard, take this slave and chain him with the others. We will have need of them all when this battle begins."

The man turned away and, as he did so, John realized why he looked so familiar. It was his eyes.

"Fernando," John said impulsively. "Has Isabella found her father?"

The man stopped and John could see his back tense. He held his breath as the man turned around.

"What did you say?" the man asked quietly.

"I asked if Isabella had found her father," John said, just as quietly. "You have the same eyes."

Again the man stared at John, but this time John held his gaze. This wasn't just another cruel soldier—it was Isabella's father, Fernando del Huesca. Shabaka glanced worriedly at John.

"Bring him to my tent," Fernando ordered the guard. "The slave too."

As del Huesca turned away, John looked at Shabaka. His friend was staring at the chained wall of slaves. Whatever his plan had been, it wasn't going to work now. John felt bad for him—he knew what it was like to have a plan go wrong—but he was also relieved. Assuming they had been ushered into the Caliph's presence, and that Shabaka had attempted to carry out his plan to kill the man, they both surely would have died. Now they were going to del Huesca's tent, and that was probably the best way to find Isabella.

John took a deep breath and followed del Huesca toward a small red and gold tent. His mind was racing. He was scared of this cruel man, but he was also elated at the way he had reacted to Isabella's name. She must have contacted him and, obviously, she hadn't killed him. John just prayed that she hadn't attempted it and failed. For the moment, at least, there was hope. As John ducked to enter the tent, he thought he heard the distant sound of horns.

"I shall look after this." As John stood up inside the tent, Fernando reached forward and wrenched Auramazdah out of his belt, pulled it a short way out of the scabbard and nodded appreciatively. "Check him for other weapons," he ordered the guard. The guard ran his hands up and down John's robe, searching for hidden daggers. Shabaka stood silently behind them.

"Nothing, sir," the guard reported.

"Good. Then leave us."

The guard slapped his open hand across his chest in salute and ducked out of the tent, but John saw nothing of this. His attention was completely focused behind del Huesca. To the man's left was a simple cot and beside it a small table on which rested an ornate helmet with a plume of deep red horsehair on the peak. A sword, several daggers and two short stabbing spears rested against the tent wall where a full-length red cloak hung from a hook. To del Huesca's right lay a scattering of large cushions, and sprawled across them was a girl.

"Isabella!" John exclaimed, stepping forward.

Fernando placed a hand firmly on John's chest. "So you do know my daughter," he said. "I fear that will be the worse for you."

"What have you done to her?" John stared past Fernando at Isabella. She was slumped on the cushions, her wrists and ankles bound with rope. A large, purple bruise discoloured her right cheek and her eye was swollen almost shut. She had not even stirred at the sound of his voice.

"So you care for her?" Fernando said scornfully. "Interesting. Are you a part of her plot?"

"Plot?" John looked at Fernando. He was holding Auramazdah and smiling, but there was no warmth in the expression.

"She came here two days ago, this daughter of mine," Fernando sneered. "It was a touching family scene. She claimed to have searched far and wide for her beloved father. She said that Pedro had forgiven me and that if I betrayed the Caliph and my men, he would meet me like a brother and reinstate all my lands." Fernando laughed harshly.

"What a fool she took me for! That weakling Pedro will *never* forgive me. The only worthwhile thing he ever had was a beautiful sister and I made her mine."

John was vaguely aware of Shabaka moving beside him, but his eyes were locked with Fernando's. They were uncannily like Isabella's, but without the calm and passion. Fernando's eyes were cold and calculating; they seemed to look on the world and everything in it as merely things that might be of use.

"I will find Pedro in this coming battle and his head will ride into Toledo on my lance. As for her"—Fernando flicked his head toward Isabella, who was staring about in a daze, unable to fathom what was happening—"As soon as her looks return, I shall present her to the Caliph for his harem. He has a liking for northern girls."

John tensed, but Fernando's twisted smile held him in place.

"Your slave I shall chain with the others, but you? What shall I do with you? Something slow because I want, between your screams, to hear your story. Unfortunately, I shall have to wait until we have destroyed this annoying crusader army, but anticipation adds to pleasure, don't you find? For the time being, I shall—"

The wide-bladed knife whizzed past John's ear and embedded itself in Fernando's neck. Fernando's eyes widened in shock and a strange, gurgling sound came from his open mouth.

John was frozen in place, but Shabaka pushed past him. He grabbed the handle of the knife and, with a vicious twist, withdrew it, freeing a frighteningly bright fountain of blood to pulse from the wound. Fernando's expression shifted to fear. He dropped Auramazdah and his hands scrabbled ineffectually at the flood. He staggered to the side, crashing into the table and knocking the plumed helmet to the floor. There was nothing to do but watch and wait. Blood sprayed a surprising distance from the dying man's wound, splattering the tent walls and floor. Fernando slumped to his knees, half leaning on the edge of the cot. He made a deep coughing sound and his arms twitched convulsively a few times before his body relaxed and the cruel eyes glazed over. John had never seen so much blood in his life.

Tearing his gaze away from the dying man, John turned and stepped over to where Isabella lay, a puzzled frown on her face. "What's the matter? Are you all right?"

She turned to look at him, but there was no recognition in her eyes. It was as if she were looking out through a fog from a long way away, trying desperately to make out the shadowy figures before her.

"What has he done to you?" John lifted her limp, bound hands.

"He has drugged her," Shabaka said, kneeling and using the bloody knife to sever the ropes. "I have seen it before. She will recover, but it will take some time."

John sat on the cushions beside Isabella and put his arm around her shoulder. She turned and smiled weakly at him.

Shabaka moved to the tent door, lifted the flap and peered carefully out. "If we live long enough for her to recover," he said, dropping the flap and retreating back into the tent. "Something is going on. I think, perhaps, the attack you talked of is happening."

"Why did you kill del Huesca?" John asked, still struggling to understand what had just happened. "He's not the Caliph."

"He is not," Shabaka agreed, wiping the dagger blade on his robes, "but he is the next best thing. Many of my countrymen have died at his hands and I have repaid part of a debt to all my brothers. The arrogant del Huesca has paid the price of not searching a poor slave before allowing him into his presence. Now we must look to our future, however short it may be."

"Captain." The voice came from outside the tent flap. John and Shabaka stared at each other. Shabaka placed a finger to his lips. "What is it?" His voice was a passable imitation of del Huesca's.

"The Northerners have crossed the mountains. Already the left wing of our army is heavily engaged and being forced back. The centre and the right are holding but there is much confusion."

As if to emphasize the soldier's words, battle horns wailed, much closer than before. John thought he could hear the faint clash of weapons.

"Call the men together and bring the horses," Shabaka shouted back.

"Yes, sir," the man responded.

"As I hoped," Shabaka said more quietly. "In the noise and confusion, he did not listen too closely to his master's voice. Now we must make a plan."

"What can we do?" John asked, feeling helpless.

Shabaka looked at the helmet and weapons, now scattered about. "You must become del Huesca," he said.

"What?" John stared at his friend as the words sank in. "I can't be del Huesca."

"No, you can't," Shabaka agreed, "at least not for long. Our only chance is to escape in the confusion and hope the crusaders win, but we need time. If del Huesca does not appear, his men will come looking for him and then we are certainly doomed. We must give them del Huesca for a short time. You are close enough to his size that, dressed in his armour, you could pass for him at a distance. So let us get you dressed for the part and I shall explain my plan."

* * *

John shuddered as Shabaka helped him pull the blood-soaked armour over his head. The padding beneath the scales was saturated and sticky, and it was still warm. John looked over at where del Huesca's body lay. Shabaka had pulled a couple of cushions over it, hiding the torso and face, but the dead man's arms and legs stuck out and a large pool of blood had collected in a hollow in the tent floor. John began wiping the blood off the scales.

"Leave it," Shabaka ordered. "We will cover it with his cloak. Let's get the helmet on."

The helmet, complete with hinged cheek plates, covered John's entire head. Intricate engraved patterns ran around the edges. The red horsehair plume rose to almost a foot in height before it flowed back over the curved neck plate. The helmet was very heavy and, even with the internal padding, a bit too big, but once it was strapped in place and the cheek plates tied down, it was enough to hide John's features from a cursory glance.

While John was busy with the helmet, Shabaka had filled a small sack with blood from the growing puddle beside del Huesca. He stepped over and handed it to John. "Tie this to the armour by your neck. Use it at the right moment."

John carefully tucked the end of the bag beneath the edge of the armour on his left shoulder.

Shabaka took a step back and looked John over. "Good," he said.

John felt far from good. He was shaking and terrified, and the smell of blood from his armour made him want to gag. Whatever sense of safety he felt came from being hidden in the tent and soon, if Shabaka's plan was to work, he would have to step out into the open and pretend to be someone he wasn't—among heavily armed men who would kill him in an instant if they suspected the ruse.

"They expect to see del Huesca, so that is who they will see," Shabaka said in answer to John's unspoken worry. "Now, we must complete the theatre."

Shabaka picked up one of del Huesca's daggers from the floor. The blade was narrow and thin. Shabaka stood on the end of the blade and snapped it off, leaving a short jagged stump sticking out from the handle. He wedged it between the plates of del Huesca's armour beside the bag of blood on John's left shoulder, close to his neck. He worked it through the padding until John could feel the edge scratching his skin. Shabaka stood back, surveyed his handiwork and nodded.

"It will do," he said.

John heard a distant scream and the closer clash of swords.

"Good," Shabaka said, "chaos is approaching."

John shoved Auramazdah into his belt and Shabaka draped him in del Huesca's cloak, hiding the bloody armour, the bag and the broken dagger. John looked over at Isabella. She still lay on the cushions, a vague smile on her face. It was probably just as well that she wasn't fully conscious. John felt a lump form in his throat. She had just seen her father murdered in front of her, felt his blood spray over her and heard the sounds of battle coming ever closer, and yet none of it seemed to have any effect. John prayed that Shabaka was right and that whatever was drugging her would wear off soon. He went over and knelt by his friend.

"Stay here," John said, slowly and clearly. "Shabaka and I will return but, whatever happens, you must not leave the tent. Do you understand?"

Isabella frowned as if she was concentrating very hard. "I understand," she said, slowly and with great effort.

"Good," John said, delighted to hear her voice again.

"She will be safe here for the time being," Shabaka said. "We must go." He picked up del Huesca's sword along with two daggers that were lying on the floor and hid them beneath his robe.

It was all John could do to make his legs take a step toward the tent flap. He was sweating from fear and the heat, and his neck muscles were already sore from the weight of the helmet.

"Hold on," Shabaka hissed. "You look like a pathetic excuse for a beaten slave. If you go out like that, you'll be dead before you take three paces. You are an arrogant killer, lord of a vicious band of mercenary soldiers who have earned their reputation as the Caliph's favourites by slaughtering his enemies without question. Act like it."

Quest

John took a deep breath and straightened his back. He pictured himself as Oddo, striding through the streets of Béziers or Bram, killing anyone who got in his way. He envisaged having that power over all lesser beings—he was immortal. It worked. John grabbed Shabaka with his free hand and pushed him roughly through the tent flap. He ducked after him and stood up. A passing soldier hesitated, a look of fear flashing across his face. He slapped his hand in salute and hurried on.

John felt powerful as he scanned the scene. It was a lot less calm than when he had entered the tent. Several of del Huesca's soldiers were around the Caliph's tent, some already on horseback. The slaves were standing now, roped closely together. John noticed there were women as well as men and that some were little more than children. Many looked around fearfully at the armed men rushing back and forth while others slouched despondently, eyes fixed on the ground at their feet. Only a few stared defiantly at the soldiers.

Pushing Shabaka ahead of him, John strode toward the slaves. One of del Huesca's soldiers hurried forward and saluted. He was in full armour and wore a helmet similar to his commander's, lacking only the cheek plates and red plume. His face was weather-beaten and a jagged scar twisted the right corner of his mouth.

"The men are gathering behind the Caliph's tent, sir," he said urgently. "The right wing and centre of the Caliph's army hold, but the left wing is collapsing. That is where the cavalry is most needed."

John fleetingly considered answering the man, but he knew his voice would give him away instantly. He strode on, and as he passed, he pushed the soldier as hard as he could in the centre of his chest. The man's eyes widened in surprise and confusion as he staggered back a step. John prayed that del Huesca's arrogance sometimes made him act in violent and irrational ways and that this would be enough to make the man hesitate instead of raising the alarm.

The desire to look back and see what the man was doing almost overwhelmed John, but that would give the game away. Instead, he shoved Shabaka extra hard and kept going toward the Caliph's tent. He was aware of men running past him and the clash of weapons sounded frighteningly close, but he kept looking straight ahead.

As they approached the line of slaves, John realized that Shabaka was leading him toward a tall man who was staring curiously in their direction. When they were close, Shabaka pretended to trip and cannoned into the slave. John heard his friend hiss something in the man's ear and watched as —in a fraction of a second—Shabaka passed him the knives he had hidden in his cloak. The man immediately passed one knife onto his neighbour and busily began cutting the rope that tied the slaves together.

John stole a glance over his shoulder. The scarred soldier was still standing where they had passed him, but he was staring suspiciously in their direction. Any moment now he would challenge them and he wouldn't be fooled a second time. John turned back to warn Shabaka, but he never got a chance. Shabaka spun around, a dagger in hand. With lightning speed, he raised the weapon high and brought it down on John's neck.

Even though John knew it was coming, it was still a shock. For a moment, he truly believed he had been stabbed, but as planned Shabaka missed, slicing the bag of blood and cutting a long slash in John's cloak instead of his throat. The back of Shabaka's hand caught the handle of the broken dagger wedged in John's armour and the ragged blade dug painfully into his shoulder. John reached up and squashed the bag he'd positioned so carefully. Blood spurted through his fingers and ran down his hand. He spun around and, pretending to clutch at the dagger hilt, tore away his cloak, revealing the blood-soaked armour underneath. Theatrically, he fell to the ground and lay twitching, as he had seen the dying del Huesca do.

Most of the guards stood frozen in shock, but the scarred soldier drew his sword and rushed over. He headed for Shabaka, but before the blow fell, John's companion dropped to one knee, drew del Huesca's sword from beneath his robe and thrust it hard into the man's stomach. The man stopped, a look of surprise on his face, but Shabaka kept going. He stood and continued to drive upwards until the sword point ripped its way out of the man's neck beside his collar bone. With a sigh, the man dropped his weapon and collapsed to the ground over John's legs.

Several of the slaves were already free and the daggers Shabaka had brought were being passed along the line, cutting more and more bonds. The big man that Shabaka had spoken to grabbed the fallen soldier's sword, ran half a dozen long strides and decapitated the closest stunned guard. Before the man's body hit the ground, the slave had grabbed his sword and passed it to one of the other freed men.

It had all happened in an instant, but now people were beginning to react. One man on horseback was shouting orders and a dozen mounted men surrounded him with drawn swords. Others from farther back were also moving in, but they wouldn't be needed; the dozen were more than enough to deal with Shabaka and the few armed slaves. John wanted to throw off the charade, to stand up and fight beside his friend, but the image of Isabella lying drugged in del Huesca's tent stopped him. Whatever happened here, he had to survive to rescue her, and the best way to do that was to continue playing dead.

John heard a horn sounding to his left and was aware of fighting quite close by, but the cheek plate on his helmet obscured his view.

The mounted men were closing in. They seemed in no hurry, but men behind them were peeling away and riding off toward the sound of the fighting that John couldn't see. A crossbow bolt thudded into the chest of the man to the leader's right, hurling him off his horse. The leader reined in his horse and looked around. Men, even the unmounted guards, were now streaming past him. Whatever the leader saw, it made him forget Shabaka and the slaves. Yelling something that John couldn't make out, he wheeled his horse and led his men off.

John couldn't stand it any more. Sitting up, he wrestled the heavy helmet off. It felt wonderful to have the breeze blow over his sweat-soaked head. The broken dagger still wedged into his armour cut him painfully. John grabbed the handle, slippery with blood, and tore it out from between the armour plates. Then he looked to his left.

Fighting was raging over a huge area. A large band of mounted knights seemed determined to hack their way through to the Caliph. John could see helmet plumes of various colours and the gleam of rising and falling swords and axes. In the centre of the band, someone was holding up a pike with the red and gold bars of the Aragonese flag swirling from it.

The attackers were being opposed by an assortment of Moorish and Northern soldiers, some on horseback but most on foot. They were fighting fiercely and they greatly outnumbered the Aragonese, but they were being forced steadily back.

Several dozen slaves were now free. The women and children were huddled in a mass with the men surrounding them. The few with swords, including Shabaka and the tall slave, waved their weapons at anyone who came close, but few paid them any attention.

Movement behind Shabaka caught John's eye. A group of warriors exited the Caliph's tent. Each carried a curved sword and wore a red turban. They were followed by a man dressed in a golden robe and wearing a turban encrusted with jewels that glinted in the sun.

Shabaka noticed John staring past him and looked over. "The Caliph," he said, stepping forward.

"No!" John shouted. "They'll kill you! You've done enough. Del Huesca is dead and you have freed your countrymen. Live to do more."

Shabaka hesitated. He turned back and knelt beside John. "You are right. God has offered me his hand, I must not presume to ask for his arm. Now we must survive."

"I must get Isabella," John said.

Shabaka nodded, spoke hurriedly to the tall slave and helped John roll the soldier's body off his legs. The fighting was much closer now and Moorish soldiers, some without weapons and many bloody, were streaming back around the Caliph's tent. Several women, dressed in expensive silk and wearing heavy jewellery around their necks and on their arms, milled uncertainly around the tent's flap, but the Caliph and his personal guard had disappeared.

John glanced back at del Huesca's tent. He was shocked to see that a minor battle was going on around it. What bothered him even more was that some of the soldiers had falcon crests on their surcoats.

"Isabella!" he yelled, drawing Auramazdah and barging his way forward. He heard Shabaka shout something, but he ignored it.

The first Falcon John reached barely had time to react. He was half turned to meet the threat when Auramazdah cut through his leather tunic and bit deeply into his shoulder. The man yelped, dropped his sword and clutched at the gaping wound. The next man was battling a large Moor and John simply pushed him aside. Then he was inside the tent.

A large rip ran down the back wall of the tent from roof to floor and the edges flapped mournfully. Isabella stood by the rent, harm in the grasp of a large man. She was struggling weakly to no effect. The man turned. The angry red scars of old burns marred his features. "Oddo," John gasped.

A twisted smile formed on Oddo's face. "What a pleasant surprise," he said, releasing his grip on Isabella's arm. "I have waited a long time to kill you." Oddo pushed Isabella away and she collapsed onto the cushions He hefted his axe. "I came to kill the traitor del Huesca and take his head to King Pedro, but I see I was beaten to it." The big man circled round the tent toward John. John noticed a pronounced limp, no doubt from the time Adso had stabbed him in the leg outside Minerve. "You wear his bloodstained armour. Was it you who killed del Huesca?" Oddo asked.

"No," John said, stepping to the side so that he kept the central tent pole between him and the mercenary. He was scared, and Auramazdah felt pitifully small in his hand. The only thing he took comfort from was Oddo's size: the man was big and would have trouble swinging his axe cleanly in such a confined space.

"Pity," Oddo said. "I would enjoy killing you more if you were not just a boy who got in the way." Oddo lunged around the central tent pole and swung his axe at John's head. He only missed by inches as John reacted instinctively with a move Adso had taught him. He dropped and rolled to the side, springing to his feet with Oddo again on the far side of the tent.

Oddo nodded appreciatively. "Perhaps this will be more fun than I thought. I think I shall take my time killing you, boy. The battle is won and only the slaughter remains. I'll leave that to my Falcons and entertain myself here with you"—Oddo leered across to where Isabella lay—"and your friend. She is very pretty."

John felt a surge of anger, but he pushed it back. Oddo was trying to annoy him and an angry man doesn't think. John needed to think. He took a deep breath and let it out slowly. He was in a crouch, balanced on the balls of his feet, Auramazdah held loosely in his right hand. The pair circled the tent pole, eyeing each other intently. John's advantages were speed and the tricks Adso had taught him: Oddo's were strength, size, experience and brutality. John willed Oddo to make a move—if he started, John could use his speed to react—but the big man seemed content to keep this circling game going.

John was debating whether he would have time to grab Isabella and drag her out through the rip in the tent before Oddo killed him when Shabaka appeared through the flap. John had been wondering where his friend had gotten to, but he'd hardly expected him to show up at this moment. Neither had Oddo.

"It seems that you have got yourself in trouble, Johan," Shabaka said with a smile.

Oddo edged round so he could watch both Shabaka and John. "So you have slaves to help you," he said to John. "No matter, slaves die as easily as anyone else."

"But you are wrong," Shabaka said, almost conversationally. "I am no man's slave."

Without warning, Oddo lunged at Shabaka. Instead of retreating out of the tent, John's friend lunged forward and threw his entire weight against the tent pole. Unable to adjust his swing of the heavy axe, Oddo's weapon only caught Shabaka a glancing blow on the shoulder. The pole gave way with an ear-splitting crack and the tent collapsed around the four of them.

John was forced to the ground by the weight of the heavy canvas. He could hear Oddo cursing, but he ignored him and crawled over to where Isabella lay. It was difficult pushing his way under the fallen canvas, over the sticky, drying pools of del Huesca's blood, around the cot and over the cushions. Eventually, John felt Isabella's ankle and hauled himself up beside her.

"John?" she asked fearfully.

"I'm here," he said as calmly as he could. "It's all right now."

"I thought you were dead," Isabella said. "What's happening?"

John felt a thrill at the sound of her voice. The drug must be wearing off. "I'll explain later. Right now we have to get out." John began to drag her toward where he thought the rent in the tent wall was. It seemed to take forever, but finally he stuck his head out into the fresh air.

The scene that met them was hellish. As Oddo had said, the battle was won. Here and there, small groups of Moorish soldiers fought hopelessly, and significant fighting was still raging off in the distance to his right, but most of the Caliph's vast force was concerned only with survival. From the vantage point of the hill, John could see tens of thousands of men attempting to flee south. They looked like a brightly coloured tide flowing over the land. Thousands of blood-enraged crusaders were pursuing them, massacring as many as possible. In some places, groups of mounted knights were cutting a swath through the fleeing horde, leaving trails of broken bodies like the wakes of deadly ships. The clash of weapons, the screams of the dying and the wail of battle horns filled the air.

John stood and began helping Isabella out of the collapsed tent. On the far side, he could see Oddo's axe, working to cut a way out.

The pair had barely got to their feet when a band of fleeing Moors crashed into them, knocking them back down. John struggled to his feet once again and stood over Isabella, waving Auramazdah. More terrified men flowed around the pair with barely a glance. John let out a sigh of relief, but the feeling was all too brief. An unearthly roar drew his attention to the other side of the tent. Oddo was on his feet, his axe raised and his eyes focused on a moving lump beneath the canvas at his feet. As John watched in horror, Oddo brought his axe down. The heavy blade sliced through the canvas and deep into the struggling body. A black arm thrust through the torn canvas, the fingers clenched in agony. John heard a muffled scream.

"Shabaka!" he yelled.

"So much for the slave," Oddo snarled, looking over at John. "Now to finish what we began."

John grabbed Isabella's arm and hauled her upright. "Come on," he shouted. The pair joined the flow of the panicked crowd. For the moment, at least, the mass of humanity was a blessing. Oddo had to fight through the press of fleeing bodies to reach them, so they managed to keep ahead of him, but a quick look back showed that he was gaining as men fell before his swinging axe and others dived out of his way.

John saw the Caliph's tent ahead and moved toward it, vaguely aware of the Aragonese banner now flying beside it. He never even saw the coils of rope dropped by the fleeing slaves. His foot caught in a loop and he flew forward onto his face, losing his grip on Isabella's arm. By the time John collected his wits and rolled over, Oddo was standing above him, his axe in his left hand and his right gripping Isabella's arm.

"This time your slave can't help you," Oddo said.

Isabella lashed out with her foot and caught Oddo on the side of his shin. The big man staggered more from surprise than the pain of the blow. Then he laughed.

"I've changed my mind," he said, looking at John but twisting Isabella's arms so that she was forced to her knees. "I think I'll let you watch this one die before I kill you."

Oddo set the blade of his axe against Isabella's neck.

"No!" John's scream had no effect on Oddo, but the imperious "Hold!" that followed it made the mercenary pause and look up.

A knight was riding toward them from the Caliph's tent. He wasn't tall, but astride his massive, armoured war horse, he was nevertheless an imposing figure.

"Simply because you and your Falcons have fought bravely in our Christian cause this day," the man said, reining in his mount in front of Oddo, "that does not give you licence to threaten the king's niece—especially when there are Moors to be killed all around."

The war horse snorted and stamped its hooves impatiently. The rider was dressed from wrist to ankle in a full suit of jet-black chain mail, and his surcoat bore a red cross of St. George surmounted by a golden crown. He carried a bloodstained sword in his right hand.

To John's surprise, Oddo lowered his axe. "I meant the lady no harm," he said sullenly.

"That is not how it looked, but for your work today you shall be forgiven. Collect the rest of your men and finish this business of killing."

"As you wish," Oddo said, although his expression suggested it was far from whathe wished. With a final, evil glance at John, he strode off.

John hauled himself to his feet and helped Isabella to stand. She was shaking and he put his arm around her waist to support her.

"And who are you—a Moor who presumes to put his arm around a Christian lady?" the mounted knight asked.

"I am not a Moor," John replied. "This is a disguise. I needed to follow Isabella here and rescue her."

The man regarded John for a long moment. His helmet had no cheek plates, so John could clearly see his face. He wore a black moustache that drooped on both sides of his mouth and his features were coarse, but glints of humour danced around the eyes.

"You might be telling the truth," the man said thoughtfully. "You wear very expensive and blood-soaked armour and your hair seems to be growing out fair. I suspect you have a tale worth hearing. Let us go to the Caliph's tent—I do not think he will be needing it again this day—and you can tell me."

The knight wheeled his horse around and rode back to the tent, where he dismounted. Half supporting Isabella, and with a last look at where Shabaka's limp arm protruded from the bloody rip in del Huesca's tent, John followed.

* * *

The inside of the tent was chaos: expensive draperies were reduced to rags, sumptuous cushions had been ripped open and lay like huge, exotic, disembowelled slugs and a gilt throne rested on its side, cracked and chipped where someone had pried out precious stones with the point of a sword.

"I'm afraid my men are none too careful with the possessions of their enemies," the knight said as he ushered Isabella and John inside. "What is the matter with the lady?" he asked John.

"She's drugged," John replied. He knew he should show more deference to this powerful man, but too much was weighing on his mind. He was exhausted after his encounter with Oddo, miserable over Shabaka's death and anxious about Isabella.

The knight tilted his head and regarded John with interest. "Do you know who I am?"

"Someone important."

"There are men in my position," the knight said thoughtfully, "who would have you flayed alive for such insolence. I am Pedro, sometimes known as the Christian King of all Aragon and Barcelona and, after today, victor of the greatest battle yet fought in the reconquest of Al-Andalus. And the only reason you still live is because the drugged girl is my niece."

"I…I'm sorry," John stuttered. He attempted a bow and almost fell over. He was relieved to hear Pedro laugh.

"I tried to persuade him to surrender," Isabella said weakly, "but he beat me. I don't remember much."

"Don't worry, child," Pedro said gently. "You kept your word to me. Rest. I will hear the tale from your strange companion."

"Is the battle over, Your Majesty?" John asked.

"All but the killing, and I have little interest in that. We came over the pass at Despeñaperros last night and took the Moors completely by surprise. They outnumbered us, but they do not have the organization nor the discipline of the Christian knights. Alfonso, my royal colleague from Castille, would say it is because God is on our side, but I fear he forgets that God was also on his side at Alarcos and that was a disaster. In any case, I shall leave Alfonso and the others to wade through a sea of blood. I am content that we have won, although I should have liked to capture the Caliph. Now sit, and tell me your story."

Pedro turned the battered throne the right way up and sat. John made himself as comfortable as possible on the remains of the cushions and Isabella sat beside him. He instinctively liked Pedro; he reminded him of an older, gruffer version of Roger Trenceval, and he felt guilty that only a few hours ago he had been prepared to give the Caliph the king's plan of attack in exchange for Isabella. He thought he'd better leave that out of his story.

For almost half an hour, despite frequent interruptions by blood-spattered knights giving Pedro reports on the progress of the slaughter, John talked. He related most of the things that had happened to him since he and Isabella had left Cordova. In addition to his attempted betrayal, John tried to leave certain things out of his narrative, but Pedro was alert and intelligent and asked clever questions. John thought he could get away with a version of events in Toledo that avoided mention of Arnaud Aumery, not knowing how the king would react to his having been threatened with torture for heresy, but Pedro pressed him to give names and details.

"A strange man," was the only comment Pedro made when John told him an abbreviated version of his meeting with Aumery. "I suspect he seeks more than just communion with God."

When John came to del Huesca's death, Pedro asked him to repeat it and then inquired about Shabaka. John found himself close to tears as he recounted how his friend had been killed by Oddo.

"The man is a brute," Pedro agreed, "but he and his Falcons fought well this morning. We came as close as we did to capturing the Caliph because of the brutality with which they led our forces to this tent. Sometimes, to arrive at God's side, we must travel a short way with the Devil.

"But I must return to the fray," Pedro said standing. "I thank you for telling me of del Huesca's end and for your devotion to my niece. You will stay with her as she recovers from the drug and then you will return with us to Barcelona and the court. I shall leave a guard on the tent for protection, but try to find some clothing that makes you look more like a Christian before you venture out. I suspect my men are not asking many questions out there or examining their victims too closely."

With a last look at his niece, Pedro strode out. For the first time since he had found her, John was alone with Isabella.

"How are you feeling?" he asked.

"Tired," she said and smiled. "My head hurts and I can't understand what's going on. I see and hear things happening, but they don't seem to make any sense."

"Del Huesca drugged you," John explained. "It's wearing off, but you should try to sleep. I think we're safe for now."

"All right." Isabella curled up in a ball on the cushions beside John and, within moments, was breathing regularly.

John looked at her. He was happier than he'd been since Madinat al-Zahra. He didn't have to think about what he was going to do next, or worry over where Isabella was. He yawned hugely. Maybe he could lie down for a moment, too—not to sleep, just to rest. The cushions were so comfortable. John lay beside Isabella and closed his eyes.

* * *

"I envy youth." Pedro's voice worked its way into John's consciousness. "To have the innocence to sleep soundly in the midst of slaughter."

John struggled to sit up and rub the sleep from his eyes. His mouth felt as if it were stuffed with wool and every muscle in his body ached. "Your Majesty," he mumbled.

"I have brought some more suitable clothing." Pedro waved his hand and a soldier stepped forward and laid a simple brown tunic and pants beside John. "Once you are dressed, this man will lead you to our camp at the foot of the pass. We will leave for Barcelona tomorrow. I fear in this heat that this valley will stink soon enough." Pedro turned and left.

John stood up and struggled to undo del Huesca's armour. The soldier watched impassively from the door. "How's your mother in Cordova?" he asked in Occitan.

John, standing in only his undershirt, stared at the soldier, who was smiling at him slyly. It was the man he had met on the other side of the mountains yesterday, one of Isabella's escorts from Toledo.

"I thought you a strange Moor, speaking Occitan as well as you did, even if you did live at Raymond's palace in Toulouse. My companion was all for following you and slitting your throat, but I says what difference does one boy make, let him go.

"I see you've found the young lady we escorted here." The soldier glanced at Isabella, lying at John's feet. "Looks as though she's not had such a good time since we sent her on her way. Are you two sweethearts?"

"No. I mean, yes." John stammered in confusion.

"Well, you should be," the soldier said. "She's a fine lass and after what you two have been through, I reckon you deserve each other. But you'd best get that tunic on and wake the lady. It don't pay to take too long doing what kings ask, and we have an unpleasant journey ahead of us."

John finished dressing as fast as he could and shook Isabella awake. She was groggy but much more aware of what was happening.

"Good day, lady," the soldier said when they were ready to leave.

Isabella stared at the man. "You! You and your miserable companion brought me here from Toledo."

The soldier laughed. "My companion did have that reputation."

"Did?" John asked.

"Afraid so. Big Moor took his head off this morning with a sword much like yours." The soldier nodded at Auramazdah.

"I'm sorry," Isabella said.

"No need," the soldier replied. "It's man's lot to die and death comes to a soldier quicker than most. I'll not miss his moaning, but he was a good man beneath it all." The man looked sad for a moment but then he shrugged. "Anyways, I now have the honour of escorting you once more, lady. My name is Peire." The soldier bowed slightly. "I know, my lady, that your name is Isabella, but what would your name be, my young Moor?"

"I'm called John."

Peire nodded. "I'm pleased to meet you and, if you're willing one day, would like to hear your story, but for now we'd best be on our way."

The scene that met John as he exited the tent took his breath away. What fighting was still going on sounded far away across the plain. Nearby lay the aftermath of the great battle. Thousands of bodies and severed limbs and heads covered the ground in all directions. Scattered among them, larger mounds and piles of still steaming glistening entrails marked where horses had died. Here and there, a sword or lance, impaled either in the ground or in a man, stood up, breaking the flatness of the scene. Crusaders, most covered in blood, walked among the dead, occasionally bending to rob something of value or finish off a wounded Moor. Already crows were arriving to feed off the bodies and they flapped away, cawing indignantly, whenever a soldier approached.

The air was heavy with the complex smell of sweat, human and animal waste and the sickly sweet, earthy odour of thousands of gallons of blood soaking into the dry ground. It took John a moment to realize that the low droning sound he could detect beneath the distant clash of weapons and the closer shouts of the victorious crusaders was the moaning of countless wounded and dying men.

"Oh God," Isabella gasped.

"I don't reckon God has much to do with this," Peire said. "It seems to me He closes His eyes when a battle's going on."

The soldier led them to where a horse and two donkeys were tethered, stamping the ground restlessly at the pervasive smell of death. "No horses to spare, so the donkeys'll have to do," he said mounting the horse.

John climbed on his mount, glad of anything that meant he didn't have to walk through the carnage. He took a last look at del Huesca's collapsed tent. At least it covered Shabaka's body and kept it from the crows. At first John and Isabella followed Peire in silence, overwhelmed by the devastation. Eventually, though, the scale of it all numbed them. John felt vaguely guilty that, amid all the horror, and even with Shabaka's death, he was happy. He and Isabella were under Pedro's protection and that should keep them safe from Oddo, at least for the time being. Also, Barcelona was close to home.

"We're going home," he said to Isabella.

"Good," she said. "I'm tired of this land, and all this death."

"It's been a bloody day and make no mistake," Peire said over his shoulder, "the Caliph had us outnumbered, for sure. Some say he had near three hundred thousand men, and we had barely one sixth part of that. Still, the surprise helped. As soon as the Moorish left flank broke, we had the victory. Worst thing an army can do in a battle is break formation and try and run away. Once that happens it's just like chasing rabbits, but a lot more bloody."

"What'll the crusaders do next?" John asked. "Keep going and sweep the Moors out of Al-Andalus altogether?"

"No," the soldier said. "Although I hear there's plenty good plunder to be had in Cordova. There's too many kings involved. Aragon dislikes Castile, Castile doesn't like Navarre, and Portugal doesn't like anyone. They only came together here because they were afraid the Caliph was about to attack them, and because the Pope called a crusade.

"Now that the kings're all guaranteed a place in Heaven and the Caliph's no longer a threat, they'll all go home and get back to squabbling amongst themselves. One day they'll come back and finish the job, but I don't reckon it'll be in my lifetime. What're your plans once Pedro's done with you?"

"Go back to Languedoc." John looked over at Isabella, who nodded her agreement.

"Maybe that's what I'll do, too," Peire said wistfully. "I miss home, even if there's just as much death there as here."

The trio fell silent as they made their way through the slaughter. Here and there, clumps of bodies showed where a party of Moors had made a last, despairing stand. These bodies were more mutilated than the others, but they were intermingled with the bodies of crusaders. John even noticed a few wearing Falcon surcoats.

What would they do when they got back to Languedoc? The first thing John wanted was to find Adso and discover what had gone on while he'd been away. He assumed that his friend had been fighting against the crusaders who had stayed in Languedoc, but he had no desire to join in that. There was enough butchery around him here to last a lifetime.

John would keep looking for Lucius' book on drawing, he was certain of that at least. Maybe the monks who had taken the book from Madinat al-Zahra had gone farther north than Shabaka had assumed. Perhaps the book, or a copy of it, was hidden somewhere among the libraries that Beatrice had told him about—the ones the Cathars kept in isolated fortresses. And then there was the Gospel of the Christ in his memory cloister. What was he going to do with that? It had the potential to hurt Aumery and the crusade, but how? For the moment, all was speculation, but John didn't mind. Isabella was safe and they were going home. But first they had to go to Barcelona.

Going Home

Montserrat
December, 1212

"We're prisoners," Isabella said angrily. "Oh, it's not the rat-infested cell you were in in Toledo and there's no torture, but it's a prison just the same."

"The world's a prison," John said glumly.

Isabella stared at her friend. "You sound like a Cathar."

"I'm not, but when I was taken prisoner before Las Navas de Tolosa I did a lot of thinking. It's wrong to imagine that prisons need walls or guards. Maybe the toughest prisons to escape from are in our minds."

"What do you mean?"

"Look at Peter," John went on. "He's always been trapped in his mind. I don't know where he is now or what he's doing, but he's likely with Aumery and probably becoming quite an important person. He has the freedom to go where he wants and the power of the Pope and the crusade behind him, but everything he sees, does or learns has to fit in with his narrow view of God and the world. He can no more see through that than I could see through the walls of the cell in Toledo. He's trapped by the way he thinks."

"I suppose," Isabella said uncertainly. "At least we're not trapped like that."

"We are," John said, "just in different ways. I'm trapped by the responsibility of carrying the Gospel of the Christ in my head. I have to find a way to use it. On top of that, I have to search out Lucius' book on drawing." He stared unhappily at the ground in front of him. He'd tried to find a simple life, as a soldier with Adso and then by escaping to Al-Andalus, but nothing seemed to work. The world seemed to have other ideas for him.

"And I'm trapped by being Pedro's niece," Isabella said. "That's what's keeping us here. I'm sorry."

John put his arm around Isabella's shoulder. "You can't control whose niece you are," he said. "Somehow it'll all work out and we'll go home."

After the battle, the army's journey north had been a slow, triumphal procession, stopping everywhere for ceremonial feasts and elaborate masses of thanks. It had been frustrating, but at least they were moving in the right direction, and John had been relieved to see Arnaud Aumery and the Falcons taking a different route via Alfonso's court in Castille. But since September, the pair had been stuck in Barcelona at Pedro's court.

King Pedro had been unfailingly kind and polite, and they had the run of the palace and its grounds. They had even been taken on hunting trips. But every time either of them brought up the subject of returning to Languedoc, Pedro had made excuses about it being too dangerous or had dismissed them with a wave of his hand. It was a comfortable prison, but a prison nonetheless.

The pair sat in miserable silence on a ledge of coarse rock high on Montserrat Mountain, overlooking the flat Catalonian plain toward Barcelona and the distant glint of the Mediterranean sea. Immediately below them, nestled between two jagged peaks, sat the sprawling bulk of the abbey of Santa Maria de Montserrat. It was surrounded by the pack mules, carts, carriages and bored guards that had accompanied King Pedro on the ten-day procession from the coast. Pedro was somewhere within the church, either kneeling in fervent prayer or deep in conversation with the monks.

"At least it's good to get out of Barcelona for a few days," John said, trying to be cheerful. Barcelona was a small city, surrounded by ancient Roman walls. Pedro's influence, both as a Christian warrior and the king of a prosperous and growing state, was becoming quite significant and Barcelona was getting bigger. Houses spilled over into untidy suburbs outside the walls, and long, sleek galleys with banks of rowers on either side worked their way in and out of the port, laden with trade goods from Italy, Greece and North Africa.

"That's something," Isabella acknowledged. "Barcelona drives me crazy. There's no life to it, just a collection of merchants trying to get rich as quickly as possible. Why do you think Pedro wanted to come here? It's a major undertaking to move the court for this long."

"He came to pray," John said. "He's always praying. I doubt if Peter prays as much as Pedro."

"Yes, but what's he praying for?"

"Advice on what to do about de Montfort," John speculated. "He can't be happy about how strong he's become in Languedoc. Pedro thinks much of Languedoc should be part of his lands, and I can't see de Montfort calmly becoming Pedro's vassal. The man's too ambitious."

"You're probably right," Isabella said thoughtfully. "I suppose that's one reason he doesn't want us to go. He certainly questions us enough about Languedoc and what we saw going on there."

"And he was very fond of his sister," John added. "I think you remind him of her and he wants to keep you close."

"All very well, but I don't want to be kept close. I want to go back to Toulouse and see what's going on. That's my home and I miss it."

The pair lapsed back into silence. John could see no way out of their dilemma. They were in the middle of Pedro's lands, so running away was out of the question. Without the king's blessing, they would be caught and brought back.

"What did you think of that odd statue in the abbey, *la Moreneta*?" Isabella asked.

"The statue of the Madonna and Child with black skin? It's strange. It reminded me of Shabaka," John said sadly.

"One of the monks told me that it was carved in Jerusalem more than a thousand years ago and that it was in a grotto here long before there was an abbey. They built the church around it."

"Just a story," John said.

"But doesn't the Gospel of the Christ say that He and Mary ended up somewhere in Languedoc? That's just across the mountains."

"Are you suggesting that they brought the statue with them?"

"Who knows, but if they did, it must have been very important to them. Maybe, like you, they thought that drawings weren't very realistic so they brought a sculpture because it was an accurate picture of Christ's mother."

John smiled. He liked the idea that Christ might have felt the same way he did about drawing. "Wait!" The implication of what Isabella had just said hit him like a hammer. "Are you suggesting that Christ's mother was black like Shabaka?"

"And Christ, too," Isabella said with a sly smile. "All the pictures of Christ today show Him as if He were alive here and now, not more than a thousand years ago at the other end of the world. Shabaka told us that his people had once been kings who ruled Egypt when it was a mighty empire. They weren't always slaves, and the land Christ lived in was part of the Roman Empire. There must have been people from all over in it."

"You're more of a heretic than I am," John said with a laugh. He was slightly shocked at what Isabella was saying, but pleased that her mood was improving.

Isabella shrugged. "In spite of my body being trapped here in Pedro's kingdom, there's always a part of me"—she tapped her head—"that can wander wherever it wishes."

"That's true," John said with a smile. He loved the way that Isabella always managed to come around to seeing the bright side of everything.

"The monk told me something else as well," Isabella went on. "There is a legend that claims that the Black Madonna marks the secret hiding place of the Holy Grail."

"If it were here, it would be in the abbey," John pointed out.

"Maybe not. There are caves all over these mountains where hermits lived, prayed and died. It might be in one of those. The problem is that there are many Black Madonnas. There's even one in Toledo, although we didn't see it. Which one hides the Grail?"

"None," John said, "and that's just as well. Aumery and the crusaders are doing enough damage without it. Imagine what they would do if they thought they had the Holy Grail and were ushering in the Day of Judgment?"

John felt Isabella shudder beside him. He put his arm around her shoulder. "So let's not go searching the caves for it, all right? Let it stay lost."

"Yes," Isabella agreed. She fell silent, staring thoughtfully down at the abbey. "That drawing of the monster you found in Nasir's library," she said at last, "do you still have it?"

"It's here in my satchel," John replied, puzzled by the change of topic.

"The woman on the beast's back is carrying a jewelled goblet, isn't she?"

John opened his satchel, pulled out the drawing and unrolled it. "She is, and it's a very valuable one. It seems to be made of gold and covered with precious stones."

"Do you think it's the Holy Grail?"

John shrugged. "I suppose it could be." He hadn't thought about the strange drawing much. "What if it is?"

"I don't know," Isabella said, reaching over to run her fingers over the drawing, "but the idea of the Grail being hidden in a cave made me think. If this is a picture of the Grail, then maybe the whole drawing is a clue, a key to where the Grail is."

The idea intrigued John, but he was unconvinced. "I don't know. There are a lot of weird things in this picture. They probably all meant something to whoever drew it. We know the artist was representing something from the Revelations of St. John, but the rest is a mystery. I doubt if we'll ever know what it all means."

"I suppose not," Isabella said. "In any case, I don't think we're going to get time to think about it now. Look." She pointed down at the courtyard in front of the abbey. A party of soldiers had just arrived and Pedro and the other dignitaries were coming out of the abbey to meet them.

"Something's happening," John said, rolling up the drawing and standing. "We'd better go down and see."

* * *

By the time John and Isabella returned to the abbey, the square in front of it was a hive of activity. Horses were being saddled, carts loaded and carriages prepared for the road.

"Looks as if we're leaving," John observed. "I wonder what news those soldiers brought?"

As they looked around, John spotted Peire. He had chosen to stay when he had been offered a place in Pedro's palace guard. Now he was covered in dust from a long journey and drawing a bucket of water from a well at the edge of the square. John led Isabella over.

"Don't even get time for a rest," Peire grumbled. "We ride hard all the way from Barcelona with the royal messenger and then turn around and head back. I could use a cup of ale and a good night's sleep."

"What message did you bring?" Isabella asked.

"Well, lady," Peire said, "I don't pretend to understand all the ins and outs of it, but it seems there was a big meeting up north in Pamiers. De Montfort, Aumery and all the bishops were there. Even the well-fed Foulques left the comforts of his palace in Toulouse to attend. But I suppose there were enough important folk in Pamiers that they ate well enough. Not the sour wine and mouldy bread we were given for the journey."

"What happened?" John asked impatiently.

"Word is that it was all a show to confirm de Montfort as lord of the lands the crusade has conquered."

"Why should that cause such a commotion here?" John asked. "De Montfort's been in control of most of the lands since Minerve fell."

"It's important here," Isabella said, "because de Montfort's been confirmed as lord of the lands by the Church. As long as he was just a military commander, Pedro could ignore him. Now that he's confirmed as lord by the bishops, the counts will have to swear vassalage to him, and some of those counts, including Raymond, owe allegiance to Pedro. De Montfort's sent out a direct challenge to Pedro. He can't ignore that."

"Lady's got it right," Peire said. "I don't understand how these rich folk work things out, but Pedro was unhappy when he heard what had happened. He raged against de Montfort, the bishops and even the Pope himself. Swore to send a delegation to Rome to have de Montfort put in his place, and if that didn't work, to head north himself to sort things out."

"Head north?" Isabella asked.

"That's what he said, head north—with words at first but at the front of a great army if needs be."

Isabella turned and grinned at John. "We're going home after all."

John returned her smile, but the thought of going north with Pedro and his army was worrying. The crusade so far had been a war of sieges and ambush. If armies became involved, it could only increase the bloodshed and suffering. John silently prayed that words would work.

PART THREE

Peter's Story

A Quest

Rome
June, 1212

Peter stood and stared up at the obelisk. It was covered in carvings of animals, birds and plants that people told him were antique writing. Peter had trouble believing that, but then the obelisk was already ancient when Caesar's legions had brought it back from Egypt. Whatever the carvings said or meant, the pillar was certainly impressive. But much more important, and the reason Peter stopped here every day as he headed for the library, was the red rock about twenty feet away.

More than a thousand years before, the Romans had set up the obelisk in the centre of a huge oval circus where slaves raced chariots and, as a special entertainment, some of the first Christians had been martyred. The red rock marked the spot where St. Peter, Christ's chief disciple and the first leader of the Christian Church, had been killed by the emperor Nero, who blamed the Christians for burning Rome. At his own request, St. Peter had been crucified upside down so that the manner of his death could not be confused with Christ's.

Afterwards, St. Peter's body had been dragged away and buried. But his followers had remembered the spot, and many years later they built a church over it. Now all that remained of the circus was the obelisk, and St. Peter's tomb lay beneath the altar of the largest church in Christendom—St. Peter's Basilica.

Peter touched the red rock, said a quiet prayer and crossed himself. Then he looked up at the imposing bulk of the basilica. The walls towered above him, making him feel insignificant and in awe of the invincibility of the true Church. The library was on the far side of the basilica, and the shortest way to it was through the great edifice itself. Peter set off along the side of the building toward the south door.

After he entered the church, Peter stopped, as he always did, in admiration of its sheer size. The nave to his right almost disappeared into the distance and soared up to the flat wooden roof, painted blue and gold to represent the stars in heaven. The walls were painted with biblical scenes or covered with golden mosaics of Christ, Mary and the disciples.

The windows were small and made Peter remember John, who talked about new churches in the north where the walls were mostly stained glass windows and the interiors were bright with the light from heaven. John had used these dazzling new churches as an argument in favour of trying new things and learning to draw differently. Peter had dismissed his friend's ideas as presumptuous, and he believed they encouraged dissatisfaction with the way God had ordered the world. However, he had to admit that more light here would help him appreciate the paintings and mosaics.

Peter walked to the centre of the basilica and turned to his left to face the simple altar that sat over St. Peter's tomb. Above it, a magnificent crucifix was picked out in gold. Peter knelt briefly and crossed himself again. As always, he said a prayer of thanks for his safe arrival in Rome.

His journey from Cîteaux last winter had been a nightmarish trek. The roads were dangerous, cluttered with refugees from the crusade and haunted by bandits. Fortunately, the robbers paid little attention to a solitary, obviously poor monk trudging south. What slowed Peter's progress the most was that every community or travelling group he came upon demanded that he stay with them for a few days to bless the sick, hear confession and supervise the burial of the dead. He had been so delayed that winter storms were already threatening by the time he reached the mountain passes.

The first storm was the worst anyone could remember and held him up in a peasant hut for two weeks. After that he had faced the seemingly endless frustration of attempting snow-filled passes only to be forced back by thigh-deep snow or another storm. After weeks of trying, Peter had to admit the error of his decision to cross the mountains directly in such a hard winter. He backtracked many miles before heading south and edging along the coast into Italy.

Then, south of Firenze, when Peter thought the worst of his trials were over, the sickness had broken out. He left immediately and believed he had escaped untouched, but four days later he collapsed by the roadside close to the small town of Assisi. A travelling party of monks found him and carried him to their chapel in the woods.

Peter hovered between life and death for weeks. He eventually recovered, thanks to the gentle monks' care, but was so weak he could barely sit up in the cot they had provided. On a diet of bread and soup he regained his strength, and the spring sun had done the rest.

Quest

Unlike the Cistercians at Cîteaux, who worked the land and sold their produce, the monks of Assisi and their leader, Francesco, owned nothing, believing that material possessions distracted one from achieving closeness with God. Peter was fascinated by the brotherhood. Their denial of material things was similar to what the Cathar heretics of his own country believed. Of course, Francesco and his followers were not heretics—they were not dualists and they did believe in the divinity of Christ and the Catholic Mass—and Peter couldn't help but admire their simple life. Surely it brought them closer to God than the ostentatious wealth of Bishop Foulques in Toulouse? The more difficult question was whether it brought them closer to God than Arnaud Aumery's quest. Six weeks later, Peter still hadn't figured out the answer.

Frequently throughout his journey, Peter had made time for quiet contemplation, imploring the voice that had spoken to him in Cîteaux to answer his questions. But throughout his trials, the voice had remained silent. Had his voice abandoned him or was he already doing what it wanted? Peter had no idea, so he simply continued on his way.

He had been in Rome since April. He had climbed each of the seven hills upon which the ancient city had been built, but had discovered no eighth hill that could make sense of the letter he had received from Father Aumery. Now he was deeply into his studies in the library, searching for clues to the meaning of his mysterious map fragment, but that search was equally frustrating.

He had found many maps in the library. Some were simple things that showed what someone had thought the world should look like—a reflection of heaven above—and of no practical use to a traveller. Others were remarkably accurate. These were sailors' maps, showing coasts and reefs in life-saving detail, but fading into insignificance away from the sea routes. Peter was slowly coming to understand that maps showed only what the mapmaker was interested in or thought important. None looked anything like the one he had received at Cîteaux from Father Aumery. Sometimes he wished the voice would return to give him a clue.

"Holy St. Peter," Peter prayed fervently, "help me understand what I do not know and guide me to success in Father Aumery's holy quest. And, if you are the source of my voices, return to comfort me in my loneliness." Peter knelt for a moment, but no one spoke to him. He stood, crossed himself once more, and left the basilica to begin his day's work.

* * *

The library next to St. Peter's was an old Roman temple, a circular building with a domed roof and a pillared entrance. The steps leading up to it were heavily worn by the passage of countless thousands of pairs of leather sandals. Peter wondered whose sandals had contributed to the wear—the sort of imagining that would have fascinated John. It was unlikely those sandals belonged to any of the early Christians, Peter thought. More probably, the feet that had trod here were those of the pagan emperors who had persecuted Christ's followers.

Peter had to admit, though, that pagan Rome must have been an impressive place. The city was much smaller now than it had been a thousand years before. Back then, it had spread along the banks of the Tiber River and covered the summits of those seven hills. Now the huge temples, palaces and public buildings lay in ruins, their vast pillars fallen like so many sticks. Only the odd building had survived intact to serve as a church or, as in the case of the one he was entering, a library.

The inside of the library was shadowy, even in broad daylight. The only light came through the open doorway and a few small, round windows set high in the wall. Rough wooden shelves lined the circumference or stood alone in the central open space. Each shelf was stacked, apparently haphazardly, with piles of scrolls and books of varying sizes that all lay on their sides. The possibility of finding anything specific depended entirely on the old monk who sat by the door and seemed to know the contents of every book and document in his care. Peter had found the old man very useful, although he had been careful not to mention anything about his quest.

Peter had read everything he could find about the Cathar heretics and their history. He had learned how their ideas had originated in the East and travelled west through a strange and mysterious sect called the Bogomils who lived north of Greece. The Bogomils and their beliefs had eventually made their way to Languedoc, where the Holy Crusade was presently trying to destroy them. None of Peter's research had told him anything about where the Grail might be, or even if it still existed. Feeling as though he'd reached a dead end in that aspect of his quest, Peter had moved on to a so-far fruitless search of the library's maps. His hope was that he would come across something similar to the fragment Aumery had sent.

Peter nodded to the old monk and made his way to the table where he'd piled the maps he was working on. Although none of them matched the fragment, Peter was in the process of copying one that he hoped might be useful. It showed the world—Al-Andalus, Languedoc, France, the Britannic Isles and the lands of the Norsemen. Italy, Greece, the crusader lands and the coast of North Africa were well drawn, but the map was damaged to the east and showed little there.

Quest

Cities were marked and named—Peter recognized Rome and Jerusalem—but many of the names were worn off or written so small that Peter couldn't make them out. Mountains and rivers were defined in such detail that Peter couldn't hope to match it in his copying. Nevertheless, he had been working hard on the map for several days. Partly it was to keep himself busy and partly it was to avoid admitting that his search here had been a waste of time.

Peter had drawn the coastlines and rivers as accurately as he could and had marked the cities that he could decipher. Perhaps in the full daylight, he thought, he might be able to see more. Peter picked up the map and his copy and walked back outside. He spread out the map on the top step with his copy beside it and stared. The original was heavily stained from repeated handling and cracked where it had been folded and refolded over the years. Peter leaned forward and peered at the names that he hadn't deciphered yet. Even squinting painfully, he could make out only the odd letter.

"This may be of help, brother." Peter was so engrossed in the map that, for an instant, he thought the voice in his head had returned, but it was just the old monk. "My apologies! I did not mean to startle you. I merely wished to offer this. The work you examine is not in the best condition."

The monk gave Peter a perfectly polished disc of clear crystal. It was two inches in diameter and half that in thickness, almost flat on one side and curved on the other. Peter held it carefully by the edges and looked questioningly at the monk.

"Look at the map through it," the old man suggested.

Peter leaned over the map and put the lens close to his eye. Everything looked blurry. He moved the lens away and, almost magically, a small section of the map leaped into clear focus—five or six times its actual size. Peter jerked his head back in surprise.

"Wonderful, is it not?" the old man said with a chuckle.

"Yes," Peter said, turning the lens around in his hand.

"It was given to me many years ago by a traveller from the East. He said it was ancient and that the skill of making such things is now lost. He also said that some men knew of a way to put more than one of these together in a tube, which allowed them to look at the moon and stars as if they were held in your hand. I should like to try that," he added wistfully.

"If God wished us to see the moon and stars as if they were in our hand," Peter replied, "He would have given us the eyesight to do so."

"Perhaps it is as well there is only the one glass and we are not tempted," the monk replied. "In any case, I do not think God would object to this glass helping my old eyes," he hesitated, "or your search, if you seek something of which He would approve."

Peter recognized that the monk was gently chastising him for his arrogance. "I'm sorry," he said. "You're right." He leaned back over the map and moved the lens into position.

He concentrated on a name beside one of the towns. "B-Y-Z-A-N-T-I-U-M," he read slowly. Peter moved the lens over. "P-H-I-L-I-P-P-O-U-P-O-L-I-S." He'd never heard of it. Peter focused on a name that was almost erased, willing it to appear before him.

"What do you seek?"

"Trimondium," Peter answered.

"What did you say?" the monk asked.

"I answered your question. I seek Trimondium."

"I asked no question."

Peter almost dropped the glass. Had he imagined it? No—the words had been clear—soft, but certainly there. His voice was back. Before he had a chance to think what it meant, the old monk nodded toward the map. "You have found it."

Peter's head swirled with confusion. Then, like a physical blow, the implications of the monk's words struck him. "What do you mean? You know where Trimondium is?"

"And so do you." The old man smiled mischievously. "There, in Thrace, where you just looked. A land conquered long ago by Philip, the father of Alexander the Great. He named a city after himself—Philippoupolis—but the Romans didn't like the name and renamed the town Trimondium."

Peter blinked. "Philippoupolis is Trimondium?"

"It is," the old man smiled. "A fascinating place, I am told. It was once the centre of the heretic Bogomils."

Peter's heart raced. The Bogomils—the link between the eastern heretics and the Cathars. He *must* be on the right trail! He only hesitated for a moment before he put the lens down and reached for the map fragment in his satchel. This was the first piece of useful information he had gained in weeks! What else did the old man know, and what possible harm could come from showing him the map?

"I was given this by Father Aumery, the abbot of Cîteaux and leader of the Holy Crusade against the Cathar heretics," Peter said, unrolling the mysterious map on top of the one he had been examining. "It has Trimondium marked, and many other places, but I do not know them and the map is like none I have ever seen."

"Then you have never seen a Roman map," the monk said.

"A Roman map?" Peter's breathing was coming fast now. He felt as though he was on the verge of some great discovery.

"The Roman Empire was the greatest the world has ever seen, dwarfing even that of Alexander or the Babylonians, who took the Jewish people into exile. To hold the empire together, they built roads, such as the Via Appia that runs out of Rome. That is what their maps show."

"But this map is not of the world!" Peter exclaimed in confusion.

"It is," the old man said, "but of the world squashed and stretched out so that it might easily be shown on a long scroll that could be carried in the pouch of a traveller. Look." He pointed to two tongues of land at the left edge of the map. Peter had assumed that they were part of an island in the sea that ran along the centre of the map. "This is the end of the very land we are in. The sole and heel of the boot stretched and turned on its side. Brindisium is the town we know as Brindisi. If your map extended but a little farther to the left, you would see Rome itself.

"This"—the monk ran his finger along the coast across the narrow stretch of sea from Brindisium—"is the land of Illyrium, and see the red line that runs from Dyrrachium on the coast? That is the Via Egnatia. From there you may travel north to Trimondium, which lies on the Via Diagonalis."

"If I take a vessel from Brindisium—Brindisi—over to Dyrrachium, I could follow the roads all the way to Trimondium?" Peter asked.

"Indeed you could, although it is a long journey and the roads are not in the condition they were at the time of the caesars."

Peter had been looking at the map as the monk talked, but now he became aware of the old man staring at him. He glanced up to see an intense, questioning expression on the aged face.

"Why do you wish to go to Trimondium?"

Peter had a sudden strong feeling that he shouldn't have shown the map to the old man. But surely that was ridiculous. He was simply curious. "Father Aumery instructed me to discover as much as I could about the Bogomils," Peter lied, "so that we might better understand the heretics we fight in the crusade."

"I see," the monk said thoughtfully. "But if you did not know the location of Trimondium before I explained the map to you, how did you know it had anything to do with the Bogomils?"

"I didn't," Peter said, his mind racing to try to explain what he was doing without mentioning the Grail. "I was reading of the Bogomils. The map was something separate that Father Aumery thought might be important. I did not realize the connection until you mentioned it." It was a weak lie, but all he could think of on the spur of the moment. In any case, it appeared to satisfy the monk.

"May I use this to finish my copy of the map?" Peter asked, holding up the lens. He was hoping to distract the man from more talk of his quest.

"Of course you may," the monk said.

"Thank you." Peter rolled up Aumery's map. He hurriedly scanned the legible names on the librarian's map and transferred them to his copy. There were some that were too worn to read, but the lens made deciphering most names easy. For the entire time that he worked, Peter was aware of the old man sitting silently by his shoulder. Finally, he rolled up the worn map and handed it to the librarian.

The old man took the map. "So you plan to journey to Trimondium?"

"Yes," Peter said, rolling up the copy as casually as he could manage and standing. He handed the lens back to the monk, who accepted it with a nod.

"It is a long journey, and I wish you good fortune. Go with God."

"Thank you," Peter said, turning away. He wanted to leave before he was asked any more awkward questions.

"You know that names change," the librarian said. "As I explained, Philippoupolis of the Greeks became Trimondium of the Romans."

"Yes," Peter said, hesitating.

"It will make your travels easier if you know some other changes. Dyrrachium is now known as Durrës, and Trimondium has changed yet again. It is now known as Plovdiv. A strange name, but I am told it is the most beautiful of all cities—built on seven hills, just like Rome."

Peter almost choked. Seven hills! The Cathar Perfect that Aumery had examined at Lavaur hadn't meant Rome—she'd meant Plovdiv! He *was* on the right track.

"Thank you again," Peter said, struggling to keep the excitement out of his voice. "You have been a great help."

"You are most welcome," the librarian replied.

Peter walked out, his mind busy forming plans for his journey. Finally, he had a direction, a clue! He had absolutely no doubt that Plovdiv was where he had to go. It was where he'd find the answer to his and Aumery's quest. Was there an eighth hill in Plovdiv? *What do you seek?* Peter marvelled at how the voice in his head had asked exactly the right question. His own unwitting answer had started the conversation that had led to all this! It was clear, then: he *was* being guided!

As Peter walked on, more sure of himself than he had been for weeks, the old man stared intently after him.

* * *

Peter gazed ahead at the Via Appia vanishing into the distance between two rows of white marble tombs. The ancient Roman law forbidding burial within city limits had turned every road leading away from Rome into a cemetery lined with the dead. Most of the tombs were pagan, but Peter was nevertheless impressed by their size—one was even a recreation of an Egyptian pyramid—and the beautiful workmanship of the statues and pillars.

Peter adjusted the satchel containing his meagre belongings, some bread and a full wineskin and settled into a regular stride that could carry him twenty miles a day for weeks on end. He glanced down at the cobbles his leather sandals slapped against with every step. They were polished to a glass-like shine by the uncountable feet that had passed this way before him, and scored with the parallel ruts of innumerable carts. Peter was reminded of the worn library steps in Rome and he felt himself surrounded by the past —dark and mysterious, yet holding the answers to all his questions. It felt good to be on the move, seeking answers to some of those questions, though he was nervous about setting off on such a long journey into the unknown. He had thought of sending Father Aumery a letter from Rome, telling of his discoveries so far, but he didn't have anything very concrete to report and he was wary of putting too many of his speculations in writing.

Peter looked up. Odd, he thought, how the lines of tombs came together in the distance until there was no road between them, yet when he reached the farthest point he could see, the road would still be as wide as it was here. It was different from the roads in paintings, which were the same width all along. Peter wondered if this was what John meant when he talked about painting the world as he saw it. But that wasn't accurate. Everyone knew that even if the road *appeared* to vanish in the distance, it really was the same width all along. And wasn't that what painting should show—what everyone knew to be true, not some trick of the eye?

That was the whole difference between Peter and his friend. Peter *knew* that God had created everything and sent His only Son to save mankind. Everything Peter thought had to fit with that. If something *didn't* fit, it was either an error or an example of the Devil tempting people. But John believed what he saw—even if it was a trick like the road disappearing—and tried to change what he believed to fit with that. Surely, that was the way to heresy.

Peter wondered where John was now. He hoped he hadn't given up his soul to the Devil and been drawn into the evil Cathar heresy. Destroying the heresy in Languedoc would be the first thing he and Father Aumery would do once Peter found the Grail. At the head of the Christian armies, they would be invincible. With the Grail, not only would they become the most important and powerful men in this world, but they would be assured of an eternal place in heaven among the highest rank of angels. It would be worth the hardships that lay ahead.

"Come, brother, and pray for your journey at the most holy chapel in Rome. Walk in the footsteps of Christ and St. Peter." Peter turned to see a short monk standing outside a rather dilapidated small church. To one side, half a dozen loaded donkeys were tethered and contentedly nibbling the grass by the road.

"What is this place, brother?" Peter asked.

"You are a stranger to these parts?" The monk stepped forward and indicated the church door with a wave of his hand. "This is the Church of Domine Quo Vadis. It was here, when St. Peter was fleeing persecution in Rome, that the apostle met Jesus. The Gospels record that St. Peter asked Jesus, 'Lord, *quo vadis*—whither goest thou?' and Christ replied, 'I return to Rome to be crucified again.' Given strength by his Lord's words, St. Peter returned to Rome and was crucified in the circus."

"I have prayed at that spot," Peter said. "But I do not recall the tale you have told from any of the Gospels."

"You think of only the four Gospels." The monk smiled. He had a round face and his cheeks glowed like two tiny apples. "I spoke of the Acts of St. Peter, which many consider to be a true gospel deserving of being part of the foundation of our Church."

"The true Church recognizes only the Gospels of Matthew, Mark, Luke and John," Peter said with a touch of annoyance in his voice. "The rest are forgeries and temptations of the Devil."

The monk looked startled, but his smile soon returned. "Of course, of course. It is but a story. But come inside and pray. The floor of our humble church miraculously preserves the imprint of the feet of Christ in marble. It is a holy place to pray for a good journey."

Calmer now, and intrigued by the mention of miraculous footprints, Peter followed the monk into the church. It was sad. Even here, by the very gates of Rome, monks who should know better were repeating stories not approved by the Church. Peter thought of John again. It was easy to see how the ignorant could be led into heresy.

The church was simple, with a few wooden seats, a cloth-draped altar and a crude crucifixion painted on the whitewashed wall. There was one other occupant, a large merchant—the owner of the donkeys, Peter assumed—kneeling in prayer in front of the altar.

Quest

The monk led Peter forward and pointed to a marble slab set in the floor. It showed the impression of two feet, facing in the direction of Rome. The marble was polished to a shine by the touch of pilgrims.

"The feet of Christ," the monk whispered.

Peter crossed himself and knelt beside the slab. He clasped his hands, gazed up at the crucifix and prayed. "Lord help me overcome the trials of the world on this journey and arrive safely at my destination. If it be Your will, allow me to find what I seek there, and use me as Your instrument to bring about the Day of Judgment when the dead shall rise and the righteous sit at Your right hand."

Peter closed his eyes and waited for a long moment on his knees. He half-hoped that the voice in his head would return to offer more advice, but all he could hear was the monk shuffling impatiently and the merchant's mumbled prayers.

Peter crossed himself again. "In the name of the Father and of the Son and of the Holy Ghost. Amen." He stood and made for the door.

"Perhaps you would wish to purchase a relic to keep you safe on your journey?" The small monk scuttled along after Peter.

"No, thank you," Peter said without turning.

"I have a piece of the shroud that our Lord's body was buried in, or a tear shed by the Blessed Virgin at the foot of the cross."

"No," Peter repeated as he stepped out into the sunlight.

"Perhaps your journey is especially long and difficult and you need some special protection," the monk whined as he tugged at Peter's habit. "I would only part with it to someone as obviously devout as yourself, but I have"—the monk lowered his voice conspiratorially—"a toe bone of St. Peter himself."

"Pigs' bones!" The voice was louder than it had ever been, roaring in Peter's head with a force that made him stagger as if from a blow. "This worm deserves the fires of Hell."

Such anger! Peter had no will of his own, only the voice hammering in his head. He spun around and lashed out, knocking the startled monk to the ground. "I do not want your sea-water tears or pig-bone relics!" he screamed, barely recognizing the sound of his own voice. The monk whimpered in terror as Peter loomed over him, fists clenched. "I do God's work and He walks beside me," he snarled, taking a step forward as if to kick the prone man. The monk cried out and covered his head with his hands. "I have no need of the false charms you peddle to the ignorant for your own profit. Repent your sinful ways or beware your immortal soul."

The anger drained out of him as suddenly as it had arrived. He was exhausted and his head ached. He rubbed his temples, staring at the man on the ground before him. What had he done? He mumbled an apology, turned away from the monk and his church and strode off down the road.

As Peter walked, he struggled to clearly recall the incident. It was true the monk was selling false relics to the gullible, but that was not unusual. Peter disapproved of the habit, but the violent anger he had felt was new. Could the voice in his head now control his emotions? No, it was more than that. He knew he had attacked the monk, but while it was happening he'd felt almost detached, as if he were watching someone else. Had he been taken over by God? Become an instrument of divine vengeance? It was a terrifying thought, but Peter felt strangely glad as well—elated even. He was special, chosen, not alone. The voice had swallowed all his doubts. As long as it spoke to him, he would be certain that he was right.

"Lead me to the Grail," Peter prayed under his breath as he walked along.

As the morning wore on, Peter thought back over his time in Rome. Something about his encounter with the monk brought it to mind, and the memories made him sad. The ruins of ancient, pagan Rome had been impressive and his search successful but, overall, the Holy City had left him with a sour taste in his mouth. Ever since he had been a child, discussing his dreams for the future with John, Rome had been the place he'd wished to go. It was the centre of the Church and the seat of all holy knowledge. After his run-in with Oddo, he had also seen it as the source of a power that would make him stronger than the likes of any mercenary. But the heart of the Church, it turned out, was just as weak and corrupt as the limbs.

The monk he had just left was not the first to try to sell Peter rubbish that was claimed to be a holy relic. At various times in Rome he had been offered pieces of the true cross, barbs from the crown of thorns, St. Augustine's elbow and one of Christ's baby teeth. The large number of simple pilgrims who flocked to Rome each year made the sale of false relics a profitable business, and the cardinals of the Church in Rome lived in palaces and dressed in vestments that made Bishop Foulques look like a pauper. Despite the ruins, Peter's overall impression of the city was one of wealth and worldly concerns.

Peter shook his head in frustration. Rome wasn't the answer he sought, so what was? Certainly, there were holy men who weren't sunk in depravity and corruption—men like Francesco and his community living on nothing in Assisi, or Father Aumery devoting himself to burning heretics and tearing his back open in religious ecstasy, or Dominic Guzman travelling the land in poverty preaching to, and arguing with, heretics. There were communities that retreated from the world in prayer and contemplation, but was it enough? If the End Days were coming, there wasn't much time. The Grail *had* to be the answer. Once it was in his possession, and with the voice instructing him, Peter would be able to cleanse the Church of all its corruption and prepare the way for the Judgment. But it was a hard road. Visions, voices, mysteries, maps, it was all complicated and frightening. For a moment—and despite his excitement at the prospect of progress—Peter almost wished that he were back at Cîteaux or with Francesco at Assisi, living the simple life of a monk.

"Go with God, brother."

Peter swung around, trying to locate the speaker. The merchant who had been praying at the church was not far behind him. The man was fat, with several chins rolling over his collar, and his face was covered in a sheen of sweat. He was riding a tired-looking donkey and leading the other five, each heavily laden with sacks of goods.

"And you," Peter replied.

"You go to Brindisi?" the merchant asked as he drew level.

"Yes."

"And then by boat to—?"

"Durrës."

"Good," the merchant said with a smile. "Perhaps we shall meet again." With a wave that almost toppled him off the poor donkey, the merchant passed Peter and continued down the road.

At Sea

Valona
July, 1212

"Hello once again, my young friend."

Peter turned to see the plump merchant who had passed him on the Via Appia outside Rome. It was early in the morning, but already the Brindisi docks were bustling with activity. Sails, bearing the coats of arms of every major city around the Mediterranean, flapped gently in the breeze. Brightly painted ships both large and small were being loaded or unloaded by sailors of all nationalities. Shouts in a dozen languages and occasional snatches of song filled the air, and the smell of fresh tar almost obscured the stale odour of fish. Peter should have been enjoying the morning, but the vibrant energy all around him seemed like nothing more than a taunt. Despite two days of searching, he had been unable to find a ship to take him to Durrës, and he saw no reason why he should have any more luck today.

Adding to his worries, the voice was back and three times in the past two days it had shouted "Beware!" inside his head. "Beware of what?" Peter had asked, once loud enough to surprise a sailor loading a cart beside him, but he had received no answer.

"I see you have caught up with me," the merchant continued. "I fear I have dallied too long amid the pleasures of the harbour. My name is Paulus."

"I am called Peter," Peter said, taking the outstretched hand. It was warm and fleshy. He smiled, pleased to see a familiar face after the long, lonely trudge from Rome and the disappointing search for a ship.

"As I recall," Paulus said, "you seek passage to Durrës. Have you had luck?"

"I have not," Peter replied. "Everyone demands so much and I have no money."

The merchant laughed and pounded Peter on the shoulder, almost knocking him over. "It is indeed true that the roads on land are free for every beggar, but those across the sea must be bought and sold. Perhaps I may be able to help you. I have taken passage on a vessel leaving on the tide this very day for Durrës. It is not sumptuous, the crew are a villainous-looking bunch and I would not trust the captain with a pennyworth of my business, but the fare is low and, as you have discovered, passage is not easily come by in this port. I should be honoured if you would accompany me."

"I should be grateful," Peter said, "but why would you pay for my passage?"

"You are a man of God. I am a lowly merchant who seeks to earn his way into heaven through good deeds. Also," the merchant smiled, "with a holy man by my side, I shall feel more at ease in the company of the vessel's other occupants."

"Thank you, then," Peter said, returning the merchant's smile.

"Excellent," Paulus replied. "That is our vessel over there." He pointed to a moderate-sized ship docked nearby. Peter estimated it was about sixty feet long. It had two tall masts, one amidships and the other rising from the raised deck at the stern. The sails were large, white and triangular, and each bore a rectangle ornamented with three horizontal gold bars separated by two red ones.

"She is an Aragonese trading vessel," the merchant explained. "See King Pedro's flag on the sail? She is broad of beam and not the fastest, but with a favourable wind she will convey us to Durrës in a day or two. We sail on the tide at noon. Do not be late—the captain suffers from the sin of impatience."

Paulus walked away, leaving Peter alone amid the bales of merchandise and the bustle of the dockside. He was glad of the offer of a ship to Durrës—and the beginning of the long road to Trimondium, or Plovdiv as the old librarian had called it—but there was something about the merchant that bothered him, and it seemed a strange coincidence that he should run into Peter and offer him free passage exactly when Peter was looking for a ship. Was Paulus any more trustworthy than the captain and crew he was to take passage with? "Is it Paulus you're telling me to beware of?" he asked under his breath, but the voice remained silent.

* * *

The tops of the waves gleamed with phosphorescence in the darkness, and the bow of the ship sliced through the black water with incredible ease. Around Peter, ropes snapped against masts and the ship's timbers creaked with the strain. Above him, the huge sails billowed in the fresh wind. They were making good time and, with luck, would be in Durrës before dark tomorrow.

Peter was thoroughly enjoying his first voyage. True, it was under ideal conditions—clear skies and favourable winds—but Peter had been surprised at, and fascinated by, how complicated sailing a ship of this size was. The crew numbered fifteen as far as he could tell. As Paulus had said, they were a rough-looking crowd, but they seemed to know their jobs. Peter had spent much of the afternoon watching them go about their business, continually weaving multitudes of ropes into unfathomable patterns, shinnying up and down the masts to adjust the sails, and measuring the ship's speed by throwing a knotted rope over the stern and timing how fast it played out. Everything was kept on schedule by a series of bells that reminded Peter of the calls to prayer at Cîteaux. The entire affair was orchestrated by the captain, a short man who was missing several fingers on his right hand and whose cheeks were scarred by pox. He stood on the raised stern deck, taking in everything from the running of the waves to the scudding of the clouds and occasionally barking orders to all and sundry.

Things were quieter now that darkness had fallen and there were only three other figures on the deck, sailors gossiping among the bales of merchandise. It struck Peter that the scenes he had witnessed today had changed very little since the Roman galleys plied these waters. The sea was constant and the ways to cross her similar, regardless of whether you were Alexander the Great setting out to conquer the world or a modern crusader heading to battle the Saracens in the Holy Land.

"Where does your journey lead you from Durrës?" Paulus leaned his fleshy elbows on the rail alongside Peter.

His pleasant reverie disturbed, Peter felt a flash of annoyance. Although he had tried to put his suspicions aside back on the docks—having concluded that his mission itself was making him wary of everyone and everything—he still felt the need for caution around this man. "I plan to visit nearby monasteries and holy sites."

"Splendid! Perhaps you will go as far as Plovdiv." Peter tensed at the mention of his real destination—how much did this man know?—but the merchant rambled on without any hint of sinister intent. "That is where I am headed and I can recommend it to any traveller. A very beautiful city, built on seven low hills in the midst of a wide plain on the banks of a charming river."

Peter feigned a lack of interest in Paulus' ramblings and allowed his eyes to wander over the sea and the ship's deck, but he was listening intently. The three sailors had disappeared from their spot among the bales.

"The narrow, steep, cobbled streets are lined with houses that the inhabitants paint a quite staggering variety of colours." Paulus continued his monologue. "Of course, there are many of the eastern faith there and a fair number of pagans."

"And heretics," Peter encouraged.

"Indeed," Paulus agreed cheerfully. "The Bogomils and others. I have often wondered why God allows such heresies. It seems to me—"

"Beware!" The voice screamed in Peter's head. He spun around to see the three sailors standing close behind them. One carried a heavy club.

"What do you want?" Paulus asked, turning to face the newcomers.

"Everything," one of the sailors answered. Before Peter even realized what was happening, the sailor had produced a knife, sliced Paulus' purse from his belt and with the aid of his companions, hoisted the man onto the rail and rolled him over the side.

"What are you doing?" Peter asked stupidly as he heard Paulus splash into the water below.

"Making ourselves a bit of a profit on the voyage." The men formed a semicircle around Peter.

"Help!" Paulus' voice rose up from the water. It sounded as if he was already quite far behind the ship.

"You must rescue him!" Peter said.

"Must we?" asked the sailor who had spoken before, a tall, strongly built man. "How about we send you over to save him?"

"But I haven't done anything," Peter said, fear rising in him.

"Wrong place at the wrong time then," the big man replied.

The three stepped forward and Peter felt strong hands grab him. He struggled, but it was no use. Something hard caught him a glancing blow to the back of his head. Dazed, he sagged forward.

"The map!" Peter's voice ordered.

Peter felt arms tighten around him. He stopped struggling and clutched his satchel. Someone tried to rip it away, but he held on. "Leave it," a voice said. "Monks ain't got nothing of value."

Peter's whole body lifted. The top of the ship's rail caught him painfully on the hip and then he was falling toward the black waves.

The shock of the cold water closing over his head revived Peter somewhat, but there was nothing he could do. He gulped convulsively and swallowed a mouthful of salt water. He had no idea what was up and what was down or whether he was sinking or floating. He kicked his legs, but they were entangled in his habit. He was drowning. What a shame, he thought vaguely as the water surrounded him. And on his first-ever voyage.

When his head broke the surface a few moments later, he was almost disappointed. Drowning had been so peaceful. But his body took over and he gasped in a lungful of air. He went under again, but this time he knew which way was up, and soon surfaced once more.

Peter felt detached from his body, dispassionately observing what was going on. I'm cold and my head hurts, he thought. Is this what dying is like?

The gentle motion of the waves was soothing and Peter calmed down. By kicked his legs, he freed them from his habit and by moving them together and waving one of his arms he found he could keep his head above water most of the time and still hang onto his satchel. By the time he was stable enough to look around, there was no sign of Paulus, and the sails of the ship were ghost-like shapes a very long way off.

"Paulus!" Peter yelled at the top of his voice. There was no reply. He shouted several more times, but succeeded only in getting another mouthful of seawater.

Now, at last, he began to worry. Here he was, lost and floating alone in the sea, in the middle of the night with no hope of rescue. His voice hadn't been warning him against Paulus, after all. The poor man had simply been what he seemed, a cheerful merchant going about his business. The voice had been trying to warn him about the sailors who were out to rob the merchant. Peter wondered how many bones lay at the bottom of this sea, and whether his own would soon join them.

* * *

The weak dawn light found Peter still struggling to keep his head above water. The sun seemed to take an age to crawl above the low hills he could see to the east. There was no warmth in it, but the light was comforting. Not that it was much help. Peter was exhausted and his feet and hands had long ago gone numb. He had a splitting headache where the one sailor had hit him, but his mind had cleared. Unfortunately, all that did was allow him to fully understand the gravity of his situation. Unless a miracle happened, he was going to drown—and soon.

Peter had prayed a lot since he'd landed in the water. At first it had been with confidence that help would appear. After all, why would God allow him to drown now, after leading him so far on his quest? But as time passed with no sign of rescue, Peter had begun to despair. What if God didn't want the Grail found? What if the Church wasn't ready? And where did his voice fit in? At least Peter knew now what the voice had been trying to warn him about, but it was a bit late. Why could it not have said, "Beware of the sailors," or "Beware of getting on a ship with Paulus?" If it had, he wouldn't now be floating in the middle of the ocean, waiting to die.

Peter closed his eyes and sighed. The idea that it would be easier to give up the struggle and sink beneath the waves was taking shape in his mind. Just relax and let the soft waters close over your head, he thought. It would be so easy—but it would be a sin. Peter coughed and tried to push his face farther out of the water. He couldn't keep this up much longer, but he would keep struggling as long as he could and let God's will be done.

The net landing on Peter's face panicked him. His first thought was that some sea monster had attacked him and he struggled furiously, waving his arms and legs as hard as he could. By the time he realized that he was in a net, and not in the grasp of some demon from the deep, he was firmly entangled and sinking fast. Flailing wildly, Peter swallowed great gulps of seawater. Now he could barely move. He tried to hold his breath, but his lungs hurt dreadfully and red and white spots of light flashed before his eyes. Were the spots of light angels coming to take him to heaven? So be it. He relaxed and drew in a long breath of water.

Peter was unconscious when the fishermen hauled their net over the side of the boat. There were three of them, and two were convinced he was either already dead or a devil and should be thrown back over the side. The third had almost drowned as a child and been resuscitated by his father, so he knew that it was possible to bring men back from the clutches of the sea, even if many considered it unlucky to do so.

The man turned a fish barrel on its side in the bottom of the boat, laid Peter over it so that the curved side of the barrel pushed into his stomach and chest and began rolling him back and forth. After a few rolls, gouts of seawater and vomit began to spray out of Peter's mouth and nose.

As Peter regained consciousness, his first thought was that he was still in the water being rolled about by the waves. But the waves had been gentle; they hadn't hurt him. He felt as if his ribs were being broken and his stomach torn out. With a convulsive retch, he vomited up the last of his stomach contents and choked in a great gasp of air.

Hands grasped Peter's shoulders and rolled him off the barrel onto his back on the bottom of the boat. It was a relief, but his belly, chest and throat hurt horribly. His head still pounded and his hip, where it had hit the ship's rail on his way into the water, ached badly. He wished for nothing more than to be dropped back into the numbing waves, but a devil was torturing him! It was rubbing his hands and feet. They had been comfortably numb, but now needles of pain shot through them and up his arms and legs.

A shocking thought flashed into Peter's brain. Perhaps he was in hell and this was eternal torment. He opened his eyes in terror. The devil pummelling his hands was bearded and dressed in a leather tunic. His hair was long and straggled wildly but his eyes were unexpectedly kind and a smile spread across the face. Words came out of his mouth, but they meant nothing to Peter. He relaxed a little: it was unlikely that devils smiled so reassuringly.

With the bearded man's help, Peter sat up against the side of the boat and took in his surroundings. The boat was a third of the size of the one he had been thrown off. It was wide and curved up slightly at the front and back. A crude mast rose from the centre and a grubby sail was furled on a crosspiece near the top. The boat had no deck, so filthy seawater, Peter's vomit and the occasional dead fish sloshed back and forth among the piles of netting and barrels on its broad bottom.

The three-man crew were heavily bearded and dressed in similar tunics and high boots. One stood at the stern, a rudder pole tucked under his arm. Another stood beside him and both stared suspiciously at Peter as the fisherman who had been torturing him continued to smile. He leaned forward and handed Peter the satchel he had almost forgotten he was clutching when the net had caught him.

"Thank you for saving me," Peter said. The idea that he wasn't dead was beginning to take hold of his tired and confused brain.

The smiling man talked excitedly in a tongue like nothing Peter had ever heard before. Peter shrugged helplessly. "I don't understand," he said.

The man turned away and spoke to his companions. A loud, three-way conversation, accompanied by much arm waving, ensued. Bemused, Peter watched. The sun was now high enough to shine over the side of the fishing boat and the summer day was warming up. Peter's various pains were easing and a comfortable drowsy numbness was creeping over him. He didn't have to struggle any more. He was safe.

Peter watched as the men gesticulated over the side of the boat at the distant land. He caught a word—was it "Valona?"—repeated several times and then he drifted off into a wonderful oblivion.

* * *

The sun was high in the sky when Peter woke. It took him a moment to work out where he was, and his first attempts at movement brought back many aches and pains. The fisherman who had saved him noticed his struggles and shouted something cheerful in his direction. Peter acknowledged it with a weak wave and struggled to his knees. They were sailing into a large bay protected by a round stone fort at the end of a narrow promontory. Ahead of them was a small town backed by a range of dry-looking mountains.

"Valona," the fisherman said, waving at the town.

Peter watched listlessly as they approached a rough stone pier. With much incomprehensible shouting between men on the shore and the crew, the fishing boat tied up. The cheerful fisherman helped Peter out of the boat and, through easily understood gestures, made him sit on a pile of nets while he and his companions unloaded barrels of fish.

Peter was happy to sit in the sun and rest. His headache had eased and his once-frozen hands and feet no longer hurt, but his throat still felt as if he had swallowed broken glass and his body ached. It was a struggle to stay awake, but Peter forced himself to think about what had happened and what he was going to do.

He was lucky to be alive. Luckier than Paulus, who was floating dead in the water. Peter had no idea where Valona was, but it wasn't Durrës, which was probably just as well. He doubted that the sailors who had thrown him and Paulus overboard would be pleased to see him. On the other hand, he was alone and adrift in a foreign land with no idea how to get to Plovdiv. Peter undid his satchel and peered inside. Everything was there. He carefully unrolled his maps. They were soaked, but the lines and the writing were still legible. He silently thanked the librarian in Rome for giving him good quality ink and rolled up his maps.

"Welcome to our shores, brother." The words were spoken in Latin, and Peter looked up, eager to see who was addressing him in the familiar language. The man was obviously a monk: he wore a black, wide-sleeved, hoodless habit, and a simple wooden crucifix hung from his rope belt. Even so, he looked more like a wild man from the forests than a member of any monastic order Peter was familiar with.

The man's face was wrinkled and weather-beaten, giving an initial impression of great age, but his eyes were bright and youthful. His hair was dark, with only a few strands of grey, and hung long over his shoulders. He wore a full beard that stretched almost to his waist. Peter struggled to stand.

"Sit, sit," the man said. "You have had quite an experience, I hear."

"I suppose I have," Peter replied, slumping back onto the nets. His throat hurt when he talked. "You speak Latin."

"Many of us do over here," the monk said with a smile. "And Greek and a host of pagan languages from the north and east. We are not savages, after all!"

"I didn't mean that," Peter said hurriedly.

"No matter. I do not take offence. My name is Nicodemus," the monk said, gathering his habit and sitting on a bollard beside the pile of nets. "The sailors called for me as your boat docked, for the very reason that my brothers and I speak Latin and you were clearly a foreigner from across the water."

"It is a pleasure to be able to speak to someone. My name is Peter. Where am I?"

"You are in the town of Valona, sometimes called Vlorë. What was your destination and how did you fall upon the mercy of our fishermen?"

Quest

"I was on a ship from Brindisi, bound for Durrës." Peter hesitated. "I travelled with a merchant called Paulus, but the sailors attacked us and threw us into the water. I fear Paulus drowned."

The monk crossed himself. "It is a much too common occurrence," he said. "Greed blinds men's eyes to goodness. You are indeed lucky that you drifted south to where our fishermen work these summer mornings. God must favour you."

"Yes," Peter agreed, although he was by no means certain.

"What is in Durrës that draws you?"

"I was simply going to pass through on my way to Plovdiv."

"Ah, Plovdiv," Nicodemus said, as if that explained everything. "The city of seven hills. It is very beautiful, and very ancient. I studied with the brothers there years ago. But it is many days' journey from here. First you must regain your strength. If you feel up to it, I shall take you to my monastery in the town here, where you may rest and recover. It is not elegant—but then our purpose is to worship God and not to wallow in earthly wealth—and we can provide simple yet nourishing fare."

"I would be delighted to accept your hospitality," Peter said, immensely relieved that the old monk hadn't questioned him further about the purpose of his journey.

Nicodemus stood and offered Peter his hand.

With an effort, Peter stood. "Could you thank the fishermen for me and give them God's blessings on their endeavours?"

Nicodemus spoke rapidly to the three fishermen, who were busy unloading their catch and folding nets. Two of them grunted and continued with their work but the one who had saved Peter stopped and grinned broadly at him. He said something to Nicodemus and waved. Peter waved back and the pair set off slowly along the dock.

"What did he say?" Peter asked.

"He said he was glad he had saved you and thanked you for your blessing. And he said 'May you find the Grail.'"

Peter almost fell over at Nicodemus' words. The horrifying thought that he might have been babbling in his delirium flooded Peter's mind, even though it was unlikely the fishermen could have understood him. "Find the Grail? What did he mean?"

"He meant nothing," Nicodemus said with a smile. "It is only a local greeting. It means may you find that which you seek."

Peter relaxed a bit. Still, it was strange. Ever since he'd left Rome, he'd had the feeling that he was in a different world, one where everyone else knew things he didn't and was somehow aware of his quest. The normal rules no longer applied, and it seemed that the closer he got to Plovdiv, the stranger things became. He shook his head gently, as if to dislodge the thoughts that crowded his mind. It was all ridiculous, of course. The events of the previous night had made him overly suspicious, or else the blow to the head had scrambled his brains more than he knew.

"Come." Nicodemus led Peter gently by the arm. "Meet my brothers and rest."

Discovery

Plovdiv
August, 1212

The six weeks of walking from Valona had been hard and monotonous. After the first few days, Peter had settled into a rhythm. Physically, he walked at a regular, mile-eating pace, day after day. Mentally, he sank into a state resembling meditation, oblivious to his surroundings and aware only of one footfall after the other. But today was different. Peter's heart beat faster and he was conscious of every rock on the road and aware of every rustle in the trees. Plovdiv, and the secrets it might hold, was close.

A traveller that morning had told Peter that his goal was a mere day's walk ahead through the hills. All morning, he pushed himself hard, breaking his usual rhythm. Around every corner he had hoped to see the city built on seven hills, but he wasn't there yet. Eventually, he forced himself to stop and eat some lunch.

As he sat with his back against the rough bark of a large pine tree, chewing on a hunk of black bread a farmer had given him the night before, Peter reflected on his strange journey. He'd spent two days resting at the monastery in Valona with Nicodemus. He and the old monk had had several interesting conversations. Nicodemus had told Peter about the Eastern Church, how it had been established by the Emperor Constantine and how the Church of Rome had slowly grown apart from it. According to Nicodemus, the Eastern, or Orthodox, Church was closer to the true intentions of Christ than Rome was. Peter didn't agree, but he was fascinated by Nicodemus' stories and surprised by how little difference there was between the beliefs of the Eastern Church and his own. If only the easterners could change a few of their beliefs, such as the denial of the existence of purgatory, he thought, they could be welcomed back into the true church with open arms. Of course, Peter had to admit that the sack of Constantinople only eight years earlier, by a crusader army on their way to

Jerusalem, had done much to sour the relationship between the two churches.

Peter had also questioned Nicodemus as much as he could about Plovdiv. "The locals claim their city is even older than mythical Troy," the old monk had explained. "And certainly, there are many buildings and theatres from Roman times, unfortunately mostly fallen into sad disrepair."

"And it was a centre for the Bogomils?" Peter asked.

"Oh yes, and for many other sects. Even, I have heard, for a few of those who still practice the ancient Greek philosophies—Cynics, Stoics and so forth. But it is a centre of importance to Christians as well. Plovdiv is the only place I am aware of that both St. Peter and St. Andrew—the apostles who founded the Holy Church in Rome and Byzantium—visited in the years after our Lord was crucified. As you know, Plovdiv is built on seven hills, although four are little more than bumps on the ground. In any case, a local story claims that there is an eighth hill, and within that lies a cave containing the tomb of St. Andrew."

The mention of both St. Peter and St. Andrew had caught Peter's attention, but the talk of an eighth hill sent a shiver through him. Could the tomb really exist? Did it contain the bones of St. Andrew and could the Grail be buried with him?

"You haven't seen the hill?" Peter had asked, struggling to contain his excitement.

"Of course not," Nicodemus had replied. "It doesn't exist. It is simply a story."

Peter had stopped prodding Nicodemus after that, but he was convinced he was getting close to some sort of discovery. He had no idea why the two most important of Christ's apostles had visited such an out-of-the-way place, unless something vital, like the Grail, had drawn them there.

By the third day in Valona, Peter had felt recovered enough from his ordeal to continue and, with detailed instructions as to his route and Nicodemus' blessings ringing in his ears, he had set off. Villagers along the way were happy enough to give bread and wine to a man of God, and monasteries often provided an evening meal and a cot for the night. Most of the monks he met spoke at least some Latin and no one seemed to mind that Peter was not of the Orthodox Church. Now, he had almost reached his goal.

Peter downed the last of his wine and scratched his ribs beneath his left arm. The creatures that lived in his habit and on his body had become particularly annoying in the past few days, and his skin was scratched raw in several places. Generally, Peter felt good. The endless days of walking had hardened him. He was still as skinny as a stick, but he had a wiry strength and the stamina to keep going along the steepest mountain trails for hours. He and his clothes, however, were showing signs of wear. His habit was filthy and threadbare in places and the soles of his sandals were nearly worn through. Peter scratched again. A wash would feel good. He knew many of the Church's thinkers said that washing was ungodly, and that a good thick layer of dirt kept diseases away, but a wash was refreshing and it did discourage the biting creatures that God had sent to torment everyone, sinner and saint alike.

Peter placed the remains of the bread in his satchel and stood up. Not long before he had stopped, he'd caught a glimpse through the trees of a waterfall to his right. That meant there must be a stream in that direction. The weather was fair and the last time he had washed had been when he had been thrown over the side of the boat. As he set off through the woods, Peter detected movement at the edge of his vision. He turned, but there was nothing there. It was probably a deer or some other wild animal particular to these parts. He hoped it wasn't a bear or a wolf. Keeping a careful eye out, Peter headed to where he thought the stream must be.

After a few minutes, the trees in front of Peter opened up and he saw the water. The stream wasn't large, but it formed a series of inviting pools where it splashed over some rocks. The clearing was wide enough to allow sunlight in and Peter was warm when he removed his habit and crouched to wash it in a pool. He pounded it against one of the smooth rocks and was gratified to see large numbers of tiny creatures drift away on the current.

"You are not alone."

Peter spun around at the sound of the voice but there was no one there. Feeling vulnerable without his habit on, he peered intently into the surrounding trees, but he saw no sign of any living thing. The voice in his head had been silent throughout his journey from Valona and its sudden reappearance surprised him.

"Do you mean that God is always with me?" Peter asked aloud. There was no reply. Keeping watch on the trees, Peter wrung out his habit and spread it over some bushes in the sun to dry. He took off his worn sandals and placed them beside his satchel, then slowly lowered himself into a clear pool. The water was cold but incredibly refreshing. Peter sank down and rubbed himself all over. He closed his eyes and held his head under, rubbing his scalp hard with his finger tips. He could feel things scurrying across his head as he worked his hands through his hair. Go with God, he thought, as he chased them into the water.

"You are not alone."

Peter exploded out of the water. A little man stood beside his habit, staring at him. He was tiny, little more than child-sized, and he looked immeasurably old. His skin was wizened and dark and he was hunched over. He wore an odd assortment of tattered rags—all different fabrics and colours—and he was barefoot. He jumped about from foot to foot and his hands were in constant motion, feeling Peter's habit, wringing each other and waving about aimlessly.

"Who are you?" Peter asked.

"A Latin! A Latin!" The little man said gleefully, his face splitting in a wide grin that showed the stumps of only three teeth. He picked up Peter's satchel.

"Don't touch that," Peter said.

The man laughed, a thin, high-pitched sound, and hurled the satchel across the clearing. "It is nothing, nothing, nothing. Material possessions are nothing."

Peter splashed out of the pool and ran to retrieve the satchel. When he turned back, the strange man was still beside his habit, doing his odd dance from foot to foot. "You're a heretic," Peter said angrily. "Are you a Bogomil?"

"Bogomil. Bogomil," the man said. "Dear to God. Am I dear to God? Ha! What God could love me?"

"God loves everyone," Peter said, feeling vulnerable at his nakedness and edging toward his habit.

"Does He? Does He? Unbaptized children who die in pain of the bloody flux? The evil man who rapes and kills the innocents between bending his knee at Mass? All those whom God condemns to an eternity of unspeakable torment in the fires of Hell? Does He love all equally?"

"Of course."

The man stopped dancing. "What a remarkable god you have. You must tell me of him."

Peter had reached the bush now. He lifted his habit. It was still wet, but the sun had warmed it. "Who are you?" he asked again, pulling the habit over his head.

"I am no one. I am nothing. But if you must, I am a dog—shameless, possessionless, free. I live with nature. Nature provides. I eat, sleep, keep warm. What else is there?"

A lot more, Peter thought but did not say. "I am called Peter. What is your name?"

"Peter. Peter." The man began his dance again. "I have no name, but if you wish you may call me Diogenes."

"Diogenes, like the pagan Greek Cynic?"

"Ah, Peter. You are more clever than you look. Why are you here? What do *you* seek?"

"How do you know I seek something?"

"Everyone seeks something."

"But if you own nothing and live only in nature, what do you seek?"

"Clever. Clever." Diogenes' strange dance sped up. "I seek truth and an honest man."

"In the forest?"

"As likely here as in the city. Where is your destination?"

"Plovdiv."

"Then I can help," Diogenes said gleefully. "Come. Come. Come." He plucked at Peter's habit and skipped off.

Peter slipped on his sandals and followed as the strange little man danced through the trees. Diogenes' continual movement, rapid-fire way of talking and outlandish statements gave Peter little time for thought. Obviously, the man was insane, but whether blessed by God or possessed by the Devil, Peter had no way of knowing.

Eventually, Diogenes led them out into a clearing on the edge of a high cliff. "There is your destination," the old man said.

Peter looked out over a broad plain toward another range of mountains in the far distance. Along the middle of the plain meandered a sizeable river, and built on a cluster of low hills on the near bank lay a town. Peter silently counted the hills. They were various sizes, some little more than mounds by the riverbank, but there were seven. "Trimondium," he said softly.

"Yes. Yes," Diogenes said, dancing perilously close to the cliff edge. "One of the mystical seven cities."

"Seven cities?" Peter asked.

"You do not know?" Diogenes abruptly stopped dancing and stared at Peter.

"No," Peter admitted. "I haven't heard of the seven cities."

"Then I shall tell you a story. Sit. Sit. Sit."

Intrigued, Peter followed Diogenes over to the trees and the pair sat.

"Do you have any food?" Diogenes asked.

Peter resisted the temptation to remind Diogenes of his claim that nature provided all he needed and took the remains of his black bread out of his satchel.

Diogenes sniffed the bread suspiciously and took a small bite. He spat. "Disgusting. Not fit for rats." He hurled the bread in an arc over the edge of the cliff.

"What did you do that for?" Peter asked.

"It was bad," Diogenes said simply. "Now, do you wish to hear my story or not?"

"I do."

"You are arrogant," Diogenes began. "Do not be offended—all men are. It matters not which god they worship, all men assume they know their god's will. Not all can be right."

Peter swallowed his objections. After all, he did have trouble interpreting his visions and voices, and he had to admit to some doubts about how God could wish men like Arnaud Aumery to tear open the flesh of their back to get closer to Him.

"All religious men assume that every day brings them closer to their god and to a more perfect state of grace," Diogenes went on, much more relaxed now that he had begun his tale. The twitching had almost stopped. "But they live on the summit of a mountain of arrogance, based on a foundation of ignorance. What do you know of those who went before you?"

"I know of the Romans and the Greeks."

"Newcomers," Diogenes scoffed. "You think you know more than all those who came before, but you do not. You know the flea, but not the body it crawls upon. So much has been lost." For a moment, Diogenes looked as if he was close to tears, but then he continued. "Much of great value has been lost. Even your Greeks—the Moors of Al-Andalus know more of their works than you do."

"You know about the Moors and Al-Andalus?" Peter asked.

"One must travel far if one hopes to find an honest man, and it is wondrous what a simple hermit can learn from those who travel the roads near his home." A flash of humour gleamed in Diogenes' eyes. "But the Greeks are only yesterday. The Babylonians who took the Jews into exile are much more ancient, yet they knew more of the revolutions of the heavenly bodies than your greatest scientist. And there were others, so far back in the mists of time that even their names are lost to us."

"What did these pagans know?" Peter asked dismissively.

"Who is a pagan?"

"Someone who does not believe in the one true God."

"Yes. Yes. Yes. So the ancients are pagans to you?"

"Of course they are," Peter replied.

"And you are a pagan to them," Diogenes said with glee.

Before Peter could object, the old man continued. "I will tell you one thing these antique men knew. There is a map of the entire world, so accurate that looking upon it is like being a god gazing down from the heavens, and so detailed that a competent sea captain could use it to sail to continents and lands that we have not yet even begun to imagine."

"Who drew it?" Peter asked, interested despite himself.

"Nameless seafarers whose world was engulfed in fire and flood long before Babylon was even a watering place in the desert."

"Noah's flood?"

"That's what you say. Many holy books talk of floods."

"But why isn't this map known? Does God not wish us to know of these places?"

"Perhaps. Perhaps not." Diogenes shrugged. "This map would make a man a modern Caesar. He could build an army and a navy and conquer the world. He would make the great Alexander seem like a small boy playing in the village square. Who should have the map?"

"The Pope," Peter said excitedly. "He could conquer the world for Christ!"

"What if this Caesar were a Moor, or a heretic—a Bogomil?"

The thought sent a shiver down Peter's spine. Five hundred years before, the Moors had come within an ace of conquering the world without the knowledge of such a map to guide them. All the gains that Christianity had made since then—all the work of the brave saints preaching to the heathen and the knights of the crusades—could be swept away. Perhaps it was better that things such as the map remained unknown.

"Knowledge is power," Diogenes said, "and great knowledge is great power. The map I talk of is but one very small piece of what can be known."

"And you know these things?"

"Some. Of others, I have heard only rumours."

"Why do you not seek out this knowledge?"

"I do not seek possessions or power," Diogenes said with a sly smile. "But you do. I can see it in your eager eyes."

Peter flushed with embarrassment. Was he that easy to read? He felt a rising anger toward this peculiar, clever little man. "I seek only power that comes from God."

"I see," Diogenes said, looking at Peter sideways. "Then let me ask you a question about this God of yours. He is omnipotent, all-powerful, yes?"

"He is," Peter agreed.

"He can do anything? If He wished on a whim He could make the sky around us rain fire, or the solid rock become water, or the trees change into birds, or"—Diogenes smiled slyly—"He could strike me dead this instant for my presumption?"

"He could do any and all of these things."

"Good. And this God, He is also omniscient, all-seeing?"

"Yes," Peter agreed once more, wondering where this conversation was going.

"He sees everything that is happening everywhere at this instant, and everything that has ever happened and will ever happen?"

"Of course." Peter answered, frustrated now. "Why are you asking this?"

Diogenes gave a little laugh. "So your all-knowing God sees every action that He is going to take in the future. Let us say that He sees that He is going to strike me dead as we sit here." Diogenes chuckled as if he liked the idea. "In the instant before He strikes me dead, God has two choices, to strike me dead or not. After all, He is all-powerful. But"—the little man waved his hand in the air—"should He decide in His infinite mercy to let me live, He is not all-seeing since He saw Himself strike me dead."

"Then He will strike you dead," Peter said angrily.

"But, but, but," Diogenes said excitedly, his arms waving about, "*if* He has to strike me dead to prove that He is all-seeing, then He cannot be all-powerful, since He cannot reprieve me."

Diogenes sat back, smiling. "Your God cannot exist, at least not as the all-powerful, all-seeing being you imagine."

"You argue that there is no God?" Peter asked, shocked.

"I merely create a situation and ask for your opinion. But perhaps I have taken you by surprise. Perhaps you would like some time to think on it. We can talk more after I have finished telling you of the seven cities."

"He is an unbeliever trying to trick you," the voice in Peter's head said. "He will get what he deserves."

"You will get what you deserve," Peter snarled.

"As we all shall, I have no doubt." The little man seemed untroubled by Peter's anger. "But let me continue with my tale.

"It is said, and who am I to deny it, that the ancients, in a past that is almost forgotten, built seven cities, each on seven hills. One you see over there." Diogenes waved a wrinkled hand toward Plovdiv. "Another, I think you know."

"Rome?" Peter's anger slowly subsided as he was drawn back into Diogones' story.

"Yes! Yes!" Diogenes clapped his hands in glee.

"What are the other five?" Peter asked.

"Some you know, I think. Jerusalem is one, or Hierosolyma as it was known. Constantinople is another, or Byzantium if you prefer. Casteddu, a city on the Isle of Sardinia. Tehran, far to the east. Makkah, the holy city of the Muslims."

"I know of all these places," Peter said. "They are on a map I found in a library in Rome." He rummaged in his satchel for the copy he had made with the old librarian's lens. He unrolled it for Diogenes.

The little man hunched forward and peered. "Yes. Yes. Yes," he said. "You say you copied this from a map in a library in Rome?"

"I did," Peter acknowledged. "A very ancient map."

"Hah!" Diogenes scoffed. "Not very ancient. A copy of a copy of a copy of a fragment of a very ancient map, perhaps. Yet it appears accurate enough. The seven cities are there: Roma, Hierosolyma, Casteddu, Trimondium, Byzantium, Tehran and Makkah. But not the eighth."

"There's an eighth city?" Peter asked, a jolt of excitement passing through him as he remembered the information Aumery had discovered from a heretic at Lavaur and passed on to him in his letter: "the eighth of seven hills." The quest Aumery had sent him on was suddenly very alive and real.

"Where there are seven there are always eight, and often nine and ten and eleven as well."

"Is there an eighth hill here at Plovdiv?" Peter asked.

"Of course. You sit upon one, and there is another behind us and more over there." Diogenes waved his hand at the mountain range across the valley.

Peter sighed. He was never going to get anything that made sense out of this man. Living the life of a hermit for so long had addled his brains.

"Kill the heretic." The voice was soft, but it was perfectly clear. Peter looked over at Diogenes, who smiled back.

"I can't," Peter said.

"Can't what?" Diogenes asked.

"Nothing," Peter said, frowning. Did the voice mean Diogenes? Was it ordering him to kill the man? Did he have to do what the voice ordered? With a start, Peter realized that Diogenes was talking to him. "What did you say?"

"I said, unless you mean the Hill of the Chalice."

"The Hill of the Chalice? What's that?" Peter asked stupidly, still thinking about the voice.

Diogenes stood and hauled Peter to his feet. He led him over to the cliff edge. "There is Plovdiv on its seven hills," Diogenes said slowly, as if talking to a not very intelligent child. "And there"—he pointed to a low, tree-covered mound much closer to the cliff on which they stood—"is the Hill of the Chalice. The eighth hill."

"The eighth hill." Peter stared. And then it hit him. The Hill of the Chalice! A chalice was a goblet used in the Holy Mass. It couldn't be a coincidence! He felt sweat breaking out on his palms. "Why do you call it the Hill of the Chalice?"

"Because there is a chalice in the hill."

"*In* the hill?"

Diogenes danced away from the cliff edge. "It was much more interesting talking to you when you didn't repeat everything I said."

"You mean there used to be a chalice—a goblet—inside that small hill?"

"No," Diogenes said slowly. "I mean there *is* a chalice inside that hill."

Peter struggled to draw a full, smooth breath. Could it really be this easy? He made an effort to steady himself before he spoke. "How do you know?"

"Because I trust what I see with my own eyes."

"You've *seen* this chalice?"

"Questions. Questions. Questions. Here is one for you. How could I trust my own eyes had I not seen it?"

Anger surged through Peter. Did this fool not understand? He stepped forward threateningly. Diogenes moved back. He wrung his hands and began dancing faster. "What does it look like?" Peter asked.

"Like a chalice," Diogenes said, then hurried on when he saw Peter's expression. "It is gold, I think, with inlaid silver and precious stones."

"Why did you not take it? It must be valuable."

"What is value? To me, it is the life of nature without the false distractions of possessions. What need have I of a cup? My cupped hands lift water from the streams quite well."

"Why has no one else taken it?"

"No one else knows of it."

"Only you? How?"

"No one else has asked me about it."

"How did you find it?"

"Questions. Questions." Peter took another step forward and Diogenes hurried on. "One day, several years past, about the time of the trees turning, there was a great storm of wind. Many trees came down. There are many hazelnut trees below us, and I knew that if one had been blown over it would be nature's gift to me as they were ripe at the time. So I went down. I was unlucky, though." Diogenes seemed saddened by the memory. "No hazelnut trees were down. I would have to climb as always. Nature does not often give up her bounty easily." Diogenes brightened. "But a great oak had come down. Acorn soup is not as good as hazelnut, but..." Diogenes shrugged.

"The chalice," Peter reminded him roughly.

"Yes, yes. I was getting to that. I was collecting nuts by the oak when I noticed that the tree's roots had grown around a great flat stone. In falling, the roots had been unearthed and had lifted the stone. I looked under, and that is when I saw the man in the tomb."

"The man?"

"Yes! The dead man beneath the tree. He lay as if asleep, but he had been sleeping a long time. He was little more than bones. The chalice rested by his head."

Could it be St. Andrew? Peter wondered. Nicodemus had talked about a cave, but stories changed over the years. Perhaps it was a stone tomb. Peter wanted to scream. St. Andrew and the Holy Grail! Forcing himself to stay in control, he continued with the conversation. "What did you do?"

"I covered him up. I managed to free the slab from the roots and let it fall back in place. Then I covered it all with earth."

"Why?"

"Why not? Let the dead rest. I had no need of this man's chalice, and if others found it, their greed would lead them to dig up the whole hillside looking for more. I would have no peace."

"Could you find the place again?"

"Of course."

"Would you take me there?"

"So you can steal the dead man's chalice?"

"Not steal," Peter said carefully. He needed Diogenes to take him to the place. "I believe that man's chalice could be very important. I think it might be what the world needs to fulfil the prophecies of Christ and bring about the End of Days as foretold in the Bible."

"You think it is the Holy Grail?"

Peter was annoyed that the old man had so easily worked out his quest. "Yes. And I believe it could be used for great good in the world."

To Peter's surprise, Diogenes burst out laughing. "Great good in the world," he repeated when he had calmed down. "There is no good in the world, just as there is no bad. These are things *we* put there in our presumption and arrogance. There is only nature and it is not good or bad, it simply is. Enlightenment comes through understanding and becoming one with nature."

Diogenes fell silent and the pair stood looking at each other. Peter had almost decided to go and search for the fallen oak on his own when the old man spoke. "But what do I care about your Grail, or good or bad in the world? I have all I need here. I will take you. Come."

Diogenes turned with surprising speed and danced off into the trees. Peter followed as best he could, his heart pounding with excitement, and wild ideas of power, glory and the end of the world swimming in his head.

* * *

Peter stood staring at the large stone slab. He was covered in sweat and dirt and breathing heavily. He had done most of the work, digging feverishly with his bare hands through the earth among the roots of the fallen oak. Diogenes had mostly danced around, constantly and annoyingly reminding Peter of how useless material possessions were. Peter had done his best to shut out the man's rantings, and his hard work had paid off. He wiped some sweat from his forehead. The slab was too heavy for a single man to lift, but it was cracked diagonally near one corner. Peter thought it might be possible to shift the broken corner and see what lay beneath.

Peter struggled to regain his breath, acutely aware of the moment. Whatever happened in the next few minutes, his life would never be the same. He had no doubt that he was where he should be. All the clues—from the statement Aumery had torn from the tortured Perfect, to the random information he had heard from the librarian in Rome, Paulus, Nicodemus and even crazy Diogenes—led here. Either the bones of the apostle St. Andrew and the Holy Grail lay beneath this stone or they did not. If they did, Peter would become the most important human on earth—the instrument of the Second Coming and the Day of Judgment, when the names of the just would be read out of the Book of Life. If there was nothing under the slab, Peter's quest, and probably his entire life, had been a complete waste. Peter prayed silently that the Grail was there.

"It's there. It's there. It's there," Diogenes chanted as if he could read Peter's mind. Peter ignored him and bent to his task.

The crack in the slab was just wide enough for Peter to squeeze his fingers in. Rather than trying to lift the broken corner, he attempted to drag it to the side. At the first try, the stone moved with a deep groan. Peter heard Diogenes laughing behind him, but it was as if he were a long way off.

Now the work was easier. Peter could put more of his hands into the crack. It was a slow business—he had to keep stopping to dig away dirt from around the slab so that the broken fragment had somewhere to slide to— but he made progress. He strained and pulled, resisting the temptation to peer into the dark crack. One final effort should do it.

"You have the strength of the Lord," the voice echoed in his head.

"I have the strength of the Lord," Peter said out loud. He tensed every muscle in his body and pulled. The broken corner rasped over the edge of

Quest

the tomb and embedded itself in the dirt. It was done. Peter closed his eyes and prayed for success.

"Look," his voice ordered. Peter opened his eyes. A golden glow was rising from the opening he had created. He gasped and crawled forward to peer in. It was there. The Holy Grail. The cup Christ drank from at the Last Supper. The Cup that had caught the blood that ran from the wound in His side when He hung on the cross to redeem the sins of the world.

Peter could barely look, the unearthly glow was so bright. He could see, though, how magnificent the Grail was: encrusted with jewels, inlaid with silver in intricate swirls and lines—and golden. Golden beyond anything Peter had ever imagined. "Thank you," he murmured.

"Take it," the voice said.

With infinite care, Peter reached down into the grave and touched the Grail. He almost expected it to burn him, but its surface was cool. Carefully he lifted it up. Even in daylight, the golden light illuminated the surrounding trees in a brilliant glow. Peter felt a strange power surge through him as he held the Grail high.

"Pretty, isn't it?" Diogenes' voice came to Peter as if from far away.

"Pretty?"

"Pretty. Pretty. Pretty," Diogenes sang.

"It is magnificent," Peter said. "Do you not see the glow? The light of God as bright as the burning bush within which the Lord appeared to Abraham?"

Diogenes laughed. "I see the glint where the natural light of the sun gleams off the gold of your pretty cup, but I see no light of God."

"Kill the unbeliever!" Pain seared through Peter's head as his voice roared its order. He turned to face Diogenes, who drew back at the wild look in Peter's eyes.

A small part of Peter's mind wanted to resist, to not kill this odd little madman. He stepped forward. "Do you see the glow?" he asked.

"I do. I do," Diogenes said hurriedly.

"He lies," Peter's voice thundered, swamping everything else in his brain. "Kill the heretic!"

Gently, as Diogenes watched, Peter laid the glowing Grail on the ground. Then, with ferocious speed, he lunged and grabbed the little man around the throat. Diogenes fell with Peter on top of him. His eyes bulged in fear as Peter drove his thumbs into his neck. Peter felt Diogenes' fists beating his sides and his legs kicking his back, but he ignored any pain that the frantic movements caused. Staring into the heretic's eyes, he pressed harder and harder.

•

Diogenes was making strange gurgling noises and his face was turning a deep red. His eyes looked as if they were about to pop out of their sockets. His mouth was open and his tongue protruded. Peter ignored it all and kept squeezing. All the while, the voice in his head chanted, "Kill him. Kill him. Kill him."

At last the voice stopped and Peter relaxed. Diogenes had stopped struggling some time before and lay limp on the ground, his open eyes staring at nothing. Peter's hands shook as awareness of his surroundings flooded back. He stood and dazedly looked around. The Grail lay on the ground beside him, its glow extinguished. Peter bent and picked it up. He noticed for the first time how heavy it was. Even without the glow, it was extraordinary: the gold, jewels and silver work were perfect.

"Thank you," Peter repeated. He bent and pulled a long strip of cloth from Diogenes' body, wrapped the Grail carefully and placed it in his satchel. He felt drained, yet more alive than he had ever been. For the first time, he felt certain about his visions. Death had appeared to him for a reason. Now that he had the Grail, *that* was what he was bringing home—not only the deaths of all heretics and unbelievers as the Grail-led armies of the Pope swept victorious across the world, but the very death of the world itself. All pestilence, evil and suffering would be banished, and the dead would rise from their tombs to be judged by Christ on the Last Day. The Devil would be defeated and the unjust cast into the fiery lake. The just, with Peter at their head, would ascend to dwell in heaven in eternal bliss at Christ's right hand. Murmuring prayers of thanks, Peter set off through the trees and back over the mountains.

A Sign

Durres,
December, 1212

Peter stood on the crest of the hill, staring down at the crescent-shaped beach below. The violent storm that had kept him huddled in an abandoned shepherd's hut all of the day before had ended, and the sky was a watery blue except for a few puffy clouds that raced overhead. Large waves still rolled in, crashing onto the beach and shaking the skeletal remains of the ship that lay, broken, on the rocks half a mile offshore. The beach itself was covered in a jumbled mass of shattered wood, torn sails and tangled rigging. A small group of men huddled at the top of the beach around a blazing fire.

Peter crouched and watched the men. Most were sailors but one was a monk. "Who are these men?" Peter asked out loud. The voice in his head remained silent.

It had been three months since Peter had walked away from Diogenes' body outside Plovdiv. Three months of walking, wandering and wondering. There were weeks at a time about which Peter could remember nothing. He would suddenly become aware, striding along a dusty road, that he had no idea what day it was or where he was. He would then have to surprise the next traveller he met by asking the date and the name of the nearest town. Peter had also fallen into the habit of talking out loud to the voice in his head. Sometimes the voice answered, sometimes not. On a couple of occasions, Peter had had quite long conversations with the voice, much to the confusion of those he met. Others couldn't hear the voice and, to them, Peter appeared to be just a crazy man mumbling to himself. His appearance only encouraged that impression. He was now skeletal—his eyes hollow, his cheeks sunken and the bones of his joints jutting out alarmingly. His hair had grown long and wild and what remained of his habit was so worn it was almost transparent in places. He had been lucky enough to be given a new pair of sandals when his old pair had fallen apart. That was the advantage of looking the way he did: people either assumed he was crazy or very holy. Either way, they gave him food and drink, if only to hurry him on his way.

On every aware moment of his journey, Peter had thought of nothing but what he carried in the satchel over his shoulder. He had wrapped the Grail in the two maps and the filthy piece of material from Diogenes' clothing, so its true nature was not immediately obvious, but Peter knew. The responsibility of carrying the most holy relic in Christendom had filled him with awe. Sometimes Peter's burden seemed so light and magical that he felt if he only jumped high enough, he would be able fly over the world to wherever he wished. At other times, the Grail was so heavy that it dragged Peter down and he could not take another step. He had to simply stand where he was until the feeling passed.

Peter's route back to the coast had been different than the journey from Valona. Partly this was due to conscious detours around mountain ranges he saw on his map, partly it was simply the way he wandered during the times he couldn't remember. Peter's route resembled string batted about by a cat.

Four weeks earlier, Peter had reached the coast, many miles north of Durrës, where he hoped to find a vessel to take him back across the sea to Italy. He had been walking south when he came upon the shipwreck.

Peter continued to stare down, wondering what to do. Absent-mindedly, he scratched the palms of his hands. Over the past few days they had begun to itch strangely, as had the soles of his feet. They were also beginning to look red, like the many marks on his body where multitudes of tiny creatures lived and fed. Peter assumed the itching was simply another effect of the annoying insects that seemed to be God's way of testing him.

"Go and talk with the monk," Peter's voice ordered.

"Very well," Peter said, setting off down a rough path to the beach.

As he approached the fire, Peter's wild appearance made some of the sailors move away and cross themselves, but the monk smiled and stepped forward. "Welcome, brother," he said in a voice that Peter recognized. "We have little, but come and share at least the warmth of our fire."

"Brother Francesco," Peter said.

The monk frowned as he studied Peter's face. Then recognition loosened his features. "Ah, yes," he said. "The young traveller whom we nursed back to health at Assisi this spring past. Peter?"

Peter nodded.

"Then doubly welcome. Does God not work in truly wonderful ways, to make our paths cross once more?" Francesco crossed himself.

"What are you doing here?" Peter asked.

"More of God's work, although not what I had intended. I was on my way, as I thought in my presumption, to preach to the heathen in the Holy Land, when God sent the storm of yesterday to alter my purpose. The winds drove our ship onto the rocks and us onto this barren shore."

"And those who drowned to a watery grave," one of the sailors grumbled. He was a rough-looking man, short but broad across the chest from years spent clambering up and down rigging and hauling on ropes.

"They rest now with the Lord," Francesco said, glancing over his shoulder at the man, "free from the trials and cares of this world." The sailor didn't look convinced and spat pointedly on the sand. Francesco ignored him and turned back to Peter. "I knew God had a purpose in sending the storm, and here you are."

Peter had a momentary doubt that God had arranged the storm to make this meeting possible, but then he remembered: he carried the Grail, which surely must be the centre of God's purpose.

"How has God brought you here?" Francesco asked. "I recall you were on your way to Rome when last we met."

"Keep the secret." The voice in Peter's head was quiet but firm.

"I was indeed in Rome, but I took passage here to find the ways of the eastern Church."

"And to preach, I hope."

"Of course," Peter lied. "Now I wish to return to my home and I go to Durrës to seek passage across the sea."

"Then we shall go together," Francesco said enthusiastically. "God intended for us to meet, and not for me to continue to the Holy Land, so I shall seek passage home with you. But first, let us give thanks for the ever-mysterious workings of God's plan that brought us together here."

The rough-looking sailor gave a low snort as Francesco led Peter a short distance away from the group. They knelt in the sand and prayed.

After, they stood and Francesco addressed the sailors. "I thank you for your role in God's plan and bless you." He made the sign of the cross in the air. "Brother Peter and I must continue on our journey. God be with you."

"If not God then the Devil," the sailor who seemed to be in charge said under his breath. If Francesco heard him, he gave no sign and began climbing the track up to the road. Peter followed, but heard the sailor address his companions. "Come on, lads, we've been blessed and there's work to do. Let's salvage what we can from this mess and see what work this land offers a group of honest sailors."

Francesco waited for Peter to catch up and together they headed south. "You travel light," the monk observed, "yet you clutch your satchel tightly to your body."

Instinctively, Peter pulled the satchel even closer. He mustn't let Francesco know what it contained. God wanted Peter to take the Grail back to the Holy Crusade, eliminate the heretics and bring about the Final Days. "It's nothing," Peter said, "just a bag in which I carry any food that God sees fit to send my way."

Peter looked at Francesco. He wasn't even carrying a satchel. He possessed nothing except his simple brown habit of coarse, homespun wool and a pair of sandals. The habit was tied at the waist with a white cord that had three knots at one end. "You carry even less," Peter observed.

"I do," Francesco said. "My goal is to emulate Christ as much as possible in everything I do. He owned nothing, therefore I own nothing. When I began the order, I gave everything I owned, even my clothing, to the poor. I began my new life naked as a newborn and I rely on the God-given generosity of others for my simple needs. You too should discard possessions." Francesco looked pointedly at Peter's satchel. "Material things are not of God and are a distraction to a life of contemplation and prayer."

Peter clutched his satchel, feeling the bulge of the Grail beneath the leather. He looked suspiciously at Francesco. He had heard Cathar Perfects say almost identical things. "What is the purpose of the three knots in the cord binding your habit?" he asked to change the subject.

"Those are to remind me of my three vows," Francesco said, lifting the cord and fingering the knots. "Obedience to authority: in the family, to the father; in the nation, to the king; in the Church, to the Pope and his bishops; and in all things, to God. Without obedience none can attain heaven."

Francesco's fingers moved to the second knot. "Chastity. Women are weak vessels and easily tempted by the Devil. Those who seek heaven should avoid all carnal association or acquaintance with them."

He lifted the third knot. "Poverty. We should love God above everything. Attachments to all other things are a diversion from our purpose here." Francesco looked once more at Peter's satchel.

The pair walked on in silence. Peter was unsure of what to make of this monk. He reminded Peter of two other groups of people who also owned nothing and travelled the land preaching: Dominic Guzman and his followers, and the Cathar Perfects. But how could that be? Guzman was a holy man, but how could someone as obviously godly as Francesco remind Peter of the vile Perfects?

"Await the angel," the voice whispered in Peter's head.

Quest

* * *

"Surely there will be one godly captain who will give a couple of itinerant men of God passage over the sea," Francesco said as he and Peter stood looking over the teeming harbour at Durrës. Long galleys with rows of upright oars along each side and squat cargo ships with furled sails and flapping coloured banners were packed in along the docks. Sailors were busy loading and unloading, and carts trundled back and forth constantly.

There were certainly plenty of ships, but given his experience at Brindisi, Peter did not share Francesco's optimism. The five-day journey down from the shipwreck had been difficult. At first Peter had been glad of Francesco's company, but after months on his own, the habits of solitude were deeply ingrained and Peter was soon wishing that his companion had not joined him. What annoyed him most was Francesco's interest in his satchel, which he claimed was the only thing standing between Peter and God. On top of everything else, Peter's voice was giving him no rest. It was continually talking to him, sometimes about insignificant things or in languages that Peter did not recognize. Occasionally, it made obscure references to angels and their coming. Peter was confused, upset and exhausted. He just wanted to get home and relieve himself of his burden.

Peter was scanning the ships for a second time, looking for a likely vessel, when he spotted Oddo. There was no mistaking the falcon on his chest or the black axe over his left shoulder. Peter went cold. Sweat broke out all over his body, and his breathing began to come in ragged gasps. From many miles away he heard Francesco's voice saying, "Brother, what is wrong? Are you taken sick?" Then the voice in his head shouted, "He comes with the angel!"

Peter watched in frozen terror as Oddo strode up from the docks straight toward him. He wore an evil grin and blood dripped from his axe. The closer he came, the larger he grew, until he was towering over Peter. "Britta has found you, my young monk," Oddo said with an echoing laugh as he lifted his axe from his shoulder.

Peter was looking almost straight up now. He tried to follow the curve of the axe head as it swept toward him but it was too much. Peter overbalanced and fell backwards onto the rough cobbles, hitting the back of his head painfully. Above him Oddo laughed, but the axe hadn't fallen. In fact, as Peter stared up, Oddo was changing: his armour grew paler, turning into a white tunic. Six wings were sprouting from his back, two forming a canopy above his head, two spread on either side as if in flight and two wrapped around his body. His face glowed with a brilliant inner light. Why had Peter never noticed that Oddo was so beautiful before?

"The seraph is here," Peter's voice boomed. Peter smiled. The seraph smiled back and Peter felt a sense of overwhelming peace. For the very first time since his visions of death had afflicted him in the square at Toulouse, he was totally content. The only thing not perfect was the itching: his hands, his feet, his side—it was unbearable.

"Why are you here? What do you want of me?" Peter asked quietly. The seraph remained silent, but Peter's voice chided him: "Do not question God."

"You have been chosen," a second voice said. He thought it was the seraph, but the brilliant face above him remained immobile. Was it another voice, then? Another voice guiding him? Sudden pain shot through Peter's hands and feet. His arms flew out to either side and his back arched. The seraph glowed brighter and brighter until Peter's eyes hurt. With a searing flash, the vision exploded into fire. Then everything went black.

* * *

When Peter opened his eyes, the seraph-Oddo figure was gone. He was lying on his back on the cobbled street by the dock, his feet crossed at the ankles and his arms spread wide. Francesco stood over him, crossing himself repeatedly, a look of shock on his face. Others had been attracted by Peter's fit and stood around staring.

Gasping for breath and still stunned, Peter struggled to sit up. He was sweating profusely and wiped his right hand over his forehead. Warm blood trickled into his eyes. Peter stared at his palm. The itching red mark had burst and blood covered most of his hand. His left hand was the same. Peter looked down at his feet. His sandals, too, were covered in blood.

"What's happening to me?" he asked, holding his hands out for Francesco to see.

"It's a miracle," Francesco said in awe. "You have the marks of Christ's suffering on the cross on your hands and feet. The stigmata."

Several of the watching sailors were crossing themselves, and others drifted over to see what was going on.

"This holy man has been blessed," Francesco said, raising his voice so the assembled crowd could hear. "His body has been chosen to exhibit the signs of Christ's passion." Francesco helped Peter to stand and pointed out his wounds. A gasp ran through the crowd and several people stepped back. "God has chosen Brother Peter for a great purpose. The Holy Father in Rome must know of this. Who will give Peter a place to rest and passage across the sea?"

"I will." A sailor stepped forward. "I sail with the tide this forenoon and will happily do God's work, if you will consent to bless my ship and journey. I sail for Bari, where St. Nicholas of Winter is buried and awaits our prayers of thanks."

"May St. Nicholas bestow many gifts upon you," Francesco said. "Show us to your vessel."

The sailor nodded and led the way through the parting crowd to a small cargo vessel tied up at the end of the pier. A dozen men were busy loading freight onto its decks. They stopped to watch as the strange passengers boarded.

"I fear I do not have any cabin space on my vessel," the sailor said, "but I shall make you as comfortable as possible on the deck."

"God will see to our needs," Francesco said. "Thank you."

The sailor settled Peter and Francesco to one side of the deck, surrounded by bales of wool that sheltered them a little from the elements. The bleeding from Peter's wounds had slowed, but blood still dripped from his palms, forming a small pool by his feet. He felt as he had after his vision in Toulouse —completely drained and confused. He didn't doubt that the vision of Oddo and the seraph meant that he had been chosen, but for what? Was it the task he was already engaged in—taking the Grail to the crusade—or something different? "What does it mean?" he asked Francesco once they were settled.

"You have been chosen," Francesco replied. "Let us offer up a prayer of thanks."

The pair knelt and prayed, although Peter's tired brain had trouble concentrating. When they were done, he asked Francesco, "What have I been chosen for?"

"Only God and you can say. Your gaze back there on the dock was on something not of this world. Did you have a vision?"

Peter briefly told Francesco what he had seen.

"The seraph said nothing to suggest what your task would be?" Francesco asked.

"Nothing," Peter said, but he hesitated and his eyes drifted to the satchel at his side.

"Perhaps it is something you already know of?" Francesco suggested.

Peter was debating telling his companion about the Grail when a sailor approached. He crossed himself and knelt. With an apologetic look, he gently leaned forward, dipped his fingers in the blood that had run onto the deck from Peter's feet, crossed himself again and left.

Others followed and soon there was a crowd on the dock, clamouring to touch the miraculous blood. The captain did his best to prevent the crowd from boarding, but many got through. Some copied the first sailor and simply dipped their fingers in the blood; others soaked pieces of cloth in it.

A couple tried to collect as much as possible in various cups. Francesco, certain these last were planning on selling the blood to the crowd on the dock, drove them away. Eventually, cleared of pilgrims, the ship was cast off.

Peter sighed and sat back. The gentle movement of the water beneath the ship's hull was soothing, and it was good not to be the centre of attention. Peter examined his wounds. They were only on the palms of his hands and the soles of his feet. Although the irregular holes remained open, the bleeding had almost stopped.

"I think," Francesco said, "that it might be best to keep the stigmata hidden. Whatever God's purpose for you, it will be impossible to fulfil if you are continually the centre of a crowd."

"How long will it last?" Peter asked.

Francesco shook his head. "I have never seen of such a thing before. Perhaps until your task is complete, perhaps forever. In any case, you are charged with some holy purpose."

Peter thought for a long time. It was one thing to keep Aumery's quest a secret, but the situation had changed. He had been visited by a seraph and marked with the signs of Christ's suffering. Also, his sickness on the road in Italy had led him to Francesco, and now a storm had led Francesco to him on the road north of Durrës. Were these events mere coincidence or parts of some larger plan? Did Francesco have a role in all this? Eventually, Peter came to a decision. "I carry the Holy Grail," he said softly.

Francesco looked hard at him. "That is what you clutch so protectively in your satchel?"

Peter nodded.

"How did you come upon it?"

As they sailed out of sight of land under a pale blue winter sky, Peter told Francesco the tale of his adventures, from Cîteaux and Aumery's letter to the tomb of St. Andrew outside Plovdiv. He told of the voices in his head, but not that they had ordered him to kill Diogenes. When Peter had completed his story, Francesco sat for a long moment and then asked, "May I see it?"

Bending in such a way that his body prevented the crew from seeing what he was doing, Peter carefully took the bundle from his satchel and unwrapped the Grail. Keeping it low, Francesco gently took it and looked closely. Then he raised his eyes to Peter.

"This is the Holy Grail that Christ drank from at the Last Supper?"

Peter nodded.

"I'm puzzled," Francesco said. "You say you have been months on this quest to find the Grail. You say that you are already charged by Abbot Aumery to return with it so that it may sit at the head of the Holy Crusade against the heretics, and afterward lead the armies of the blessed Pope Innocent against the unbelievers and introduce the Last Days and the Judgment." Peter nodded and Francesco continued. "What then is the meaning of the stigmata and the seraph?"

Peter shrugged. "I don't know."

Francesco stared at the Grail, turning it slowly in his hands. Sunlight glinted off the precious stones, and the complex whorls that decorated the golden surface appeared to dance. Perhaps, Peter thought, he had been chosen to give the Grail to Francesco. Maybe this simple monk who owned nothing was the one destined to use it to bring about the End Times. Peter's heart sank. Through everything, it had been the image of himself, holding the glowing Grail aloft at the head of the victorious crusader armies, that had kept him going. The thought that it might be someone else's task was crushing. The Grail was power, and power was what Peter wanted—needed.

"Kill him!" The voice rang in Peter's head, just as it had by the grave outside Plovdiv. Every imaginable emotion swam across Peter's face as he wrestled with the voice's order—anger, surprise, joy, disgust, sadness, fear. An argument raged in Peter's mind and he had no idea if it was silent or if he was screaming. His hands clenched and unclenched spasmodically.

"No," Peter said out loud, trying to fight down an urge to grab Francesco by the throat.

Francesco looked up at him.

"I won't kill him," Peter said. "He's gentle and kind."

"You must," the voice roared. "I order you."

"But he does me no harm."

"He desires the Grail. He wants to steal our power."

"But if it is God's will that he have the Grail—"

"It is *not* God's will," the voice thundered. "It is our destiny to carry the Grail to the Last Days when the dead shall rise, wrapped in the rags of their grave clothes, and be judged. Our destiny!"

"I'm not sure," Peter said helplessly.

"I am," Francesco said softly. Moving so fast that Peter had no time to react, Francesco lifted the Grail and hurled it over the side of the ship.

For an instant, the world stopped. The voice in Peter's head fell silent. He couldn't hear the seagulls' calls or the wind in the ship's rigging. The deck beneath his feet and the waves sweeping alongside the vessel's hull vanished. The sun exploded into blackness and Peter fell. He was spinning in a black void, twirling in nothingness, forever. Then he screamed and leaped for the ship's rail.

Peter felt Francesco's arms around his waist, holding him back from following the Grail into the ocean. He struggled, but Francesco was surprisingly strong. Over the side Peter saw only white-capped waves racing by. He slumped back onto the deck and wept.

"Why?" he eventually managed to ask.

"Do not ask me why," Francesco responded. "Better to ask, if that were the true Grail and you or I were destined to use it to bring on the Day of Judgment, why was I not smitten before I could throw it, or why did it not float above the surface of the waves?"

"What do you mean?" Peter's tears were clouding his eyes, and his thoughts were still jumbled.

Francesco sat beside Peter and put an arm around his shoulders. "I mean, my friend, that it was not the Holy Grail."

"You're lying," Peter shouted. Surely Francesco was wrong! The feeling of power Peter had had after he killed Diogenes and imagined marching triumphantly through the Last Days of earth before the Judgment was too strong. It had to be the Grail, didn't it? Doubt grew in Peter's mind. "How do you know for certain it is false?"

"There are many reasons," Francesco said with a calming smile. "Firstly, as I said, I was allowed to cast it into the depths where it is lost to man. If your Grail was genuine and it is man's destiny to use it, I would not have been allowed to do what I did.

"Secondly, you did not discover it in the tomb of St. Andrew. True enough, he did go to Plovdiv to preach with St. Peter, but after their time there they went their separate ways, St. Peter to his destiny in Rome and St. Andrew to spread Christ's word in the East. He was crucified in Patras and his bones carried to Byzantium, where they are venerated to this day."

"Then whose grave did I open?"

"Some heathen lord. I have seen the swirling markings on the cup before, on the works of the northern pagans." Francesco removed his arm from Peter's shoulder and turned to face him. "But, finally, think on this. Christ and His apostles were poor. They were itinerant preachers who lived as I strive to, owning nothing. They broke bread and drank wine together in the house of the water carrier in Jerusalem. Do you think they sat at a silver table and drank from jewel-encrusted golden chalices?"

"I don't know."

"They did not," Francesco said gently. "They broke bread with their hands at a plain wooden table and they drank from the plain earthenware cups provided by their host. The Holy Grail must be something that would not look out of place in a simple tavern."

Quest

Peter's head swam with confusion. What Francesco said made sense, and he trusted this pious man who appeared to see the world so clearly. But it was hard to accept what Francesco said. If the golden cup Peter had spent months searching for was not the Grail, was his quest a waste of time? Had all his suffering, both physical and mental, been for nothing? And what about the stigmata? Were his voices and visions meaningless—or worse, the work of the Devil? Was it the Devil who had made him murder poor old Diogenes?

"I murdered a man," Peter said hopelessly, the words rushing from his mouth. "He was a harmless old fool who led me to the cup and I killed him. The voice in my head told me to and I thought it was the voice of God, but was it the voice of the Devil? Am I cursed—damned forever?"

"Perhaps it was the Devil's voice," Francesco said gently, "but that need not mean you are irredeemable. God is infinitely merciful. If you do penance you will be forgiven."

"How? What should I do?"

"That is for you to discover. Pray and you will be guided."

"I shall throw away everything as you have done and preach," Peter said with determination, "although I already have almost nothing—just an old map—but I will cast it over the side now."

Peter reached into his satchel, but Francesco held his arm. "Don't be hasty. It is not enough to simply throw away your possessions. I gave all my wealth to the poor and needy. What you discard must do some good."

"What good is an old Roman map and a sketch I made in Rome?"

Francesco shrugged. "I don't know, but when the time comes, you will."

Peter sighed deeply. "You are right, but I can start preaching immediately."

"Did you not tell me that you were on a quest for Father Aumery?"

"Yes, but it has turned out to be a quest for a false Grail."

"That does not matter. Father Aumery did not know that. You still owe obedience to him as your superior in the Church. You must return and tell him of your quest and do whatever else he asks you. When he releases you, you may leave and preach."

"But is there nothing I can do now?" Peter asked. He felt utterly empty and exhausted.

"Rest," Francesco said. "You are starved and worn out. Sleep. I shall stay by you and pray that the Lord lifts your burden."

Peter lay against Francesco's shoulder and closed his eyes. He was confused and scared, yet he felt calmer than he had in a long time. There was something about this simple monk, something that made him feel that everything would be all right.

The last thing Peter felt before he fell into a dreamless sleep was Francesco, gently stroking his filthy hair.

Answers
1213

Reunited

Toulouse
February

John sat on the steps across from the Château Narbonnaise. A light rain was falling and a chilling wind swirled around the square, but he didn't mind. He was home. This was where his strange adventure had begun almost seven years before. Seven years! It was hard to believe so much time had passed, and yet it was a short time for the world to change so radically. Peaceful Languedoc had been convulsed by war, and its economy and culture shattered. Thousands had died as the cities fell to de Montfort's northern crusaders and hundreds more had perished on Aumery's bonfires. John had learned more than he had ever imagined possible, fled to a foreign land only to have war follow him there, and he had had Isabella to share it all with.

John smiled to himself as he looked over to where Isabella had sat with their friends on the steps below so many years before. Across the square, William of Arles had performed by the château doors and offered John the chance to leave here and learn. It had been a strange and difficult journey, but not one he would change.

A frown crossed John's face as he looked at the step where Peter had sat. His friend's journey had begun that day as well. Where had it taken him? John had heard nothing of Peter since the siege of Minerve, two and a half years ago. The only thing he could be certain of was that Peter's journey had taken him to a very different place.

John shrugged. He wasn't responsible for Peter's life, only his own, and that seemed to be taking a turn for the better. John and Isabella had returned home as part of Pedro's retinue to attend the Council of Lavaur in January. In an attempt to establish who should have power in Languedoc, everyone had been there—Arnaud Aumery, Simon de Montfort, Bishop Foulques and a host of minor counts and clerics. Even William of Arles had been in the town and John had spent many happy hours catching up on his news. William had collected stories wherever he went and was a font of knowledge about all aspects of the crusade, so John and Isabella were soon well informed about everything that had happened in their absence.

The only person John hadn't seen in Lavaur was Adso.

William had said their friend had been there, but had left before John arrived. William was here in Toulouse as well and had seen Adso, so it was only a matter of time before John bumped into him.

The council at Lavaur had gone well. True, Pedro had been snubbed by the northern crusaders, made to wait and then denied an opportunity to address the council directly, but it had not mattered. Pedro's envoys had been to Rome and convinced Pope Innocent that the heretic threat was over and that the continuing war was simply a power grab by de Montfort. Letters had arrived from the Pope ordering Aumery to desist in his heretic burning and de Montfort to abstain from attacking any lands whose lords owed allegiance to Pedro. The crusade was over. Perhaps now life could return to normal.

Since Lavaur, John and Isabella had been part of Pedro's triumphal tour of his lands. After his stunning victory at Las Navas de Tolosa, Pedro was the most powerful Christian king in the world. Everywhere he went, his party was feasted and entertained, and crowds, delighted that the war was over, cheered and threw flowers. Every lord, from Raymond in Toulouse to the counts of Foix and Comminges, and every small community along the northern foothills of the Pyrénées, bowed a knee and swore allegiance. It had been a triumphal procession and it was to end here in Toulouse before Pedro returned to Aragon.

That was the only darkness on John's horizon. Pedro would want him and Isabella to accompany the royal party back to Barcelona. If they did that, who knew when they might see home again? Being back in Toulouse had made things clear for John. He wanted to live here now that calm had returned. He would be able to search for the drawing book in peace and, with any luck, he might be released from the responsibility of using the Gospel of the Christ against the crusade. But it was difficult to refuse kings.

"So, 'ere's the traveller back from the 'eathen lands."

John stood up and turned. "Adso!" The friends embraced. "It's good to see you again," John said. "I looked for you at Lavaur, but William told me you'd already left."

"It's a busy life when you're as important as me," Adso said with a laugh, "but, fortunately, I 'ave some time and I spotted a tavern just around the corner. Will you join me in an ale and tell me your story?"

"I am to meet Isabella here later, but I have time for a story, if you will tell me yours."

Side by side, the pair strolled over to the nearby tavern. They settled into an alcove and ordered two jugs of ale.

"So," Adso began after he had taken a swig, "'ow was Al-Andalus? I 'eard from William that you got caught up in the big battle down there."

"We did," John said, "but there's much more than that." John proceeded to tell the story of his and Isabella's adventures over the previous two and a half years. He showed Adso the strange drawing he had found at Madinat al-Zahra and the sword, Auramazdah, that he had bought in Toledo. Adso was fascinated by the sword and insisted on swinging it about dangerously in the tavern. "Fine piece of steel," he commented. "Far too good for the likes of you."

Adso made John repeat the story of Las Navas de Tolosa, in particular the bits concerning Oddo. "'E's a devil, that man," he said with a shake of his head. "One day, 'e'll get what 'e deserves. I just 'ope it's me that gives it to 'im."

"Now, tell me your story," John asked when he had finished.

"Not near as exciting as yours," Adso apologized, before he launched into a detailed account of his time with Bertrand, the betrayal, and the discovery of the body in the tomb at Rhedae. He was ashamed of his long fall into depression and drink, but it was part of the story so he told it, ending with his rescue by William and Esclarmonde.

"I sort of work for 'er now," Adso explained. "Being a Perfect, she can't move about much, so I'm 'er eyes and ears."

"Hopefully she'll soon be able to move around with greater ease," John said. "With Toulouse, Foix and Comminges confirmed as Pedro's domain, even if de Montfort keeps hold of the lands around Carcassonne and Béziers, there should be a significant refuge along the foothills of the mountains."

"I 'ope so." Adso drained his jug of beer and stood up. "But I must be off. Esclarmonde asked for a report on 'ow active Bishop Foulques' Angels are these days. As far as I can see, they're keeping low. And you must be off to meet that girl of yours. Say 'ello and that I 'ope we can all get together afore Pedro drags you two back to Aragon."

"I will."

The pair stepped into the chill wind, pulled their tunics tighter and went their separate ways.

* * *

John had barely got himself settled back on the edge of the square when he caught sight of a tall, skinny figure heading for the doors of the château. For a moment, he couldn't believe what he was seeing, but there was no mistaking the gangly frame and the long, thin face.

"Peter," John shouted as he stood up and ran down the steps.

Peter stopped and tilted his head. The voices in his head had changed after that day on the ship with Francesco. The first one—had it been the voice of the Devil that had ordered him to kill Diogenes and Francesco?—had stopped altogether. Now he heard only the gentle voice of the seraph, whispering isolated words and phrases, and then only rarely. Still, Peter could never be certain that the other voice, or a completely different one, might not one day address him again. But this voice sounded familiar.

"Peter, is it really you?" John stopped a couple of paces in front of his old friend and waited for Peter to recognize him. He was happy to see Peter again, but images of their last meeting raced through he head: Umar dying in a pool of blood by the well in Minerve, Peter dashing out the door to escape. Umar's death had been an accident—Peter hadn't intended to kill him—but his childhood friend *was* with Aumery and the Catholic Church and had become very harsh in his thinking. Was he even worse now? Was Aumery here?

"It's me," Peter said, staring at his friend. He tried to calculate how long it had been since they'd seen each other. Had it been Minerve? He was just as confused as John. So much had happened in his life since then that he had almost forgotten what had gone on before. It seemed like a different world. "What are you doing here?"

"I'm with King Pedro. But let's sit and talk! What have you been doing since last we met?"

"I don't have time," Peter said, glancing at the doors of the château. "I must speak with Bishop Foulques so he can prepare for Father Aumery and de Montfort's arrival."

John looked nervously around the square. "They are here?"

"They will arrive tonight, but preparations must be made."

"Of course," John said, relaxing a bit, "but surely a few minutes with an old friend won't slow down the process too much?"

"I suppose not." Almost reluctantly, he joined John on the bottom step.

"What have you been doing? I see you still wear the Cistercian habit."

"Of course," Peter said. "One does not take orders lightly, and it is a commitment for the full span of life on this earth." Even as Peter said the words, he felt guilty at sounding so certain. He remembered how lightly Aumery had made him a monk, simply so that he could negotiate the surrender of Carcassonne.

"I have been travelling in the East," Peter continued. He gave John an abbreviated account of his year at Cîteaux, his time in Rome and his travels to Plovdiv. He talked about the attack by the sailors and about Nicodemus, but omitted the voices and Diogenes. "On my return journey," he added, "I travelled part way with a remarkable monk called Francesco. He has set up an order based on poverty and obedience. They own nothing and travel around preaching to simple folk."

John bit his tongue to stop himself saying that they sounded like Cathar Perfects. "He reminds me of the black-clad monk, Dominic," he said. "The one that we heard debate the Cathars in St. Sernin the night we came to hear William the troubadour in this very square."

"There are similarities," Peter agreed, "and I intend to become like him once I have finished my duties to Father Aumery."

"Give up all your possessions?" John asked lightly.

Peter had a moment of regret as he visualized the golden cup arcing over the side of the boat into the sea. "I have very little." An idea surfaced in Peter's mind. "Do you still have an interest in drawing?"

"I do," John replied with a smile. "Do you still think it the work of the Devil?"

"I never thought it the work of the Devil," Peter said indignantly, but then he responded to John's smile. "I simply thought your pursuit misguided and your time—time you could have spent coming to know God—misspent. But I have something that might interest you." Peter pulled the maps from his satchel and handed them to John. "This one is a fragment of a Roman map. It is stretched out, but once you recognize that and can read a few of the names, it makes sense."

John took the map carefully and examined it. "It's fascinating! Are these lines between the towns roads?"

Peter nodded. "I have walked some of them. It is yours now. Keep it. And this one too." Peter handed John the sketch he had made of the map in the library in Rome. "It's just a copy I made, but it might interest you. I used it in my travels, but no good came of it. I was told that, among other things, it shows seven cities that were each built on seven hills. Plovdiv where I went was one—but it is also called Trimondium—and Rome another." Peter's brow furrowed as he tried to remember the other names Diogenes had told him. "Hierosolyma, Byzantium, Makkah, the holy city of the Moors, and...," Peter closed his eyes, but nothing came to him. "There were two others, but I have forgotten them. There was also an eighth, but I was not told its name."

"Thank you," John said. "Are you sure?" He looked at the second map. It was a rough sketch, but it seemed vaguely familiar.

"I do not know what all I have told you means, but the maps have brought me only pain and trials. If they will do you good, then you will be helping me get rid of all my worldly possessions and know God better." Peter's tone was serious, but he was happy. This was what Francesco meant when he said that good had to come from giving your possessions away. John would enjoy the maps and Peter was now free of them.

John glanced up at Peter to see him smiling. He smiled back. "I will treasure them." This was almost like old times. "But you haven't told me what brings you here."

"After I returned from the East, Francesco persuaded me to accompany him to Rome to pray. While I was there, it came to a Cardinal Grazanni's notice that I was intending on travelling back here. He gave me some copies of letters to give to Father Aumery. I did this at Narbonne, and now I come here to tell Bishop Foulques that there is to be a council tomorrow."

"What was in the letters?" John asked, vaguely nervous at the mention of another council.

"I don't know," Peter replied. "They were not for me to read. But I must go soon. Tell me quickly of your doings."

John briefly outlined his travels in Al-Andalus and with King Pedro. He gave no details of Isabella's relationship to King Pedro, but he did notice a sadness cross Peter's face at the mention of her name. As he talked, he noticed Peter rubbing the palms of his hands as if they itched.

"What's the matter?" he asked once he had finished his story.

Peter looked embarrassed, but held out his hands. There was an irregular red mark on the centre of each palm. "They appeared on my way back from the East. These and one on each of the soles of my feet. Sometimes they open and bleed, but mostly they just itch." Peter hesitated, unsure if he should go on. "Francesco said they are the stigmata, the marks of Christ's suffering on the cross. He says they mean that I have been chosen, but I do not know for what."

Peter fell silent and John stared at him. Could these marks be a sign from God? If they were, did it mean that the course Peter had chosen after his visions was the right one and that John's search for knowledge was just an empty waste of time? John opened his mouth to ask more, but he was interrupted by Isabella's voice from behind.

"There you are. I've been—" She stopped abruptly as Peter turned and stared up at her. "Peter. What are you doing here?"

"I've just been telling John that," Peter said stiffly, tucking his hands inside the sleeves of his habit. "I must go." He stalked off toward the château.

"I didn't mean to scare him off," Isabella said, sitting beside John. "It was just such a surprise to see him after all this time."

"I know," John agreed. "He's here to prepare for a council tomorrow. Aumery and de Montfort are coming."

"Aumery! We must leave."

"We'll keep a low profile and we'll be safe enough under Pedro's protection," John said. "Besides, I want to know what happens, and Peter's not the only old friend I met. Adso's here. We had an ale and caught up on each other's news. He says hello and hopes we can all get together."

"That would be good," Isabella said, but her brow was creased with worry. "If we can. John, did you talk much to Peter? Why is there going to be another council? Did he say?"

"He didn't. He brought letters from Rome for Aumery and de Montfort, but he doesn't know what's in them." John tried to move the conversation away from the strange council. "Peter seemed more relaxed than I remember." John spoke quickly and as cheerfully as he could, giving Isabella a short version of what Peter had told him. He was happy to see her features relax as she was drawn into the tale.

"And he gave me these," John continued, holding out the maps. "He's trying to give up all his material possessions, and he though I might like them. This one's an old Roman map, but the other one Peter copied in Rome. It bothers me. It looks familiar."

"Of course it does," Isabella said, tilting the manuscript to see it better. "It looks like that drawing of the monster you found in Madinat al-Zahra."

"That's it!" John exclaimed. He rummaged in his satchel, pulled out the rolled piece of vellum and held it beside the map. "You're right! The monster is based on the map. Al-Andalus is the head, Languedoc and France the body, and Italy the foreleg. The rear stretches down to the Holy Land and the tail must be the lands of the Norsemen. The wild woman might even be the Britannic Isles. It is fascinating—but why draw a monster based on a map? And what do the seven snakes' heads with the letters beside the eyes mean?"

"I don't know, but the dots with the numbers beside them are cities. Look, seven of the cities on the map match the golden dots on the monster: Roma, Hierosolyma, Casteddu, Trimondium, Byzantium, Tehran and Makkah."

"The seven cities built on seven hills," John said excitedly. "Remember the book of Revelations where it described this monster? St. John mentioned the seven heads that are the seven mountains on which the woman sat. Maybe that has something to do with it."

"Maybe," Isabella replied, shrugging.

"Peter could only remember the names of five of the seven cities on seven hills, but the other two must be Tehran and Casteddu. I've never heard of them. He also mentioned an eighth city, but he didn't know the name."

"Some of the names are changed or unusual," Isabella said thoughtfully. "Hierosolyma is Jerusalem now, and I've never heard of Casteddu, Tehran *or* Trimondium."

"Trimondium is where Peter travelled in the East." John stared for a long moment at the documents, his eyes moving back and forth between the map and the monster. Words with numbers beside them. He counted the number of letters in each name. It wasn't that; there were always more letters in the word than the number. Maybe the number referred to a letter in the name beside it. A pattern leaped out at him. "Look!" he said, his voice rising with excitement. "If you take the letter from the city name that corresponds to the number beside it, you get the same letters as the ones beside the seven eyes. Trimondium is VII, so that's the D; Byzantium is IV that's A; Roma and Hierosolyma are both I, so that's R and H; Casteddu is V, that's E; Makkah is III, that's K; and Tehran is II, that's E—D, A, R, H, E, K, E. Those are the same letters as beside the eyes. But what does it mean?"

"That's right. D, A, R, H, E, K, E." Isabella said, listing the letters thoughtfully. "It's not a word in any language I've ever seen, but look," she moved a finger over the drawing of the monster. "The VII beside Trimondium gives us the letter D, so let's draw a line between Trimondium and the eye with the D beside it. The IV beside Byzantium gives us A, so draw a line from Byzantium to the eye with the A. The lines cross at the monster's neck. If you do the same for the other five cities and eyes—R to Roma, H to Hierosolyma, E to Casteddu, K to Makkah and E to Tehran—all the lines intersect at about the same place."

John moved his finger over the drawing, tracing the lines. "You're right. So where would that intersection be on the map?"

"It's somewhere in Languedoc," Isabella said, "but it's not precise enough to tell exactly where. It can't be coincidence, though. The drawing must be the key to the map! What do you think is at the point where the lines cross? Is it the eighth city Peter talked of?"

"I've never heard of a place called Darheke," John said. "What can it mean?"

"I don't know. Maybe that's where the drawing book that you've been searching for for years is hidden," Isabella suggested with a smile.

"Don't tease me," John said. "If Lucius' book exists, I'll find it eventually, but I doubt if Peter's map and an old, weird drawing will lead me there. We'll probably never even find exactly where the lines intersect. There's no city marked in that spot on the map, Darheke means nothing to us and the map's too small. The spot where the lines cross could be any of a hundred places."

"You're right," Isabella acknowledged. "It's interesting, but it doesn't mean anything. Even the writing doesn't help. *Septumdecim denique libri*, seventeen of the final book, tells us that the monster is from the Revelations of St. John, but it has nothing to do with the map."

"And *ungere qua oculus et septem opportunus*—anoint where the eye and seven meet. Darheke is where the lines between the eyes and the seven cities meet, but how do you anoint a place, even if you do know what it is?"

Isabella shrugged helplessly. "I don't know, but I don't think staring at it any more will help. Maybe when we see Adso we can ask him if he's heard of a place called Darheke."

"Good idea. He's done a lot of travelling around recently." John stood, rolled up the drawing and the map and replaced them in his satchel.

As the pair left the square, John was deep in thought. He was glad he had been able to distract Isabella from thoughts of the council tomorrow, and he had enjoyed working out the puzzle of the map and the drawing, but a dark sense of foreboding was weighing heavily on his mind. Why another council? Aumery and de Montfort's arrival couldn't auger well.

* * *

The following day, John and Isabella stood among the crowd that filled most of the main hall in the Château Narbonnaise. They had met up with Adso the night before and shown him the mysterious map and drawing, but he had been just as confused as they were. In any case, the puzzle had slipped in importance as de Montfort and Aumery arrived in the city and word spread rapidly that another council was to take place. Many of the people in the hall today wore worried expressions, and wild speculation was rampant. Not surprisingly, the presence of Simon de Montfort, Arnaud Aumery and a bodyguard of arrogant, swaggering crusader knights made people nervous.

"I wish I knew what they were talking about," Isabella said.

"Me, too," John agreed, "but they haven't been in there long. If they're going to argue about something, this could take all day."

The pair had been standing in the hall for more than an hour. They had arrived with King Pedro's entourage. Nothing had happened for a long time as an increasingly frustrated and angry Pedro had waited for de Montfort and Aumery to arrive. Finally, less than ten minutes earlier—dressed in all their finery and surrounded by Oddo and his Falcons—they had come. Now there was nothing to do but worry and stare at the two armed Falcons who guarded the wooden door behind which the meeting was going on.

"That Oddo terrifies me," Isabella said.

"Terrifies *you*..." John attempted a smile but failed. "It's me he swore to kill outside Minerve, and I have a suspicion that Oddo doesn't take vengeance lightly. On top of that, I think Aumery would like little better than to get me back into one of his torture chambers. It was good to see Peter and Adso yesterday, but I wasn't thrilled to see the others arrive last night."

"There you are." Adso pushed through the crowd to stand beside John and Isabella.

"Where else would we be?" John asked.

"I thought you'd 'ave left by now. Nothing good's going to come of this. They can only want a second council because the Pope's gone back on what 'e promised Pedro at Lavaur, and that's bad news for all of us."

"Perhaps de Montfort's come to pay homage to Pedro as his liege," Isabella speculated.

John choked back a bitter laugh. "That man pays homage to no one. He *demands* homage. But we're still under Pedro's protection and I want to see what happens this morning."

"'As anything 'appened yet?" Adso asked.

"Not yet," John said. "They haven't been in there long. It could take all day."

"That's right enough," Adso agreed. "Once important men get to talking they don't know when to stop. But listen, I've been thinking about that Dar'eke puzzle you showed me yesterday."

"You remember a place called Darheke?" Isabella asked eagerly.

"No. There's no such place, it's—" Adso was cut off as the doors swung open violently. The startled guards turned to look into the room, as did everyone else in the hall.

Pedro stood, framed in the archway, his back to the hall. "You try to steal the lands of those who pay lawful homage to their king," he shouted, his voice echoing around the otherwise silent rooms. "I am King Pedro the Christian of Aragon. I led the reconquest of Al-Andalus from the heathen Moors and you paltry northern scum presume to take my lands while hiding behind the screen of a holy crusade. De Montfort, you will not build an empire here. Foix and Comminges are mine, and Raymond of Toulouse pays vassalage to *me*. If you persist in travelling this path, it will mean war, and I shall cross the mountains with a host that will make the slaughter at Las Navas de Tolosa look like a Saturday afternoon fair."

Pedro turned and strode through the crowd. People fell over each other to get out of his way, and his retinue scrambled to collect their scrolls and scuttle after him. A babble of conversation erupted in his wake.

"War? Did he say war?" John asked disbelievingly. "Pedro's prepared to lead his army against de Montfort?"

"And Aumery and the Pope, it seems," Isabella added. "What went on in there?"

She got her answer almost immediately as Aumery and de Montfort appeared in the doorway. Contrary to Pedro's demeanour, they seemed calm. A slight smile even played around de Montfort's lips.

"You see how the supposed Christian king of Aragon regards the word of the Blessed Pope Innocent," Aumery said. His voice was soft and everyone strained to hear what he was saying. "His Holiness was tricked by emissaries of this King Pedro into thinking that our work here was done and that we simply toiled on for personal gain. We have corrected this misapprehension and informed his Holiness that this putrid city of Toulouse is the viper's bloated belly of this still-living heresy, and that it is stuffed with rotting and disgusting refuse. Neither it nor the hotbeds of vile heresy that are Foix and Comminges can be allowed to survive if we are to purify this realm and the world in preparation for Christ's Second Coming.

"Pope Innocent has written a new letter to King Pedro." Aumery theatrically pulled a scroll from his habit and unrolled it. He read aloud to the stunned crowd. 'We are astounded to learn of the lies by which your ambassadors obtained letters from our hand in favour of the counts of Foix and Comminges. They are protectors of heretics and yet they have not sought absolution and reconciliation. Instead, they have continued in their wickedness and in the protection of heretics. We believe that protectors of heretics are more dangerous to the faith than the heretics themselves and thus we renounce our letters of before and reinstate the Holy Crusade to rid the land of Languedoc of this foul heresy. Any who stand in the way of this holy work shall suffer the blight of excommunication in this world and the fires of Hell in the next."

Aumery rolled the letter and replaced it in his habit. His eyes scanned the hall triumphantly, as if daring anyone to challenge him. He was met by total silence. John was so horrified by what he had heard that he forgot to duck out of the way and Aumery's strange eyes locked on his. The stare lasted for only a second before the eyes moved on, but in that time they communicated triumph and hatred, and a shiver ran down John's spine. A moment later, Aumery, de Montfort and the others crossed the hall and left. John noticed Peter among the entourage who hurried after them, but his childhood friend never looked up.

A babble of excited conversation erupted behind them, but John couldn't have felt less like talking. He was devastated. All the hopes he had nurtured of a return to peace and safety had been dashed. The crusade would continue, and now it would be a full-scale war between de Montfort and King Pedro. "Will there never be peace?" he said to no one in particular.

"Not until every Perfect is dead and this land is securely part of de Montfort's kingdom." Isabella sounded as miserable as John felt.

"Told you no good'd come of this meeting," Adso said. "But afore we all fall to wailing and weeping, there's something I 'ave to tell you. Come on."

Adso led the way out of the château onto the steps of the square. He sat in a shadowed corner and waited until his friends joined him.

"Dar'eke isn't the name of a place," he began.

"But the lines intersect at a place," Isabella interrupted. "If the letters don't tell us the name, what do they tell us?"

"The letters *do* tell us the name of the place," Adso continued with a smile, "just not in the order you put them. The letters beside the eyes aren't meant to be read in order, they're jumbled up. I lay awake most of last night with those letters swimming around in my 'ead."

"What did you come up with?" Isabella asked.

"The letters spell Rhedae," Adso announced triumphantly, "the place I scratched around in with that monk Philip."

John hadn't been paying much attention—what did it matter, all of these maps and letters; the world was about to go to war—but the mention of Rhedae, a real place, caught his attention. "Rhedae must be close to where the lines we drew on the monster intersect."

"Very close," Adso agreed.

"But," John said slowly, "it doesn't work. There are seven letters in Darheke and only six in Rhedae. The K is missing."

"That kept me awake for another couple of hours," Adso said. "K is the first letter of the Greek's name for Christ, Kristos, and—"

"He was the Messiah!" Isabella interrupted. "The anointed one! Of course, that makes sense now."

The mention of the anointed one triggered John's memory. "*Ungere qua oculus et septem opportunus*. The words written at the bottom of the drawing: Anoint where the eye and seven meet." John's bleak mood had vanished. "Where the eye and seven meet is where the lines intersect—Rhedae, if Adso's right."

"'Course I'm right," Adso said.

John ignored him and continued. "'Anoint where the eye and seven meet' isn't an instruction. *Ungere* means the anointed one."

"It means Christ is where the eye and seven meet, in Rhedae," Isabella said, "and that's what the K means as well. K, Kristos, at Rhedae!"

The three fell silent as the implications of what they were working out sank in.

John pulled the Gospel of the Christ out of his memory cloister and scanned it. "The Gospel of the Christ says that He came to Languedoc. Perhaps he went to Rhedae?"

"No!" Adso's anguished cry made them turn and look at him. "Per'aps 'e died there."

"You discovered Christ's tomb," John said in wonder.

"And I burned 'is body," Adso added miserably, his head sinking into his hands. "I can 'ear the Devil laughing already."

"It was an accident," John said without much conviction. He felt totally overwhelmed. He had no proof that any of this was true, but it did all seem to fit a pattern. John silently wished that Beatrice or Umar were here. They knew so much. They would be able to confirm what the three had worked out.

"You won't go to hell," Isabella said to Adso. "At least not for that."

Adso raised his head and stared at Isabella.

"If the Catholic Gospels are true, then Christ rose from the dead on the third day in Jerusalem and the body you found at Rhedae can only be that of some local lord. If John's Gospel of the Christ is true, then it's possible that you found Christ's tomb, but then he wasn't the son of God. Either way, the Devil will have to find a different reason to take you."

"There's more'n enough of them," Adso said softly. "But there's something else."

John and Isabella watched as Adso retrieved a curved fragment of pottery from his pouch. It was grubby and unremarkable.

"What's that?" John asked. "A souvenir from your drinking days?"

"No," Adso said sheepishly, "although I broke it one day in a gutter." He smiled wryly. "It's part of a goblet I found beside..."—he hesitated, unable to bring himself to say that it had been Christ's body—"in the tomb. I wondered why someone important enough to be buried up there only 'ad this ordinary clay cup. If it was Christ, do you think this was the 'Oly Grail that I broke?"

John gaped at Adso in shock, then burst out in hysterical laughter. It was easier to laugh at Adso's drunkenness than to dwell on the fact that everything he had been taught might be a lie. Isabella and Adso stared at him while he struggled to get himself under control. "At least," he said eventually, "we don't have to worry about Aumery conquering the world at the head of the crusader host. I doubt if many people would have followed a common clay cup, even if you hadn't broken it."

John began laughing again and this time, the others joined in. Eventually they quieted down and Isabella spoke. "The writing you copied onto the rim of the cup. What does it say?"

Adso held out the fragment and tilted it so that the light caught the writing:

Χριστός ο άνθρω_ος ο ריקא

"It was carved beneath the alcove where the body lay. The first two words are in Greek, *Xristos anthropos*. William translated them for me. They mean Christ man, but 'e had never seen the third word before."

"Christ man," Isabella said. "That could mean, 'This is the tomb of Christ the man.'"

"It could," John said warily. "We can make everything fit if we try hard enough. The last word, ריקא "—he stared hard at the fragment—"is written in different letters. I recognize them. It's Aramaic, the language that Christ spoke." John studied the writing. "Did you copy it down accurately?"

"'Course I did," Adso said indignantly. "I may not be able to read, but I can copy as well as you can draw."

John's brow furrowed in concentration. There had been some Aramaic in the books Umar had told him. The old man had had to write down the words to show him. There had also been some in the Gospel of the Christ. John closed his eyes and the pages of the ancient book flashed before his mind's eye. What Adso had written on the cup was familiar. He'd seen it before, or something similar. There it was! *"The end days come not,"* John murmured, reading what he saw. *"The Father has deserted us. We poor men are alone. I have been a fool. Christ the man is a fool."*

John opened his eyes. "The last word means 'fool.' It's from the Gospel of the Christ. He's telling us that he was human and a fool."

"So the Cathars are right," Isabella said. "Christ was just a man."

"A lot of good it'll do them," Adso said bleakly. "Now that the fighting's starting again, the bonfires'll just get 'igher."

"And we have no proof of any of this," John added. "If we tell anyone, they'll just laugh and say it's a hoax."

"If we tell anyone," Adso said, "we'll be the first onto the bonfires."

"What do we do?" John asked.

"Nothing," Isabella said. "The Cathar secret exists only in our heads, and we'll be killed if we tell anyone. We can keep it, but I don't know what good it'll do."

"If only I 'adn't been so clumsy," Adso moaned. "If we could take people to the tomb and show them Christ's body and the Grail, they'd 'ave to believe it."

"No they wouldn't," John said. "Isabella's right. Even if we had proof, no one would believe. The Church is too strong. Aumery and those like him would kill anyone who knew the secret and destroy all the evidence, even if it took a dozen lifetimes."

The three sat miserably on the steps. They had discovered answers that they couldn't even have imagined a few months before, but there was nothing they could do with them. John wondered if Beatrice and Umar had known all this. Certainly they had known the Gospel of the Christ and the story it told, but had they known the location of the tomb at Rhedae? Someone had, because Aumery's torture had discovered the clues that sent poor Philip on his quest, but had any one person known all the pieces? Was this part of a single great secret that John, Isabella and Adso were stumbling toward, or was it just a collection of isolated pieces of information that blind luck had allowed them to put together?

"What'll we do?" Isabella spoke the question in all their minds.

"Well," Adso said ruefully, "I've done enough damage. I'm getting out of this town afore Bishop Foulques' Angels start celebrating."

"Where to?" John asked.

"Back to the 'ills. Esclarmonde will want to know what 'appened 'ere, and I'm certain she'd be interested in the story we've just worked out, if she doesn't know it already. Then I suppose I'll go back to fighting. It's all I know and it looks as if the war's about to begin again." He stood and stretched. "What about you two? You going back to Aragon with Pedro?"

John and Isabella looked at each other. "What do you want to do?" he asked.

"I want to stay here," Isabella replied. "This is my home."

John's heart sank. He didn't particularly want to go back to Aragon, but Aumery's look had scared him. The man obviously wasn't going to forget that John had escaped him in Toledo; now John had two of the most powerful men in the crusade dedicated to torturing or killing him. At least in Aragon he would be safe from Aumery and Oddo for a time. But there was no way he was going to leave Isabella. "We're staying here," John said with a weak attempt at a smile. "I still have to find Lucius' book."

Isabella gave him a hug.

"Well, I wish you two lovebirds the best of luck."

"Thank you," Isabella said. "The same to you, and be careful."

"You too," Adso said as he turned and strode off across the square. The two friends watched until he disappeared round the corner of the château.

"What now?" John asked.

"Count Raymond won't allow de Montfort and Aumery to stay in Toulouse, so we'll be as safe here as anywhere once they leave. This city won't fall easily, certainly not before Pedro can bring his army up here and defeat de Montfort."

"And if de Montfort wins?"

"He can't win," Isabella said with certainty. "He has enough knights to besiege a small fortress like Minerve, maybe even in time Toulouse itself, but you saw Pedro's army at Las Navas de Tolosa. It defeated a Moorish army many times its size. De Montfort's finished. By September everything will be over. The crusade will be defeated and we'll be able to live in safety in our own home under King Pedro's protection."

John smiled. Isabella's certainty was infectious and he hoped with all his heart that she was right. All he needed to do was avoid Oddo and Aumery until Pedro returned with his army. "Let's go and find something to eat—somewhere we can wait safely until the crusaders leave."

Isabella returned his smile and, arm in arm, the pair set off down a narrow alley beside the city walls.

Book III
Rebirth

A Great Victory

Toulouse
July 23, 1213

"Our great victory at Pujol is complete." The scarlet-clad herald on the balcony of the Chateau Narbonnaise threw his arms wide and was rewarded by wild cheering from the crowd packed into the square below. "In response to a cowardly threat to ravage our harvests, the knights of your beloved Count Raymond and the Counts of Foix and Comminges, and"—the herald paused dramatically—"the people of the City of Toulouse"—the crowd roared its approval—"set forth to teach those in Pujol, the flower of the crusader army, a lesson they would not soon forget.

"Our noble army, armed with siege-machines, battering rams and endless courage, mined the walls and filled in the moat, heedless of the fire, stones and crossbow bolts hurled at them. The arrows flew as thick as dust in a summer wind as our soldiers, wading through rivers of blood, scaling mountains of corpses and racing through avenues of flame, stormed the citadel of that usurper Simon de Montfort." The crowd jeered lustily. "The town was laid waste and the souls of sixty verminous knights dispatched to the everlasting tortures of the deepest pit of hell. De Montfort, arriving too late to help his minions, wept at the defeat." Wild cheering broke out once more.

"Only three knights of Pujol survived," the herald went on when the mass before him quieted, "and they languish in the dungeon, awaiting Count Raymond's pleasure."

"Give them to us," a tall, dark-haired man in the crowd yelled, encouraging a chorus of agreement. "We'll know what to do with them, right mates?"

Cries of "Kill them," "Hang them," "Burn them," rang out.

The trumpeters on either side of the herald stepped forward and clear notes echoed over the square.

"Toulouse!" the herald yelled.

"Toulouse!" the crowd answered.

Three times the herald called out Count Raymond's battle cry and three times, each louder than the one before, the crowd answered. Then the herald was gone.

John stood silent on the edge of the crowd, looking over the seething mass of people. Men were still shouting incoherently and several fights had broken out. A large body of townsfolk, led by the dark-haired man, split from the main crowd and disappeared down an alley beside the Chateau.

"When I met her on the battlements at Béziers," John commented thoughtfully, "Beatrice said that the citizens who were rushing out the open gate to fight the crusaders were only proving that they had more of the Devil in them than their enemies. In all the years since, I don't think I've seen anything to suggest that she was wrong."

"Beatrice was right in most things," Isabella said. "But the whole world isn't like that. What about Umar and Nasir?"

"True," John acknowledged, "but gentle folk with peaceful intent are few and far between these days."

"That they are," Adso agreed, "but in my experience, gentle, peaceful folk don't last long in times such as these. It's only the strongest and most violent who survive."

"Like Oddo?" John asked.

"Like Oddo," Adso agreed, a frown darkening his face.

"I've wondered for the past five years whether it was Oddo I saw killing Pierre of Castelnau outside Arles. It was certainly a left-handed knight, and there are few of them around."

"That was after the debate at St. Gilles?" Adso asked.

"Yes," John confirmed, "although it wasn't much of a debate. Aumery and Pierre simply insulted Count Raymond and then excommunicated him. Raymond certainly threatened the Papal Legates, and Aumery made a big fuss about Raymond's guilt afterwards, but no one ever proved anything."

"I was in Toulouse when Raymond returned from St. Gilles," Isabella said. "He was certainly in a foul mood, but he was also worried that Pierre of Castelnau's death would be used to convince the Pope to declare a crusade. Raymond even asked to be tried for the murder so that he could prove his innocence, but his request was ignored."

"It don't sound as if 'e were guilty," Adso commented, "but then you can never trust what lords and bishops say. I don't think Oddo'd lose any sleep over a single murder."

"I agree," John said, "but even if Raymond were guilty of organizing the murder, why would he pick Oddo to do his dirty work for him? The man's a mercenary, but he's fighting on the side of the crusade."

Rebirth

Adso shrugged. "The doings of important folk're too complicated for a simple soldier, though there might not 'ave been a crusade if Pierre 'adn't been killed."

The three fell silent, pondering the long-ago crime. It was Isabella who spoke first, addressing Adso. "After your ambush outside Lavaur failed and Bertrand was killed, you made a promise to find and kill Oddo. Do you still hold to that?"

"I took an oath," Adso said miserably. "Not only did I promise Bertrand, but I swore after Oddo's Falcons murdered that simple monk Philip at Esperanza that I would avenge 'im." Adso laughed sardonically. "Lot of good that did. I ended up doing exactly what Oddo had sent the Falcons 'oo killed Philip down there to do. I destroyed the Gospel of the Christ."

"Don't be so hard on yourself," Isabella said. "The Good Christians don't believe in oaths. They say that Christ spoke against them in the sermon where he fed the people with loaves and fishes."

"I say this unto you," John said, reaching into the memory cloister and calling up the Gospel of Matthew, "do not swear at all, either by heaven, since that is God's throne; or by earth, since that is his footstool; or by Jerusalem, since that is the city of the great King. Do not swear by your own head either, since you cannot turn a single hair white or black. All you need say is 'Yes' if you mean yes, 'No' if you mean no; anything more than this comes from the Evil One."

"Is there anything you don't 'ave crammed into that memory of yours?" Adso asked.

"Plenty," John said with a smile. "There will always be more books containing more knowledge and more wisdom."

"And I suppose you'll keep on searching for them until you wear out either your eyes or your mind?"

"I will," John replied.

"And I will take any chance that comes my way to kill Oddo, until I get too weak to 'old a sword or until 'e kills me. Oh," Adso hurried on before John could interrupt, "I won't seek 'im out and rush blindly at 'im with sword raised. If God wants me to fulfil my oath, 'E'll provide an opportunity and I'll take it. Meanwhile, I'll just watch and wonder at the madness around me."

Adso nodded down to the square. Much of the crowd had dispersed, but the party that had disappeared down the alley was back. They were dragging three bloodied figures. As John and the other two watched, three horses were brought forward and one prisoner was tied behind each. One man fell to his knees and prayed loudly for mercy. The other two stood and stared arrogantly at the rabble around them.

When the captive's hands were tied, one of the men stepped forward and hit each of the horses a sharp blow in the rump. The kneeling man was immediately dragged away. The other two tried to keep their feet but soon fell to the cobbles.

The crowd that had remained in the square, and those who had returned to see what the commotion was about, made way for the horses and encouraged them to ever greater speed as they galloped wildly around the square. The three bodies bounced and dragged on the uneven ground, limp and bloody.

"Are those the three knights captured at Pujol?" John asked. "How did those men get them out of the dungeon so quickly?"

"I imagine someone gave them a key," Isabella said.

"Why?" John asked. "Wasn't there enough blood at the battle?"

"There's never enough blood," Isabella answered, her voice much softer than usual.

"Nothing like the sight of blood to get a crowd excited," Adso grumbled. "Besides, I 'eard that all that stuff the 'erald said about climbing over mountains of bodies was just for the crowd to 'ear. I 'eard that it wasn't the great victory we've been told, just a rabble 'oo walked into the town and, when they found they couldn't get at the knights in the keep, offered them safe passage if they surrendered."

"There was no battle?" John asked.

"Not what you, the great survivor of Las Navas de Tolosa, would call such," Adso said.

"So the herald was lying."

Adso burst into a laugh that quickly degenerated into a fit of coughing. John and Isabella waited patiently until it had passed and their friend could continue. "Never did manage to throw off that damned cough. Sleeping sodden and drunk in the gutter for all those months weren't the best rest cure. Anyway, as I was about to say, why should lying surprise you? Everybody lies or, at best, exaggerates what suits them. Only difference is that princes, counts, popes and bishops lie to more people."

"I do not lie." The trio turned to see William of Arles standing behind them. He looked thinner and older than John remembered, and his brightly-coloured troubadour's costume was faded and frayed at the edges.

"You!" Adso exclaimed. "You're a troubadour. You lie more'n most."

William performed an elaborate, ironic bow. "I will admit to altering a few minor facts in the interests of a good story, however, I do so only to tell a deeper and broader truth."

Rebirth

Adso snorted loudly, but William continued. "And what is truth? Pilate asked Christ that very question, but did not wait to hear the answer. Do you believe the truth that the herald proclaimed or the truth that you heard? The Catholic Church proclaims the truths they wish us to hear, but there are different truths in the documents John holds in his memory. As my friend said, we can only choose the truths that suit our own needs. Only God knows the whole truth."

"Then I shall ask 'im when my time comes," Adso remarked.

"And you imagine in your arrogance that He will tell you," John said. "You, the bumbling fool who set the body of Christ on fire."

"It was an accident." Adso said sheepishly. "Besides, we don't know for sure that's 'oo it was."

"Wait," William held up his hand. "Did I hear you aright? Burned the body of Christ? This sounds like a tale too good to miss."

"And I am sure these two will be happy enough to tell you in excruciating detail over a mug or two of ale," Isabella said. "But what brings you to our troubled city?"

"Troubled indeed," William agreed, "but no more so than the sorry times we find ourselves in. I came here because there is nowhere else to go and because this is where everything will happen and I fear that this year will see a resolution to this mess once and for all. Word is that King Pedro's army is on the move."

"About time," Adso said. "'E's been talking about it long enough. But you're right, William. Soon as King Pedro brings 'is army up 'ere to sort de Montfort out, we'll be able to go back to the life we 'ad afore this all started."

"We can never do that," William said. "Too much blood has been spilled and too many bonfires have been lit. Whatever happens this year, this land is changed forever."

"But at least we'll be rid of de Montfort," John said. "Pedro defeated a much larger army than the crusaders at Las Navas de Tolosa and this time he'll be supported by Count Raymond's knights and those of the Foix and Comminges. At least the bonfires will stop."

"I wouldn't be so sure." The three men stared at Isabella. "We decided earlier that Beatrice was usually right, and she said that the Church hated and feared us so much that it would never give up until the last Good Christian was dead. With what you hold in your head, John, you should know that better than anyone."

The group's focus moved to John, who shrugged helplessly. "No one will believe what I remember, and even if they did, they would simply kill me to keep it secret. All I want is to find Lucius's book on drawing and go somewhere quiet to practice."

"I wish you luck," Adso said, "but, at the very least, when de Montfort and Oddo're dead and Aumery's scuttled back to whatever 'ole he crawled out of, it'll be much 'arder for the crusaders to get their bonfires going. Things'll be better then and I'll fight with anyone, Aragonese king or not, to achieve that. Now, did someone mention ale and stories? That's just what I need to soothe my cough."

"I believe it was the fair Isabella," William said, slapping Adso heartily on the shoulder. "And I cannot think of a better idea."

As the four moved away from the square, John hesitated and looked back. The three knights of Pujol were little more than bloody shapes that had left red smears across the cobbles. Would it ever end?

A Small Defeat

Carcassonne
July 23, 1213

Peter struggled to keep up with Arnaud Aumery as he strode along the stone corridor. They had been summoned by Simon de Montfort, but that wasn't what was on Peter's mind. As they hurried along, they continued a conversation that had begun before the summons.

"That misguided fool in Aragon is meddling in our affairs," Aumery said. "We must not let it distract us from our God-given task. Do not doubt that the crusade will continue whatever King Pedro does. God will see to that. Things may change, but that is nothing. They have changed already. Today it is not like the days when we began this great task. Then there were but a handful of Papal Legates struggling to carry out God and Pope Innocent's work to stem the tide of heresy. Now there is an army of God's soldiers, and the Holy Inquisition gains strength every month. Dominic Guzman's Black Friars, even though they do not yet have the Pope's approval, are growing in number and strength. They dedicate themselves to a life of poverty, preaching and prayer, and root out heresy wherever they find it."

Peter knew that Aumery was right. The Black Friars seemed to be everywhere these days, preaching and denouncing heresy, and there was no way the crusade would cease, not as long as Pope Innocent supported it and de Montfort was intent on building his empire.

Peter almost yearned for Dominic's Black Friars to take over the role of seeking out and destroying the heretics. That would release him from his obligations and allow him to seek answers to the troubling questions that had been plaguing him since his return from the east. What was the meaning of his voices and the stigmata, and what did God have planned for him? The voices had been quiet lately and the stigmata were now little more than minor red patches on his hands and feet, but both loomed large in his mind.

"Will you continue the search for the Grail?" Peter asked.

Aumery stopped and spun round so fast that Peter almost cannoned into him. "Never mention that out loud," he hissed. "Speak only of the Cathar Treasure and reply vaguely if anyone asks."

"I shall," Peter said, unsettled by Aumery's reaction and the wild stare in his bulbous eyes.

"Good." Aumery continued walking and Peter fell in at his side. "Of course I shall continue the search," Aumery went on. "I remain convinced that the Cathar Treasure is the key to bringing on the Day of Judgement. I shall continue working for the crusade at de Montfort's side and you shall be my eyes and ears, scouring the land for clues as to the treasure's whereabouts."

Peter's heart sank. He was not to be released from Aumery's influence as easily as he had hoped, and he was not as certain as he had been that the Grail could be found without difficulty. His experiences in the east and his conversations with the strange yet obviously holy Francesco had seen to that.

The palms of Peter's hands itched uncomfortably. He scratched and his fingers came away with blood under the nails. He sighed and tucked his hands into the wide sleeves of his habit. So far he had managed to keep the stigmata hidden from everyone, except Francesco and John. He regretted mentioning it to his old friend, but there was nothing that could be done about that now.

Aumery stopped outside a curtained archway. He took a deep breath to compose himself and pushed through the curtain. Peter followed.

The room was the same one in which Peter had negotiated the surrender of Carcassonne with Roger Trenceval. That had been in the first year of the crusade, a lifetime ago, it seemed, and Trenceval was long dead. Peter felt a twinge of guilt at the role he had played in the young count's betrayal, but he pushed it back. He had been unaware of Aumery's trap and, in any case, he had been engaged in God's work.

Simon de Montfort stood in the centre of the room, deep in conversation with Oddo. He turned as Aumery and Peter entered.

"Ah, Father Aumery," de Montfort said with a smile.

Aumery bowed slightly. "You wish to discuss some matter?"

"Indeed. I have just received word that the Aragonese king, Pedro, has issued a call to arms and that his army is assembling in preparation for crossing the mountains to attack us."

"Surely this is not a surprise after the council at Toulouse in February. Pedro made no secret of the fact that he would resort to arms if you maintained your claim to Foix and Comminges."

"True enough, although I had hoped that cooler heads in Pedro's court might prevail and dissuad him from such a rash venture."

"It's not rash to go to war when your army's three times the size of your enemy's." Oddo rested his stare on Peter. His mouth twisted into a sneer that stretched the scar tissue on his cheek and exposed several yellow teeth. Peter shuddered and lowered his eyes.

"Perhaps," de Montfort continued, "and that is why I have asked you here. We are outnumbered, and while Pedro can expect his forces to increase with the knights of Toulouse, Foix and Comminges, we can count only on what few crusaders trickle south this year.

"There will be a great battle here before the end of this summer, and its outcome will determine the future of this land. If we win, the crusade wins, and you and the Black Friars can cleanse the land of heretics without let or hindrance. However, should we lose, an outcome that seems increasingly likely as Pedro's army grows, the crusade is finished. Languedoc will become a part of Pedro's lands and the vile heresy of Catharism will flourish unopposed."

"And my role in this will be?" Aumery asked.

"Our knights are valiant, but it is God who will win this battle for us. I cannot imagine Him sitting aside and watching all the good work we have already accomplished go to waste. The only danger is that He does not see us as worthy. Therefore, I would beg that you collect all the bishops of the land, including that fat fool Foulques, and accompany my army when the time comes. With God at our head and the prayers of all Christendom supporting us, we shall triumph."

Aumery stood silent for a moment. Then he said, "I will do it. If it is God's will that you triumph over Pedro, then I must do all in my power to further that end."

De Montfort bowed slightly. "I thank you."

"I have heard," Aumery said, "that much of the countryside is in turmoil and that many minor lords who previously swore allegiance to you and the crusade now slip back into their old ways and bow a knee to Raymond of Toulouse."

"It means nothing," de Montfort said. "They bend with the wind and a gale is coming."

"Word goes around that Pujol was taken by the rabble from Toulouse."

"It was," de Montfort said with a shrug, "but it is of little consequence. There were but three knights in the town. It is but a small defeat that none will remember after we have overcome Pedro."

"Pray hard," Oddo said, "but if God wishes us to triumph in the coming battle, He will lead my Falcons and me to Pedro, and He will guide my beautiful Britta"—he fingered the blade of his axe lovingly—"through the misguided Aragonese fool's skull."

Peter shuddered at the sight of Oddo's axe, and at the man's harsh contempt for the most powerful king in Christendom. Peter had learned much from Aumery and from his travels, and he was no longer the weak, uncertain boy who had argued with John on the banks of the Rhone Rover outside Arles five years previously. He was a fully ordained priest in the service of God and Pope Innocent and he was supported by all the power that that implied. Yet the naked aggression and the violence in Oddo's tone still intimidated him. He felt the itch growing on his palms and tucked his hands deeper into the sleeves of his habit. With a surge of relief, he followed Aumery out of the room.

"Well," Aumery said, "it appears that the continuation of your search for the treasure must wait on the affairs of man."

"Will de Montfort win?" Peter asked.

"You doubt that God is on our side?"

"No. No. Of course not," Peter said hurriedly, "but God was on King Pedro's side at Las Navas de Tolosa. Has He now abandoned him?"

"Of course. At Las Navas de Tolosa, Pedro fought on the side of right against the heathens, but that victory made him proud and greedy. Now, for personal gain and aggrandisement, he fights on the side of heretics against the Holy Church. Of course de Montfort will win. But not without some help."

"Our prayers?" Peter asked.

"Of course." Aumery smiled humourlessly. "And I must begin the prayers now. I suggest you do the same."

Aumery strode off down the corridor, leaving Peter with his doubt and a fervent wish that he could simply withdraw from all the confusion that surrounded the affairs of men. If only he could find quiet and solitude, then he might attain peace and discover what everything meant, including what God wanted of him.

A Summons

Toulouse
September 9, 1213

The streets of Toulouse reminded John of the festivals he had loved so much as a boy. Jugglers and tumblers performed wherever there was space and the walls of the Chateau Narbonnaise were draped with scarlet banners bearing the golden cross of Toulouse and the gold bars of Aragon. Aragonese, Basque, Catalan and Gascon knights swaggered through the streets in their brilliant red, blue and gold liveries.

"How many knights do you think my uncle brought?" Isabella asked John. The pair were strolling through the crowds outside the Chateau after having watched King Pedro and his retinue go inside to meet with Count Raymond.

"Adso said this morning that he had watched them come down the road yesterday and had counted over eight hundred," John replied. "If you add the knights of Toulouse, Foix and Comminges, there must be fourteen or fifteen hundred mounted knights all told. Then there's twenty or thirty thousand vassals and Toulouse militia. De Montfort doesn't have a hope."

"How many knights does he have?"

"Hard to say. It depends on how many answered the call to the crusade this summer. Maybe half as many as King Pedro and only about a thousand foot soldiers. I think the problem's going to be forcing de Montfort into a battle. If I were him, I'd keep away from Pedro and let his army march all over the countryside until they're exhausted and have to go home. Then I'd attack them as they crossed back through the passes."

"You mean there might *not* be a battle in the next few days?" Isabella sounded disappointed.

"I don't know. I'm only saying what I would do, and I'm not a count or a king. Do you really *want* there to be a battle, with all the death and suffering that means?"

"I want this all to be over, and if it takes a battle to finish it, then yes, I want a battle. Besides, knights are born and brought up to fight, so let them do it. It's the innocents caught up in this war that I feel sorry for: the farmers whose families starve because their crops have been destroyed, the children who are orphaned because their parents were in the wrong place at the wrong time, and the women raped when a city falls."

"And the Good Christians forced onto the bonfires." John added.

"Them, too," Isabella agreed. She was about to add something else when the pair were distracted by a soldier hurrying toward them. His livery identified him as one of King Pedro's bodyguards.

"My Lady," the soldier said, bowing before Isabella. "I bring a request for you to attend the presence of his illustrious majesty, the most Christian King Pedro of Aragon and Barcelona." The soldier looked up slyly. "And I bring greetings from an old friend."

"Peire!" John and Isabella said simultaneously, recognizing the soldier they had become friends with at Pedro's court in Barcelona.

"We heard that you chose to accompany Pedro back to Aragon after the council in Toulouse, and now you are back. It's good to see you. And"—John gestured at Peire's fancy uniform—"you have done well for yourself."

Peire spread his arms wide to show off his bright livery to its best advantage. "The King's personal bodyguard. We get the best food, best quarters, and"—Peire winked broadly at John—"the ladies do love the uniform. But"—he turned to Isabella and assumed a more formal expression—"I do bear a request for your attendance at the King, and I have been some considerable time in searching you out. We should proceed."

"Both of us?" Isabella asked as Peire led the way toward the Chateau.

"The King did send me to seek out his niece, but he said if she was not alone that I should bring along the fair-haired Moorish impersonator."

"What does he want with us?" John asked.

"What do kings ever want?" Peire asked thoughtfully. "To be obeyed, worshipped and powerful. But I think in this case he merely wants to visit with his favourite niece."

"I'm his only niece," Isabella said.

Peire shrugged. "He was sad that you decided to stay."

"He could have forced me to go with him."

"He might have, had he not cared for you so much."

The three climbed the steps to the Chateau in silence. Inside, the main hall was a riot of colour. Banners covered every square inch of wall and thick carpets were strewn over the floor. A long table groaned under the weight of every imaginable food, and a vast fire roared in the ceiling-high fireplace at one end. Servants darted here and there among the sumptuously dressed guests and the noise of conversation and laughter filled the air. King Pedro sat in a chair on a raised platform at the opposite end of the hall from the

Rebirth

fire. To his right, on a slightly lower platform, sat Count Raymond, and flanking, lower yet but still above the lesser knights and retainers, were the Counts of Foix and Comminges.

As Peire led the way over, Pedro noticed them and beckoned. "Isabella, it's good to see you once more," he bellowed. "This time I have brought my army to show you."

Everyone looked toward the focus of the King's attention and John felt acutely uncomfortable.

"And you have brought the young master of disguises with you. Perhaps we might persuade him to dress up as a Moor later for our entertainment." The King roared with laughter and everyone dutifully followed. John wished the floor would open and swallow him. "Come and sit by me and tell me of your adventures this past summer."

As John and Isabella settled themselves at Pedro's feet, Count Raymond leaned over and said, "Your Majesty. We must plan our attack on de Montfort. The seasons move on and time is short."

"Yes, yes," Pedro said with a dismissive wave. "As you mentioned earlier, de Montfort has some thirty knights at the town, what was its name?"

"Muret," Raymond replied. "A force of my knights and the Toulouse militia have been besieging them there this past week."

"Of course. Tomorrow I shall lead my army to Muret. De Montfort cannot afford to lose so many knights. He must come to their aid. Then we shall defeat him and end this presumption once and for all. But that is the work of tomorrow. Tonight we dine, drink and talk. Where are those minstrels I ordered?"

John watched with interest. Every previous time he had seen Count Raymond the man had been in charge, the most powerful lord present. Now he was in the presence of his king and he cut a different figure—quieter, respectful and subservient. Nevertheless, John detected a hint of annoyance in Raymond's furrowed brow. He wasn't happy with Pedro's easy dismissal of military matters in favour of revelry.

John glanced around the hall. It was noisy and seemed chaotic, but there was an order to what went on. Everyone in the room, from King Pedro down to the lowliest servant, knew their place, knew who was above and who was below them and how they should address and be addressed by those more or less important. The world was ordered as it should be, just as the battle, if it were to happen, would be fought according to the established rules of chivalry and honour.

Peter would approve of the structure, John thought, and say that it was ordained by God, but John wasn't so sure. Was this complex web of duty and responsibility as secure as it seemed? Was there a different, less rigid, way of ordering human affairs? John didn't have an opportunity to pursue the thought.

"You will accompany us tomorrow to Muret," Pedro said. It wasn't a question but a statement of fact.

"Of course, Your Majesty," John and Isabella replied.

"Excellent. Then you shall see how we handle that upstart de Montfort. Afterwards, you shall accompany us back to Barcelona. Next year I plan to take my armies south to reconquer Cordova from the Caliph. Then who knows? Sevilla, Granada? There will be a great Christian empire from Africa to Toulouse and Carcassonne, and Aragon will be at its heart with Barcelona as its capital. And the heart of Barcelona will be my cathedral that will house the body of the holy martyr Saint Eulalia. Do you know her story?"

"I'm not familiar with the story, Your Majesty," Isabella said. John remained silent, struggling to keep up with Pedro's stream of words.

"The blessed Saint Eulalia was a thirteen-year-old girl, pure in Christ, who was tortured by the heathen Romans. She underwent thirteen tortures when she refused to renounce her Christianity, one for every year of her age. They included hideous mutilations and being rolled down a hill in a barrel with knives stuck in it, all of which she suffered in silence. When at last her head was cut off, a pure white dove flew from her bleeding neck. I shall build her the most magnificent church in Christendom. My scribe"—Pedro clapped his hands and a thin, bearded old man stepped hurriedly forward—"has been to the north where he has collected drawings of the newest ways of building churches." Pedro broke off and fixed his gaze on John. "You like drawing, I recall."

"I do, Your Majesty," John replied, confused by the abrupt change of topic.

"Good. Good. Alessandro will show you he what he has found." Pedro turned to Isabella. "Now, dear niece, tell me of your adventures this past summer."

With that, John was dismissed. The old man scuttled round to the side and beckoned him urgently. John bowed to Pedro, who ignored him, and followed the scribe, wondering what he was to be shown.

"Come, come, come." Alessandro spoke rapidly, in short bursts. His voice was high-pitched and his hands were continually in motion, as if attacking each other. Under his left arm he carried a worn, leather folder. "Too noisy. Too noisy. Need peace. Need quiet."

Alessandro led John into a small side room, bare except for a long oak table. The old man placed the folder on the table and opened it.

"Are these the drawings for King Pedro's cathedral?" John asked.

Rebirth

"What?" Alessandro sounded surprised. "No, no, no. These are of what has been done, is being done, in the north." The old man's skinny fingers picked at the vellum pages while he provided a running commentary. "Saint Dennis, only an abbey, but complete. Chartres, Laon, Paris, great cathedrals. Almost done. All are here, all in the new French style."

Most of the pages were detailed, elaborate plans, with dots where pillars supported roofs and lines for walls. Some were church fronts with doors, windows and sculpted figures drawn in. Others were sketches of details, jumbled together on single pages, a window and a statue here, an arch and a vaulted ceiling there. Some seemed to be almost doodles—people in different poses, mason's tools, mazes, animals and mythical beasts.

"See. See. That's the key," Alessandro said, pointing at a strangely pointed arch between two sturdy pillars. "The pillars take the weight and between can be glass, allowing God's light to flood the church."

John had heard about these new churches with their walls of windows that transformed the dark, cave-like interiors with which he was familiar. It was the architectural equivalent of what he wanted to with his drawing, if he ever found Lucius' book. He examined the drawings with interest. They were wonderfully detailed and intricate, but they were flat. Of course, they were showing flat objects, walls and plans, but John wished for something that would show him what one of these new churches would look like as he entered the great west door. Then he saw it, the very last vellum in the folder. He gasped and reached out for the sheet.

"Ah, that is Laon. It is a strange illustration, is it not? It is not for the mason. It will not help pile one stone atop another. Yet I brought it for its novelty."

As Alessandro chattered on, John became lost in the drawing. He lifted it almost reverently by the edges and tilted it so that it caught the rays of light streaming through the room's narrow window.

The sketch was very rough and poorly done. Only the major features were shown and they were not well drawn. The lines weren't clean or even straight in many cases, and details were missing or just suggested by a scratch or two. Yet it was still the most wonderful thing John had ever seen.

The view was of what you would see if you entered one of these new churches and took a step or two to the right. The nave, lined with pillars and flanked by narrow aisles, stretched into the distance toward the transept and choir. The pillars supported pointed arches that opened into the aisles, but rose above the openings to impossible heights where they spread into arches that formed a vaulted roof. The impression was like being in the cathedral itself.

"It's impossible," John gasped, laying the drawing back on the table reverentially.

"No. No," Alessandro said. "That is how it looks. The arches and buttresses, which you cannot see, as they are on the outside, allow for the walls to be built to a quite remarkable height."

"I mean the drawing," John said. He touched the picture, almost expecting his hand to sink into it. "It's so...real."

"It is unusual, I grant you that, but real? It is badly drawn, not nearly as good as the masons' drawings and, for all its strangeness, it is still merely ink on vellum and not the thing itself."

"Who did this? Are there more?"

"More? More? Is a single wonder not enough?"

"More than enough," John said. "But who did it?"

"A man from hereabouts, I was told. At least he spoke Occitan and claimed to have come from Queribus."

"Queribus?"

"That is what I said," Alessandro said testily. "It is a fortress in the mountains by the border with Aragon."

"I know."

"Then why did you ask?"

John felt the conversation slipping out of control. "I don't know. I'm sorry. Look, what was the man's name?"

"He was called Dario. An Italian name, I believe, although after Darius, the great king of Persia."

"*Was* called?" John asked.

"Unfortunately, yes. The poor man went to heaven some months prior to my visit to Laon. It seems he was sitting sketching in the choir of the cathedral, which is yet to be completed, while masons worked above. A large piece of stone fell and crushed him."

John felt a wave of sadness. Already he had been imagining a journey to meet the creator of this wonderful drawing, and sitting at his feet to learn. Now the one man who seemed to know exactly what John craved to learn was dead. "Are there other drawings by Dario?"

"I daresay," Alessandro shrugged. "I saw none."

"May I copy this drawing?" John asked.

Alessandro glanced toward the main hall, from which the raucous sound of laughter and singing came. "I do not see the harm, if you are quick."

"I will be," John said. With shaking fingers, he took the notebook that Beatrice had given him and a piece of charcoal out of his satchel and set to work.

Rebirth

* * *

John sighed. It was all he could do not to rip the pages out of his notebook and crumple them up in frustration. He had been working feverishly for nearly an hour, copying Dario's drawing over and over, but with no success. He would draw the pillars, marching off into the distance, but as soon as he attempted the arches, something went wrong and the picture looked flat. If he worked on the arches first, then, when he drew the pillars, they appeared to wander all over the place. And he hadn't even attempted the roof. There was something he was missing, a piece of information, a trick. John sighed again. It made sense, he supposed. If drawing this way were easy, someone other than this mysterious dead man from Queribus would have managed it.

"We must get back." Alessandro had been getting increasingly nervous over the past while.

"I suppose," John said. "I can't do this. I need more."

"Ah, my young friend," Pedro said when John and Alessandro reappeared in the hall. "Did you like my drawings? Will my cathedral be the most magnificent in Christendom?"

"It will, Your Majesty," John replied with a bow. "It will be a wonder of the world."

Pedro laughed. "And you and Isabella shall watch it grow. But now rest. You will come with me tomorrow to Muret and see how King Pedro of Aragon deals with upstart usurpers. Alessandro will show you to the royal suites."

"Thank you, Your Majesty," John said, bowing again.

Isabella, who had been sitting by Pedro's throne stood. "Yes, thank you, uncle."

Pedro smiled and waved his hand in acknowledgement and dismissal.

"The old man had an incredible drawing," John said excitedly as soon as he and Isabella had been shown to the royal suites. "It was of one of the new-style cathedrals in the north and it did everything I have been trying to do with my drawing. It wasn't a very good drawing, but looking at it was like being in the cathedral itself. I tried to copy it, but it didn't work. There's something missing and the man who drew it is dead."

As he rambled on, John noticed that Isabella was struggling to show an interest in what he was saying.

"Are you all right?" he asked. "I'm sorry to go on so. What did you and King Pedro talk about?"

"Nothing much. He asked about our time here, but his mind kept wandering. I'm worried about him," Isabella said. "He seems different from the last time we saw him."

"But that was only a few months ago. How does he seem different?"

"I'm not sure. More arrogant, certainly. He used to be quieter and more thoughtful. Now he's surrounded by people who always agree with him and are continually telling him that he's the most important and powerful King in Christendom. He seems to believe them. Several times, Count Raymond tried to discuss tactics for the upcoming battle, and Pedro simply brushed him off. He seems to think that all he has to do is show up with his knights and de Montfort will collapse in terror. Eventually, Count Raymond gave up and retired to his chambers."

"Well, Pedro does have a point. His army is overwhelmingly superior to de Montfort's. It should be an easy victory."

"I know," Isabella acknowledged, "and you're probably right. I worry too much. Tell me more about the drawing."

"It's of the new cathedral in Laon. It was wonderful and I tried to copy it but I couldn't. I thought I could go and learn from the artist, but he died in an accident."

"He couldn't have been the only person in the world who could do this kind of drawing."

"I hope not," John said, "but I've never even heard of anything else like this drawing. The artist came from round here. Queribus, Alessandro said."

"Then that's where we should go."

"But there's not much at Queribus," John said. "Just a small fortress on top of a rock."

"Adso's rescuer, Esclarmonde and several other Cathars are there, and at Peyrepertuse along the valley. Besides, do you suppose this mysterious artist might have learned from a book?" Isabella said with a sly grin.

"Of course!" John's face brightened. "Why didn't I think of that? *Perspectiva*! Lucius' book on drawing must be at Queribus or nearby."

Isabella smiled broadly at John's sudden enthusiasm. "*Might* be at Queribus or Peyrepertuse," she corrected, "although I doubt if your artist took it with him on his travels."

"But how can we go to Queribus? Pedro wants us to go with him to Barcelona after he has defeated de Montfort." John's enthusiasm waned as he saw his goal slipping away once again. "Why does this war keep getting in the way of what we want to do?"

"Perhaps Pedro will let us go to Queribus on the way to Barcelona," Isabella said, without conviction. "Or maybe one of us. I could accompany Pedro and you could go to Queribus."

"I don't want us to be separated," John said. "Too much can happen these days. We should stay together. Maybe Pedro will be happy after the battle and let us go."

"Maybe," Isabella said. "In the meantime, we should get some rest. I have a feeling the next few days will be busy."

"They will be," John agreed. He gazed into Isabella's eyes. Even after all this time together, her beauty still overwhelmed him—the tiny dimples at the corners of her lips when she smiled; the long smooth sweep of her forehead; the sparkle in her dark eyes that concealed a depth John felt he could drown in—wanted to drown in. He leaned forward and kissed her.

"It'll be all right," he said when they drew apart, although he doubted that it would.

A Mass

Fanjeaux
September 10, 1213

"Last night my wife had a dream." Simon de Montfort, dressed in full battle chain mail, stood on the steps of the tiny church in the centre of Fanjeaux. The sun was sinking low over the distant hills and the shadows around the square were deepening. Crusader knights crowded the small square in front of de Montfort and spilled down the narrow streets in all directions. To one side, Bishop Foulques, Arnaud Aumery and Peter watched. Opposite, Dominic Guzman and five of his black-clad monks stood like a small convention of crows. Oddo and two of his heavily armed Falcons stood behind.

"In the dream, blood poured from her arms," de Montfort continued in a voice that drowned out the rattle of equipment. "In a fright, she woke me. She said the dream was an omen, a warning of disaster to come, and that I must retreat to Carcassonne and take refuge there. I told her I would do no such thing." De Montfort paused for effect and the crowd waited in silence.

"I do not believe in omens or auguries," he continued. "I am not weak and superstitious like the Aragonese King Pedro. Nor am I like Count Raymond, who pretends to see the future in the random flights of birds. I am Simon de Montfort, Lord of this land, and I rule in the name of the Holy Mother Church and with the blessings and by the grace of Pope Innocent III."

Peter felt his palms itch and scratched nervously.

"King Pedro and the heretic Raymond," de Montfort continued, "march this day to attack our garrison at Muret. Tomorrow we shall march there and destroy them. We cannot fail. God marches with us and we shall be led by this." De Montfort indicated to Bishop Foulques, who in turn waved to a priest standing beside him. The priest lifted a long, narrow bundle wrapped in spotless white linen. Reverently, Foulques and the priest unwrapped it. The tension in the waiting knights was palpable. The itching in Peter's hands and feet had become almost unbearable and he dug his thumbs into his palms viciously. He didn't notice that Aumery, the only person in the crowd not gazing expectantly at Foulques, was watching him with interest.

Finally, the package was unwrapped. Foulques held a splintered, black piece of wood above his head. It was about two feet long, squared off at one end and jagged and broken at the other.

"Behold," Foulques announce majestically, "a fragment of the True Cross upon which our Lord Jesus Christ suffered his passion for us. This wood was pierced by the same nails that pierced Christ's hands and feet. It is anointed with the blood of our Saviour."

The crowd gasped and many knights fell to their knees and clasped their hands in prayer. Instinctively, Peter crossed himself. Flecks of blood flew from his hands as he moved them in the air before him.

"With this holiest of relics to lead us," Foulques went on, "we cannot fail in our blessed mission. Now, let us enter God's house and pray."

Holding the piece of wood high, Foulques turned and led the way into the small church. De Montfort and the others followed. Peter tucked his bleeding hands into the sleeves of his habit and joined them. Aumery held back and stared after him.

* * *

"And therefore, in the name of His Holiness Pope Innocent III, we announce the excommunication of Count Raymond of Toulouse, the Counts of Foix and Comminges, and any who follow them in their heretical ways and lead the innocent into the fires of Hell." Bishop Foulques finished announcing the excommunication. He stood behind the small church altar on which lay the dark piece of wood. Lit torches blazed along the walls, dispelling the gathering evening gloom. Every lord, knight, priest and monk who could fit into the church was kneeling before him. Peter knelt near the back, the hard stone floor hurting his knees. The itching in his hands had eased, but he kept them deep in his sleeves and held tightly against his body.

Peter was awed to be in the presence of a piece of the True Cross. The thought that Christ had been nailed to, and suffered on, that broken piece of wood before him almost took his breath away. He was nearly overcome with dizziness at the thought that His blood had soaked into this relic that he could almost touch. It was like the moment when he thought he had uncovered the Holy Grail outside Plovdiv.

"Kiss the Holy Cross." The voice in his head was so faint that Peter wasn't even certain he had heard it, but the idea fitted so perfectly with what he craved that he moved to stand.

"Kneel." He heard Aumery's voice, whispering urgently, in his ear. Peter sank back onto the cold store floor. As he did, someone at the front of the worshipping crowd stood. It was Simon de Montfort. The metallic hiss of his sword leaving its scabbard echoed loud in the silent church. De Montfort stepped forward and laid his weapon on the altar. He knelt once more, bowed his head and crossed himself.

"Merciful and bountiful Christ," he intoned. "I am unworthy, yet You have chosen me as Your instrument in this Holy Crusade. I dedicate my sword on Your altar and swear by the fragment of the True Cross on which You suffered for us that I shall not rest until I have proven myself worthy and cleansed this land of the vile corruption of heresy." He stood, lifted the sword from the altar and kissed the blade. "I receive from You the instrument of battle."

Turning to the kneeling crowd, he held the sword high. It glinted in the flickering torchlight. "Let us go forth and do God's work."

A rumble of agreement passed through the knights as they stood. Foulques lifted the piece of the cross and led the way out of the church. Peter stood and watched him pass, fighting down an impulse to reach out and touch the relic. He was about to follow when he felt Aumery's hand on his sleeve, holding him back. When they were alone, Aumery spoke. "A very nice performance."

"Performance?" Peter asked.

"Of course." Peter could see Aumery's teeth glint in the torchlight. "Tomorrow, de Monfort goes to war. He is at a disadvantage and he must be certain that those who follow him are as dedicated as he. They will die for God before they will die for him."

"But they follow a fragment of the True Cross."

"Indeed they do," Aumery added thoughtfully. "I wonder where this holy artefact has been all these years?" Before Peter could ask whether Aumery was questioning the authenticity of the relic, the older man shrugged and continued. "In any case, we must give thanks that it has been discovered in time. It is unfortunate that they do not follow the Grail."

Was this a criticism of his failure in the east, Peter wondered.

"But I think we have another miracle, closer to hand." Aumery went on.

"What do you mean?" Peter asked, his brow furrowed in puzzlement.

"Look." Aumery pointed to the floor where Peter had been kneeling. Two dark spots stained the stone flags. Instinctively, Peter looked down at his feet. Blood soaked the edges of his sandals.

"Let me see your hands," Aumery ordered.

"No." Peter's response was immediate and instinctive.

"Do not deny me." Aumery's voice rose. "I command you in the name of God, show me your hands."

Peter closed his eyes, pulled his hands out of his habit sleeves and held them out, palms forward. He heard Aumery gasp, "The stigmata."

The sounds of movement made Peter open his eyes, Aumery was on his knees with his hands clasped in prayer, gazing up at him with a look of rapture in his staring eyes. "You are blessed. You have been chosen."

Peter didn't feel blessed. Yes, he had been chosen, but for what he had no idea, and Aumery on his knees before him was embarrassing. "I...I don't know," he stammered.

Aumery stood up and leaned so close to Peter's face that he could feel the spittle on his cheek when the monk spoke. "You don't *know*?" Peter jerked back at the sudden scorn in Aumery's voice. "You snivelling wretch! You have been chosen before others who have suffered much more in Christ's name and you do not know. Is it not obvious? You must lead us to victory over the arrogant King Pedro and the heretic Raymond."

Peter's hands shook with nerves. What should he do? Was Aumery right? Was he blessed with the stigmata for this purpose, or was there something more? He clenched his fists. A roaring thundered in his ears and flashes of light exploded behind his eyes. He pressed his bleeding fists to his temples. He heard Aumery's voice as if from a great distance, "What is happening?" he asked. "Is it a vision?"

When the other voice came it was almost a physical force—a blow causing Peter to stagger backward. It wasn't the gentle voice of the Seraphim he had been hearing since he had been with Francesco. No. This was the original voice—the one that had ordered him to kill Diogenes—the one that brooked no denial.

"False idols!" the voice boomed. "I suffered for mankind, not a worldly empire. Look to the End of Days."

Peter's eyesight began to cloud at the edges. After a few moments, it was as if he were peering down a long, dimly lit tunnel. At the very end he could see the fragment of the cross on the altar. Stumbling forward, Peter knocked Aumery aside. As he moved unsteadily toward the altar, the wood seemed to rise up into the air. He reached out to grasp it. The wood felt oddly malleable. As Peter held it, the relic softened and shrank until it was no more than a dark ball that he could hide in the palms of his cupped hands. Yet it felt strangely heavy.

Peter opened his hands. The dark ball erupted into a column of blinding light that widened in the air to form a cross of light.

"Behold my suffering!" Peter's voice ordered.

A darker shape formed on the cross of light, resolving itself into a human figure. Blood ran freely from the places where large, ugly nails impaled the hands and feet, and from a jagged wound in the figure's side. Peter fell to his knees. He wanted to flee, but he had no power over his body. Wide-eyed in terror, he gaped at the face looming over him. The eyes were hooded and there was a smile on its lips. Even though the mouth never moved, Peter heard a voice echo round his head. "The answer lies in the wilderness. Seek the King." A flame appeared in the centre of the figure's chest. The fire grew until it consumed the body and was almost too bright to look at. Then it swirled into a spiral and shot upwards as if drawn by some irresistible force.

Peter gasped and slumped to the floor, hitting his head painfully on the corner of the stone altar. When he came to, Aumery was crouched over him. "Did you see it?" Peter croaked weakly.

"See what?" Aumery asked, a puzzled frown crossing his face.

"Christ on the cross. The fire. I lifted up the relic and it became a cross of light with our Lord suffering upon it."

"I saw nothing," Aumery said. "You clutched your temples and staggered to the altar, mumbling strange words I could not make out. Then you fell to your knees before collapsing to the floor."

"But the True Cross...I changed it."

Aumery's stare moved above Peter's head. "The True Cross is gone. Foulques took it when he and the others left. The altar is empty."

Peter struggled to his feet. He felt as weak as a newborn lamb and had to hold on to the edge of the altar to keep his balance. Aumery was right—the altar was bare. Peter took a deep breath and felt the cold, hard, empty surface. His hands left bloody smears on the stone. What had the figure's words meant? "The answer lies in the wilderness. Seek the King." What wilderness? Who was the King? Was it Christ or some earthly leader?

"You had a vision." Aumery crept closer to Peter, his voice soft and greedy. "Tell me about it."

A wave of disgust flowed through Peter. Whatever they meant, his voices and visions were his own. He had no desire to share them with this fanatic monk.

Peter suddenly saw Aumery clearly. The man sought power, worldly power, and that was what had been so attractive to Peter at the beginning. He had been shy and uncertain, awkward with other people—he thought briefly of his relationships with John and Isabella—and humiliated at Béziers by the brutish mercenary Oddo. Aumery's offer to take him under his wing and involve him in the quest for the Holy Grail had offered him a way out.

"My visions are mine and God's," Peter said, standing straight and meeting Aumery's disquieting stare. "Too long now I have been in your thrall. You gave me the power of the Church for a shield and for that I am grateful, but that power is worldly. In that, if nothing else, the heretics are correct." Aumery was staring hard at Peter, but he remained silent.

"You and the black brothers work tirelessly in rooting out this foul Cathar heresy and you will be blessed in heaven because of it, but I do not believe that Christ would place a sign as simple as the Grail, or"—Peter glanced over at the altar—"the Holy Cross, in our imperfect hands."

It was the first time Peter had ever challenged Aumery, or spoken to him as an equal, and it frightened him. Aumery was a man who commanded the armies of the Pope and who shamelessly manipulated those around him to his own ends. With a shudder, Peter remembered that, back at the beginning, in 1208, Aumery had even suggested to Peter that he had been involved in organizing the murder of the Papal Legate Pierre of Castelnau. Peter thought it best not to mention that suspicion.

"Each of us must find our own way to God, and only when enough of us have done so will we prove that we are worthy and Christ will usher in the End of Days. The Grail is a chimera, a fantasy we hope exists to make our lives simple, but it doesn't exist. We must all struggle for perfection. Of course we have a duty to destroy the heathen and the heretic, but that will all be for nought if we are not purified within ourselves. You seek God through the ecstasy of mortification of the flesh." A vivid image of blood spraying off Aumery's back as he swept a coarse, knotted rope over his shoulder flashed into Peter's mind. He pushed it back and continued. "I do not yet know where my path leads. Perhaps my visions and voices will tell me, but I must find peace and quiet so that I may listen."

Peter fell silent, exhausted by his outburst. He half expected Aumery to rage at him, call him a coward and unworthy to wear the monk's habit, but he did not. He stared unblinkingly at Peter for a long moment and then, in a chilling, silky voice, he said, "You are still a child. I have lived many years and seen the depths to which weak men can sink. I have done many things that have shocked people—some you know of and some you cannot even suspect—but every word I have spoken and every act I have performed was in God's name. If I believed it necessary, I would swim though an ocean of blood and climb a mountain of corpses without a second thought. This earthly life is nothing but a collection of snares set by the Devil to trap us. If a few thousand deaths will help to cleanse it, then so be it. I will do my part."

Aumery fell silent once more. Peter craved escape but the strange eyes held him. Eventually the monk continued. "I have not been blessed like you with voices and visions to guide me, but I have battled hard and will continue to do so until God sees fit to extinguish the breath in this poor body. I hoped once that you would walk by my side and help carry my burden, but now I see you must go your own way. I think you are wrong, but I shall not prevent you. But remember this. Satan also spoke to Our Lord in the desert. Be sure you know to whose voice you listen.

"I wish you well and now I must go. Foulques has some fool idea of sending an emissary to seek a resolution with King Pedro and avoid bloodshed. The man is an idiot. His faith is weak, but he has the ear of the Pope and must have his chance, even if nought will come of it." With a final hard look at Peter, Aumery turned and left.

Completely drained, Peter fell to his knees and prayed. "Please help me understand," he whispered. "Help me find my way." His only answer was silence. After a moment, he stood and left the church.

The square was empty, the corners deep in shadow. Peter looked to the east, where the crusader army was camped beneath Fanjeaux's walls. He could hear the shouts of the knights, the clank of their equipment, and the snorting and stamping of their great warhorses. Already, hundreds of campfires were casting a glow that reflected off the low cloud.

Peter turned and faced west. It was quieter in that direction and the last rays of the sun were painting the clouds on the horizon a fiery red. "That's where I must go," Peter said out loud. He had no idea whether the king of his voice was King Pedro or not, but he had a very powerful sense that his destiny lay at Muret. Aumery had planted the seed of the idea that a monk might be able to prevent the seemingly inevitable bloodshed between Catholics. If that were so, it would not be one of Foulques' minions, but someone pure enough in heart to sway the mind of the Christian King.

Peter didn't consider himself pure, but perhaps the stigmata might have an effect. Was this the task for which he had been chosen? He couldn't be sure, but there was only one way to find out. Peter walked down the church steps and headed toward the west gate and the setting sun.

First Blood

Muret
September 11, 1213

Adso stood beside John on a low hill across the Louge River from Muret, To their left the muddy waters of the much wider Garonne River swirled past on their way to Toulouse. Muret sat where the two rivers joined, its heavily-walled citadel and cathedral crammed onto the narrow neck of land overlooking the confluence. To the south, the lower town spread over a wider flat area. A small wooden bridge crossed the Louge and a much larger one, also of wood, spanned the Garonne, linking the town to the east bank.

The morning sun was warm enough to raise tendrils of mist from the swampy ground south of Muret's walls where thousands of the Toulouse militia sprawled in a heaving, stinking mass. Mangonels and trebuchets, barged down from Toulouse, were set up haphazardly on any mound that promised a firm footing. Adso gave a deep, guttural cough that seemed to originate in the very depths of his lungs, cleared his throat and spat onto the grass.

"Are you all right?" John asked.

Adso nodded as he regained his breath. "It's just the smell of that rabble," he said with a weak smile. "Even for an army, they stink."

"They do," John agreed. "I'm glad we're up there." He waved his arm toward the hilltop almost two miles away where the cream of Pedro and Raymond's army was camped under a sea of swirling red, blue and gold banners. "Do you think Pedro will attack today?"

"Pedro won't. 'E doesn't want to waste 'is knights on Muret. 'E'll sit up there and wait for de Montfort to come to 'im. But that lot"—Adso swept his arm wide over the militia camp—"I don't reckon anyone can control them. They know that there's only thirty knights in Muret and the walls're not much to speak of. They might decide to attack any minute."

As if to confirm Adso's comment, a mangonel banged and a rock flew out and crashed into the wall beside the town gate, leaving a jagged hole. Other mangonels fired and the trebuchets joined in. The aim wasn't great, not nearly as precise as the work of the huge trebuchet that had destroyed the water supply at Minerve, but enough rocks hit the walls and gate to make it obvious that there would soon be a breach. A disorganized rabble of armed men drifted out of the camp and stood watching the siege engines work.

"Will de Montfort come?" John asked.

Oh, 'e'll come," Adso replied. "'E 'as to. If 'e don't beat Pedro and Raymond, 'e's finished. 'E'll go back to being a landless lord with no prospects. "'E 'as to win or die."

"And if he wins the crusade'll be over."

"Maybe. Certainly, I can't see the Pope 'aving an easy time raising another crusade if this one's defeated and we're under King Pedro's protection. But remember, Beatrice always said they would never give up until the last Cathar was burned. And," Adso went on before John could respond, "as my Dad used to say, don't count chickens 'til the eggs 'atch. Pedro's got to win the battle yet."

"That won't be a problem. Pedro and Raymond have at least twice as many knights as de Montfort can possibly call on, and I saw what Pedro's knights did to a much larger army at Las Navas de Tolosa. The crusade doesn't stand a chance."

Adso sucked his teeth noisily. "Per'aps, but remember, Oddo's Falcons fought *for* Pedro at Las Navas, and now they fight for de Montfort."

"But there's no more than forty or fifty of them," John interrupted. "They won't make a difference."

"Maybe not," Adso acknowledged, "but I seen strange things 'appen in war. Still, let's assume you're right and Pedro wins. What're you and the lovely Isabella going to do once this is all over? Back to Barcelona?"

"That's what King Pedro wants," John said glumly.

"It's 'ard to refuse kings, right enough," Adso commented. "But if you don't go with Pedro, what'll you do?"

"Same as I was doing before, looking for books and learning them. Beatrice gave me a gift in teaching me the memory cloister, and I have a responsibility to use it. Besides, I think Lucius' book on drawing might be down at Queribus or one of the remote fortresses in the mountains. I still want to find that and learn to draw differently."

"And you'll drag poor Isabella around with you?" Adso said. "I can see William of Arles composing a romantic ballad on the wonderful way you 'ave of wooing a fair lady."

John laughed. "But what about you? What'll you do?"

Rebirth

"Oh, I don't know. Fighting and drinking are all I know and I seem to 'ave been doing both forever. Maybe I'll try something different. Find a woman 'oo can put up with me and settle down in a quiet village somewhere."

"Good luck finding someone to put up with you," John said, slapping his friend on the back.

The pair fell silent, but John noticed a worried frown furrowing Adso's brow. "What's the matter?"

"Oddo," Adso replied. "I took an oath to kill 'im or die trying, and I suspect 'e's on 'is way 'ere as we speak."

"Then keep out of his way."

"Can't do that," Adso shook his head. "I told you I wouldn't search 'im out, but neither will I run away if our paths cross."

The pair stood in silence, watching the rocks crash into the walls of Muret. John was wondering how to cheer up his friend when he spotted Isabella heading toward them. He smiled to himself. As long as they were together, he would be happy.

"I knew you two wouldn't leave here as long as there was fighting going on," she said when she finally reached them, "so I brought some bread, cheese and wine." John and Isabella embraced.

"Enough of that," Adso said, pulling himself out of his dark mood. "Just 'cause she's the best woman in the world and 'as brought us lunch, there's no need to go all romantic. That's the job of the troubadours."

John and Isabella laughed and the trio sat on the grass and shared out the food. As they ate, the Toulouse militia gathered below Muret's shattered walls and, with a great roar, surged forward.

"Proving they have more of the devil in them than their enemies," Isabella commented quietly.

* * *

"That didn't take long," John remarked as he finished the last of the wine Isabella had brought. The siege engines had made short work of the wall around Muret's lower town and the militia was fighting there now, pushing the defending knights through the narrow streets toward the upper town and the last refuge of the citadel. The distant clash of arms and the screams of the wounded and dying reached the trio on the hill. Tendrils of smoke rose from the beginnings of fires across the town.

"It'll take longer if many of the knights make it into the citadel," Adso remarked. "That's built stronger. I doubt if they've got much food, though. Not that it matters, de Montfort'll be 'ere from Fanjeaux soon enough and what 'appens in Muret won't be worth a troubadour's oath."

"Except to the poor people who are dying there just now," Isabella said bitterly.

"True enough," Adso agreed. "But people dying isn't a strange occurrence in this sorry land these days. Anyway, we'd best be 'eading back to camp and leave the rabble to their pleasures."

With a last look at the town, Adso turned and strode north toward the fluttering banners of the Aragonese army. Isabella followed, but John hesitated, staring over the river into the distance. He frowned and squinted at a smudge of brown on the road to Fanjeaux and Carcassonne.

"What's that?" he asked, loud enough to bring Isabella and Adso back to his side. By the time they too were looking east, the smudge had resolved itself into a dust cloud rising above a squad of rapidly moving horsemen.

"I'll wager that'll be the vanguard of de Montfort's army," Adso said quietly.

"Already?" Isabella asked.

"They're moving fast and Fanjeaux's less'n forty miles away," Adso said.

"We should get back to the camp," John suggested.

"No 'urry." Adso was shielding his eyes and peering at the rapidly approaching men. "These'r just the first. The army proper'll take all afternoon to get 'ere. Won't be a battle 'fore tomorrow at the earliest. If the militia 'old or destroy the bridge over the Garonne, it might be days yet."

John felt sweat break out on his back. He had known there was going to be a battle, but to see the enemy army approaching so fast filled him with dread. Automatically, his hand wandered to his side and rested on Auramazda's handle. He loved the magnificent sword he had bought from the blacksmith in Toledo, and had worked hard learning the fancy tricks Adso had taught him were possible with a well-balanced blade like this. However, there was a world of difference between practicing with a friend and fighting against an enemy intent on killing you.

"Let's go," John pleaded, feeling horribly exposed on the hill, even though the riders were still some way off and on the other side of the Garonne. He took Isabella's hand and the pair started back. This time it was Adso who hesitated.

"Just wait one more minute," he said. John and Isabella paused.

"Goddamn," Adso swore eventually.

"What," John asked.

"Look," Adso ordered. "'Oo are those riders?"

John looked hard. The horsemen were more distinct now. They were knights in full armour and the man to the fore carried a banner that swirled and snapped in the wind. John couldn't make out the crest, but Isabella could.

Rebirth

"Falcons," she breathed.

Just then the wind caught the banner and swirled it out to one side. John saw the red bird clutching the black axe in its talons.

"And I'll wager that's Oddo leading them," Adso said. He coughed and spat. "Looks as if I'm going to 'ave to fulfil that oath after all."

In silence, the three turned and headed back to the camp. Behind them, the militia too had noticed the advancing riders and were abandoning their attack and streaming back out of Muret toward their camp in the swamp. Even at that distance, John heard a ragged cheer from de Montfort's knights in the citadel.

* * *

"That rabble is useless for anything other than slaughtering helpless wounded men." Count Raymond paced angrily back and forth outside the royal tent in the hilltop camp as the sun lowered toward the western horizon. "They didn't even attempt to defend or set fire to the bridge. They allowed de Montfort to walk into Muret unopposed."

"We do not need them." King Pedro lounged on a gilded throne beneath the awning of his gloriously decorated tent. He held a silver goblet filled with wine in his right hand. "My knights will take care of that upstart de Montfort." Pedro waved his hand dismissively and wine spilled from the goblet onto the ground.

John and Isabella stood to one side, watching the scene and wondering why they were there. Pedro had summoned them to his tent and then ignored them. It wasn't the first time this had happened. Often they had to stand around while Pedro finished business, listened to a troubadour's song or flirted with one of the ladies-in-waiting who always seemed to be hovering nearby.

Isabella was right. Pedro *had* changed since John had first met him on the battlefield of Las Navas de Tolosa. His arrogance had grown to the point where he was unwilling to listen to advice from anyone. Also, he seemed increasingly interested only in enjoying himself, drinking, arranging assignations with the women who continually fawned over him, and throwing lavish parties that went on until dawn. John felt a flash of sympathy for Raymond, who frequently made practical suggestions that were dismissed out-of-hand by the Aragonese king. He tried to make another one now.

"Of course you are right, your Majesty. Your knights, and mine, will make short work of de Montfort, but there may be a way we can use the despicable behaviour of the rabble to our advantage, to make our task even easier."

"How so?" Pedro asked disinterestedly.

"Because the bridge over the Garonne was not destroyed, de Montfort has moved his entire force into Muret. I estimate he must have close to eight hundred knights and several hundred foot soldiers in there. It must be uncomfortably crowded within those walls."

"So?" Pedro spilled some more wine and a page hurried to refill his goblet. "Why should I care about de Montfort's comfort? His head will be on a pole beside my tent soon enough." Pedro laughed and those nearby dutifully followed his lead.

"You should care not one whit, Your Majesty," Raymond agreed patiently. John could see the Count was working hard to defer to the King's frivolous mood. "But consider, if *we* now destroy the bridge over the Garonne, and the smaller one over the Louge, de Montfort will be trapped. He and his army will be bottled up with food for no more than a day or two in a partly ruined town that will become a disease-ridden cesspit within a week. He can expect no reinforcements, so we can sit in comfort and watch his army disintegrate until it is too weak to resist. We need not risk the life of even a single knight."

"My dear Count," Pedro said, his voice soft and his eyebrows rising in an expression of extreme condescension. "You have been fighting dirty little battles against de Montfort and his like for too long. You do not understand real war. Where is the honour in what you suggest?"

John was close enough to see Raymond's jaw muscles clench as he struggled to control his temper, but he remained silent and allowed Pedro to continue.

"There *must* be danger. I and my knights must face the possibility of death for there to be any glory. I did not bring my army here to watch de Montfort rot in Muret. I came to add laurels to my name and fame to my royal house and to Aragon. You, my dear Count, may sit in comfort and safety and watch, but come tomorrow morning, when de Montfort sallies forth from the town, I shall don the armour of an ordinary knight and go and destroy him in an honourable and noble way."

For a moment, John thought Raymond was going to rage at the king, but he managed to restrain himself. "Very well, Your Majesty," he grumbled before turning on his heel and stalking off. Pedro didn't even seem to notice Raymond's departure; he simply signalled for more wine. John exchanged a puzzled look with Isabella.

Eventually, Pedro looked up from the suggestive banter he was conducting with a dark-eyed lady-in-waiting and noticed the pair. "Ah, my niece and her young friend," he said, beckoning them closer. "Are you excited about the battle tomorrow?"

"Yes, Your Majesty," John answered dutifully. Isabella remained silent.

"Splendid. Splendid. That is as it should be. You"—Pedro waved his goblet towards John—"if you are to marry my niece, you must acquire honour. You must prove yourself in battle. Tomorrow you will fight by my side. You will show the world that you are worthy to join my noble house."

John's mind was reeling. He had heard everything Pedro had said, but the words had reached him as if through a haze after the mention of marrying Isabella. He glanced at his companion and saw that she was as bemused as he was.

"M...marry, Your Majesty?" he stammered.

"You do not wish to marry my niece?" Pedro was instantly stern. "I do not take insults to myself or my family lightly."

"No. No. I mean, yes." John felt his face flush with embarrassment.

Pedro guffawed loudly and slapped his thigh, spilling more wine. "I have seen how you look at her," he said with a wide grin, "and how she looks at you. Normally, I would not permit a member of my family to marry such a low commoner as yourself, but I am feeling generous today and"—he leaned conspiratorially close to John—"she is only a niece. What do you say?"

"Thank you, Your Majesty," John managed to blurt out. He glanced over at Isabella and was disturbed to see that a dark frown now wrinkled her brow.

"Excellent!" Pedro exclaimed. "The details, dates, dowry and so forth can wait until I have disposed of de Montfort. Certainly it will be a splendid occasion—a feast about which the troubadours will sing for a generation. But"—Pedro looked John up and down, mild distaste lowering his brows—"if you are to be a member of my royal family, certain standards must be maintained." He snapped his fingers. A page scuttled forward and handed the king a leather pouch. Pedro took it, weighed it thoughtfully in his hand and tossed it at John, who almost dropped it. "Keep that bag safe," Pedro said. "There is sufficient gold in there for you to live at the standard befitting your position. I suggest you use the first of it at the royal armoury so that your appearance does not disgrace the court in the battle."

"Battle, Your Highness?" John asked.

"Good God, will I have a dolt for a nephew? Tomorrow, Isabella will stay safe in the camp while you and I go out and seek glory on the field of battle. You must prove yourself in war and for that you must look the part. The armourer will see to it that you do.

"After de Montfort is dead and the celebrations over, you shall accompany me to Barcelona where I shall arrange a suitably magnificent wedding. More wine." Pedro's attention left John as abruptly as it had found him. He began stroking the lady-in-waiting's hair and whispering in her ear.

"Thank you, Your Majesty," John mumbled as he retreated. Isabella fell in beside him and the pair walked around the tent.

"What did you mean by that?" Isabella's voice was dangerously quiet.

John stopped and faced her. "Mean by what?" he asked nervously.

"Agreeing with my uncle that you would marry me, as if I were a side of lamb being bought and sold in the market. If you think I will calmly do as you and Pedro bid when I am not even consulted, you are both very much mistaken."

"What was I supposed to do?" John asked helplessly. "He's a king. I was as shocked at what he said as you were."

"So now you're shocked by the idea of marrying me?"

"Of course not!" John said hurriedly. "I didn't have time to think! But kings can order people to do whatever they wish."

"That's the whole problem. You don't think."

John could see tears welling in Isabella's eyes. "Look," he said, stepping closer. "After the battle tomorrow, we'll decide what to do. We could run away," he finished weakly.

"Tomorrow," Isabella shouted, hitting John hard on the chest, "you'll be in the thick of it with my stupid, arrogant uncle. There won't be an 'after the battle'. You'll be killed."

Isabella's tears were flowing freely now. John reached out and held her close. She buried her face in his shoulder and John could feel warm tears flowing down his neck. "It's all right," he said, although he didn't feel it was. "I'll be careful."

Isabella pushed herself away from John and wiped her eyes. "Careful? How can you be careful in a battle? You're not even a soldier."

John felt a twinge of annoyance. He had a glorious sword and Adso had taught him a good deal about fighting. He considered himself a soldier, but he decided it was best not to say that at the moment. "We could run away tonight," he suggested.

Isabella shook her head. "That won't work. Pedro hates not to have his way. After de Montfort is defeated, he will search for us and, once he finds us, even if he doesn't throw you in a dungeon, he will never allow us to marry."

John was about to argue that they would indeed be able to escape, when he realized what Isabella had said. "I thought you didn't want to get married," he said.

"Idiot." Isabella hit John on the chest again. "You don't listen. I never said I didn't want to marry. What annoyed me was Pedro's and your stupid arrogance in assuming that I don't have any say."

Rebirth

"That's not fair," John objected. "Pedro's arrogant—he's a king, after all—but I'm not. What could I do, argue with him? That would only have made him angry, and who knows what he would have done then."

"You're right, I'm sorry." Isabella visibly relaxed and stepped back from John. "We're lucky. Neither of us grew up with close families to organize our lives and betroth us to someone we'd never met when we were seven years old. We've been free to make choices that most people can't. I suppose what really annoys me is my uncle Pedro suddenly appearing and assuming that he can organize my life without even asking me."

Isabella looked up at John and smiled. "I *do* want to marry you, but not the way Pedro wishes." She hurried on before John could get over his stunned feeling of happiness and say anything. "I don't want Pedro to smugly hand me over to you as a possession, or to have a slimy cleric like Foulques standing by mouthing how pleased his corrupt church is that I am now duty bound to produce as many babies as possible to swell the ranks of the faithful."

"I want to marry you as well," John said, taking advantage of the pause in Isabella's speech. He was by no means certain what she meant by marriage if not the traditional kind.

Isabella's smile broadened and she leaned forward and kissed him. "I'm glad," she said. "but we've been through a lot together and we've done it as equals. I won't let that change just because Pedro or the Church says it should. I want a Good Christian marriage."

For a moment John was speechless. "But Beatrice told me once that the Good Christians don't believe in marriage. It's of this world and therefore the work of the devil. She also said that children were bad because they trapped another soul in this evil world." He scratched his head. He was happy that they were talking of marriage—he wanted nothing more than to spend his life with Isabella—but he was worried about the course the conversation was taking. He didn't want Pedro's wedding any more than Isabella did—they *were* equals, he was certain of that. On the other hand, he wanted to have children one day, a son or daughter to teach all the things he had learned and would still learn.

"The Good Christians believe that when Christ talked of marriage He meant a spiritual union of two souls," Isabella explained seriously. "Yes, they do see children as a way of trapping souls in the prison of this world, but they also recognize that the only way for a soul to be saved and to spend eternity in Paradise is for it to be trapped in a human body and be released through the *consolamentum*. Children are a necessary evil."

John wasn't sure he wanted to regard any children he might have as necessary evils, but he was glad Isabella seemed open to the idea. "So how do we get married as Good Christians?"

"We don't," Isabella said with a mischievous smile. "We already are."

"We are?" John asked.

"Our souls have been joined since we first laid eyes on each other. I've known it since then. It just took you longer to realize it." Isabella laughed and embraced John. "We don't need Pedro or anyone else."

John felt unreasonable happy as he returned Isabella's embrace. Gradually, however, the dark cloud of the coming battle intruded. "What about tomorrow?"

Isabella released John. Her worried frown was back. "Perhaps you're right and we should run away tonight," she said. "Maybe de Montfort will win tomorrow."

"You can't seriously want that." John said. "I know Pedro's unbearably confident, but he has reason to be. His army's huge. It'll take a miracle for any outcome tomorrow other than total defeat for the crusade. Despite our personal difficulties, that's the outcome we want. This land has suffered enough."

"I suppose you must fight tomorrow," Isabella said miserably. "I cannot see any way around it."

"And then we will run away," John added. "We will beg to return separately to Barcelona. Perhaps we can use my search for books as an excuse. Once Pedro is safely across the mountains with his army, we will head north. We have enough coin to travel so far that Pedro will never find us." He hefted the bag the King had given him. It clinked heavily.

Isabella reached over and took the bag. She undid the ties at the neck and looked in. She tilted the bag and several gold coins fell into her palm. "This will take us to the edge of the earth," she said.

"Then you had better keep it safe. It's probably best not to go into battle with a bag of gold on one's belt."

"It's a lot of coin," Isabella said thoughtfully. "Should we take it?"

"It was freely given and, as Pedro said, we *are* family. Besides, what seems like a lot of coin to you and me is little to a king."

"I suppose you're right," Isabella said. She handed John three of the coins and retied the bag. "I'll keep it safe, but you will need some to visit the armourer."

"Thank you. I'll get a good thick helmet to protect my head. Now, I think it's time that—" John was distracted by a lone figure approaching out of the gathering gloom. The man was tall and gangly and dressed in a monk's habit.

"Peter!" John exclaimed. "What are you doing here?"

Last Chance

Muret
September 11, 1213

The figures emerging from behind the tent were just two strangers until one of them spoke.

"Peter," a familiar voice said. "What are you doing here?"

Peter struggled to focus his gaze. With the exception of a few hours in the back of a farmer's cart, he had been walking for a day and night. He had drunk from village wells and been given a piece of bread by an old woman, but he was weak, tired and hungry. "John?" he asked.

"Yes, it's me—and Isabella. What are you doing here in the middle of King Pedro's camp? I thought you would be with de Montfort and Aumery."

Peter's mind was working very slowly. "I'm in King Pedro's camp?"

"You are," John replied. "That's his tent behind us. How you got past the guards I don't know, though I suppose you don't look like much of a threat. Why are you here?"

"To stop the war. I must speak to the king." Peter struggled to get the words out. He had begun with clear idea but exhaustion clouded his brain.

"How are *you* going to stop the war?" Isabella asked, taking Peter's arm. "Do you have a message from de Montfort?"

"I have a message from God. Where is the king?" Peter's hands were shaking and his eyes darted back and forth nervously, but he was determined.

"The king is busy," Isabella said gently. "You look worn out. Come and sit with us and rest. We'll get some bread, cheese and wine."

"I must speak with the king," Peter shouted, shrugging off Isabella's grasp. "Where is King Pedro? I have a message from God."

Peter started advanced toward the king's tent, but stopped short when John stepped in front of him. "Isabella's right," John said. "This isn't a good idea. Come and rest and we can decide what's best to do."

"No!" Peter's voice was almost a scream. He *had to* see the king. His voice had demanded it. "God does not wish me to rest. I must speak with the king.

Do not stand in my way." He shoved John hard in the chest, pushing him to one side.

Ignoring John—who stood with his jaw hanging open in shock—Peter headed for the royal tent. Peire and another heavily armed guard appeared to bar his way.

"Let me by," Peter yelled. "I would have words with the king."

"I don't think so," Peire replied.

Peter tried to push past, but the two men held him easily. "King Pedro. King Pedro," he bellowed, "God would have words with you."

Peire's firm expression changed at the mention of God. He glanced questioningly over at John, who shrugged helplessly.

"Don't hurt him," Isabella asked, coming up to stand beside Peter. She put a hand on the monk's shoulder, but he ignored her and continued his struggling and shouting. John stepped forward, intending to help calm Peter, but before he could do anything, the tent flap was thrown open and King Pedro, his favourite lady-in-waiting hanging off his arm and flanked by more guards, appeared.

"Who calls the king in God's name?" he asked, smiling as if he thought the whole scene was a great joke organized for his entertainment.

"I do," Peter said.

"And who might you be?" Pedro inquired. "I see you have already met my niece and her young man. What do you want with me?"

Peter had given no thought to what he would actually say when he got to the king, but the words flowed freely now. "I come to order you to desist from this folly. Christian should not kill Christian. Go to de Montfort and decide how best you may aid this Holy Crusade in banishing foul heresy from this land. God will dispense worldly powers as He sees fit."

"Wretch." Pedro's smile vanished as he spat the word out. He pointed a bejewelled hand at Peter. "You, a filthy, itinerant monk, presume to *order* me, the greatest king in Christendom? I will have your head, as I shall that of de Montfort, on the morrow."

"Uncle, he is a man of God." Isabella stepped toward Pedro. "He has safe-conduct."

"Monks who travel with armies and who do the bidding of upstarts such as de Montfort need and deserve no safe-conduct." Pedro let his gaze rest on Isabella. His expression softened. "But you are right, my dear. He *is* a man of God, however misguided he may be in his allegiance."

"My allegiance is to God," Peter interrupted. "As yours should be."

Pedro flashed his captive a withering glare. "You are lucky that my niece speaks on your behalf, and that I am in a generous mood. You are free to go."

Rebirth

Pedro nodded to Peire and the other guard, who stepped away from Peter. "I suggest that you go and pray, but do not waste your prayers on de Montfort. He has but a few hours before he stands to be judged before Christ."

"Now, young John." Pedro's attention abruptly turned away from Peter, his manner suddenly relaxed and charming. "We shall go and drink some wine and discuss how we shall make you a hero suitable for my niece. Isabella, you may retire to your tent."

Pedro took John's arm, and with him on one side and the simpering lady-in-waiting on the other, turned back to the tent. John stole a glance over his shoulder to where Isabella and Peter stood, dismissed.

"Sorry, lady," Peire mumbled as he and his companion retreated to the tent door.

Peter stared glumly after the royal group. The conviction that he had to see King Pedro and that his task was to prevent war had grown on his long walk from Fanjeaux. He had been certain that God would put words in his mouth that would convince the king, but it had not happened. God had deserted him and he had been humiliated. Why then had his voices told him to seek out the King?

"Come," Isabella said, interrupting his thoughts. "I'll get you something to eat and drink."

"No." Peter wanted no comfort. He didn't deserve any after his failure. He had failed at everything: his pitiful attempt to stop the coming battle, his quest to find the Holy Grail, his struggle to become powerful enough not to fear Oddo and—he looked at Isabella—he had even failed to win this beautiful woman all those years ago in Toulouse. "I'm a failure," he confessed, his shoulders sagging.

"No, you're not," Isabella said, thinking that he was referring to his encounter with Pedro. "My uncle is a headstrong man who has become overly arrogant since Las Navas de Tolosa. No one can change his mind once it is made up."

"Not even God?" Peter asked.

"It seems not," Isabella said. "Or else God does not wish his mind changed."

"Perhaps," Peter acknowledged. He took a deep breath. It calmed him. It was good to talk to Isabella. Maybe she would understand what was tormenting him. "But that is not all I meant," he continued. "I have failed at everything I have attempted all through my life. I thought the Church would give me power and confidence, but I was wrong. The Church cannot give us what God does not wish us to have." He hesitated, wondering how much to tell Isabella. Her smile encouraged him.

"My journey to the east was a quest," he began hesitantly. "I went at the behest of Aumery to seek out the Cathar Treasure."

"The Cathar Treasure?" Isabella asked. "What is that?"

"Aumery believes it is the Holy Grail. That it was in the land of the heretic Bogomils and that we are destined to find it and use it to bring on the End of Days. That is why I went to Plovdiv." A frown crossed Peter's face. "Or was it Trimondium? Or Philippoupolis?" Peter was finding it increasingly hard to keep his thoughts in order. He was utterly drained and couldn't remember why he was trying to tell Isabella this story. His gaze drifted aimlessly away from Isabella and he fell silent.

Isabella knew of Trimondium/Plovdiv from the map that Peter had given John, but not much of what Peter was saying made sense. "Did you find the Holy Grail?" she encouraged, wondering how this fitted in with the story Adso had told about the cup in the cave at Rhedae.

Peter ignored her question and began speaking in a monotone, as if no one were listening. "Paulus died. My voices warned me, but I did not understand. I killed Diogenese, the poor fool, because my voices told me to. Was it the Devil speaking? The shipwreck on the beach...Francesco...No," Peter clenched his fists in anger. "He threw the Grail away." He relaxed again. "Then the Seraph came." He smiled off into the distance and stopped talking.

Isabella watched her old friend struggle to make sense of his jumbled thoughts. She had no idea who these people were, although she vaguely remembered John saying something about a Francesco when he had told her about Peter's journey to the east. The fluctuating emotions flitting across Peter's face were disturbing, but she couldn't think of anything to say, so she waited for him to continue.

"I thought St. Andrew guarded the Grail beneath a tree." Peter shuddered and went on. "But I was wrong, misguided, foolish. Francesco is right—give up all and live like Christ in the wilderness. Isn't he?"

Peter's stare swung back to Isabella. His look was utterly desolate, his eyes so helpless and pleading that Isabella was brought close to tears. "I don't know," she said, a choke in her voice.

"Of course not." Anger flashed in Peter's eyes. His stare was cold and frightening, and Isabella stepped back at the sudden change in his expression. "You don't know. You're just like all the rest. I was wrong to ever think that I loved you. I'm alone. But I don't understand. Have I been listening to the Devil? Have I been seduced by honeyed words? Penance must be mine, but what?"

Peter pushed violently past Isabella, almost knocking her to the ground, and staggered away. She regained her balance and stared after the bedraggled figure stumbling into the darkness. She was worried about Peter's confused speech, shocked at his mercurial change in mood and stunned at his confession of love. Was he insane? Had the vision of death in the square at Toulouse seven years earlier been but the beginning?

Isabella thought of chasing him, but what good would it do, even if she did manage to catch up? Peter's mind followed its own path and she doubted if anything she could say would change that. Besides, she had other things on her mind.

Isabella sighed and looked back at her uncle's tent. The sound of music and laughter spilled out of the doorway with the flickering light of the torches. Even had they planned on escaping that night, it would no longer have been possible. Pedro's revels usually lasted all night and John's chances of slipping away, now that Pedro seemed to have taken an interest in him, were slim. She turned and walked slowly back to her tent.

* * *

No one paid any attention to the solitary monk wandering through the camp, and Peter ignored the soldiers eating, drinking, singing and shouting around him. Soon he was away from the tents, alone in the dark on a low ridge. To his right he could see the fires of de Montfort's army crammed within the walls of Muret and the sprawling camp of the Toulouse militia outside. He had no desire to go to Muret. He simply wanted to be alone with his confused thoughts.

Peter wandered aimlessly for several hours, sometimes on higher, dry ground, sometimes up to his knees in marshy swamp. Once, he found himself beside the Garonne River, its dark surface gleaming like tarnished silver in the almost full moon that appeared intermittently through the ragged clouds.

At one point, Peter found himself in a large swamp. It seemed to go on forever and, whichever way he turned, the cold water engulfed him, and the black mud, like some malignant monster beneath the earth, threatened to suck him down. Every step was a nightmare as he laboured to heave one leg out of the clinging mire only to have the other sink even deeper. He had almost resigned himself to a slow, miserable death in the clinging mud when the ground firmed beneath him and he struggled onto dry land—cold, wet, shivering, scared and utterly worn out.

Barely aware of what he was doing, Peter collapsed against a large rock. Sharp edges scraped his back, but he barely noticed. What was happening to him? Why he was here? What did his voices mean? He was so tired he could barely frame the questions, but the idea that he was descending into madness, being toyed with by the Devil, was growing in his mind. But how could he know for sure? His voices had guided him on his quest, admittedly enigmatically at times, and yet his quest had been a failure. But had it? It had led him to the gentle Francesco, whose simple life with its vows of poverty and goodness was attractive. Might that meeting have been the real goal?

Peter's voices had also led him to kill Diogenes, but was killing a pagan a sin? His visions had shown him the glowing Seraph at Durres and the bleeding Christ on the cross at Fanjeaux. Those must be images from God, mustn't they? Then there was the stigmata, the marks of Christ's suffering appearing on his own body. Surely the Devil couldn't cause that. Or was it all some hideous trick, a game played by the devils who possessed him?

Peter closed his eyes and clasped his hands before him. "Help me understand," he prayed. "Tell me what I must do. Help me know how I am to serve you." Peter was distracted by a dry fluttering sound near his right ear. Thinking it was an insect of some sort, he swatted with his hand. A sharp pain drove through his palm.

Crying out, Peter opened his eyes. The air around his head was filled with a swarm of small creatures. Each was about the size of his hand and all had round, scaly bodies, long tails and evil talons on the ends of two hawk-like legs. Two glowing red eyes burned out of each squat face and a needle-sharp nose protruded above fleshy, slavering lips. The demons hovered and dove through the air by beating pairs of black, leathery wings. As Peter stared in growing fear, one of the creatures dove swiftly toward him and plunged its sharp nose into his shoulder. It was like being stabbed with a long, red-hot needle. Peter screamed, twisted away and beat at the horror. It flapped off, but was instantly replaced by another that stabbed him in the side.

Peter leapt to his feet, beating the air around him frantically. It did no good. For each monster he knocked away, another attacked. His wounds didn't bleed, and they healed over instantly, but the pain was excruciating. Peter flailed wildly and wept at the torture. Eventually, he fell to the ground and curled into a ball, huddled miserably at the foot of the rock.

After what seemed like a lifetime, the pain stopped and the sound of the leathery wings faded, only to be replaced by a raucous cawing. Peter forced himself to uncurl and open his eyes. A huge bird, larger than any eagle he had ever seen, perched on the rock above him, staring down with malevolent golden eyes. Its wings were folded behind it and it clasped the rock with long, curved claws. Where a feathered tail should have been, the body of a snake writhed and thrashed angrily.

Before Peter could grasp what was happening, the bird lowered its wickedly curved beak and tore a strip of flesh from Peter's arm. The pain was almost unbearable, yet the bloody wound healed over before his

Rebirth

astonished eyes. Again and again the head dropped and the beak tore at Peter's body. Each time the pain was near intolerable, and each time the wound healed magically. Peter tried to move but he was paralyzed; he could only scream in agony and fear. Eventually, with a loud screech, the monster spread its broad wings and lifted into the night sky.

Before he had time to enjoy the relief, Peter was assaulted by a new torment. All around him, large slime-covered worms broke through the ground. They slithered toward him and, using rows of razor-sharp teeth, bore into his body. Peter could feel the beasts moving within him and see the throbbing lumps as they moved beneath his skin. His whole being was a mass of insufferable agony. He screwed his eyes shut and beat himself with his fists.

A blinding flash of white light startled Peter and revealed an old, skinny man. He wore a grey beard to his waist and was dressed in a tattered monastic habit. He held a scroll in his right hand, and above his prominent cheekbones, watery blue eyes stared compassionately at Peter. "I shall not be in thy power," the man said in a sepulchral voice.

"Saint Anthony," Peter breathed, recognizing the saint who had lived his life in the desert and suffered the torments and temptations of the Devil. His faith had been all that had sustained him in his trials. Peter took a deep breath and repeated three times, "My life belongs to God. You have no power over me." Almost instantly, the worms disappeared and the pain vanished. With a sigh of relief, Peter sagged back against the rock and offered up a prayer of thanks for his deliverance.

What had his torments meant, he wondered. Were they a sign that his voices were from the Devil or not?

"Your faith is strong." Peter's eyes snapped open to see a tall, elegant man dressed in a cardinal's robes standing before him. His voice was soft and wonderfully soothing.

"Thank you, Father," Peter said. "Saint Anthony came to me and gave me strength."

"Ah, Saint Anthony," the cardinal said with a smile. "He is strong. But you are as well, Peter. You resisted demons and worms that would have devoured lesser men. You deserve a reward."

Peter frowned. Something was wrong. Before his tired mind could work out what, the cardinal reached into his robes and pulled out a purse. He undid the string and tipped the small sack, releasing a flood of gold and silver coins that glinted in the moonlight as they poured over Peter's legs.

"Here is your reward, Peter," the cardinal said, his voice softly compelling. "Think of the good, of the poor you could help with these riches. And of the power." The shimmering flow continued from the pouch, almost burying Peter's legs. "With wealth such as this, you could rise rapidly in the Church. Perhaps you could even aspire to the Papacy itself. Think what you could do—a second Peter to rise to be Bishop of Rome! Perhaps a sign that the End of Days has arrived."

Peter thrust his hands into the growing pile of coins. They felt cold. There was the wealth of kings here. What could he not do with this? A doubt shadowed Peter's mind. "How did you know my name and what had tormented me?" he asked.

"I know many things," the cardinal said softly.

"What is your name?"

The cardinal's smile broadened. "I have many names."

"Tell me some," Peter ordered.

The smile faded and a nervous expression crossed the man's face. "I have been known in many times and places as Mechembuchus, Belial, Azazel, Angra Mainyu." The smile returned. "What would you choose to call me?"

"And Aaron shall cast lots over the two goats, one lot for the Lord and the other lot for Azazel," Peter quoted from the book of Leviticus. "You are the Wicked One, the Lord of the Flies, Beelzebub, Lucifer, Satan. Be gone!"

Instantly, the gold and silver vanished, but the cardinal remained where he was. A look of pure hatred flashed over his features, making Peter cringe, but it was immediately replaced by the seductive smile. Slowly the smile widened and the features softened. The cardinal's robes fell away to reveal a lavish green velvet dress, studded with sparkling gems. The most beautiful woman Peter had ever seen stood before him, bedecked in the opulent clothes and the jewelry of a princess. "Hello, Peter," the woman said in a familiar voice that made Peter feel weak and short of breath. "It's good to see you again."

"Isabella," Peter gasped. He was having difficulty drawing enough air into his lungs. "Is it really you?"

"Of course it is," the vision breathed quietly, the dark eyes destroying Peter's will and melting his heart. "I've always loved you and I've come back to you now. I see the error of my ways and I want to find God. Will you forgive me and teach me?"

The voice washed over Peter. It seeped through his skin and knotted his insides. He felt utterly helpless, completely in thrall of this wonderful figure before him. Could it be possible? Did Isabella really love him? Had she come back to spend the rest of her life, eternity, with him?

Isabella held out a perfectly formed, pure white hand. "Come with me, Peter. You can be mine—forever."

Rebirth

Peter reached up until his fingers almost touched the outstretched hand. Forever. There was nothing he wanted more. He gazed rapturously up at the smile that promised so much, but something was wrong. This wasn't the smile of love; it was the smile of a predator about to devour its prey. "Nothing human lasts forever," Peter breathed.

The smile faded and the glowing skin of Isabella's face rotted and fell away, just as it had done years ago in his vision on the steps of the Chateau Narbonnaise in Toulouse. An embittered scream issued from the twisted, worm-laden jaws and the figure before Peter collapsed into a cloud of dust that disappeared in the night breeze.

"No," Peter whimpered as his limp hand fell back on his lap. "Isabella," he moaned, but it was no use. She was gone. Peter knelt beside the rock in the darkness, clasped his hands and prayed as he had never prayed before. He had survived the torments of demons and resisted the lure of worldly riches and power, but he missed Isabella dreadfully. Even knowing that she had been a phantasm, a temptation of the Devil sent to lure his immortal soul into eternal damnation, he wanted her back.

With eyes closed to hold back his tears, he prayed to God, Christ, Mary and every saint he knew to send him release from his suffering. He prayed so hard he felt neither discomfort nor cold, and he prayed so long that he didn't notice the dawn lighten the sky to the east or the armies array themselves for battle around him.

Preparations

Muret
September 12, 1213

John woke up slowly as the increasing light and heat become uncomfortable. His head hurt, his stomach was turning somersaults and his mouth felt as if he had been dining on dry sand. Gradually, memory returned. Pedro had ushered him into the tent and seated him on cushions beside his throne. He had plied John with wine and embarrassed him when John felt he'd had enough and ceased refilling his goblet.

"Drink," Pedro had ordered. "If you wish to wed my niece and join my royal household, you must be able to drink and carouse as well as fight."

John had refrained from pointing out that while he would like nothing more than to wed Isabella, he had no desire to join Pedro's court and grow old in Barcelona. He'd stayed silent and drank when ordered to.

Pedro had been in good spirits, laughing uproariously at the jesters, sharing shouted boasts about what he was going to do in the coming battle with his knights, and whispering to his lady friend. From time to time, he would make asides to John, about how beautiful Isabella was, how like her mother she was and how grateful he was that John had been instrumental in killing del Huesca at Las Navas de Tolosa. John nodded companionably and only spoke when asked a direct question.

At one point, Pedro had asked to see John's sword and almost killed a page swinging it wildly around. Fortunately, he had returned it before any damage was done.

"A fine blade," Pedro said, his words beginning to slur with an excess of wine. "A strong axe or mace blow will break it—nevertheless, I'll wager it will put a few of de Montfort's mercenaries to sleep tomorrow."

John had tried to slip away to a number of times, but Pedro had always caught him, ordered him back to his cushioned seat, and poured more wine into his goblet. Sometime in the small hours of the morning, when the revelry still showed no sign of slacking, John had slipped into deep, dreamless sleep, oblivious to the noise around him.

Now he was awake, but he felt awful. Keeping his eyes screwed almost shut, John looked around. Most of the revellers were like him, sprawled out on cushions or the ground, either looking around or still snoring loudly. A group of musicians lay huddled in a corner, embracing their instruments. A large black hunting dog sprawled by the entrance gnawing on an enormous ham bone, and several smaller beasts rummaged among the cushions and bodies searching for discarded scraps. There was no sign of Pedro.

Painfully slowly, John dragged himself to his feet. He stood for a long moment with his eyes closed, until the pounding behind his eyes eased a little. He cursed Pedro and his party and stumbled toward the tent door. He would find Isabella, but first he would drink the large clay water jar outside the tent door dry.

The brightness of the morning sun sent needles of pain through John's skull, but the cold water felt wonderful as he poured it over his head and washed the sour taste out of his mouth and throat. He felt almost human enough to seek out Isabella when two knights in battle dress appeared round the side of the tent.

"Where's the king?" the first, a huge man whose belly strained against the chain mail that covered his stomach, demanded.

"I don't know," John replied.

"Well, get in there and find him," the man ordered, jerking his thumb at the tent, "de Montfort's on the move."

"What?" John asked stupidly.

"Good God, we've found an idiot," the soldier said. "De Montfort's leaving Muret. The battle's about to begin." The big man pushed past John and strode into the tent. A dog yelped as it was kicked out of his way.

De Montfort was coming out to give battle. In a few hours the crusade would be over. Excitement and elation overwhelmed John's physical misery. He rushed round the tent and peered out over the open ground to Muret, almost two miles away. Sure enough, a line of mounted men, their polished helmets and chain mail glinting in the morning sun and their bright banners flapping in the breeze, was winding its way around the northern extension of the town walls and crossing the bridge over the Louge. On the nearby plain, they were being organized into three compact units. John could see the large falcon banner waving above the second unit.

"So it's true then." John turned to see Adso staring toward Muret. His friend was already dressed in his old, battered chain mail tunic and wore a dented round helmet that exhibited patches of rust. He carried a long sword, much heavier than Auramazdah, and had his favourite dagger tucked into

Rebirth

his leather belt. He didn't look very knightly, but John knew from the hours they had spent practising together what an efficient fighter he was.

Behind Adso the camp was rapidly coming to life as knights emerged from tents, shouting for their horses and equipment, and pages swarmed around them frantically adjusting their armour and passing them helmets, grieves and weapons. John could see that the knights closest to him wore smiles of greedy anticipation.

"I must find Isabella," John said. He began to head back into the camp, but almost immediately cannoned into a group of men coming round the side of the king's tent. They were led by Pedro, who was half dressed in a suit of black chain mail. He was flanked by Peire and another guard, and a group of young pages bustled around him, strapping on his sword and adjusting his equipment. One approached carrying the magnificent surcoat bearing the coat of arms of the King of Aragon. Pedro waved him away.

"Today," the king said, "I fight beside my men as an ordinary knight. Bring me my plain helmet."

"A king should be recognized by his men." Count Raymond had appeared from around the tent. "They must have a rallying point should they be hard pressed."

"You always look at the worst," Pedro scoffed. "The only hard pressing will be on them." He pointed at de Montfort's army, still forming up on the plain. "Look how puny they are. This will only be a light sport to give us an appetite for breakfast. I dress as an ordinary knight so that I may fight as one and so gain more honour. I do not wish the enemy to run away when they see King Pedro of Aragon, the most powerful king in Christendom, approach." The knights around Pedro laughed dutifully.

"Very well, Your Majesty," Raymond acknowledged. John could hear the stress in the count's voice as he fought to control his temper. "What is to be the order of battle? Who shall have the places of honour and how shall we respond to de Montfort's movements? Shall I send orders for the militia to harass de Montfort's men as they prepare and advance? Where would you wish my knights and me to fight?"

"Questions, questions, questions! I do not wish the rabble from Toulouse to participate. This will be a matter of honour, not a street brawl. My knights shall have the places of honour and dispose themselves as they see fit. You and your knights shall hold back as the rearguard."

"Sire?" Raymond's eyes widened in shock. "Rearguard? That is my enemy down there. This is my land we fight on. I demand a position of honour."

"No, my dear Count," Pedro said with a smile, "you demand nothing. This is my land. You merely hold it in fief. I am tired of your continual carping. The glory of today shall be mine and you shall follow behind."

John could scarcely believe the insult Pedro had just delivered. Technically, the king was right. In the complex web of loyalties that enmeshed them all, Raymond did owe allegiance to king Pedro, but Raymond was a powerful lord in his own right, the equal of the French king in Paris, and Pedro had shown little interest in his Languedoc lands until he had felt insulted by de Montfort and Pope Innocent.

In battle, a lord's position in the front line denoted his relative importance. Traditionally, the right of the line was the most honorable, followed by the left and then the centre, but there were many subtleties around who stood beside whom and how close one stood to the king. The rearguard was the least worthy or honourable position, almost a mortal insult.

For a moment, the two men glared at each other. All around them, soldiers stood immobile, watching. The guards' hands moved to their sword hilts. If Raymond struck Pedro, he would be dead in an instant. Abruptly, Raymond turned on his heel and stalked off. Everyone let out a collective sigh of relief.

"Now, my young friend." Pedro turned to John, apparently oblivious to the recent tension. "Let us get you arrayed for battle so that you can share in the glory and do my niece proud. Bring your friend," Pedro indicated Adso, who had been hovering in the background. "He can be your companion, just as Alexander the Great fought with his companions by his side."

For a moment, as Pedro regarded him silently, John hesitated. What choice did he have? He wanted to go and find Isabella, but how could he deny Pedro's request? He was still struggling to find a way out when Adso stepped forward.

"Thank you, Your Majesty," he said, bowing low. "It is an 'onour indeed to be recognized by a king as great as you. I shall protect the young lord's back as 'e wins immortal 'onour defeating your enemies."

"Excellent," Pedro laughed. "Now come, we must prepare. See, de Montfort hurries to his destruction." Everyone turned to look over the plain below. De Montfort was indeed hurrying. Already the bulk of his army had exited Muret and knights on horseback were riding about busily organizing the troops. Pedro moved off and his guards swept John and Adso along in his wake.

* * *

"What were you doing, fawning to King Pedro like that?" John said angrily. "I don't want to go to battle. I want to find Isabella and get out of this mess."

Rebirth

The pair were in a large tent filled with piles of assorted equipment. The armourer hurried about, attending to the last-minute needs of various lords. When John and Adso approached, he had accepted a gold coin and gestured for the pair to help themselves. Much of the equipment was of Moorish design, the spoils of the battle of Las Navas de Tolosa, John supposed. The most important of Pedro and Raymond's knights owned their own armour, but sometimes the lesser knights required some piece of equipment to replace a loss or a damaged item and it was easier, faster and cheaper to get one from here than to have the armourer make something new. Of course, all the fine armour and weapons had been taken long ago or been claimed as spoils by individual knights, but there was still much to choose from. Several of the poorer knights were rummaging around, looking for specifics. The large guard was standing by the door, watching John and Adso suspiciously.

"You still 'aven't learned. 'ave you?" Adso replied. "You can't argue with kings. It only annoys them and an 'appy king is always better than an un'appy one. You should be thanking me."

"I suppose," John acknowledged grudgingly. He held up a chain mail shirt and examined it. It looked in fair condition, although there was a hole in one side and a tear on the left shoulder with some rust, or very old bloodstains, around it. "But I don't want to fight in this battle and I'm worried about Isabella."

"Isabella's safe back in camp. We'll get this battle done, give de Montfort 'is due and then you two lovebirds can go and live your quiet life wherever you want."

"I hope so," John said, pulling the chain mail over his head. It felt cold and heavy, but fit remarkably well over his padded, sweat-stained tunic. He pulled the coif over his head.

"'Ere, this looks about the right size." Adso handed John a battered conical helmet. "It's seen a bit of work, but it's better'n nothing." He turned away and coughed harshly.

"Are you all right?" John asked.

"Fine," Adso waved a hand dismissively.

John took the helmet. It was simple and unpolished, without even a strip descending to protect his nose. It was plain, except for some marks around the rim that John recognized as Moorish writing. "It must be from Las Navas de Tolosa," John mused. "I wonder what the writing says."

"Probably asking for protection against the swords of the infidels," Adso speculated. "Apparently, it didn't work so well. 'Ope you 'ave better luck."

John placed the helmet on his head. It was heavy, but that was good, it meant it was strong and would give him maximum protection. It was a bit small, but John managed to work the padding around so that it sat securely.

"You look lovely," Adso said. "Now, 'urry up, de Montfort must 'ave just about finished lining up 'is army. There's work to be done. Buckle on that sword and let's go. And don't look so worried." Adso smiled and patted his friend on the back. "I'll look after you."

John picked up Auramazdah and strapped it to his hip. He noticed his hand was shaking. John had been in battles before—at Béziers, Minerve, Las Navas de Tolosa—but this was different. Those other times he had got caught up in the battles either because he couldn't get out of the way or because he was trying to do something else, such as rescue Isabella at Las Navas de Tolosa. This time he was consciously preparing to go into the middle of the most important battle of the crusade, to kill or be killed. This wasn't for him; it was what Adso did—or Oddo, John thought with a shiver. "I'm scared," he said, quietly.

"Me too," Adso said.

"You don't look scared."

"That's only 'cause I've done this plenty of times. Look, this is the worst time in any battle, the waiting afore it begins. Your mind imagines the most awful things that could 'appen. That's why everyone tries to keep busy afore a fight. Keep the mind occupied."

"What are you occupying your mind with?" John asked.

"I imagine winning," Adso said with a wink. "I picture myself after it's all over wearing the magnificent armour I've stripped from a dead enemy lord, surrounded by prisoners I can ransom for a fortune and telling the story of my exploits to an 'orde of adoring, beautiful women."

John couldn't help himself, he laughed out loud. "I'll just imagine myself leading a quiet life with Isabella."

"You never were any fun," Adso said. His smile faded. "But this time's different."

"How so?"

"There won't be any gleaming armour or beautiful women after this."

"What do you see yourself doing, then?"

Adso was silent for a moment. "I see myself standing over Oddo's body, holding up 'is 'ead for all to see," he said grimly. Adso fell silent and stared into the distance.

"Come on. We can't keep kings and counts waiting," John said, in a weak attempt at levity. He was worried by his friend's sudden change in mood and by his ever-present cough. It had been particularly bad the past few days,

Rebirth

and Adso looked pale and drawn. "They can't start the battle without us," John said as cheerfully as he could manage.

Adso showed no reaction. "It's not real," he said, as if talking to himself. "I usually 'ave no trouble imagining the spoils of war, but I can't see Oddo. 'E keeps slipping away. What does it mean?"

"It means nothing," John said, placing his arm around Adso's shoulder, "nothing at all. If Oddo's here, you'll find him and kill him."

Adso blinked and shook his head. "Of course," he said, his smile returning. "'E ain't no match for me. I'm braver, quicker and smarter. Come on, let's go."

John followed Adso out of the tent. His own fear was gone, replaced by worry about his friend.

Outside, Peire, dressed magnificently in the royal colours of Aragon, stood holding two horses. They were huge beasts, draped in brightly coloured cloth and each carrying a heavy wooden saddle. They snorted steam into the cool morning air and stamped their vast hooves impatiently.

"The King bade me deliver these to you so that you may ride into battle suitably mounted," Peire said with a smile. "He waits over there." He indicated a chaotic mass of mounted knights milling about beneath a waving forest of red and gold banners.

"I've never ridden anything larger than a donkey," John said, staring at the great beasts in horror.

"Principle's the same," Adso said cheerfully, "but these animals're certainly a step up in the world for the likes of us. Where'll you fight today?" he asked, turning to Peire.

"My place is beside the king," Peire replied. "I suppose the time has come when I have to work for all these magnificent clothes, the good food I've eaten and the beautiful women I've known." He smiled broadly. "Still, whatever happens today, I can't complain. These past months at King Pedro's court, I've lived a life I could never have imagined back in Toulouse. I'm only sorry my miserable friend from the road to Las Nava de Tolosa couldn't be here. It might even have cheered the depressing sod up a bit." Peire stepped forward and clenched Adso's and then John's hand. "I wish you both luck."

"And I you," the two said simultaneously. "I doubt you'll 'ave to work too 'ard today for your keep," Adso added.

"I hope not, but if we don't get a move on, we'll be in more danger from King Pedro than de Montfort."

Peire waved to a page, who scuttled forward and placed wooden stools beside each horse. Even standing on the stool, John had to stretch his leg up to reach the stirrup, grab the saddle pommel and haul himself onto the horse's back. He felt as if he were on a mountain top. The ground seemed fearfully far below him, yet he felt secure. The saddle was solid and rose behind him to hold him in place. An exhilarating sense of raw, potential power surged up from the restless animal beneath him. He felt immortal. "This is the way to fight," he said, looking over at Adso, but his friend wasn't paying attention. He was staring out at the scene before them.

In contrast to the disorganized mass of knights around King Pedro, Simon de Montfort's army was drawn up in three perfectly disciplined rectangular squadrons. They stood still, over a mile away in front of Muret. The Toulouse militia hovered off to their left, a great sprawling mass of humanity like a dark, stinking sea that washed around the walls of the town. They were too lightly armed to harm the heavily armoured knights, and too scared to try.

A smaller group of knights milled in front of the squadrons around de Montfort's banner and the flags of Carcassonne, Narbonne and the red crusader cross. De Montfort was dismounted, giving final orders to his commanders. When he was done, he tried to mount his charger, but the stirrup broke and he tumbled to the ground. A chorus of raucous laughter broke out among the Aragonese on the hill. Unfazed, de Montfort mounted from the other side while a page hurriedly repaired the break. Then he rode forward and addressed the squadrons. John couldn't hear what he said, but the sound of cheering drifted up in the morning air.

"De Montfort's stirrup breaking's a good omen," John said.

"Don't believe in omens," Adso replied sullenly.

John glanced over. "What do you mean?"

"I mean, a stirrup is nothing. Look 'ow disciplined de Montfort's men are and 'ow Pedro's mill about as they please."

"True," John acknowledged, "but de Montfort still has only half as many men as us, and look, he's splitting his force." John pointed down the hill to where de Montfort had joined the third squadron and was leading it to the north along the river. "He's running away."

"Don't you believe that. 'E knows that 'e either wins today or dies. 'E's got some plan."

"It doesn't matter," John said, although he was disturbed by Adso's comments. "It leaves only two of his squadrons to fight. That can't be more than five or six hundred knights. We must have almost two thousand up here."

"Numbers's not everything in a battle," Adso observed.

"Don't be so miserable!"

Adso ignored John. "Look at the second squadron. That's where Oddo is."

Rebirth

John squinted at the two masses of knights moving slowly forward. Sure enough, a large group in the centre rode beneath a large banner bearing the red falcon grasping the black axe. The knight at the front held his axe resting on his left shoulder.

"Come on. Whatever de Montfort's doing down there, we should join Pedro," Peire said. "It's best not to seem to ignore the honour of riding into battle beside him."

Adso grunted, but he rode off toward the gathered knights with Peire close behind. John grasped the reins and breathed a silent prayer that he would be able to control his charger. The destrier snorted and stamped but did what its rider's hands and knees told it.

The three pushed their way into the crowd and toward the royal banner. Several knights around it were dressed in the royal livery of Aragon, but King Pedro himself still wore simple black chain mail and a plain helmet. He looked nothing like the king who laughed, spilled wine and caroused all night. He wasn't a large man, but mounted on a horse even bigger than John's, he looked imposing. "Well," he said as John, Adso and Peire reached him. "The time has come to teach this upstart a lesson. I wish you luck today, John." Pedro raised his voice. "For God, honour and the glory of Aragon, forward!"

The great mass of the Aragonese knights began moving down the hill away from the camp. Like the crusader army, it too was divided into three squadrons. The squadrons were much larger than de Montfort's but had nothing like the same structure. The banners of the Counts of Comminges and Foix fluttered over the leading host and each was surrounded by the cream of those two courts, but the rest of the mass had no shape. Individual knights chose where they wanted to ride and the mass was more like a crowd at a country fair than an army going to battle.

Behind them, and separated by a strip of open ground, came Pedro's Aragonese army with the king, John, Adso and Peire at its centre. Behind them, after an even greater gap, came Count Raymond and the Knights of Toulouse.

"No infantry," Adso grumbled quietly as he rode beside John.

"De Montfort hasn't any either."

Adso continued, as if talking to himself. "Nothing like a line of pikemen or a few dozen crossbow bolts to break up a charge. It might not be 'onourable, but there's no 'onour in being dead, as far as I can see."

"For God's sake," John whispered urgently, "keep your voice down and your depressing thoughts to yourself." He struggled to suppress his anger at his friend. No, he didn't want to be here, and certainly king Pedro could have done things differently, but they still had overwhelming superiority of numbers. John simply wanted to get this done. He glanced over at Adso, who staring back at him with a sad expression.

"Be careful," Adso said with a weak attempt at a smile. "Kings ain't worth dying for. If this all goes wrong, get out and 'ead back to camp. Find Isabella and get as far away from 'ere as quickly as you can." He coughed harshly and spat. John thought he saw a flash of red at the edge of Adso's mouth, but his friend wiped it away before he could be sure.

John was still trying to think of something to say to Adso when he was distracted by shouts from the leading squadron. Swords and axes were being waved in the air as the mass broke into a gallop toward the advancing crusaders. Even John knew this was wrong; they were charging too soon. The crusader knights were still over half a mile away and moving at a brisk trot. The knights of Foix and Comminges would be tired after galloping that distance flat out. The correct thing to do was what de Montfort's men were doing: walk, then slowly increase the speed to a trot, then a canter, and only break into a full gallop at the last minute. That way the horses were fresh and the power of the impact maximized.

King Pedro shouted something and the Aragonese broke into a trot. John didn't have to do anything, his destrier increased its pace to keep up with the other horses around him. Sensible not to gallop, John thought, but the gap between the first and second groups was increasing.

John felt his heart rate increasing as the beat of thousands of hooves on the hard ground intensified. Around him knights were drawing swords and hefting axes and maces. He drew Auramazdah. It felt small compared to the heavier weapons designed to smash heads beneath solid helmets and bodies through strong chain mail.

But it was too late to worry about that. The distance between the galloping front group and the Crusaders, who had now reached a canter, was narrowing fast. John felt sweat breaking out beneath his clothes. His mouth was dry and he had a strong urge to relieve himself, but he was helpless, borne along in the midst of this mass of humanity bent only on killing its enemies.

John felt incredibly powerful. His great mount felt unstoppable and the jangle and clank of equipment and armour, overlaying the deep thunder of the hooves, was like a protective blanket wrapped around him. He stole a glance over at Adso. His friend had drawn his sword and was staring grimly ahead. On the other side of him, King Pedro had a look of insane glee on his face as he swung a huge, studded black mace on the end of a chain above his head. Peire rode just behind the king, his sword drawn.

Rebirth

John's apprehension, even his desire to avoid the battle and run away with Isabella, had vanished. He felt strong and invulnerable. The thrill of the imminent fight flooded through him. There was nowhere on earth he would rather be at this moment.

The crusaders at last broke into a gallop and, even over the thunder, John could hear the roar of battle cries—"Montfort!" "Auxerre!" "Saint Dennis!"—answered by those around him screaming—"Toulouse!" "Comminges!" "Aragon!" John could feel his face twisted into a wild grin. "Toulouse!" he yelled.

Adso pushed in front of John and struggled to the front of the group. Before John could respond, the compact, disciplined mass of the Crusaders' lead squadron slammed into the leading group of Pedro's army with a sound like an entire forest being felled at once. Screams, curses and battle cries mixed with the metallic crash of weapons on armour. Through the swirling dust, John could see swords and axes rising and falling. His teeth were clenched so hard his jaw hurt. He felt as he never had before—elated, ecstatic, overjoyed. All thoughts of learning, drawing and even Isabella vanished in the overwhelming euphoria of battle.

John prayed that the forward group didn't destroy the crusader army before he had a chance to do his bit. "Toulouse!" he screamed again into the chaos around him. Then, "You were wrong, Beatrice! It's not the Devil that makes us do this. It is God!"

God's Will

Muret
September 12, 1213

In the strengthening daylight, Peter stood up slowly and looked around. He was stunned by how much time had passed while he wrestled with his visions and prayed. He felt exhausted and confused. Every muscle in his body ached and his habit was stiff, caked with the foul mud of the swamp. His hands and feet itched and a deep rumbling seemed to reach him through the very earth itself. It took some time for an awareness of his surroundings to penetrate his befuddled brain. In front of him, two armies were charging on a collision course; the rumbling was the sound of thousands of hoof beats.

Peter could see the tents of the camp on a hill in the distance to his right. In front of the camp rode a mass of knights beneath the banners of Toulouse. Much closer and riding faster were the knights of Aragon, and ahead of them, at a full gallop, a third group, seconds away from crashing into the first of two well-organized squadrons of knights riding from Muret. Slowly, full realization dawned. De Montfort was leading his army out from the safety of Muret to give battle to the much stronger army of King Pedro and Count Raymond.

"Stop!" Peter screamed, but his voice was lost in the rising tumult of noise. He flung his arms wide and stepped forward. The two armies met with a thunderous roar. Beneath a gleaming forest of swords, axes and maces, the dense mass of de Montfort's knights drove into their enemy, chopping, hacking and crushing anything in their way. Horses and men screamed in an unearthly cacophony that rose above the clamour and din of battle. A riderless horse, its saddle soaked in blood, broke away from the fight and galloped past Peter.

De Montfort's knights were outnumbered, but because they were a disciplined compact body, only Pedro's knights close to them could fight. The crusaders drove inexorably on.

"Why am I here?" Peter shouted into the noise. He was sickened by the carnage and felt betrayed by his voices. "If you did not bring me here to prevent this, then why? Am I to be but a helpless witness?" Peter walked slowly toward the battle. The itching in his palms and his feet was intense now, but he kept his arms spread wide and kept going. God wished him to do something. He could only go on and meet his fate. More horses passed him, some bearing knights with no visible wounds.

Already the crusaders had battered through the forward mass of Pedro's army, clearing a way for the second squadron to push through. Peter hesitated as he caught a glimpse of the man leading the crusaders, who were now forming up to charge the Aragonese kights of Pedro's second rank. Standing high in his stirrups, waving his axe above his head and yelling commands, Oddo dominated the battlefield.

Peter's belief that he was ordained to do God's work vanished. Whatever confidence he'd had in himself withered. He forgot every lesson that Aumery had taught him and was suddenly back in the square at Béziers, a terrified boy forced to kiss the gore-encrusted blade of Oddo's axe. He fell to his knees.

"Why did you bring me here to face this man again?" he whimpered. "Have I not suffered enough? Can I not be released to find my own way?" Tears streamed down his cheeks. "If I am not worthy then let me die, but why torture me so? Or if I must suffer, stretch me on the rack or break my bones in the screws, but do not bring me back to face this monster again."

There was no response to Peter's pleading. No visions appeared and his voices remained stubbornly silent. Peter gulped in great breaths of air and forced himself to stand, but that was all he could do. Still with his arms wide, he watched as Oddo gave a last scream and led his Falcons at the advancing Aragonese horde. They crashed through the front line and a wild melee developed, moving ever closer to the royal standard.

Peter didn't know what he wanted to happen. Should Oddo win and the crusade triumph, or should King Pedro overcome the mercenaries? The first was undoubtedly what God wanted. It would mean victory over the heretics, but it would also leave Oddo free to do what he wanted and Peter would live forever in fear. If Pedro triumphed so did heresy, but it would mean Oddo's death and Peter would be free. He watched in horrified fascination as the fighting ebbed and flowed around the Aragonese standard. It looked as if Pedro was winning. The fighting was brutal, but Oddo was making no headway. Every time he fought to clear a path to the king, other knights pushed in to fill the gap and protect their monarch. Slowly but surely, Oddo's Falcons were being cut down. Soon, only Oddo would be left and then, weakened by exhaustion, he must succumb to the numbers. Peter couldn't help but feel a tiny thrill at the prospect. Then a noise behind him drew his attention.

Peter turned to see another army. It had filed through the swamp that had almost trapped him the night before and was now forming up on the solid ground. There were two hundred knights, and leading them, beneath his fluttering banner of a white lion rampant on a red background and dressed in his war-worn armour, was Simon de Montfort. Peter stood, unable to move, his arms still spread, and watched.

At a shouted command from de Montfort, the knights urged their war horses into a walk. They formed a solid wall, knee to knee, their raised swords, axes and maces forming a glittering crown of death. Another command and the walk increased to a trot. The knights were coming straight at Peter. The ground shook beneath his feet as if all the devils in hell were trying to escape. He noticed tiny, meaningless details: the way the horses' eyes rolled white and the double puffs of steam forced from their flared nostrils; the sharp, metallic sounds of equipment banging against armour; the way the fringe of coarse hair above the horses' massive hooves rose and fell with each step that brought the army ever closer to trampling Peter into the earth. He took a deep breath and closed his eyes, resigned to the end.

The sound of hooves grew until it seemed to vibrate in Peter's very soul. A shudder passed through him, but he held his ground. He heard shouted commands and the noises became confused before they died away. He heard a loud snort and felt warm, wet breath on his face. Peter opened his eyes and stared into the wild face of Simon de Montfort's war horse. He raised his head to see de Montfort move his sword to make the sign of the cross in the air before him. On either side, other knights lowered their weapons and bowed their helmeted heads. Those farther away strained to see what was going on. Peter heard isolated words and phrases shouted between them.

"Stigmata."

"The signs of Christ's suffering."

"God is with us."

"Miracle."

Peter turned his head to look at his outstretched hands. Blood poured from deep wounds in his palms. He looked down. His feet and sandals were soaked in red.

De Monfort rose to stand upright in his stirrups. "If ever we needed proof that we shall triumph in God's name this day, it is here before our very eyes.

He has sent us a sign, the marks of Christ's suffering for all to see on this young monk. He will lead us to victory."

Peter stood immobile, stunned by the implications of de Montfort's words. Was he being asked to lead them? De Montfort leaned forward in his saddle and spoke quietly. "This is your moment, boy. Lead us."

Peter remained frozen.

"Now," de Montfort hissed. "Turn around and lead us. Seek the king."

De Montfort's voice reminded Peter of the voices in his head. Seek the king. He had to obey. Slowly, he pivoted around to face the battle raging before him. Keeping his arms stretched wide, and with blood dripping onto the ground on either side, he took his first tentative steps toward his destiny.

* * *

Even through his insanity, a part of John's brain was rationally aware of what was going on. Above the pounding of his heart he heard the shouts of command and the clash of weapons. Through his wildly staring eyes he watched the mass of crusader knights plough through the first group of Pedro's army like a deadly ship forcing its way through a thick sea. Horses and men fell screaming and bloody before the onslaught. Others struggled to get out of the way. In mere minutes, the Crusaders sliced though the front mass of knights and flooded into the space in front of the Aragonese.

John's first emotion was delight. He *was* going to get his chance. Then he noticed the man leading the crusader knights toward him. He was big, wearing full chain mail and a helmet that covered his head and left only a horizontal slit to see through. His surcoat bore a red falcon with a black axe grasped in its talons, an axe very similar to the bloodstained weapon the man held raised in his left hand. Oddo was coming straight at him.

Terror and mad joy fought to dominate John's emotions. In that instant nothing but the battle mattered, not the memory cloister or the book on drawing or even Isabella. The world was unbelievably simple: run away or fight; go or stay; live or die. With an animal scream that John barely recognized as coming from his own throat, he urged his mount forward.

Around him others struggled to reach the enemy, the great horses snorting and jostling for space. Out of the corner of his eye, John caught a glimpse of Pedro's black chain mail off to his right. Ahead he could see Adso in the thick of the fighting where the Falcons had thrust into the Aragonese troops. John was glad to see there weren't many of them. Others were streaming across the open space where the first group of knights from Comminges and Foix seemed to have broken into two groups. The open ground between the swirling melees was covered with bodies, some still struggling to crawl away from the carnage. Riderless horses plunged about

Rebirth

in confusion and fear, and mounted knights, many without weapons, streamed away to either side. De Montfort had won that battle, but it didn't matter. His forces had spent most of their strength on the first group. Pedro still had two groups left, including the veterans of Las Navas de Tolosa. They would have little trouble destroying the crusader knights piecemeal as they broke through, and the first band to be destroyed would be Oddo's Falcons.

John dug his heels into his horse's flanks and the beast reared forward, but the crush was too great and they made little progress. John rose up in his stirrups and stared ahead. Oddo stood out in the centre of the confusion, always ploughing forward with his Falcons battling beside and behind him. The Aragonese knights gave way before his furious onslaught, but they were too many. As Oddo cut into them, more swept around, attacking his Falcons from behind. Men on both sides fell, but the Falcons were few. Soon Oddo and a handful of survivors would be surrounded, cut off from any help. Then it would only be a matter of time.

John could see Adso. He too was struggling to get to Oddo, but he was much closer than John; only a few Aragonese knights separated the two men. John tried once more to fight his way forward, this time to help his friend. He had just begun to make some progress, when he gradually became aware of a commotion off to his left.

At first he thought the band of knights standing on the edge of the swamp were Count Raymond's men come forward from the camp to help in the final phase of the battle. Then he saw de Montfort's banner fluttering in the wind and the blood-red cross on the surcoats. He had a moment of doubt, but then he realized the new arrivals would make little difference. They were too few to affect the outcome. But why did they just stand there?

John saw Peter as his old friend turned toward him, a solitary figure in a monk's habit with his arms spread wide. He couldn't make out Peter's features at that distance through the dust in the air, but there was no mistaking the tall, gangly figure. What was he doing here, caught between two sides in a battle? As he watched, Peter began a slow walk toward him, and the crusaders spurred their horses into a walk.

John's brow furrowed in puzzlement. What was going on? He glanced back toward Oddo and Adso. The two men were close now and the fighting raged around them with no let up. He turned back to de Montfort and Peter. Incredibly, the Aragonese knights in front of them were falling back, pushing backward into the side of the mass. Some were even peeling off and riding away.

Peter kept coming at a slow, steady pace, and the Aragonese kept falling back, getting in each other's way in their eagerness to keep away from the strange walking monk. A figure to the fore of de Montfort's knights stood up in his stirrups and raised his sword. A roar of "Montfort" reached John above the clamour of battle as the knights surged forward. They split around Peter and crashed into the confused and disheartened Aragonese like two deadly arrows plunging into the unprotected flank of a deer.

Men fell screaming to the ground. Some attempted to fight back, but the majority thought only of escape, and Pedro's army began to melt away. John caught a glimpse of Peter, still walking forward in the dusty space that was left around him, before he turned back to Oddo. The Falcons were fighting with even greater fury as the Aragonese faltered at the realization that they were being attacked on two sides. Oddo's bloody axe rose and fell with terrifying regularity.

John caught sight of Adso, staring to the side, trying to see what was going on. Oddo was only one man away and that man collapsed as the Falcon's axe sliced deep into his shoulder.

"Adso!" John screamed, but he was too far away either to warn or help. Too late Adso realized the danger and turned back. He swept his sword up but it clanged harmlessly off Oddo's helm. The big man's axe swung round and bit deeply into Adso's side. John watched helplessly as his friend dropped his sword and slid off his horse.

"No!" John shrieked. He dug his spurs into his horses' flanks, urging it forward. The going was easier now as the confusion in the Aragonese ranks spread and knights turned in all directions to meet the different threats. John was barely aware of the men around him. All he saw through a red haze of rage was Oddo, triumphantly raising his axe to dispatch another enemy.

A man with a falcon on his chest reared in front of John, who slashed madly with Auramazdah, felt it sink into something soft and saw the man, open-mouthed and bloody, flash by. Everything that Adso had taught John about remaining calm in battle vanished. Fury ruled him. He slashed and stabbed to right and left, not knowing whether he was killing or maiming, or even if he was striking friend or foe. His only goal was to reach Oddo and kill him. How he did this was irrelevant.

Close by and to his right, John heard a voice. "To me, Aragon. I am the king." He ignored it. Oddo was close now. A Falcon rose before him and swung a massive mace. Instinctively, John ducked, but the heavy weapon caught Auramazdah and the blade shattered two thirds of the way along its length, sending a shiver up John's arm. He barely noticed as he swung Auramazdah back and the razor-sharp edge took the Falcon's arm off below the elbow. There was no pattern to the fighting now; men struggled, screamed and died all around. Panicked and wounded horses charged

Rebirth

aimlessly about, trampling the living and the dead. Any cohesion the Aragonese had had was gone. Falcons and de Montfort's men fought everywhere, slashing lines through chaos.

Oddo was very close now, towering over John. He was busy dispatching a knight to his left, but in a second he would swing around and see John. Suddenly, the broken Auramazdah seemed a pitifully inadequate weapon when matched against Britta, and John a pathetic excuse for a soldier when matched against Oddo's cold, killing wrath. John hesitated. Oddo finished his axe stroke, leaving the decapitated man to fall from his saddle. The Falcon turned back. His helmet swung round and, through the slit, John caught a glimpse of icy, triumphant eyes. The same eyes that had stared at him with such hatred after John had burned the man's face outside Minerve, when Oddo had sworn to kill him next time they met. The same eyes that had gleamed in triumph as they had ended Shabaka's life in the ruins of Fernando del Huesca's tent at Las Navas de Tolosa. John's wild anger vanished, overwhelmed by terror. Adso had failed to kill this man. What chance did he have?

"I am Pedro, your King." The voice was clear and close by. "To me, Aragon."

Oddo's head snapped round. He had led his Falcons through the enemy army just for the glory of killing the king and now here he was, only a few yards away.

John saw his opportunity. He lunged clumsily at Oddo with every ounce of strength he could muster. He vaguely realized that this was his one chance. If this lunge failed, John died.

Auramazdah slipped past Oddo's shield. The jagged point tore into the Falcon's side just below his armpit. John drove his sword home as hard as he could. The thin, broken blade disappeared up to the hilt.

Oddo roared. His shield whipped back and caught John a painful blow on his forearm, tearing the sword from his grip. John caught a glimpse of the axe sweeping down and flung himself from the saddle, losing his helmet in the process. The axe bit deeply through the wooden saddle. John's horse screamed in pain and reared up on its hind legs, pulling the embedded axe with it and hauling Oddo off his own mount. The mercenary crashed to the ground amidst the flailing hooves of the pain-maddened destrier. John curled into a ball as the great hooves smashed against Oddo, crushing chain mail into flesh and breaking bones.

John wrapped his arms round his head and huddled into the smallest possible shape. The hooves crashing into the ground beside him thundered in his ears. Dust swirled up and choked him as he gasped for air. Pain exploded in the right side of his chest as his ribs caught a glancing blow from an iron-shod hoof. Then the war horse fell, like an ancient tree crashing to the earth.

John's right leg had stretched out involuntarily when he'd been kicked in the ribs, and now the destrier landed on it. The bone-crushing wooden saddle missed the leg, but the horse's shoulder landed on his foot and ankle, twisting it agonizingly to one side. His own scream was the last thing John heard before his world went black and silent.

*　*　*

When John awoke, he was aware only of pain and misery. He gulped the grit-filled air and prayed that the agony would stop. After what seemed like an eternity, his torment lessened. The pain in his ribs eased to a dull ache, although his skin stung sharply and he could feel warm blood running down his back. The burning torture of his twisted leg faded and he began to take notice of the world around him.

The fighting had moved away. The clash of weapons on armour and the reverberation of hooves was still loud but not as threatening. Knights rode past, but paid him no attention. John tentatively tried moving his trapped foot. Needles of pain shot through his ankle, making him draw a sharp breath. Thankfully, the pain faded rapidly as soon as he stopped trying to move. Very slowly, taking as much weight as possible on his arms, John raised himself up. The effort exhausted him and he sat for several moments with his eyes closed, recovering.

When he eventually opened his eyes and looked around, John's first impression was that he was back in the aftermath of the battle of Las Navas de Tolosa. The battlefield was much smaller and there were tens of thousands fewer casualties, but there were the same mutilated bodies of men and horses and the same pitiful screams of wounded knights and animals. As if by magic, the scavengers who always followed an army had appeared and were already killing the wounded and taking whatever they could.

Holding his right arm tightly against his torn side, John turned as far as the pain would allow. What he saw was the complete victory of the hated crusade. The banners of de Montfort, various northern lords and the red cross of the Pope were everywhere. The survivors of the Aragonese army streamed back in rout toward the camp; those who lagged were mercilessly set upon and slaughtered by their pursuers. There was no sign of Count Raymond and the Toulouse knights.

Nearer to hand, Oddo's body lay on its back on the far side of John's horse, Auramazdah's hilt protruding from his side. The horse itself was still alive but only just. Exhausted by its wild struggle, it lay quietly, its head twisted

Rebirth

back, its nostrils flaring and closing as it breathed shallowly, and its eyes rolling sightlessly in its head. Oddo's axe was still embedded in its back beneath the splintered saddle, and dark red blood pumped slowly onto the ground. A rear hoof twitched spasmodically.

John reached forward and pushed the horse's neck above. A quiver ran under the skin, but the weight stayed solidly atop his trapped foot. John pushed harder. The same thing happened. John lay back and thought. There was no way, even if the pain in his leg allowed it, that he could stretch forward far enough to exert sufficient force to move the horse. He was thoroughly trapped, unable to move until some scavenger arrived to kill him and steal whatever he thought of value.

John frowned and willed his mind to focus. The horse twitched convulsively, slightly lifting its neck and causing its former rider to flinch in agony. An idea began to form in John's mind. Reaching around his waist, he was relieved to find his dagger still tucked into his belt. He pulled it out and leaned forward. "Sorry," he said out loud. He hesitated only for a moment before he plunged the dagger into the horse's neck. The dying beast whinnied loudly and tried to pull away from this new torture. The weight of the huge neck lifted from John's foot. He screamed again, but managed to push himself backward, dragging his limb clear before the neck came crashing back down.

Breathing heavily, John gave himself a moment to recover. When his breath no longer came in ragged gulps, he tucked his dagger back in is belt and tried to stand. It took him several attempts and cost a lot of sweat and cries of pain, but eventually, he stood shakily on his good, left leg. Hopping awkwardly, he rounded the horse's head and reached Oddo. Grunting with the effort, he lowered himself onto his good knee and looked at his enemy.

Oddo was a mess. In addition to the wound that John had administered, the man's left thigh was broken, and his leg twisted away from his body at a crazy angle. Flailing hooves had torn away his Falcon surcoat and ripped great holes in his chain mail and flesh, exposing the whiteness of ribs. There was a large dent in the crown of his helmet.

As John stared, he was shocked to hear Oddo groan. It seemed impossible that the man was still alive. John slid around and hesitantly pulled at Oddo's helmet. It came away easily to reveal a hideously bruised and blood stained face. There was a noticeable depression in the top of his skull.

Oddo's eyes flickered open. For a moment the wounded man's gaze wandered aimlessly, then settled on John. With obvious effort, Oddo's lips moved. John couldn't hear the words, nor could he fully believe that life still flickered in such a ravaged body. Oddo's lips curled in either a snarl or a grimace of pain. Despite the fear and hatred of this man that John had felt over the past three years, he began now to feel the first stirrings of pity. No one should suffer like this.

Oddo's right arm rose surprisingly fast and his hand fastened onto the neck of John's mail shirt. John tried to pull back, but the grip was strong. Slowly but inevitably, he felt himself drawn down toward Oddo's bloody face. Terror made him weak and his struggles ineffectual. The thought that this dying man still had the will and power to kill him, as he had sworn to do at Minerve, made John feel sick.

Oddo hauled and John put up a futile resistance until their faces were mere inches apart. Oddo's lips moved once more. "Kill me," he said.

John couldn't believe he had heard correctly. Oddo was too powerful. He shook his head. "Kill?" he asked.

The grip on John's mail tightened and Oddo's eyes burned into him. "You are weak." John strained to make out the slurred words. "But you are lucky. You were lucky at Minerve." Oddo stopped talking and his eyes closed. If not for the vice-like grip, John would have thought Oddo was dead. Then the eyes snapped open once more and the leader of the Falcons grimaced as he took a deep breath and gathered his remaining strength. "You were lucky today. Be strong now and end my suffering. Kill me."

John shook his head helplessly. The rage he had felt during the battle was gone, washed away by the pain of his injuries. Then he had been ready to kill anybody or anything that got in his way. Not now. Now, in cold blood, John doubted he could kill anyone, even someone he hated and feared as much as Oddo.

"I will give you something in exchange," Oddo said through gritted teeth.

"What?" John asked nervously. Was this some kind of twisted trick? What could this shattered man offer him?.

"I will give you Aumery."

"Aumery?" John struggled to understand. "What do you mean?"

Oddo flinched as another wave of pain engulfed him. "That man is the Devil and I would enjoy little more than seeing him cast down into the deepest pit of Hell. But that is one pleasure I shall miss," Oddo said when he had regained control. "But you need not. You hate him because he hates you and all those like you who know things he does not wish known. He will not rest until you and all those like you are dead. I will give you his doom." Oddo sighed and closed his eyes, exhausted after his long speech.

John stared down at the ravaged face. "Why do you wish to hurt Aumery? He leads the crusade. You are allies."

Rebirth

"Allies!" Oddo opened his eyes and spat the word out. "My only ally was my power, wielded through Britta and my Falcons. I feared neither man nor beast in this world. Now I stand on the threshold of the next world and that is the place Aumery draws his power from. I do not believe in Aumery's God. There is an older one for warriors who rules an afterlife of battle, but that skinny, rat-faced monk is the only man who has never shown me fear. I will sit more comfortably in the warrior's heaven knowing that I have finally made him suffer."

John was intrigued by Oddo's speech. The man was as much a heretic as those he had helped burn. "How can you give me Aumery?" John asked.

Oddo smiled. "Revenge is sweet, is in not?" Without allowing John to reply, he continued. "Aumery had Pierre of Castelnau killed by the river outside Arles after the meeting with Raymond at St. Gilles."

"It *was* you," John said, remembering the left-handed knight charging from the trees almost six years before.

Oddo nodded weakly, his face twisted with pain. "He paid me well and arranged for my Falcons to work for de Montfort."

"And you have proof?"

Again Oddo nodded. "There is a letter."

"Where?"

"Swear that you will do what I ask in return," Oddo said.

John hesitated. Could he do what Oddo asked? Was it really that much? Oddo was obviously suffering horribly and near death. It would be a mercy. "I will."

"Swear."

"I swear."

The grip on John's neck relaxed a bit. "The abbot at St. Gilles has it. Show it in the right places and Aumery is destroyed. Now I grow tired. Do what you promised."

Slowly, John drew his dagger and held it before the dying man's face. Oddo's smile returned. "The neck," he said.

Still John hesitated, drained after the emotional turmoil and madness of the battle. Too much had happened and there'd been no time to sort it all out..

Oddo's lip curled and his smile changed to a sneer. "Your friend wasn't weak like you. He was a worthy adversary. He came to kill me but, instead, Britta tasted his blood."

The image of Oddo's black axe sinking into Adso's side filled John's mind. He raised his dagger and sliced it deep into the side of Oddo's exposed neck.

Warm blood spurted out. Oddo sighed. "Thank you," he murmured as his hand dropped away from John's neck.

John pushed away as hard as he could, forgetting his crushed foot. He screamed and collapsed back onto his knee. The blood had stopped flowing from Oddo's neck and his eyes were glazed. Oddo was dead. The story that had begun when John and Beatrice had watched the mercenary storm through the gates into the bloodbath of Béziers was over. All the dead, including Adso, were avenged. Now there was only Aumery.

Carefully, John stood up, balanced on his good leg and looked around. What fighting remained was far away around the camp. When he looked the other way, toward Muret, he saw that a large body of de Montfort's knights were busy slaughtering the Toulouse rabble outside the walls of the town. Hundreds were running in every direction and hundreds more were throwing themselves hopelessly into the swift waters of the Garonne. It was a slaughter.

John scanned the bodies nearer at hand. A pair of scavengers was working on a cluster of bodies off to his right, unceremoniously hauling black chain mail off a knight. Swearing loudly, they dragged the body into a sitting position. John was shocked to recognize King Pedro's face as the head lolled around. Only hours before, this lifeless corpse had been the most powerful king in Christendom.

There was sadness as well. This was, after all, Isabella's uncle. True, he had become overly fond of drinking and carousing, had grandiose plans for his kingdom, and would have trapped John and Isabella in a life they didn't want in Aragon, but he didn't deserve to end up this way. No one did.

John picked up a broken spear and, using it as a crutch, continued his search. He found Peire's body, twisted and bloody, before he saw Adso lying by himself about fifteen feet away. Oddo's axe had nearly cut him in half.

"No," John sobbed as he hopped painfully over and knelt by his friend's head. Adso's face looked almost peaceful except for a smear of dried blood around his mouth. John wondered if it was from his coughing or his wound. Certainly Adso hadn't been well recently. Perhaps all he had suffered and the cough that wracked his body from time to time had weakened him and slowed his reflexes just enough to give Oddo the fatal advantage. Whatever the reason, John would never again hear his rough accent, laugh at his disrespectful jokes or learn from his worldly wisdom.

John squeezed his eyes shut to prevent the tears but it was no good, they came anyway. Memories flooded his mind: Adso leading John and Beatrice out of the gate at Béziers; helping him carry Umar's body in Minerve;

teaching him to use a sword; adding a key piece to the map puzzle. John gulped as the sobs wracked his body. His closest friend was dead.

"Ain't no use bawlin' over him," a coarse voice said. "What's dead's dead. Take his weapons or let us."

John looked up. Through the blur of his tears he saw a rough, bearded man dressed in mismatched pieces of armour, leaning on a long gnarled staff and carrying a large sack over his shoulder. John stood and poked the man viciously in the chest with the jagged end of the broken spear shaft. The man jumped back, dropping the sack and the staff. "Hey! What're you doing?"

John aimed the spear at the man's throat. "If you or any of the other scum touch this man's body, I swear I will come back and cut off your ears." John prodded the man's neck and a tiny spot of blood appeared. "Do you understand?"

"I understand," the man said stepping farther back. "We won't touch this un. There's plenty here for everyone."

"Do you swear on your eternal soul?"

"I won't touch him. May I rot in hell for eternity if I do."

"Good," John said. He lowered the spear and rested his weight on it. "Don't forget," he reminded the man as he turned way. "I have to go to the camp and look for someone, but I'll be back. If this body is touched, I'll find you and carry out my promise."

The man nodded sullenly, picked up his sack and slouched off. John had no idea if his threats would do any good, but he had no choice. He had to find Isabella.

Putting as much weight as possible on his makeshift staff and swinging his left leg forward rapidly with each step, John found that progress across the battlefield wasn't too difficult. His foot throbbed continually and every step hurt his bleeding side, but he had to keep going, he had to find Isabella. Adso's death weighed heavily on his mind. He didn't know if he could survive if something had happened to Isabella, too. He limped along, taking comfort from the fact that most of de Montfort's knights had joined the slaughter of the Toulouse militia down by the river, leaving the tattered remnants of Pedro's camp almost deserted.

Aftermath

Muret
September 12, 1213

There were fewer bodies scattered around King Pedro's camp and fewer signs of fighting. Many of the sumptuous Aragonese tents were ripped open or collapsed, and broken furniture, torn cushions and discarded equipment were strewn everywhere, but this was largely the result of hurried flight and scavenging, not battle. The knights, pages and grooms left to guard the camp had fled as soon as it became obvious who was winning on the hillside outside Muret.

Numerous ragged men, a few women and a handful of knights were either sorting through the debris or making off laden with spoils. Most kept well clear of John and any who did approach, thinking the wounded man might be easy pickings, were encouraged to search elsewhere by his angry expression and a threatening wave of his spear.

Gut-wrenching worry at what might have happened to Isabella dominated John's emotions as he searched the devastated camp. Waves of blazing anger at the futility of the death and destruction he had seen, and a mind-numbing, hollow sadness when he thought of Adso, occasionally overwhelmed him and brought him to a shuddering stop as he fought back the urge to either shriek or weep. Through it all, the throbbing pains in his torn side and twisted foot were constant reminders of his body's fragility.

John moved around the camp much more slowly than he wished. He wanted to run, to search everywhere until he found Isabella, but the scattered debris and the uneven ground made progress frustratingly slow. John felt like screaming in aggravation, but limited himself to shouting Isabella's name. He didn't hear a response until he had worked his way close to the piled remains of King Pedro's royal tent. Ignoring the pain as his foot banged against objects in his path, John hobbled as fast as he could around the tent.

Isabella was sitting with her back propped against a pile of red canvas. Her clothes were blood stained and ripped into tattered rags that she struggled to hold across herself as modestly as possible. Where her skin showed, it was scratched and bleeding, and her face was pale and tear-stained. A man's body lay beside her, the handle of a dagger protruding from his back. Isabella looked up and smiled weakly.

Terrified that she was seriously wounded, John lunged forward and collapsed beside her with a cry of pain. "Are you all right?" he asked, touching her cheek.

"Yes, I think so," she said, nodding slowly. "It's just a few scratches. Are you all right?" she added looking at his foot.

"I'm fine," John lied. "My horse fell on me, that's all."

The pair embraced and for an age the chaotic world around them ceased to exist. Eventually, they pulled apart. John stared into Isabella's face. "I was so worried about you," he said. "I didn't know where you were."

"I thought you were dead," Isabella said quietly. "I heard the fighting and then the man came." Her eyes brimmed with tears and she buried her head in John's shoulder. He held her tight and stroked he hair until the sobbing eased. "What happened?" he asked when she had calmed down.

Isabella wiped her face, leaving streaks of dirt across her cheeks. She adjusted her rags as best she could and sniffed loudly. "The battle's lost, isn't it?"

John nodded.

"I realized it when Count Raymond's knights fled through the camp," Isabella said. "I was about to come looking for you when the crusaders arrived. I had no trouble hiding from them—they were busy going after Raymond's men—but they cut down a lot of the tents as they passed through, and killed any stragglers they could find. I was hiding under cushions in Pedro's tent when it came down on top of me. It was just like being back at Las Navas de Tolosa."

Isabella shuddered at the memory and John squeezed her shoulder.

"Anyway," Isabella went on. "I waited until it got quiet and then crawled out. The knights had mostly gone, but the scavengers had already moved in to rob the bodies and ransack the tents."

"Those vultures don't take long," John said. "They were on the battlefield almost before the fighting stopped."

"They're brutes," Isabella said with a violence in her voice that surprised John. He waited patiently until she continued. "I was so scared that you were dead that I didn't even see that man"—she nodded toward the body on the ground beside her—"until he grabbed me. He was a devil. His breath stank worse than anything I've ever smelled and he said filthy things. I fought him, but he was strong and he punched and scratched. He ripped my clothes and forced me down here beside the tent. Then..."

Isabella lowered her eyes and fought to control her sobs. John held her and fought not to scream out, "What happened? What did the monster do?"

Isabella took in a trembling breath and looked up. Her eyes met John's and he was surprised at how calm they had suddenly become. "Then I killed him," Isabella said simply.

"What?"

"He forced me down onto the ground. I was hitting him, but it wasn't doing any good. Then I felt the handle of the dagger at his belt. I hauled it out and stabbed down into his back as hard as I could. He screamed. It was a hideous animal noise. I wanted him to stop, so I stabbed him again and again. He jerked backward and tried to reach the dagger, but I just kept stabbing. There was blood coming out of his mouth and nose. At last he stopped fighting and collapsed."

Isabella took another long breath through clenched teeth and blinked. "He's the first person I've ever killed," she said. "It was horrible."

"Death *is* horrible," John said, "but he deserved it. He was an animal. Much better men than him have died today. Did he...? Are you...?"

John's questions tailed off in embarrassment.

"I'm all right," Isabella said and kissed him on the cheek. "Just a few bruises and scratches. But what happened to you? Where's Adso?"

"Adso's dead," John said. "Oddo killed him."

"No," Isabella said as she closed her eyes and swallowed hard. "Not Adso."

"I'm afraid so. I saw it happen. Peire's dead too. So's King Pedro. I'm sorry."

"Does everyone have to die in this hellish war?" Isabella asked bitterly. She looked up nervously. "Where's Oddo?"

"He's dead as well. I killed him."

"You killed Oddo?" Isabella looked up at John as if seeing him for the first time.

John nodded. "I was lucky."

"At least that's one good thing that's come out of all of this. I don't suppose you managed to kill Aumery as well?"

"No," John said, "but Oddo told me something before he died that might destroy Aumery. I'll explain later." John remembered something else. "I saw Peter as well."

"Is he all right?" A worried frown crossed Isabella's face.

"As far as I know. We lost the battle because de Montfort brought a group of knights through the swamp and they attacked us in the flank while Oddo's Falcons attacked our front. The strange thing was that Peter seemed to be leading them. He was walking through the battle untouched. He had his arms spread wide and he seemed to be bleeding."

"He was wounded?"

"I don't think so. It appeared to be his hands and feet that bled. Everyone moved away and gave him room as he walked. Our knights were almost frightened of him."

"I hope he's all right."

"So do I. But what are *we* going to do now? We can't stay here. It'll only be a matter of time before de Montfort's knights return."

"We could go to Toulouse," Isabella suggested.

"I don't think there's much point. The crusade has won. Toulouse will fall, maybe not this year, but soon."

"Then nowhere's safe."

"In Languedoc, no," John said, "but we don't have to stay here. Do you still have the bag of money Pedro gave us?"

"Yes. The brute who attacked me wasn't after money."

"Good. Then we can go far away."

"Not until you have healed," Isabella said, looking at John's foot and the blood that had seeped through his clothing. "We need somewhere closer where we can we can disappear. Perhaps Queribus, Montsegur or Pereypertuse. They're a long way, but they'll be safe for a while."

"Good idea. We should get started before de Montfort's army returns."

Isabella nodded. "You're right. But there's something I have to get." She stood up and began lifting the folds of Pedro's tent.

"Can I help," John asked.

"Just hold this up so I can find my way out," Isabella said, handing him the folds of heavy canvas. Isabella ducked through the rip in the tent and disappeared.

John looked around as he balanced on one leg and waited. He could see the lump Isabella made as she moved around the tent. He looked over at the man she had killed. What an extraordinary person she was—smart, beautiful and strong. He was lucky that she saw something worthwhile in him. Despite everything that had happened—the bloodshed, the crusader victory, losing Adso—John felt stupidly happy. Isabella was all right and they were together once more. She was the only thing he didn't think he could live without and all he wanted was to be with her.

John looked over the battlefield. He could plot the course of the fighting from the density of bodies scattered over the countryside—a mass where Oddo and his Falcons had fought their way through the first squadron of Pedro's army; a second group where both Oddo and Pedro had met their end, and where Adso lay; and a scattering of dead marking the lines of retreat for the Aragonese army. Farther away, a second landscape of death marked the area where de Montfort's knights were still hunting down and slaughtering the Toulouse militia.

There were more scavengers now and several knights had returned to search for spoils or wounded enemies they could ransom. Soon they would be working their way through the ruined camp and then it would be much harder to escape. "Hurry up, Isabella," John said under his breath.

A solitary, familiar figure off to John's right caught his eye. It was a tall, gangly monk, standing stationary with his arms by his sides, gazing off over the flat countryside toward the distant darker line of hills to the northeast.

"Peter," John shouted. He had to call several times before the figure hauled itself out of its reverie and looked around. Slowly, as if in a daze, Peter came over. John was shocked to see the look of his childhood friend. He was filthy, his habit caked in mud and his hands and feet covered in blood. His eyes were dark-rimmed and had a distant stare, even when directed at John.

"What happened to you?" John asked. "I saw you in the battle. You were bleeding."

Peter lifted his hands and stared uncomprehendingly at them. They were caked in blood that cracked and flaked off as they moved. "Stigmata," Peter said absently.

"How?" John asked.

Peter ignored the question and continued to spout apparently disconnected words and phrases. "Chosen. Seduced by the Devil. Monsters with wings. Seraphim. Diogenes. Francesco. Isabella." While he spoke, Peter's eyes flicked randomly around. Eventually they rested on John's face and the brow above them furrowed in worry. "Why me?" he asked.

John shook his head helplessly. "I don't know."

"No one knows God's will," Peter said.

Encouraged by the fact that Peter's stare was now focused on his face, John continued. "You mentioned Isabella's name. She's all right. She's here."

"Dreams. Seductions of the Devil."

John tried a different approach. "Adso was killed in the battle."

"We all die," Peter stated matter-of-factly, his gaze drifting away once more. "Death is nothing."

"Oddo as well."

Peter's eyes snapped back to focus on John. "Dead?"

"Yes," John answered. "I killed him."

"Killed him?" Peter reached forward and grabbed John's shoulders. "Are you certain?"

"Yes. I saw him die."

Peter released a long sigh and let his arms drop to his sides. "I am free, at least, of Britta."

John had no chance to think of anything else to say before Isabella reappeared out of the fallen tent. She was pulling John's satchel behind her. When she stood up and noticed Peter, she dropped the satchel and struggled to arrange her ragged clothing into some semblance of modesty.

Peter stared so long at Isabella that both she and John began to feel distinctly uncomfortable. John was about to say something when Peter reached down and hauled his mud- and blood-encrusted habit over his head. He stood, holding it in front of him, his skinny body pale in the weak sun.

"It is all I have," Peter said in a monotone. "I give it to you to cover your nakedness."

Peter's troubled face relaxed and he sighed deeply. Suddenly, he looked much younger, almost like the boy who had been John's closest friend all those years ago in the Priory of St. Anne in Toulouse. "To be truly free, I must give away everything I own to someone who will benefit. I gave John the old maps because that is his interest. Now I give you my habit to preserve your modesty. It is not much." Peter looked down at the filthy garment in his hands and the beginnings of a smile flickered across his features. "But perhaps it will be of use to you. Please take it."

Isabella smiled back at Peter, reached forward and lifted the habit from his outstretched arms. "Thank you." She slid the habit over her head. "It is perfect."

It was far from perfect—the hem dragged on the ground and Isabella's hands disappeared in the folds of the sleeves—but her smile enlivened Peter. He beamed and looked happier than John could remember seeing him since the day of his fateful vision on the steps of the Chateau Narbonnaise.

"I am reborn," Peter said, a gleam in his eye and a thrill in his voice. "As naked as the day I came into this corrupt world, I carry nothing with me. I am free to do penance for my past sins."

"How will you live" John asked.

"God will provide." It was the sort of thing Peter would have said before, but then it would have sounded pompous. Now it was a simple statement of fact.

"Where will you go?" Isabella asked.

"To the hills." Peter waved a hand toward the dark line on the horizon. "There are many caves in the valleys above Minerve. I shall find a suitable one in which I shall live and pray. When I am worthy, I shall preach."

A part of John envied Peter. He seemed so certain of what he was going to do and how to do it. John's hope for a settled existence had been crushed by de Montfort's victory. Adso was dead and the horrors of the crusade would continue. Oddo was dead, but Aumery was still out there, and John had to decide if he was going to do anything about that. Oddo had given him a weapon and, if he didn't use it, wherever he and Isabella went, John would always be living under a threat. If Aumery ever got his hands on John, all he could expect was a long, excruciating death in the torture chamber or on the bonfire. John was weighed down by the secrets in his head. Peter *was* lucky.

"Go well," Isabella said.

"Yes," John agreed. "Good luck and God bless you."

Peter nodded acknowledgement of their good wishes and turned toward the distant hills. John and Isabella watched as the tall, skinny, pale figure picked his way through the debris of the destroyed camp.

"We must leave as well," Isabella said. "The crusaders will be back soon."

And Aumery, John thought, but he said, "Yes, let's go." The pair turned away from Peter's retreating back and set off, hand in hand, in the opposite direction.

Home

North of Carcassonne
November 12, 1213

Although he had begun his journey to the hills with nothing, Peter had collected various items as he travelled. He had sought none of them, but the tall, solitary figure moving so purposely through the landscape had attracted attention. Despite saying or doing nothing to suggest it, everyone he came in contact with assumed he was holy and was eager to help him on his way.

On the day after the battle, in a tiny village south of Toulouse, an elderly woman had approached Peter, kissed his blood-encrusted hands and presented him with an old, threadbare, brown robe to cover his nakedness. Later that same day, a farmer had offered him a length of rope to tie around his waist. Peter had thanked the man and tied three knots in the rope, as he had seen Francesco do, to remind himself of the three vows of obedience, poverty and chastity. Food was also not a difficulty, as those who met Peter seemed happy to provide more than his meagre appetite required.

As he progressed, Peter settled into a contented rhythm of walking and accepting the hospitality and generosity of strangers. When asked to, he blessed people and performed the functions of a priest, hearing confession, praying for the sick and, once, performing extreme unction for an innkeeper's dying child.

The more time passed, the more Peter felt at ease. His voices remained silent and his visions stayed away. He had only fragmented memories of the night before Muret and a sketchy idea of his role in the battle, and he was happy enough not to remember. Best of all, he felt no obligation to Arnold Aumery. His role in that strange man's quest and attempt to bring on the Last Judgement was complete. If God wished the End of Days to come, they would do so without Peter being their instrument. All Peter wanted was to lead a solitary life of contemplation, meditation and prayer.

Peter followed an irregular route, but always working his way east toward Minerve. He was in no particular hurry and was convinced that he would end up where he was supposed to, regardless of how he got there. If he was honest with himself, he enjoyed the walking. It was a simple life and it reminded him of his time in the east, but without the onerous responsibility of the quest. He felt free and confident that God would provide for his needs. Gradually, he began to understand the sense of peace that had seemed to emanate from Francesco.

By November, Peter had woven his tangled route into the rough gorges and hills that he had seen nearing every day for several weeks. The first chills of approaching winter could be felt when the sun dropped below the horizon and the cold intensified as he climbed out of the plain. Three days earlier he had passed Minerve. The siege, and Peter's part in it, seemed such a long time ago. Several buildings in the town still showed signs of the damage done by de Montfort's siege engines and the gates of the castle protecting the entrance had been torn down, but the inhabitants went about their business calmly enough. Peter saw no sign of any heretics, although as he entered the town he had noticed that someone had strewn fresh-cut herbs over the spot where the Perfects had climbed their funeral pyre.

From Minerve, Peter had walked north, through smaller and smaller villages where a family or two struggled to claw a living from the harsh soil. Now he was standing at the foot of a craggy limestone cliff in a narrow gorge. The day had been sunny and warm and the people in the tiny village at the mouth of the gorge were generous with bread and cheese, but the shadows around Peter were deepening and he shivered in the chill air.

In front of Peter, a rugged goat path led up the cliff to a narrow ledge that appeared to front a black cleft in the rock that might provide shelter for the night. Peter mumbled a prayer of thanks and started up.

It was more of a scramble than he had expected, but after half an hour's work, he stood on the ledge and peered into the darkness of a narrow cave. He had a moment of apprehension that the cave might already be occupied by some dangerous creature, but trusting in God, he ducked low and entered.

The cave entrance was not wide, Peter could touch both walls with his outstretched hands and the space appeared to taper toward the back, but it was tall enough for him to stand upright, the floor was smooth, and the rock walls radiated the last of the heat they had collected from the day's sun. Peter knelt and offered fervent thanks. He was home.

Prospects

Peyrepertuse
January 3, 1214

John stood on the battlements of Peyrepertuse. He shifted his weight onto his left leg. The right one had healed well over the past months but it still ached if John stood on it too long. The bones in his foot, some of which John suspected the horse had broken, had mended, but left his foot now turned a little inward, giving him a slight limp. The torn skin, where the horse's iron clad hoof had raked along his side, had also healed, leaving a hard knot of scar tissue that prevented him from lifting his right arm high above his head. The limp was annoying and the limitation on the movement of his arm meant that he would never be able to wield a sword effectively, but John didn't mind. Auramazdah was broken and left on the battlefield. It was a small price to pay for surviving the debacle at Muret.

John was wrapped in a heavy cloak against the cold and wore a loose fitting, floppy felt hat that he'd pulled down over his ears. He stared down into the valley, white from last night's snow. The grey walls of the castle dropped away below him to merge with the twisted rock of the unscalable cliff on which the fortress sat. On the valley floor, thin wisps of smoke rose from scattered farmhouses, each encircled by a patch of flat, white land, laboriously cleared from the surrounding forest.

This must be how God feels, staring down on all the puny achievements that we think are so important, John thought. He had been thinking a lot about God recently, wondering how much He involved Himself in the affairs of individuals. He had no doubt that the Diety *could* answer specific prayers and involve Himself in day-to-day events, the problem was the inconsistency of it all.

John accepted that God may well have decided that the crusade would win, and even that He might have used Peter as an instrument to help de Montfort defeat Pedro at Muret, but why had He allowed methods that caused such a vast amount of suffering to innocents? The women and children slaughtered at Béziers, the farmers' families who starved to death because the crusaders ravaged their lands, and the countless helpless individuals who had been raped and murdered by the instruments of God's will had all prayed fervently for rescue and safety in which to live their simple lives in peace. Many had been good Catholics who attended mass and lived a better Christian life than Crusading knights like Oddo, yet their pleas had been ignored. The more John thought about it, the more the Cathar idea that the entire world and everything in it was the work of the Devil seemed to make sense.

"What are you looking so thoughtful about?" Isabella asked. She was standing beside John, dressed as heavily as he was in a long green cloak. Instead of a hat, she wore a dark brown woollen scarf tied under her chin.

"I was just wondering why God allows evil things to happen to innocent people."

"Just?" Isabella let out a short laugh. "If you could answer that question you could be Pope."

"Look." John ignored Isabella's comment and pointed down at the tiny figure of a farmer dragging a sled laden with firewood across his fields toward his house. "See that farmer? He's probably a Catholic. He's struggled to pull a living from the land. I'll bet his wife's busy right now in their warm kitchen, preparing dinner while their children play in the thresh at her feet. They're good people. They've done nothing wrong, and yet one day the soldiers of the crusade will come through here, destroy their crops, steal all their food and, if they're unlucky, kill the man, rape the wife and leave the children as orphans. It's all so hideously unfair! Why would a merciful God allow that to happen?"

"Because it is not the work of a merciful God." John and Isabella turned to see Esclarmonde approaching along the wall. Despite the cold, she wore only the black hoodless habit of the Cathar Perfects.

"Are you not cold?" Isabella asked.

"Of course I am, my dear," Esclarmonde said with a smile. "But it is merely the body that is cold and that is the Devil's creation. The soul is warm. And that answers your question," she turned to face John. "The Devil created everything material, the farmer below, his firewood, the dinner on his table, his wife and the thresh in which his children play, just as certainly as the swords and axes in the hands of the knights who may one day come and destroy his farm and kill his family. This world is corrupt and evil, as the past few years of suffering in this sad land must prove to any with eyes."

"I suppose so," John acknowledged, "but there is also so much beauty in the world. At the moment, that scene below us is idyllic. Can the Devil create something like that?"

"It is only idyllic in your eyes," Esclarmonde said. "You see a farmer with wood and a house and you imagine the rest. Perhaps he beats his wife to prove his authority. Maybe she is a nagging shrew, never satisfied with his hard work. Possibly his children are sickly and will die. Perchance his landlord is a grasping and greedy man who keeps the family on the verge of starvation from one winter the next. The devil is in everything."

"But I have to believe in beauty," John said, "and that it might be possible for me to capture that in my drawing. I don't think I could ever become a Good Christian and take the *consolamentum*. I'm sorry."

"Don't be sorry," Esclarmonde said. "I can see why Beatrice chose you for the memory cloister, and it was not because she thought you would make a Good Christian. You have an independent mind and that gives you the strength to go your own way regardless of what I, or Pope Innocent, say. Long after the bonfires have claimed all of my kind and destroyed all we carry in our heads, you and the knowledge you have acquired will be safe.

"Speaking of which, how are you enjoying the books in our small library here?"

"They are wonderful," John said, although in truth he was disappointed. The library at Peyrepertuse was tiny, only a handful of scrolls and John had read half of those before. When he and Isabella had arrived in October, after a long, hard journey from Muret, he'd hopes of finding *Perspectiva*, but there had been no sign of it. Nevertheless, he had busied himself with what there was in the small, dark library in the castle cellar. He had begun the final, short scroll that day. "I have learned much and added it to the cloister. I think I shall be finished in a day or two."

"And then?" Esclarmonde asked.

John let his gaze drift the three miles along the valley until it rested on the dark hump of rock that guarded the southern entrance. He focussed on a separate pinnacle of rock, on which the black silhouette of a stone tower stood out against the backdrop of more grey, snow-laden clouds. Queribus, the place where the mysterious artist had learned to draw the incredible picture of Laon Cathedral before his life had been so tragically cut short. Was that where *Perspectiva* lay? It had been hard, when he discovered that the book was not at Peyrepertuse, for John not to descend immediately and go to Queribus, but he'd forced himself to stay. He had a responsibility to put whatever he could in the memory cloister. The works at Peyrepertuse would not take long to commit to memory and, if *Perspectiva* was at Queribus, it would still be there when he had finished. Now he was almost finished, and eager to move up the valley, as soon as the snow allowed.

"I'll go to Queribus and learn what they have there," he said as calmly as he could manage.

"And Puilaurens, Montsegur and the other places where books are hidden?" Esclarmonde asked.

"If there is time," John said, knowing that if he found the book at Queribus, learning what it contained would occupy him for a long time to come.

"There will be time," the Perfect said with certainty. "De Montfort and the Pope have won the war but it will take many years to finish it. De Montfort's first priority will be Toulouse and then he will concentrate on gaining and keeping the loyalty of all his important subjects. They will bow a knee quickly enough to him, but he must establish his authority so strongly that, once his back is turned they will not fall back into the old ways. That will take many years, and in that time he will not concern himself with a few isolated castles in the mountains. Our turn will come, but we are safe for the time being."

The trio fell silent, each occupied with his or her own thoughts. Isabella spoke first, asking a question that made the other two stare at her. "What's the Cathar Treasure?"

"You know that we do not value or hoard gold or material possessions," Esclarmonde said before the silence grew too long.

"I know," Isabella said. "It's just that when I met Peter before the battle he talked about it. He was confused and hard to follow, but he did say that Aumery thought that the Cathar Treasure was the Holy Grail, the cup that Christ drank from at the Last Supper. That was why Peter went to the east; he was following some clue Aumery had given him."

"We don't believe in Christ's divinity, so his cup has no value to us," Esclarmonde said.

"Besides," John added, "if the Grail did exist, Adso probably broke it after he discovered the body at Rhedea."

Esclarmonde nodded agreement. She had been fascinated when John and Isabella had related Adso's story of how he thought he might have burned Christ's body and found the Grail but then broken it when he was drunk in an alley.

"But it doesn't matter what we believe," Isabella went on. "It's what Aumery believes that's important. Now that de Montfort has won, he has no distractions. If he truly believes that the Cathar Treasure is the Grail and that possessing it will bring on the Day of Judgement, he will leave no stone unturned, or heretic not tortured or burned, until he finds it. And, sooner or later, he'll discover or work out that the most likely place for the Grail to be hidden is in one of these isolated castles in the mountains."

"So we may not have as long as we think," John said thoughtfully.

"Then we must do what we can, while we can," Esclarmonde said.

"So there is no such thing as the Cathar Treasure?" Isabella asked, bringing the conversation back to her original question.

"I never said that," Esclarmonde responded with a sly smile. Isabella and John stared at her.

"What do you mean?" John asked.

"Everyone assumes that treasure must be material—a chest of gold, precious jewels, a lost map, a holy relic—but they are wrong. The Cathar Treasure, as you call it, is here"—Esclarmonde tapped her forehead—"and here and here," she leaned forward and tapped John and Isabella's heads in turn.

"You mean the memory cloister?" John asked. "The Gospel of the Christ?"

"No. I mean what those things can lead to."

"I don't understand," Isabella said with a frown.

"Material things are of the devil, Angra Mainyu. Immaterial things are of God, Auramazdah," Esclarmonde explained. "So wood is of the Devil, but fire, which comes from wood, is of God."

"I understand that," John said, "but how does it relate to what I hold in my mind?"

"Consider William the troubadour. He travels the land seeking facts upon which he intends to base an epic song of this troubled time. The facts he learns are nothing in themselves, simply fragments of information about this evil world."

John and Isabella nodded as they concentrated on following what Esclarmonde was saying.

"As William gathers more and more facts, he notices that they relate to each other, that they form a pattern. *That* is knowledge. He now has a framework, like the wooden scaffolding put up around a building. When he discovers a new fact, he knows where to fit it into this scaffold in his mind.

"If his mind is open and he accepts all facts, not merely the ones he agrees with, his knowledge grows. William begins to comprehend the ideas underlying the crusade—what we the Good Christians believe and what the Catholics believe. The facts he has learned no longer exist in isolation. He has developed an understanding of *why* the facts that he has learned happened.

"If he perseveres with this process, his understanding broadens. He comes to know the ideas of the Moors, or perhaps the strange peoples who are said to live far to the east. With enough understanding, William attains wisdom, an understanding that is greater than the peoples or the events he has been learning about. From facts about this corrupt world he has risen to wisdom, comprehension of what is true and right regardless of the circumstances. That is spiritual and comes from God."

"You are saying that what we hold in our minds is wisdom?" John asked slowly.

"No," Esclarmonde smiled broadly. "Far from it, in fact, but it is a start. You may never achieve wisdom in a single life, but the facts, knowledge and understanding you acquire can be passed on and help proceed toward wisdom in the future."

The three stood silently as the first large flakes of the next snowfall drifted. John was deep in thought. The Cathars not possessing the Grail was no surprise. They would have no use for it, and given Adso and Peter's experiences, it probably didn't even exist. Could it be that it was nothing more than a wildly unrealistic hope in Arnaud Aumery's fanatical mind? What intrigued John was the thought that the books he held in his mind were part of something much larger. He had assumed that works like the Gospel of the Christ stood alone and had value only for the damage they could do to the Catholic Church if they were believed. Now he was beginning to see the gospels and the other books he knew, such as Lucius's *Scultura* and the mathematics book by Aristarchos of Samos, as small pieces of a much larger puzzle, a puzzle that might not be completed until long after he was dead. It was a humbling thought, much like the way the great cathedral builders must feel when they began a project that they could not hope to live long enough to see completed.

The snow was becoming heavier now. The far end of the valley and Queribus had disappeared in a grey swirl and flakes were resting on hair and clothing. "So," Isabella said slowly, breaking the silence, "a wisdom that does not yet exist is the Cathar Treasure?"

"Exactly," Esclarmonde replied. "That and the information, knowledge and understanding that we all hold in our minds and which are the building blocks of that wisdom."

"No wonder Aumery is having trouble finding it," Isabella said with a smile.

"That doesn't make him any less dangerous," John added, thinking back to the torture chamber Aumery had shown him in Toledo. "Torture for a non-existent idea is just as agonizing as torture for hard information or a real cup."

"You worry too much," Isabella admonished. "Aumery's not going to bother us. We're safe for the moment, so let's just appreciate that and get on with collecting facts, building knowledge, achieving understanding and creating future wisdom."

"Spoken like a true Good Christian," Esclarmonde said, "but if we are not to lose all this enthusiasm in a drift of snow, we should return inside. I doubt if Aumery will arrive to seek the Grail this night."

Library

Queribus
February 20, 1214

Queribus was less impressive than Peyrepertuse, merely a small stone keep and a few attached buildings crammed onto the peak of a rock pinnacle that rose vertiginously from the summit of a broader hill. Other thick-walled, squat buildings, constructed from blocks of the hill's rough limestone, were scattered lower down the slopes and housed a thriving community of Good Christians and a number of refugees from the crusade.

Pereypertuse, perched along its knife-edged ridge at the far end of the valley, was easily visible from Queribus on clear days, but John had little chance to appreciate the view. The library at Queribus, housed in an oddly shaped vaulted room in the keep, was larger than John had expected. Almost twice as many dusty leather-bound books and ribbon-tied scrolls as at Peyrepertuse were piled on a shelf against one wall. On the far side of the single, strangely off-centre pillar that supported the ribs of the roof, an angled reading desk sat against the opposite wall where it caught the light from the lone large window. John sat reading at a stool at the desk.

When he and Isabella had arrived, he'd quickly scanned the scrolls looking for *Perspectiva*. None of the faded labels attached to the wooden cylinders around which the documents were rolled identified the contents as Lucius' book. This was a great disappointment, but there was always the chance that one of the scrolls was mislabelled. John had been searching for the book for so long and in so many places that he was philosophical when faced with a setback. If *Perspectiva* wasn't here, there were still other libraries to search.

John worked his way systematically through the pile. As he unrolled each scroll, he had a moment of hope that this might be it, but so far he had been let down. As at Peyrepertuse, John had already memorized a lot of the books, although the copies here appeared to be older than the ones he had seen in other places.

Isabella had left John to his work and pursued her own interests, talking to the Good Christians, listening to their stories and learning about the history of their beliefs. John didn't mind being alone. The memory cloister demanded his undivided attention and his reading was easier as a solitary task.

In the six weeks since he'd arrived at Queribus, John had gotten through about three quarters of the library—Greek plays, Latin poets, lost gospels, but nothing as controversial as The Gospel of the Christ or as complex as Aristarchos' mathematics book. It was late afternoon and John was tired. He had just finished a scroll by an early Greek Christian called Quadratus. The document was an appeal to the Roman Emperor Hadrian to allow the Christians to live and worship in peace. John found it interesting that Quadratus claimed to have met and learned from some of Christ's Apostles and that some of those whom Christ brought back from the dead were still alive, but there was little particularly important or controversial in the text.

John limped across the room and replaced Quadratus's work on the shelf. He was lifting the next scroll when he noticed the end of another document placed along the back of the shelf instead of lying across it like the others. He pulled it out, wondering if it was worth beginning something new this late in the day or if he should just leave it where it was and begin fresh tomorrow. Three things made him carry the scroll over to his desk with mounting excitement.

First, it was extremely old and made of much finer vellum than most of the works John had read. He felt the material between his fingers and marvelled at its smoothness and quality. This must have been an expensive document of great importance to someone long ago.

Second, despite its age, the scroll was tied with a much newer ribbon and was considerably cleaner than the others. Mostly, the books and scrolls here were thick with dust and neglect, as if it had been generations since anyone had looked at them. This one looked as though it had been read relatively recently.

Third, it was unlabelled.

John's hands shook as he untied the ribbon. Forcing himself to breath normally, he unrolled the first length. John stared at the scroll so hard he forgot to blink. Only when his eyes started stinging and tears formed did he close his eyes. He was almost afraid to open them again in case his imagination had been playing tricks on him and the wonder he had been looking at had somehow vanished.

The text was beautifully written in a neat, careful hand. The writing was blocky in the Roman style and the roll was divided into pages, although they

Rebirth

were longer that the pages of any book John had seen. Almost deafened by the pounding of his heart, he unrolled more. The lines of text were broken by exquisitely detailed drawings, sometimes almost filling a page. The drawings were of a wide variety of subjects—animals, humans, buildings, streets—but many were covered by a web of straight construction lines that seemed to disappear into the surface.

This was it: *Perspectiva*. John had expected Lucius' work to be a book like *Scultura*, but that work must have been a later copy. This was much older, possibly even the original written in Lucius' own hand. The shock was almost physical. John's hands shook. His heart raced. This was the thing he had been searching for ever since Beatrice had told him of its existence four years earlier in Minerve. Even his first, cursory glance told him that it was everything he could have hoped for. The drawings were magical, much better and deeper than even the drawing he had seen of Laon Cathedral.

John rolled the scroll between his hands, mesmerized by its images. This was his dream, a new way of representing the world, pictures that looked as if the viewer could walk into them. Would he be able to learn this wonderful technique? The text between the drawings looked complex and was sprinkled with mathematical symbols and words that didn't look familiar. The drawings themselves were covered with lines, letters and shapes. It all looked hideously complicated.

John continued rolling his way through the scroll, his excitement turning to concern as he realized the magnitude of the task before him. The scroll was long and increased in complexity as it went. Maybe this was beyond him, too difficult. Then he reached the end. The last page was a picture without any construction lines or numbers, and it took John's breath away. It showed a Roman theatre. The view was from the top of the rows of seats where the audience sat, sweeping down and around to half enclose the stage, which was backed by tall pillars. Figures, human and animal, stood, sat and reclined at numerous places on the steps. Behind the stage, the landscape stretched away to a distant temple and vanished to the far horizon. As John leaned close he almost felt he might tumble down the steps onto the stage.

Lucius had obviously put all the tricks and techniques he outlined in the book into this drawing, and used all his skill and craft to produce the most perfect picture he could. It was designed for those daunted by the complexity of the instructions that had come before, to show what could be done if one persevered. In the instant he saw the drawing, John knew what he would do. There was no doubt. If it took the rest of his life, he would learn what Lucius knew and practice until he could produce a picture as magnificent as this.

John rolled the scroll back to the beginning and began reading.

"My name is Lucius of the Macrinus family and I respectfully dedicate this modest work to my patron, Appolonnius Sulla, in but small gratitude for his support and encouragement. Having decorated his villa outside Rome in this style, I respectfully submit this treatise on the art of drawing as a lesson that, if it be studied and applied with rigour, will allow the student the ability to represent the world around us on a page or wall with a fidelity heretofore impossible. So, dear reader, I welcome you to my ideas and wish you speed and luck on the journey upon which you are now embarking."

John recognized the words as being similar to those at the beginning of *Scultura*. The familiarity made him feel as if her were meeting with an old friend and gave him comfort as he began what he was certain was going to be a long and arduous task.

* * *

Isabella found John several hours later, hunched over the scroll and muttering to himself. He was squinting uncomfortably in the weak light of a single wax-draped candle, his eyes only inches from the document's surface.

"Not only will you go blind if you continue to try and read in this light," Isabella said as she approached, "you will also starve to death if you don't come to the refectory to eat."

John didn't respond. He just leaned over his desk, mumbling to himself. Isabella stepped forward and touched him on the shoulder.

John jerked upright, almost knocking Isabella over. "Hey," she said, "it's me. That must be something really interesting you've found."

John stared at Isabella. His eyes were red-rimmed and he looked at her as if he were coming out of a deep, dream-filled sleep and only gradually recognizing where he was. "I'm sorry," he said eventually. "I was concentrating. See," he leaned to one side to allow Isabella a view of the scroll. "I've found Lucius' book on drawing."

Isabella scanned the section of the scroll open on John's desk in increasing wonder. "Is this really it?"

John nodded.

"I'm so happy." Isabella hugged John. Then her brow furrowed in concentration. "It looks complicated."

John took a deep breath and rubbed his eyes and stretched. He felt the scar on his side pull tight and the ache in his foot. "It is. That's why I was so involved. I was trying to make sense of it. Look." John rolled the scroll to the end to show Isabella the remarkable picture. In the flickering candle light, it almost seemed as if they were looking through a window onto a real scene.

"It's astonishing," she said in wonder. "Is that really possible? Can you learn to draw like that?"

"I hope so," John said, "but it's going to be even more difficult than I thought it would be. It'll take a long time. There's a lot of mathematics involved."

"When you have learned how to do this"—Isabella indicated the drawing of the theatre—"will you teach me?"

"Of course," John said with a smile, "and I know what my first drawing is going to be."

"What?"

"It's a secret. You'll have to wait and see."

"That's not fair." Isabella hit John playfully on the arm.

In the ensuing silence, John looked up from the drawing to see that Isabella's expression had become serious.

"What's bothering you?" he asked.

"It's five months since Muret."

"Yes," John agreed, "but I think we still have a lot of time before the crusaders turn their attention here."

Isabella nodded thoughtfully. "You're probably right, but what about what Oddo told you?"

John knew immediately what Isabella meant. Since their arrival at Peyrepertuse, they had talked a lot about whether the letter that could be used to destroy Aumery was actually with the Abbot at St. Gilles, or whether it was merely a fiction that Oddo had invented to get John to end his suffering.

When John had first told Isabella the story of Oddo's death, she had favoured the fictional version. Why, she had argued, would Oddo offer something as powerful as the letter to John, whom he hated and whom he had sworn to kill? John had agreed that Oddo had hated him, but he had also despised him as weak, so the mercenary felt superior. Oddo couldn't feel superior to Aumery because the monk didn't fear him. Oddo's power depended on him being feared so, John contended, Aumery was a threat and, therefore, Oddo hated him much more than he did John. Add to that Oddo's desire for a quick, clean death, and his decision to offer John the letter made sense.

Of course, there was no guarantee that the letter contained what Oddo said or whether it had been protected all these years by the Abbot of St. Gilles. The only way to know if the letter still existed and what it contained was to go to St. Gilles. Strangely, it was now Isabella who was keenest to travel. Although John was more convinced that the letter existed—he had seen the truth in Oddo's dying eyes—he was less keen to rush to find out. He felt safe here in the mountains and, if he was honest with himself, frightened of venturing out onto the plain, where the chances of capture or simply misadventure were much greater.

"I can't leave here now. I need time with Lucius' book," John pleaded.

"I know," Isabella said, "and you can have it. It's still winter, not a good time to travel, but can we agree on a time to set off? How long do you think learning Lucius' book will take?"

"I have no idea," John said with a shrug. "To learn everything? Months. Years." John spotted the concerned look on Isabella's face. "But there are different levels of learning. Perhaps to grasp the simplest it might only be a few weeks. Why the rush? The crusade will ignore us for a long time."

Isabella nodded. "Yes, but as we discussed at Peyrepertuse, Aumery, in his search for the Grail, might not give us as long. A letter in his hand ordering Pierre of Castelnau's murder, if shown to the right people, will stop him. It might save many lives and prevent much suffering."

John knew what Isabella said was true. If using the letter to hurt Aumery would stop him torturing people for the location of the Grail, it was important. "It's a long way to St. Gilles and the travel will be much easier when the spring comes. Even without Lucius' book, I don't think we should leave before April or May."

"I agree," Isabella said. "I'm not trying to rush you. Spring will be fine. Now, come on," Isabella tugged on his sleeve. "It's too late to do any more work tonight and I've saved you some bread and cheese."

"Thank you," John said. He looked longingly back at the scroll. It was hard to stop, but Isabella was right. His head hurt with the effort of squinting in poor light. Reluctantly, he carefully rolled the scroll and tied it with the ribbon. He tucked it under his arm and turned to the door.

"Are you not going to put in back where you found it?" Isabella asked.

John shook his head. "Now that I've found it, I'm never going to let it out of my sight again. Everywhere I go, Lucius goes as well."

"So, I am no longer the only person in your life," Isabella said with a mischievous smile. "I'll have to compete with Lucius. I must admit it's a bit offensive. I had thought that any competition would come from a beautiful damsel, not a long-dead Roman." She took John's arm and they moved toward the door.

John stopped in the archway and looked at Isabella. "You will never have any competition, beautiful damsel or dead Roman," he said seriously. "I mean that. I love you."

"I love you, too," Isabella said. As they kissed, John turned awkwardly to move the scroll safely to one side.

"See," Isabella said with a laugh as she pulled back. "Already Lucius comes between us."

Celebration

Queribus
May 8, 1214

"Do you know the one thing I really miss?" John mused. He and Isabella were sitting side by side on a smooth rock beneath the walls of Queribus, looking south across the valley at the snow-covered peaks of the Pyrenees Mountains. There was no snow around Queribus any more. After a lot of snow in January and February, the spring had been mild and the early afternoon sun provided some warmth. Nevertheless, they both wore thick woollen cloaks against the chill breeze that blew off the mountains.

"The hot afternoon sun at Madinet al-Zahra?" Isabella guessed.

"Well, yes," John acknowledged, "but I was thinking of the taste the rich meat just sliced from the pig on the spit over the fire and dripping with hot juice, smell the fresh baked bread, the music of the troubadours and the laughter and applause of the crowd."

"That's more than one thing." Isabella nudged her friend playfully in the ribs.

"I know," John agreed with a laugh. "I suppose what I mean is, I miss feast days. I know that the Good Christians say that all the festivities around religious days are just a way for the Church to extract more money from the poor, but I do miss the celebrations. I used to love the Easter parade in Toulouse and the jugglers and conjurers in the street on the Feast of the Assumption."

"I miss those things as well," Isabella agreed, "but perhaps we're just missing the simpler times. Times before the crusade, when people could enjoy themselves and not worry if they would still be alive on the next feast day."

"Perhaps," John said. "It was certainly a different world before de Montfort's knights came here, killing and burning."

"It was the Feast of the Assumption, six years ago, when everything began to change. That was when Peter had his visions outside the Chateau Narbonnaise."

"I remember," John said. "That was also the day that William offered me the chance to travel with him and his musicians."

"And caused me a lot of work trying to track you down over the following years," Isabella said with a laugh.

"I'm glad you did," John said, kissing her on the cheek. "But you're right, they *were* simpler times. Even after Peter's visions, we had no idea that the crusade was coming, and for ages after the massacre at Béziers, we all went on believing that the knights would give up and go home. We had no idea how much they hated us."

"At least Muret ended the war," Isabella said.

"Yes, but not the fighting. That'll go on until all the castles that house any Good Christians are destroyed, and I imagine the burning of heretics will go on long after that."

"So, there's not much hope for Esclaromonde and those like her?"

"No," John agreed. "Sooner or later, the inquisition will hunt them down, torture and burn them."

Isabella was silent and thoughtful for a moment. "It's time to move on," she said eventually.

"It is. I've made a lot of progress with Lucius' book and there will be other opportunities after we've been to St. Gilles. The weather's good enough for travel. We should set off soon."

"What will we do if we find the letter?"

"That depends on what it says. If it's as damning as Oddo suggested, just making it known to the Church authorities might be enough. Then we can escape."

"Let's hope so. But where?"

"Wherever we wish," John said. "The coin Pedro gave you could last us for a few years if we are careful and don't get robbed on the road. But I really have no idea where we should go. Is anywhere safe these days?"

Isabella shrugged. "We need to go somewhere you can continue learning your drawing."

"I've been thinking about that," John said. "At first I thought the north would be good, after all, that's where they are building these wonderful cathedrals and where the first drawing came from, but the north is also where the crusade comes from and I want to escape that. Then I remembered a place that William the troubadour told me about. It's north of Rome, a town called Firenze. It's wealthy, from selling sheep and wool, I think William said, but they are paying artists to paint churches, palaces and the houses of the rich merchants. I might be able to make a living there, and there will be other artists that I can learn from."

"And teach," Isabella said, smiling.

"I don't think I'm ready to become a teacher yet."

"But you are. Remember, Esclarmonde said the knowledge we have has to be used to build wisdom in the future. That places a responsibility on us. It's not enough to just keep knowledge alive and safe from all the powerful people who want to burn books and destroy the learning that they don't agree with. We have to pass on knowledge on to others."

"True," John agreed, "but we'll have to be very careful who we talk to. I get the feeling that the Church will be looking for heretics everywhere, not just in Languedoc."

"The Inquisition?"

John nodded. "Dominic Guzman's Black Friars are becoming more powerful all the time."

"We will have to be careful, but this Firenze sounds like a good place to start," Isabella said, hugging John round the waist. "As long as we're together and safe, I don't care where we go,"

The pair sat in happy silence, thinking about the uncertain future. Eventually, Isabella spoke. "I've got you a present for you." She reached under her cloak and produced a small book.

"Thank you." John took the book and opened it. The pages were filled with Isabella's small, neat script. "What is it?"

"You know that while you've been lost all winter in the library, reading and practising your drawing, I've been talking to Esclarmonde and the other old Good Christians."

John nodded.

"Well, they've told me some extraordinary stories about the Zoroastrians and the Bogomils, and all the different groups that were around a thousand years ago. The Good Christians going to the bonfires here are not unusual. They are just the last of the groups who think differently from the Catholic Church."

"You've written down a history of the Good Christians?" John thumbed through the pages.

"Yes, and all the other groups they have told me about. I've also added a history of the crusade up to the battle of Muret. I thought that, if the Church eventually succeeds in killing all the heretics and burning all the books, there should be some written record."

"You learned all this from talking to the old Good Christians?" John asked, impressed that Isabella had discovered something he hadn't come across in all his readings.

"Not everything's in dusty, dry books," Isabella said with a smile. "There are live people in the real world and they know things as well."

"All right," John said with mock contrition. "I admit you've always been better with people than me."

"I've written down all the stories. Now all you have to do is read my book and remember it. It's my contribution to the memory cloister."

"It's like a little library," John said. He was overwhelmed that Isabella had spent so much time and gone to all the trouble to produce this present for him. He had assumed she was simply filling in time in all her talks with the Good Christians. "I'll look forward to reading it. Thank you very much." He kissed her. "And I've got a present for you." He dug a small roll of vellum out of his satchel. It was tied with a purple ribbon.

"We'll never be Good Christians," Isabella said as she untied the ribbon, "as long as we hold onto material things." She unrolled the vellum and gasped. Covering the piece was the most incredible drawing she had ever seen.

It was the inside of a building, but it looked like a forest. Dozens of pillars, joined at the top by rounded arches, covered the surface and vanished into the distance. Each pillar was different and the decorations on the arches and the ceiling above them were drawn in wonderful detail, but that wasn't what had taken her breath away. The picture looked incredibly real. If she were somehow able to shrink down to the size of her thumb, Isabella was convinced she could walk into the drawing and disappear in the distance where the spaces between the pillars vanished. "Where did you find this?"

"I drew it," John said, thrilled at the effect his drawing was having on Isabella. "It's the Mezquita, the mosque in Cordova where I first met Shabaka. You weren't allowed in and it was so astounding that I swore I would remember it and that, when I found Lucius' book and taught myself to draw, it would be the first thing I would create. I wanted you to see it. I know this isn't as good as being there, but it'll give you an idea of what it was like."

"It's magnificent," Isabella said, turning the picture to examine it from different angles. Eventually, she tore her eyes away from it and looked up at John. "And it's better than being there and seeing it. It's the most incredible drawing in the world, better even than the one at the end of Lucius' book, and you drew it for me."

John beamed with pleasure. He never felt happier than when Isabella was happy.

"I mean it," Isabella said. "There *is* nothing else in the world like this and no one who can come close to doing what you have done. You'll change the world! Imagine a church in which all the walls, and even the ceiling, are painted like this. People would flock to see it. It would be more famous than St. Sernin in Toulouse or," she hesitated, searching for a suitable example, "St. Peter's in Rome."

"It's just a drawing," John said, embarrassed at Isabella's passion.

"Don't ever say that," Isabella scolded, becoming suddenly stern. "God has given you an extraordinary gift. He created you with a love of drawing and with the conviction that you could draw a different way. He gave you the strength to hold onto that belief even in the midst of war. He showed you the drawing of that cathedral in the north, left clues in your path that brought you here. He allowed you to find Lucius' book and gave you the time to learn what it could teach. Everything that has happened to us since that day on the steps of the Chateau Narbonnaise has led us here, to you and this drawing."

John blushed, but before he could stutter out a denial, Isabella went on. "This is what Esclarmonde meant. You can change the very way we see the world. That's the true Cathar Treasure. Even if every Good Christian is consigned to the flames of the Inquisition, the drawings and paintings you will spend the rest of your life creating will be a beacon for the future. Artists not yet born will look in wonder at your work in the same way you looked at Lucius drawing. They will be amazed, but they will learn. One day, everyone in the world will understand what you have done and all artists will paint in the same style as the great master, John of Toulouse."

"Or John the Lame," John interrupted, trying to ease his embarrassment with a joke.

"Paintings will become like windows onto any world the artist wishes to imagine," Isabella went on, ignoring John's comment. "The painted walls of great halls will expand forever and the ceilings of cathedral naves will blossom upward to heaven itself. John, you are the future."

John sat and stared at Isabella. Her face was lit from the left by the golden light from the setting sun and a strand of dark hair lay across her cheek. Her eyes blazed with excitement, and the passion in her face as she spoke made her look more beautiful than he had ever seen. "I want to paint you," John said.

Isabella frowned at the sudden change in topic. Then she laughed out loud. "See," she said when she had calmed down, "I'm right. You're an artist. You can't help yourself. Here I am busy telling you that you are the most important person in the entire world. Most people would be flattered, embarrassed or angry. All you can think of is the next thing you want to draw."

"I am flattered," John said, "and embarrassed, but I can't believe that I'm all the things you say I am. I'm just an orphan from Toulouse who has been very lucky. Very few people find even one thing that they love, I have found two: drawing and you. Yes, I will keep drawing and painting and learning as long as my eyes can see and my hand can hold a charcoal, and I will never stop loving you, but that is enough. The future will take care of itself, with or without me and Lucius' book on drawing."

The pair embraced for a long moment. At last, Isabella pushed John away and looked back at the drawing. "Tell me how you did it," she said.

"It's not easy to explain," John replied, "and there are still many things I don't understand. This is a simple drawing. There are much more complicated scenes in the world that I couldn't even come close to attempting."

"But what gives the drawing its depth?"

"That's what Lucius calls *perspectiva*. He made up the word but it comes from *perspicere*, which means to see through. He got the idea from drawing scenes as he saw them through glass. What he ended up with was different from other paintings and he tried to express it with numbers and lines. He started with his eye, perhaps an arm's length in front of the glass he was drawing on. Then he imagined a line from his eye through the spot he was drawing on the glass, to the actual object in the distance. He did this over and over again. It took him years to work it out. The mathematics he came up with is complicated, I don't completely understand it yet, but I will."

"But why do you need to do all that? Can't you just draw what you see on the glass?" Isabella asked.

"Yes, but then you couldn't change the size or draw something you weren't really looking at. I couldn't have drawn the Mesquita for you."

Isabella nodded in agreement. "So *perspectiva* is a way of doing that?"

"Yes," John continued, "Lucius made up some rules to use. You know how things seem smaller the farther away they are?"

"Like the sides of a straight road seeming to come together on the horizon?"

"Exactly. That's *perspectiva*. Lucius called the place where the two sides of the road appear to come together the *evanidus cuspis*, the vanishing spear. All the lines that are going in the same direction as the sides of the road must come together at that point. It doesn't matter whether it's a road or the edges of the walls of a building."

"That sounds simple. Why don't more artists use it?"

"Because it's more complicated than that. It's simple if all you want to draw is one road. What if you're walking along that road and you come to a fork? There's a second road branching off to the left. It too narrows as it goes away. So now you have two different sets of lines going in different directions toward two vanishing spears."

John held up his hand to prevent Isabella interrupting. "Now imagine that there's a building between the two roads. Two walls of the building are parallel to the two roads. The edges of the walls going in the same direction as the roads will have the same vanishing spears, but what about the back wall, the front wall, the vertical edges, the roof? Each new set of lines has its own vanishing spear."

"Stop. Stop," Isabella implored. "You've convinced me it's complicated. I suppose this explains all the lines that Lucius drew all over his drawings."

"Some of them," John said with a sly smile. "Those are his lines of *perspectiva*, but there's also something he calls *planta brevis*."

"To make something short?" Isabella asked. "What does that mean?"

"I don't know," John shrugged. "I haven't worked that one out yet. And this doesn't even begin to say how to draw nature, where there are very few straight lines or vanishing spears. My drawing of the Mesquita was simple. The tops and bottoms of each line of pillars are like the edges of a road turned on its side, they all go toward the same vanishing spear. All I had to do was draw them, fill in some pillars and draw arches between them. It'll take years of practise before I can draw something like Queribus, with all the different bits of the fortress at different angles, built wherever there was room on the mountain top."

"It's a lifetime's work."

"I think so," John said. "Lucius tries to explain it all using mathematics. I recognize some of the symbols he uses from Aristarchos' book, but I don't have a clear idea what it all means. I'll have to become a mathematician to understand that."

"Then that's what we'll do." Isabella sounded determined. "This spring we'll go to St. Gilles, find the letter Oddo told you about, use it to destroy Aumery, and then we'll run away to Firenze and you'll become the most famous artist in the world."

John laughed. "It sounds simple."

"It will be." Isabella stood up. "But not if we sit out here all day. Let's find a fire to warm ourselves by."

"Good idea," John said. He massaged his aching foot, stood up and led the way along the narrow path at the foot of the wall. John couldn't remember ever being happier. He had everything he had ever wanted: Isabella, Lucius' book, safety, a plan for the future. He felt a vague twinge of guilt that he could be so happy amidst so much destruction and chaos, and he missed Adso terribly. More worryingly, there was a tiny, nagging part of his mind that kept telling him that things couldn't be this simple. Nothing in the past—his work for Roger Trenceval, his flight to Al-Andalus, Muret—had worked out as he had hoped or planned. Would his future now be different? John pushed his doubts away. Of course things would be all right. He was finished with the crusade. One more thing to do: find Aumery's letter, if it ever existed, put it in the right hands, and he and Isabella would be free to live their lives in peace. That's how it was going to work out, wasn't it?

Old Friends

Arles
June 6, 1214

John was trying hard to imagine what the amphitheatre must have been like when the Romans built it a thousand years ago. It wouldn't have had the four towers that had turned it into a fortress where the populace could find refuge in troubled times, or the collection of ramshackle buildings that seemed to sprout from the exterior walls like strange growths of nature. Inside, according to old books that John had memorized, twenty thousand people had once sat on stone terraces that were now cluttered with dilapidated houses between which old men smoked, women gossiped and grubby children ran. The arena floor itself no longer saw gladiatorial combat or chariot races, being mostly covered with more houses and shops. Only a small space was left in the middle to serve as a village square.

"It's like a separate town," Isabella said as she surveyed the huge oval structure from the top of the southernmost tower.

"It was once," John said. "Arles was an important Roman centre, but when they left, almost everyone else did, too. Those that stayed moved in here and turned it into a fortified village within the ruins of the larger town. They were very troubled times."

"Worse than the times we find ourselves in?" William asked. John and Isabella had searched out their troubadour friend in his home town, where he was living quietly now that his profession was not welcomed by the crusader lords.

"I think so," John said. "Today, things are bad where there is fighting and where the crusader army goes and, of course, for any Cathars, but there are many places, like Arles, that are untouched by the war. After the Romans left there was war everywhere. Roving bands of barbarians and moors could descend on your village at any time and destroy everything. This place must have been a haven, safe from all but the strongest army."

"I wish I'd lived here in Roman times," William said wistfully. "I can see myself standing down there singing, with an audience of thousands in rapture at my talents."

"From what I understand," Isabella said, "you would be more likely to be food for some vicious and exotic animal."

"And that would be more entertaining than your singing," John said, ducking theatrically when William aimed a punch at his head.

"I am surrounded by the Philistines, unappreciated even in my home town," William complained, pretending to be on the verge of tears. "But my day will come," he said, perking up. "The great epic poem that I am working on will be recognized for the masterpiece it is. A work to be recited alongside the immortal Homer."

"And what is it about?" Isabella asked.

"I write about what I know. My epic is called A Chronicle of the Good Christian Wars. It is a tale of these sad times created from what I have seen and the stories I have found as I travelled the land, and that is why I wish to talk to you two before you move along. John, you have much that is useful stored in that cloister you call a memory, and Isabella, John mentioned that you had been talking with many old Cathars during your sojourn in the mountain fortresses."

"I have," Isabella acknowledged, "and I will happily tell you all I discovered, but it might not be necessary. I wrote everything down in a book. Of course, John now holds that book in his head, so he may be persuaded to lend the original to you. We can collect it when we return from St. Gilles."

"Of course," John said. "It's full of wonderful stories and written in a way that will bring you to tears or laughter whenever the great writer intends." He smiled at Isabella, who kissed him on the cheek.

"Good God," William said, his face wrinkling in mock disgust. "Love is a painful thing for those not engaged in it. But I thank you and shall take good care of the book until you return. When do you plan to go to St. Gilles?"

"Tomorrow," John said. "It is a walk of only twelve miles or so."

"How long do you plan to stay?"

"That depends on what we find. Isabella thinks we should stay for a few days and try to become friends with the Abbot before we ask about the letter. I think she's right; that will increase our chances of seeing it."

"What if the Abbot won't give it up or denies its existence?"

"I suppose that will depend on whether he knows what the letter contains," John said. "I hope he doesn't and, now that Oddo's dead he will have no reason to keep it. If he has read it, he may well have destroyed it already or given it to Aumery. In that case…" John shrugged.

"If you do manage to lay hands on the letter, then what? It seems to me that this document could be very dangerous to anyone who carries it."

"We hope not as dangerous as it will be to Aumery," Isabella said.

"We've talked a lot about who we should take the letter to," John said. "The danger in giving it to someone here is that they might be under Aumery's power and would simply give the letter to him."

"Which would not be good for you," William interrupted.

"Exactly," John went on. "That's why we'll take the letter to Rome. Pierre of Castelnau was a Papal Legate, so Pope Innocent won't be happy to discover that his murder was arranged by the man he has since put in charge of the crusade."

"It's a long journey," Isabella said, "but we think that's the safest way to do it."

"You're probably right," William agreed. "I wish you luck. I have never liked the fanatic, but I have heard of another reason why the world will be a better place without him. Now that the crusade has succeeded, his name is being bandied about as a possible cardinal, perhaps even a future pope."

"Pope!" John and Isabella exclaimed simultaneously. "That's impossible."

"I wish it were, William said, "but it's very possible. His elevation to cardinal is almost assured, which means he will go to Rome. You know how manipulative he can be. Once at the centre, he could well build enough support to be a realistic candidate when Innocent dies."

"We *must* stop him," John said. "Aumery on the throne of St. Peter in Rome! It's a horror that doesn't bear thinking about."

"I agree," William said. "He really would turn the world into the devil's playground that the Good Christians think it is. I wish you well in your task, and I shall look forward to hearing the details of how you progress."

"And we will tell you," Isabella said, "although you may have to come and find us to obtain those details. After we have been to Rome, we plan to go to Firenze so John can practice his drawing."

"It is a beautiful town where the troubadour's talents are still appreciated. I shall seek you out there."

"We shall look forward to it." Isabella stepped forward and embraced William. "Until then, let us hope we may all avoid the troubles that plague our land."

"Indeed." William returned Isabella's embrace, stepped back and shook John's hand. "Be careful at St. Gilles."

"We'll be on our way to Rome in a week," John said.

The three friends descended from the tower and separated, William to the room where he lived while he worked on his epic song, and John and Isabella to the inn to prepare for their departure in the morning. No one noticed the black-clad monk standing in the shadows watching.

The Letter

St. Gilles
June 13, 1214

John stood lost in thought on the steps of the west front of the Abbey church of St. Gilles. He never tired of looking at the wealth of extraordinary carvings that surrounded the three doors. Strange beasts and monsters carried on their backs the fourteen ornamental pillars, some of which had been quarried from ancient Roman temples. Biblical scenes were carved in intricate detail amidst a profusion of stone vegetation, and skinny saints peered down from their recessed alcoves. Above the main door, Christ sat surrounded by the symbols of the four gospel writers, an angel for Mathew, a winged lion for Mark, a winged ox for Luke and an eagle for John. What about all the other gospel writers, John wondered. Surely they deserved to be commemorated in stone as well as in his memory cloister.

"The battle between good and evil." John turned to see Abbot Olivier walking toward him up the steps. He was a short, squat man who gave off a sense of strength and power, even through his flowing habit. This fitted with some gossip Isabella had heard claiming that Olivier had been a mercenary soldier who'd fought against the English King Richard Coeur de Lion at Freteval before taking Holy Orders and rising in the Church. John could easily picture the man as a soldier. On the surface he was friendly and cheerful, but underneath, John thought he detected a hardness and Olivier peppered his speech with military terms.

"With Christ triumphant, of course,," John said. For the past week, John had been busy building a relationship with Olivier. He had presented himself as a simple pilgrim, preparing to set out for Santiago de Compestela to give thanks for surviving the violent events of the past few years. The Abbot had been fascinated by John's detailed accounts of the siege of Béziers and the battles of Las Navas de Tolosa and Muret, but John had kept well clear of mentioning the memory cloister or any of his contacts with heretics. John thought that Olivier considered him a friend and he was only waiting for an appropriate moment to introduce the topic of Aumery's letter to Oddo.

The only difficulty with the week had been that it had been a lonely undertaking. As a pilgrim, John was welcome to stay in the monastery, but that was not possible for Isabella. She was living in an inn across the square from the abbey church and they had agreed that it would be best if they met as little as possible so as not to arouse suspicion. On only two occasions had John managed to sneak away after dark and quickly tell Isabella how things were progressing.

"Unquestionably," Olivier agreed. "I have much enjoyed your visit with us here, but I imagine you are keen to be on the road to Santiago. After all, you marched but a short day from Arles and you have bivouacked with us for a week. Your journey will take many months at this rate."

"I *am* keen to be on my way," John replied with as much enthusiasm as he could muster. He was telling the truth. He couldn't use the pilgrim's cover story to stay at St. Gilles much longer without arousing suspicion, but he had seen no opportunity to bring up the subject of Oddo's letter in a way that would not provoke awkward questions. He had tried a couple of times, but Olivier had always led the conversation away from the topic John most wanted to discuss. "And I must admit to being slothful," John went on, "but you have such a fine Abbey here." He nodded toward the rich carvings on the west front. "It must be an ideal place to spend your life in the contemplation of God."

"Indeed it is," Abbot Olivier said with a smile. "I have enjoyed my years here, but..." he paused thoughtfully for a moment before going on, "there have been times when, just as you have succumbed to sloth, I have given in to the sin of envy."

"What do you mean?"

"The holy crusade has done, and is doing, great work in God's name. Do you not agree?"

"Of course."

"It must have been a wonderful thrill for you to be a part of that work at Muret."

"It was," John agreed, pushing back the vivid image of Adso's broken body. "Who did you envy?"

"I have not always been a man of God," Olivier mused, apparently ignoring John's question. "Before I saw the light, I was more a follower of Ares or Mars, the pagan gods of war. I was a soldier for hire, a mercenary who killed for gold on the orders of any petty prince who could pay. Then God spoke to me and I saw the error of my ways. I threw off my armour and took Holy

Rebirth

Orders. As you see, God has rewarded me with the fortunate position I hold here. However, when I see the sword and axe wielded in God's name, the old talents stir within me and I wonder if I would be of more use abandoning the cloister and leading men in battle."

John's mind was racing. Olivier was opening up more than he had done in the past week. This was the chance to work the conversation around to the subject of the letter, but how? John was still wrestling with that question when Olivier answered it for him.

"In the battles you witnessed, how did the Falcons perform?"

"What?" John asked, taken aback by the question.

"Oddo's Falcons? Surely you have heard of them. They are the spearhead of de Montfort's army. I heard that they played a significant role at Las Navas de Tolosa and Muret. Was this the case?"

"Yes," John said, struggling to keep the surprise out of his voice. "They almost captured the Caliph in Al-Andalus and led the way to King Pedro at Muret. Why do you ask? How do you know of them?"

"Everyone knows of them," Olivier said. He fell silent and his gaze drifted into the distance. "I more than most," he added softly.

Suddenly, John made the connection. "You said you were a mercenary. Were you a Falcon?"

Abbot Olivier's eyes flicked back to focus on John. They were cold. "You're a clever young man. That can be a dangerous characteristic."

He knows everything about me, John thought. Before he had a chance to consider what he was going to do, Olivier's face softened into a friendly smile. "I was more than *a* Falcon," he said. "I created them. Twenty years ago, for the French king, Philippe II, who wished to build an army to drive the English from his lands. Unfortunately for him, the English were led by Richard, the one called Lion Hearted, fresh from carrying the cross to the Holy Land. Philippe's army was crushed at Freteval, although my Falcons fared well enough.

"In the succeeding years, we learned the arts of war in the employ of many and developed a reputation for bravery and success. Scarce a month passed when we were not employed by some ambitious lord or other. But I tired and God opened my eyes to the horrors my men and I were perpetrating, and I recognized that my immortal soul was in jeopardy. The others did not see it this way—they saw only the gold that was flowing into our pockets—so as the twelve hundredth year since Our Lord's birth turned, I renounced my past and looked to my eternal future."

"And Oddo became leader of the Falcons."

Olivier nodded. "He had been with me since the beginning. He did not agree with me, but he respected my decision, so we went our separate ways. Although, as I said"—Olivier's lips curled in a wry smile—"a part of me still wishes to take up a more physical battle for Christ at the Falcons's head."

"Did you see Oddo much after you took holy orders?"

"Only rarely. Oddo's work took him far afield; however, he sometimes would stop by if passing this way." Olivier stared piercingly into John's eyes. "I believe he was even here the time you visited."

A chill ran down John's back. The only previous time he had been to St. Gilles had been as part of Roger Trenceval's entourage at the meeting with the Papal Legates in 1208. John hadn't seen Oddo then, but if the mercenary had been there then, it strongly supported John's idea that he had been the left-handed knight who had killed Pierre of Castelnau. John had wanted the subject of Oddo to come up in conversation, but not like this. All of a sudden he seemed to be hurtling toward the unknown.

"How did you know I'd been here before?" John asked. Curious as to why Olivier was suddenly opening up to him.

Olivier's face relaxed into a smile. "You looked familiar when I first laid eyes on you, but I couldn't remember where I had seen you before. It bothered me all week, but this morning I remembered. You were with Count Raymond's delegation that came here to debate with the Legates."

"I was a scribe for Roger Trenceval," John explained, trying to give away as little as possible.

Olivier nodded thoughtfully. "A most unfortunate event. Had Count Raymond seen the error of his ways, much of the recent unpleasantness might have been avoided. In any case," Olivier continued before John could think of a response, "I seem to recall that you left with the Papal delegation after Raymond issued his threat against Pierre and were present at the martyr's murder."

"I was," John admitted, feeling that he was getting in much deeper than he wanted. How much did this man know?

"I also recall that, on his return with poor Pierre's body, Father Aumery loudly accused Count Raymond of planning the murder. Of course, Raymond denied it, but what else could one expect from such a protector of heretics? After much screaming and shouting, Raymond and his entourage retreated to Toulouse. Father Aumery appeared strangely elated by the event of that sad morning. He is an odd man and I fear that his fanaticism might occasionally blind him to God's will."

Olivier paused and John nodded, not trusting himself to speak.

"He immediately dictated a letter to His Holiness Pope Innocent, describing the events and requesting that firm measures be taken against Raymond."

John vaguely wondered if it had been Peter's hand that had written the letter Aumery sent to the Pope beginning the crusade. His wondering was interrupted by Olivier. "You did not return with Father Aumery?"

"No, I didn't," John said warily. "I went to Béziers."

Olivier scratched his chin thoughtfully. "Father Aumery claimed that you held Pierre's donkey steady when the murderer attacked."

"No," John's mind spun in confusion. "I mean, yes. I was by Pierre when he was killed, but he called me over. I saw the knight and tried to pull the donkey out of the way, but the knight was left-handed, so I pulled the wrong way. Aumery accused me of helping in the murder and I ran."

Olivier looked at John. "It is probably best to run when you incur Father Aumery's wrath. The knight was left-handed, you say?"

"He was," John replied, wondering if he'd made a huge mistake.

"Did you get a good look at him?"

"He wore a helmet that covered his face."

"I didn't ask about his helmet," Olivier said.

John sighed. This wasn't going as he had planned. Not that he'd had a good plan. He had hoped the Abbot of St. Gilles would be mild-mannered and wrapped in his spirituality, without a knowledge or particular interest in the letter he had been asked to hold. That wasn't the case. John made a decision. "Was Oddo the knight who murdered Pierre of Castelnau?"

Olivier's expression didn't change as he continued to stare at John, who became increasingly nervous under the penetrating gaze.

"You have not been completely honest with me," he said eventually.

John shook his head.

"What was your purpose in coming here?"

John took a deep breath. There was no point lying now. Starting with Aumery accusing him of murder on the riverbank at Arles and leaving out only the detailed contents of the memory cloister, John told Olivier the story of his life. He talked about the good people he had met and the land that he loved and how they were being destroyed by Aumery and de Montfort. He told what he knew from Peter and Adso about Aumery's mad quest for the Grail. He talked about the heretic bonfire outside Minerve, the hundred mutilated knights of Bram and the slaughter at Muret. He described his meetings with Oddo outside Minerve, at Las Naves de Tolosa and Muret, and he recounted how he had killed Oddo in exchange for the information about

Aumery's letter. He was exhausted when he had finished and could only stand and stare at Olivier, whose brow was wrinkled in deep thought.

John had convinced himself that not only had he lost any chance of getting his hands on the letter, but he would be lucky to escape from this situation with his life, when Olivier broke the silence. "Would you like to read the letter?"

"Yes," John managed to force out, barely able to believe what he was hearing.

Olivier turned and walked along the west front of the church. He had almost reached the corner before John roused himself from his shock and rushed after him. They crossed the cloister and entered Olivier's cell. It was a typical monk's chamber, with a single high window in the opposite wall from the door, a cot with a single blanket on a straw-filled mattress, a reading desk with an open Bible on it and a small table on which sat a basin and a jug of water. Only two things struck John as unusual: the wall above the bed was painted with a bright picture of Christ sitting in judgement above the damned and the blessed on the Day of Judgement and, leaning against the wall at the head of the bed, was a huge, beautifully polished, two-handed sword. Without a word, Olivier went to the bed, lifted the corner of the mattress, extracted a sheet of parchment and handed it to John.

With shaking hands John took the parchment and unfolded it. He glanced up at Olivier, who nodded encouragement. John looked down. The handwriting was spidery and the capitalization of odd words gave the document an untidy appearance. The text was broken into four blocks. John's heart raced as he began to read:

> In the name of God and the much Loved and blessed Pope Innocent III, His earthly King, greetings to Oddo of Saxony from Arnaud Aumery, Abbot of Citeaux and Lowly sword in the Interminable fight against heresy and wickedness.
>
> As Ever, In Earnest duty, I Respectfully put quill to Parchment On this Feast day of Saints Cornelius and Cyprian in the year of our Reverent Lord, 1207.
>
> A mutual Companion in God intimated to me that you Are a man of No Little Skill and Uncommon discretion. God has A Task for you for which you shall earn both Earthly and heavenly reward.
>
> Be In the Good Abbey Of Saint Gilles, One Day's Slow journeying from the City of Arles, 40 Long Nights after the feast of Saint John Damascene.
>
> Yours in God.

Arnaud Aumery

John read the document again with a horrible sinking feeling. He had no doubt that it was as Oddo had said, a letter from Aumery setting up the murder of Pierre of Castelnau, but it didn't say so clearly. Aumery would be able to claim that it had a completely innocent purpose and, with Oddo dead, who could contradict him? It had been too much to hope that Aumery had been stupid enough to write everything down clearly.

"You seem disappointed," Olivier said.

"I had hoped for more," John said.

Olivier smiled. "Perhaps you don't look hard enough."

John stared at the document, but nothing jumped out at him. The only unusual things were the capital letters, but they were random. Simply a quirk of Aumery's writing.

"What do you see?"

"Nothing," John answered with a shrug.

"You are not well versed in the ways of cryptographia? Look at the first block of writing. How many capital letters do you see?"

John counted carefully. "Fifteen."

"And how many of those are where they should be?"

John went through the writing again. The capitals on God and Pope Innocent were what he expected. "There are eleven where I would expect them and four where I would not."

"What are those four?"

John ran his finger along the line looking at each word in turn. "The L in Loved, the K in King, the L in Lowly, and the I in Interminable," he said. "L-L-K-I. It means nothing."

"Can you make a word out of those four letters?" Olivier asked patiently.

John shifted the letters around in his head. It didn't take him long. "Kill," he gasped. A chill ran down his spine.

"Now what of the second block of writing?" Olivier encouraged.

John squinted at the page. "E-I-E-R-P-O-F-R," he said slowly. John closed his eyes and rearranged the letters. He couldn't make a word.

"Two words," he heard Olivier whisper. Almost instantly, the answer jumped out at him. "Pierre of..." Without any prompting, John attacked the third block of text. Long before he had read out all the letters he knew what it was going to say. "Castelnau. Kill Pierre of Castelnau. Aumery hid the instructions in the letter!"

"He did," Olivier agreed.

Already John had the letters from the final block. "I-G-O-O-D-S-C-L-N. Gold coins," But what did that mean? Then he noticed that the 40 was written larger than the words around it. "It's a contract," he said breathlessly. "Aumery is telling Oddo that he will pay him 40 gold coins to kill Pierre of Castelnau. And the feast days. Aumery wrote the letter on Saint Cornelius and Cyprian's day, 1207. That's September 16. He told Oddo to travel for 40 nights after the feast of Saint John Damascene. His day is December 4." John made a quick calculation in his head. "That would have Oddo arriving at St. Gilles on January 13. Pierre of Castelnau was killed on January 14."

John shivered, even though the evening was warm. It all fitted. In the right hands, this was more than enough proof to destroy Arnaud Aumery. John looked up at Olivier. "You obviously understand what this letter means. Why are you showing it to me?"

"First, tell me what you would do with this letter if it were yours."

"I would take it to Rome," John said without hesitation, "and show it to the most important Cardinal I could find. Pope Innocent himself if that is possible."

"To what purpose?"

"To bring down Arnaud Aumery."

"But he is a man of God," Olivier objected.

"He is not," John said angrily, no longer concerned about what Olivier thought of him. "God would not countenance the things that Aumery has done. He ordered the deaths of ten thousand people inside Béziers, most of whom were good Catholics, innocent of any taint of heresy; he has led the crusade on a path of horror and destruction through this land in pursuit of his fanatical goal of slaughtering every heretic here; and he has tortured countless men and women in his mad quest to find the Holy Grail. He works in the name of God, but he seeks worldy power."

"Could much the same not be said of Simon de Montfort?" Olivier asked calmly.

"Of course," John agreed, "but he is a temporal Lord seeking to carve out a kingdom for himself and his son. That is what Lords do. He uses the name of God but he does not hide that what he does is for his own ends. Aumery conceals his ambition behind a cloak of godliness, and he will stop at nothing." John waved the letter at Olivier. "As this proves, he planned the murder of a Papal Legate to further his own ends."

"Are you any better than him?" Olivier asked. "You would play God and use this letter to destroy him."

"No, I will not destroy Aumery. I will allow other men in Rome, perhaps closer to God than he, to decide his fate."

Abbot Olivier stared thoughtfully at John for a long moment. "That sword," he said at length, pointing to the weapon at the head of his bed. "That was my killing weapon when I created the Falcons. I cannot imagine the number of heads it has cleaved or limbs it has severed. I brought it with me when I renounced the life of a mercenary as a reminder that the power of God is infinitely greater than the power of man. I have been tempted many times in these turbulent years to take up my sword again, but I have always resisted. It has not been easy. Unless you have been a soldier, I do not believe you can understand the thrill of matching your skills against another in a life and death struggle, or the sense of joy and freedom that overcomes one in the heat of battle."

Olivier gazed at the sword. John remembered the wild sensations that had overcome him at Muret as he battled toward Oddo. It was anger and, yes, Olivier was right, joy. "I understand," John said.

Olivier turned back from the sword and nodded to John. "That feeling was the most difficult thing to give up when I renounced that life. Oddo and I were like brothers. We fought side-by-side against overwhelming odds on countless occasions and, if I am honest, I have never experienced happiness greater than when we stood, scarred and bleeding, back to back, with the bodies of our enemies piled around us. I have struggled to renounce that; Oddo never did. Perhaps there was more of the brute in him, perhaps more honesty."

Olivier smiled ruefully. "Whatever it was, Oddo changed when he fell in with Aumery. When he came here that January more than six years ago, I tried to talk him out of doing Aumery's deed but he wouldn't listen. He laughed at me and told me this monastic life had made me soft. He may have been right there, but at least I have not been in debt to the uncompromising vision of that fanatic Aumery.

"Don't misunderstand me. No one forced Oddo to do the work he did. He enjoyed the killing and the power it brought. He liked de Montfort. They understood one another and the limits and uses of earthly power. They had similar gaols and went about achieving them in similar ways. It was Aumery who bothered Oddo. He owed allegiance to powers not of this world. When God orders you to do something, the limits of earthly power are not important and Oddo did not like that loss of control. Oddo could not control Aumery through fear and I suspect he hated him above all others for that."

John listened with rapt attention. What he was hearing confirmed what Oddo had told him at Muret.

"He came to visit me for the final time in the weeks before Muret," Olivier continued. "He seemed uncharacteristically troubled, and that's when he gave me the letter. He told me to keep it safe, swore me to secrecy and instructed me to use it if anything should happen to him.

"I assumed that the letter was some kind of will and that my old friend was worried about the upcoming clash with King Pedro, although worry before a battle was not like Oddo. However, after he left, I read the letter and realized its import. It also brought to mind something Oddo had said. We had been talking about King Pedro and the upcoming fight. Oddo had no doubts that the crusade would be victorious—after all, he had seen both armies close up. I asked him, since victory over Pedro would mean the effective end to the war, would he be content afterwards using the Falcons simply to keep watch over de Montfort's lands, chastise minor lords who stepped out of line and catch and burn the occasional heretic?"

Olivier's broad brow wrinkled with worry before he went on. "I was being light-hearted, assuming Oddo would disparage that kind of work and talk of his plans to take his men north. There are still lucrative opportunities there—selling mercenary services to Philippe, who is still struggling to throw the English, and their new King John, out of his lands. Instead, Oddo flew into a rage. He said working for de Montfort would be paradise compared to working for Aumery and that he would rather cut off his legs than do that man's bidding. He truly hated him. Of that I am certain, but I suspect he also feared him and worried that Aumery might wish him ill when the crusade no longer needed Oddo's services. After all, if Aumery was planning to rise high in the Church, I'm sure Oddo knew some things that could damage the man's reputation if known in the right places. The existence of the letter in a safe place would ensure Oddo's safety."

John pondered what Olivier was telling him. It made sense, and it explained why Oddo would use the letter to destroy Aumery. "The letter can destroy Aumery. Why did Oddo not use it himself?"

"For the same reason that I have not used it," Olivier replied. "Using the letter would also destroy Oddo. Even if the letter were used effectively, Aumery would make certain that Oddo would go down with him. And remember, Aumery is a part of the Church with some powerful friends. He might be discredited in a scandal, but Oddo would be tortured and burned. If he or I used the letter, we would be signing his death warrant."

"But now that Oddo's dead, you are free to use the letter?"

Olivier nodded. "And I have been debating how best to do that. My position within the Church makes it awkward and greatly increases the risk that Aumery will discover anything I do. You do not have that problem. You may travel freely, to Rome, and seek audience with high members of the Church who owe no allegiance to Aumery. That is why I am giving you the letter."

John was stunned. He had what he had come for, but the talk of death unnerved him. If Oddo had not been able to stand up to Aumery, the man was even more powerful than John had thought. "Who should I give the letter to?" John asked.

"This is a time of shifting loyalties," Olivier said. "No one is certain. However, there is a Cardinal Ugolino di Conti who helped me when I was seeking a way to God. He was unimportant then, but he has risen to a position of power in Rome. There is even quiet talk of him being a future Pope. He is a godly and an honest man who seeks to reform the Church, rid it of corruption and return to the simpler ways of the old days. I have heard that there is a monk in Italy, a Francesco from the town of Assisi, who is trying to establish an order of penitent monks who strive to live like Christ, owning nothing and wandering the land preaching and doing good. This Francesco does not sound like a corrupt man and Cardinal di Conti supports him. Perhaps he is the cardinal you should seek out in Rome for help."

The name Francesco triggered a memory in John of something Peter had talked about in his quest to the east. "I have heard of this Francesco," he said. "Perhaps he and those who support him are the ones to go to." John folded the letter carefully and slipped it inside his tunic.

"When will you go?" Olivier asked.

John looked out the window. There was already a reddish tinge to the clouds in the west. "If I may stay here tonight, I will be gone at first light."

"Of course you may stay," Olivier said with a smile. "I hope I have not placed too heavy a burden upon your shoulders."

"You only gave me what I sought," John said. "And for that I thank you most deeply. Any weight it carries is my own doing."

"Often it is the thing we seek most that is the hardest to bear when it is found. I wish you luck and I shall pray daily for your success and safe return." A bell tolled in the church. "The Compline bell calling me to prayer. I shall begin prayers this very hour."

"Thank you," John said, "for everything."

Olivier patted John on the shoulder and led the way outside. He turned left toward the Church. John followed, but instead of entering the church, he skirted the impressive west front and headed for the inn across the square. He had a lot to tell Isabella before they set off. The figure lounging by the entrance to a nearby alley watched his progress with interest.

* * *

"It scares me," Isabella said after slowly reading the letter for the third time. She was sitting on the edge of her cot in her room at the inn with the letter on her lap. John, who was perched on a stool by the hearth, had just finished telling her the details of his conversation with Abbot Olivier. "Are you certain it's genuine? It is in Aumery's hand?"

"I have seen no one else who writes in such a thin, stretched-out way. It is genuine. But what scares you? I thought you would be thrilled that it exists and that we have it."

"I am thrilled and I cannot wait to begin our journey to Rome, but Aumery is not stupid. He also strikes me as a suspicious man." Isabella returned her gaze to the letter as she continued thoughtfully. "He wrote this letter and he has not destroyed it with his own hand, therefore, regardless of what Oddo may have told him, he cannot be certain that the letter does not still exist. He knows that the letter is very dangerous to him, but also that it was equally dangerous to Oddo. So, Aumery was safe as long as Oddo lived. Now Oddo is dead and I would wager that Aumery has searched everything Oddo owned very thoroughly. He hasn't found the letter, so there are only two possibilities: one, Oddo destroyed the letter, or two, he hid it somewhere. The first is not a problem for Aumery, the second might be."

John marvelled at the way Isabella thought. It was so clear and she was making connections that had completely escaped him. "You worked all this out?" he asked.

Isabella looked up, a frown of mild annoyance at the interruption on her face. "Yes," she said shortly. "I haven't had much else to do, sitting in this room for the past week." She looked back down at the letter as if her thoughts were written there. Abashed, John sat in silence waiting for her to continue.

"So, let us assume," she went on eventually, "that Aumery is looking for the letter, if only to confirm that it no longer exists. Mercenaries have few friends. Aumery would have begun with the other Falcons. They know nothing about the letter, but they told him about Oddo's old companion who is now abbot at St. Gilles."

"Maybe they didn't say anything to Aumery," John suggested. He too was beginning to get scared. He had thought that the difficult part would be getting the letter. Now Isabella's thinking suggested that Aumery might be after the letter as well.

"Aumery has the authority of the Church and the power of the Inquisition behind him," Isabella said slowly. "Do you think many of the Falcons would have resisted his questions for long?"

John winced at the memory of the torture chamber Aumery had shown him in Toledo.

"Aumery knows that Abbot Olivier is Oddo's friend. He may also consider the possibility that Oddo gave the letter to de Montfort, but I suspect there's little he can do about that at the moment. Let us assume the worst—Aumery suspects that, if the letter still exists, Oddo may have given it to Olivier for

Rebirth

safekeeping. It's too much of a possibility to ignore. Obviously, he hasn't been here and found the letter, but who knows when he might arrive. We need to leave as quickly as possible."

"We'll go at first light tomorrow."

"I think we should leave tonight."

"Tonight?"

"I'm scared, John. I've been sitting here all this week doing nothing but thinking of Aumery and what he would do if he caught us with the letter. I imagine Aumery's lurking round every corner. I almost faint every time I see a monk. Yesterday, a party of knights rode through town. They weren't even Falcons, but I managed to convince myself that they were here to catch us and drag us back."

"All right," John said. The worry in Isabella's eyes bothered him. "The moon's near full and it's a clear night. We should be able to travel. But first I need to return to the Abbey to get my satchel and books. We'll leave as soon as I get back. Don't worry." He stood and stepped over to Isabella. "Once we're on the road, no one will be able to find us. We'll be safe." He leaned down and kissed her.

"I'm sorry," she said. "I know it's probably just a silly worry because I've been alone and helpless these past days. I just have a bad feeling. I'll be fine once we're on the road."

"I'll be right back," John said. "You collect your things and we'll be on our way before you know it." He hugged Isabella and hurried down the inn stairs onto the street.

It was almost dark and the night was cloudy. Travelling would be hard, but at least no one would see them. Could Isabella be right? Was Aumery searching for them?

A whinny from a side alley brought John's heart to his throat. He could just make out a horse standing placidly between the shafts of a hay cart. Odd that the farmer hadn't unharnessed it and put it in a stable for the night. John shook his head. Isabella's nervousness was getting to him. It was just a farmer who had dallied too long in the tavern and left his horse unattended. John hurried forward. The sooner they were on the road the better.

He never saw the figure step from the doorway as he passed. He felt a sharp pain in the back of his head and his knees buckled. John had a fleeting image of the ground rushing up to meet his face, then everything went black.

* * *

Isabella sat in the inn, waiting. She would be glad to leave St. Gilles, not only because it might be a dangerous place, but also because she was tired of it. It was not a large town and, just to escape the confines of her room, she had walked every street and alley a dozen times each. She knew every shopkeeper by name, had played knucklebones with most of the town children and given alms to every beggar.

One man in particular interested her. He was an old soldier who had lost a leg and the use of his left hand at Las Navas de Tolosa. He was the gatekeeper at the west gate, where he lived in a single room, little more than an alcove, cut into the wall itself. His job was to open the gate in the morning and close it in the evening and answer any calls for entry or exit during the hours of darkness. He spent his free hours begging from passing travellers but, unlike most beggars, he didn't rush off to drink every silver coin he was given but liked nothing more than to converse with anyone about their journeys and experiences. He reminded Isabella a little of Peire and she enjoyed talking with him about Al-Andalus and swapping stories about their time there. She would miss him. Maybe one day she might return and exchange more stories with him. What was his name? Had he even told her? She couldn't remember.

A shout in the street interrupted Isabella's reverie. John would be back soon; she should get ready to leave. Isabella gathered her few possessions and packed her satchel, taking care to hide the letter as best she could. Then she sat and waited. She was puzzled that John was taking so long. Probably he had fallen into conversation with Olivier, but she wished he would hurry so they could get going.

In time, puzzlement turned to annoyance, which eventually gave way to worry and fear. Where was John? He knew how anxious and eager to be off she was. Had Olivier changed his mind? An hour after John left, Isabella picked up her satchel and walked into the night.

Women weren't allowed into the monks' living quarters in the abbey, but a sharp pull on the heavy bell rope hanging outside the door eventually brought a young monk to the street. He looked surprised and a little uncomfortable to see Isabella.

"I need to speak with Abbot Olivier," she said.

"Women are not allowed near the dormitory or cells," the monk said nervously. "There is a Refectory for pilgrims on the far side. You may eat and warm yourself there."

"I am not a pilgrim," Isabella explained patiently. "I wish to speak with Abbot Olivier."

"The Abbot is at prayer."

"I know my hours," Isabella said, a note of annoyance appearing in her voice. "Compline is past and it is not yet Matins. It is important that I speak with your abbot. Tell him it is about the letter."

Rebirth

The monk looked uncertain, but turned away.

"Tell him I will wait in the chapel of St. James in the church," Isabella added, not wanting to stand out in the street for long. The young monk looked back over his shoulder and nodded. Then he was gone.

Isabella hurried around the corner and through the small door in the west front of the abbey church. A few candles cast a wavering light over two worshippers, deep in prayer even at this late hour. Isabella ignored them and slipped down the side aisle until she came to the chapel decorated with scallop shells, the symbol of St. James. She entered the chapel and knelt before the alter. Instead of praying, she worried. When she left the inn, she had half hoped to bump into John hurrying back with some excuse about being drawn into a conversation by Abbot Olivier, but the streets had been dark and silent. With every passing minute, Isabella's fear grew. Something was wrong. She squeezed her eyes tight shut.

Olivier's hand on her shoulder almost made Isabella's heart stop. "I did not mean to frighten you," he said, "but you wished to speak with me?"

"I did. I do." Isabella rose from her knees and sat on the rough wooden bench in front of the altar. Olivier joined her. "Have you seen John?" she asked.

Olivier stared at Isabella for a long moment. "I spoke with him before the last Compline bell," he said slowly. "Are you a friend?"

"Have you seen him since then?" Isabella asked, ignoring Olivier's question.

"No, I have not. Is there a problem? You mentioned a letter."

Isabella rummaged in her satchel and produced Aumery's letter. Olivier glanced at it. "I gave this to John," he said. "How did you come by it?"

"He came to see me after you spoke with him at Compline," Isabella explained. "He showed me the letter and then left to return here and pick up his satchel. We were to leave tonight, but John has not returned. I came to see if he had been delayed."

Olivier stroked his chin as he gazed at Isabella. "And you are his friend?"

"I am. My name is Isabella. We have travelled together to many distant places." Isabella gave Olivier a very brief outline of her time with John. "I came here with him and stayed at the inn in town while he stayed here."

"John did not tell me he travelled with a companion. Do you know what he intended to do with the letter?'

"Yes. I was going to travel to Rome with him."

Olivier nodded thoughtfully. "It is possible that he returned without me seeing him. The first thing is to see if he has retrieved his satchel. Wait here." Olivier rose and left the church by a side door.

Isabella sat and waited nervously. Whatever had happened to John, he had not been held up in conversation with Olivier. Either he had been waylaid on his way here or on his way back, but by whom? She gasped at a sudden thought. They had been so wrapped up in the importance of the letter that they had only considered Aumery a potential threat, but, if that were the case and he had attacked John, why did he not come looking for the letter when he discovered his victim wasn't carrying it? Maybe John had been the target of a common thief. Perhaps he was lying injured, or worse, in some nearby dark alley. Why hadn't she searched for him as soon as she realized he was taking too long?

Cursing her stupidity, Isabella stood just as Olivier stepped into the chapel. He was carrying John's satchel in his right hand. "All his possessions are here," Olivier said, offering Isabella the satchel. "He never returned to collect them."

Isabella took the satchel. A quick glance confirmed that John's books were in it. John must have been attacked on his way to the Abbey. He would never have abandoned Lucius' book on drawing. "I have to look for him," Isabella said.

"Let me get you some food for the road. Perhaps there is a lay brother who might wish to accompany and help you." Olivier offered.

"Thank you. No," Isabella bustled past the Abbot. The image of John lying helpless and bleeding in a filthy alley overwhelmed her. "I have to go now." She strode down the aisle and out the church door.

Olivier stared after her long after the door closed. Everything seemed to be happening so quickly. Had he done the right thing in giving John the letter? With a sigh, Olivier turned and knelt before the altar of St. James. He bowed his head and prayed fervently.

Journeys

St. Gilles to Montpellier
June 14, 1214

John came to slowly in a strange, dark, shuddering world. He was lying on his side on a hard, moving surface that sent needles of pain through his head and his hip with every jolt. His wrists and ankles were bound behind him and seemed to be attached to each other as his knees were bent sharply back and he couldn't straighten his body out. He gasped for breath and inhaled a lungful of dust and dry straw that made him cough painfully. The smell of the farmyard—warm rotting hay and a vaguely nauseous animal smell—was overwhelming.

John lay still and breathed slowly, trying to gather his confused thoughts. Where was he? He was obviously tied up in the back of a farm cart, buried under a pile of old straw, probably the cart he had seen in the alley at St. Gilles. He had been knocked unconscious by a blow to the back of his head, which still hurt. It was probably still night, as John couldn't see the least flicker of light through the straw. The cart was on a journey, travelling slowly over a bumpy road; John could hear the creak of the wooden wheels and the clop of the horse's hooves. Who had captured him and where he was being taken were more difficult questions to answer.

Where was Isabella? "Isabella," John whispered urgently. "Isabella, are you here?"

"Silence!" a gruff voice ordered from above.

Unless Isabella was unconscious, John was alone. Despite his own situation, relief surged through him—Isabella was safe.

The letter! John jerked violently and then lay still until the pounding in his head eased, replaced by black depression. It had all been a waste of effort. Aumery had outsmarted him. John's brow furrowed as he struggled with a memory. Something wasn't right. Isabella wasn't here, and the last time he had seen her, she'd been sitting on her cot with the letter on her lap. The letter was safe as well. So was his satchel of books.

This didn't make sense! Whoever had attacked him and thrown him into the cart hadn't been after the letter. If the letter was their goal, they would certainly have searched him when he was unconscious. Realizing that he wasn't carrying it, they would have searched elsewhere, the Abby of St. Gilles or the inn.

John shivered at a thought. Perhaps they *had* searched the inn, found Isabella, taken the letter and killed her. No, John thought, that made no sense. If it was only the letter they wanted, why was he still alive?

Any way he looked at it, he was the object of the abduction. But why? And who?

As John lay miserably wrestling with increasingly unlikely scenarios, a few pinpricks of light grew in the straw above him. John had been attacked shortly after Olivier had answered the Compline bell. If the pricks of light indicated dawn, it must now be close to Prime. If they had been travelling at a slow, steady pace all night, they had gone perhaps fifteen miles. That took them farther from St. Gilles than Arles, so that wasn't their destination.

John squinted up through the straw, trying to work out the direction from which the light was coming. Since it was dawn, that would tell him where east was. The cart gave a particularly violent jolt and shuddered to a stop. Had they arrived? John heard a man swear and felt the cart sway as he jumped down. Straw was pulled aside and John blinked in the early sun.

The man was dressed in the black, hooded habit of one of Dominic Guzman's monks, but John couldn't imagine him leading a life of contemplation and preaching. The man's face was square and unshaven, and his nose, obviously broken at least once, was skewed to one side. His eyes were small and deep set beneath dark brows. The man grabbed John's tunic in a meaty paw and hauled him painfully onto his knees. "Drink," he ordered, holding up a wine skin and directing a stream of water at John's mouth. Spluttering and coughing, and trying to ignore the pain in his head, John drank as fast as possible. The water was wonderfully cold and washed the straw dust out of his mouth. Too soon, the man said "Enough," and removed the wine skin.

"Who are you? Where are you taking me?" John gasped.

"Shut up," the man said, shoving John hard on the shoulder. John fell on his side and banged his head on the wooden floor of the cart. Darkness engulfed him as the straw was thrown back into place. John felt the cart sway as the man climbed back up, and heard him flick the reins to get the horse going once more.

The water had helped clear John's head and while he had been on his knees, he had noticed the sun. It had climbed over the hills almost directly behind them, so they were travelling west, away from Arles. John pictured a rough map in his head. If they kept going west, they would reach Montpellier that night. A week more would take them to Toulouse, although that seemed improbably far. If they swung south, following the coast, Narbonne and Carcassonne were possibilities within a few days. Of course, there were also countless smaller places that could be their destination. John had no idea if any of the ones he'd thought of made any sense, but he felt slightly better knowing in which direction they were travelling. His captor, whoever he was, also seemed to have some interest in keeping him alive.

Throughout the day, John bounced uncomfortably in the cart and tried to sort out why he'd been abducted. However he imagined it, he always came back to Aumery. But if not for the letter, then why? Nothing that John could imagine ended well.

Twice more they stopped and John was given water. The first time, when the sun was almost directly overhead, they stopped for longer and John could hear the horse eating. Between the stops, John worked on his bonds, but only succeeded in chafing his wrists. Eventually, his legs and arms went numb and John concentrated on lying as comfortably as possible. His headache had improved as time passed but the skin over his hip bones and shoulders was worn raw. He prayed silently that they weren't headed for Toulouse.

The middle of the day had been oppressively hot under the straw, but it was cooling down and John had a sense of the light fading when he noticed that the rumbling of the cart wheels had changed in pitch and become more regular. He puzzled over it for a minute before he realized that they were driving over cobbles instead of uneven country roads. John concentrated. He could hear other horses passing by, and distant shouts. Gradually the noises increased until John became convinced that they were moving through a large town. Suddenly, the cart lurched to the right, travelled a short way and stopped.

John expected the water routine to be repeated, but nothing happened. He listened as hard as he could, but the street noises from before were muted and farther away. If this was a large town, it had to be Montpellier. John had been here once before, when he was travelling with William of Arles. Montpellier was a prosperous town and a centre of learning. The town belonged to Aragon through the marriage of King Pedro to Marie of Montpellier, but since both were dead, John assumed the town had now passed to their only son, James, who hadn't even been born when John and William had passed through the town seven years before. John imagined that having the young son of the defeated King Pedro in charge would make Montpellier a battleground in the struggle for power, but he had no idea whether the town was sympathetic to the crusade or the Cathars. Certainly, it had not yet been attacked by de Montfort.

John's thoughts were interrupted by the straw being harshly pulled away. He knew it made no sense to go to the effort of kidnapping him and bringing him all this way just to kill him, but that didn't stop his heart racing when he saw the big monk leaning over him with a dagger in his hand. The man roughly hauled John over onto his stomach, sliced through the rope binding his wrists to his ankles and dragged him off the end of the cart.

John fell to the ground, where he lay helpless. His knees, after being bent back for so long, ached horribly and any attempt to straighten out hurt dreadfully. His feet and hands had long since lost all feeling. The monk bent down, released John's ankles, put his hands under John's shoulders and pulled him upright. John's useless legs gave way and he collapsed back down as soon as he was released. The monk lifted him again. John collapsed.

It took several more attempts before John could stand, and even then he had to lean heavily against the cart. He was sweating profusely from the pain and effort. His hands and feet began to hurt as the blood forced its way back into them.

"Cut my hands free so I can hold onto the cart," John begged.

The monk shook his head.

"Cut his hands free," a soft, high-pitched voice ordered. "I doubt he will run away just yet."

John spun around so fast at the sound of the voice that he lost his balance and fell over. The monk reached down and cut the rope tying his wrists together. Slowly, using the wheel, John dragged himself upright and peered over the back of the cart. The figure standing smiling back at him confirmed what he'd thought when he heard the voice, and his worst nightmare. "Aumery," John breathed.

"Indeed," the Abbot of Citeaux confirmed. His mouth was smiling but his strange, staring eyes were cold and emotionless. "I have been looking forward to meeting you again. We never had the chance to finish our discussion in Toledo."

John shivered at the memory. "So you kidnapped me and brought me here."

Aumery shrugged. "Would you have come if I had asked politely?"

"No," John acknowledged. Then he asked the questions he had been agonizing over all day. "Why am I here? What do you want with me?"

"I wish only to talk. As I am certain you are aware, Muret has assured that the crusade will ultimately be successful. There is a young monk who is compiling a history of this great event and I believe you have some stories that might be of interest. But listen to me. I prattle on while you stand there in discomfort. You must be tired and hungry. Please let me offer you some meagre hospitality."

John stared at Aumery suspiciously. He didn't believe a word the man said, but he was relieved that he hadn't been immediately taken to the torture chamber.

"Henri," Aumery addressed the black-clad monk, "be so kind as to assist our guest to the refectory, and be gentle." Aumery turned and strode away and Henri stepped forward and supported John.

As John undertook his stumbling journey, he had a chance to look around. Despite the gathering dusk, he could make out most of his surroundings. The cart had come to a stop in the centre of a square courtyard. Apart from the arch through which they had entered, the courtyard was completely surrounded by a rough stone building, two stories high. Doors and windows interrupted the stonework and three sets of wooden stairs gave access to the upper floor. The roof was thatched and faint candlelight flickered in several windows. Aumery disappeared through a door in the wall opposite the entrance arch.

Almost gently, Henri helped John toward the door. Progress was slow and it gave John time to think. He was scared and still confused by the violent wrench from his life. He was worried about Isabella; what was she thinking about his disappearance? He was distrustful and terrified of Aumery, yet a tiny part of his mind hoped and prayed that he had been telling the truth about simply wanting to talk. It seemed unlikely.

* * *

Isabella slumped down miserably in a patch of moonlight beside the west gate. Sometime before, she had heard the Lauds bell, so dawn would be coming soon. For hours she had walked up and down every street and alley in St. Gilles. She had looked in every filthy, dark corner, talked to every drunken beggar she could find and searched every foul tavern. One drunk had followed her out of a tavern and accosted her. John's book-filled satchel catching him on the side of his head had discouraged any further advances.

Now she had run out of ideas. She was exhausted, thirsty, hungry and her feet ached. She was also convinced that John was not in the town, but if he wasn't, where was he? If he had been kidnapped, in which direction had he been taken? Was John already in Arles, on his way to Toulouse, on a boat heading downriver to the sea, or somewhere else she couldn't even think of? She felt like weeping, but she forced back her tears. She had to stay strong if she was going to find John.

"You are about early, Lady." The voice startled Isabella, but she recognized it as belonging to the crippled gatekeeper. He was a shadow sitting on a stool in the doorway of his tiny room.

"I've been searching all night," Isabella said.

"We all search for something, Lady," the soldier said. "What is it *you* seek?"

"My friend," Isabella answered, choking back a sob.

"Friends," the solder said pensively. "Good things to have. I've lost mine to battles, bottles and the pox. Would the friend you speak of be the one who rescued you at Las Navas de Tolosa?"

"Yes. We were to leave tonight. He went to the Abbey to get his satchel"—Isabella indicated the bag over her shoulder—"but he never got there. He's vanished."

"I presume he is not the sort who might be seduced into one of the all-too-common dens of drink and pleasure?"

"No, not John. I've searched for him everywhere. He's not in St. Gilles."

"At what time did he disappear?"

"Not long after the Compline bell." Isabella stared hard at the soldier. "Do you know something?"

"Maybe, maybe not," the man said, leaning forward into the moonlight. The shadows cast by old scars crossed his cheeks. "Last night as I closed the gate between Compline and Matins, a farmer bid me hold until he had driven his cart through."

"Surely that's not unusual. He must have been returning home after a day's business in town."

"What I thought, exactly, although the hour was late to begin a journey of any length. However, two things struck me as odd about this farmer. First, his cart was loaded with hay. In my experience farmers bring hay from the country to the city rather than the other way around. And second, the man was wearing a monk's habit."

"Was he skinny, with odd, pop-eyes?" Isabella asked, her voice rising with excitement.

The gatekeeper shook his head. "No, Lady. He looked used to hard work, like a farmer. Or a soldier," he added after a moment's thought.

"Did he say where he was headed?"

"He said naught, except an order for me to hold on closing the gate until he had passed. And never even a coin for my trouble."

"Which direction did he go?"

"West, Lady. I'll wager he'll make Montpellier, unless he's a real farmer with odd habits. After that, who can say? Narbonne, Toulouse, all the way to Paris if he turns north."

Rebirth

Isabella thought for a long moment. Could this farmer have anything to do with John's disappearance? The timing was right and a farmer dressed as a monk taking a load of hay out of the city at nightfall was odd. Besides, she had no other clue. Her choices were to stay in St. Gilles and hope John showed up, or go and try to find him. The first option—more worried inactivity—would probably drive her crazy. At least the second gave her something to do. "Thank you very much," Isabella said, reaching into her purse and tossing the gatekeeper a gold coin.

"Thank *you*, Lady," the gatekeeper said, pocketing the coin.

Exhaustion forgotten now that she had a task, Isabella hurried back through town to the inn. She found the innkeeper already in the stable. She collected the donkeys and paid him a coin for his trouble. She prepared the beasts for travel, bought some bread, cheese and wine, and was back passing through the west gate in full daylight as the Prime bell rang out over the town. "I wish you all God's luck in finding your friend," the gatekeeper shouted after her.

* * *

"I'm afraid the wine is not the best, but the harvests have not been good since the troubles began." Aumery smiled and topped up the dark red liquid in John's goblet. John took a drink to wash down his last mouthful of bread. The wine had a slightly bitter taste, but it was better than most of the things John had drunk on his travels.

John put the goblet down beside his pewter plate. He was having trouble keeping his eyes open. He was sitting on a bench at a rough table in the room Henri had led him to. Across the table Aumery sat, saying nothing except to offer more food and drink as John's plate and cup emptied. The food had been simple, coarse bread, hard white cheese and cold slices of venison, but John had been hungry and thirsty. As he had eaten, John's pains had lessened and he had gradually been overcome by a drowsy calm.

"Wild cherries?" Aumery pushed a wooden bowl of small red fruit across to John. "They are sweet this year."

John blinked the tiredness out of his eyes and reached out for a handful. The juice that exploded into his mouth as he bit down tasted wonderful. His body felt better than it had in a long time, but his mind was still fearful. What did Aumery want and what would he do to get it?

"I hope my hospitality has improved your condition," Aumery said. "I really must apologize for the methods employed to bring you here, but there was little choice. I hope this"—Aumery swept his arm over the laden table —"compensates for your discomfort in some small part."

"What happened to Isabella?" John asked. "Is she all right?"

"Your young lady friend? As far as I am aware, she is fine. She is of no interest to me."

"Why am I of interest? Why am I here?" John was having trouble putting his thoughts into words. The food, the wine and the warmth on top of his exhaustion made his mind sluggish.

"You are here to teach me," Aumery said.

"Teach?"

"You think, just because I am here to destroy the heretics, that I have no interest in learning from them?" Aumery's mouth curled in a slight smile. "Knowledge is valuable, powerful. Of course, that which contradicts or threatens the one true Church's teaching must be suppressed and destroyed, but there is much that can be of use to those of us who see it. Even Brother Dominic, who has struggled tirelessly to combat the foul heresy that poisons this land, has used the Cathar Perfect houses as a model for the convent he has established in Toulouse.

"One day, and I pray it will be soon"—Aumery crossed himself—"every Cathar will be dead and their bodies ashes. All their lying books will be destroyed and their corrupt ideas and practices lost. That will be a wondrous day, but I have set myself the task of determining that, along with all the evil, nothing of value is also lost.

"The Cathar lies are persistent and stretch far back to a pagan time before the light of Christ illuminated the world. Every pagan must be brought into the fold of the One True God before the Day of Judgement dawns. That will be part of the task set to Dominic's brotherhood. Those who do not believe, through ignorance or because they have had no chance to experience the blessings of Christ, are not at fault. Paradise will be theirs when they are taught the right way. However, those who are shown the light and deny it, or follow false gods, especially those who dwell within the bosom the Church, must be eradicated. The flames rising from their bodies must be a signal, a warning to all others that the way of Christ will not be denied."

As Aumery spoke, his voice rose in pitch and his eyes gleamed with a fanatical light. It scared John, but he stared fascinated at the man none the less. Where did he fall in this scheme of things, John wondered. He was a Christian, baptised and confirmed in the Church. True, he hadn't confessed or been to mass in some time, but for all his sympathy with them, he didn't consider himself a Good Christian. Was that enough to warrant survival in Aumery's new world, a world that would be a huge leap closer if this man ever became Pope?

Aumery fell silent and relaxed. He watched John for a long time. The examination made John nervous and he ate cherries and drank his wine to distract himself from this strange man's stare. It became increasingly hard to keep his eyes open.

"You are tired," Aumery said eventually. "I have been thoughtless in imposing my chatter upon you. We have much time and I look forward to talking with you at length once you have recovered your strength."

As if by magic, Henri appeared at John's side. "Take our guest to the prepared room," Aumery instructed. Then he turned back to John. "We will talk tomorrow. For now, I bid you a good night."

In a daze, John stood on his aching legs and followed Henri out and along a lit corridor. He was ushered into a small monk's cell, very like the one he had occupied at St. Gilles, except the only item of furniture was a cot, packed with straw. John sat on the cot as Henri closed the door, cutting off the faint light for the hall. He heard the loud click of a key turning in the lock.

All John wanted to do was lie down on the cot and sleep, but he forced himself to take in his surroundings. The walls were smooth stone and the beamed ceiling was high above his head. He could see a tiny patch of star-filled sky through a narrow window set high out of reach in one wall.

John stood and stepped over to the door. It was heavily built and solid, with no window. Gingerly, he lifted the heavy iron ring that served as a handle. He turned and pushed. The door didn't move.

John returned to the cot and lay down. He was a prisoner, albeit a comfortable one at present. Nevertheless, he could think of nothing he knew, no knowledge he had—the forbidden books in the memory cloister, the letter from St. Gilles—that he could talk safely to Aumery about. Sooner or later, the pleasantries would be dispensed with, and John knew from his conversation with Aumery in Toledo what came after that. He had to escape, but how? No answer had presented itself to him before, moments later, John sank into a deep, dreamless sleep.

Captive

Montpellier
June 15, 1214

"I trust you feel refreshed from your sleep." Aumery sat at the table where John had eaten the night before. Henri had fetched John sometime after dawn and brought him back here. John did feel refreshed after a long, deep sleep, although the area on his hip that had been rubbed raw still stung and his head hurt. His leg and arm muscles ached, but no worse than if he had over-exerted himself the day before, and he could walk unaided.

"It is too early to break fast, but come and sit." Aumery indicated the bench opposite. "We shall talk."

Nervously, John joined Aumery at the table. He had spent time, before Aumery had summoned him, wondering what he would say, but he hadn't been able to come to a conclusion without knowing what Aumery wanted from him. He had resolved to say as little as possible, at least until he had a clearer idea.

"Are you a Good Christian?" Aumery asked, taking John by surprise.

"I try to be," John said.

"You try to be a heretic?" Aumery asked.

John realized his misunderstanding. "No," he said hurriedly. "I am not a Good Christian, a Cathar. I meant only that I try to be good and that I am a Christian."

Aumery smiled. "I am simply playing with you. I do not believe you are a heretic, but are you overburdened by sin?"

"No more than others."

"Which is, of course, too much in this sinful world. But I was thinking more of the specific." Aumery leaned forward and held John's attention with his expressionless eyes. "You have consorted with heretics and the protectors of heretics. You worked for the notorious Roger Trenceval; you were seen in the company of the Cathar Perfect, Beatrice; you knew the old heretic, Umar of Cordova; you travelled to the heretic lands of the Moors of Al-Andalus;

you were among the Caliph's minions at the battle of Las Navas de Tolosa; and you fought on the side of the misguided King Pedro at Muret. All of these, taken together, are enough to question your faith and put you in the hands of the Inquisition."

John shuddered at the mention of the Inquisition, but stayed silent. He was shocked at the amount Aumery seemed to know about his activities over the past six years, and yet he was puzzled by one omission. After Oddo had murdered Pierre of Castelnau, Aumery had accused John of being a part of the assassination. Aumery clearly knew John had had no part in it, but John was still surprised that he hadn't brought up that allegation as part of the litany of accusations.

"Do not look so worried," Aumery went on. "You are young and youth is foolish. Mistakes are made in the early years of life and we do wrong to count those important at a later time—always assuming that the youth grows into an honest and God-fearing Christian man. I do not intend to involve the methods of the Inquisition," he paused significantly, "unless I am forced to do so."

John wanted to scream out, "What do you want of me?" but he forced himself to stay silent until Aumery continued.

"As I mentioned last evening, a young monk, Pierre des Vaux de Cernay, works on a history of these times and you know things he should hear."

"What things?" John could maintain his silence no longer.

"I can tell Pierre about the siege of Minerve, but from across the river. You were within the walls. Similarly, you were in King Pedro's camp at Muret; I was not. Pierre's goal is to write a true and accurate account of the wondrous victory of the crusade, in all its aspects. Unfortunately, the Perfects are not inclined to discuss it with us." Aumery's lips curled into a smile that sent a shiver down John's spine. He flashed to an image of Beatrice leading the Perfects onto the vast funeral pyre at Minerve. "You are not a Perfect," Aumery went on, "as we have established. I am certain you will be happy to tell us of your experiences."

"I will tell what I can," John said carefully.

"Excellent," Aumery replied, rubbing his hands. A young monk, dressed in the brown habit of a Cistercian and carrying a rolled parchment, quill and ink bottle, entered the room, nodded respectfully to Aumery and stared hard at John. John was surprised at the anger in the man's pale face.

"Well timed," Aumey said. "Please join us, Pierre. I am sure you will discover much of interest from our friend here."

"If anything of interest may be learned from a heretic," Pierre said irritably.

Rebirth

"Now, Pierre," Aumery said calmly. "We must sometimes put aside our feelings in the interests of gaining knowledge."

"No worthwhile knowledge can be gained from heretics," Pierre said as he sat on the same side of the table as Aumery and busied himself arranging his writing equipment on the surface before him. "Their voice is that of the Devil and our task to silence it."

"As you see," Aumery said, addressing John, "our young friend has clear ideas on good and evil, which is admirable, but which does not always allow for the complexities of human nature."

Pierre grunted unpleasantly but said nothing.

"So let us begin," Aumery said agreeably. "You grew up in Toulouse at the Priory of St. Anne? Perhaps that would be the place to start."

John's mind was spinning. He had no idea how his childhood had anything to do with what Aumery or Pierre might want to know, but at least it was safe topic. He told them everything he could remember about growing up with Peter as his friend and Mother Marie as his teacher.

* * *

As dusk fell, Aumery called a halt to the questioning. Pierre packed up his things and left, and a lay brother brought food in. As they ate in silence, John puzzled over the day. It had been more like a long conversation between friends than an interrogation. John had told Aumey much, about growing up, his time with William of Arles and Roger Trenceval, Minerve, Las Navas de Tolosa and Muret. He had spoken slowly and been very careful not to say anything that might incriminate anyone living, but Aumery had not pressed him for information, merely asking politely for more detail and occasional clarification. Pierre had been more of a problem, continually making asides about the evils of heresy and the pointlessness of leaving even one heretic alive.

Only twice had Pierre specifically intervened. After John had told about his experiences in Al-Andalus, he had asked, "Did you witness any miraculous occurrences at Las Navas de Tolosa?"

"Miraculous occurrences?" John asked, puzzled by the question. "What do you mean?"

"I cannot expect a heretic to understand," Pierre grumbled under his breath. "God wishes us to be victorious and I must record all the times that He has aided our blessed venture by His intervention. Did you witness a miracle?"

"No, I didn't," John said, although he tended to think that his and Isabella's mere survival in the midst of the battle was something of a miracle in itself.

Pierre had repeated the question when John had talked about Muret. On this occasion, John half suspected that he *had* witnessed a genuine miracle in Peter with his bleeding hands leading de Montfort's knights to victory, but he kept quiet for two reasons—he hoped Peter had escaped and found what he had been searching for and he was reluctant to do anything that would help the unpleasant Pierre.

"I shall retire now," Aumery said when they had finished eating. "We shall talk more tomorrow. I bid you a good night." Aumery stood and walked from the room. Immediately, Henri entered and escorted John back to his cell.

Sitting on the edge of his cot, John pondered what the strange day had meant. Surely Aumery hadn't gone to all the trouble of kidnapping him and transporting him to Montpellier just to hear the story of his life, however much it might add background detail to the story of the crusade. John was still nervous, but he felt much more relaxed than he had the day before. His thoughts turned toward escape. His imprisonment wasn't onerous; he was comfortable and well fed. On the other hand, it was imprisonment.

Noises from the street drifted in through the high window of John's cell. He could hear carts clattering by, the shouts of street vendors and, in the distance, singing. John envied the people outside, busy getting on with their lives without the responsibility of the knowledge he carried in his head. How nice it would be to live somewhere peaceful. To get up every morning with only the prospect of practising his drawing in front of him. To stroll through a quiet town with Isabella by his side.

What was Isabella doing now, John wondered? What had she done when he didn't return to the room at the inn? He hated the thought of her sitting worried in St. Gilles with no idea what had happened to him. He had to try and escape, but how?

The singing was right outside his window now. The voice was slurred, but recognizable.

"This William of Arles,
The master of all.
He plays with such skill,
That the valley and hill,
Both resound with the sound of his music.
His verse is so sharp..."

"William!" John shouted, leaping to his feet. The singing continued.

"When accompanied by harp,
That his listeners are held in a thrall."

"William! It's me, John." John shouted louder. The singing continued.

Rebirth

"His voice, I've heard tell
Is as clear as a bell..."

"Like a frog that is trapped in a well," John roared out the last line of the song William had sung out on the night of Peter's vision in the square at Toulouse eight years before. With no break, the voice outside continued.

"I sing of the glorious troubadours
And the wonderful styles they espouse."

The door of John's cell was flung open and Henri stood there. "Silence." He spoke softly, but in a tone that left no doubt in John's mind that obeying the order was the intelligent thing to do. The door closed.

John looked up at the window. If he stretched, he could almost touch the lower sill. If he jumped he could reach higher, but the sill was sloping and gave no purchase. The sound of the slurred singing faded.

John listened until the singing vanished under the general hubbub of the street, then slumped despondently back onto his cot. The voice had belonged to William of Arles, he was convinced of that, but it had sounded different, as if the owner had drunk too much ale. That, the street noise and the thickness of the walls of John's cell meant that William had not heard his shouts.

John punched the mattress of his cot in frustration. He didn't think William would have been able to help him, but it would have been a way to get a message to Isabella to tell her he was all right. Now that chance was gone and John doubted that Henri would allow him another. John lay back and miserably watched the sky darken through the tiny rectangle of his window.

* * *

The day before, Isabella had travelled slowly, riding one donkey and leading the other. She asked everyone she met if they had seen a farmer's cart driven by a monk and worried constantly that her quarry had turned off on one of the many minor side tracks. She was also troubled that she might be following the wrong lead. What if John wasn't with the cart but being taken in some totally different direction? Rationally, she knew she was following the best clue and had no other choice, but doubt lingered, gnawing at her confidence. She trotted into Montpellier late on the afternoon of June 15, almost twenty-four hours after John had arrived.

Montpellier was a hilly town of narrow lanes lined with prosperous merchant houses. It was bigger than St. Gilles but much smaller than Toulouse. Isabella's first stop was at a respectable inn where she stalled and fed the donkeys, ordered a room and ate some bread and cheese. Then she spent the remaining daylight exploring the town. Her first task was to visit every town gate and ask the gatekeeper if he had spotted a cart driven by a monk in the past day. She was encouraged to discover that the cart had been seen entering by the eastern gate but that no one had seen it leave. It proved nothing, but the thought that John might still be in the town and close by encouraged her.

Until twilight darkened the streets, she wandered around, peering into archways and asking about the cart. She arrived back at the inn tired and with no more information than when she had begun. Over a bowl of thin soup, she planned her next step. Obviously this aimless wandering was not going to bear fruit. Isabella needed a system. Until now she had been travelling in a straight line following something specific. From here, until she found John or convinced herself that he was not in Montpellier, she would need a plan. Chewing pensively on a tough piece of mutton from the soup, she pushed the latter thought from her mind. John had to be here. She had no idea what she would do if he wasn't.

Isabella mopped up the last of the soup with a piece of bread and sat back. What did she know? Assuming John *was* here, he probably wasn't still in the cart. She would continue to ask about it because locating it would give her another clue, but she needed a different approach. The monk, if he was even a real monk, was not much help. He may have stood out driving a farmer's cart, but on the streets of Montpellier, monks were a common sight and she had no description of him other than that he reminded the gatekeeper in St. Gilles of a farmer or a soldier.

Was there anything else she knew or could guess? John had to have been kidnapped on Aumery's orders. Nothing else made sense. Did that mean that Aumery was in Montpellier? Not that she could go around asking for him—that would draw too much attention—but there was no Abbey or cathedral in the town and few churches. Isabella doubted that Aumery would recognize her, she had had no contact with him in Toledo, which would be a help. As an idea began to take shape in Isabella's mind, she spotted a familiar figure entering the inn and looking around. "William!" she shouted, loud enough to turn the heads of most of the patrons.

William of Arles came over to Isabella's table, a broad grin on his face. "I have been in many taverns," he said, "but never one where I have been hailed by a beautiful woman."

Isabella laughed. Seeing William was like having a huge weight lifted from her shoulders. "What are you doing here?"

Rebirth

"I went to St. Gilles to see that you two children hadn't got yourselves into too much trouble," William said as he sat down and ordered a mug of ale. "When I couldn't find you, I talked with the gatekeeper." William grinned at Isabella's puzzled expression. "I have discovered over many years of travelling that there are two reasons to always be kind to gatekeepers: no one knows better than they the comings and goings of everyone from Lords to peasants, and if you need a gate opened in a hurry in the middle of the night..." William left the last thought hanging.

"Anyway," he continued, "the gatekeeper told me he had seen you leave—you are remembered if you are pretty and tip with a gold coin—and that you were following a hay cart to Montpellier, so I came here. Where is John?"

"I don't know," Isabella said. "I'm not even certain he's here." Briefly, she told William what had happened in St. Gilles, and showed him the letter.

"A powerful, and potentially very dangerous, piece of parchment," William commented thoughtfully when Isabella had finished. "But I think you are right. Whoever kidnapped John, and that fanatic Aumery is our best guess, wasn't after the letter. Otherwise I doubt if either of you would still be alive. The first step is to find John."

"I've been wondering about that," Isabella said, "but I can't think of a safe way to make inquiries. Everything attracts too much attention and that's the last thing I want." Ever since John had failed to return to the inn, she had been fighting off a mounting sense of loneliness. William's arrival was a Godsend.

William drained the last of his ale. "Sometimes," he said with a sly smile, "attention is the best way to hide." Before Isabella could ask what he meant, he continued. "You are staying at the inn?"

Isabella nodded. "In the room at the back by the stables."

"I suggest you return there and wait. I will investigate and let you know what I discover."

"How?"

William winked broadly. He stood up, stumbling awkwardly and knocking his ale mug to the floor. "I sing of the wonderful troubadours," he slurred as he staggered across the tavern, bumping into people and drawing a chorus of curses and a few wildly aimed blows. Isabella watched, wide-eyed, as he lurched out the door and disappeared.

* * *

John had finally drifted off to sleep, some time after night fell. He kept waking up, plagued by strange, disconnected dreams in which knights and monks battled on a desolate plain lit by the red glow of dozens of funeral pyres. In the last dream, John woke to the sound of rain spattering the ground. It took him some time to realize that the rain was in fact pieces of dirt and small stones falling onto the cell's packed earth floor from his window.

John sat up abruptly. A small pebble struck him on the head. "John." He heard a soft voice from outside that made his heart race. He glanced at the door of his cell. "Isabella," he hissed as loudly as he dared. A voice replied, but too quietly for him to make out the words. John looked up at the window, too high to reach. He would have to shout and Henri would hear him. He glanced frantically round the cell. Of course!

John tore the mattress off his bunk. As gently as possible, he lifted the wooden frame of his cot and leaned it against the wall beneath the window. By clambering up it, he could stand near the top and put his head in the window alcove. It felt shaky, but if he reached forward he could stretch his arm out into the open. He felt another hand grip his, a small hand, then Isabella's face appeared not a foot away from him. Light was coming from below where someone was holding a flickering torch.

"How did you find me?" John asked in wonder.

"The gatekeeper at St. Gilles pointed me here and William did the rest." John remembered the singing from earlier. It had been William and he had heard John's response. He hadn't wanted to draw attention to himself, but he had brought Isabella back later. "How are you?" Isabella asked.

"I'm all right," John replied. He gave a brief description of how he had ended up here and the strange goings on with Aumery that day. "I don't know what he wants. He's treating me well and only talks about generalities."

"He wants something more," Isabella said. "You can be certain of that."

"I suppose so," John agreed, "but it's not the letter. Do you still have it?"

"I do." Isabella shook violently, clenched John's hand and looked down.

"What are you standing on," John asked, realizing that the window must be at least as high off the ground outside as in.

"William," Isabella said.

"You're standing on William?"

"On his shoulders. I don't know how long he can keep holding me up. We must be quick. Can you escape?"

"I don't think so. The cell's locked, and the man who kidnapped me is on guard all the time. What is this place I'm in?"

"I'm not sure. William asked around but no one seemed to know much. It's not a monastery or abbey, but there are monks coming and going all the time."

"The only way I will get out of here is if Aumery lets me go," John said, thinking his way through the problem as he spoke.

"How do we do that?" Isabella interrupted.

"The letter."

"But by the time I take it to Rome and get back, months will have passed. Anything could have happened to you."

"Don't go to Rome," John said. "Find someone closer."

"Who can I trust?"

"Bishop Foulques in Toulouse."

"Foulques!" Isabella's eyes widened in surprise. "I can't trust him. He's a self-interested slug."

"Exactly," John explained. "His self-interest is the key. He hates Aumery almost as much as Oddo must have, and he'll see the letter as his chance to bring him down. In exchange for that, he'll force Aumery to let me go."

Isabella thought for a long moment. She wobbled as William adjusted his position. "It might work. The problem will be getting Foulques to listen to me. First, I'm a woman and don't count for anything as far as he's concerned, and second, he knows I used to be an attendant to Lady Eleanor. He despises Count Raymond and Eleanor almost as much as he hates Aumery."

Isabella was right: Foulques would pay no attention to a woman with heretic sympathies. William? No, a troubadour would be only marginally better and John had no right to involve him more in this. An idea struck John like a bolt of lightning.

"Peter," he said. "He's a monk, so he can get access to Foulques. We don't agree on much, but he's my friend."

"We don't even know where he is," Isabella said uncertainly.

"Yes, we do. He told me he was going to find a cave to live in near Minerve. A hermit should be easy to find, and Minerve is almost on the way to Toulouse."

"But he's..."

"Mad," John finished. "He might be, but that's an advantage. Peter has an extraordinary sense of what's right and what's wrong, and I'll wager he'll think Aumery is close to the devil when he reads the letter. He'll help us."

"All right." The conviction in John's voice almost convinced Isabella. "But the journey will still take days. What will happen to you?"

"I don't know. I'll keep telling Aumery as much as I can without saying anything too dangerous and, if I see a chance to escape, I'll take it."

"I'll do it," Isabella said with a sigh. "I don't see any other way." She squeezed John's hand. "I'll be as fast as I can. Please be careful. I'll ask William to stay in the inn. If you do manage to escape, find him there."

"You be careful as well." John leaned as far as he could into the window alcove and kissed Isabella's hand. She tried to lean forward, but the window itself wasn't big enough to allow her head through. "I love you," she said. Then she wobbled violently. Her hand slipped out of John's and she disappeared.

"Isabella! Are you all right?" John leaned as far into the window as he could.

"Yes," a voice came from below.

"She landed on me," William added. "I shall come by as often as I can."

"Thank you," John said. "Isabella. Be careful."

"And you. I'll be back as soon as I can."

"I love you," John said. He listened to the pair's fading footsteps until there was nothing but silence. Then he climbed back down and replaced his cot. He lay down. It had been wonderful to see and talk to Isabella and to know she was fine. He felt good about the plan they had worked out. The only difficulty was that it would take time to carry out. The question was, would Aumery, and whatever plan he was following, give them enough time?

A Changed Man

Minerve
June 18, 1214

Isabella dismounted and led her grey pony and her spare mount along the rough track leading up the narrow valley. The sun hadn't yet cleared the hills on her right, so it was still cool in the deep shadow along the path, but the tops of the cliffs on her left were already bathed in light. Somewhere up there, Isabella hoped, was the cave that had become Peter's home.

With a startling crash, a wild boar burst from a thicket ahead of Isabella and disappeared up the trail, sending a scattering of small stones skittering back down. The pony jerked hard on the reins in fright. Isabella stroked his head and spoke calmly. Roland—Isabella had named her pony after the hero of one of William's favourite songs—had become her friend on the two-day journey from Montpellier. He was not a large horse, nothing like the size of the destrier John had ridden into battle at Muret, but he was sturdy and good natured. Isabella had bought him and the spare mount, which she hadn't named, from a horse seller that William knew. She had exchanged the donkeys and paid a high price for the two animals, but she had been in a hurry to be on her way and horses were faster. Roland had certainly proved to be worth every denier.

They had arrived late last evening and Isabella had been pleased to discover that everyone in town knew of a tall, skinny hermit who had settled into a cave to the north the previous winter. He had become something of a local celebrity, and townsfolk regularly visited him to seek blessings or advice and to leave offerings of food.

Isabella had left Minerve before dawn and, from the directions she had received, thought she must be close to Peter's cave by now. The ease with which she had found Peter made her feel happier than she had since leaving Montpellier. All the way to Minerve, she had felt that she was abandoning John to whatever Aumery had in store for him. She knew that using the letter to discredit Aumery was the best way to help John, but she couldn't shake the idea that she was running away, just when John needed her most. Fantasies of bursting into the building in Montpellier, overpowering the guards and Aumery and freeing John, had played themselves out in her mind in the long hours of travel. She knew that her dreams were impossible and that if there was a chance to escape John and William would make the most of it, nevertheless she felt guilt at leaving Montpellier. At least now she was trying to achieve something: persuade Peter to help in the next stage of her task.

She scanned the sunlit side of the valley. Almost immediately she saw him, a dark figure sitting on a ledge in front of the black opening to a cave. He was still some way up the valley but there was no mistaking her childhood friend's skinny frame. Tethering Roland and his companion to a low bush, Isabella began to climb the steep path that led to the cave.

Peter must have seen and heard Isabella long before she reached him, but he gave no sign. He sat cross-legged with his hands on his lap, staring over the valley. As Isabella got close, she noticed that there was a slight smile on Peter's lips. He was dressed in a ragged brown habit, secured at the waist by a greasy piece of rope with three knots tied at one end. If anything, he looked skinnier than when she had last seen him. Isabella placed a loaf of bread, a round of cheese and a wineskin of water before him, and sat by his side.

Eventually, Peter turned his head and regarded his visitor carefully. "Hello, Isabella," he said. "God has provided food. Will you break your nighttime fast with me?"

"I will," Isabella replied. "Thank you."

Peter picked up the bread and broke off a chunk. He repeated the procedure with the cheese and handed the bits to Isabella. He broke off two much smaller pieces for himself and bent his head in a quiet prayer of thanks.

They ate in silence, Isabella munching contentedly while Peter nibbled like a bird. When he was done, he collected the crumbs from his habit and scattered them to one side. "Ants must eat, too," he said. They both took drinks from the wineskin and Peter offered a second short prayer of thanks.

"You seem contented," Isabella observed.

Peter carefully considered her statement for a moment. "Yes," he agreed. "God has seen fit to grant me a contentment these past few months that I have not known before. My needs, simple as they are, are met and there is ample time for prayer, meditation and contemplation. What more could a man of God seek?"

Rebirth

"I am glad you have found what you sought. After Muret you were troubled." Isabella was amazed at the change in Peter. When she had last seen him, he appeared on the brink of madness and she had been concerned that she might find him a jibbering idiot. Instead, he now exuded a calm confidence that swept over her and removed all the tensions of the past few days.

"I was." Peter glanced down at the palms of his hands. "My torments have eased greatly, but that is not to say that God's purpose for me is any clearer, only that I may have found the right way to allow it to become known. But I am being rude. You did not journey all the way here to listen to a solitary hermit talk of his life. What of you and John?"

"It is because of John that I came to see you. He needs your help."

"Perhaps if I had listened more to John all those years ago, I might have found myself at this point substantially sooner, but who can tell? Perhaps God makes us walk difficult paths for His purpose and had I not struggled exactly as I have, I would not have reached here at all. But listen to me ramble on. I fear it is a consequence of a lonely life." Peter smiled apologetically. "Of course I shall help John in any way I can."

"Do not be so hasty to agree until you have heard my request." Isabella took the letter out of her satchel and passed it over to Peter. He read it, his face creased in a frown. When he had finished, he looked up. "What does this mean?"

"Look at the capital letters that do not fit," Isabella instructed. Peter studied the document hard. "They spell out 'kill Pierre of Castelnau' and instruct when. It means that Arnaud Aumery, Abbot of Citeaux, Papal Legate to Pope Innocent III and leader of the crusade against the Cathars, ordered Oddo to kill Pierre of Castelnau on the riverbank outside Arles after the meeting at St. Gilles."

Peter's mind shot back to that cold, January morning. Images flashed in his head: spots of blood flying off Aumery's back as he whipped himself, the foul smell of Pierre's breath, the thundering hooves of the charging knight, the strange sucking sound the lance made as Aumery pulled it out of the dead man's body. And John, standing in shock beside Pierre's donkey as Aumery accused him of heresy and murder. A revelation, as vivid as his visions of death in Toulouse, swept over Peter.

"God forgive me," he wailed, struggling onto his knees and clasping his hands before him in prayer. "I see now. That is where I left the path."

Isabella stared at Peter, a sinking feeling in her heart. Was this a return to the madness? Peter's eyes were closed tightly and he was mumbling prayers at a furious rate. "What happened?" Isabella asked. "What's wrong?"

Peter continued praying for a long moment, then he opened his eyes and looked up. He was smiling broadly. "Nothing's wrong," he said. "I have simply come to see where I went wrong."

Isabella shook her head, obviously no closer to understanding.

"The morning Pierre was killed," Peter explained, "John was standing at the donkey's head as the lance struck. Afterwards, Aumery accused him of aiding the knight in the murder. John appealed to me"—Peter sighed—"and I said nothing. I was confused and angry. John and I had just had an argument and I didn't want to upset Aumery. I knew John was innocent, that he would never have anything to do with a murder, but I said nothing. I let my fear overcome what I knew in my heart was right."

Isabella reached over and placed her hand on Peter's arm. "What could you have done?"

"I could have, should have, done what was right and spoken up for my friend. It might not have done any good," Peter shrugged, "but for Satan to triumph, he requires only that good men stand by silent and do nothing. God requires every one of us to do the best we can at every point in our lives and I failed. All the troubles in my life since then stem from that morning and my weakness."

Isabella tried to say something to comfort Peter, but he held up his hand for silence and went on. "Later, Aumery as good as told me he had ordered Pierre's murder, but I chose not to believe him. I pursued what I thought I wanted—Aumery's power. That would protect me from people like Oddo and make my life simple." Peter laughed bitterly. "I was a fool. I convinced myself that since Aumery's power came from the Church it must come from God, but the Church is an edifice built by man and therefore flawed. The only power comes direct from God and He will not be denied.

"The quest for the Grail, the voices, poor old Diogenes, they were all challenges from God. He wished to see the depth to which I would fall, and I did not disappoint Him. I became as evil as Aumery. I killed a man outside Trimondium."

Throughout his speech, Peter had become more and more gloomy, but now he brightened. "But God is infinitely merciful. He sent Francesco to cross my path and show me another way. I understand now what Francesco is attempting. He and his followers are forging a new connection between man and God, one that is personal and does not rely on the Church. Once enough people form a personal link to God, the corrupt power of the Church will wither and die. I have taken that way and now here you are, offering me a second chance. John needs my help and in giving it, I can wipe away the sin of that long ago morning. I can wipe the slate clean. Perhaps, I can also

Rebirth

destroy a tiny part of the Church's corruption. What does the letter have to do with John, and what would you wish me to do?"

Isabella stared at Peter. He had done a better job at convincing himself to help John than she could. "After the murder, Oddo left the letter with the Abbot of St. Gilles for safe keeping. Before he died at Muret, Oddo told John about the letter and we went to get it. We intended to take it to Rome to show to the Church authorities, but John was kidnapped by Aumery's man five days ago in St. Gilles. He was taken to Montpellier, where he's being held prisoner. I want to use the letter to get John released."

"And what would my role be in this scheme?"

"I don't have time to go to Rome, but there are people in the Church here who dislike Aumery and would use the letter to hurt him. The difficulty is that I'm a woman. No one would listen to me."

"So you would like me to take the letter?" Peter smiled. "And this person in the Church who does not like Aumery, would that be Bishop Foulques?"

"Yes," Isabella replied.

Peter nodded. "Foulques is corrupt in the worst way. He symbolizes everything that is wrong with the Church today, everything that Francesco"—Peter hesitated—"and I, would like to change."

He's going to refuse, Isabella thought with a sinking feeling. Before she could think of something to say, Peter continued. "But perhaps it is a question of degree," he stared across the valley, deep in thought. "Foulques's sins are by no means unique. They are common in the Church today and excising the sins of one man will do little to resolve the underlying problem. Aumery, on the other hand, is a different creature. His evil is unique and his power potentially limitless. Foulques is and always will be a provincial bishop, enjoying the minor benefits that his local corruptions bring him. Aumery was instrumental in convincing Innocent to undertake this crusade and now he has overseen its successful military conclusion. His star is in the ascendant. I suspect his goal might even be the highest position in the Church."

"I have heard that as well," Isabella agreed. "Would that not be a much higher degree of sin than Foulques's gluttony?"

"It would."

"Then we must use the letter to discredit him," Isabella said

Peter smiled. It was a gentle, friendly expression. Isabella was amazed at how much Peter had changed. The months of solitary meditation had erased the madness and replaced it with a calm intelligence and compassion. Perhaps it had always been there. Perhaps Isabella was seeing the real Peter, the boy who had once been John's best friend.

"A choice of evils," Peter said. "I will take the letter to Foulques in Toulouse. He will hold it over Aumery's head. It will not be enough to destroy him, but it will be enough to prevent his rise to the top. Foulques will keep the letter safe in his possession and use its threat to keep Aumery in line. But don't worry," Peter held up a hand to prevent Isabella's interruption. "The letter's existence will ensure that Aumery never rises to the Papacy and I will make certain that Foulques uses it to free John. It will be a small way to exert his new power and underline to Aumery who is in charge."

"Thank you," Isabella said with relief.

"It is early yet for thanks," Peter said. "I assume the reason you brought a second horse is so that we may ride to Toulouse." When Isabella nodded, Peter continued. "Then I suggest that delaying here serves no purpose. Shall we be on our way?"

The pair scrambled down the hillside. Isabella felt unreasonably happy. The meeting with Peter had gone far better than she expected. Most importantly, she wasn't alone. She would do what she had to do to save John, alone if necessary, but it felt wonderful to have someone beside her who believed in what she was trying to do. Now all she needed was time.

Inquisition

Montpellier
June 18, 1214

John woke from his fourth night of captivity to the sound of William singing in the street outside. He smiled to know that his friend was still out there. John would rather be outside with him, but his imprisonment had not been too onerous so far. He hadn't seen Aumery since the first day of questions and had spent all his time in his cell. Twice a day, Henri brought in food and emptied the bucket in the corner. The food was not remarkable, but it was wholesome and the quantities were sufficient. He could live here for a long time, and that was what bothered him.

John had no idea what Aumery wanted and the options had been gnawing at him during his enforced idleness. He could think of three possibilities, three things he had that Aumery might want. The most obvious was the letter, but the way Henri had kidnapped him suggested that he didn't suspect that John and Isabella had the letter. The alternatives were that Aumery wanted what John knew about the Grail, or what he held in the memory cloister, in particular the Gospel of the Christ. John wasn't certain how dangerous any of this information might be if he gave it to Aumery, but he had no desire to find out. Despite Aumery's apparent friendship on the day of John's arrival, and his apparent lack of interest since then, John didn't trust the man at all.

John's cell door opened and Henri beckoned to him. John stood and followed him out. To his surprise, they headed in the opposite direction from the room where he had previously met Aumery. The pair walked to the end of the corridor, where a gloomy set of steps led down into a short corridor. Even in daylight, flaming torches were needed to light the way.

John's heart sank deeper the farther they went. By the time they reached the end of the corridor, John was sweating despite the chill air. He knew what he was going to see before Henri opened the heavy door and pushed him in.

The room was smaller than the one Aumery had shown him in Toledo and the walls glistened damply in the torchlight. An empty fireplace took up most of one wall, but the others were bare. There was a small, roughly-carved table with a bench on either side in the centre of the floor. The room looked innocent enough—there was no strappado hook in the ceiling or red-hot pokers by a fire—but John was horrified to see a single implement placed prominently on the table. It was about the size of John's hand and composed of two solid pieces of wood held apart by two coarse wooden screws. Tightening the screws would bring the pieces of wood together, slowly crushing whatever was placed between them.

"Not as well appointed as the room I showed you in Toledo." John turned to see that Henri had been replaced by Aumery. "But I fear we lag behind our southern neighbours in that respect."

John's mouth had gone dry and he had trouble speaking but he managed to croak out, "What do you want from me?"

"Conversation," Aumery said softly as he ushered John farther into the room and closed the door. Aumery sat down. "I enjoyed our conversation three days ago and I am sorry we could not continue it sooner, but here we are. Please sit." He indicated the bench opposite.

John was relieved to sit. He wasn't sure how long his shaking legs would hold him. "What do you want to talk about?" he asked, staring nervously at the torture implement lying beside him and tried not to imagine its uses.

Aumery laughed. "You see how poor we are here. No strappado hook. Not even a fire in which to heat irons. Just this rather crude device, although I must admit it can be effective." He picked up the implement and turned it thoughtfully in his hands. "It is called a thumbscrew, but it need not be limited to that digit. It works equally well on any part of the hand."

Aumery put the thumbscrew down and stared at John, who had difficulty meeting his strange, emotionless eyes. "Your tales the other day were most interesting, although I don't think Pierre was very impressed. He has a rather narrow view of the world." Aumery shrugged. "But he is young. I should very much like to know more and I am certain you have more to tell."

"I don't know what you mean," John forced his dry mouth to form the words.

"Come. Come," Aumery said. His voice was friendly, but his hands drifted to the thumbscrew and began tapping it against the table. To John the sound was deafening. "Let us have a conversation about the Cathar Treasure."

"I don't know anything about any Cathar Treasure." John tried desperately to hold his voice steady, but he couldn't keep the quaver out of it. "The

Cathars believe that worldly possessions are evil. Why would they have treasure?"

"Treasure need not be gold and silver, and it may be held for a number of reasons. For example, a treasure may be something that is of value to someone else, not the person who holds it. I do not expect you to give me the Cathar Treasure, merely tell me any stories you might have heard of it."

John's mind was racing. Was it the Grail Aumery was after? It had to be. He had sent Peter far to the east to search for it. What should John tell him? Who would his stories hurt? Adso was dead, the body he had found at Rhedae burned, and the Grail, if that was what it had been, destroyed. The drawing and the map were safe with Isabella and, in any case, they only showed the way to Rhedae and there was nothing left there. Perhaps Adso's story might convince Aumery that the Grail no longer existed. Maybe then he would let John go.

Aumery sat quietly with his hands clasped beneath his chin, while John thought things through. A faint predatory smile played on the monk's lips. John felt as though the other man could look inside his head. He understood now that torture didn't have to be violent. Often, time was the most effective weapon. He had worried constantly over the last two days when he had no contact with Aumery and now every second seemed like an hour. John made a decision. "There's a place called Rhedae," he began.

* * *

John's story took all morning. Mostly, Aumery listened in silence, but occasionally he asked a pointed question. He seemed particularly interested in what Peter had told John about his journey to Trimondium and was disappointed that John didn't know where Peter was and that Adso was dead.

"So," Aumery said after John could think of nothing else to add, "you claim the map was the key to the drawing and that together with the clue I obtained and gave to poor Philip, it pointed the way to the cave at Rhedea where Christ and the Holy Grail were buried?"

"I think any map was a key to the drawing, but yes, I think the body that Adso found was Christ and the cup the Grail."

To John's surprise, Aumery laughed out loud. "That is the problem with heretics," he said once he had calmed down. "Everything you hear is equally possible. A few coincidences and a scrap of paper and you have Christ's body burning in a cave in Languedoc."

Aumery pounded his fists on the table, making the thumbscrew shake and John jump. "Heresy!" Aumery screamed, his face instantly dark with violent anger. "You would deny the Gospels, the very word of God. How dare you!

The word of God is the only absolute truth. All else must flow from that. Any contradiction is a lie, placed in our minds by the Devil to tempt us into Hell." Aumery stood and leaned over John. "Christ died on the cross for our sins. To claim otherwise is a heresy demanding purification in the righteous flames of the Inquisition. Be gone. Get out of my sight. And think well on your sins before we meet again."

Aumery straightened and stormed out of the room. John turned to see that Henri had entered. Impassively and without violence, the monk took John by the arm and led him back up to his cell. When the door closed, John threw himself onto his bunk. He was shaking with fear at Aumery's outburst, but as he calmed, he thought over what had happened. Aumery's mercurial changes of mood made it immensely difficult to know how to react to the man. Obviously, the story about Rhedae and the Grail hadn't pleased him. What was next?

Almost as soon as he thought it, John's cell door was flung open and Henri advanced toward him. Before John had a chance to stand, the big man grabbed him by the shoulders and hauled him to his feet. Half dragging him, Henri led the way back to the room they had left only minutes before.

Aumery had returned and was once again sitting at the table, his cunning smile back in place. Henri pulled John in and forced him down on the bench. This time, instead of leaving, Henri sat beside John. He placed a powerful arm around him, pinioning John's left arm to his side. With his free hand, Henri placed John's right hand on the table, inches from the thumbscrew. "What do you want?" John asked, his voice barely audible through fear.

"What I have always wanted," Aumery replied, "information. First, did your stupid friend, Adso, see what was written on the scroll held by the body in the cave?"

"No," John said, momentarily surprised by the question. "It crumbled in his hand."

Aumery nodded and stroked his chin. "So you say."

"I have told you all I know about the Cathar Treasure." John knew his voice sounded weak and whiny, but he couldn't help it. He was terrified.

"I think we've had enough of your little stories," Aumery said. His voice was calm, almost companionable. "I have sat through the tales of your adventures with that Toulouse harlot, and your heretic fantasies of our Lord Christ in a cave in the mountains. Now it is time to tell me the truth. What is the Cathar Treasure?"

John was so shocked and annoyed at hearing Isabella called a harlot that it took him a moment or two to understand Aumery's question. He ignored it.

"How dare you insult Isabella," he said angrily. "She is a better person than you and all your corrupt priests."

Aumery's smile broadened. "Spoken like a true heretic, but you did not answer my question."

"I have told you all I know."

"I'm afraid you have not. I fear you have told me only as little as you think may satisfy me and that is not near enough." Aumery nodded to Henri, who lifted John's hand off the table. John struggled, but he was powerless in Henri's vice-like grip.

Aumery reached out and John clenched his fist as hard as he could. He was surprised when Aumery began stroking his fist gently. "Force will do you no good. I notice that your left hand is already damaged. Was that from the hot coals you scarred Oddo with at Minerve? No matter, we will begin with the right hand. That is the one you use when you practice the arts in that pagan Roman book you told me about—is it not?

"As you see, Henri is far stronger than you, and I do not mind which part of the hand I begin with." As he continued stroking, Aumery picked up the thumbscrew. John tried to pull his hand away, or even turn it, but it was frozen in Henri's grip. With the speed of a striking snake, Aumery rapped John hard on the thumb joint with the thumbscrew. Surprised by the blow and the sudden pain, John cried out and relaxed his thumb from his fist. In an instant, the digit was between the two wooden blocks of the screw.

"Now," Aumery said quietly. "Let us see what you are made of." Gradually, he began tightening the screws. John tried to move his thumb, but the joint was held fast between the bits of wood. The pain intensified as the joint was increasingly compressed. Aumery worked slowly and methodically, tightening first one screw and then the other. John felt sweat forming on his forehead. He clenched his teeth and closed his eyes.

"This is nothing yet." Aumery's calm voice came to him through the haze of pain. "I only apply pressure to the sides of a straightened joint. I am told, by those who would know, that when the screw is applied to a bent joint, the agony is ten times worse, and," Aumery paused, "you have fourteen joints on each hand."

Sharp arrows of pain shot up John's arm and he could feel the sweat running into his closed eyes. He had stopped struggling. It required everything he had to bear the pain. It seemed impossible that the torment could get any worse, but it did. As Aumery's voice calmly enumerated the joints in the hand, he continued tightening the screws.

Something gave inside the thumb with an audible crack. John screamed.

"Ah," Aumery said with interest. "I suspect that was a bone. Pieces do break off the edge of the joint from time to time." He gave the screws another turn and John screamed again. He was soaked in sweat and weeping uncontrollable. His breath came in shallow gasps. "I'll tell you anything you want to know," he managed to choke out.

"Oh, no," Aumery replied. "You will tell me *everything* you know." Another crack and another scream,

"Yes. Yes," John shouted. "Anything, just stop." His appeal had no effect. The screws kept tightening inexorably and the pain increased beyond what John thought possible to bear.

"You may not be aware, but there is a common misconception in these unfortunate circumstances," Aumery said, as if he was imparting a mildly interesting piece of information. "Many think that this process of inquiry that you and I are engaged in requires me asking questions and you answering them." He twisted the screws an excruciating quarter turn more. "It is believed that the infliction of pain, and the promise that the pain will cease, ensures truthful answers. There are two flaws with this idea. First, how does the questioner distinguish a convincing lie prepared in advance from the truth? Impossible. Second, the accuracy of the answers depends upon the questioner knowing exactly which questions to ask and phrasing them the right way. These are both significant difficulties when dealing with intelligent fanatics such as these heretics.

"I do not believe that you are a fanatic"—another quarter turn—"but you are undoubtedly intelligent. I find therefore a different technique works more effectively. I shall apply pain and you shall talk to me. You will tell me everything you know, from the dreams you had as a child to your darkest, innermost secrets. And you will tell me everything and, by the time we are finished, I shall know your mind as clearly as my own.

"I admit it is a long process, but it is effective. The trick, of course, is keeping you alive long enough to empty you of all knowledge. But then, as I mentioned before, you have fourteen joints on each hand and we have only begun with the first. Joints in the hands are undeniably useful, but they are not, in my experience, essential to life."

Aumery stopped talking, but continued tightening the screws one quarter turn at a time. John talked. He babbled about the memory cloister and recited parts of ancient books. It made no difference. Bones cracked, the thumbnail peeled away as the digit became distorted by the pressure and John screamed.

Eventually, Aumery stopped and loosened the screws and examined the disfigured lump that had been John's thumb. He nodded approvingly.

Rebirth

John was only barely conscious. The agony of his thumb was immense, enveloping his entire body. Henri let him go and John sagged against the monk, cradling his crippled hand against his chest.

"That's enough for today," Aumery said. "I find that patience is a virtue in this process and we have time. We shall talk more tomorrow."

Henri put his hands under John's armpits and John shrieked as his thumb banged against his chest. Henri half led, half carried him back to his cell. He spent the rest of the day lying on his cot trying not to move. The slightest jolt sent needles of pain surging up his arm and made him gasp for breath.

As the hours passed, the thumb swelled to twice its normal size and blackened. Where John's thumbnail had been, raw flesh oozed blood. Henri brought food but John ignored it.

As night fell, John began to feel slightly better. Either the knife-edged sharpness of the pain was receding or he was becoming used to it. He discovered that by using his left hand to hold his right forearm tightly against his chest and carefully keeping the ruined thumb turned outward, he could move about slowly. Every time he jarred it was agony, but John managed to nibble on some of the bread and cheese. He lay on his cot and thought.

Aumery's promise of continuing the torture tomorrow terrified John, but what was even worse was that there didn't seem to be a specific question he could answer to end the horror. Aumery appeared to simply want to continue torturing until John had told him everything he knew, and John was convinced that he would continue until he was certain there was nothing else to tell. That would take forever and then what? Would Aumery kill him, have him burned alive as a heretic? After a few more days of torture like today, he would probably welcome death in the fire. John shuddered at the thought.

Eventually, John fell into a fitful sleep. He woke up frequently, sometimes in pain when he moved his hand and sometime sweating in terror at the black dreams that haunted him. "Isabella," he cried out as the sun rose, "come back."

Favours

Toulouse
June 21, 1214

"My child, it's good to see you once more." Bishop Foulques swept through the door, his voice rich with insincerity. He was not wearing the formal attire of his office, but his robe was obviously expensive and decorated with crosses picked out in gold thread. The folds of flesh hanging from his cheeks and chin glistened with fat, which he wiped at with the voluminous folds of his sleeve. "You must tell me of all your adventures."

Isabella distrusted Foulques's false cheerfulness. He had never paid her a moment's notice when she had lived at Count Raymond's court and she was certain he only did so now because he thought he might gain something from it. "I would be delighted to, Your Excellency. Thank you for agreeing to meet with us."

Isabella and Peter had waited in the entrance hall of the Chateau Narbonnaise all morning. To begin with no one had paid them any attention, ignoring Peter's polite requests for an audience with Foulques. Isabella had quickly become discouraged and angry, but Peter had remained calm and asked everyone who passed when they could meet with the Bishop. He had been given every imaginable excuse—his Excellency had not yet risen, he was attending to his toilet, he was dining—but Peter had persisted, quietly and politely requesting an audience and suggesting that he had some information of importance and value. Finally it had paid off and they had been ushered into a small side room with no furniture and bare brick walls.

"Always a pleasure to meet with such an attractive young lady." Isabella shivered as Foulques's eyes scanned her. She felt as if her clothing had suddenly become as transparent as water. Foulques ran his gaze dismissively over Peter's dirty, unshaven face and grubby, torn habit. A sneer flashed across his features before he turned back to Isabella and his lecherous smile returned. "What is it I can do for you?"

Isabella had assumed that Peter would do the talking, and was disconcerted that Foulques insisted on addressing her, but she took a deep breath and said, "I have come from Montpellier, where a friend of mine is being imprisoned by Arnaud Aumery." At the mention of Aumery's name, Foulques raised his eyebrows, but remained silent. "I believe Aumery plans to torture my friend and I…"

"Why?" Foulques interrupted. At Isabella's confused expression, he continued, "Why would Aumery torture your friend?"

"Because…" Isabella hesitated, unsure how to continue. "Because he knows things that Aumery wants," she finished weakly.

"The location of the Holy Grail?"

Isabella gasped. "You know?"

Foulques laughed. "Aumery's quest to bring on the Day of Judgement is well known. What is your friend's name?"

"John," Isabella replied, wishing that Peter would join in and help.

"Would this John," Foulques asked, licking his lips, "be the boy who I seem to remember was the scribe for Roger Trenceval at St. Gilles?" Before she could answer, Foulques went on. "And if so, would he also be the boy that Aumery accused so loudly of assisting in the murder of Pierre of Castelnau?"

"Yes," Isabella said. She was nervous at Foulques's questioning and upset by how much he seemed to know. She felt a bead of sweat form between her shoulder blades and run down her back. "But he had nothing to do with the murder. That's why we're here."

"So you say," Foulques waved a bejewelled hand dismissively. "But even if your protestations are true, I doubt if this John is a shining example of Christian virtue and righteousness. Why should I care if Aumery wishes to practice his methods of persuasion on some unenlightened heretic?"

Confused thoughts swirled around Isabella's mind. This was all going horribly wrong. She regretted not planning what to say more carefully, but she had assumed Peter would do the talking and he hadn't said a word yet. However, now he did break his silence and what he said shocked Isabella.

"You should not care one jot, Your Excellency," Peter said, stepping forward. "This John is unimportant. I do not believe he is a heretic, although you are correct in saying he is not a good Catholic. However, I do *know*, beyond a shadow of a doubt, that he took no part in the murder of Pierre of Castelnau."

"Know?" Foulques said. Peter had his undivided attention now. "You were Aumery's creature at St. Gilles. I recognize you, but how can you possibly know what was in this John's mind when he held the reins of Pierre's donkey?"

"I can know because I grew up with John and, for all his doubts and theological errors, he would never knowingly be a party to murder. And," Peter hurried on before Foulques could interrupt, "I have proof."

"Proof?" Foulques was enthralled now.

Peter nodded. "Proof that John had nothing to do with Pierre of Castelnau's murder. And, more importantly, Your Excellency, this proof also uncovers a great evil at the highest level in the leadership of our holy crusade." Peter fell silent to allow Foulques to digest this information. It had to be obvious to him that the reference to leadership of the crusade must be a reference to Aumery.

"What is this proof?"

"A letter, Your Excellency, to one Oddo of Saxony, ordering him to murder Pierre."

"And this letter was written by," Foulques hesitated, pulling absently at his fleshy chins, "this 'highest level in the leadership' of the crusade?"

"Indeed it was, Your Excellency."

"How did you come by this letter?"

"It was kept by Oddo and given to the Abbot of St. Gilles for safekeeping."

"You have this letter?"

"Not on my person." Isabella shivered. Peter was telling the truth, but the letter was in her satchel and it suddenly felt very heavy.

"And there can be no doubt about the content of this letter?" Foulques asked. "It cannot be read any other way than that you describe?"

"It cannot, Your Excellency. It is a truly damning document."

"And you can lay your hand on this document with ease?"

Peter nodded. He stood silent while Folques pondered. "What makes you think I would want this letter?" he asked eventually.

"I am certain that Your Excellency is as shocked as I was by the existence of this document and the evil it exposes within our Church. I am but a poor priest, struggling to come closer to God, but you have the power to cleanse the Church of this sin."

Foulques stared at Peter, who held his gaze. Although it had never been spoken explicitly, both knew that Peter was offering Foulques power over his enemy, and that there would be a cost.

"So, you wish to exchange the life of your friend in Montpellier for this letter?" Foulques placed his hands in an attitude of prayer and buried the tips of his fingers in the folds of his chins. "You wish to bargain for the life of a possible heretic. You are a priest of the Church. It is your holy duty to deliver this letter to me without condition in order that I may cleanse the Church."

Peter remained silent and held Foulques's stare. Isabella felt as tense as a coiled spring. It was all she could do not to leap forward, fling herself at Foulques's feet and beg for John's release, but she waited.

Eventually, Foulques spoke. "Very well. Bring me the letter and I will see what I can do to get your friend released."

Isabella opened her mouth to protest, but Peter beat her to it. "Thank you, Your Excellency," he said smoothly, "but I fear time is pressing. Father Aumery's enthusiasm in rooting out heresy is well known and every moment that we delay, we run the risk of the death of an innocent burdening our consciences."

"What do you propose?" Foulques had dropped all pretence at friendship.

"Perhaps if Your Excellency could write a letter, sealed with your ring and in the name of the blessed Pope Innocent, ordering the immediate release of John, it could be taken to Montpellier by fast dispatch rider."

"I will go as well," Isabella could contain herself no longer. "Give me a fast horse and I will accompany the dispatch rider."

Both men turned to stare at her. It was Peter who broke the ensuing silence. "That is a good idea. When we hear that John is released, I shall retrieve the letter for Your Excellency."

"You do not trust me?" Foulques asked coldly.

Peter opened his eyes wide in surprise. He knelt before Foulques and kissed the Bishop's ring on the fat finger. "Your Excellency, I beg forgiveness if I have unwittingly given offence by suggesting such a thing. My trust in you is complete and unfailing. It is Father Aumery's good faith that I distrust."

"Very well," Foulques said, mollified. "I shall write the letter and arrange for its delivery. The rider will leave this afternoon. And I hope"—he turned to Isabella and leered—"that you will come back and express your gratitude once your friend is released."

"Thank you, Your Excellency," Isabella whispered. "I am forever in your debt."

Foulques nodded in agreement. "You may wait here while I make arrangements." With an imperious swirl of his expensive robe, the bishop left the room.

Isabella's knees felt weak and she sagged down to sit on the floor. Peter crouched beside her. "Are you all right?" he asked. "Will you be able to keep up with the rider?"

"I will," Isabella said, drawing a deep breath. "I have to. I'm just so relieved. I didn't think Foulques was going to agree."

"He was always going to agree. He's a greedy man and we offered him something he wanted. I just hope you can get back to Montpellier in time."

"So do I."

"Once John is released, give Oddo's letter to the dispatch rider to bring back to Foulques. You take John somewhere safe. Do not, on any account, return here. I will wait until the rider returns."

Isabella looked at Peter. Not once on the journey here from Minerve, or throughout the discussion with Foulques, had he seemed anything other than completely calm. "You were wonderful with Foulques."

Peter smiled shyly. "God was with me."

"You seem so content."

"Loneliness has taught me much," Peter said. "All my life, I have wanted what other people had: Mother Marie's contentment at the Priory of St. Anne, Oddo's power over others, Aumery's certainty that he was right." Peter hesitated for a moment. "Even John's inquiring mind. I envied him, you know. He's comfortable with what he doesn't know and is happy just trying to learn things. I'm not like that. I need structure and I thought Aumery and his certainty could offer me that."

"And you don't any more?"

"No," Peter shook his head slowly. "Francesco taught me that, although I didn't realize it at first. I have always thought that the visions that have plagued me were either sent as torment by the Devil or as a test of my faith by God. Perhaps God does not work in such an obvious way. Perhaps the visions were in my head and God simply sat back and waited for me to resolve them myself. To do that, I had to stop wanting anything, and that meant that I had to see that everything I have ever wanted in this world has led to harm and evil. I wanted to be engulfed in the security of the Church and that made me deny John's innocence when Pierre of Castelnau was murdered. I wished for Oddo's power so I betrayed Roger Trenceval and spied in Minerve. I craved Aumery's certainty and that led me to kill poor old Diogenes.

"There is much else that I don't understand." Peter paused and stared at the palms of his hands. Faint red blotches marked where he had bled. "The stigmata. Was it something my mind created all unknowing or was it God telling me that my journey of discovery was almost over?" Peter shrugged. "In any case, Francesco taught me that the way to God is through solitary contemplation, and my time alone in the cave at Minerve taught me how to do that. I have found my God. He does not give me earthly power or the knowledge of how to bring on the Day of Judgement but, as you say, He has brought me contentment.

"I shall resolve whatever I can from my past life, as I am doing here with John, and, when I am ready, I shall leave my cave and begin preaching as

Francesco does, owning nothing, expecting nothing and travelling simply with God." Peter fell silent, a gentle smile on his thin lips.

"And I am certain you will be a fine preacher who brings much comfort to many troubled souls."

Isabella felt ridiculously happy that Peter appeared to have found peace and freedom from the visions that had so tormented him. She was wondering if she should say anything else when Foulques bustled back into the room, followed by a harassed-looking scribe carrying a roll of parchment. The pair stood up.

"I have your letter," Foulques announced. He waved a bejewelled hand and the scribe scuttled forward and held the parchment out to Peter, who took it and studied it.

"Thank you, Your Excellency," Peter said when he had finished. "This is perfect."

Foulques took the parchment and rolled it while the scribe set up a small candle on the floor and melted some red wax. The scribe poured some wax on the parchment and Foulques pressed his bishop's ring into it. "There," he said. "I have fulfilled my part of the bargain. A dispatch rider and a spare horse wait downstairs."

"Thank you, Your Excellency," Isabella said. She looked over at Peter, who nodded and said, "God speed."

The scribe led Isabella out of the room.

Rescue

Montpellier
June 23, 1214

They had made extraordinarily good time on the 90-mile-long road from Toulouse to Montpellier. The large horses that Foulques had supplied had covered almost 30 miles on the first afternoon, easily as far as Isabella's pony could have covered in a long day, 50 miles on the second day, and the final 10 miles on the third morning. Despite the speed, every second had seemed like a year to Isabella. Her companion's insistence on resting the horses and feeding themselves was infuriating, as was his reluctance to travel in the dark, particularly on the final night when they were so close. His rationale made sense—the horses suffered much less if they were rested, and travel on rough roads in the dark was dangerous—but that didn't make the journey any less agonizing.

When Isabella wasn't concentrating on staying on the horse's back, and when she lay awake on a cot in some inn, she fretted about what might be happening to John, and even if Aumery would obey Foulques's letter and allow him to go free. The gut-wrenching thought that Aumery might already have killed John tore through her at unexpected moments and tortured her nights. Thoughts of John, broken on some hideous machine, thrust Isabella into the depths of tearful despair and to the heights of an incandescent rage at Aumery and the Church that promoted such cruelty. If John was dead… Isabella didn't know what she would do. She would find out soon enough: ahead lay the inn where William of Arles had promised to await her return.

"William," Isabella yelled as she dismounted. "Where are you? What has happened?" Her one hope was that John had been released or escaped and found his way to William. He hopes were dashed the instant she saw the look on William's face.

"What happened?" she repeated as she ran toward the figure coming out of the inn door, a terrible dark knot of fear settling in her stomach. "Is John still alive?"

"Alive, yes," William acknowledged as he took Isabella's hands and began to lead her inside.

"No," Isabella said. "I have the letter from Foulques. We must go now and release John."

William looked hard at Isabella. He glanced up at her companion, still sitting astride his mount. "Very well," he said at last. "I shall have the landlord attend to the horses and see to rooms for your return."

The dispatch rider dismounted and came and stood by Isabella. "How is he?" Isabella asked William, her brow furrowed with worry.

"To tell the truth, I do not know. Every morning and evening, I have walked the alley by his cell singing the agreed song. Sometimes he has responded."

"What did he say?" Isabella interrupted.

"Nothing. Some days he made no sound, on others it was simply a shout or a cough. I suppose he did not wish to alert the guard." William hesitated. "Once he did say a word."

"What?"

"Two days ago, in the morning, he said 'help me.'"

"We have to go," Isabella said, fighting back tears.

"He shouted back this morning," William said, "but I couldn't make out if he was saying anything or not."

Isabella nodded and turned to the dispatch rider. "Come on," she ordered.

William watched as the pair turned the corner. "I hope you are not too late," he said under his breath.

* * *

"So, the fat slug, Foulques, wishes me to release the heretic, John." Aumery looked up from the letter in his bony hands and stared at Isabella. His emotionless smile terrified her. "Very well, follow me." Aumery turned and left the room. Isabella was too stunned to move and had to run to catch up with him in the corridor. Could it be this simple?

Aumery led the way down to the cellar, where a large monk stood outside a heavy door. "Henri," Aumery said, "it seems our guest will be leaving us. Our hospitality is not to his liking."

Henri stared back impassively for a moment, stepped forward and unlocked the door. Isabella pushed past him and entered the room.

Her first emotion was an immense flood of relief. John was alive. He sat, hunched over, on the far side of a bare table. "John," she said. John raised his head. Isabella gasped. John's face was frighteningly pale and his filthy hair was plastered across his forehead with sweat. His face was pinched in a look of confusion and his eyes scanned the room aimlessly, struggling to focus on who was speaking.

"It's me, Isabella," she said, stepping forward.

"Isabella?" John asked in wonder. "Have you come back?"

"I've come back to get you, like I promised." Isabella moved round the table and reached out to John. He shrank back and whimpered. "Don't touch me."

Isabella's relief at finding John alive vanished. Something was horribly wrong. "Don't touch you? Why? What's wrong?"

With agonizing slowness, John lifted his hands from beneath the table and held them out. Isabella let out a shuddering breath and grasped the edge of the table as her knees turned to water. The things on the ends of John's arms were barely recognizable as hands. They were swollen to almost twice their normal size, and livid red patches alternated with older, black bruising. Worst of all, the fingers were twisted into impossible claw-like shapes.

John looked up at Isabella, tears streaming down his face. "I thought you weren't going to come. I wanted to die."

Isabella gulped but she couldn't swallow the sobs that rose from deep within her. "I came as fast as I could," she said helplessly. She reached out and gently wiped the tears from John's cheeks.

Isabella looked up to see Aumery standing in the doorway. He was smiling. "What have you done?" she asked, feeling anger begin to replace her misery.

"Your friend and I have had many interesting conversations," Aumery replied calmly. "He has many interesting things in that memory of his."

"You will rot in Hell for this." The venom in her voice surprised even Isabella.

Aumery blinked, then his smile returned. "On the contrary, it is you and your friend who will rot in Hell. I do God's work."

"If this is God's work"—Isabella glanced down at John's ruined hands—"then I want no part of your God."

"So you are a heretic as well," Aumery said. "I should have you both consigned to the flames, but you appear to have friends in high places. Besides, I do not think there is anything left in your friend's head that I have not discovered."

Isabella tensed. If that were true, then Aumery knew The Gospel of the Christ and the other forbidden books in the memory cloister. He knew about Adso's adventures at Rhedae and the Cathar Treasure.

"You look nervous," Aumery said, his tone suddenly conversational. "Do not worry. I have little interest in the fantasies that heretics claim to be gospels. In any case, they now only exist in the head of your crippled friend, and who will believe him? Even if the scroll in the cave at Rhedae was the so-called Gospel of Christ, your companion, Adso, did my work for me and it is destroyed. As for the Cathar Treasure, knowledge can indeed be a dangerous thing, but soon, when the flames have claimed the last Cathar heretic, there will only be the true knowledge of the Church. Thus purified, the armies of the True God will cut through the unbelievers like a scythe through ripe corn."

A look of regret flashed over Aumery's face, but then he went on. "I had hoped that the Holy Grail would lead us on that great day, but it was not to be. Perhaps the easy answers are always sent merely to tempt us. In any case, I am done here." Aumery swept his arm around dismissively. "Take your friend and go."

Isabella reached down and placed her hands gently on John's shoulders. He flinched at the touch. "We can go now," Isabella whispered in his ear. "Can you stand?"

John nodded slightly. With Isabella's help, he stood and stepped away from the table. Holding his hands carefully before him, he stumbled round the table and toward the door. Aumery stood in the way.

"Just one further thing," he said, looking at Isabella with his strange, emotionless eyes. "There is something I need you to give me before I can let you go."

Isabella froze. Aumery had said he knew everything in John's mind. That meant he knew that Oddo had preserved his incriminating letter and that John and Isabella had it. The letter lay in Isabella's satchel, along with John's books and drawings. If she had to give it up then their release would mean nothing. "What?" Isabella managed to ask through her suddenly dry mouth.

"The books," Aumery said.

It took Isabella a moment to understand what he meant. "Lucius's book on drawing?"

Aumery nodded. "Also the one on sculpture and the mathematical one that supposedly proves the heresy that the earth is not the centre of God's universe."

"But they are ancient books from long before the Gospels. Surely what they contain cannot be heretical."

"Knowledge is heretical," Aumery announced.

Isabella didn't know whether to be relieved that Aumery didn't mean the letter or shocked at what he had just said. "Knowledge?" she said stupidly.

"You, with your heretical ideas, will never understand. Away from the light of Christianity there is no knowledge. The books scribed by pagans and unbelievers are mere chicken scratches in the dirt; there is no God-revealed truth to guide the hand. But if that were all they were, then there would be no harm in the pages you carry with you so carefully." Aumery closed his eyes and tilted his head back. His hands clenched spasmodically in front of him. "The body is corrupt and weak, and there are few of us with the strength of spirit to scourge that weakness." Aumery brought his head back down and his eyes sprang open. "It is the duty of those of us with strength to protect the rest. All knowledge that does not come direct from God must be destroyed, on bonfires that will make Nero's conflagration in Rome seem but a spark."

Aumery's eyes blazed with a fierce passion. "And," he continued fervently, "those who disseminate false knowledge; those who seduce the innocent away from God's truth with fantastical tales of the Earth spinning around the sun or of a new way to draw the world that leaves no room for God; those who do not see the Truth of Christ's teachings, they must join the books within the purifying flames. When only the Pure survive, then will God's world dawn."

Isabella stared in horror, overcome by Aumery's utter insanity. He was proposing nothing less than the destruction of everything, and everybody, not approved of by the Pope and his Church in Rome. Only a very few would be allowed to live in Aumery's world and his madness would determine who. She thought of all the people she had known and what she had loved in them—Beatrice and Umar's peaceful wisdom, Shabaka's nobility and Adso's bravery. She remembered the beauty she had seen—the Mezquita in Cordova, the vast majestic ruins of Madinet al-Zahra and the exquisite, intricate detail of the golden tile that John had exchanged for the equally wonderful Auramazdah. None of that meant anything in Aumery's doomed world. Isabella wanted to scream—*this is not God, this is lunacy. You are worshipping death, not life*. Instead she lowered her gaze, slowly withdrew the books from her satchel and passed them to Aumery's eager hands.

Isabella raised her head and met Aumery's stare. The monk stepped aside. "Do not think that you escape," he said as they passed him in the doorway. "Your turn will come soon enough."

Gently, Isabella helped John along the corridor, up the steps and out into the safety of the street. John turned to face her. "I didn't tell him," he said. He looked weak and frail, but there was a strength in his eyes.

"Didn't tell him what?" Isabella asked.

"I didn't tell him we had the letter to Oddo."

The look of pride on John's pain-ravaged face brought Isabella to the verge of tears. She couldn't imagine what it had cost him over the past days not to divulge that simple piece of information. "You did well," she said. "I'm sorry I had to give up Lucius's book."

John Wilson

"It doesn't matter," John croaked, attempting a weak smile. He held up his wrecked hands. "I don't think I can draw any more."

Plans

Montpellier
July 7, 1214

"It's been two weeks," John said. "If my hands were going to rot it would have begun by now. Perhaps Aumery's reluctance to draw blood helped in some way."

John, Isabella and William sat at a table in the inn where all three were lodging. Their first inclination as soon as they got John back there was to flee as far from Aumery as possible, but it was obvious that it would be at least a few days before their injured friend would be capable of moving far. The worry was removed the following morning when William reported that Aumery, in the company of several monks and considerable baggage, had set out on the road west.

"Going to Toulouse," William surmised, "to have it out with Foulques."

"He'll get an unpleasant surprise," Isabella said. The day before, she had given the dispatch rider the damning letter and he had set off back to Toulouse. The letter would have been in Foulques's hands for several days before Aumery arrived. Isabella regretted not being able to see Aumery's face when Foulques produced the letter. If she could be certain of one thing about the fat bishop, it was that he would make the most of the moment and Aumery would squirm and wriggle like a worm impaled on a fish hook.

"But you're still in a lot of pain," Isabella said.

"Yes," John agreed, "but it's going to be a long time until the pain stops—if ever." He looked down at the hands on the table before him. The swelling had gone down a lot, except over some of the finger joints. The angry redness had mostly gone, replaced by black bruising that faded in places to a deep, sickly yellow. It was the fingers that were hardest to look at. Not one rested in a natural position.

John's right hand was the worst. As it had healed, the fingers had curled inward until they formed a loose parody of a fist with the useless thumb tucked under the first and second finger. The only finger that John could move at all was the small one on the outside, which was bent but could be moved up and down without unbearable pain.

The left hand looked better. Aumery had not worked as diligently on that one, and the fingers were less tightly curled and all had some movement; however, the knuckles where the fingers joined the hand were smashed and John couldn't make a fist or even clench anything firmly.

Isabella had bathed the hands and wrapped them in warm cloths, which had eased the agony a little. She had also fed John every meal since his rescue. At first he hadn't been interested in eating, but his appetite gradually improved. He had put some weight back on and looked generally much healthier than when she had found him. Now he was ready to move on.

"We can't stay here forever," John said. "Aumery could come back any day. We have no way of knowing what went on between him and Foulques. Our power went with the letter, so we have to find somewhere safe to hide."

Isabella knew John was right, but the thought of moving long distances scared her. "Where could we go? Back to Queribus or Pereypertuse?"

"Somewhere like that," John said. "Esclarmonde said that Montsegur was a good place. It's impregnable. She helped to rebuild the castle there, and it protects a larger community of Good Christians than at the other places. I think it would be safe for a long time."

"It's such a long way," Isabella said.

"I think you will find," William contributed, "that anywhere safe is a long way from here. The only alternative I can see is going in the opposite direction, completely away from the war."

"That won't work," Isabella said. The thought of wandering aimlessly with John in the condition he was in was even more frightening than a single long journey. There was certainly an attraction to being somewhere safe, if they could only get there. "All right," she said eventually. "Montsegur it is. Will you come with us, William?"

William thought for a moment and then nodded. "I shall. I too need somewhere safe if I am to write my epic poem of the crusade. Montsegur will do as well as anywhere and I daresay I can ferret out a few worthwhile stories from the other refugees. What will you do there?"

"I don't know," John said, staring miserably at the hands that couldn't even hold a spoon let alone a charcoal or brush. "Survive, I suppose."

"You can draw," Isabella said.

"With these?" John lifted his hands miserably.

"I will be your hands," Isabella said. "Lucius's book is still in your head and there's nothing wrong with my hands. You can tell me what to do. It'll be slow, but I can learn."

"You would do that?" John asked, raising his eyes to look at Isabella.

"Of course I will," she said, "and I will try and learn the mathematics book and the sculpture book."

John smiled. For the first time since Henri had hit him over the head in the alley in St. Gilles, John could see a glimmer of hope for the future. "Let's go, then."

"Well," William said, standing. "Now that our futures are decided, we should get some rest. Tomorrow, I shall find a cart to take us to our new home. Goodnight."

As William left, Isabella turned to John. "Are you sure that you'll be all right for such a long journey?"

"I will," John said with as close to a reassuring smile as he could manage. "The travelling will be painful, but it's painful just sitting here. I want to feel safe again. And be with you."

"So do I," Isabella said. She kissed John on the cheek. "Together we'll be the greatest artist there has ever been."

John laughed. "We will," he said, "and we'll remember. Whether it will mean anything to anyone, *we* will remember what we have see and done and learned. As long as we do that, Aumery and the others will fail."

The Last Night

Montsegur
March 15, 1244

"A life is made from many hours and every single one wounds you, but of them all only one kills you—the last one. I have been blessed to live for more than half a hundred years. I cannot complain that the last hour of so many is finally with me." John smiled weakly.

Isabella knew that what John said was true. For two weeks now, he had been too frail to even rise from the cot on which he lay. She had tended to him, but he had barely eaten and the skin stretched over his bones had taken on an almost transparent quality. He was dying.

She smiled back at him. "You're looking more like Peter every day."

John attempted to laugh, but all that came out was a feeble croak that quickly degenerated into a wracking cough. When it had passed, his eyes focussed on Isabella, her still-beautiful face framed by greying hair. "Every day, you look more like Beatrice," he said softly.

"I can think of no one I would rather grow to be like," Isabella said. "I wish I had known her better. That was a long time ago, wasn't it?"

"It *was* all a long time ago," John said. He lay on a cot in the small house that clung to the hillside below the imposing walls of the castle at Montsegur. The house was a part of the community of Cathars and refugees from the crusade, and it had been John and Isabella's home for the past 30 years. The crusade had officially ended fifteen years before but, since then, Dominic Guzman's black-clad inquisitors had been busy searching out and burning heretics. The king of France had also taken an interest and his army now surrounded this final Cathar refuge.

John was propped up on a straw-filled pillow and his twisted hands lay on the thin blanket on his lap. His eyes appeared huge above the ledges of his cheekbones and they were unnaturally bright.

It had been difficult for Isabella, watching John fade, but she took comfort from the sense of peace and acceptance that exuded from the man with whom she has shared her life. Despite his physical deterioration, John's mind was still sharp, although gaps were appearing in his memory. The forgetting bothered John—his memory had been such a huge part of his life—but he accepted it as part of dying, just as he accepted the progressive weakening of his body. John could still talk, although his voice was barely above a whisper and he had to rest often, so he and Isabella spent long hours reminiscing and wondering about the future.

"Are we all that is left?" The wrinkles on John's brow deepened as he concentrated. "I can't remember very well. Adso's dead, isn't he?"

"Yes," Isabella said gently. "At Muret. Oddo killed him and then you killed Oddo."

"With my sword," John said.

"Auramazdah."

"Yes, I remember. It's odd. I walk along the memory cloister and it's all crumbling. Every day a new bit has fallen down, taking some memory with it. Most of the books have gone, and most of the people. I remember de Montfort died at Toulouse." John suddenly brightened.

"At the siege in 1218," Isabella said. "He was killed by a rock from a mangonel. The city still fell."

John nodded slowly. "Aumery. What happened to him?"

"Nothing." There was still a hint of bitterness at the mention of Aumery's name, even after all these years. "The Pope made him Archbishop of Narbonne and he died peacefully in his sleep seven years after de Montfort. I suppose that's all we could hope for. The Church looks after its own. At least we prevented him rising to cardinal or pope. I hope he's suffering all the torments of Hell for what he did to you."

"If there is a Hell," John said. "Perhaps Beatrice was right and Hell is this world. I don't think Adso even thought there was a God. Maybe he was right." John fell silent and his gaze drifted down to the ruined hands on his lap. As they had healed after his torture, he had regained limited use of a couple of his fingers, enough to hold a spoon or knife and feed himself. After hours of frustrating labour, he had managed to hold a charcoal in a way that allowed him to draw, but he could not manage any fine movements and the results, after hours of painful effort, were crude at best.

"I won't miss the pain," he said quietly.

"They hurt all the time?"

"Every day," John replied. "I'm tired."

"I'll let you sleep," Isabella said.

John shook his head weakly. "My soul is tired." With a great effort he lifted his head and looked at Isabella. A thin smile played on the edges of his lips.

Rebirth

"Sometimes I think that all that is left to bind my soul to this poor remnant of a body is your love."

"Then you will live forever," Isabella said.

John's smile broadened. "I think not." He closed his eyes.

For a moment, Isabella thought he had slipped away, but then she saw the almost imperceptible rise and fall of his chest and relaxed. She stood up, kissed him on the forehead and quietly left the room.

Once outside, Isabella climbed the steep path that ran beside their house toward the towering walls of the castle itself. She settled in her favourite spot, a flat rock outcrop that projected from the most northerly angle of the castle walls. The spring sun was low in the western sky, but high enough that Isabella could feel a slight warmth against her left cheek.

Montsegur was a long, narrow hill, running roughly east to west. The fortress and the village lay on a bulbous nob at the west end. From there the hilltop widened out and sloped gradually down to the east before narrowing once more. The eastern extremity sported a much smaller castle called the Roc de la Tour.

Isabella looked down at the French army, thousands strong, that was camped on the valley bottom far below. They had been there for almost ten months. Ten months of siege, fighting, hardship and fear, but it would be all over tomorrow. Ever since Christmas, when the French had managed to climb the cliffs around Montsegur and conquer the Roc de la Tour, the defenders' fate had been sealed. Gradually the attackers had worked their way west along the hilltop until they were able set up a mangonel that could bombard the main castle on the west end. The defenders did not have the men or resources to prevent them and two weeks earlier, on March 2, Montsegur, the final major stronghold of Catharism and the last refuge of any who questioned the Church, had surrendered to the French knights below.

In a rare gesture of humanity, the besiegers had allowed the defenders two weeks' grace before they entered the castle. It had been a strange two weeks, with no fighting, but with the doom of the more than two hundred Perfects hanging over everyone. If Isabella leaned out and peered round the corner of the castle wall, she could see the massive funeral pyre that had been built on the closest flat ground to the castle entrance.

In the two weeks of unexpected peace and quiet, several inhabitants had escaped, braving the tortuous climb down the cliffs in the dark and sneaking through gaps in the army below. Isabella did not have that option, since John was nowhere close to strong enough to make the journey, but she was in no danger. All those who were not Perfects would be questioned and sent on their way.

John had tried to get Isabella to leave; she was the only one who remained who knew about Lucius's revolutionary books on drawing and sculpture and Aristarchos's text that claimed the earth spun around the sun. Over their many years here, John had taught Isabella as much of the books as he could. He had even spent countless painstaking hours teaching her to draw and she was now a fair artist in her own right. Not relying on her flawed memory, Isabella had written down all that John had tried to teach her and had, tucked in a hole in the wall by the hearth in their home, John's sketch book, the drawing of the Mezquita that he had given her, and roughs of both Lucius's and Arsitarchos's books. Tomorrow Isabella would be allowed to walk down the hill, but she would have to leave all the papers behind. Getting John down worried her as well, and where would they go? John wasn't strong enough to travel any distance and the last thing she wanted was for him to die on some crude cart on a rough track in the middle of nowhere.

The noise of a small rock skittering down the hill disturbed Isabella. To her left, a tall, skinny man was carefully making his way along the narrow path at the foot of the castle wall. He was wearing the travel-worn brown habit of a Franciscan monk.

"Peter!" Isabella exclaimed, standing. The pair embraced on the narrow ledge. "How did you get up here?"

Peter smiled. "Getting up here is easy. It's getting down that's tricky. It's good to see you again. How's John?" Peter had visited several times over the years, most recently in the summer four years previously. After helping secure John's release from Aumery, Peter had travelled to Assisi where he had become a close friend of Francesco and journeyed with him to Egypt and Rome. He had been with Francesco when he had received the stigmata in 1224 and by his cot two years later when he died. Peter was also present in the summer of 1228 when Pope Gregory IX pronounced Francesco's sainthood and laid the foundation stone of a magnificent basilica in Assisi. Since then, he had travelled and preached and visited John and Isabella whenever he passed through Languedoc.

"John is dying," Isabella said. She surprised herself by how calmly she made such a bald statement. "He is very weak and he thinks he will die tonight." Isabella paused and looked sadly at Peter. "I hope he is right. He cannot live long and a peaceful end here would be a blessing compared to the turmoil that tomorrow will bring."

"I shall pray for him," Peter said. "May I speak with him?"

"Of course. His body is failing, but his mind, apart from his memory, is strong." Isabella led the way down to the tiny house.

John was awake when the pair entered his room. "Peter," he said, his pale face breaking into a wide smile. He tried to raise himself but the effort was too great and he slumped back onto his pillow, fighting for breath.

"Be easy, my old friend," Peter said, placing his hand gently on John's shoulder. "Rest."

"There will be time enough for rest soon," John said. "Tell me what you have been doing."

"I have been back to Assisi," Peter related. "The building work on the basilica progresses well. I wish you could see it. The master mason is using the new ideas from the north to create magnificent windows that will let in the light of heaven."

"I wish you could draw me a picture of it."

Peter laughed. "Drawing was always your talent. Mine was wrestling with my visions and my God."

"And your God has triumphed?" John asked.

"With Francesco's help, yes. I find it difficult now to think back to the tortured soul who struggled with those visions all those years ago. Was it me who did and was a part of those terrible things?"

"Has God forgiven you?"

"I hope so. I have worked tirelessly to earn forgiveness. Which reminds me, have you heard that the strange preacher, Dominic Guzman, the one who began that order in the black habits, has been canonized?" Isabella shook her head and John blinked. "Yes, he's Saint Dominic now."

"Perhaps you will be a saint one day," John said slowly.

Peter laughed again. "I doubt if God's forgiveness will extend that far. But he did bless me with the chance to meet an old friend of yours and use my poor head to carry a message to you, although I cannot say that I agree with all the sentiments expressed in it."

"A message," John asked. "From whom?"

Peter took a deep breath, closed his eyes and recited:

"The mounted knights in armour came.
From the northern lands by way of Arles,
They came to Béziers.
The cry was 'Kill them all,'
And the summer sun was black with smoke,
And the Orb ran red with the blood of thousands.
God worked hard sorting souls that day."

"William!" John exclaimed, before he broke down coughing. Isabella dipped a cloth in a nearby bowl of water and wiped his brow.

"I met him in Italy," Peter continued when John had settled. "He was very old, but still as rude as ever. As you see, he did write his epic. There is much more but that is all I could hold in my cluttered head."

"I was there, in Béziers," John said wistfully.

"So was I," Peter added, "and so were Aumery and de Montfort and Oddo."

"And Beatrice and Adso," John added. "We really are the last."

"We were the first and now we're the last." Peter leaned forward to John. "Do you wish me to hear your confession and pray with you?"

"Thank you, but no," John said.

"You haven't..." Peter hesitated awkwardly.

"No," John said. "I haven't taken the *consolamentum*. I'm not a Cathar. I shall take my chance, even if, as Adso told me he heard once, God has six arms filled with weapons to destroy the world."

"And if there is nothing?" Peter asked.

"Then there is nothing," John replied. He closed his eyes for a moment, gathering what little strength he had left before continuing. "I have a final request of you. Peter. Will you stay in Montsegur tonight?"

"I will," Peter said.

"Then, tomorrow morning, will you have my body carried and placed on the fire with the Perfects."

Isabella gasped.

"Do not be sad," John instructed. "I will be dead and I cannot think of better company for my body to be with than the gentle folk who will ascend the pyre in a few hours."

"I will see to it," Peter said.

John sighed and visibly relaxed. "Thank you. What will you do when this is all over?"

"The same as always," Peter replied, "travel and preach as long as God allows me."

"Convert everyone to the one true belief?"

"Even now, you still try to goad me," Peter said with a smile. "Yes, I will continue to try and enlighten those who live in darkness, but if my life has taught me one thing, it is that God and the Church are not as Aumery envisioned them. I encourage no one to rip their flesh as he did, nor do I believe there is a single easy answer like the Holy Grail. God, like the world around us, is infinitely more complicated than we would like to believe and I am more inclined to listen to others than I once was. Even unrepentant unbelievers like you."

Rebirth

"Do you remember the discussions we used to have as boys in Toulouse?" John asked.

"Fondly," Peter replied.

"It would be good if there was time for more of them. I wish you well."

"And I you. Whether you want me to or not, I shall pray every day for your soul."

"Thank you," John said. His gaze drifted over to Isabella.

Peter took the hint. "Farewell, my friend." He turned and slipped quietly out of the room.

John and Isabella sat in silence for a long time, their eyes locked. The shadows cast by the setting sun crawled slowly up the walls of the small room. Silent tears ran down Isabella's cheeks.

"I wish I could dry your tears," John said eventually.

Isabella sniffed and wiped her eyes. "It really is the end, isn't it?"

"Yes," John said, "I shall not see the night through." John smiled at Isabella to prevent her protests. "It's true, my love, and I have a final request of you. When my spirit leaves this poor vessel of a body, I would have you take the copies you made of my books and escape with the others down the mountain tonight."

"How do you know?" Isabella asked.

"I am dying," John replied. "I am not deaf. I have heard the talk in the next room, Amiel Aicart, Hugo and Poitevin are to be let down the cliff on ropes tonight. They are the last three who have the memory cloister. They hold many lost and forbidden books, Poitevin even has a version of the Gospel of the Christ, but none have the three books you know. Remember what Esclarmonde said about the Cathar Treasure. The four of you are it. You carry the knowledge, understanding and wisdom that is all that remains."

"I cannot leave you," Isabella said through tears.

"You will not be leaving me," John said. "I shall be leaving first. You will simply be saying farewell to the useless husk that was me."

Isabella thought for a long time. "Very well," she said eventually. "If you die this night, I will go, but I will not leave while there is one beat left in your heart.'

Her answer seemed to satisfy John who nodded, but the effort of talking had drained him, and he now appeared to collapse in on himself. "I'm very tired," he said. "I should like to sleep."

"I'll sit with you," Isabella said. She leaned over and kissed John on the lips. "I love you."

"I love you," John replied. "Good night."

John's face in sleep seemed calmer than Isabella had seen it in a long time. She sat in the darkening room watching the almost imperceptible rise and fall of John's chest. Eventually it was too dark to see anything, but Isabella didn't move to light a lamp. Even though she could no longer make out John's shape on the cot, she knew the exact moment his heart stopped beating.

Legacy

Near Florence
April 15, 1273

The shepherd boy sat on a rock in the warm spring sun, watching the old woman slowly move up the valley toward him. She rode a donkey that appeared almost as old as she was; it must have taken the pair many hours to work their painstaking way up from Florence. He wondered if she was a witch come to cast a spell on him, but he doubted that witches travelled so slowly on such decrepit animals.

At last the woman reached the boy and dismounted. The donkey stepped to the side and began nibbling disinterestedly on a clump of grass. The woman nodded to the boy. She was even older than he had thought. Her face was a complex mass of incredibly deep wrinkles and was surrounded by a halo of long, completely white hair. She wore a grey travelling cloak and carried a worn leather satchel over her shoulder. Despite her advanced age, the eyes that the woman focussed on the boy were still clear and bright.

"Good afternoon," she said in heavily accented Italian, "my name is Isabella."

"Good afternoon," the boy replied. "Why have you come so far into the hills? What do you wish?"

"To sit in the sun, and perhaps a drink of water," Isabella replied.

The boy unhooked a wineskin that hung from a nearby tree and passed it to Isabella, who took a long drink. "Thank you," she said, passing the skin back. The boy offered her a piece of dry sausage, but she declined. "When a body gets to be my age," she said, "it does not require much sustenance."

Isabella sat on a nearby flat rock and looked around. The hills were dry but the scattered sheep seemed content finding patches of young grass to feed on. Soon, as the weather continued to improve, the boy would take them farther into the hills. She was lucky she had found him this early in the year.

The air was fragrant with the smell of wild sage and rosemary, and that took Isabella back many years to her childhood in Languedoc. Idly, she began to softly hum a tune that William of Arles used to play.

"Old woman," the boy prompted. "Did you come all this way to serenade me?"

"No. No," Isabella said. "My apologies. My mind is old and sometimes wanders."

"Why then did you come all this way to seek me out? Your accent is not from round here and I do not think your aged bones needed the exercise."

"Indeed not," Isabella said. "I come from a place you have never heard of, Languedoc. I wonder if there will come a day when no one has heard of that land. But that will be no concern of mine. As you say, I have come a long way and, if you will bear with me, I would tell you a brief story."

The boy nodded, intrigued by his strange visitor. Shepherding the family's flock was a lonely occupation for a young boy with intelligence and imagination, and anything that broke the monotony was welcome.

"Once, long ago when I was young in the land I come from, I loved a boy called John. He loved me, but he also loved learning. Together we travelled far and wide learning everything we could. The times were troubled and many of the things John held in his head were dangerous to know. He suffered greatly for that and, many years ago now, he died and the wonderful books he held in his head died with him, except for three. He taught those three to me and for nearly thirty years, I have searched for the right people to pass on the wisdom of these books to. I came to Italy because I heard it was a country where people loved learning.

"One of the three books that I learned and copied was about mathematics. My first journey took me to Persia, where they love that art. There I met a remarkable man, Muhammad ibn Hasan Tusi. He was much taken by what I could tell and show him about the movement of the heavenly bodies and planned to build an observatory to better understand these things.

"More recently, I found myself in Pisa, where came upon a remarkable father and son, Nicola and Giovanni Pisano. They are sculptors struggling to find new ways to represent the world in stone. They were much impressed with the second book, *Scultura*, by the ancient Roman, Lucius. That left only one book, also by Lucius, on drawing. The Pisano's told me that Florence was host to many artists, and so I came here.

"What I heard of Florence was true, but I found that those working there had little interest in new ideas. I was ready to move on when I happened upon an artist, Giovanni Cimabue. He was happy with the old art but told me of a shepherd boy who had talents for drawing beyond his years."

Rebirth

The boy nodded acknowledgment. "I know Giovanni. He gives me charcoal so that I may draw on the rocks. It helps pass the time."

"May I see some of your work?"

"You are sitting on my latest masterpiece."

Isabella took a moment to understand what the boy was saying. Then, with a laugh, she stood and examined the rock she had been resting on. It was covered with black, line drawings of sheep, birds and animals.

"These are good," Isabella said, "but they do not live."

"Live?" the boy asked scornfully. "They are but lines on a flat rock. How can they live?"

Isabella delved into her satchel and pulled out the picture of the Mesquita in Cordova that John had drawn for her. The boy stared hard at the sketch. "What magic is this?" he asked in wonder

"No magic," Isabella replied. "It was drawn by my friend John, many years ago. It is merely the product of a technique studied and practised over many years. It is not perfect. There are many things John did not fully understand or could not pass on to me."

The boy tilted his head this way and that, trying to grasp how the drawing had been done. Tentatively, he put out his hand and touched the surface of the rock. "What is this magic called?"

"Perspectiva."

"Can you teach it to me?"

"No. That would take many years that I do not have left, even if I were skilled enough. You must learn it yourself."

"How?"

"Because you are a talented and a curious boy, and because I journeyed up here to give you the third book." Isabella pulled a pile of tattered sheets from her bag. "It is only my poor copy of a much better original and I fear some of the pages have suffered over the years, but what you need to know is set out within if you but take the trouble to search it out and apply yourself."

The boy held the pages reverently. He scanned the drawings.

Isabella turned to leave.

"Wait," the boy called after her. "Why do you give me this gift?"

Isabella stopped. "I have seen the horrors to which a narrow belief in God can lead. I know how many corpses pile up when men use God to increase their own worldly power. Our only protection against this evil is knowledge and wisdom. I have taken what little knowledge John passed on to me and tried to place it where it might do the most good in building future wisdom. Yours is the last piece of the Cathar Treasure. It is a new and better way to see this wonderful world. I hope you use it well."

Isabella retrieved the donkey and climbed onto its back. She turned to the boy. "Cimabue told me where to find you, but he did not tell me your name."

"I am called Ambrogiotto di Bondone," the boy said with pride, "but most simply call me Giotto."

Isabella nodded and began her long ride back down the hill. She was smiling. Already, behind her, young Giotto was reaching for a piece of charcoal and looking for a convenient flat rock.

If you enjoyed **The Heretic's Secret Trilogy**, you might enjoy others of John's titles. Here's a sample of his novel set around Henry Hudson's doomed last voyage.

The Final Alchemy

A Novel of Murder, Magic and the Search for the Northwest Passage

MELANOSIS

Robert Bylot sat in a high-backed wooden chair, a threadbare blanket wrapped around his shoulders, waiting for death. His head was surrounded by unkempt white hair and a five day growth of beard, and his wrinkled skin sagged as if already beginning its inevitable decay. He had eaten a light supper of antipasto, a habit from the continent which his aged digestion found much suited to its taste, and was chewing on a freshening finger of fennel as he settled his stiff bones by the low fire to warm them before sleep beckoned.

Bylot's life had been long and, by the autumn of 1669, he was ready for it to end. He yearned to slip quietly into the next world, but life clung to him like the wisps of white hair on his head. Each night he went to bed wondering if the temporary death of sleep would be but the antechamber to eternity. Each morning he awoke to the noises on the street outside reminding him that he had to face another day. It was always a disappointment, but never a surprise.

In the empty years since Penelope's death and the fire that had destroyed his beloved city, Bylot had experienced a growing sense that his journey was not complete. Something was missing. Some event or revelation that would assuage his guilt, make meaningful the jumbled events of his life and allow him to rest. If this was not the case, why then was he being allowed to live so long past his allotted span?

As he waited, lonely in his meagre rooms on Wapping High Street, close by the river on which he had launched so many of his dreams, Bylot wondered what this event might be, what form it would take and when it would arrive. He never suspected that it would be heralded by a simple knock on his door.

At first, Bylot was loathe to answer the knock. He was as comfortable as he ever was these days and did not wish to descend the stairs to the noisome street simply to face some drunken sailor who had mistook his door for one of a pleasure house. But the sound was persistent. Grumbling, Bylot rose stiffly, descended the narrow, creaking stairs and peered out on the cold night. A light, wetting rain fell and, nearby, Bylot could hear the water of the Thames lapping against its banks.

"Master Bylot?" the hooded figure on the step asked.

"Aye" Bylot responded, "who wishes to know?"

"Master Bylot, explorer, and lately Mate on the bark *Discovery*?"

"Aye. Much lately I fear, but that is I." Bylot was intrigued now by his mysterious visitor. He had not been called an explorer in many years and mention of the *Discovery* brought back memories he would rather have left buried.

"I bring a wondrous document from afar. Would you indulge my entry from this damnable night?" The voice was soft but clear. It suggested some intelligence, yet possessed an element of low cunning. Bylot suspected it was not unfamiliar with cajoling and flattery, often to its own benefit.

"Come in," Bylot said stepping aside. It was not his habit to allow strangers into his small home, especially in the dead of night, but the man's reference to the past interested him and he was beyond caring what evil might befall his frail body.

The man entered and the pair climbed to Bylot's apartments in silent darkness. There, in the dim light of the fire, the visitor removed his cloak and hood to reveal the shabby attire of a sailor. The garb surprised Bylot. The tone of voice had led him to suspect the clothing more of a gentleman, or at least of a street charlatan. With the flickering fire behind his visitor, Bylot could make out little of the man's features, but his posture suggested that he was examining his host intently. Feeling at a disadvantage, Bylot indicated the spare chair by the hearth.

When both were settled, Bylot took his turn examining the man. He was close to thirty years of age and had a care-worn, clean-shaven, squarish face topped by prematurely thinning brown hair. His eyes were a pale, watery blue and they regarded Bylot with an expression of smiling superiority. There was to the mouth an almost feminine cast and the lips were continually moistening by darts of a sharp tongue. The man carried a small bundle, wrapped in oil-cloth in his right hand.

"What is your name and what do you want with me?"

"I am Robert Gilby," the man began, "but newly returned from the northern wilderness of the Americas in the ketch *Nonsuch* under the Captaincy of Zachariah Gillam."

"I have heard of your voyage. In search of trade in furs to compete with the French were you not?"

"Aye, and with some fair measure of attainment too."

"That is not what I heard. The word is that your sponsors will not retire on the proceeds of this voyage. How then, with no profit to show, can you count a commercial venture a success?"

"The attainment is not in and of itself but rather in that it proved what is possible. The success is in the future this endeavour will lead to—but it is little concern of mine what befalls some company of adventurers. I simply voyaged as a diversion."

Bylot wondered who that diversion had left in London searching vainly for stolen purses or lost honour.

"I did my work," Gilby continued, "counted my pay as profit, and saw something of that part of the world. In truth, I saw much of interest and not a little that leads me here to this business tonight."

"And what business might it be that would concern me?"

Gilby regarded his host shrewdly for a long moment. "Since you have heard of our voyage, you will know well enough that we over-wintered in the sea called for Thomas Button or sometime your first master, Henry Hudson?"

Bylot nodded.

"Well, 'tis a God forsaken place and no mistake. We built a fort from the logs abundant there by a river we named Rupert on the shores of the bay named for old Captain James. We built in part upon the foundations of a rude dwelling said by some to have been constructed by Englishmen some sixty years previous. I think you know of this place?"

Bylot's mind flashed back to the winter of 1610. A ship lay, drawn up upon a barren shore, beside a rough timbered house from which a thin stream of smoke escaped. Discarded equipment lay all around, poking blackly through the blanket of snow. Bent, ragged figures went about a variety of tasks. A tall figure in a fur-collared coat stood some way off and gazed across the ice to the west.

"I might," Bylot said noncommittally.

"Well," Gilby went on, "the season became wondrous cold, but we were well victualed and passed a snug enough time. Come spring the local savages came in trade and we filled our holds with an abundance of fine beaver pelts. The best kind we found were those already worn, for then the coarse hair was naturally eroded, leaving but the fine and saving one step for the hat maker. I fear there will be some savages who will feel the chill winds this winter for want of an extra layer of pelts."

"I am glad of your comfort and thank you for this lesson in the milliner's arts, but I do not see that it should be a concern of mine."

"Patience," the man continued through a lopsided smile which exposed several broken teeth. "All things come to those who wait.

"We traded with upwards of ten score savages this spring past. We were never without sight of some and they took to entering our dwellings most inconveniently before Captain Gillam discouraged them. They were peaceable enough and I took to observing them for interest's sake.

"One in particular caught my eye. He was an old man, much about your own years I would judge, bent near double with the cares of a harsh life in the wilderness. He drew no attention to himself, yet he was in constant attendance upon our dealings. Every day he could be found off to one side, watching, with no greater presence than a mote caught in the corner of one's eye. I took to being heedful of his attitude and movements. None of our doings escaped him, and yet he took no part nor seemed to wish for more than simply to observe.

"At length, he noticed my attention to him. Rather than being a discouragement, my curiosity seemed to please him and he attached himself to me where possible, at a goodly distance but always there. I neither threatened nor encouraged, preferring to await what would.

"We completed our trade as the ice departed from the shore and we organized for our return. The old man was so much a common part of the surroundings that I rarely gave him a moment's thought, busy as I was with preparations for sail.

"On the morning of the tide that was to bear us away to a home all were eager enough to see again, a large number of savages; men, women and children, both old and young, congregated in their primitive finery to bid us farewell. I was busy with bundle of pelts some little distance from my companions when I became aware of the old man by my side, much closer than previous. I stopped work and looked directly at him. He was swarthy as any savage and certainly the owner of their unpleasant odour. He was dressed in their habit of leggings and a loose shirt of animal hide. He had a rough leather pouch hanging from a belt around his waist. His hair was grey and long and plastered down with some foul-smelling animal fat. He shuffled towards me, as I suspected, for one last chance to beg for trinkets and baubles."

Gilby paused here in his story. Bylot fidgeted with impatience. The location his visitor spoke of had long held a place in his heart and Bylot almost envied him his journey there. "What did he want?"

"I see you wish to hear my tale now," Gilby said with a suggestion of a sneer on his lips. "You shall, and then we will see about some business.

The Final Alchemy

"The old man approached until he was as near as I am to you. I would have been loathe to allow such a close approach had I not taken an interest in the man, so I stood my ground and waited. I have seen many wonders in my travels, but what transpired next surprised even me. Instead of the begging hand or the offered worthless tool, the old man spoke, and not the sing-song gibberish of his people, but the King's English."

Gilby paused once more to increase his effect. Bylot's mind was a turmoil of possibilities. The past was roaring back to overwhelm him, but what did it mean? "For God's sake, what did he say?"

Gilby smiled and tortured him more. "It was not easy to understand his rude speech—at first, I did not even recognize it as my own language, so rough and arcane was its mode—but with repetition, I began to make something out of it. The first thing he said was, 'Did any live?'"

"What did he mean by that?" Bylot interrupted.

"I know not," Gilby replied. "I asked, but got no response other than repetition of the phrase wrapped in the gibberish of the savage tongue. I fear that a life in the wilds had unhinged his mind."

"Was anything else he said intelligible?"

"Little that I could make out with certainty. There were a few words and phrases I could understand with effort; 'Desire Provoketh,' 'God's Mercy,' and 'Michaelmass' were most often repeated, but meant nothing to me. There were also sounds which might have been attempts at our speech, I suspected I heard 'discovery' at one place in his discourse but it was not repeated. The old man seemed particularly keen that I learn his name even though it meant as little to me as the others I had heard. The savages thereabouts place much stock in names and exchange them freely amongst each other and with strangers."

"What was his name?"

"As close as I could make out and transposed into the spelling we found most useful for recording the utterances of the savages for trade, it was *Dja-khu-tsan*."

"And he uttered nothing else?"

"Nothing, but repetition of what I have told you and the unintelligible language of his people.

"Now that I was over my surprise at his first words, I saw he was nothing but an old mind-weakened savage. Truly, he must have had some contact with an English party and had picked up a few words with which he was trying to impress me, but it was also obvious that I could learn nothing of import from him.

"I turned to go, as it was near the turn of the tide. As I did so, the old man reached forward and grabbed my arm. His grip was surprisingly strong, his fingers like the thin talons of a large bird. I was annoyed at him laying on a hand and I turned back, raising my free hand to strike him away. My blow never fell. Certainly the man cowered away in fear, but he did not loose his grip and his other hand offered me a book. This book."

Gilby held up the package he had been keeping by his side. Bylot reached over to take it, but he drew it back.

"Not yet," he said. "This is the hub of the business I would conduct with you, by which we shall both profit, and I would finish my tale."

Bylot doubted whether his profit was much in Gilby's mind. None-the-less, he nodded acquiescence.

"Well," Gilby sat back deliberately, placed the package in plain view on the arm of his chair, and locked his fingers together below his chin. "I at once realized the possible import of what the old man held. It was not of savage generation, they having no writing to speak of, therefore it must have come to this place through abandonment or loss by some explorer. As I knew, Captain James suffered no loss in this region. Unless it were some unrecorded voyager, the only other civilized visitors to these parts had been the unfortunate Master Hudson greater than a half-century previous. That expedition I knew had been surrounded by much mystery. If this document, so strangely offered to me in the wilderness, held any answers to those mysteries, I might be able to derive some benefit from it.

"Not wishing to weaken the position of my bargaining through informing the savage of my interest in what he held, I retained a stern appearance and spoke harshly to the effect that he should unhand me forthwith. To my surprise he did so and, to my even greater surprise, he made no attempt to bargain, but placed the book in my hand, turned away, as I thought with a sad expression on his visage, and shuffled off into the trees. I placed the book from sight, completed my chore and made way back to my companions.

"I was, I frankly admit, excited by this odd turn of events, yet, what with the bustle of setting sail and the cramped confines of our quarters which precluded any privacy, we were several days at sea before I found the opportunity to even examine my new possession in security."

Again Gilby paused. Bylot's mind was racing. "Desire Provoketh," "God's Mercy," and "Michaelmass" were all names he remembered only too well. They were names given by Henry Hudson to features he discovered all those years ago. "*Discovery*" was the name of Hudson's ship. The savage could only have come by them from contact with one of Hudson's crew. And the book—

Bylot had not seen it, yet he was certain what it was. It was his past come back to haunt him. A deep past, one buried beneath the equanimity of his life with Penelope. But Penelope was gone and now this man and this book were here, like a ruined city of the ancients, buried and forgotten in sand until its streets and walls are uncovered by wind.

Bylot was disgusted by Gilby's utter lack of interest in anything other than a profit, yet he was in his power. This was what he had been waiting for, but he had to sit and endure Gilby's silly games. With a remarkable effort, Bylot sat stone-faced preparing himself for what he knew was coming. Eventually, Gilby continued.

"I am not well-versed in the arts of reading," he said. "I can decipher a broadsheet or the Lord Mayor's proclamation well enough, better than some I daresay, and in my line of work, that has always more than sufficed." Gilby licked his lips and leered across at Bylot. "After all, my usual acquaintances are more familiar with the card and blade than Master Spenser's Faerie Queen.

"None-the-less, upon examining the old native's book, I immediately apprehended its import. It has been much ill-used over the years, not being placed with its companions in some learned man's library press. Much is stained, many words are now unreadable even to those more skilled than I, and entire pages are destroyed by the vicissitudes of fate. Still and all, what little I could decipher convinced me that it is of some value.

"Upon my return, I planned to seek out some antiquarian of wealth who might be prepared to part with a few crowns for the privilege of reading these pages. However, chance placed me one night in the company of some friends in the Pie Tavern. I was, I admit, the worse for too much ale and porter and was elaborating upon my late voyage to all who would listen. I of course did not mention my find, but one old patron listened with uncommon attention. As I finished my tale, he approached and engaged me in conversation. It seems that the tavern was close by where you once lived and you also were much in the habit of confiding your adventures to this very same person. Thus it was that I learned of your continued tenure on this Earth and conceived of the idea of our current business. You are not an easy man to find Master Bylot but, as you see, I have sought you out."

"What is the book?" Bylot asked with scarcely controlled impatience, although he was convinced he already knew the answer. Part of his mind was back, fifty-eight years in the past. He had just entered the Great Cabin at the stern of the Discovery and was standing before the table on which lay the mysterious map that had led to so many of their troubles. Henry Hudson, hunched over and looking gaunt and older than his years, sat across from him dressed in the long red coat with the fur collar that he habitually wore.

"Ah, Robert. I was about to send for you," Hudson intoned in a voice shorn of all feeling. "I have a favour to ask of you."

"Anything."

"Will you keep this safe for me?" Hudson stood shakily and handed Bylot a book.

"Certainly. But why can you not keep it with your charts and papers?"

"I fear these are uncertain times. You will stand by me, Robert?"

"Of course."

"Good."

A wave of guilt swept over Bylot as he thought how poorly he had carried out that promise to his old friend.

"Oh!" said Gilby with feigned surprise, interrupting Bylot's memories, "have I not mentioned that. How remiss. Here, read for yourself." He unwrapped the book and held it forward. Bylot fixed his glasses on his nose and leaned forward. His heart raced dangerously fast in his old breast.

The cover of the book was dark and heavily stained. It took Bylot a moment to adjust his eyes to the contrast, but he could soon make out words written upon the cover in quill and ink in a curling hand. It was a hand he recognized. Some letters were unreadable, but Bylot could guess them well enough from memory.

"I see from your expression that I have come to the right person. Surely this volume must be worth a few guineas. They will not mean much to such as yourself, but will greatly ease the lot of a poor sailor like myself. Shall we say 5 guineas?"

It was outrageous, but Bylot was too weak to argue. Rising and shuffling dazedly to the other room he retrieved his purse, extracted the required sum and returned.

"Damn you, Gilby. You are a thief and a villain, and you deserve not one farthing of this money, yet I will pay it none-the-less, if only to see the memory of brave men preserved."

Gilby laughed. "Aye, if you wish. I care not what you do with these old scratched words."

Bylot handed over the money and Gilby placed the journal in his shaking hands.

"Now be gone. You have caused enough upset to memory for one night."

"Well, I believe I shall be on my way." Gilby stood and retrieved his cloak. "I thank you Master Bylot and I shall toast your health afore non."

The Final Alchemy

Then he was gone. A quick blast of cold air from the street door and Bylot was alone. No, not alone. He would never be alone again. Too many ghosts had been released. They hovered around Bylot's rooms, tormenting him and dragging him back into the past.

Bylot saw Hudson's face, looking up at him from the open boat as it drifted farther away amongst the ice floes. Obviously the old savage of Gilby's acquaintance had had some contact with Hudson's ill-fated party after they had disappeared from the ken of civilized men. Bylot could imagine the desperate conversation of starving men eager to trade for food. It was not difficult to understand how the names told by Hudson could become imbued over the years with some savage magic and remembered long after they had been pointed out and told from a rude map. What he found less understandable and more disturbing was the phrase "Did any live?" How had that survived across the years in the mind of a savage? To whom did it refer if uttered, as it must have been, by one of Hudson's party? Was it simply a meaningless phrase retained parrot-fashion and regurgitated with the others, or did it carry some other meaning from the past? It disturbed Bylot because it echoed something that someone else had said to him and which he had remembered every day of his long life since.

A second wave of guilt swept over Bylot. There were so many questions. Could Henry Hudson and some of his men have survived one more winter? Did they sit, desperate, starving skeletons, on the barren shore of Michaelmass Bay in the summer of 1612 and watch in vain for the ship that Bylot had promised would come? Did they curse him as he cursed himself? Did they, in their final desperate moments, guess that it was the dream that had drawn them all there that had seduced Bylot from his promise and led to their betrayal and abandonment?

Bylot gazed into the embers of the dying fire. The white ash where it cooled was like snow—the snow that blanketed the ice floes that dotted the grey swells around a ship and covered the heaving deck. Bylot stood, wrapped against the cold, and gazed resolutely forward—to the west. He would not—could not—look south where the same snow might be covering the shivering bodies of a tiny group of his closest friends.

Continue **The Final Alchemy** by picking up your copy at any Amazon site.

Reviews

"...this book is a true, well-crafted page-turner...If you've ever wondered how the continents and the particular slab of rock you live on came about, you will love this book. Even if you don't, you'll still love it. Highly recommended." Ghost Mountains and Vanished Continents: North America from Birth to Middle Age

- Amazon reviewer

"The extracts from the diary describe intimate wartime experiences of death and destruction in gruesomely dispassionate terms . . . it's a story of unmitigated horror, highlighting more than any textbook the futility of war . . . This unique compilation of firsthand impressions of the Great War will be a valuable resource for adults and teens with an interest in this turning point in world history." A Soldier's Sketchbook: The Illustrated First World War Diary of R. H. Rabjohn

- Kirkus Starred Review

"And in the Morning joins other outstanding novels about the First World War—an invaluable resource for libraries and classrooms."

- Jeffrey Canton, Quill & Quire

"Equal parts philosophical debate and historical fiction, this book... presents a compelling and thoughtful story of war that should appeal to a wide range of readers." Flames of the Tiger

- Quill & Quire

"This absorbing, well-crafted tale...is a haunting description of the tragedy and irony of war...In this vivid narrative, the awful cacophony of war comes to life...the skilled author succeeds without moralistic preaching in highlighting the harsh reality, the utter misery, and the heartbreak of war in this intricate but fascinating book." Four Steps to Death

-VOYA

For more information on John Wilson, visit:
http://www.johnwilsonauthor.com

A Selection of Books
By John Wilson

Lands of Lost Content: A Memoir
Once upon a time, a shy kid from Skye almost drowned in nostalgia as he sat in the corner of a high-ceilinged room listening to fabulous tales of earthquakes, rebellion and crocodile hunting in a magical lost world. He grew up and survived his troubled teenage years in gang-ridden Paisley, field work in war-torn Rhodesia, near-death helicopter experiences in northern Canada and several encounters with bears. A mid-life crisis encouraged him to realize the importance of that childhood nostalgia and, using a life-long passion for history and his real-life adventures, he became a successful storyteller and author of fifty historical novels and non-fiction books for kids, teens and adults. He is still searching for that lost world, but this is the tale so far.

North with Franklin: The Lost Journals of James Fitzjames
Somewhere on a barren Arctic shore in the summer of 1849, knowing he was dying, a British Naval officer wrapped his journal in sailcloth and buried it beneath a lonely pile of frost-shattered stones. He was the last of the 129 doomed men of Sir John Franklin's lost Arctic expedition. His name was James Fitzjames and for four years he had carefully recorded the expedition's achievements, hopes and, as things began to go horribly wrong, the descent into madness and eventual death of his closest friends. This is his journal.

Ghost Mountains and Vanished Oceans: North America from Birth to Middle Age
This book is more than the story of how a continent formed over 4 billion years. Told in readable, entertaining prose and filled with personal and geological anecdotes, Ghost Mountains and Vanished Oceans tells the story of our world, and in doing so, it tells our story.

The Alchemist's Dream
"In this engrossing historical adventure, John Wilson paints a vivid picture of a bygone era involving Henry Hudson's fateful search for the elusive Northwest Passage, an alchemist, mysterious passengers, and enigmatic maps. The Alchemist's Dream fascinates from start to finish." (from the

Governor General's Award jury). In the fall of 1669, the Nonsuch returns to London with a load of fur from Hudson Bay. It brings something else, too—the lost journal from Henry Hudson's tragic search for a passage to Cathay in 1611. In the hands of a greedy sailor, the journal is merely an object to sell. But for Robert Bylot—a once-great maritime explorer—the book is a painful reminder of a past he'd rather forget. As Bylot relives his memories of a plague-ridden city, of the mysterious alchemist John Dee, and of mutiny in the frozen wastes of Hudson Bay, an age-old mystery is both revealed and solved. Set against the thrilling backdrop of the quest for the Northwest Passage, The Alchemist's Dream is a riveting tale of exploration, ambition, and betrayal.

The Third Act (soon to be a major live-action movie)
The Third Act deals with the intercultural struggles faced by Chinese students studying in North America in the present day and by an American playwright, Neil Peterson, caught up in the Nanjing Massacre of 1937. The contemporary story focuses on three Chinese friends (Tone, Pike and Theresa) who grapple in their own ways with the pressure to succeed in an unfamiliar culture. The historical tale concerns Peterson's effort to find his literary voice and save the woman he loves amidst the chaos and horror of the fall of Nanjing in the Second Sino-Japanese War. The two stories are tied together by a play that Peterson attempted to write after his return to America. The students in the present day get caught up in putting on a performance of the missing third act of Peterson's play, and in doing so they are forced to confront their cultural and personal pasts and futures.

The Ruined City: book 1 of The Golden Mask (The inspiration for the upcoming animated feature, Heroes of the Golden Mask)
Howard is a lonely, geeky tenth-grader dealing with a father who's had some kind of breakdown, a flaky, overprotective mother and frightening waking dreams. Then he meets Cate, a strange girl who convinces him that he is an Adept, which means he can communicate through dreams with other dimensions and, under certain circumstances, travel between them. Howard discovers that our world is only one of several dimensions swirling in time and space, and that one of the others, peopled by unimaginably powerful monsters, is approaching Earth for the first time in millennia. The last time the dimensions coincided, our world was saved by the breaking of a powerful golden mask in the Chinese city of Sanxingdui. Together, Howard and Cate travel through time and space, meeting other Adepts and avoiding

lurking monsters, in a quest to find the three fragments of the golden mask and prevent it from falling into the wrong hands.

A Soldier's Sketchbook: The Illustrated First World War Diary of R. H. Rabjohn
A unique First World War diary, illustrated with more than a hundred stunning pencil sketches, for children learning history and also for adults interested in a new perspective on the war and authentic wartime artefacts.

Shot at Dawn
Sentenced to death for abandoning his unit, during the night before his execution, a soldier recalls the events leading up to his arrest.

Graves of Ice
The last survivor of Sir John Franklin's doomed search for the Northwest Passage remembers his hopes and fears as he sits awaiting a rescue that will never come.

And in the Morning: Somme 1916
Flames of the Tiger: Berlin 1945
Four Steps to Death: Stalingrad 1942
Lost in Spain: The Spanish Civil War 1936
Flags of War: Shiloh 1862
Battle Scars: Libby Prison 1865
Germania: The Roman Empire 9 A.D.
Where Soldiers Lie: India 1857

The Caught in Conflict Collection is an imprint of fast-paced, historically accurate, morally-complex quick reads for Adults and Teens. They can be read in any order.

Lost Cause (The SEVEN Series)
Steve travels to Spain and uncovers his late grandfather's involvement in the Spanish Civil War.

Find out more about these and other titles by John Wilson at **www.johnwilson.com**

All of John's 50 books are available through Amazon.

Printed in Great Britain
by Amazon